THE RIVERDALE PONY STORIES

AMANDA WILLS

The Riverdale Pony Stories

THE LOST PONY OF RIVERDALE

1

---

oppy McKeever hoped with a passion that she was dreaming. Her family was sitting around the kitchen table looking at her, their faces full of smiling expectation, yet she felt nothing. She looked at each of them in turn, willing herself to feel something – anything – so she could join their happy trio. Her dad was treating her to his full-wattage BBC beam, her stepmother's cerulean blue eyes were appealing for her approval and her brother was fidgeting on his chair, barely able to keep a lid on his excitement. And still she felt nothing. She chewed her bottom lip and wondered how best to break the news.

'I'm sorry,' she said at last. 'I'm not going.'

Her dad and stepmother exchanged a look and Charlie stood up so quickly his chair rocked back and landed on the tiled floor with a clatter that sent Magpie, their overweight black and white cat, scurrying for cover. Poppy used the diversion to sneak another look at the estate agent's brochure on the table. The pictures showed a cottage sitting squarely at the end of a long gravel drive. Its walls were built from uncompromising grey stone and two dormer windows jutted out of the heavy slate roof like a pair of bushy eyebrows. The yellow paint on the small front door was flaking.

'It looks like an old woman's house. And anyway, it's too far away,' she muttered crossly, although her dad and Caroline were too busy with Charlie to hear.

Poppy slid down her chair until she was almost eye-level with the table and regarded her family. It was alright for them, she thought mutinously. They all loved an adventure and couldn't understand why she clung like a limpet to the status quo. But eleven-year-old Poppy knew from bitter experience how someone's life could be turned upside down in a heartbeat. It was only natural that she hated change.

Her dad had dropped the bombshell after dinner. He'd put on his special fake newsreader's voice. Usually his imitations were so over the top they made Poppy giggle. Not today.

'Welcome to the six o'clock news. Here are the headlines. It's all change for the McKeever family -' he began.

Charlie interrupted the broadcast. 'Why? Are you getting divorced?' The question was asked with relish. Half his friends at school had parents who'd split up. To six-year-old Charlie it meant having two bedrooms and a constant supply of guilt-induced presents. But her dad and Caroline couldn't keep the grins off their faces. They were even holding hands, for goodness' sake. Whatever the news was, it wasn't a divorce.

'No, you ghoulish boy, we are not getting divorced. It's good news. The McKeever family is leaving leafy Twickenham behind to begin a new life in the country!' her dad announced, squeezing Caroline's hand and smiling encouragingly at the children.

'Cool!' whooped Charlie, his fist punching the air.

'*What?*' Poppy demanded. Surely they weren't serious?

'We've bought a cottage in Devon, right on the edge of Dartmoor. I know it's a surprise but we didn't want to get your hopes up until everything was signed and sealed,' her dad said.

Under the table Poppy pinched her thigh. Her worst fears were confirmed. She was definitely awake. 'But I like living here. I don't want to move.'

'Don't be silly – you'll love living on Dartmoor. It'll be a new start for us all,' her dad added, giving Poppy a meaningful look. She wriggled uncomfortably in her chair. She knew exactly what he was referring to. But moving to the other end of the country wasn't going to miraculously make things better between her and Caroline. She hid behind her long fringe and said nothing.

'The cottage is called Riverdale. It's absolutely beautiful. Look, here are some photos.' Caroline pushed the estate agent's brochure towards her. 'The woman we're buying from has lived there for years but the house and land were getting too much for her so she decided to sell. We're so lucky to have found it. It must have been fate.'

'I don't care about fate. I don't want to leave Twickenham. I feel close to Mum here,' said Poppy bluntly.

The smiles faded from the three faces in front of her and she felt a prickle of guilt when she saw Caroline's wounded expression.

Then her dad dropped a second bombshell.

'You might change your mind when you hear the whole story, Poppy. The house has a sitting tenant.'

Curious in spite of herself, Poppy asked grumpily, 'What do you mean?'

'The owner of the cottage is moving to a warden-assisted flat. She has an ancient pony and as part of the sale we had to agree that he could stay at Riverdale.'

Poppy had a stubborn streak and had been fully prepared to dig her heels in over the move but suddenly all her objections melted away like frost on a sunny winter's morning.

She sat up in her chair. 'A pony? What's his name? How big is he? Is he too old to ride?'

'I don't know, sweetheart, the estate agent was a bit vague. And the pony was at the vet's when we looked around the house so we didn't get to meet him, quiz him about his age or take his inside leg measurements.'

Poppy played with a strand of her hair and thought. Their house in Twickenham was the last link with her mum. It was a connection she guarded fiercely. And yet waiting for her at this shabby-looking cottage in the middle of nowhere was the one thing she had dreamed of all her life – her own pony. She took another look at the photos. One showed two fields either side of the drive and a ramshackle crop of outbuildings at the back. On closer inspection she noticed something she hadn't seen at first. In one of the fields there was a blurry grey blob. The pony was too far away for Poppy to make out any details, but in her imagination he became the 14.2hh dappled grey of her dreams.

'But you can't ride, Poppy. You've never even sat on a horse!' an incredulous Charlie cried. Some people are born diplomats. Poppy's blond, blue-eyed half-brother was not one of them. Tact had never been one of his strong points. But as usual he was spot on.

'It doesn't matter. I could soon learn. Anyway, I know more about them than you do,' she retorted.

That was true at least. Poppy had an almost encyclopaedic knowledge of horses. One of her most prized possessions was a dog-eared box-set collection of books about riding and pony care that she'd unearthed at the bottom of a box of junk at a boot fair the previous summer. Inside the shabby green cardboard case were four well-thumbed books that had helped feed her obsession. Thanks to the books Poppy knew exactly how to look after a pony, in theory at least, from worming him to making a poultice. She knew the difference between a snaffle bit and a kimblewick, a running and a standing martingale. She'd memorised the chapters on teaching horses to jump and riding across country. And this was despite the fact that the closest she'd ever been to riding was having a turn on the donkeys at the beach in Broadstairs.

'I assume that means you're coming with us?' said her dad cheerfully. With an imperceptible nod of the head Poppy stood up and walked out of the kitchen with as much dignity as she could muster after her complete about-turn.

THREE MONTHS later Poppy pulled the final cardboard box towards her, tore off one last strip of brown parcel tape and carefully stuck the lid down. She looked around her bedroom. There was hardly a square foot of carpet that wasn't covered in boxes. Otherwise the room was bare. All her worldly possessions were packed and ready to go. Her clothes for the morning – a pair of faded jeans and her favourite sweatshirt – were folded neatly on yet another box at the end of the bed. Her dad wanted to leave straight after breakfast to avoid the worst of the traffic. Poppy still wasn't sure she wanted to leave at all, but she hadn't really had a say in the matter. Her dad and Caroline had decided that life in the country would be much better for the children. Healthier, safer, more like the childhoods they remembered, they kept telling her.

She picked up the battered Mickey Mouse clock from her bedside table and set the alarm for seven. Her eyes fell on the photo next to the clock. Taken shortly before her fourth birthday, it could have been one of those pictures newspapers use after a tragedy, with the caption 'In happier times'. It was winter and their small garden was blanketed under a layer of powdery snow. Poppy and her mum had spent the morning building a snowman. His head was slightly wonky and he was wearing the policeman's helmet from Poppy's dressing up box at a rakish angle. Poppy and her mum were standing to attention either side of him. They were wrapped up in coats, hats and gloves, their usually pale faces rosy with exertion. They were both laughing into the camera. Her dad must have said something funny at the exact moment he had clicked the shutter but Poppy couldn't remember what it was. In fact she wasn't sure if she could even remember her mum with any clarity any more. Photos were a physical reminder of her features but when Poppy tried to visualise Isobel the image was too fleeting to evoke the sound of her voice, the feel of her touch, what she was like. She sighed, picked up the photo, wrapped it in an old scarf and put it in her rucksack, ready for the morning.

As she climbed into bed Poppy thought about their new life in Devon. Her head was a tangled mess of sadness, trepidation and excitement that she was too tired to unravel tonight. Magpie landed with a soft thump beside her. He circled around on the duvet making himself comfortable before finally settling down. Tomorrow life was going to change forever. It was Poppy's last thought before she fell into a dreamless sleep to the sound of Magpie purring.

2

P oppy was up before six, woken by the butterflies in her stomach. She could hear Caroline singing along softly to a song on the radio in the kitchen below. She dressed quickly and went downstairs. Caroline smiled as she came in and flicked the kettle on.

'Hello, sweetheart. You're up early. I couldn't sleep either. I've been awake since five. There's only toast, I'm afraid. Everything else is packed and ready to go.'

'Toast is fine,' said Poppy, brushing her long fringe out of her eyes. 'Where's Dad?'

'In the shower. And Charlie's still asleep. I'm making the most of the peace and quiet to get the last few jobs done.'

Caroline busied herself making toast, her back to Poppy. 'How are you feeling about the move? I know it'll be hard to say goodbye to the house but you'll love Riverdale, I promise.' How did Caroline know what she would love and what she wouldn't, Poppy thought, aggrieved. She said nothing. Misinterpreting her silence for sadness, Caroline continued, 'And I know you'll miss your friends, especially Hannah, but you can keep in touch by email and phone and she can come to stay in the holidays if her mum agrees.'

'Maybe,' Poppy muttered, through a mouthful of toast. She knew Caroline was making an effort to talk and she was being monosyllabic in return, but she couldn't help herself. It was the way it had always been. There was a time when Poppy had been chatty, carefree and confident in the knowledge that she was at the centre of her parents' world. Not any more. Her mum had been gone for almost seven years and these days she had both Caroline and Charlie competing for her dad's attention. No matter how hard Caroline tried to include Poppy she felt like she'd been sidelined, left forgotten on a lonely railway siding like one of Charlie's wooden trains. She finished her breakfast, took her plate over to the sink and dashed upstairs to clean her teeth before Caroline could say any more.

SIX HOURS later the McKeevers were stuck in crawling traffic on the A303, in the wake of their lumbering removal lorry. Poppy had lost count of the number of times Charlie had asked if they were nearly there. She stared out of the window, daydreaming about cantering along grassy tracks and soaring over huge cross country fences, a set of pricked grey ears in front of her. Her dad and Caroline were arguing about his next assignment - an eight week posting to the Middle East. Her dad was a war correspondent for the BBC. A familiar face on the news, he reported from the frontline of the world's most dangerous trouble spots, from Iraq to Syria. Wearing his trademark beige flak jacket and often over the sound of distant shell-fire, Mike McKeever brought the horrors of war into people's front rooms from Land's End to John O'Groats. He was due to leave Riverdale the following afternoon.

'Why do you have to go so soon? Couldn't you have at least arranged to have a week off to help with the move? I don't know if I'm going to be able to do it all on my own.' Caroline's usually calm voice rose as she turned to face her husband.

'I know, I'm sorry. You'll be fine. I'll be back before you've even realised I've gone.'

'By which time it'll all be sorted. As usual,' she grumbled.

Poppy was proud of her dad but she missed him desperately when he was away. She'd much rather he was a postman, or a mechanic, or worked in a bank. Anything really, as long as it meant he'd be safe and home for tea every night.

Fields gave way to houses as they approached Plymouth. They followed the removal lorry as it turned off the A38 onto the Tavistock road, the final leg of the journey. Riverdale was a thirty minute drive from the market town and by 3pm they were nearing their destination, the village of Waterby.

'We need to take the second right after the church,' reminded Caroline. They drove straight on for a mile and a half and then turned left down a track just past a postbox. 'Look, kids - there it is!'

Poppy's first impression of Riverdale was of a slate-roofed stone building with an almost melancholy air, which stood in the shadow of a small tor. The car had barely crunched to a halt on the gravel drive before she had undone her seatbelt, itching to be the first out. As she slammed her door shut behind her she heard Charlie's gleeful tone, 'Mum! Magpie's just been sick all over his basket. Yuck, that's so gross!'

'You've found us then! I was beginning to think you'd got lost.' Poppy spun round at the sound of a disembodied voice that appeared to be coming from the wooden porch at the front of the house. 'I'm Tory Wickens. Welcome to Riverdale!'

A white-haired woman whose face was hatched with a lifetime of wrinkles stepped slowly out of the porch with the aid of two sticks. 'I wanted to be here to welcome you to Riverdale. Couldn't say goodbye to the old place without seeing who was taking it on. And you must be Poppy. You'll no doubt be wanting to meet Chester. I need to show you how he likes things done.'

Her dad had parked the car and he and Caroline came up and shook the woman's hand. They started chatting about the journey while Charlie struggled to pull Magpie's basket out of the car and Poppy paced impatiently from foot to foot.

'Can we please go and see the pony now?' she asked, after what seemed like a lifetime of pointless talk about whether the A303 was quicker than the motorway.

'Pony? Oh, you must mean Chester. Of course, silly me,' said Tory. She beckoned Poppy through the open front door.

The photos of Riverdale hadn't done the house justice, Poppy realised as she followed Tory along the hallway. There were doors leading off the hall to a lounge and a dining room. Both rooms were empty but light streamed in through tall windows and Poppy could see dust motes whirling in the shafts of sunlight. Floral sprigged wallpaper was peeling in places and there were darker rectangles where Tory's pictures must have once hung. But the rooms were large and felt homely despite the faded decor. Tory continued her slow progress through the hall to the kitchen. There was a pillar box red range in the chimney breast and dark oak units lined the walls. The back door was straight ahead and Poppy felt her pulse quicken as they stepped through it to the outbuildings at the back of the house. Like the house, the buildings were built of stone and tiled with slate.

'There are two stables and a small barn where you can store hay and straw. There's enough in there to tide you over for a month or two. That door between the two stables leads to the tack and feed room. It's only small but it's plenty big enough for Chester's things,' Tory said.

She saw the barely suppressed excitement on Poppy's face, smiled and pointed to the stable on the left. 'That's Chester's stable. I've just given him some hay. Why don't you go and say hello.'

Poppy walked the few steps to the stable door. The upper section was wide open and a horseshoe had been tacked to the wooden beam above it. A leather headcollar hung on a hook to the right of the door. The sun felt warm on Poppy's back as she leant over the closed bottom half of the door and peered into the gloom beyond. Straw was banked up around the walls of the stable and she could make out a metal rack on the wall that was half-filled with hay. It took a few seconds for Poppy's eyes to totally adjust to the darkness and when they did she thought she must be imagining things. She looked into the shadows again. Inside the stable, munching on the hay, was not a dappled grey 14.2hh pony but a small, hairy, long-eared donkey.

'But where's Chester?' Poppy asked Tory.

'That's him, pet. That's my Chester. He's a beauty, isn't he?' the old woman replied proudly. At the sound of their voices the donkey turned around, saw Poppy's silhouette over the stable door, curled his top lip and gave an almighty hee-haw.

3

D isbelief and disappointment swept over Poppy. She felt Tory
looking at her, the old woman's snowy eyebrows raised in
concern. Tory watched the expression on Poppy's face change
from excitement to shock. The girl looked crushed.

'Did you think Chester was a pony? Oh, love, he's my donkey. I've had
him since he was a foal. I've told him all about you. He's very pleased that
you're going to be looking after him from now on.' Tory called softly to
the donkey, who came over and nuzzled her outstretched hand.

Tears threatening, Poppy mumbled an apology and ran back through
the house and out of the front door. Charlie was sitting on the doorstep
with the cat basket on his lap, talking to Magpie. Her dad had started
unloading the car and Caroline was issuing orders to the removal men.

'Dad - you said there was a pony here. It's a donkey! You lied to me!
How could you?' The lump in her throat stopped her saying any more but
tears started sliding down her cheeks. She brushed them away with the
back of her hand.

'A donkey! A donkey! Poppy's pony's a donkey! Wait until Hannah
finds out! Serves you right for being such a show-off,' crowed Charlie
from behind Magpie's basket.

'Charlie, that's enough. Poppy, I don't understand. The estate agent was a bit vague but he definitely said it was a pony, at least I thought he did.'

Poppy refused to meet her dad's eyes as she kicked the ground viciously. Caroline broke the silence. 'Still, a donkey - how sweet. I know we were all expecting a pony but surely a donkey is better than nothing?'

Poppy rounded on her stepmother. 'You don't understand. You never do! What use is a donkey? I can't ride that - I'd be a laughing stock. I hate you!'

Shocked by the venom of Poppy's outburst, Caroline flinched and turned away. Poppy stormed off down the drive, her back rigid with tension. Halfway down the track she paused for a moment before climbing over a five bar gate into the larger of Riverdale's two paddocks. She headed towards the far side of the field, where grass gave way to a band of thick woodland. She needed to get as far away as possible. Once she'd reached the post and rail fence that marked Riverdale's boundary she sat down, facing the trees.

Poppy knew better than most how unfair life could be and if she was being honest she knew this latest disappointment wasn't the end of the world. As her dad was fond of saying, worse things happen at sea. Yet she felt bereft. All her life she had fantasised about having her own pony. While some children had imaginary friends, Poppy had had an imaginary Welsh Mountain pony called Smudge when she was younger. She'd made him a stable behind the shed at the bottom of the garden and spent hours constructing cross country courses using bricks and bamboo canes. Eventually she outgrew Smudge but she never outgrew her passion. Some of the luckier girls at school had riding lessons every Saturday morning and she'd eavesdropped conversations about their exploits and the different ponies they rode, longing to be just like them. Her best friend Hannah wasn't interested in horses. She wanted to be a pop star when she grew up and couldn't understand Poppy's fixation. Then her dad had told her about the pony at Riverdale and she'd spent the last three months believing that her dream was finally going to come true. How stupid she'd been.

Half an hour later her dad came to find her.

'I thought I'd give you time to calm down,' he said mildly, sitting on the grass beside her. Poppy still felt a huge weight of disappointment but now she'd cooled off it was tinged with shame at her outburst, which she knew had been totally uncalled for. She'd felt an instant liking for Tory and the old woman must have thought she was a spoilt London brat. And Poppy felt increasingly uncomfortable when she remembered how hard she'd been on Caroline.

'Tory's been asking after you. She feels that it's somehow her fault. And Caroline was only trying to cheer you up. There was no need to take it out on her, Poppy.'

Her dad looked tired and Poppy felt mortified. She hated upsetting him.

'I'm sorry, Dad. I'll go and apologise to them both. It's just - it's just I was so excited. And now there's nothing for me here. I'd rather be in Twickenham.'

'Don't be silly, of course there is. For starters, you need to come and learn how to look after Chester. You wouldn't leave him at the mercy of your brother would you?'

Poppy managed a weak smile. 'No, I suppose not. Charlie would probably end up using him for jousting practice or something. You go first. I'll be over in a minute.'

She sat for a few moments more, thinking about Chester the donkey and the pony that never was. One day she'd probably be able to laugh at the afternoon's turn of events, but not quite yet. She took a deep breath and prepared to face the music.

As Poppy stood up and brushed the dust from her jeans something caught her eye and she glanced into the wood. She thought she saw a flash of white in the trees. She paused, looked again, but there was nothing there except dark brown, tightly woven branches, heavy with leaves. Shrugging her shoulders she set off back across the field to the house.

4

_____

By tea-time the removal men had unloaded all the furniture and Poppy had been overloaded with enough information on Chester's likes and dislikes to write, 'The A to Z Encyclopaedia on Donkey Care.'

'By rights donkeys don't like living on their own but there again Chester has always had -' Tory paused, gave a quick shake of her head and carried on. 'You need to turn him out after his breakfast every morning and his stable needs to be mucked out every day. He needs fresh water in his stable every night and you also need to make sure the trough in the field is kept topped up

'He loves his salt lick and he has a scoop of pony nuts a day, half in the morning and half when you bring him in for the night. There's a sack in the dustbin in the tack room. It'll see you through until you get a chance to go to Baxters'. That's the animal feed place on the Tavistock road,' Tory added, seeing Poppy's puzzled face.

'I've also left you his headcollar and his grooming kit. I've no use for them where I'm going.' Tory was leaning heavily on her two sticks and her eyes had grown misty. 'Anyway,' she said, visibly collecting herself. 'Use the dandy brush for his body and the body brush for his head. You might need to take the curry comb to his tail - he's a terrible one for getting knotted in thistles. And you also need to make sure you pick out his feet twice a day. They say a horse is only as good as his feet, and the same goes for donkeys.'

Poppy was glad of her books. At least she'd be able to work out which brush was which. But Tory hadn't quite finished. 'He'll also need his feet trimming once every couple of months. He's not due for six weeks but I've left the farrier's phone number with your mum.'

'Caroline's not my mum, she's my stepmother,' Poppy replied automatically. Tory looked at the thin, pale-faced girl and felt a wave of sympathy. It must have been a rollercoaster of a day. 'Here's Chester's headcollar. Why don't I show you how to put it on and you can have a go at grooming him. He'd like that,' she said.

The donkey came up, nuzzled Poppy and obligingly held his head perfectly still while she grappled with the leather straps and, under Tory's directions, put the headcollar on. As she picked up the dandy brush and started tackling the donkey's thick grey coat she asked, 'What did you mean when you said earlier that Chester wasn't on his own?'

'Nothing for you to worry about, pet.'

Poppy could have sworn the old woman suddenly looked shifty, although she had no idea why. The rhythmic sweeping of the dandy brush and Chester's occasional friendly nudges had a calming effect and for the first time that afternoon Poppy felt her spirits rise.

'I really am sorry about before. I didn't mean to be so ungrateful. And I promise I'll look after Chester properly.'

'I know you will, pet. I'll go back to the flat happy now I know he's in good hands. I'll miss both him and -' she looked over towards the woods and stopped abruptly.

'Well, it would be lovely if you could come and visit Chester - and me. It would be nice to have a friend here,' Poppy told the old woman.

'I'd like that, pet. And you're always welcome to come and see me in my rabbit-hutch of a flat. But be careful of Mrs Parker. She's the warden and she's a formidable character. I've rubbed her up the wrong way already and I've only been there five minutes.'

They spent the next hour working together companionably, grooming and feeding Chester and settling him down for the evening. With Tory guiding her, Poppy picked out the donkey's feet and untangled at least five burrs from his tail. By the time they'd finished Tory's nephew had arrived to drive her back to her new flat. Clasping Poppy's hand as she stood propped up on her sticks by his car Tory said, 'Goodbye Poppy, see you soon. And thank you for looking after Chester. He means the world to me.'

Poppy smiled. 'Thank you for letting him stay at Riverdale. He can be my pretend pony. Who needs the real thing anyway?'

Charlie was unpacking his action heroes in the hall and Caroline was busy finishing tea when Poppy returned indoors.

'Your dad's upstairs making up our beds. Why don't you come and help me lay the table. Dinner will be ready in a minute,' said Caroline, drying her hands on a tea-towel.

Poppy looked at her stepmother. Caroline was tall, blonde and blue-eyed - the polar opposite of Poppy's mum, Isobel, who had been green-eyed, dark and petite. Poppy knew deep-down that Caroline wasn't your archetypical wicked stepmother. She was kind and patient and always put the children first but from the first day her dad had introduced them Poppy had felt prickly and defensive. She couldn't even begin to explain why. But she noticed the way Caroline would suddenly scoop Charlie up into a hug, smothering his apple-pink cheeks with butterfly kisses. She tried not to feel jealous when Caroline tickled her irrepressible brother until giggles convulsed his whole body or when she stroked his hair absentmindedly while she was reading the paper or watching television. The pair had such a close bond and they strongly resembled her fair-haired father. Poppy, who was the spitting image of Isobel, felt like the cuckoo in the nest.

As she leant over to unpack the knives and forks from one of the dozen or so cardboard boxes in the kitchen, a fan of dark hair hiding her face, Poppy mumbled an apology to Caroline. Fortunately her stepmother wasn't one to hold a grudge.

'That's OK, sweetheart. Your dad and I were just worried about you. I know how excited you were about the pony. Right, let's get this show on the road. Can you tell the boys dinner's ready?'

Before she went to bed in her new room at the back of the house, Poppy slipped out to say goodnight to Chester. It was a still night and the silence felt alien after the 24-7 noise of London. The donkey was quietly munching on some hay but when he saw Poppy's head poke over his stable door he came over and gave her a nudge.

'Tory said you like Polos. I'll make sure we get some tomorrow. Do you miss her?' Poppy asked, as she stroked the donkey's velvety nose. The expression in his soft brown eyes was unreadable but he gave her another nudge, as if to say, 'Yes, of course I miss her, but you'll do,' and Poppy felt a mixture of gratitude and protectiveness towards her new charge. An owl hooted, followed by the distant sound of a horse neighing. Chester lifted his head and gave a plaintiff hee-haw in return.

'Must be one of the Dartmoor ponies. I didn't realise they would be so close,' Poppy said, half to herself. 'I'll take Charlie exploring tomorrow. It'll be fun to have real wild ponies on our doorstep.' And she kissed Chester's nose, crept back into the house and took herself off to bed.

5

The first thing Poppy saw when she opened her eyes the next morning was her favourite photo of her mum. She'd unpacked it the previous night and it was back in pride of place on her bedside table. When Caroline came into her room a few minutes later, Poppy was lying on her side, staring at the picture with such a look of yearning on her face that Caroline felt the familiar jolt of inadequacy somewhere deep in her stomach.

'Breakfast's nearly ready and it's a beautiful morning!' she said brightly, pulling open Poppy's curtains to reveal a cloudless blue sky. 'What are you going to do today? I need to drive into Tavistock and hit the supermarket but you two can stay at home if you want. Your dad'll be here getting ready for his trip - the flight's at eight tonight so he's going to need to leave by three.'

'Um, I thought Charlie and I might spend the morning exploring properly. I heard a neigh last night so I think we must have a herd of Dartmoor ponies quite close. I want to see if we can find them,' said Poppy, as she swung her legs out of bed and reached for her jeans.

'Good idea. Make sure he stays out of trouble. I could do without a trip to casualty today.' Poppy nodded. If there was a tree to fall out of or a river to fall into Charlie was always the first to oblige. As a result he'd been a frequent visitor to the accident and emergency department at West Middlesex University Hospital.

When she suggested to Charlie that they spend the morning exploring together his blue eyes shone in excitement.

'Cool! Can I bring my Nerf gun, just in case we meet any predators?'

'No! You'll give the Dartmoor ponies a heart attack! They'll never let us near them,' shrieked Poppy, who was beginning to doubt the wisdom of inviting him along.

'Some people say there are big cats living wild on Dartmoor you know. Dad told me,' Charlie said, sticking out his chin.

'Maybe, but the noise you make they'd run a mile anyway. Why don't you bring your bow and arrows instead?' she suggested.

'Alright,' he grumbled. 'But I have been practising tracking and stalking. The big cats won't know I'm there until I spring onto their backs.' He demonstrated by taking a flying leap from his chair to the back of the nearby sofa. Poppy looked at Caroline and they raised their eyebrows in unison. Charlie's passion for danger was fuelled by his addiction to wildlife and survival programmes. While Poppy followed top riders like Pippa Funnell and Ellen Whitaker and spent hours watching Badminton, Burghley and the Horse of the Year Show, Charlie's heroes were Bear Grylls, Steve Backshall and Ray Mears and his ambition when he grew up was to track and film clouded leopards in the foothills of the Himalayas.

The two set off shortly after Poppy had fed and groomed Chester and turned him out in the smaller paddock to the left of the house. The paddock was bordered by a much larger field of pastureland that belonged to the farm next door and was grazed by a herd of black-faced sheep. There was a public footpath from the road at the bottom of Riverdale's drive leading diagonally across the sheep field and Poppy and Charlie started their exploration by following it. At the far side of the field they came to a second unmade lane that ran parallel to the Riverdale drive but was more roughshod than theirs.

'I didn't notice this driveway yesterday. I bet it leads to the farm Tory told me about. She said a girl about my age lived there,' said Poppy.

'Does she have a brother?' asked Charlie, bending down to inspect the ground, his bow and arrows slung casually across one shoulder. 'Yes, that's definitely sheep poo,' he said with satisfaction.

'Sherlock Holmes has nothing on you,' said Poppy drily, as she looked behind him to the field of sheep. 'I don't know if she has a brother, Tory didn't say. She just said I should go over and say hello once we'd settled in.'

Poppy would have loved to have been the type of girl who thought nothing of casually rocking up on a stranger's doorstep and introducing herself. Charlie had inherited their dad's gregarious nature and didn't think twice about bowling into new situations and making friends. But Poppy was often paralysed by her shyness. Knowing her luck she'd stand on the farmhouse doorstep and be rendered mute, opening and closing her mouth like a demented goldfish.

They re-traced their steps and crossed the Riverdale drive into the field to the right of the house. It was four times the size of Chester's paddock and in Poppy's opinion was the perfect size for a pony. The field was flanked by the dense woodland that Poppy had seen the day before. Charlie led the way, climbing over the post and rail perimeter fence and disappearing into the trees. Her usually boisterous, noisy brother turned back to look at her, holding his index finger to his lips as he warned her to be quiet. She followed as silently as she could as he led her soundlessly through the undergrowth. Eventually they came to the bank of a gently flowing stream.

'No wonder the house is called Riverdale,' whispered Poppy.

'Let's follow the river upstream,' breathed Charlie. Life in Devon seemed a long way from suburban Twickenham and the potential for adventure appeared limitless. They came to a bend in the stream where it widened out and the water slowed pace. A small sandy beach in front of them was too much for Charlie to resist and he raced over, pulling off his trainers and socks, whooping with glee as he ran, his silent tracking temporarily forgotten. Poppy joined him and they paddled in the icy water until they couldn't feel their feet. As they sat on a boulder drying their toes Charlie tugged at his sister's sleeve.

'Look, there's a hoofprint from one of your Dartmoor ponies,' he said, pointing to the sand in front of them. It was a shallow print, about the size of Poppy's hand, facing the water. The ponies must come here to drink, she thought excitedly.

Charlie seemed to read her mind. 'It's like an African watering hole only in Dartmoor. They probably come to drink here at dawn and dusk, like the animals do on the savannah. We could come and watch them one night.'

'Fantastic idea, little brother. Shall we carry on?' Charlie nodded in assent and they continued to follow the river. As the trees thinned out, Poppy realised they had reached the moorland at the base of the tor which towered over Riverdale. In front of them was a small herd of seven Dartmoor ponies. Some bay, one chestnut and a couple of greys. When they heard the two children they looked up from their grazing. Before Poppy and Charlie could get any closer they ambled off together around the far side of the tor.

Charlie strode purposefully over to where one of the ponies had been standing and peered down at the ground.

'That's a bit weird. Come and have a look,' he beckoned to his sister. The grass was marshy and at first Poppy wasn't sure what she was supposed to be looking at.

Seeing her puzzled face Charlie explained, 'Look, see the hoofprints in the mud. They're tiny - much smaller than the one we saw by the river. That must have been made by a bigger pony, maybe even a horse.'

Poppy felt a fizz of excitement which made the hairs on the back of her neck stand up. 'Very clever. Who needs Steve Backshall when you have ace tracker Charlie McKeever as your guide?' she teased him, wondering whether the mystery hoofprint had anything to do with the flash of white she thought she'd seen in the wood.

'No sign of any big cats though. I wanted to find at least a pawprint - maybe even the carcass of a dead sheep,' said Charlie glumly.

Halfway up the tor they found a boulder to sit on and Poppy produced two chocolate bars from the pocket of her sweatshirt. From their vantage point they gazed at their new home, spread out before them in the sunshine.

'I think I'm going to like living here. I thought I'd be missing Twickenham by now but Riverdale almost feels like home already,' mused Poppy. Charlie scrambled off the boulder. 'Same. Come on, let's go back now. It must be nearly lunchtime. The chocolate was nice but I'm still starving.'

By the time they reached the house Caroline was unpacking bags of shopping in the kitchen. Charlie rushed straight in and began regaling her with tales of their morning's adventures. As she walked to and fro finding space in the cupboards for the various jars, tins and packets Caroline occasionally ruffled his thatch of blond hair. Poppy hovered in the doorway, feeling excluded as usual, a feeling that was compounded when her dad came downstairs, joined Caroline and Charlie in the kitchen and started teasing Charlie about his big cat obsession.

Caroline unpacked the last of the shopping and looked over at Poppy. 'I overheard a strange conversation when I popped into Waterby Post Office to buy stamps this morning.' She described how she'd been standing in the queue behind two old farmworkers. 'They were talking about the annual drift. Did you know hundreds of Dartmoor ponies are rounded up off the moor every autumn before being taken to market?'

Poppy nodded. She'd read about the drift in one of her pony magazines. It was a tradition that had been going for generations.

'Anyway,' Caroline continued, 'One said to the other, 'I wonder if they'll finally manage to round up the Wickens' colt this year.'' Her attempt at a broad Devon accent was met with smiles from her husband and son.

'And the other one said, 'Colt? He must be ten if he's a day.''

By now Caroline had everyone's attention. 'So the first one said he reckoned that the colt must have had help hiding from the drift all these years. And the second one seemed to find that funny because he was laughing when he replied, 'Aye, but what'll happen now that the help is stuck in an old people's flat in Tavistock?' Bit strange, wasn't it?' said Caroline, giving Poppy's shoulder a quick squeeze. Poppy shrugged off her stepmother's hand.

'If you say so,' she shrugged again and left the three of them to their game of Happy Families.

6

All too soon the taxi arrived and it was time to say goodbye. As the driver loaded the bags into the boot Poppy's dad gave her a hug, kissed Caroline and shook Charlie by the hand.

'I'll be back before you know it,' he told the three glum faces. That's what he always said, Poppy thought, but it didn't make the time go any quicker.

'Keep smiling, kids, and don't forget to watch the news for the McKeever messages!' he told them. Years ago her dad had developed a secret code meant for the family when he delivered his news reports. Poppy's code was a plaited leather friendship bracelet which, worn on his right wrist, meant he was thinking of her. She'd made it for him when she was eight. A royal blue handkerchief in his breast pocket was Charlie's special message to remind him that he was the man of the house in his absence. He communicated with Caroline by a pair of sunglasses perched on top of his head. Poppy had never been privy to that particular message but she'd noticed that it always made Caroline blush.

He blew them all kisses as the taxi drove away and Poppy, Charlie and Caroline walked back inside, feeling deflated as they always did when he left on an assignment.

'I'm going to design a big cat trap,' announced Charlie, setting off upstairs to his bedroom.

'I suppose I'd better make a start on dinner. Want to give me a hand?' Caroline asked Poppy.

She shook her head. 'Do you mind if I go and sort out my room? There are boxes everywhere and I can't find anything.'

'You go ahead. I'll give you a shout when dinner's ready.'

Poppy's bedroom was a perfect square, set in the eaves below the cat-slide roof at the back of the house. From her window she could see the stables and barn with the tor looming darkly in the distance. She looked around the room. The removal men had stacked the boxes in one corner. Caroline had unpacked her clothes and her dad had threaded her fairy lights around the wrought iron bedframe but otherwise the room was bare. She was relieved that Tory's weakness for floral wallpaper and carpets was less pronounced there. She actually thought the delicate flowers, the colour of amethyst, looked pretty against the cream wallpaper. The oatmeal carpet was flecked with brown and opposite the bed was an old cast iron fireplace.

Box by box, Poppy began unpacking her books, photos, posters and mementos, becoming absorbed in her work as gradually the room began to take shape. Her favourite posters were stuck to the walls and books were arranged in a tall, oak bookcase. A patchwork blanket, knitted by Caroline in rainbow colours the previous winter, was carefully folded at the end of her bed and a matching cushion was plumped up on an old wicker chair next to the window.

At the bottom of the final box, protected by layers of bubble wrap, was another boot fair find. The bronze racehorse may have seen better days but Poppy loved it. To her it captured the very essence of freedom and speed. She looked around the room for a suitable home for it and settled on the fireplace. As she placed the galloping thoroughbred on the mantelpiece her fingers brushed against something silky. A tiny triangle of red material protruded from a narrow gap between the mantle and the wall. Poppy tried to pull it out with her fingers but the material was too small and smooth to grip. She thought for a moment then disappeared into the bathroom to ferret around in Caroline's make-up bag. She returned with a pair of tweezers which she used to tease the fabric from its hiding hole.

'Oh!' Poppy exclaimed. It was a red rosette with the words Brambleton Horse Show in gold lettering around the edge. The ribbon was faded and smelt so musty it made her sneeze. She turned the rosette over. On the back someone had written *September 24, 2006.* Poppy had been four in 2006. She shuddered. It wasn't a year she wanted to remember.

Before she could begin to wonder who the rosette had belonged to she heard her name being called. Caroline poked her head around the bedroom door.

'There's a visitor for you, Poppy,' she said.

An auburn head appeared, followed by the body of a girl about Poppy's age, with hazel eyes and a Cheshire cat-sized grin on her face. Poppy stuffed the rosette in her pocket and stared in silence.

'I'm Scarlett,' the girl said. 'You must be Poppy. Tory told me a girl was moving into her old house and she said I ought to come and say hello once you'd settled in. I live at Ashworthy, it's the farm next door.'

Poppy silently thanked Tory for sending the freckle-faced girl to Riverdale. She would never have plucked up the courage to knock on Scarlett's door.

'I'll leave you two to it,' Caroline said, retreating downstairs with a satisfied smile on her face. She was aware that other children thought Poppy was aloof, although she knew it was just shyness. A bubbly no-nonsense farmer's daughter was just what Poppy needed to bring her out of herself, Caroline thought.

In the bedroom Scarlett began giving Poppy the third degree.

'What's it like living in London?' she demanded. 'Have you been to the Natural History Museum? My brother Alex went there on a school trip once, said it was awesome. What about the London Eye? Did you see any of the Olympics? I would have given my right arm to have gone to Greenwich Park to see the eventing but I had to make do with watching it on the telly. How are you enjoying looking after Chester? He's so sweet - I've known him all my life. Do you ride? I bet the riding schools in London are amazing. They ride in Hyde Park, don't they?'

Poppy was finding it impossible to get a word in edgeways but as Scarlett paused for breath she said shyly, 'No, I've never learnt to ride, although I've always wanted to. Do you have a pony?'

'Yes, Alex and I both have Dartmoor ponies, Flynn and Blaze, although Alex is far too big to ride Flynn these days. For the last couple of years he's just been turned out in the field getting fatter and fatter, poor thing. Flynn that is, not Alex!' Scarlett laughed loudly at her own joke. Then she looked around the bedroom, seeing the riding magazines, pony books and posters. 'So you obviously love horses.'

Poppy nodded.

'But you've never ridden?'

'Only donkey rides on the beach.'

Scarlett looked at Poppy with concern. 'That's terrible.' She paused for a second before a thought struck her. 'I know! I could teach you to ride. You'll have the whole summer holidays to learn. Flynn is the perfect gentleman, a proper schoolmaster, he'd look after you beautifully, and goodness knows he needs the exercise.'

Poppy's heart soared.

'Yes please,' she breathed, all shyness forgotten, 'When can we start?'

7

_____

Poppy had to wait a week until Scarlett's school broke up for the summer before they could begin lessons. Scarlett was also in her final year at primary school and both girls were due to start at the secondary school in Tavistock in September. So Poppy spent the week getting to know Chester. The donkey stood patiently for hours while she practised putting on his headcollar and taking it off again, tying quick release knots and picking out his feet. She gave the tackroom a spring clean, sending spiders scuttling as she brushed away ancient webs. She talked Caroline into driving to Baxters' Animal Feeds and spent a blissful hour among the horse paraphernalia, spending her pocket money on a smart grooming kit for Chester. Caroline bought her a skull cap with a navy and pink silk.

On Saturday morning Poppy walked to Ashworthy along the footpath at the front of Riverdale, her new hat under her arm, feeling equally nervous and excited. She'd spent so many years daydreaming about riding, imagining herself cantering along bridleways with the casualness of a cowgirl or at horse shows being presented with trophies so shiny she could see her face in them. What if she was useless? What if she was so incompetent she never got the hang of it? Taking a deep breath, she knocked on the front door. The sound set off a round of barking and she could hear a boy say, 'Meg, be quiet! Oh, I think there's someone at the front door.'

When the door opened, Scarlett was standing there clad in jodhpurs and a checked shirt, a smile on her freckled face.

'There you are! We wondered who it was. Only the postman uses the front door. We always go around the back. But how would you know that – it's the first time you've been here? Anyway, come in and you can meet everyone.'

Scarlett kept up a stream of chat as she led Poppy through the house. Ashworthy was the kind of farmhouse that Poppy had read about in books but never believed actually existed. The house had low ceilings, mullioned windows and the aroma of baking. It was shabby and threadbare in places but Poppy loved it. Scarlett's mum, Pat, was in the kitchen, chopping vegetables and dropping them into an enormous saucepan which sat like a witch's cauldron on the Rayburn. A black and white border collie appeared, her tail wagging so quickly it was almost a blur. The dog woofed a greeting, pushing a wet nose into Poppy's hand and giving her palm a soggy lick. She stroked the dog's silky ears.

'This is Meg. She seems to like you already. Oh, and that's Mum,' added Scarlett as an afterthought.

Pat smiled. 'I've heard all about you, Poppy. It's so nice for Scarlett to have someone her age next door. How are you settling in?'

Scarlett's mum was as freckly as her daughter and had the same open, friendly face. Poppy instantly felt at ease. They chatted for a while until Scarlett grew impatient and dragged Poppy outside to meet Flynn and Blaze. Flynn was a rotund, dark bay gelding who made a beeline for Poppy's pockets looking for a titbit. Blaze was a chestnut mare with a flaxen mane and tail, whose fox-red coat matched the exact shade of Scarlett's hair, as if by design.

'Doesn't your brother ride any more?' Poppy asked, as she stroked Flynn's brown nose, trying to calm the butterflies in her stomach.

'He's thirteen,' Scarlett said, rolling her eyes, as if his age explained everything. 'He used to be fun but these days he's so boring. He's only happy when he's got his head in a book. Right, shall we get started?'

Poppy finally summoned the courage to broach an issue that had been bothering her all week. 'My stepmum has bought me a hat but I haven't got any jodhpurs or boots.' She looked down at her jeans and trainers in despair.

'Minor details. I'm sure we can find some. Mum never throws anything away. You start grooming Flynn and I'll go and ask.'

She returned a few minutes later with a pair of Alex's old jodhpurs and boots which fitted well enough and they spent a happy morning with Scarlett teaching her friend how to tack Flynn up, mount and dismount, the correct riding position and how to hold the reins properly. Scarlett clipped a leadrope to Flynn's snaffle bit and led him and Poppy around the farm, giving a running commentary as they walked sedately through fields and along tracks. Poppy felt exhilarated. Flynn was as round as a Thelwell pony but he was alert and forward going and Poppy had the feeling he was enjoying himself as much as she was.

Over the next three weeks Poppy learnt the basics of riding under Scarlett's knowledgeable, albeit occasionally impatient, tutelage. The two girls spent every morning at Ashworthy. For a couple of days, Poppy remained on the lead rein. But eventually Scarlett taught her the aids, how to use her hands, legs and seat to start, halt, back and turn the long-suffering bay gelding. It was the sort of thing that was second nature to Scarlett, who had learned to ride almost before she could walk. By the end of the first week Poppy had fallen off four times but had mastered a sitting and a rising trot, although she was still too nervous to trot without stirrups. After two weeks she had successfully managed a couple of canters and Scarlett was muttering about trotting poles and cavellettis.

'You do have a natural seat,' said her friend, looking at Poppy with a critical eye as she sat on Flynn at the end of a lesson. 'And I don't mean to sound big-headed, but I do think I'm a born teacher,' she added modestly.

'You're a hard taskmaster, that's for sure,' replied Poppy, who'd discovered muscles in places she didn't know existed. She had bruises on her backside and blisters on every finger. But despite the aches and pains and occasional falls she was having the time of her life. She'd barely been at home since meeting Scarlett and her newfound friendship eased the loneliness she usually felt when her dad was away.

She'd finally met Scarlett's brother, Alex. Tall and thin, with auburn hair a few shades darker than his sister's, he had mumbled a greeting and not said a word since.

'He's so rude!' Scarlett had complained, although Poppy recognised the signs and suspected he was just shy.

The McKeevers had been at Riverdale for a month when Pat invited them to Sunday lunch. Caroline had spent the first three weeks at their new house in a frenzy of activity, ripping up carpets, sanding and varnishing floorboards, stripping wallpaper and whitewashing walls. After transforming the house she'd started digging a vegetable patch while Charlie spent hours making dens and honing his tracking skills in the fields around Riverdale. Most evenings the children sat with Caroline after dinner and watched the six o'clock news in case their dad was on and every few days he rang from the Middle East for a short chat.

The lunch was a welcome distraction and when they arrived the three McKeevers were greeted by the sight of an enormous joint of Ashworthy lamb served in the centre of a huge pine table, surrounded by dishes of roast potatoes and parsnips and Pat's home-grown vegetables. Charlie was his normal ebullient self, firing questions at Scarlett's dad, Bill. 'Can I have a go at shearing one of the sheep? What do you do with all the cow pats? Have you ever seen a big cat?'

'As a matter of fact I think I have,' Bill replied between mouthfuls. 'It was during lambing last spring. It was so cold there was still snow on some of the higher tors. One night I was out at midnight helping one of the ewes deliver twins. Meg started barking at the line of trees at the edge of the field. I shone my torch over to see what she was fussing about but all I could see was a pair of eyes shining back at me in the torchlight.'

Scarlett, Alex and Pat had obviously heard the story a dozen times and carried on eating. Charlie had stopped, his fork raised half-way to his mouth, his eyes as wide as saucers.

'Dad, it was probably just a fox,' said Alex. Poppy looked up, surprised – it was the longest sentence she'd heard him utter.

'I know, that's what I told myself. Lord knows I've seen enough foxes in my time. But the eyes were spaced too far apart. And the reaction of the sheep was strange. They ran from that side of the field in a blind panic. I just can't explain it. Anyway, whatever it was disappeared as quickly as it had appeared and I've not seen anything like it since.'

Charlie was agog and Poppy could practically see his brain whirring, dreaming up madcap schemes to track down the Beast of Dartmoor.

Talk turned to Riverdale and how the McKeevers were settling in.

Caroline seemed subdued, Poppy thought, watching her normally chatty stepmother. She looked tired. Not surprising really. She hadn't stopped since they'd moved to Devon.

'How long did Tory live at Riverdale?' Poppy asked.

'All her married life and then she stayed there on her own after her husband died fifteen years ago. Douglas was a lovely man. It must have been lonely for her but she refused to move into the village,' said Pat.

'Did she never have children?' Poppy thought of the red rosette she'd found in her bedroom.

'Yes, she has a daughter, Jo, but they haven't spoken for a long while,' Pat answered.

'Why not?' Charlie asked, through a mouthful of roast lamb.

'Nothing for you to worry your head about, love,' Pat said, as she stood up and started piling second helpings onto everyone's already heaving plates.

After the meal, Poppy and Scarlett were sitting on the post and rail fence around Flynn and Blaze's paddock watching the ponies graze. Poppy asked if her friend knew what had happened to cause the rift between Tory and her daughter.

'No, Mum won't tell me. Says it's none of my business. I asked Tory once but she looked so sad I wished I hadn't. I never asked her again.'

The conversation was quickly forgotten as the girls started discussing the next day's lesson, when Scarlett was going to start teaching Poppy how to jump. Flynn, whose rotund belly was beginning to fade away with all the work he was doing, came over and nuzzled their pockets for a Polo.

'Caroline's really cool, you are so lucky to have her as a stepmum,' said Scarlett suddenly.

'What?' asked Poppy, who had been wondering how many times she was likely to fall off in her jumping lesson the next morning.

'My mum's great, I know. She's a brilliant cook and I know she loves me but she's stuck in a time warp - she's never even used a computer for goodness sake! Caroline's so fashionable and she knows all about music and stuff. It must be great to have someone like her as a mum.'

Poppy looked Scarlett straight in the eye. 'I'd rather have my own mum, Scarlett. Caroline doesn't love me, not like she loves Charlie. Not like your mum loves you. Not like my mum loved me.'

Her friend took a deep breath and finally asked the question she'd being bursting to ask since the day they met.

'What did happen to your mum, Poppy?'

8

Poppy had always felt responsible for her mum's death. Although she had difficulty remembering details of her mum's face - the exact shade of her green eyes, the curve of her smile - she had regular flashbacks to the accident in which every agonizing moment played out in her head.

They were walking home from school one bitterly cold afternoon not long after the snowman photo had been taken. Poppy's right hand was clasped safely in her mum's and in her left she held her beloved stuffed rabbit, Ears. They had crossed the main road at the top of their road when Poppy realised she'd dropped the rabbit. She slipped like an eel out of her mum's grasp and darted back into the road to rescue him. Her mum turned and screamed, 'Poppy, no!' and ran towards her. Poppy could still remember the look of absolute terror on Isobel's face when she saw a speeding car bearing down on them.

The next few minutes were a blur of disjointed sounds and images. The sickening squeal of brakes as the car shuddered to a halt. A flash of red as her mum was thrown over the bonnet. Howls from the young driver as he realised what he'd done. The screech of sirens as police cars and an ambulance arrived.

Poppy saw her four-year-old self standing at the edge of the road, clutching Ears to her chest, not understanding what had happened. Her mum was lying on the pavement a few feet away. She had run over and tried to shake her awake. But her mum hadn't moved.

'She's sleeping,' Poppy told the paramedics over and over again. They gently lifted Isobel onto a stretcher and covered her face with a blanket. Poppy pulled the blanket off. 'Don't do that. She won't be able to breathe.'

A group of mums and children stood silently watching the paramedics lift the stretcher into the ambulance. A familiar figure burst through them and gathered Poppy into her arms. It was Sarah, Hannah's mum. They usually walked home together, the four of them, but that day Sarah had stopped to speak to one of the teachers about a school trip.

'Where are they taking my mummy?' Poppy asked her.

Sarah's face was wet with tears. 'Oh, my darling. Mummy's badly hurt. They've got to take her to hospital. You can come home with us and I'll phone your daddy.'

For once Scarlett was silent as Poppy recounted the events of that day.

'I still thought she would be OK,' Poppy remembered. 'No-one told me what had really happened. My dad was in Iraq at the time and it was two days before they could find the Army unit he was based with and tell him about the accident. He flew straight home but it felt like ages before he got back.'

Isobel had taken the full force of the impact protecting Poppy from the car. Countless well-meaning bereavement counsellors had told Poppy over the following months that it wasn't her fault. She didn't believe any of them.

'After all, if I hadn't run into the road my mum wouldn't have died, would she?' Poppy said flatly.

Scarlett didn't know how to answer so tried to change the subject. 'How did your dad meet Caroline?'

Poppy gazed towards the moor. 'He refused to go abroad for the first year after Mum died so he could be at home for me. I had a childminder called Shirley who looked after me before and after school and in the holidays, but Dad was home every night. Then Caroline started working at the BBC. He said they became friends first and then he realised he was falling in love.' Poppy pulled a face. 'He started inviting her around to our house. She tried to be friendly, but she wasn't Mum. I hated seeing them together. One day he picked me up from school, took me to our favourite cafe, bought me a milkshake and told me he had some 'exciting' news. Caroline was having a baby and he'd asked her to marry him.'

At Caroline's insistence Poppy had been the bridesmaid at their wedding. Dressed from head to toe in cream silk to match Caroline's elegant wedding dress, Poppy had spent the entire day missing her mum while all around her were smiling and celebrating her dad's second chance at happiness.

'Then Charlie was born, Caroline gave up work to be at home with us and my dad started going away for work again. I always felt like the odd one out but when it was just the three of us it was even worse. Luckily there was always Hannah.'

'She was your best friend in Twickenham?' Scarlett asked, trying not to feel jealous. 'Does she ride?'

Poppy laughed, 'No, horses are far too muddy and she'd hate mucking out. She hasn't even got a pair of wellies. Hannah's ambition is to win X-Factor. But we've been best friends since forever.' The last remark was more to convince herself than Scarlett. Poppy had emailed Hannah once or twice a week since the move to Riverdale but whereas her emails were filled with the exploits of Flynn, Blaze and Chester, walks on the moor with Scarlett and Charlie and updates on the house and Caroline's fledgling vegetable patch, Hannah talked about clothes she had bought, music she was listening to and her new group of friends. As the days flew by they grew further and further apart. Poppy supposed it was bound to happen.

She glanced at Scarlett, who was chewing on a piece of grass. Bubbly, generous Scarlett, who had welcomed her into her life with open arms. Poppy felt lucky to have found such a good friend.

'To be honest, I have much more in common with you than I do with Hannah these days. At least we're as pony-mad as each other. And you don't want to be a pop star, do you?'

Scarlett grinned and shook her head vehemently. 'I can't imagine anything worse. I'd love to win Badminton maybe, but not X-Factor.' Her face became solemn and she said quietly, 'Thank you for telling me about your mum, Poppy. I'm so sorry about what happened. But you really mustn't blame yourself. It was the driver's fault, not yours.'

Poppy looked unconvinced. But Scarlett's next words threw her completely.

'Caroline does love you, you know. It's completely obvious to me. Surely you can see it too?'

'You're barking up the wrong tree there. She puts up with me because she has to. No more than that.'

9

C harlie's obsession with big cats was growing by the day. With Poppy's help he'd Googled news stories of reported sightings on Dartmoor and was convinced Bill hadn't seen a fox while lambing the previous spring.

'It could have been a puma or a jaguar, or maybe even a panther, which is another name for a black leopard,' he informed Poppy and Caroline over breakfast one day towards the end of August. The holiday was slipping through the children's fingers like sand and they only had a dozen days left before they started at their new schools.

'Poppy,' whispered Charlie, as Caroline bent down to empty the dishwasher. 'It's going to be a full moon tonight. Can we go to the river later, see who turns up for a drink?' He winked conspiratorially at her.

'OK, little brother. I'll come along and hold your hand, in case there are any beasties about,' she smiled.

For the rest of the day Charlie was fizzing with excitement. Caroline was suspicious. 'I know he's up to something. You don't know what he's planning do you? I've got a horrible feeling it's something to do with this wretched big cat he's convinced is living on the doorstep.'

Poppy couldn't hold her stepmother's gaze as she replied evasively, 'I don't know. He hasn't mentioned anything to me.'

'Sweetheart, you would tell me if you knew, wouldn't you? I don't want him to do anything silly.'

'Don't worry. I promise I'll keep an eye on him.' That much was true, at least.

'Thank-you, darling,' said Caroline, giving Poppy such a sweet smile she felt the usual twinge of resentment. Caroline was never as worried about her safety as she was about Charlie's.

That evening Charlie went straight to bed without any of his usual time-wasting tactics, adding to Caroline's unease. But she was too glued to the ten o'clock news watching Mike's poignant report on a suicide bomber who'd destroyed a school in Afghanistan to hear the click of the back door as the two children let themselves out.

Charlie had insisted they both cover their faces with the camouflage face paints that their dad had brought home from one of his trips to the Middle East. He'd been given them by a British soldier he'd interviewed in the desert.

'I knew they'd come in handy one day,' whispered the six-year-old, his face streaked with brown and khaki-green, his ultramarine eyes glittering with excitement.

It was a cloudless night and the full moon cast a benevolent light on the pair as Poppy once again followed her brother across the field, over the fence and into the wood.

This time, in place of his bow and arrow, Charlie carried a pair of bird-watching binoculars around his neck and the small digital camera he'd been given for Christmas in his pocket. The spindly beams of light cast by their head torches helped them pick their way through the under-growth until they reached the river. They turned left to follow it upstream, scrambling over fallen branches until they came to the bend where the river widened out.

Before they reached the small sandy beach Charlie stopped, motioning Poppy to follow suit.

'We don't want to get too close,' he murmured. 'We need to find some-where good to hide.'

Poppy looked around, her gaze settling on a fallen oak tree with a girth so wide they could easily take cover behind it. She pointed and they crept silently towards it, slithered over the tree and positioned themselves as comfortably as they could behind it. Charlie grinned at Poppy and pointed at the luminous dial of his wristwatch. It was ten to eleven and Caroline was probably in bed by now, oblivious to their exploits.

At first it was exciting listening to the sounds of the night and watching the bats swoop over their heads to drink from the stream. Twice they heard the long, eerie screech of a barn owl. The sudden noise was so close it made them both jump. After half an hour Poppy had cramp in one foot and even Charlie the expert tracker was beginning to get restless.

'Five more minutes,' she said softly. Charlie nodded and once more they settled down to wait.

Charlie was the first to hear a rustle in the undergrowth and he clutched Poppy's arm. The sound was coming from the far side of the river and they strained their eyes to see. Behind the undergrowth and interwoven branches was a ghostly shape which gradually began to take form as it drew closer. Charlie's grip on Poppy's arm grew tighter and she realised she was holding her breath as the shape finally emerged from the trees. Poppy felt the hairs on the back of her neck stand up.

It wasn't a puma or a jaguar. It was a dappled grey pony, which stopped and sniffed the air cautiously before stepping forward to drink from the river. The pony was bigger than Blaze and Flynn and was of a much finer build. He had dark grey points and a tail so long it brushed the floor. He drank thirstily, his coat briefly turning silver in the moonlight. Poppy gazed at the pony, wondering where he'd come from and how he'd ended up in their wood. She was surprised he couldn't hear her heart hammering.

She was so focussed on the pony that she didn't see Charlie reach into his pocket, take out his camera, point it and click. For a split second the flash lit the air and the pony half-reared in shock, whinnied and wheeled off into the trees.

Poppy rounded on her brother. 'Charlie, you idiot! Look what you've done!'

'Sorry Poppy, I didn't mean to scare it away. I forgot about the flash.' He looked so crestfallen she didn't have the heart to say any more.

'Anyway, we've seen loads of Dartmoor ponies since we moved here. Why are you so upset about this one running off?' he asked.

'That was no Dartmoor pony,' replied Poppy, standing up to let the blood flow back into her cramped foot. 'I don't know where he's come from or why he's living wild but I intend to find out.'

10

The next morning Poppy was so convinced that the pony was a figment of her imagination that she'd gone into Charlie's bedroom, found his camera and checked that the photo he'd taken actually existed. After scrolling through various out-of-focus images of her and Caroline and a few of Chester, she came to the photograph she was looking for. Charlie had captured the pony half-rearing in the moonlight in the moment before he turned and fled. Although the image was fuzzy Poppy could make out his flared nostrils and brown eyes full of fear. The sight made her heart twist painfully.

'Where could he have come from?' she asked Scarlett later that morning, as the pair tacked up Flynn and Blaze before setting off on a gentle ride on the moor. Poppy loved hacking out. Flynn was such a gentleman that she overlooked his tendency to grab a mouthful of grass whenever he thought he could get away with it.

'I've no idea but I bet I can guess who does,' Scarlett replied.

'Tory!' Poppy answered. She'd spent the morning wondering if the old woman knew more than she was letting on. Her evasiveness and the wistful way she'd looked into the wood suggested she might know something about the mysterious grey pony. Poppy was desperate to quiz Tory about him.

As luck would have it she didn't have to wait long. After weeks of sun the weather finally broke the next day and, faced with the unappealing prospect of a rainy Saturday afternoon at home entertaining an energetic Charlie, Caroline had suggested they go into Tavistock for a trip to the library followed by a cream tea.

'While you two are in the library, could I go and see Tory? I want to show her the photos Charlie took of Chester after I gave him that bath,' Poppy asked, holding her breath while Caroline considered the request.

In Twickenham her stepmother never let the children out of her sight but she'd become much more relaxed since they'd moved to Devon. Poppy was eleven and about to start secondary school after all. She needed some independence.

'Good idea. I'll drop you off at Tory's flat and then we can meet in the cafe opposite the town hall at three o'clock. I've got her address here somewhere.'

Caroline fished about in a drawer in the oak dresser until she found the scrap of paper she was looking for.

'Here it is. Right, shall we go? Charlie, have you got your library books?'

The windscreen wipers were going nineteen to the dozen as Caroline drew up outside the block of sheltered flats where Tory lived.

'Tory's flat is number twelve. Give her our love and we'll see you at three,' Caroline said. Poppy pulled on her hood and made a run for the flats. As she splashed through puddles to the disabled ramp at the front of the building, the strident tones of a woman's voice made her start.

'Hello! Can I help you?' It sounded more like a threat than a question. The woman stuck her head out of the entrance door and looked at a rain-sodden Poppy with distaste, as if she was something the cat had dragged in. 'I'm Mrs Parker and I'm the warden here. You're not one of those dreadful hoodies are you?' she said, peering closely at Poppy. She was, Poppy guessed, in her late fifties and had a helmet of tightly permed grey hair that didn't move when she looked Poppy up and down. She wore a heavy tweed skirt of a nondescript brown and a fawn-coloured twinset with an obligatory string of pearls. Unfortunately the lady-of-the-manor look was ruined by her pink, fluffy, rabbit-shaped slippers. Mrs Parker caught Poppy staring at her feet and the girl's perplexed expression seemed to antagonise her further.

'Well, do you have a tongue in that head of yours?' she asked sharply.

'I'm Poppy. I'm a friend of Tory's. Can you show me where her flat is, please?' Poppy attempted a winning smile.

'I might have known,' Mrs Parker muttered, opening the door wide enough for Poppy to step inside. The warden's helmet of hair remained motionless as she turned and pointed along a dimly lit corridor.

'Down there, second door on the right. She's in - I can hear her television from here. Well, what are you waiting for - Christmas?' Mrs Parker asked rudely, as Poppy stood rooted to the spot. 'And I don't want any trouble from either of you!' With that, she turned on the heel of her slippers and stalked off in the opposite direction.

Poppy pulled back her hood, sending raindrops scattering, and walked along the corridor, stopping when she saw a ceramic plaque painted with the number twelve and a pretty border of pink roses. She knocked softly and then with more force so Tory would hear her over the sound of the television. Her friend opened the door a crack and, seeing a bedraggled Poppy standing outside, opened it wide, a broad smile on her weather-beaten face.

'Poppy! What a lovely surprise. Come in, you look absolutely soaked. Sit down over here. You can tell me how Chester is while I make you a drink. I'm missing the old boy dreadfully. Did you meet Mrs Parker? See what I mean? She has me down as a trouble-maker, all because I've started organising a poker night in the residents' lounge every Friday. It's very popular but the old dragon doesn't approve, says it's lowering the tone. And it's not like it's strip poker! This place needs livening up a bit if you ask me.'

Poppy sank gratefully into one of the two armchairs in Tory's front room and looked around her while Tory turned off the television and went into the kitchen to put the kettle on. Tory's lounge had a window overlooking a small courtyard. Doors led off to a galley kitchen, a tiny bedroom and an even smaller bathroom. There was a faint smell of toast. Poppy got the impression that more furniture than there was room for had been shoehorned into the flat. The two armchairs were covered in a busy floral fabric and each was draped in lace antimacassars. Against one of the magnolia walls was a glass-fronted dark wood cabinet filled with porcelain figurines. An old oak gate-leg table with barley twist legs stood between the two armchairs, its surface covered in framed photographs.

As Tory chatted away in the kitchen, Poppy stole a look at the pictures. One, a sepia portrait of a young couple looking seriously into the lens, must have been Tory and Douglas on their wedding day. There was a photo of the couple and a small girl aged about five standing in front of Riverdale. She must be Jo, the daughter Tory had fallen out with. Other pictures showed Tory's family through the passing of years and Poppy was beginning to lose interest when a photo half hidden at the back caught her eye. She reached out to have a closer look and what she saw made her stomach flip over. The photo showed a girl on a dappled grey pony being presented with a red rosette by a man in a hacking jacket. Peering closer, she could just make out the words Brambleton Horse Show around the edge of the rosette. As Tory shuffled slowly in with Poppy's tea she guiltily tried to put the photo back in its place but in her haste toppled over the two frames in front of it.

'I wondered if you'd notice that,' said Tory, gently placing the mug on a small stool next to Poppy's armchair.

'It's the same pony I've seen in the wood, isn't it Tory? You know where he came from, don't you? Please tell me.'

Tory picked up the photo and sat down heavily in the other chair. She looked at the girl and pony and her face sagged in sadness.

'Yes, I do know where the pony came from, pet. But it's a long story with no happy ending. Are you really sure you want to know?'

11

'I used to be a bit of a rider myself in my day,' Tory began, settling herself into her armchair as the rain pounded against the window.

'You didn't tell me that,' said Poppy, taking a sip of the milky tea, feeling its warmth spread through her. She held the mug in both hands as Tory smiled.

'Nothing major but I used to compete in local shows and hunter trials. A couple of times I even entered the showjumping classes at the Devon County Show on my mare Hopscotch. She was a chestnut thoroughbred, a beautiful horse, so willing and nice-natured. You would have loved her. When our daughter was born I assumed she would be as pony-mad as I'd been but Jo suffered badly from asthma and being around horses often brought on an attack. Perhaps because of this she was always nervous around them and, of course, they picked up on it. It wasn't a happy combination.

'Then, 18 years ago, Jo's daughter Caitlyn was born. Almost from the time she could walk Caitlyn lived and breathed horses and would pester her mum into bringing her to Riverdale to spend time with Hopscotch and Chester. Hopscotch was virtually retired by then but I used to put Caitlyn up on her and take them both onto the moors on the leading rein for hours at a time. Cait looked like a pea on a drum but she loved it.

'When she was about six I was given Sparky, a roan Dartmoor pony, on loan as a companion for Hopscotch and Chester and, of course, he soon became Caitlyn's pony. Jo wasn't best pleased but Caitlyn adored him and the two of them joined the pony club and competed in gymkhanas and local horse shows.'

Poppy tried not to feel envious of Caitlyn, who'd had the kind of pony-filled childhood she'd always dreamed of.

'Eventually Caitlyn grew too big for Sparky. Jo didn't want her to have a bigger pony and was keen for her to give up riding altogether to concentrate on her schoolwork, but I disagreed. Cait was a really instinctive, gutsy rider and I felt sure that with the right pony she could compete at a county level, if not higher.

'Then I heard about a shipment of ponies that had come over from Ireland and were being sold at the next horse sale at Newton Abbot. I drove over there in my horsebox one April afternoon thinking it was worth a try.'

'How long ago was that?' Poppy asked, intrigued.

'Let me think. It must have been six years ago now. Caitlyn was 12 at the time. I didn't tell her or her mother what I was doing. I didn't want to get Cait's hopes up and I knew Jo would try to talk me out of it. So I turned up at the sale and there was the usual mix of coloured colts and mares with foals at foot with the odd riding pony thrown in. The Irish ponies were listed last. They were all nice-looking ponies, mainly Connemaras that had been backed but needed bringing on.

'But the last pony really caught my eye. He was a 14.2hh dappled grey with a handsome face and lovely conformation. He was very nervous and skittered around the ring shying at everything. But he had the kindest eyes. I had a gut feeling he was the right pony for Caitlyn.'

Poppy knew the answer but she asked anyway. 'Did you buy him?'

'Yes. I got him for a song because it was the end of the day and I think people were worried he was a bit flighty. Jo was so cross she wouldn't speak to me for a couple of days but Caitlyn was on cloud nine. She fell in love with him in an instant. And that's what we called him - Cloud Nine, or Cloud for short.'

'What was he like?' asked Poppy.

'He was gentle with me and Cait but he was a different pony around men. When the farrier came to shoe him he went berserk in his stable and it took over an hour for him to calm down. I'm sure he must have been treated roughly at some stage. But he and Cait clicked straight away. We spent the first few weeks gaining his confidence, just grooming him, tacking him up and taking him out for hours on long reins. All the handling paid off and when Caitlyn did finally ride him he went like a dream.

'Soon they were jumping at local shows and winning their classes easily. Cloud would do anything for Caitlyn. They trusted each other completely. She was desperate to follow in my footsteps and compete in a hunter trial. Her mum was dead set against it. She said it was too dangerous but I talked her around.'

Tory picked up the photograph of the girl and her pony again as if drawing strength for the final part of her story. 'We found a novice hunter trial for her in Widecombe. She was so excited she and Cloud practised for hours jumping fallen trees and ditches on the moors. After weeks of dry weather the day of the competition was as wet as today.' Tory looked at the window where the rain was still beating a steady drum against the glass.

'The course was as slippery as a skid pan. Jo pleaded with Caitlyn not to compete but I convinced her they would both be fine, that Cloud had studs in his shoes, he was a really careful jumper and that he'd look after her.'

Poppy could hardly bear to hear what happened next.

'They set off well and Cloud was jumping out of his skin.' Tory gave a half sob before carrying on. 'Every hunter trial has its bogey fence and this one was a drop fence followed by a ditch three quarters of the way around the course.'

Poppy had seen drop fences at Badminton and Burghley. Often a log or brush fence, they looked straightforward but had a steep drop on the other side so horse and rider landed on a lower level than the one they'd taken off from.

'The bank on the other side of the fence had been completely churned up and those horses that hadn't refused were slipping down it,' remembered Tory. She and Jo had been standing close to the fence as Cait and Cloud galloped towards it. Tory remembered the pony's ears flick back as he hesitated for a second before taking off.

'I don't know what happened next, no-one really did. Whether he had been spooked by something in the crowd or by the height of the drop I don't know, but Cloud suddenly twisted in mid-air. As he landed he lost his footing and somersaulted over, throwing Cait underneath him.'

Five years later the scene was still imprinted on Tory's memory as if it had happened that morning. Cloud had struggled to his feet and given an almighty shake. Below him Cait was lying motionless on the ground. Jo had screamed and together they had run over, Tory repeating under her breath, 'She's just winded herself, she's just winded, she'll sit up in a minute.'

But thirteen-year-old Caitlyn never did sit up. Within minutes an ambulance, its blue lights flashing and its sirens screaming, arrived and a screen was erected around the young rider, shielding her from the crowds as the paramedics carried her still body onto the ambulance and away.

By now the tears were streaming down Tory's lined cheeks. 'Her death was all my fault. I should never have encouraged Cait to enter the competition. If it wasn't for me she'd still be here. She would have been eighteen by now. She had her whole life ahead of her and because of me she never even reached her fourteenth birthday.

'Jo blamed me for Cait's death and I don't blame her. She's not spoken to me since. I would do anything to turn back the clock, Poppy. I lost a daughter and a granddaughter that day.'

'What happened to Cloud?' Poppy asked quietly.

'One of the course officials took him back to the lorry and by the time I got back he was shivering with cold or exhaustion - or both. You probably think I'm being sentimental when I tell you that his heart was broken that day. I think he knew what had happened. We both felt responsible for Caitlyn's death.'

Tory explained how she had taken Cloud back to Riverdale but that the pony's spirit had been destroyed. She recalled how, in a fug of misery, she had sold him to a pugnacious man called George Blackstone in the hope that it would appease Jo.

Blackstone, who farmed the far side of the valley, was a member of the local hunt and prided himself on his horsemanship skills. But he wasn't a kind man and Tory told Poppy how she had watched, powerless, as Cloud sank into deeper despair. The pony didn't even have the energy to fight back as Blackstone, realising he'd been sold a dud, took his frustration out on him.

'Selling Cloud to Blackstone was a terrible mistake, I quickly realised that,' said Tory. 'I knew I had to do something - I owed it to Cloud. I tried to buy him back several times but Blackstone flatly refused - he was convinced he could, as he put it, 'knock some sense into the pony'.'

Poppy suspected that Cloud must have been the colt the two old farmhands had been talking about in the post office the day Caroline had popped in for stamps. 'How did Cloud end up living wild?' she asked Tory, not imagining that Blackstone would have ever set him free.

For the first time since she'd begun her story the old woman looked at Poppy with something resembling a glint in her eye. 'Let's just say he was liberated one night.'

The loud chimes of the antique clock on Tory's mantlepiece made Poppy jump and she realised with surprise that it was three o'clock.

'Oh no! I'm supposed to be meeting Caroline and Charlie at three. I'd better go or I'll be really late.' She looked at Tory. 'Thank-you for telling me about Caitlyn and Cloud. I'm sure Charlie and I have seen Cloud drinking from the stream in the wood next to Riverdale although he galloped off as soon as he saw us.'

'I'm glad. I worry about him. And there's nothing I can do to help him stuck here.'

Poppy thought again of the conversation Caroline had overheard in the post office. Something about the annual drift. But she didn't have time to think about it now. 'I'm going to have to go, Tory. But please come and see me and Chester soon. I need to know if there's anything I can do to help Cloud.'

Poppy felt a rush of affection for the old woman and she reached over and gave her a hug. Tory beamed, although her eyes had grown misty again. 'You're a lovely girl, Poppy, and you remind me so much of Caitlyn. Now, off you go before Caroline starts worrying you've been kidnapped by aliens, and watch out for Nosy Parker in the hallway - the interfering old bat's probably listening at the door.'

The next morning it was still raining and Caroline suggested that Poppy invite Scarlett over for lunch. Poppy was upstairs daydreaming about Cloud when she heard her friend at the back door and by the time she had jumped down the stairs, two at a time, Scarlett was deep in conversation with Caroline in the kitchen. They were talking about the girls' new school and Scarlett was regaling Caroline with outrageous stories about the children from her primary school who would be in their year. Caroline had seemed down in the dumps recently but her face was animated as she listened to Scarlett's colourful descriptions of her former classmates and she laughed out loud as Scarlett told a story about a particularly obnoxious boy called Darren who had once fed chalk dust to the class goldfish. I never make her laugh like that, thought Poppy despondently, as she pasted a smile to her face and walked in to join them.

'Do you two want to give me a hand with the vegetables?' Caroline asked. The three of them spent the next half an hour at the kitchen table shelling peas, slicing runner beans and discussing the pros and cons of their new burgundy and navy school uniform. Poppy's was hanging up in her wardrobe, a glaring reminder that the summer holiday was almost over.

After lunch Poppy finally managed to get Scarlett on her own when the two of them went to muck out Chester's stable. She was bursting to recount the previous day's conversation with Tory.

'That explains everything. No wonder Tory and her daughter fell out. Poor Tory, she must have been heart-broken. I suppose I would only have been about five at the time, otherwise I would have remembered it,' said Scarlett. 'One thing that puzzles me though,' she continued. 'How did Cloud avoid being rounded up with all the Dartmoor ponies in the drift every year?'

'I'm pretty sure Tory used to hide him in Chester's stable while the drift was on,' said Poppy, who'd thought of little else all night. 'Which means Cloud must still trust her, despite everything.'

'But why hide him? Why didn't she just come clean and give him a permanent home where he'd be safe and cared for?' asked Scarlett, puzzled.

'Because George Blackstone still owns him, I suppose. According to Tory he wouldn't sell Cloud back to her after Caitlyn died, even though she pleaded with him to. Perhaps he still thinks he can make a competition pony out of Cloud.'

Scarlett knew the belligerent farmer of old, and suspected that he'd refused to sell the pony back to Tory out of sheer pig-headedness, but she kept the thought to herself.

'What about this year though, Scarlett?' wailed Poppy. 'What's going to happen to Cloud now Tory's in Tavistock? He'll be rounded up and sent back to George Blackstone who'll pick up where he left off five years ago, trying to 'beat some sense into him'. I can't let that happen.'

'Don't panic. We just need to come up with a plan. I'll find out when the drift is - my dad'll know - and you need to speak to Tory again and tell her we need to know how she managed to catch Cloud.'

'Who's Cloud?' piped up a voice from the stable door and Poppy's heart sank right to the bottom of her borrowed jodhpur boots. Who knew how much of the conversation Charlie had heard.

'No-one for you to worry about, little brother. Come on Scarlett, we're done here. Why don't you go inside and dry off while I go and catch Chester.' She grabbed the donkey's headcollar from its peg and headed for Chester's paddock, irritated to see that Charlie was following her.

'Is Cloud the white pony we saw by the stream?' he asked, running to keep up with her as she strode across the field, her head bent against the driving rain.

'None of your business. And anyway, you never call a horse white, it's always grey,' she said, knowing she was splitting hairs but hoping it would put him off the scent. No such luck.

'It is my business. And if you don't tell me I'll tell Mum about the pony and it'll be her business too,' he replied, smiling evilly at his sister.

Poppy knew she had lost. Charlie was as tenacious as a fox terrier. She stopped and turned to face her brother, sighing loudly. 'Alright, I will tell you but not now. Tonight, I promise. But you've got to give me your word that you won't breathe a whisper of it to anyone, especially Caroline. And I mean that, OK?'

She tried to look as menacing as she could but Charlie wasn't exactly quaking in his wellies. Instead, while nodding vigorously, he was trying hard to suppress a jubilant smile. Typical, she thought, as she caught Chester and led him to the shelter of his newly mucked-out stable. She would now need to baby-sit Charlie as they tried to rescue Cloud from the drift. As if she didn't have enough to worry about.

Satisfied he wouldn't be missing out on any excitement, Charlie disappeared back indoors. Poppy tied Chester up inside the stable and began rubbing him down with an old towel.

'Did you help Tory look after Cloud?' she murmured to the old donkey. He turned and looked at her with his clear brown eyes and Poppy got the sense that he had been very much involved in the annual rescue operation. She remembered back to their first night at Riverdale when she'd heard a horse's lonely whinny and Chester had returned the call. The two had been stablemates for almost a year before Caitlyn's death. As she scratched the donkey's ears absentmindedly she realised he probably held the key to saving Cloud from the drift and a life of certain misery with George Blackstone.

THE RAIN WAS STILL BEATING its relentless tattoo against the windows of Riverdale that evening as Poppy, Charlie and Caroline settled down after dinner to watch the six o'clock news. Her dad was giving a live broadcast from the Middle East.

'When is Dad coming home?' asked Poppy, who was cheered to see her leather friendship bracelet peeking out from his right cuff.

'We were hoping he'd be back before you both started school but he texted this afternoon to say he might have to do another couple of weeks,' said Caroline, her eyes fixed on the television screen. After his report the presenter turned to a story about a reported sighting of a puma-type animal in the Peak District.

'See!' shouted Charlie, bouncing up and down on the sofa. 'There are big cats in the wild. It's not just me who thinks so.'

'I'll read Charlie his story tonight if you like,' Poppy offered a grateful Caroline, who had purple shadows under her eyes.

'That would be brilliant, thanks Poppy. Make sure he cleans his teeth and washes his face. You know how allergic he is to soap.'

'Will do. Come on Charlie, let's get you to bed. What do you fancy tonight - The Lion, The Witch and The Wardrobe or Spongebob Squarepants?'

'Spongebob, of course!' replied the six-year-old, following his sister out of the room.

Fifteen minutes later Charlie's face had been scrubbed clean, his teeth had been brushed and he was sitting in bed sucking his thumb, a long-held habit only the family were ever allowed to witness. He took his thumb out briefly to ask, 'Now will you tell me about Cloud?'

Poppy gave him an edited version of the pony's history and how he had come to be roaming wild on the moors. 'Now we need to work out how to keep him safe from this year's drift, otherwise Blackstone will get his hands on him again and either sell him or, even worse, keep him.'

'Couldn't you just buy him?' asked Charlie, with all the logic of a six-year-old.

'I've got about two pounds fifty in my piggy bank, Charlie. I spent all my money on Chester's new grooming kit,' she reminded him.

'We need to find a way to capture him then, don't we?' He went quiet, his thumb firmly in, as he pondered the challenge. 'I know!' he said, sitting up suddenly. 'I can creep up on him upwind, and when I'm close enough I'll spit a sleeping dart through a straw into his bottom. You can get a headcollar on him while he's knocked out.'

Poppy's raised eyebrows were enough to tell Charlie it wasn't going to happen.

'Alright then, we'll dig a massive pit, cover it with branches and put a bucket of Chester's pony nuts in the middle. Then when Cloud comes over for a nibble, he'll drop down into the pit.'

Poppy tutted. 'There's a saying Dad uses sometimes. Softly, softly, catchee monkey.'

Charlie looked baffled. 'But we want to catch a pony, not a monkey.'

'You twit! It means I need to be patient if I stand any chance of catching Cloud. He's lost all faith in humans - apart from Tory - so I'm going to have to gain his trust and that could take ages.'

'Please let me help you, Poppy. I promise I'll do whatever you say, and my tracking skills might come in useful.' Poppy sincerely doubted it, but she had a feeling Charlie meant what he said, and it might be useful to have an extra pair of hands if Scarlett wasn't around.

'OK then. But you must give me your word you won't tell Caroline,' she reiterated. She knelt down in front of his bookcase, tracing her fingers along the book spines until she came to Spongebob Squarepants.

'Why don't you ever call her mum?' said a small voice from the bed.

'Because she's not my mum and never will be.' Poppy glanced at her half-brother, still sucking his thumb and looking at her solemnly with Caroline's big blue eyes.

'But your mum's dead so she's the only one you've got. You don't even seem to like her very much most of the time.'

'You're too young to understand,' said Poppy, neatly side-stepping the question. 'Come on, shall we see what's happening in Bikini Bottom?'

Scarlett fulfilled her promise to find out about the drift and put Poppy in the picture the next morning as they groomed and tacked up Flynn and Blaze.

'Every autumn all the Dartmoor ponies are rounded up so their owners can check them over to make sure they are healthy,' she explained. 'Foals born the previous spring are separated from their mothers and the foals are sold at market. So are any ponies that look like they might not survive another winter on Dartmoor. The hardiest ponies are returned to the moor to breed.'

'How do they round the ponies up?' Poppy asked, fascinated.

'They use local people on quad bikes, horseback and on foot. It's quite a task because sometimes as many as three thousand ponies need to be rounded up, Dad said.'

'No wonder Tory decided to hide Cloud. He'd have been completely traumatised and would have stuck out like a sore thumb among all those Dartmoor ponies. He's at least a couple of hands higher,' said Poppy.

'When are you next seeing Tory?' Scarlett asked.

'Tomorrow. Caroline has invited her to tea. I can't wait to ask her how she managed to catch Cloud every year.'

'Well, Dad says this year's drift is less than a month away, which doesn't give us very long.'

When Poppy arrived home after her ride she let herself in through the back door and went in search of a carrot for Chester. She could hear Caroline talking on the phone in the lounge and, without thinking, inched closer to the open door.

'I just feel as if there's this huge black weight bringing me down. And I'm so tired all the time, Lizzie. I can hardly get out of bed in the morning and by nine o'clock in the evening I'm asleep on the sofa. That's not like me.'

Lizzie was Caroline's older sister. A secondary school teacher in Bromley with two teenage sons, she was straight-talking but a lot of fun. Although weeks could go by without them seeing each other, the two sisters were close and spoke every couple of days on the phone.

Poppy held her breath as Caroline listened to Lizzie's reply.

'I thought moving to Devon would be a new start. Don't get me wrong, Lizzie, I love the house and Poppy and Charlie adore it here, it's been so good for them both, but I'm lonely. I miss Mike, I miss you and I miss my friends. I've started talking to the sheep, for goodness sake!' But her attempt at a laugh turned into a sniff.

Poppy could imagine Lizzie in the untidy kitchen of her town house in Bromley 250 miles away. She'd be sitting on the small sofa that looked out onto her immaculately-kept garden. Gardening was one of Lizzie's passions. Housework was absolutely not.

'Charlie's convinced there's a big cat living wild on the moors and is constantly dreaming up madcap schemes to find it and Poppy spends all her time with Scarlett - the girl from the farm next door I told you about?'

Poppy stiffened at the sound of her name.

'No, nothing's changed. I thought leaving Twickenham might be a clean break for us all but she's still so prickly with me. Whatever I do or say seems to be the wrong thing. It's like she's still punishing me for Isobel's death, after all these years.'

There was silence again as Caroline listened to her sister's reply.

'I know, I will. And I promise I'll go and see the doctor if I still don't feel any better in a couple of weeks. Anyway, I'd better make a start on dinner. Thanks for listening to my woes and give my love to Stuart and the boys. Bye Lizzie.'

Poppy was busying herself by the vegetable rack rooting among the potatoes and onions for a carrot by the time Caroline came into the kitchen. She was wearing yesterday's rumpled clothes and her hair, usually so shiny, needed a wash.

'Hello Poppy, did you have a good ride? How was Flynn today - did he go well for you?' Caroline asked brightly, the light tone of her voice contradicting the weary sag in her shoulders as she sat down at the kitchen table. Perversely her stepmother's well-intentioned enquiries irked Poppy, who located two good-sized carrots and straightened up.

'What's this - twenty questions?' The words came out before she could stop herself. Even to her own ears she sounded surly.

'Sorry sweetheart - I was only asking. What do you fancy for dinner? I've only got mince so it'll have to be spaghetti bolognese or cottage pie but you can choose.'

'Um, bolognese, I guess. I'm going out to groom Chester.'

Poppy heard Caroline sigh as she flung the back door shut behind her. As she stomped out to Chester's stable she thought about the conversation she'd overheard. How dare Caroline call her prickly? She missed her mum, that was all, and the sooner Caroline realised she could never replace Isobel the better, as far as she was concerned. Her stepmother was always so annoyingly cheerful and capable it was difficult to believe she was lonely and maybe even a bit depressed. Poppy dismissed the thought. She was just exaggerating, knowing she'd get a sympathetic reaction from her sister. A nagging feeling told her Caroline wasn't the type to go fishing for sympathy but she ignored it, gave Chester a gentle pat on the rump and started brushing the burrs from his tail, all thoughts of her stepmother forgotten.

～

CAROLINE MADE an extra effort for Tory the following day. She baked a chocolate cake - Charlie's favourite, Poppy thought sourly - and made a quiche which she planned to serve with lettuce and tomatoes from the garden. Tory caught the bus to the end of the drive and was delighted to see a small welcoming committee made up of Caroline, Poppy and Charlie waiting to help her up to the house.

Poppy and Caroline took an arm each and as they walked Tory's head tracked back and forth, taking in the paddocks, the wood and the tor, which was basked in sunshine.

'I know it's only been a few weeks but it feels grand to be back,' said Tory, as they finally made it to the front door and Caroline helped her off with her coat.

'Charlie and I have a surprise for you,' Poppy said. 'Sit here and close your eyes.' She motioned to a wrought iron bench in front of the house. 'Come on, Charlie.'

The two children had spent the morning giving Chester the grooming of his life. Poppy had weaved red ribbons into his thick mane and tail and Charlie had brushed his hooves with oil until they glistened. Charlie proudly led the donkey round to the front of the house. 'You can open your eyes now!'

'Oh my, don't you look handsome!' Tory told Chester, ferreting around in her handbag for some Polos. The donkey accepted one graciously.

'Thank you Poppy and Charlie, what a lovely surprise. Chester looks so well, you've obviously been looking after him beautifully.'

Poppy smiled and Charlie gave a little bow. 'All part of the Riverdale service, madam,' he said with a grin.

For the rest of the day the house buzzed. Poppy realised how quiet it had been over the past few weeks with Caroline so listless. Even Charlie, naturally so exuberant, had been less boisterous than usual, perhaps picking up on his mum's downcast mood. But Tory cheered everyone up. Despite being 'absolutely ancient' as she described herself, she had an incorrigible sense of fun and made them laugh with tales of colourful local characters and recollections of the many happy years she and her husband, Douglas, had spent living at Riverdale.

Later Tory and Poppy sat on the bench at the front of the house, enjoying a cup of tea and a slice of cake as they caught the last rays of the sun. Breaking the companionable silence Tory said, 'I've been having a long chat with Caroline this afternoon.'

The stone wall behind them felt warm to the touch and there was a background hum of bees as they buzzed lazily around two lavender-filled terracotta pots on either side of the bench. 'She seems very low. Nothing like the woman I met the day you all moved in.' Tory took a sip from her mug and looked out across the valley.

Poppy kicked her heels against the ground and shrugged. 'She's probably just a bit lonely. Missing Dad and her friends in London, I expect.'

'No, I think it's more than that.' Tory looked Poppy in the eye. 'I remember when I was your age. I thought the world revolved around me. All children do, I suppose it's a survival instinct. Teenagers are probably the most self-absorbed of the lot, although some old people can be just as selfish - I suppose we all come full circle in the end,' she mused.

With a little shake of her head she carried on. 'Of course, once you have children that all changes. Women like Caroline think of everyone else first, they have to be totally selfless. I'm sure your mum was the same.'

Poppy nodded. In the years since her death Isobel had taken on the status of a saint in Poppy's eyes. She had subconsciously provided Caroline with an impossible act to follow.

'Native Americans have a saying - don't judge a man until you have walked a mile in his shoes,' Tory continued.

Poppy wondered where the conversation was heading. She had a sneaking suspicion she wasn't going to like it.

'Have you ever walked in Caroline's shoes?' Tory asked, and Poppy pictured herself staggering down the bumpy Riverdale drive in Caroline's favourite red killer heels. Suppressing the image she shook her head.

'What I'm trying to say,' persevered Tory, 'in a long and convoluted way, is this. I know you miss your mum and always will, but have you ever stopped to think about Caroline and how she is feeling?'

'Why do people keep on at me about Caroline? First Scarlett, then Charlie and now you. I thought you were on my side!'

'I am, pet. I'm just trying to make things better for everyone. I hate to think of Riverdale as an unhappy house.' Tory took a deep breath in a nothing ventured, nothing gained kind of way and changed tack. 'Caroline was telling me today about Isobel's accident. It must have been so hard for you when she died.'

Poppy nodded. She knew Tory understood what it was like to lose someone you loved. But the old woman's next comment hit her in the solar plexus. 'I may be wrong but I get the feeling you blame Caroline for Isobel's death.'

'That's not true! Dad didn't even meet Caroline until after Mum died. The only person I blame is me! Mum was run over because I ran back into the road, didn't Caroline tell you that?' Poppy's eyes flashed dangerously.

'She told me it was an accident, pet, and that if anyone was to blame it was the driver who was going too fast on a busy road so near a school.'

Poppy continued kicking the ground viciously as Tory ploughed on. 'Blaming yourself is no good - the guilt will just eat you up. You've got to accept it wasn't your fault and move on, Poppy.'

'You sound like one of those awful bereavement counsellors Dad made me see after Mum died! Pathetic do-gooders who couldn't do any good because they couldn't turn back the clock, could they?'

'I know, pet, no-one can turn back the clock. But you should know that Caroline feels…'

Poppy never did find out how her stepmother felt as before Tory could finish she had stalked off to her bedroom, banging the door shut as ferociously as she dared and refusing to come down to say goodbye when Tory's nephew turned up half an hour later to take her home.

That night Poppy dreamt about the accident. Her four-year-old self held Ears in one hand and the other was clasped firmly in her mum's. But her hand felt different and when she looked down at their shadows her mum's was tall and willowy, not small and slim. They crossed the road, heading for home, and reached the pavement on the other side. She realised she'd dropped the rabbit, slipped out of her mum's grip and ran back into the road. But when she looked up, Ears dangling from her fist, the face staring back at her, white with terror, wasn't Isobel's. It was Caroline's.

'Mummy!' shouted four-year-old Poppy in the dream, and Caroline took two steps forward and swept her into her arms and to safety. They both spun around to look as the speeding car flashed past. Poppy pressed her face into Caroline's neck, breathing in the familiar scent. She felt safe and loved. Caroline murmured into her hair, 'Oh Poppy, my darling girl. Everything will be alright. I promise.'

1 4

‘So, basically, you ran off in a strop without asking Tory anything about Cloud?’ demanded Scarlett the next afternoon. Poppy was sitting, cross-legged, on the red and royal blue rug on her bedroom floor. Scarlett was sprawled on her bed, leafing through old editions of Poppy's pony magazines. Charlie, who had been allowed in under the strict conditions that he only spoke when spoken to and didn't breathe a word of their conversation to Caroline, was sitting on the wicker chair by the window playing on his DS. Magpie lay curled in a ball on the carpet, his substantial stomach illuminated by a shaft of sunlight.

‘I know. I was an idiot, you don't have to tell me,’ groaned Poppy, who had felt slightly out of kilter since she'd woken up, the previous night's dream refusing to fade from her mind's eye. ‘The trouble is I'm not sure when I'll next get a chance to talk to Tory. She probably won't even want to see me after the way I stormed off yesterday. We're never going to find out how she managed to catch Cloud.’

Scarlett had stopped listening. Her eye had been caught by an article in one of the magazines. ‘Look at this! How to be a Horse Whisperer,’ she read. ‘It's a whole feature on gaining the confidence of even the most nervous of horses.’ Poppy jumped up and joined her on the bed and they pored over the article.

‘What does it say then?’ asked Charlie, glancing up from his DS.

Magpie lifted his black and white face and looked at the two girls with interest.

'That a horse won't trust you until he has confidence in you. That you've got to think about how he feels and the things he fears. Look, there are lots of tips...don't make eye contact, turn your back to him so he gets curious and seeks your attention, talk or sing to him so he gets used to your voice. If he heard me singing he'd run for the hills. Mum says I'm tone deaf,' said Scarlett gloomily.

'What you need is some direct action. You're not going to get Cloud to trust you by sitting in your bedroom talking about it,' said Charlie, ever the pragmatist.

'But we go to Granny's tomorrow! We won't be back until the day before term starts,' moaned Scarlett, who was not looking forward to the family's annual pilgrimage to her grandparents' draughty farmhouse in Wiltshire.

'Sorry Scarlett, but for once Charlie is right. I need to start if we stand any chance of catching Cloud before the drift. I'll text you to let you know how we're getting on. You'll be back before you know it.'

Scarlett had been summoned home for tea and Poppy and Charlie walked with her back to the farm, taking a handful of carrots with them for Flynn and Blaze. Scarlett was subdued and for once it was down to Poppy to keep the conversation going.

'You know Scar, you won't miss anything. It's probably going to take weeks to get anywhere near Cloud, let alone catch him,' she told her glum-faced friend.

'I know. It's just that I hate going to Granny's. I miss Blaze heaps when we're away and now I won't be able to help you with Cloud. It's so unfair!'

Poppy nodded sympathetically and gave Scarlett a brief hug. 'I'll text, I promise,' she said. 'Come on, Charlie. We'd better get going.'

'You'll need someone to go with you though, won't you?' said her brother, his blue eyes turned hopefully towards hers as they walked across the sheep field to Riverdale.

Poppy sighed. 'I suppose so. But you know the rules, little brother.'

'Yes, the rules. No talking, no moving, no making any noise, no breathing. I know, I'll play dead, then I'm bound to stay out of trouble.'

'Ha ha, very funny. Shall we go tonight?' She paused. 'What should we tell Caroline?'

'Leave that to me,' replied Charlie, who had the satisfied look of a man with a plan.

'Mum?' he said, tracking Caroline down in the kitchen where she was standing by the sink looking blankly out of the window. Poppy found her utter stillness unnerving but as Caroline turned to face them her face cleared and she smiled.

'Oh, there you are, you two. What have you been doing?'

'That's what I wanted to tell you. We've been reading about badgers,' Charlie said, producing a book on British wildlife from behind his back with a flourish. 'We've been looking at their habitat and how to spot signs that they have a sett nearby. What badger poo looks like and stuff like that,' he explained earnestly, his blue eyes fixed on Caroline's. 'We were wondering if we could go out into the woods after tea and see if we can find any. Badgers, that is, not badger poo. Although, of course, if you find the poo you'll find the badgers.'

'Yes, I get the picture,' laughed Caroline. She thought for a moment. 'Yes, I don't see why not, as long as you take your phone Poppy, you don't go too far and you're back before it gets dark.'

Poppy looked at her brother with a mixture of astonishment and admiration. Six years old and totally unfazed at fabricating stories. How did he manage it?

They set off just after six o'clock, armed with binoculars, phone, camera and Charlie's wildlife book.

'Hold on, I've just remembered something,' said Poppy. She darted into the tackroom next to Chester's stable, emerging seconds later with a scoop of pony nuts in a bucket. 'I'm sure Chester won't mind. They are for his friend, after all,' she whispered.

'Shall we go to the little beach where we saw him before?' asked Charlie, who was bouncing along beside his sister. There was nothing Charlie loved more than direct action.

'Yes, I think that's probably as good a place as any,' Poppy answered and they crossed the field in front of the house, climbed the fence and disappeared into the wood.

Twenty minutes later they arrived at the clearing. Recent rain had turned the meandering stream into a fast-flowing river, which whooshed noisily past them.

'Let's put the bucket of nuts on the beach, go and hide behind that tree again and see if he comes,' said Poppy, feeling sick with nerves.

They crouched down behind the tree and waited. It was a windy evening and the branches sighed and creaked around them. The light was beginning to fade and as the sun set to the west it cast long shadows that rippled and danced across the woodland floor. Charlie grew fidgety. Poppy nudged him to be still.

'Sorry,' he whispered. 'But I need the toilet.'

She sighed loudly and stood up. 'Great. Look, go over there behind that bush. And try and be quiet about it, will you?'

When Charlie returned, a leaf sticking out of his hair, he sat down and started silently flicking through his book on wildlife. Every now and then he stopped, licked the pad of his index finger and held it up to the wind, nodding sagely. Poppy didn't know whether to hug him or throttle him. Instead she fixed her eyes on the line of trees in front of them and stared so hard that the leaves dissolved into a blur of green. She checked the time on the glowing face of her phone.

It was just as she was beginning to lose hope of Cloud ever turning up when there was a crackle in the branches and a sliver of silver through the leaves. Poppy felt her heart pounding. Even Charlie had let his book fall to his lap and was staring intently ahead.

They both watched breathlessly as Cloud poked his nose out of the trees. He sniffed the air, looking this way and that. Satisfied there was nothing to harm him he stepped slowly out into the clearing. Poppy and Charlie looked at each other and smiled. Poppy held her finger to her lips and Charlie nodded. He was determined not to do anything that might scare the pony this time.

Cloud was thinner than Poppy remembered and his coat looked dull. As he walked forwards, stopping every few paces to sniff the air, she saw he wasn't putting his full weight on his near hind leg. He hobbled over to the bucket, his neck stretched and his nostrils flared as he sniffed it. He was poised for flight and Poppy's heart was racing. Perhaps the smell of the pony nuts was too much to bear, perhaps he smelt the lingering scent of his old friend Chester, but after a few moments he began to eat noisily until the last nut had gone before taking another few uneven steps forward and drinking from the river.

The branches behind the two watching children rustled and Cloud looked up. He gave a start when he saw two pairs of eyes staring back at him from the other side of the river and Poppy immediately lowered her eyes, motioning Charlie to do the same. She held her breath, expecting him to turn on a sixpence and flee, but the pony stood watching them warily for a minute or two before limping slowly back off into the woods.

'I'm worried about him. He was lame, did you notice? And did you see how thin he looked?' Poppy asked her brother as they trudged back home through the dusk.

'At least he didn't run away as soon as he saw us, like he did before. So that's good, isn't it?' countered Charlie.

It was a start, thought Poppy as she settled down to sleep that night, the dead weight of a gently snoring Magpie pinning her feet down. But they still had a long way to go.

15

The following day Caroline drove Poppy and Charlie into Plymouth to buy school shoes, rucksacks, pens and pencil cases, yet more reminders that their holiday was almost over. Poppy had visited her new high school briefly during their first week in Devon and had left feeling overwhelmed at the size of both the school and the students. They had been shown around by the head boy, Jordan White. Jordan was so long and lanky he looked as if he'd been stretched on a rack in some medieval torture chamber. Charlie had spent the entire morning staring with interest at an angry cluster of spots on his chin. Poppy had squirmed with embarrassment when the puzzled six-year-old had asked the sixth-former, 'Isn't Jordan a girl's name?'

She wondered how on earth she'd ever manage to find her way around the countless corridors and classrooms with their unfamiliar odour of sweaty trainers and school dinners. She was beyond glad that Scarlett would be starting with her.

As they drove home across the moors, Poppy noticed for the first time that the trees were beginning to turn from vivid green to ochre. It wouldn't be long before the swallows disappeared and autumn arrived in their place. She thought of Cloud, facing the harsh Dartmoor winter not only lame but underweight, unlike the round, hardy Dartmoor ponies, whose coats were becoming thicker as the days grew shorter.

'So, are you two planning to go badger-watching this evening?' Caroline asked, as they crunched up the drive to home.

'Oh, yes please Mum.' Charlie cast a sidelong look at his sister. 'We found a hole in the roots of a tree that looked like it might be the entrance to a sett but even though we looked and looked we couldn't find any fresh poo, so it must be an old one.'

'At least it shows there must be badgers about. It's just a case of tracking them down,' said Poppy, who felt that Charlie's apparent interest in badger-watching was the perfect cover to see Cloud. When Charlie asked for something Caroline rarely said no.

That evening they ventured out to the wood an hour before dusk, Charlie taking two steps to Poppy's one as she strode purposefully across the field.

'I think we'll put the bucket in the same place, but tonight we'll sit on the tree instead of hiding behind it. We need him to start getting used to us,' Poppy told her brother.

'Cool. I've brought some pictures I've drawn of some panther paw prints so we can look for them as well,' Charlie produced a crumpled sheet of paper from deep inside the pocket of his shorts.

'You're not still on about that are you? We haven't even seen a badger in the woods, let alone a big cat.' Seeing the indignant look on her brother's face Poppy decided there was no point antagonising him. 'OK, on the way there and back we'll keep an eye out for paw prints, but while we're waiting for Cloud we need to be quiet and still. We can't afford to scare him.'

Charlie dipped his head in assent. Soon they reached the bend in the river and Poppy placed the bucket on the small beach. This time she'd added a scoop of soaked sugar beet to the pony nuts to give Cloud extra energy. To her surprise they only had to wait for ten minutes before the pony ventured out into the open. He headed for the food and wolfed it down, only looking up once he had licked the bucket clean. Keeping her voice low and reassuring Poppy began talking to him. She felt self-conscious at first but Cloud pricked his grey ears and watched her without moving. So she prattled on until her steady monologue became part of the familiar noises of the wood.

After what seemed like hours but was probably only minutes Cloud lowered his head and drank from the river. He gave them one last look, then, with a swish of his tail, turned and hobbled off. Poppy looked at Charlie, her green eyes shining. 'He's getting used to us, isn't he? He watched us for ages without moving. He knows we want to help him, I'm sure of it!'

But Charlie had more pressing matters on his mind. 'Yes, it's brilliant, Poppy. But can we please start looking for big cat prints now?'

~

OVER THE NEXT three evenings they gradually sat closer and closer to the bucket and when Cloud arrived Poppy kept up her chatter so he got used to the sound of her voice.

He was still hobbling but his stomach looked slightly rounder and his coat a shade less dull. He looked at them inquisitively as Poppy talked and she felt as though she was making real progress. She texted Scarlett every morning to update her, and wished the last precious days of summer away in her impatience to see Cloud each evening. She felt as though she was walking around in her own little bubble of happiness.

But on the fourth night Poppy's bubble was broken. She and Charlie arrived in the clearing and she placed the bucket on the beach, confident that Cloud would turn up as usual. But half an hour passed, then an hour, with no sign of the pony.

'Where is he?' she wailed, looking around desperately. 'I thought he was beginning to trust me. Is it something I've done wrong?' Perhaps he'd been hit by a car, caught by George Blackstone or fallen down a ditch and broken his leg…

She couldn't bear the thought of leaving in case Cloud was in danger. But it was getting late and she knew Caroline would be worried. She finally admitted defeat and they trudged back home.

'I'm sure he's OK,' said Charlie. 'He probably went off exploring and didn't realise what time it was. It happens to me all the time.'

But Poppy was on edge all evening and after a fitful night's sleep woke early. She let herself out of the house and ran all the way to the clearing. She could barely believe it when she found the bucket was empty. It gave her a glimmer of hope and made her more determined than ever to try again that night.

Charlie spent the day sneezing.

'No badger-watching for you tonight I'm afraid, angel. You need an early night,' said Caroline, as they sat down at the kitchen table to eat plates of pasta. Usually Caroline made her own pasta sauce but tonight it was out of a jar.

'Can I still go? I'm sure it's only a matter of time before we see a badger,' said Poppy, her face turned expectantly towards her stepmother.

She could see Caroline wavering and pressed home her advantage. 'It's not far into the wood from the Riverdale fence. And I'll take my mobile with me.'

'OK, but only for half an hour. It looks like rain and I don't want you going down with a cold as well, not with school starting so soon,' she said.

Rolling grey clouds were chasing each other across the horizon like a herd of monstrous sheep as Poppy left the house. Once in the clearing she sat with her back against an oak tree, just a few feet from the bucket. For an agonising half an hour, worry gnawed at her insides. Then she heard a familiar rustle in the undergrowth. She was sure it was the sound of a large animal making its way closer. The rustling stopped. Poppy held her breath and waited. Branches crackled and Cloud appeared. He saw Poppy and walked straight over to the bucket. Exhaling slowly, Poppy began talking to him as he munched away quietly.

'I'm going to stand up ever so slowly and see if you'll let me stroke you. I'll be quiet and gentle and I promise I won't hurt you. I want to help you, Cloud, but you have to trust me.' He looked at her, his flanks rising and falling with each breath and his ears flicking backwards and forwards. Something about the girl's voice stirred a deeply buried memory. This girl brought him food in a bucket that smelt of his old companion, the donkey who'd always made him feel safe. Cloud's leg ached and he felt tired. He could smell the first faint traces of winter in the air and he didn't feel ready for the long, cold, dark months ahead. He stood still as Poppy approached infinitesimally slowly, her eyes cast down, her voice calm and gentle. He flinched as she raised her hand to his flank but remained still as she stroked him softly, still talking to him. The outside world disappeared, leaving just the brown-haired girl and the dappled grey pony set in sharp relief against the emerald green backdrop of the trees.

'That's it, there's a good boy. You are so brave,' murmured Poppy as she stroked Cloud's neck and ran her hand over his withers and ribs. She felt him relax imperceptibly under her hand and he lowered his head and looked at her. A jolt of pure euphoria shot through her body and she struggled to keep her voice steady. She remembered the packet of Polos she had brought with her but as she slowly reached into her pocket for them the silence was pierced by the harsh ringtone of her mobile phone. Cloud's head shot up, he turned on the spot and cantered unevenly off into the woods. Poppy's elation shrivelled to dust and she looked in frustration at the screen.

Riverdale calling. Caroline! Furious and resentful, she pressed the green key. 'I was finally getting somewhere and you've just frightened the living daylights out of him,' she hissed without thinking.

'Sweetheart, I'm just checking you're OK. It's getting late.'

The hurt in Caroline's voice irritated Poppy intensely. 'There was no need to phone. I'm perfectly fine,' she snapped.

'Don't be like that, Poppy. I was worried about you. Are you on your way back yet? And who did I frighten the living daylights out of, anyway?'

Poppy reminded herself why she was supposed to be in the wood. 'The badger, of course. I saw him close up for the first time,' she lied.

'Charlie will be fed up he missed it but I'm glad you've had an exciting evening. Anyway, come home now. I don't want you out there on your own too late.'

Poppy felt like stamping her feet or hollering to the skies but knew it wouldn't make any difference. As usual Caroline had borne the brunt of her anger. She picked up the bucket and took one last look at the curtain of trees through which Cloud had disappeared. A slight movement caught her eye and she squinted in the half-light, struggling to see what it was. Two soft brown eyes on a ghostly grey face were staring back at her through the branches. Her heart sang as she realised that Cloud was still there.

'You brave, brave boy. I am so proud of you. And I'll see you tomorrow, Cloud,' she told him.

By the time Poppy opened the back door she was whistling cheerfully, her earlier frustration forgotten. Feeling benevolent towards Caroline she called, 'I'm back! Would you like a cup of tea?'

Her stepmother walked into the kitchen and leant against the doorframe as she watched Poppy. 'That would be lovely thanks, sweetheart. I was just going to make one myself.'

71

'How's Charlie feeling? Did he -? Hold on, have you been *crying*?' asked Poppy, noticing Caroline's red-rimmed eyes.

'No, not really. Well, yes. A little,' Caroline admitted. She looked discomfited and Poppy was lost for words. In all the years she had known Caroline she'd never seen her stepmother shed a single tear.

'What's wrong? It wasn't because I was cross when you rang, was it?' Poppy was incredulous.

'No. Well, not really. I've just been feeling a bit down recently and little things seem to set me off. It wasn't your fault. It's me.' Caroline shrugged her shoulders and avoided Poppy's eye as she crossed the kitchen to lift two dirty mugs off the draining board before rinsing them half-heartedly under the cold tap. Poppy looked around. Her head had been so full of Cloud that she hadn't noticed until now that the kitchen was a state. Their dinner plates were still on the table and the remains of the pasta sauce had congealed like a sticky red scab around the edge of the saucepan. Caroline followed her gaze and shrugged again. 'I know. It's a bit of a mess, but I was just coming out to tackle it.'

Poppy said firmly, 'No, you go and sit down. I'll sort this lot out and I'll bring your tea through in a minute.'

To her horror Caroline looked as if she might be about to burst into tears again, so Poppy turned and started clearing the table, feeling helpless in the face of her stepmother's distress. Poppy knew Caroline well enough to know something must be very wrong and she had no idea how to fix it. As she loaded the dishwasher she wished her dad was home. He always knew what to do.

T he bright autumnal days had been replaced by a relentless September mizzle that settled on the moors like a heavy over-coat and matched Caroline's bleak mood. Poppy was feeling under pressure. There were four days left before term started and the thought of school made her sick with nerves. To make matters worse the annual drift was just over three weeks away and although she knew she was gaining Cloud's trust it was a slow process and she was no nearer to catching him.

A sneezing and coughing Charlie was banned from joining Poppy on her nightly 'badger watch' until he was over his cold. One afternoon as he sat on the end of her bed, a string of green mucus hanging from each nostril, he asked her why she didn't tell Caroline about Cloud.

'She likes horses. She used to ride when she was your age, remember?'

Poppy wasn't sure why she kept Cloud a secret, if she was honest. Caroline probably would have understood and tried to help, although the way she was at the moment she didn't really seem to care much about anything. On the plus side her stepmother's malaise meant that Poppy was enjoying much more freedom than usual. On the down side the house was a tip, the washing basket was overflowing and they were existing on frozen ready meals and jars. In Twickenham Caroline had fed the children nothing but healthy, organic food and they'd snacked on pumpkin seeds and fruit. These days she just slapped whatever happened to be in the cupboard or freezer into the oven. This week they'd had turkey twizzlers, oven chips and baked beans for three nights running. Charlie was in heaven, but Poppy was missing the ready supplies of houmous and fresh vegetables. She had a spot on her forehead and a couple of nights ago had even Googled the symptoms of scurvy.

'I will tell her. Just not yet,' promised Poppy.

The next morning Charlie was feeling better and was itching to get out after being cooped up inside for so long. The rain had stopped and Poppy suggested they take a picnic lunch onto the moor. She wanted to see if they could find Cloud and Charlie was desperate to discover a paw print. Caroline, pleading the onset of a migraine, was curled up in bed with the curtains drawn when Poppy crept in. It was so out of character that Poppy was beginning to wonder if her stepmother had lost the plot.

'Caroline, would it be alright if we took a picnic up onto the tor? I promise not to let Charlie do anything silly.' Poppy spoke slowly and with emphasis, as if she were talking to a half-wit. Grateful to be left in peace Caroline said they could go as long as they stayed within sight of Riverdale and had Poppy's phone with them.

There wasn't much in the cupboards but Poppy cobbled together a picnic of sausage rolls, crisps, half a packet of bourbon biscuits and the last of the raisins, in the hope that they would provide at least a small dose of vitamin C. She packed the food into her rucksack along with a couple of bottles of water, Charlie scooped up his binoculars and camera and they set off.

'The ground is nice and soft so we should be able to see any prints quite easily,' said Charlie, as he hitched the camera strap up his shoulder.

'Can you also keep an eye out for Cloud's hoofprints? I'm sure he can't stay hidden in the wood all day. He must come out and graze sometimes. I was wondering if he ran with a particular herd of Dartmoor ponies,' Poppy said.

They skirted around the edge of the wood at the base of the tor, inspecting the ground as they walked as if they were forensic officers examining a crime scene. Charlie found a smudged hoofprint in the mud that could have been Cloud's but could equally have belonged to one of the larger Dartmoor ponies. They came across the same herd they had seen when they first moved to Riverdale, but there was no sign of the dappled grey pony.

'Shall we have our picnic now?' suggested Poppy, and they settled down in the shelter of a large boulder. She shared out the lunch and watched her brother with amusement as he dived on the food as if he hadn't eaten for weeks. She stretched her legs out in front of her as she leant back on the boulder. 'Can I borrow your binoculars, Charlie? I'll see if I can see Cloud.'

Poppy adjusted the lens until the view in front of her swam into focus and she started scanning the moor, sweeping from left to right as she looked for Cloud's familiar grey shape. But the vast expanse of green and purple moorland was deserted. Not a sheep, a rambler or a pony in sight. Even the crows had stopped wheeling overhead. The air was still and silent. Odd, thought Poppy, as she reached for a handful of raisins and munched thoughtfully.

'It feels a bit weird up here today, don't you think?' she asked her brother, who was lying on his front watching a grasshopper rubbing his spindly legs against gossamer wings.

He shrugged. 'What do you mean?'

'Like the calm before the storm. It's as if something's waiting to happen. Don't worry, I'm probably just imagining things.' She handed Charlie the binoculars and he trained them on the grasshopper. The insect sprang away in a series of staccato leaps, making him jump.

A mosquito buzzed angrily and Poppy waved it away. The air felt sticky and she could feel a slick of sweat across her forehead. 'Come on, let's make a move,' she told her brother. But Charlie was sitting as still as a statue, staring at the top of the tor. When she followed his gaze her hand flew to her mouth. Tucked behind another huge boulder was a black, distinctly feline-shaped head with small pointed ears and a jutting jaw.

'Look at that!' breathed Charlie. Poppy motioned to his camera. 'Take a picture. Quickly!' she said in sotto voce. He lifted the camera, zoomed in as far as he could and pressed the shutter a dozen times. The animal looked in their direction then jumped with a neat spring onto the rock.

'Oh no, the battery's run out,' said Charlie. He swapped the camera for his binoculars and they watched as, with a flick of its long tail, the panther-like creature bounded off the rock with one graceful leap and disappeared behind the tor. Brother and sister looked at each other in disbelief.

Charlie was the first to speak. 'Poppy, this is just amazing. A big cat, living on our tor! Tell me I'm not dreaming. You did see it too, didn't you?' he asked her, suddenly uncertain.

'I saw something, goodness only knows what, but it did look like a cat,' she admitted. 'We need to go home and look at those photos.' She shoved the remains of their picnic into her rucksack and they scrambled down the rock-strewn hill towards Riverdale.

Caroline was in the kitchen tidying up unenthusiastically.

'Mum! You're not going to believe this! We've found a big cat,' shouted Charlie.

'Really? Well, that is exciting. Was it a lion, a tiger or a leopard?'

'No, we really did see one, didn't we Poppy?' He glanced at his sister for reassurance and Poppy looked at Caroline. 'We saw something large and black. I don't know what it was but it definitely wasn't a sheep or a Dartmoor pony. But Charlie's taken some pictures so we can show you.'

Caroline was glad of a distraction after spending the morning trying and failing to shift the feelings of lethargy and unhappiness that at times threatened to drown her. She took out her laptop, booted it up and slipped in the memory card from Charlie's camera. Together they watched the screen as Caroline downloaded the photos. There was the tor, so familiar to them by now. Charlie pointed to the boulder where they had seen the animal. 'Look! There it is,' he cried with relief.

Indistinct though it was, they could definitely make out the cat-shaped head. Poppy gasped. 'There - look. You can see its tail.' And sure enough, a long black tail stuck out from the side of the rock.

'Well I never,' said Caroline in amazement. 'That really is extraordinary. I wonder if it could be a panther or something?'

'Of course it is!' replied Charlie hotly. 'I told you there were big cats on Dartmoor and I was right. This must be the same one Scarlett's dad saw. He'd believe me,' he said, his bottom lip wobbling.

'I believe you, Charlie,' said Poppy quietly. Although they had been a couple of hundred metres away she was in no doubt that what they'd seen was some kind of large cat.

'What do we do now?' demanded her brother, who was jumping from one foot to another, his blond hair tousled and his blue eyes shining.

'What do you mean?' Caroline asked, puzzled.

'Well, do we call the police or the zoo - or do we start building the big cat trap I designed ages ago?'

'I suppose we could call the Tavistock Herald,' Caroline suggested. She had started out as a junior reporter on a local paper before moving to the BBC and knew they loved a big cat story - especially if there was a photo involved. The fact that a six-year-old had been behind the lens was the icing on the cake.

'Yesssss!' Charlie punched the air with his fist. 'Fantastic idea, Mum. Can we do it now?'

'Sweetheart, it's gone five o'clock. There won't be anyone in the newsroom until the morning, but we'll do it then, I promise.'

The intrigue brightened Caroline's mood and they spent a happy evening playing Monopoly and eating crisps in front of the fire. It was almost like old times and Poppy felt some of the unease she had been feeling about her stepmother's frame of mind lifting.

'I really must do a big food shop tomorrow. We'll pop into the Herald offices afterwards if you like,' Caroline offered and Charlie beamed.

'Is there any chance I could go and see Tory while you two are at the supermarket? I wanted to apologise for not saying goodbye when she came for tea. With school starting on Monday I'm not going to get another chance for ages,' Poppy said.

'Yes, that's fine. But I still don't understand what happened between the two of you. I can't imagine Tory upsetting anyone; she's so lovely.'

Poppy swallowed. Admitting she was wrong was not something she was good at. 'It was my fault. She was trying to help and I was mean to her. But I don't want to talk about it,' and, avoiding an inquiring look from Caroline, she picked up the dice, threw them and landed herself in jail.

T his time Poppy was prepared when she turned up at the old people's flats and walked straight bang into Mrs Parker.

'You're back, I see,' said the warden, who was wearing a fitted Royal blue suit with hefty shoulder pads that matched her newly blue-rinsed hair.

'Yes, I certainly am,' said Poppy firmly. She'd decided that morning to take no nonsense from the old battleaxe. 'So is Tory in?'

Mrs Parker was taken aback by the girl's assertiveness. 'Well, I dare say she is as her ladyship hasn't stepped foot outside her flat for the last week. She even missed her card night on Friday. Not that it was any loss. I convinced everyone to try a few hands of bridge instead of that dreadful poker she insists on playing. So much more *appropriate*,' she sniffed.

'She's not ill is she?' asked Poppy, lines of concern furrowing her forehead.

'No, she's not ill, but she's not herself,' conceded Mrs Parker. 'Not that she'll tell me what's wrong, of course. Says I shouldn't stick my nose in, I ask you. Perhaps you'll have more luck.'

Poppy headed down the corridor towards Tory's front door. She knocked and waited. She heard the volume of the television being turned down and the sound of shuffling. She rehearsed her apology one last time.

Tory opened the door. 'Ah, Poppy. Come in.' Poppy felt that the welcome was more muted than before and she cursed herself for her behaviour. After all, her friend had only been trying to help. She started gabbling an apology but Tory held up a hand to silence her.

'It's alright, pet. Everyone says things they don't mean every now and then. The fact that you've come to say sorry is enough for me. Let's forget it ever happened.'

Flushed with gratitude, Poppy realised that she could learn a lot from Tory. She sat down and they chatted about the weather and school and Poppy told Tory about the cat-like animal they had seen the previous day.

Tory wasn't surprised. 'I've never seen any big cats myself, but it's true that people used to have leopards and panthers in private collections. Then local councils decided they needed licences to keep them and I dare say a few were released into the wild. I bet Charlie's pleased.'

'You're not wrong there. He's beyond excited. He hasn't stopped talking about it, and now he's convinced he's going to be front page news in the Herald. He'll be unbearable,' said Poppy, not minding in the least.

She thought of Caroline staring mindlessly out of the kitchen window and remembered why she had come. 'Tory, I need to talk to you about something.'

'Is it Cloud?'

'No. Actually I want to ask your advice about Caroline.'

Tory raised her eyebrows. This was a turn up for the books. 'What's the matter, pet?'

'You were right and I'm sorry again for storming off. I've noticed Caroline hasn't been herself and since the day you came to lunch she's been even worse. The house is a tip, she's feeding us non-stop junk food and I keep finding her just staring out of the window. She always used to be so cheerful. Annoyingly cheerful, most of the time. But it's like we've got her identical twin living with us. She looks the same, she sounds the same, but this one doesn't seem to care about anything. And she's forgotten how to smile.'

Poppy breathed out deeply, relieved to have voiced the concerns that had been building over the past few weeks.

'I think she's probably suffering from depression,' said Tory matter-of-factly. 'Has she ever been like this before?'

'Never. But I had a friend at school whose mum was depressed and had to take tablets for it. She called them her happy pills.'

'They're called antidepressants. I had post natal depression after Jo was born, although we didn't call it that in those days, it was just the baby blues.' Poppy looked at Tory in surprise. 'It's more common than you think, you know. But it is treatable. We'll keep an eye on her for a couple of weeks and if she's still no better perhaps we need to convince her to go to see her GP.'

Poppy smiled at Tory gratefully. 'Thank you. I didn't want to worry Dad – he's too far away to do anything anyway. And Charlie's too young to notice anything's wrong. He's just happy to have chips for tea every night.'

'I'm glad to help, pet. And if you are in the slightest bit worried about Caroline phone me. Don't feel as though you have to sort it all out on your own. I'll do whatever I can to help. Now, should you be making a move? I don't want to make you late for Caroline and Charlie.'

Poppy said goodbye, glad that she and Tory were friends again, and set off for the café where she had arranged to meet her stepmother and brother.

'They're going to send a reporter and a photographer to interview us tomorrow!' Charlie said, the moment she sat down.

'Us?' she replied, puzzled. This was Charlie's obsession, not hers.

'You were there, too. I'm only six so they want you there to collaborate my story,' he said importantly.

'Corroborate,' corrected Caroline gently and Poppy stole a quick look at her stepmother. There were still dark shadows under her eyes and she looked wan, but at least she seemed to be interested in the big cat story. Perhaps she was over the worst.

Later that afternoon Poppy cornered Charlie in his bedroom, where he was making a complicated three dimensional version of his big cat trap with Lego and K'Nex.

'You need to help me clean the house before the people from the Herald come tomorrow. It's a pigsty,' she told him.

Normally the mere suggestion of helping around the house invoked a storm of protest, but Charlie was so excited about the reporter's arrival that, for once, he was happy to oblige.

'I'll do the kitchen. You can make a start on the lounge. We'll get up early tomorrow and do it. It'll be a nice surprise for Caroline,' said Poppy.

Unaccountably the thought of helping her stepmother gave her a warm, fuzzy feeling. It was too weird for words.

18

Charlie was as good as his word and the next morning he was already sitting at the kitchen table eating a bowl of cereal when Poppy came in from feeding Chester. She gave him the beeswax polish, a duster and a set of instructions.

'The first job is to tidy up. The old newspapers can go in the recycling bin and put any grubby clothes you find in the washing basket. I'll put a wash on later.' Poppy eyed a dirty sock, lolling like a diseased rodent under the sofa. 'Bring the dirty mugs, glasses and plates into the kitchen and plump up the cushions on the sofa and chairs. Then you can dust. Once you've done that I'll bring you the vacuum cleaner. By the time you've finished the place should look like new. Got all that?'

'Yes,' said Charlie, counting the jobs off on his fingers. 'I'm to put the grubby clothes in the recycling, polish the glasses and plump up the news-papers. Only joking,' he added hastily, seeing the exasperated expression on his sister's face.

It took almost an hour for Poppy to load the dishwasher, wipe down the surfaces, clean the sink, empty the bin and sweep and clean the kitchen floor. She was pleasantly surprised when she went into the lounge to inspect Charlie's handiwork. The wooden floor gleamed and the rug in front of the fire was no longer covered with crumbs. Cushions had been plumped and the mess tidied away. Charlie was beaming with pride.

'Well done, little bro. Caroline will be pleased.'

'I certainly am.' Caroline's voice made Poppy jump. She was standing at the doorway, with a smile on her face that for once reached her eyes. 'The kitchen and lounge look amazing. Aren't you two good to me. Come here, let me give you both a hug.'

Charlie ran straight into her arms. Poppy hesitated. Being the outsider was her default setting, the part she had chosen to play. But Caroline beckoned her close and she found herself walking slowly over, as if pulled by an invisible thread.

'Thank-you, darling, I expect it was all your doing. What a lovely surprise,' she murmured into Poppy's hair as she held the two children close.

'It was Poppy's idea. I just did what I was told, as usual,' admitted Charlie with a grin. 'I did a good job though, didn't I? Did you see how shiny the floor is now?'

For once Poppy allowed herself to relax into her stepmother's embrace. The three of them clung together until Charlie started fidgeting and wriggled out of their arms. Caroline took Poppy's face in her hands and tilted it up to hers. 'You don't know how much that means to me. Thank-you, sweetheart,' she said softly, and kissed her forehead before letting her go. Poppy wasn't sure if Caroline was referring to the clean-up operation or the hug, but realised that for once it didn't actually matter.

A rap at the door sent Charlie into orbit. 'They're here! They're here! Quick, where's the photo?' he shouted, and they swung into action, Caroline going to answer the door, Poppy grabbing the laptop from the dining room and Charlie bouncing off the walls in excitement.

The reporter and photographer from the Tavistock Herald were waiting on the doorstep with polite smiles on their faces.

'Mrs McKeever?' inquired the shorter of the two. He glanced down at his notebook. 'And you must be Charlie and Poppy. I'm Stanley Smith, though people call me Sniffer. And this is our photographer Henry Blossom, though people call him Henry.' No-one smiled at the joke.

'Pleased to meet you,' said the photographer, who was a tall, thin man with a camera slung around his neck, a camera bag on his shoulder and a long-suffering expression on his face. Caroline shook their hands and they followed her into the lounge, Charlie and Poppy in their wake.

'So, we'll have a chat and then go out onto the moor to see where you said you saw this 'ere puma, shall we?' said Sniffer, winking at Charlie.

'I didn't say I saw the cat, I actually saw it. And I don't think it was a puma, I think it was a jaguar,' answered Charlie with spirit, and Poppy saw shades of their dad in her brother. Charlie may have only been six, but he wasn't about to be patronised by a middle-aged hack from a local paper, not when his dad was a famous war correspondent for the BBC. Sniffer didn't endear himself to either of the children when he shoved a sleeping Magpie off the comfiest of the armchairs so he could sit down. The cat shot him a look of pure disdain and stalked off to the corner of the room, where he proceeded to wash himself, stopping every now and then to look daggers at the reporter.

'Tell me what happened on Thursday then, Charlie,' Sniffer said, thumbing through his notebook until he reached a blank page.

Charlie recounted how they'd decided to have a picnic on their tor. 'Usually there are sheep everywhere but on Thursday there weren't any. I thought that was a bit strange.'

Poppy couldn't remember Charlie saying as much at the time, but she kept the thought to herself. She didn't want to rain on his parade.

'Anyway, we were just about to go when something caught my eye. I saw the head of a big cat poking up from behind this huge boulder. I told Poppy to look and I got out my camera and took some photos. Then the cat jumped onto the boulder and we got a really good look at it. It was massive!' said Charlie.

'Unfortunately the camera battery ran out before the animal jumped onto the rock, but Charlie did manage to take a few pictures before it packed up,' said Caroline, swivelling the laptop so the two men could see the screen. They both leant forward, poring over the photos. Within seconds the scepticism vanished from Sniffer's face.

'Interesting, very interesting,' he said, half to himself. He turned to Charlie. 'You could have something here, young man. I have contacts on the nationals and they love a genuine big cat story. We might get some mileage from this.'

'Don't forget where your loyalties lie, Stanley,' said Henry. 'The Herald has the exclusive.'

Fortunately Caroline knew the ways of local journalists who liked to make a bit of extra cash selling stories to the national newspapers. 'And you'll not be forgetting that these are Charlie's pictures, taken on Charlie's camera and are therefore his copyright,' she said pleasantly.

A nasty expression flitted across Sniffer's face, although Henry Blossom looked at her admiringly. 'Too true, Mrs McKeever,' he said, in his gentle Devon burr. 'I'll make sure no-one takes advantage of him,' he added, eyeing his colleague pointedly. Caroline smiled her thanks and the five of them headed outside and up onto the tor, where Henry took pictures of Charlie and Poppy by the boulder where they'd seen the big cat.

'When will the story be in the paper?' demanded Charlie.

'I want to show the photos to the head cat keeper at the local zoo first to get his take on them. But the story should make the next edition,' replied Sniffer.

'Cool! Do you think I'll end up on the telly like my dad?'

Sniffer stood stock still, his eyes fixed on Charlie. He reminded Poppy of a hound that had just picked up the scent of a fox. 'Who's your dad then, young man?' the reporter asked, thinking privately that this story was getting better and better.

'Mike McKeever. He's a war correspondent for the BBC,' Charlie said proudly.

Sniffer took a pen from behind his ear and made a few more indecipherable squiggles in his notebook. 'Good, good. Right then, Henry. We'd better be heading back.'

'Are you sure you wouldn't like a cup of tea first?' asked Caroline.

'Aye, that would be champion, Mrs McKeever,' said Henry Blossom, slinging his camera bag over his shoulder and giving Caroline a wide smile. Poppy noticed that he had a lop-sided gait, the result of years spent hefting about bags laden with lenses.

Back at the house Caroline switched on the kettle and disappeared into the lounge to light the fire. Henry and Charlie joined Poppy in the kitchen. Sniffer stood outside the back door among a pile of abandoned wellies trying, without much success, to get a signal on his mobile phone. Poppy was setting out a row of mugs and dropping a teabag in each when she heard a cry and an almighty crash from the lounge. Her stomach flipped over. Henry and Charlie stopped talking and were rooted to the spot. Poppy dropped the teabags and rushed into the lounge. Caroline was lying on the wooden floor, clutching her left wrist. Her face was white. 'I think I've broken my arm. It's the floor – it's so slippery,' she gasped.

Poppy took a look and flinched. Caroline's hand was bent at an unnatural angle to her arm and her wrist was already starting to swell. She looked as if she was about to pass out. Suddenly the reassuring presence of Henry Blossom loomed behind them. 'Oh dear. What have we here?' he said in his gentle voice.

Assessing the situation in a flash, he started giving instructions. 'Right Poppy, where's the phone? I think we're probably going to need an ambulance. Charlie, you go and find a blanket for your mum. We don't want her going into shock.'

He knelt down beside Caroline. 'I think it's safe to say you've broken your wrist. And a proper job you've made of it too, by the looks of things. We're going to call an ambulance. You're going to need to go to hospital. And the paramedics will be able to give you something for the pain.'

'What about the children?' whispered Caroline, as Henry took a patchwork blanket from Charlie's hands and wrapped it gently around her shoulders.

'Don't you worry. I'll stay with them until we get something sorted. I'll get Sniffer to ring the boss and let her know. She'll understand. Is there anyone else who can look after them until you get back from hospital?'

'My husband's in the Middle East. I could ask my sister but she has children of her own and lives in Bromley anyway. It would take her hours to get here.'

Poppy thought. 'What about Tory? She'd come and look after us.'

'Tory Wickens? Do you have her number, Poppy? I'll give her a ring once the ambulance is here and arrange for her to come over,' said Henry.

Satisfied with the arrangements Caroline slumped down against the sofa and they waited together in silence for the ambulance.

19

The next few hours passed by in a blur. The ambulance arrived and two cheery paramedics took charge, strapping Caroline's wrist into a sling and giving her gas and air for the pain. Henry Blossom was as good as his word and phoned Tory, who promised to ring her nephew at once to bring her over. Sniffer prowled around the lounge, picking up photos of the McKeevers and examining the family's assorted curios and ornaments, from fossils found by the children to Caroline's collection of old Chinese vases. Poppy watched the journalist, seeing the room through his eyes. Caroline had spent a week painting the walls and sanding and waxing the floorboards. Two huge squashy damson-coloured sofas, a battered leather armchair and their eclectic collection of painted furniture were arranged around the open fireplace. Patchwork throws and cushions the colour of jewels made the room warm and welcoming. Poppy realised with a jolt that Riverdale already felt more of a home to her than their house in Twickenham ever had.

Her stepmother's face was still ashen as the paramedics accompanied her to the ambulance. Grimacing with pain at every step, Caroline thanked Henry, who had promised to stay with Poppy and Charlie until Tory arrived. Caroline turned to the children, who both looked slightly shell-shocked. 'Goodbye, angels. I'll be back as soon as I can. Be good for Tory, won't you?'

'Of course we will!' said Charlie, slipping his hand into Poppy's. 'Anyway, Poppy will look after me, won't you Poppy?' He looked at his big sister trustingly.

Poppy smiled into his blue eyes, so like Caroline's, and her heart gave a funny twist. She squeezed his hand and replied, 'It goes without saying, little brother.' She looked shyly at Caroline. 'I hope everything goes OK at the hospital. Will you ring and let us know how you get on?'

'Of course I will, sweetheart. Don't you worry about me – I'll be fine.' And she stepped gingerly into the ambulance and was gone.

'Your mum's a brave lass,' observed Henry. For the first time in her life Poppy didn't feel the urge to correct him. 'Yes, she is,' she said quietly.

While they waited for Tory to arrive Poppy finished making Henry's cup of tea and went into the lounge to straighten the rug where Caroline had fallen. As she walked over to the window she, too, almost lost her footing. The floor was as slippery as an ice rink. She looked at the gleaming wooden floorboards and suddenly everything was clear. Poppy tracked her brother down in his bedroom, where he was morosely lining up his action heroes in height order.

'Charlie – when you tidied the lounge this morning, how did you clean the floor?' she asked gently.

'I hoovered the rug and used that polish you gave me on the wooden bit of the floor of course,' he said, not looking up from his toys.

'I thought so,' said Poppy. 'Probably best not to use polish on the floor again next time. Makes it a bit slippy,' she added, as tactfully as she could. 'I think I'd better go and wash it off before Tory arrives. We don't want her taking a tumble as well.'

Charlie was humming tunelessly to himself, his head bent over the Incredible Hulk and his red Power Ranger. Poppy left him to it. There was no point making him feel guilty for causing Caroline's fall – he'd only been trying to help. Caroline would see the funny side, she felt sure.

Poppy's stomach was beginning a low level rumbling by the time she heard the crunch of gravel and a knock at the front door. She flew into the hall and threw the door open. There on the doorstep was Tory, leaning on her sticks, a look of concern on her weathered old face. Behind her, her nephew was unloading carrier bags from the boot of his car.

'Hello Poppy, I thought you might not have much in the house so we popped into the supermarket on our way. That's why we're a bit late.'

'Fantastic! I'm starving. In fact I'm so hungry I could eat a Dartmoor pony!' said Charlie, who had appeared in the hallway. 'Only joking – it would probably be a bit chewy. What have you got us for tea?'

Henry had followed Charlie into the hall. Poppy noticed that he walked with a stoop even when he wasn't carrying his camera bag.

'Hello Tory, long time no see,' he said, holding out his hand.

'Come here, you daft twit. Give me a hug,' Tory commanded, and Henry, looking slightly abashed, did as he was told. Tory watched the children's astonished faces with amusement. 'I've known Henry since he was a baby,' she said. 'His mother was a great friend of mine. I met Margaret in the maternity ward and Jo and Henry were born within hours of each other. We always hoped they'd end up getting married but it wasn't to be,' she said wistfully.

They chatted for a while until Tory's nephew started making noises about getting back before it got too dark and Henry reluctantly stood up and said he should also make a move.

'Now are you sure you're going to be OK looking after the children, Tory? Will you be able to manage the stairs?' he asked.

'I lived here on my own until the beginning of July, Henry Blossom,' she replied tartly. 'We'll be absolutely fine. Poppy can show me where everything is, can't you, pet?'

They waved the two cars off and went into the kitchen where Tory, with Poppy acting as her sous chef, cooked sausages and mash with peas and onion gravy.

'That was yum,' declared Charlie, yawning extravagantly. He stuck his thumb in his mouth and watched sleepily while Tory cleared the table and Poppy began loading the dishwasher. Poppy felt a wave of responsibility sweep over her. Both children were so used to their dad's trips abroad that his absences were part of the fabric of family life, but Caroline was a permanent fixture. The only time Poppy could recall her stepmother being away for any length of time was when she went into hospital to have Charlie six-and-a-half years ago.

Poppy remembered how excited everyone had been, how they assumed she was looking forward to the baby coming. Truth was, she'd dreaded it. The thought of another girl coming into their home and commanding all her dad's attention was beyond endurance. When she found out the interloper was a boy it was a little easier to bear and, despite initial resistance on her part, her baby brother gradually wormed his way into her affections. Charlie was an easy baby with a gummy smile that sent old ladies into clucky raptures. But he only had eyes for one person – his big sister. His blue eyes followed Poppy adoringly around the room and as soon as he could crawl he became her shadow. Occasionally having a kid brother got on her nerves but after five years as an only child it was nice to always have someone to play with, even if the games did tend to involve trains and super heroes.

'Come on Charlie. Let's take you to bed before you fall asleep at the table,' she said now, and he followed her obediently up to his room.

By the time she came back down half an hour later Tory was settled on one of the sofas with some knitting, the clicking needles the only sound. Poppy looked at the clock on the oak beam above the fireplace. It was almost eight o'clock and too late to go and see Cloud now. The day had been so filled with drama that she hadn't given the pony a second thought for hours, she realised guiltily.

'We never did get a chance to talk about Cloud, did we? Have you seen him again?' Tory said, as if reading her mind.

Poppy played with a strand of her hair while she deliberated whether or not to tell Tory about her attempts to catch the pony and hide him from the drift. Deciding they both had Cloud's best interests at heart she took the plunge and told Tory about her forays into the wood under the pretext of badger-watching, the pony's poor condition and the buckets of food he had wolfed down.

'The last few times I've really felt I've made progress. He's let me stroke him and I'm sure he's beginning to trust me. But the drift is only two weeks away and I start school on Monday. I'm running out of time,' she said despondently. Tory stopped knitting and her eyes took on a faraway look. Poppy thought back to the conversation Caroline had overheard in the post office all those weeks ago. Tory must have hidden the pony every autumn to stop him being rounded up with the rest of the Dartmoor ponies.

'Tory?' she began, biting her bottom lip until it turned white.

'Yes, pet?' The needles resumed their rhythmic clicking.

'I know you'd have hated it if Cloud had ended up back at George Blackstone's farm. I was wondering…did you hide him here at Riverdale?'

Tory stopped knitting again and looked at Poppy. She reminded her so much of Caitlyn and it was clear to her that Poppy and Cloud had some kind of connection, just as Caitlyn and Cloud had once had. Taking a deep breath, Tory made a decision she hoped she wouldn't live to regret.

'Yes, pet, I did. Saving her beloved Cloud was the one thing I could still do for Caitlyn, so that's what I did.'

'But he's so nervous around people. How on earth did you manage to catch him?'

Tory smiled sadly. 'Think about it logically, Poppy. The answer is right under your nose.'

20

'What do you mean?' asked Poppy.

Tory laid her knitting on her lap. 'I think I told you that when Cloud first arrived at Riverdale he was incredibly nervous around people?'

Poppy nodded.

'Gaining his trust took a long time. He spent the first few days cowering in the corner of his stable. Caitlyn spent hours sitting in there with him, trying to tempt him closer with carrots and Polos, but he wouldn't go near her. I was beginning to think I'd made a terrible mistake, although Caitlyn refused to give up on him. But then someone you know very well helped us make the breakthrough.' Her eyes twinkled.

'Chester?' breathed Poppy.

'Yes,' smiled Tory. 'Of course he was much younger in those days and loved to be at the centre of things. While Caitlyn sat in the corner of Cloud's stable Chester would rest his head over the stable door, watching this dappled grey bag of nerves in the corner. Chester had an amazingly calming effect on Cloud and as time went on Cloud gradually came out of his shell and started to trust us all. By the time Caitlyn was able to handle Cloud he and Chester were inseparable. Chester was by Cloud's side when we first tacked him up, when we long-reined him, lunged him and when Cait eventually rode him for the first time.' Tory could still picture the pony and donkey standing side by side at the paddock gate as they waited patiently for Caitlyn to arrive at Riverdale.

'It meant that when Cait and Cloud started competing we always had to take Chester too, but Chester didn't mind – he thought it was a great adventure. He became a familiar sight at all the local shows and loved the attention. And as long as Cloud had Chester and Caitlyn he was alright.'

'So how did Chester help you catch Cloud?'

'That first autumn after Caitlyn died I knew I had to hide Cloud from the drift so he didn't end up back at Blackstone's. So I went out onto the moor to try to catch him.'

Poppy held her breath.

'I'd seen him in the distance once or twice so I thought he had stayed fairly close to Riverdale, whether to be near Chester or in the hope that Caitlyn would come back for him one day I'll never know.' Tory sniffed loudly. 'But try as I might, he wouldn't let me near him. Then one night not long before the drift I was lying awake in bed worrying what to do when I heard Chester braying and suddenly I had the answer.'

'So you took Chester out onto the moor to see if Cloud would follow him home?'

'That's exactly what I did. The very next morning Chester and I went to the end of Riverdale wood. You know where the trees start to peter out at the foot of the tor?'

Poppy nodded. It was close to where she and Charlie had seen the big cat.

'Apart from a few sheep it was deserted but I had a funny feeling that Cloud would turn up. We waited for over an hour before he finally appeared. I think he'd been hiding in the trees watching us for a while. He and Chester were so pleased to see each other and when I started leading Chester home Cloud followed, all the way back into Chester's stable where he stayed until after the drift. That's how I caught him.'

'But why did you let him go again once the drift was over?' demanded Poppy.

'It was the right thing to do. He belonged to George Blackstone, don't forget. Keeping him would have been theft. But every year Chester and I led him back to Riverdale and kept him safe.'

'What did you think would happen to him this year, Tory?'

The old woman sighed. 'It's been worrying me for months, pet. What with leaving Riverdale, missing Chester so much and fretting about Cloud I haven't really been myself.' She looked close to tears.

'Couldn't someone have helped you?' Poppy asked more gently.

'I thought about trying to talk to Jo, to see if she would, but she hasn't spoken to me for years and she still blames Cloud for Cait's death anyway. She wouldn't throw a bucket of water on him if he was on fire. I can't stop thinking how disappointed Caitlyn would have been in me.'

Poppy wasn't a demonstrative child but Tory looked so desolate that she reached over and hugged her. Tory batted away a couple of tears that were rolling slowly down her lined face and muttered, 'Don't mind me, pet'. She smelt of talcum powder and peppermint and her jumper, the colour of heather, felt as soft as down against Poppy's cheek. She only drew back when she realised that one of Tory's knitting needles was poking uncomfortably in her ribcage.

'You have me now. I'll take Chester out onto the moor to see Cloud and we'll bring him back to Riverdale together.'

Tory was about to reply when the phone rang. 'It'll probably be Caroline,' said Poppy, dashing over to the oak sideboard and grabbing the handset.

'Poppy, it's me,' said her stepmother. She sounded echoey - as if she was standing in the middle of a vast aircraft hangar. 'They've brought a phone to my bed. I'm in the orthopaedic ward. It's full of young men who've fallen off their motorbikes. But they're all very chatty,' she added inconsequentially. Poppy wondered how many painkillers Caroline had been given.

'So how's your wrist?' she asked.

'Oh, that. They've X-rayed it and it's a clean break, luckily. They finished plastering it about half an hour ago. I am now officially plastered,' she laughed. Poppy raised her eyebrows. 'But unfortunately I must have banged my head when I fell because they say I've got mild concussion. Anyway, enough of me. How are you and Charlie?'

'Oh, Charlie's happy – he's gone to bed on a full stomach. I'm keeping Tory company,' she smiled at her old friend, who had taken up her needles again and was poised to start clicking. 'Do you know when you'll be back?' Poppy asked, thinking of her plans for the morning.

'They're going to keep me in for the night because of the concussion. Will you all be OK? I'm going to try and ring your dad now to see if there's any chance he can come home early. In fact I'd better try now before I run out of credit. I'll ring you again in the morning to let you know when I'll be back. Night night darling.' And the phone went dead.

'Everything alright?' Tory asked.

'Yes, she seems a bit spaced out but otherwise fine. Much more cheerful, actually. It sounds as though she should be back some time tomorrow. So I've decided. Chester and I are going to bring Cloud home tomorrow morning before she gets back.'

Before she went to bed Poppy let herself out of the back door, slipped on her wellies and went to see Chester. She flicked a switch and the single bulb hanging from the roof cast a yellow glow over the stable where he stood chewing hay.

'You and I have an important job to do tomorrow,' she told the donkey, rubbing his velvety soft nose. A kaleidoscope of butterflies was sending her stomach into turmoil as nerves and excitement started to build.

Chester, completely oblivious to the rescue mission ahead of them, eyed her calmly and carried on munching.

21

Poppy woke late after a fitful night's sleep. When she'd finally managed to doze off she'd dreamt of black panthers stalking grey ponies to a soundtrack of rushing water. Opening the curtains she realised why – heavy rain was falling in sheets from a thundery grey sky. The tor was completely concealed by low cloud curling around the trees at the edge of the Riverdale wood. Poppy gave an involuntary shiver. It was what Caroline called Hound of the Baskervilles weather. Unable to shift a sense of unease that had inexplicably settled on her like the mist on the tor, she followed the smell of toast downstairs and into the kitchen where Tory was unloading the dishwasher.

'Hello Poppy, there you are. I thought I'd leave you to lie in. Thought you needed a decent night's sleep after the dramas of yesterday,' she said.

Poppy glanced at the clock on the oven. Ten to nine. 'Has Charlie had his breakfast already?' she asked, sitting down at the kitchen table.

'No, pet. I didn't want to disturb him either. Poor lamb looked all in last night. He's having a lie in, too.'

'Crikey. I don't think I've ever known Charlie to stay in bed past seven o'clock. Usually he's the first up.'

Poppy yawned and smiled her thanks at Tory as the old woman placed a plate of buttered toast in front of her, although the butterflies in her stomach made the thought of eating impossible.

'I don't think it's a good idea to go out on the moor today, Poppy. Dartmoor can be a dangerous place at the best of times, but in weather like this it's treacherous. I'd never forgive myself if anything happened to you or Charlie while I'm looking after you both.'

Poppy was silent. There was no way a bit of rain was going to stop her rescuing Cloud, but she didn't want to worry Tory. 'Perhaps it'll brighten up later,' she ventured.

'Perhaps,' replied Tory, unconvinced. 'What would you like to do this morning? Shall I teach you poker?'

'Yes, that would be fun. Thanks for breakfast but I'm not really hungry. I'll go and clean my teeth and then feed Chester,' she said.

On her way back from the bathroom Poppy glanced into Charlie's bedroom and saw the silhouette of his sleeping shape under the Thomas the Tank Engine duvet cover that, aged six, he now considered too babyish for words. She went back downstairs, fed Chester, then spent a companionable hour with Tory learning about flushes and five card draws, poker faces and tells. When ten o'clock had been and gone and there was still no sign of her brother Poppy put down yet another losing hand and said, 'Tory, before you beat me again, I'm going to check on Charlie. I won't be a minute.'

She crept into Charlie's room and peered into his bed. Expecting to see his tousled blond head on the pillow, his thumb in his mouth, she gasped in shock when she saw the head of his biggest teddy bear instead. She whipped off the duvet and found Caroline's fluffy cream dressing gown laying rolled up where her sleeping brother should have been. She looked wildly about the room as if he was going to jump out of his wardrobe and surprise her with a triumphant 'Gotcha!' But there was no sign of the six-year-old, just the usual jumble of dirty clothes, bits of Lego scattered like fallen leaves and the line of action heroes he'd set up the previous afternoon, their moulded plastic faces inscrutable. Her eyes fell on a piece of paper on his pillow. It must have slipped underneath the bear's head when she pulled off the duvet. Scrawled in Charlie's spidery handwriting was one word. Poppy.

She grabbed the note, unfolded it and, with mounting anxiety, read:

Deer Poppy,
    I don't think sniffer bel, beleaf, beleived me when I said I had seen a real live

big cat. I have gone to find it and get a better picture for the paper. I have taken
some sausages to use as bait. I will be back before tea.
    Charlie

Poppy grabbed a handful of the dressing gown and lifted it to her cheek. The soft towelling smelt of Caroline and she clung to it, wishing her calm, capable stepmother was downstairs and not in a hospital bed ten miles away. Magpie padded softly into the room and jumped up next to Poppy. The cat had an uncanny knack of making an appearance whenever anything interesting was happening. His two stomachs swinging beneath him, Magpie regarded Poppy with interest, waiting for her next move.

'You know what they say about curiosity, Magpie,' muttered Poppy under her breath.

What should she do? The moor was no place for a daredevil six-year-old on a day like today. She didn't want to worry Tory, of that she was certain. She had no idea how long Charlie had been gone but he may not have got far. In an instant she made up her mind.

'I'll go after him,' she whispered to the cat, who was now settling down for yet another nap, making himself comfortable on Caroline's dressing gown. He tucked his head beneath his tail and within seconds was snoring softly, his stomachs rising and falling in time to his breathing. Poppy ran into her room, grabbed her thickest fleece top and pulled on another pair of socks. She could hear the television in the lounge. Tory was obviously watching daytime TV. Perfect. She stole down the stairs, took her waterproof coat and wellies and quietly opened the back door.

Her heart sank when she heard the television go silent. 'Poppy, is that you?' called Tory from the sofa. Poppy took a deep breath, slipped off her boots and walked into the lounge. Smiling brightly, she said, 'Charlie's still comatose. I'm going to muck out Chester's stable before the weather gets any worse. Then perhaps we can have another couple of hands of poker?'

Tory looked out of the lounge window. Although mid-morning it was as dark as dusk. 'Alright, pet. Don't be long though. You'll get drenched.'

Practising her best poker face Poppy nodded. 'OK. I'll be as quick as I can,' she promised, her fingers crossed behind her back.

She grabbed a couple of lead ropes from the tack room and the torch she kept on the windowsill in case there was ever a power cut. She didn't really know why – it just made her feel a bit better prepared. Like a Girl Guide or one of the Dartmoor search and rescue people, only on a bad day.

'Wish me luck, Chester.' The donkey gave her a friendly nudge and she set off into the gloom. The rain was sleeting down. Poppy pulled the hood of her jacket over her head and wished she'd worn waterproof trousers. The boulder where she and Charlie had seen the big cat seemed as good a place as any to start her search, so she set off towards the tor, her chin tucked into her chest.

It was hard going. There was no wind but the fog and rain were all-consuming and visibility was down to three or four metres. Following her instinct she found the spot where she and Charlie had eaten their makeshift picnic just a few days before. It felt like a lifetime ago. She started calling his name, but the swirling fog deadened the noise so she stopped shouting and kept walking, stumbling over rocks and tussocks. The ground was so marshy in places that once she almost lost her boot to the peaty mire which threatened to swallow her rubber-clad foot like quicksand. She looked out for familiar landmarks but realised the fog was playing with her senses when she walked past the same twisted tree twice. Or was it a different tree? She couldn't tell any more.

Poppy felt a bubble of panic rising in her throat but she knew she had to carry on until she'd found Charlie. The two lead ropes hung like chains around her neck and her mud-covered boots felt as heavy as lead. She was saturated from head to foot. Keep walking, she told herself.

She had lost all sense of time and when she turned on the torch to look at her watch she realised with frustration that she'd left it in her bedroom. She had no idea if she'd been on the moor for one hour or three. Tory must have twigged that she had gone by now. She must also have seen Charlie's empty bed. If she'd read his note she would have put two and two together and realised that Poppy had gone in search of her brother. Would she have called the police or the search and rescue people by now? Were they at this very moment preparing to launch a search for the two children? Poppy felt terrible for putting Tory in such a difficult situation. She trudged on. By her reckoning she had walked around the base of the tor and was heading deeper onto the moor. She and Charlie didn't know this area as well as they knew their own tor and the Riverdale wood.

Poppy almost jumped out of her skin when a long, black face loomed out of the mist. She stifled the urge to scream, realising with relief that it was one of the black-faced sheep that grazed the moor. The animal gave her a baleful stare before turning and running off into the bracken. She tried to steady her breathing. She knew she needed to stay calm.

The fog seemed more impenetrable than ever. What hope did a six-year-old have in this? Poppy tried not to think about life without her brother – it was inconceivable. She knew Caroline would be heartbroken if anything happened to Charlie. But instead of wallowing in jealousy, Poppy remembered Tory's advice and tried to see things through her stepmother's eyes. Charlie was the apple of his mum's eye but how did Caroline really feel about her? What must it have been like to take on someone else's child? Poppy knew she could be reserved and self-contained. Caroline had described her as prickly. She'd been outraged at the time but knew deep down it was true. She'd always blamed her step-mother for not being Isobel. Caroline had tried so hard to break down the barriers Poppy had put up. Poppy wouldn't have blamed her if she'd thrown in the towel years ago. But she never had.

Was it too late, she wondered as she tramped on through the fog. Caroline had been so sad recently. Would she ever forgive Poppy if Charlie was hurt – or worse? Poppy started bargaining with herself. If she could bring her brother back safe and sound everything would be alright. She and Caroline could try again. But that was all well and good, she thought grimly, as she tripped over yet another slab of granite lying in her path. First she had to find him.

After walking for what seemed like hours with no sign of Charlie, Poppy was beginning to feel tearful. She could hear the catch in her throat when she tried shouting his name. The rain seemed fractionally lighter and Poppy tried to convince herself that the fog was beginning to clear. But she knew she was kidding herself. Maybe she should return to Riverdale and make sure Tory had called for help. Then she realised with a sinking feeling that she'd lost all sense of direction and had no idea how to get home. Exhaustion washed over her. She found a boulder and sat down while she tried to marshal her thoughts. Under its blanket of mist the moor was deathly quiet. Poppy slumped with her head in her hands, wondering what to do. She loved Dartmoor but today it seemed the creepiest, most dangerous place on earth. To make matters worse she couldn't shake the feeling that she was being watched.

She turned around slowly, hoping to see the face of another sheep and not a black panther on the prowl. Her heart hammered in her chest. Her eyes widened in shock as she saw two eyes staring intently at her through the mist.

22

Poppy thought she must be hallucinating. She shook her head, swivelled round on the boulder and looked again, expecting to see nothing but fog. Not so. Standing about five metres away was the head of a ghost horse, looking straight at her. Cloud? No, it couldn't be. Poppy rubbed her eyes, but he was still there when she opened them. Squinting into the mist she could just make out the outline of his body. Not a phantom at all.

'Cloud!' Poppy whispered. She slid off the boulder and walked slowly up to him, her hand outstretched. He stood still, lowering his head as she came close, letting her stroke him.

Tears streamed down her cheeks.

'I can't find Charlie, Cloud. He's gone. I don't know what to do,' she sobbed into his damp neck. She felt him begin to move away from her. 'Please don't leave me, Cloud. I'm so scared,' she hiccupped through her tears. The pony stopped. She walked towards him, but as soon as she reached him he set off again, walking a few paces into the mist before stopping and turning to look at her. It was as if he wanted her to follow him.

After about half a mile Cloud came to a halt. Poppy stood next to him, her right hand resting lightly on his withers. In front of them was a sheer drop, a cliff of granite left by quarrymen two centuries earlier and now as much a part of the Dartmoor landscape as the tors that towered, unseen, above them. In the mist Poppy couldn't tell how deep the quarry was. She could hear Cloud breathing. She looked at him, hoping she wasn't about to send him galloping for the hills. She took a deep breath and yelled as loudly as she could.

'CHAR-LIE!'

The sound reverberated around the old quarry. Cloud stiffened beneath her hand, but didn't move. She called again, louder this time. As the echoes died away she thought she heard something. She called once more. This time she definitely heard an answering shout coming from the bottom of the quarry.

'Poppy! Is that you?'

'Charlie! I'm here! What happened? Are you OK?'

'I'm alright. I was looking for the big cat when I fell down this cliff. I haven't hurt myself but I couldn't climb back up again. I thought I might be here all night.' His voice sounded ragged and Poppy felt her heart contract.

'Don't worry, I'm here now. And guess who helped me find you?'

'Was it Cloud? He was with me before. He came right up to me and I stroked his nose. I didn't find the big cat but I did find Cloud for you.'

Poppy looked at the pony and then down into the quarry. Below her feet the rain-sodden grass gave way to a giant slab of granite which marked the edge of the quarry.

'Charlie, how far down did you fall, can you remember?' she called.

'Um. You know how high the roof of Chester's stable is?'

Poppy thought, that's not so bad.

'About four times as high as that.'

Oh.

'But the bottom was more of a slope than a drop. I was doing my stuntman roll, otherwise I would've probably stopped sooner.'

'Your stuntman roll?' she asked incredulously. Only Charlie could be thinking of stunts at a time like this.

'It's to stop you breaking any bones. You tuck up, then roll down the hill.' Poppy could only assume her brother was giving a practical demonstration to the nearest sheep. But this wasn't getting them anywhere.

'Charlie, listen. I'm going to come down to get you. I've got a couple of lead ropes to help get you up safely.' She looked at Cloud again. His solid strength was so reassuring she couldn't face the thought of leaving him. It was probably the last chance she would have to catch him and return him to Riverdale before the drift. She couldn't bear the thought of him back at George Blackstone's farm. But she had to help Charlie.

Poppy clung to the pony's neck and whispered, 'Stay safe, Cloud.' He whickered softly and she reluctantly let him go. She took a couple of steps forward and sat on the edge of the quarry. She felt the unyielding stone beneath her as she turned onto her front and slithered down. For one terrifying moment she felt nothing but air beneath her feet as she dangled like a string puppet over the edge of the cliff. Her fingers curled around the root of an old gorse bush and she held on desperately while her feet struggled to find a foothold among the seams of granite.

'Poppy! Are you coming?' Charlie shouted from somewhere below.

'Yes. I'm on my way,' she called back, resisting the urge to look down. Her feet found a crevice and she edged her way along it until she felt a slab of stone sticking out like a shelf. She stepped onto it gratefully. Her arms and legs felt like jelly and her fingers were numb.

'Not far now!' she called to her brother in a voice that sounded a lot braver than she felt. Once more she turned over and inched her way over the drop.

'I can see your wellies!' cried Charlie.

If Charlie could see her feet Poppy calculated that she couldn't have too far to fall. She took a deep breath and let go of the rock shelf, waiting for the ground to hit her. When she landed it was onto a gorse bush which ripped her waterproof coat. She felt its thorns tear her cheek as she tumbled onto the boggy grass beneath. Charlie ran up to her, appearing out of the fog like a tornado. He had painted his face with streaks of green and black and was wearing his camouflage trousers and a green water-proof coat. He would have been impossible to spot even on a clear day.

'Poppy!' He launched himself at her. She opened her arms and held him tightly. His face felt icy. He wriggled out of her grasp and looked at her, his blue eyes widening. 'You're bleeding!'

'Am I?' She felt her cheek. It was wet. She looked at her scarlet hand and back at Charlie. 'I'm fine,' she answered. 'But are you OK?'

'I ate the sausages I was going to use as bait for the big cat but they've made me really thirsty and I forgot to bring a drink. And I'm freezing. I think I'd like to go home now,' he said. Together they looked up at the side of the quarry. The sheer granite looked as impenetrable as the walls of a castle. Poppy thought carefully. Even with the two lead ropes she doubted they would be able to climb even half way up the cliff. How on earth were they ever going to get out?

'Hold on a minute. Did you say Cloud came to you when you were down here?' she asked.

'Yes. He came so close I was able to stroke him. He wasn't frightened at all.'

'There's no way Cloud could have made it down that drop. It means there must be another way out of the quarry.' Poppy rubbed her cheek again and considered. 'If this was a quarry they must have got the granite out somehow. I bet there's a path, maybe even an old railway track. We just need to find it.'

Shivering, Charlie looked at his sister. 'Maybe we could look for Cloud's hoofprints? They might show us the way.'

'Yes, that's a good idea. Wait - I have a torch somewhere.' She fished about in the pocket of her waterproof. 'Here it is. I thought it might come in useful.'

Together they searched for Cloud's hoofprints, using the beam of the torch to light the ground. But the peaty soil was so waterlogged it would have been impossible to make out the footprints of an elephant, let alone a pony.

Poppy began to lose hope that they'd ever find their way out.

'I'm so tired. Can't we find somewhere to sit down for a while? Just until the sun comes out?' Charlie wheedled. Poppy knew she had to keep her brother moving. She took his hand. His teeth had started to chatter.

'You're freezing. Take my coat, that'll warm you up a bit. Let's sing a song to keep us going. You choose.' And so to Ten in a Bed they carried on tramping through the fog away from the granite cliff-face. Occasionally a startled sheep would leap out of their path and once they heard the plaintiff caw of a rook flying overhead. Progress was slow. Charlie, normally so full of bounce, was lethargic. Every now and then he would plead with her to stop for a rest. Finally she relented and they found a boulder to perch on.

'Just for five minutes,' she told him firmly, wrapping her arm around him in an attempt to keep him warm. 'I wonder if the search and rescue people are out looking for us,' she thought out loud. 'Maybe they're only minutes away. I expect they have one of those big St Bernard dogs with them with a barrel around his collar filled with chocolate.' She attempted a smile.

'Do you think they might be? I hope so. I miss Mum.'

'So do I,' said Poppy, knowing it was true.

'Do you think we'll ever get home?' he asked sleepily.

Poppy gave her brother a squeeze. 'Of course we will. I promised Mum I'd look after you, didn't I?' She'd tried the word experimentally. It didn't sound as awkward as she'd thought it might. A few minutes later, as she rubbed her hands together in a feeble attempt to warm her freezing fingers, she noticed his head droop forward.

'Charlie!' she said urgently. 'Don't fall asleep. We need to keep moving.' She pulled him to a standing position and held onto him as he started swaying. She took his hand and they stumbled on through the fog. Then suddenly she stopped.

'Wait a minute. Isn't this the rock we had our picnic on? We can't be far from Riverdale.'

Charlie, still shivering, shrugged his shoulders. He looked utterly defeated. 'I don't want to walk any more. I just want to go to sleep,' he whined, his bottom lip wobbling.

Feeling increasingly desperate Poppy tried to adopt Caroline's calm manner. 'Charlie, we are nearly home, I promise. Just a little bit further, then you can go to bed with a lovely hot water bottle. Think how nice that'll be.'

A cry pierced the gloom but Poppy dismissed it as another rook, wheeling overhead. They continued trudging wearily on. But the call was followed by another, louder this time. Poppy listened hard with blood pounding in her head, her senses on full alert. Please let it be help, she thought. For Charlie's sake.

23

Inspector Bill Pearson dunked a digestive biscuit into his mug of tea as he studied a map of Dartmoor, which had been hastily blue-tacked to the wall directly opposite him. Usually the room, on the top floor of the police station, was where officers kept their kit in lockers and spent their breaks microwaving meals and watching sport on a flat screen in the corner. Today the television was silent. The room had been set up as an incident room, a nerve centre where the police were co-ordinating the search for the two missing children.

The 999 call to say the brother and sister had disappeared from their home near Waterby had come in to the force control room at just before eleven o'clock that morning.

The children had now been missing for two hours and, with the weather on the moor deteriorating by the minute, the search for them was being treated as a critical incident.

Inspector Pearson had been put in charge of the search by his chief inspector and was expecting a long shift. He was due to go home at four o'clock but with two children missing on the moor in weather like this he knew the odds of finishing on time were long, to say the least.

Ignoring the buttons straining across his large stomach he reached for another biscuit.

'How many have we got on the moor now, Woody?' he asked the man sitting next to him.

Sergeant Wood was as thin as Inspector Pearson was round. He looked disapprovingly at his superior as the inspector took a large bite of the soggy digestive.

'Well, boss. We have all our available late shift officers and three Dartmoor search and rescue teams on the moor, two of them with dogs. They're searching a three mile radius of the house, although they're looking to extend that if we haven't found the children before it gets dark.'

'What about the chopper? Surely the thermal imaging camera's going to be our best bet?' asked the inspector.

'The helicopter's grounded because of the fog, boss. The search is going to have to be done on foot.'

'That's going to make things tough. What do we know about the two children?'

'They were being looked after by a friend of the family who has been staying with them while their mother's in hospital. Mrs McKeever broke her wrist yesterday, by all accounts, but is due home this afternoon.'

'They're not having a very good week, are they?' remarked Inspector Pearson.

'The boy, Charlie, left the house some time before ten this morning. He's six. According to the family friend his sister Poppy, who's eleven, discovered her brother had gone walkabout and went looking for him on her own. We think she's been missing since about half past ten.'

Inspector Pearson looked at the clock. One o'clock. The rain was still drumming against the window. Dartmoor was no place for children on a day like this.

'What about a media appeal?'

'We're working on that, guv. The on call press officer has been briefed. We're just waiting for the go-ahead from the mother. Then we'll get someone down to the house to pick up some recent photos of the kids.'

'Do we have someone at hospital with the mother?' he asked.

'Yes, boss. PC Bodiam has been there since about half past eleven.'

Inspector Pearson looked at the map again. By Dartmoor standards Riverdale wasn't particularly remote, but it edged on to an isolated part of the moor where the terrain could be dangerous. Add to that the worsening weather. The temperatures plummeted at night at this time of year. If the children weren't found before nightfall they didn't stand a chance, he thought grimly.

The next couple of hours passed quickly in the makeshift incident room. Every half an hour briefings were given and the inspector updated on the progress of the search. More cups of tea were made and more digestive biscuits were dunked. North east of Riverdale police officers and volunteers from the Dartmoor Rescue Group, in their trademark red jackets, scoured the landscape for any trace of the two children. At just after three o'clock hopes were raised when one of the trained search dogs found a small digital camera. The information was radioed to PC Claire Bodiam at Tavistock Hospital who asked Caroline McKeever if either of the children had a camera, and if so, what make and model.

'Yes,' Caroline replied quietly. 'I bought Charlie his own digital camera for Christmas last year so he could take his wildlife pictures on it. It's a Canon, although I have no idea what model it is. But it's silver, if that's any help.'

PC Bodiam nodded and relayed the message back to the incident room. She smiled reassuringly at Caroline, who was white with worry.

'It looks as if it is Charlie's camera they've found,' she confirmed. Seeing the fear on Caroline's face PC Bodiam tried to set her mind at rest. 'It's good news, Mrs McKeever. It means the search teams are definitely in the right area. I'm sure it won't be long before we find Poppy and Charlie.'

But another hour passed and there was still no sign of the children. Back in the incident room Inspector Pearson was about to incur the wrath of his wife by texting her to say he would be late home. Just as he started tapping out the message his radio crackled. He held it to his ear. Over the airwaves a voice shouted, 'We've found them, guv!' He deleted the text message with relief. 'Are they alright?' he asked.

'The lad is showing early signs of hypothermia and will need to go to hospital. We've just radioed for an ambulance. The girl is fine,' replied the police officer who had been leading the search teams up on the moor.

'Good job. Has anyone let the mother know?'

'PC Bodiam is next on my list to call, guv.'

Inspector Pearson was puzzled. 'What on earth possessed the children to do a disappearing act on the moor in this weather?' he asked.

'They'd gone looking for big cats apparently, guv,' the radio crackled.

The inspector raised his eyebrows. 'I might have known. Sniffer Smith was on to the press office a couple of days ago asking for a police comment on a sighting of the so-called Beast of Dartmoor. For something that doesn't even exist, that damn creature has a lot to answer for.'

24

Poppy couldn't stop shivering. Tory sat her down in front of the fire in the lounge and wrapped her in her duvet to warm her up, but her body refused to stop trembling. Charlie, who was bundled up in his Thomas the Tank Engine duvet next to her, was trying to sip a mug of hot chocolate through chattering teeth. Tory, watching them anxiously, said, 'It's probably the shock. You'll both be as right as rain after a good night's sleep.'

Henry Blossom stood by the window, keeping an eye out for the lights of the ambulance. Poppy could hear the quiet murmur of chat coming from the kitchen, where the two remaining members of the police search team were making cups of tea. She'd been surprised to see Henry when they'd finally arrived back at Riverdale, exhausted and chilled to the bone. 'He was the first person I called when I realised you and Charlie had gone. I didn't want to phone the police straight away in case you were both tucked up in one of the outbuildings, or had gone up to the farm together. Henry searched the grounds for me while I went over the house. That's when I found Charlie's note, realised what must have happened and called the police,' Tory had explained.

Her grey hair was mussed up as though she'd spent all day running her hands through it in worry. But her brown eyes were as kind as ever.

'I'm truly sorry for disappearing without telling you and causing everyone such trouble,' Poppy said for about the tenth time that afternoon.

'It's alright, pet. I know you were worried about Charlie. At least you're both safe. All's well that ends well. That's what my old mum used to say.'

'My mum had another saying,' smiled Henry from his post by the window. 'What doesn't kill you makes you stronger. Oh look, here's the ambulance at last.'

Charlie was so tired he could barely keep his eyes open but rallied when he heard that it had finally arrived.

'Cool! My first ride in an ambulance! Though I've been to the hospital near our old house loads of times,' he informed Henry proudly. 'Do you think they'll use the lights and sirens?'

'They only use blues and twos for emergencies I'm afraid, Charlie,' Henry replied, glad to see the six-year-old smiling again. Both children had been subdued since they'd been home and looked lost without Caroline. He was glad they'd soon be reunited with her at the hospital in Tavistock.

Tory was allowed to ride with them in the back of the ambulance and Charlie spent the half hour journey in heaven being shown defibrillators, spine boards, inflatable splints and the burns kit. Poppy chatted quietly to Tory, describing how Cloud had found her in the fog and led her to Charlie.

'I probably could have caught Cloud but I was so worried about Charlie – I had to put him first,' said Poppy, her eyes downcast.

'You did the right thing, pet,' said Tory, patting her gently on the knee. 'Cloud has run wild on the moor for years, he can look after himself. Look how clever he was today, leading you to Charlie. He'll be fine, I know he will.' Poppy attempted a smile and tried to believe her.

Before long they drew up outside the hospital and the two paramedics helped them down the ambulance steps and into the minor injury unit where Caroline was waiting for them, her arms outstretched, a look of pure relief on her face. Charlie was usually quick to rush into his mother's arms but this time Poppy beat him to it.

'Thank God,' Caroline murmured into Poppy's hair as Charlie joined in the hug, Caroline gingerly holding her broken wrist above his head.

'I've been so worried about you both. You two mean the world to me, you do know that, don't you?'

Poppy looked into her stepmother's blue eyes and nodded. 'Yes, I do. And I'm sorry - for everything.'

'What do you mean? If you hadn't gone after Charlie God knows what would have happened to him up on the moor on a day like today. You saved his life, Poppy.'

'I didn't mean for today. I'm sorry for the last six years. For everything.'

'Shhh. It's all forgotten. I think today is the perfect day to start all over again, don't you?'

Poppy nodded gratefully and smiled at her stepmother, who hugged her again.

Charlie broke the silence. 'Is Dad coming home?'

'He's tried to get permission from his newsdesk to come home early and they've said they'll do all they can but we don't know when he'll be back I'm afraid, sweetheart. I've managed to get a message to him that you're both OK and he sends his love,' Caroline replied, and, realising a doctor was hovering in the background, let the children go.

Once they'd been checked over and declared fit to return home Tory called Henry Blossom, who had volunteered to drive the four of them back to Riverdale.

'I've got an idea,' Caroline said, with a twinkle in her eye. 'Shall we stop off on the way and treat ourselves to a fish and chip supper?'

'Oh, yes please!' shouted Charlie. 'This has been the best day ever! I get to meet loads of real live police, stroke two proper search dogs, ride in an ambulance *and* have fish and chips for tea. It's been awesome!'

The three adults and Poppy exchanged looks before bursting out laughing. Charlie scratched his head and looked at them. 'Did I say something funny?'

T hey were just finishing their fish and chip supper when there was a thump on the back door.

'It's only me!' yelled Scarlett. 'I'm back from gran's and wanted to talk to Poppy about school.'

Scarlett stood stock still as she took in the presence of Tory and Henry Blossom and noticed Caroline's broken wrist.

'Well, you've obviously had a much more exciting week than me,' she commented. 'Gran's was sooo boring. She thinks cross stitch is an exciting hobby and her television stopped working when they went over to digital. We spent most of the time visiting ancient aunties and looking around stately homes. It's been gruesome. I'm so glad to be home, even if we do start Year Seven tomorrow.'

Poppy swallowed. She'd pushed all thoughts of secondary school to the back of her mind but now it was just hours away. She looked at Caroline. 'Is it OK if we chill out in my room for a bit so I can fill Scarlett in on all the dramas?'

'Of course, sweetheart. I'm going to get Charlie to bed and then crash in front of the television. Henry's taking Tory home.'

The two girls dashed upstairs to Poppy's room. Caroline had already pulled the curtains, laid out clean pyjamas and switched on the fairy lights, which twinkled merrily over Poppy's bed. Scarlett sat on the wicker chair by the window. 'Right. I want to hear *everything*,' she said.

Twenty minutes later Poppy had brought her friend up to speed. 'I wish I'd been here to help,' Scarlett said fervently.

'So do I,' said Poppy. 'I was terrified something had happened to Charlie. And I feel so guilty about leaving Cloud. If it wasn't for him we'd probably still be on the moor. I can't stop thinking about it.'

'The drift is two weeks away. There's still time to catch him,' Scarlett pointed out. 'Anyway, I'd better make a move. Mum only let me come if I promised I wouldn't be longer than half an hour. Are you all ready for the morning?'

'Yes, my uniform, PE kit and new shoes are in the wardrobe. I just need to sort out my rucksack.' Poppy went quiet. She knew Scarlett wouldn't judge her. 'Actually, I'm dreading it,' she admitted.

'Don't worry. We'll stick together and I'll introduce you to the girls from my primary school. A few of them are lame but most of them are really nice. You'll be fine. Don't forget, the bus goes from the bottom of the lane at ten to eight. So let's meet at the postbox at twenty to and we'll walk down together. Mum's told Alex he's got to look after us. He's over the moon, as you can imagine,' Scarlett giggled.

When Scarlett had gone Poppy lay on her bed staring at the ceiling and wishing she was as sociable and outgoing as her friend. Caroline stuck her head around the bedroom door.

'Pat's just phoned to say she'll take Charlie to and from school for me until I can drive again. Isn't that kind of her?'

Poppy nodded. 'And Scarlett and I are going to walk to the bus stop together in the morning.'

'That's a good idea. Why don't you come down and say goodbye to Tory and Henry and I'll run you a nice hot bath. You mustn't be too late to bed tonight.'

∼

POPPY FELT as though she'd been asleep for a nano second when her Mickey Mouse alarm clock woke her with a shrill ring the next morning. She threw off the duvet, jumped out of bed and looked out of the window.

The day before the tor had been completely concealed by fog. This morning it was bathed in mellow autumn sunshine.

Downstairs in the kitchen Caroline was singing. She broke off when Poppy walked in. 'How are you feeling, sweetheart?' she asked, her blue eyes full of concern.

'Much better, thanks. I finally feel warm again,' Poppy said, reaching for a box of cereal.

'Good. Charlie's still in bed. I thought I'd let him lie in.'

Poppy raised her eyebrows. 'Are you sure? That's what I thought yesterday and he turned out to be your dressing gown.'

'No, he definitely is. I heard him snoring. Unless he's invented a snoring sound effect and is now halfway across Dartmoor looking for his wretched panther.'

'I wouldn't put it past him,' said Poppy. She caught Caroline's eye and they started giggling. The giggles bubbled into laughter and soon they were both laughing hysterically at the thought of Charlie rigging up a snoring soundtrack before creeping, SAS style, back onto the moor.

'As your dad's not here perhaps he had to make do with recording Magpie snoring,' snorted Caroline, wiping tears from her eyes.

Poppy clutched her stomach and dissolved into giggles again. Her dad could snore for England. She tried taking deep breaths but every time she looked at Caroline they broke into peels of laughter. Poppy remembered the day Scarlett had made Caroline chuckle with stories of school and how jealous she'd been, watching from the sidelines. It felt so good to laugh with her stepmother. She realised that the only person leaving her out of everything had been herself.

Before she knew it she was walking reluctantly down the Riverdale drive in her new school uniform. The navy blazer felt scratchy around her neck and her new shoes rubbed her ankles uncomfortably. Poppy had worn polo shirts at primary school and after their fit of the giggles Caroline had shown her how to knot her new navy and gold striped tie.

'If you can do a quick release knot you'll soon get the hang of this. You look so grown up, Poppy. Let me take a photo so I can email it to your dad. He'll be so sad he's missed your first day at secondary school.'

The bus ride into Tavistock was nerve-wracking and even Scarlett seemed intimidated by the too-cool-for-school sixth-formers, even though she could vaguely remember some of them from her primary school. In a whisper Scarlett filled Poppy in on everyone's family histories so that by the time the bus pulled into the layby outside their new school she knew whose great aunt had married her first cousin and whose dad had been arrested for sheep rustling.

In fact the day Poppy had been dreading for weeks whizzed by. The two girls were delighted to discover they were in the same form but horrified when they were given their fortnightly timetables, which contained tortures like double science and maths. Their form teacher was a tall, thin, anxious-looking man called Mr Herbert. Some of the boys had already nicknamed him Filthy. Scarlett introduced Poppy to her friends from primary school and the girls trailed around endless corridors searching for the right classrooms whenever the bell went. There was a certain camaraderie among the new Year Sevens. They'd spent the last year strutting around their primary schools with all the confidence of very big fish in very small ponds. Suddenly everyone, even the most self-assured among them, felt as insignificant as sprats, back at the bottom of the pecking order.

At lunchtime Alex came to find them to check they were OK. Being in Year Nine gave him a certain amount of kudos and a couple of the Year Seven girls sitting near them tittered nervously as he chatted to Scarlett and Poppy about their morning.

'Scarlett, is that really your brother? He's so good-looking,' said one dreamily as Alex walked away.

'You're joking, right? You don't have to live with him and his sweaty trainers. He's a complete and utter pain in the –'. At that moment the bell went and they gathered up their lunchboxes and trundled slowly out of the canteen in a river of navy blue and burgundy.

By Thursday Poppy and Scarlett were beginning to find their way around the school and were getting to know more of their classmates. Charlie had started at Scarlett's old primary school the previous day and had already made firm friends with a boy called Ed, whose dad was the local farrier. The evenings were getting darker and Poppy had at least an hour's homework every night. She hadn't had a chance to see Cloud all week and fretted about him constantly.

On Friday the Tavistock Herald published its story about Charlie's big cat sighting alongside a shorter article about the search operation for two children who had gone missing on the moor the previous weekend.

Charlie produced the paper with a flourish the minute Poppy let herself in the back door after school. She flung her rucksack under the kitchen table and settled down to read. The big cat story took up most of page three. Next to Charlie's picture of the cat were Henry Blossom's photo of Charlie and Poppy and a file picture of a black panther with the caption, *Could a creature like this be roaming Dartmoor?*

EXCLUSIVE: Boy captures Beast of Dartmoor on camera

By Stanley Smith

A six-year-old Waterby boy has astounded big cat experts after capturing the clearest photo yet of the so-called Beast of Dartmoor.

Charlie McKeever was with his 11-year-old sister Poppy on the moor near Waterby last Thursday when they saw the black panther-like creature.

'The cat was massive and we were both absolutely terrified,' said Charlie, whose dad Mike McKeever is one of the BBC's top war correspondents.

'We weren't terrified,' said Poppy indignantly.

'I know. Sniffer Smith seems to have embellished most of the quotes,' Caroline replied drily. Poppy continued reading.

The quick-thinking Waterby Primary School pupil grabbed his digital camera and took this photograph seconds before the cat leapt from the boulder and disappeared onto the moor.

Big cat enthusiast John Clancy, who has been tracking the fabled Beast of Dartmoor for the last five years, said the image was irrefutable evidence that the big cat existed.

'Thanks to a brave six-year-old we can at last prove to the sceptics that there is a black panther living on our doorstep,' he added.

But Tavistock Police Inspector Bill Pearson was quick to dismiss the sighting. He told the Herald: 'I really don't know why people continue to get so excited about the so-called Beast of Dartmoor. Call me cynical but it's probably just someone's overweight black moggie that's strayed too far from home.'

Have you seen the Beast of Dartmoor? We'd love to hear your story. Email the newsroom now.

'We're famous, Poppy!' said Charlie. 'Everyone at school's going to think we're so cool.'

Poppy quickly scanned the second article about the search and rescue operation. Inspector Pearson was quoted as saying he was glad the outcome had been a happy one while issuing a stern warning about the dangers of Dartmoor. He hadn't released their names to the press and she was relieved to see that Sniffer hadn't made the connection. But her name was still plastered all over the local paper. She hated the limelight and couldn't imagine anything worse than being the centre of attention, especially at school. The very suggestion made her feel sick.

Seeing her concern Caroline squeezed Poppy's hand. 'Don't worry, sweetheart. By Monday people will be wrapping their fish and chips and lining their cat litter trays with the Herald. It'll be old news. Now, what would you like for tea?'

2 6

Poppy's head was filled with thoughts of Cloud when she awoke the next morning. The drift was exactly a week away and she knew the weekend would be her last chance to catch him and bring him home to Riverdale. She picked up her mobile phone from the bedside table and texted Scarlett.

Hi Scar, any chance we can go for a ride on the moor and see if we can find you know who? P x

The screen flashed with a reply within seconds.

Course. Be here for ten. I'll be by the stables. C U later! S ;-)

Poppy hadn't ridden for a couple of weeks and it felt great to be back in the saddle. Flynn seemed as pleased to be out as she was and looked around with his bay ears pricked as they followed Scarlett and Blaze along the rocky track that led from Ashworthy to the moor. Scarlett chattered about school while Poppy scanned the horizon looking for Cloud's dappled grey coat. They headed towards the Riverdale tor and as they drew nearer were bemused to see a huddle of people at the foot of the tor, looking and pointing to the cairn at the top.

'Who on earth are they?' cried Poppy. 'Cloud's not going to come near with that lot hanging around.'

Scarlett swung around in her saddle to get a better look. The group was mainly middle-aged men with cameras around their necks. A couple were filming with camcorders.

'Do you know what, I think they've probably come to look for Charlie's black panther,' she told her friend. 'I expect they read the story in yesterday's Herald.'

Poppy's heart sank. 'Typical. We might as well give up now. Cloud will be miles away.'

'Let's at least ride over to Riverdale wood and see if he's there. You never know,' said Scarlett. But although they saw a couple of small herds of Dartmoor ponies there was no sign of Cloud.

It was the same story the next day. Even more people had turned up hoping to get a glimpse of the famous Beast of Dartmoor. Poppy felt so frustrated she could have wept. With school the next day she knew that any chance she had of saving Cloud from the drift had all but disappeared.

Caroline sensed her despair as they sat down to roast chicken that evening. She waited until Charlie had gone to bed before she tackled Poppy.

'Something's up, I know it is. Are you worried about school tomorrow?'

'No, it's not that,' Poppy replied miserably.

'You know you can tell me anything, don't you Poppy? I'm on your side.'

Poppy looked at Caroline across the kitchen table and managed a weak smile. 'I know you are. I should have told you sooner. I don't really know why I didn't. But I don't want to keep secrets from you any more.'

Over the next half an hour Caroline listened quietly as Poppy told her about Cloud. How she'd glimpsed the flash of white in the woods they day they moved to Riverdale and the first time she and Charlie saw him by the river. She recounted how her suspicions that Tory knew where the pony had come from had been correct. Caroline looked shocked when Poppy described the hunter trial where Cloud had fallen in the mud, trapping Caitlyn beneath him, and how the pony had ended up at George Blackstone's farm before being set free by a heartbroken Tory.

'You know Charlie and I kept going to watch the badgers? We weren't. We were out looking for Cloud,' said Poppy, not daring to meet her stepmother's eyes. 'Every year Tory used Chester to lead Cloud to Riverdale where she kept him in the stable hidden from the drift,' she continued. 'That's what I was going to do last Sunday when you were in hospital. I had everything planned. Then Charlie went missing and I knew I had to go looking for him instead. But Cloud found me in the fog and led me to Charlie. It's Cloud who saved Charlie, not me.'

When she finally raised her eyes to Caroline's face she could see only concern so she ploughed on. 'And the drift is next Saturday, so I'm too late to save Cloud now.'

Caroline looked at her stepdaughter. Poppy's shoulders were slumped and her green eyes were forlorn.

'Oh Poppy, I had no idea. I could have helped, you know. You may not believe it but I was as pony-mad as you when I was your age.'

'You never said.'

'You never asked, sweetheart,' Caroline replied. 'And I was lucky enough to have my own pony. I didn't like to rub your nose in it.'

'What was your pony like?' Poppy asked.

Caroline's face took on a faraway look. 'His name was Hamilton and he was a fleabitten grey, not dappled like your Cloud. He was 14.2hh and the love of my life.' She looked at Poppy and smiled. 'You go and sit by the fire. I'll be with you in a minute.'

The lounge was warm and cosy and although she couldn't shake the wretchedness she'd felt all weekend Poppy felt glad to be cocooned inside after the strain of the last few days. Caroline re-appeared with a tatty old shoebox tied up with a faded red ribbon. She sat down on the sofa beside Poppy and attempted to open the box one-handed.

'Let me help,' said Poppy. 'What's inside?' she asked as she leant in to get a closer look.

'Just some photographs I thought you might like to see.'

Photo after photo showed a handsome grey pony, ears pricked as he looked over his stable door, caked in mud while he grazed in his field, pulling hay from a net tied to a five bar gate. She riffled through the pictures. There were photos of the pony jumping over small fences, being shampooed, having his mane plaited and new shoes fitted.

'Is that you?' Poppy asked Caroline, pointing to a photograph of the pony nuzzling the ear of a slim blonde girl about Poppy's age.

'Yes. And that's Hamilton. I think I was about twelve when that photo was taken. You can see his stable in the background.'

'He was beautiful. He reminds me a bit of Cloud,' said Poppy, a catch in her voice.

'He was. And he was such fun. We had a ball together, we really did. For three years he was the most important thing in my life.'

'What happened to him?' Poppy asked.

'You remember my dad used to work for an oil company before he retired?' Poppy nodded. 'When I was fourteen he was posted overseas and your Auntie Lizzie and I were sent to boarding school. My parents said we had to sell Hamilton. He went to a nice family but I was absolutely devastated. I never rode again.'

Poppy reached over and gave her stepmother a hug. Caroline held her close. 'I really do understand how you feel,' she said, wiping a tear from Poppy's cheek.

'I know you do. It's just so unfair. I know something awful will happen to Cloud and there's nothing I can do to help him. He trusted me, I know he did. And I've let him down.'

'Don't give up hope, Poppy. We'll go out early on the morning of the drift. You never know – you still have time to bring him home to Riverdale.'

Poppy seriously doubted it, but she supposed there was at least a chance. She tucked her legs up and sank back into the sofa, resting her head on Caroline's shoulder.

'I'm glad I've told you about Cloud,' she mumbled.

Caroline kissed the top of her head. 'So am I, sweetheart. So am I.'

27

'Dad phoned after you went to bed last night,' Caroline informed the two children at breakfast the next day. 'His newsdesk has finally agreed to send in another correspondent to replace him. He's flying out on Saturday night and should be home some time on Sunday.'

'Hurray!' shouted Charlie, his mouth smeared with raspberry jam. 'Did you tell him I'm headline news?'

'No, not yet!' Caroline laughed. 'I thought you'd want to tell him yourself.'

Caroline looked happier than she had for weeks, Poppy thought as she shrugged on her blazer and let herself out of the back door. Scarlett was waiting for her by the postbox and as they walked to the bus stop together Poppy realised with surprise that she was actually looking forward to school. A couple of her new classmates gave her some gentle ribbing about the story in the Herald but she followed Scarlett's advice and played along with them and her five minutes of fame were soon forgotten.

At lunchtime their talk inevitably turned to Cloud and the drift. It was all Poppy thought about these days.

'I'm going try one last time to find Cloud before they start rounding up the ponies on Saturday morning. Caroline's going to come with me,' she told her friend.

'I don't believe it,' groaned Scarlett. 'Mum's dragging me and Alex to Plymouth for the day on Saturday. Says we both need new clothes for the winter. There's no way she'll let me come with you instead. Normally I'd love a day's shopping but I'd much rather help you catch Cloud.'

Privately Poppy thought that the fewer people who were looking for Cloud the better, but hurting her friend's feelings was the last thing she wanted to do so she grimaced convincingly and said, 'That's such a shame. But I promise I'll text you if we do find him.'

Saturday morning finally arrived, mild and sunny. By nine o'clock Poppy, Charlie and Caroline were ready to go. Poppy ran into the tack-room, grabbed an old rucksack and swung it over her shoulders before looking over the door of Chester's stable.

'I'm keeping you in today,' she told the old donkey. 'I don't want you being upset by all the noise and commotion of the drift. You'll be safe in here.' She blew him a kiss and joined Caroline and Charlie. They set off towards Waterby, where the ponies would be herded into a temporary corral before they were sorted. As they walked they could hear the distant sound of neighing and the roar of quad bikes. Poppy could feel her stomach churning. They passed flat-capped farmers in checked shirts and tweed jackets, their craggy faces inscrutable as they headed for the moors, walking sticks in hand.

'Scarlett said that some of the people rounding up the ponies are on horseback and others ride quad bikes,' said Poppy, slightly out of breath as they marched up a steep lane that led to one of the bigger tors behind Waterby.

'Look!' cried Charlie, as they rounded a corner and the moor stretched out in front of them. In the distance they could see a small group of Dartmoor ponies picking their way through the rocks as they headed towards the village. The herd, driven by three women on cobs and a boy in his late teens on a quad bike, was soon joined by another gaggle of ponies that cantered down a grassy path flanked by gorse bushes. Their coats already thickening in preparation for a harsh Dartmoor winter, the ponies flashed past Poppy, Caroline and Charlie. Poppy's eyes skimmed the dark bays, blacks, chestnuts, skewbalds, piebalds and red and blue roans. There were two grey ponies in the group, but neither was Cloud and she breathed a sigh of relief.

For the next couple of hours they watched as more and more ponies trickled down from the highest parts of the moor, forming a mass of streaming manes and heaving flanks. There was still no sign of Cloud and Poppy could feel her spirits rise. He knew the moor so well. Maybe he had managed to hide from the drivers.

'Well, hello!' said a familiar voice, and the three of them turned to see Henry Blossom standing behind them, his camera around his neck, his camera bag attached, as always, to his stooped right shoulder.

'How are you all? Not planning another adventure on the moor I hope?' he asked, looking at Charlie with a grin.

'No,' answered Charlie, sheepishly. 'We're watching the ponies. Why are you here?'

'I'm covering the drift for the Herald – we do every year,' he explained. He looked behind to where Sniffer Smith, notebook in hand, was talking to one of the rugged old farmers. 'This year Sniffer is planning to write a feature and flog it to one of the Sunday papers. Always has his eye on the main chance, that one.'

Poppy glanced at the journalist, who was now heading towards them. Sniffer was as unpleasant as Henry was likeable, and she didn't trust him one inch.

'Shall we go?' she said under her breath to Caroline who, seeing Sniffer approaching, agreed at once. They said hasty goodbyes to Henry before turning and walking off.

'What do you want to do now, Poppy? Stay and watch the ponies as they come off the moor to see if we see Cloud?' asked Caroline.

'If I was Cloud I'd be hiding in the Riverdale wood,' announced Charlie suddenly. 'It's so overgrown the quad bikes and horses and riders wouldn't be able to get in. We could go and have a look.'

'That's actually a really good idea, Charlie. If we walk quickly it shouldn't take us more than half an hour to get there,' said Poppy.

'But what are we going to do if we do see him?' Caroline asked.

Poppy looked over her shoulder at her rucksack. 'I've got a headcollar and leadrope in here, plus a scoop filled with Chester's pony nuts. It's been digging in my back all morning. I just hope Cloud trusts me enough to let me catch him.'

Half an hour later they reached the edge of the wood. Caroline followed the two children as they plunged into the trees, struggling to keep up as they ducked and weaved around branches and over fallen logs.

'You seem to know the wood pretty well,' she panted, as they all stopped in front of a fallen tree trunk.

'Must be all that badger watching,' grinned Poppy, as she scrambled over, Charlie following closely behind. Eventually they reached the river and followed it down to the small beach where Poppy and Charlie had first seen Cloud. There was no sign of him today.

'What should we do, Poppy?' asked Caroline quietly.

'I think you and Charlie should go and sit on that log and I'll stay here by the river with the pony nuts and headcollar. I've a feeling Cloud will come to us.'

'How can you be so sure?'

Poppy's green eyes were shining. 'Because I'm pretty certain that for the last ten minutes he's been following us.'

2 8

Poppy's conviction that Cloud was nearby started to waver when he didn't immediately appear from behind the trees. When he still hadn't showed after another ten minutes the fleeting elation she'd felt drained away to be replaced once again by nerves. Caroline gave her an encouraging smile from the log where she was stationed with Charlie. Poppy could see her brother was getting fidgety. Any minute now he'd realise he was hungry and then it would only be a matter of time before they had to abandon their rescue mission and head back home.

Just as she was about to admit defeat she heard the branches behind her rustle. Spinning around she almost cried out with relief when she saw Cloud's familiar grey nose poking out from behind the russet and gold leaves of a beech tree. She looked over at Caroline and Charlie, pressing her finger to her lips. Charlie gave her the thumbs up and she could see Caroline crossing her fingers for luck.

Poppy started talking softly to Cloud, hoping he wouldn't sense the nerves that were making her voice wobble. He emerged slowly from the trees and at once she could see that something was very wrong. His flanks were dark with sweat and he was trembling with fear. Yet he looked straight at her, his brown eyes locked on hers, as she held out the scoop filled with pony nuts. As he approached she realised with shock that Cloud was now so lame he couldn't put any weight on his near hind leg.

'You poor, poor pony. What's happened to you? Did you get caught up in the drift?' she crooned softly as he hobbled towards her. Still talking, she stretched out her arm. Cloud hesitated and Poppy thought for a moment that she'd lost him. But then, as if he'd made up his mind to trust her, he whickered, walked forward and started eating the nuts.

Poppy ran her hand along his neck and he leaned into her. She put the scoop on the floor and with one hand on Cloud's neck slowly reached for the headcollar by her feet with the other. She put the leadrope around his neck while keeping up her monologue. Her fingers were shaking and she fumbled trying to undo the buckle of the headcollar. She glanced over at Caroline and Charlie, who were watching intently. The pounding in her ears almost drowned out the constant background rumble of quad bikes and neighing horses.

The buckle now undone, Poppy slowly edged the noseband over Cloud's muzzle. His ears twitched back and forth but he didn't pull away and as she pulled the strap over his poll with her left hand she felt a surge of triumph.

But just as she started to do up the buckle an explosion, as loud as the crack of a gunshot, pierced the air. Poppy jumped out of her skin, letting go of the headcollar, which slithered to the floor by her feet. Cloud half-reared in fright, turned in mid-air and fled back into the trees. Poppy sank to her knees, her head in her hands. Caroline and Charlie rushed over and Poppy felt Caroline's arm around her shoulders.

'What was it?' she cried, tears running down her cheeks.

'It sounded like a quad bike backfiring. I'm so sorry, Poppy, but Cloud's gone,' said Caroline.

'That's it, then,' Poppy said, blinking back the tears. 'It's all my fault. I dropped the headcollar and now he's going to get caught. I've failed him.'

'Don't say that, sweetheart. It's not your fault. No-one could have done any more than you.' Caroline held out her arms. 'Come here.'

Poppy's legs felt like jelly but she stood up and went to Caroline and they clung together, Poppy's head tucked under Caroline's chin, until Charlie started grumbling that he was starving.

Caroline stroked Poppy's hair, lifted her chin and looked directly at her. 'Don't give up hope, angel. I know it doesn't feel like it now, but these things have a habit of working out in the end, you'll see.'

Once Poppy would have let rip, accusing her stepmother of not understanding or getting it all wrong as usual. But things had changed - she no longer felt angry with Caroline. Instead she nodded mutely, misery descending as she thought how Cloud, with his poor damaged leg, would never escape being caught now.

'Would you like to see the last of the drift?' Caroline asked gently.

'No,' Poppy replied. 'I think I'd just like to go home.'

HALF A MILE away the last few stragglers were being rounded up by two men on quad bikes. A small herd of ponies, led by an old bay stallion who had witnessed countless drifts during his long life on the moor, had been discovered grazing on the edge of the Riverdale wood. The herd, half a dozen mares and their yearlings and foals, followed the stallion, delicately picking a path through the gorse and bracken that marked the end of the wood and the beginning of the moor.

'I think this is probably the last of them,' shouted one of the quad bike riders, a middle-aged man whose close-cropped hair was flecked with grey.

His younger companion was about to agree when he saw another pony emerge from the wood. 'Hold on - look what the cat's just dragged in!'

The two men stopped revving their bikes and watched a dappled grey pony approach. He was limping badly, his head nodding in pain every time he took a step. His flanks were dark with sweat and his mane and tail were matted.

'Good grief!' exclaimed the older man. 'He's in a sorry state. I'm not sure he's going to keep up with the rest of them. We might have to take it slowly.'

One of the mares whinnied and Cloud whickered in return. 'He's not a Dartmoor pony but they seem to know him alright,' said the younger rider.

'I wonder –' mused his companion. A couple of years ago, over a pint of beer, one of the old farm hands had told him about the Connemara pony that had killed Tory Wickens' granddaughter at a local hunter trial. The pony had never been caught in the annual drift. Everyone had assumed it must have died during one of Dartmoor's unforgiving winters. Apparently not.

The younger rider, itching to get home, started revving his bike and the grey pony hobbled over to join the rest of the herd.

'Come on! We'll be here all night unless we get a move on,' he yelled. The older man nodded. He turned his quad bike and started driving the ponies towards Waterby. Although the grey pony was now surrounded by the herd he stuck out like a sore thumb. He stood a couple of hands higher than the native ponies and was obviously of a much finer build. He had a noble look about him.

The quad bike rider had the distinct feeling that if they managed to get this interloper to the village in one piece it was going to cause quite a stir.

B y four o'clock that afternoon the temporary corral at Waterby was thronging with horseflesh. The drift was the one and only time of the year that so many Dartmoor hill and the purebred Dartmoor ponies were seen in one place – usually they were dotted across the moor in their own small herds. Leaning against the rails of the corral were the farmers, also brought together from far flung corners for the annual ritual.

Henry Blossom was taking photographs of the bustling scene while Sniffer Smith chatted to a couple of the older farmers, whose eyes were roving over the ponies looking for their owners' individual marks.

'Remind me, how do you tell who owns which ponies?' Sniffer asked the two farmers, pen poised over his notebook.

'There's some who favour ear cuts and others cut their ponies' tail hair in different patterns, but mine all have ear tags,' answered one gruffly.

''Course, the foals are all born between May and August so they have no mark, but they stick so close to their dams we know which are ours,' added the other, eyeing Sniffer with interest as the journalist turned his words into shorthand squiggles on the page of his notebook.

'And what happens now?' Sniffer queried.

'Once we've sorted the ponies they'll go back to their own farms where they'll be checked over and wormed. We'll wean the foals and decide which ponies to send back onto the moor and which to send to market,' explained the second farmer.

His companion added, 'Aye, it's usually the colts and the older ponies that go to market. The hardiest go back on the moor to breed.'

As they talked a whisper went up among the people leaning against the rails. Sniffer - who was hard-wired to detect a good story a mile off – pricked his ears and looked around, trying to identify the reason for all the excited murmuring.

'What's everyone talking about?' he asked the old farmers, who were chuckling quietly to themselves.

'Well, lad, it's not your Beast of Dartmoor, but it's almost as infamous around here,' said the first, giving Sniffer a toothy grin before pointing to the latest ponies being driven into the corral by two men on quad bikes. Sniffer stared at the newcomers but all he could see were more of the same. He looked at the two men quizzically.

The second farmer took pity on him. 'Look at that grey pony, right at the back of the corral. That's the pony that escaped from George Blackstone's yard all them years ago, that is. Caught at last, the same year Tory Wickens moved out of Riverdale. Funny that,' he smirked.

'I don't really see the relevance,' said Sniffer. 'Perhaps you could enlighten me?' But before the farmer could explain Henry Blossom walked up, told Sniffer it was time they headed back to the office and steered him firmly in the direction of their car, which was parked on a verge nearby. Once the journalist and photographer had driven off down the lane towards Tavistock the two old farmers resumed their ponderings.

'I wonder what old George'll make of it all. He always thought there was cash to be had with that pony and you know how he likes his money-making schemes.'

His companion hooted with laughter. 'Blackstone's so tight moths fly out of his wallet every time he opens it. But I wouldn't have thought he'll be making much from that one. It'd be kinder to put the poor thing out of its misery, if you asked me.'

They both looked at the grey pony standing at the back of the corral. His head low, his ears flat, he exuded exhaustion from every pore. At the other end of the corral farmers had begun sorting their ponies. As soon as their marks were identified they were sent into smaller pens with a hefty slap on the rump. From the smaller pens they were herded up the ramps of waiting livestock trailers before being transported back to their farms.

'Where is George, anyway?' asked the first farmer, scanning the faces lining the corral for their neighbour.

'Looks like he's sent Jimmy instead,' said his companion, pointing to an unassuming-looking lad a few feet away. 'Blackstone's probably back at home counting his money and dreaming up his next get rich quick scheme.'

'Do you remember that time he tried selling bottled Dartmoor spring-water to the tourists?' said the first farmer, taking a pipe out of his pocket and planting it in the corner of his mouth.

'Aye. You mean the water he was getting straight from his kitchen tap? He'd sell the coat from his own mother's back if she was still alive, God love her.'

'I hope he does right by that poor pony. You know me, I'm not usually sentimental, but look at it. It hasn't had much of a life, that's for sure.'

They both watched as Jimmy, George Blackstone's faithful farm-hand, started driving his employer's ponies into one of the smaller pens. The old bay stallion bore the Blackstone mark, a small nick to the left ear, as did his mares. Jimmy walked behind them, a walking stick in each hand to propel them into the pen. Only once they were all in did Jimmy notice Cloud for the first time. He'd still been at school when Blackstone had bought the Wickens' pony but remembered the accident. The girl who died had been a pupil at his school, although a few years younger than him. He'd heard how Blackstone had been incandescent with rage when his new purchase had escaped and how, to the farmer's intense annoyance, the pony had somehow managed to evade capture in the drift year after year.

I wonder, he thought to himself. What if this is the famous Cloud Nine? The pony was eyeing him warily. Jimmy had the uncomfortable feeling it was reading his mind. He couldn't see Blackstone's mark so, lunging forward, he tried to grab the pony's left ear. But Cloud was too quick and, with teeth bared, he snaked his head away and squealed in anger. Smarting with humiliation and feeling the eyes of a dozen dour hill farmers on his back Jimmy retreated to the side of the corral to consider his options. He felt stuck between a rock and a hard place. This pony, almost certainly Blackstone's, had plainly gone feral and was going to be a nightmare to get back to the farm. But Jimmy had been on the receiving end of George Blackstone's vicious temper more times than he cared to remember and he had no intention of incurring the farmer's wrath by failing to bring the pony back with the rest of his herd.

Squaring his bony shoulders Jimmy set off once again. Before the pony could react Jimmy raised his walking sticks in the air and roared, 'Gerrup you old donkey!'

The two old farmers watching the scene unfold saw a spark of fight flare briefly in the pony's eyes. But as one of Jimmy's sticks connected heavily with the pony's rump the spark died. Acquiescent, Cloud limped into the pen and Jimmy punched the air and whooped in victory. The pony watched defeated as the jubilant farmhand tied the gate tightly shut with a length of orange baler twine.

Dusk was falling as Jimmy drove back to George Blackstone's farm. Cloud and the rest of the ponies stamped restlessly in the back of the lorry as he negotiated the potholed track to the farmyard. The yard was empty. Jimmy swung through the gateposts and parked by the side of an open barn. He jumped out of the cab and strode over to the back door of the farmhouse. His arrival set Blackstone's two border collies off in a frenzy of barking. Tied to a post inside the barn, the dogs strained against their ropes in their eagerness to reach Jimmy, who usually had a treat and a kind word for them.

The Blackstone farm was a gloomy place. It had been a thriving business when George's parents were alive and the yard and farmhouse had been as neat as a pin. But over three decades it had slowly fallen to rack and ruin. George Blackstone was as mean as he was idle, and hadn't spent a penny on the place in years. Buildings were patched together with old timber and hope and the field next to the barn resembled a tractor graveyard, a place where the farm's once fine fleet of vehicles had given up and died.

Jimmy paused for a second by the back door. He hoped Blackstone would be pleased that he'd returned Cloud but you never knew. It had been a long day and the last thing he needed was a tongue-lashing. He rapped on the door and let himself in.

'Jimmy, is that you?' barked a querulous voice from the depths of the old farmhouse. Jimmy's heart sank to the bottom of his mud-splattered boots.

'Just coming, Mr Blackstone. And I've a surprise for you!' he replied, shaking off his wellies in the filthy hallway. George Blackstone was sitting by a smoky fire in what had once been his mother's best parlour. But her beloved knick-knacks had long been sold off and the once cream walls were now yellowed with nicotine. A half-drunk bottle of whisky and a dirty glass sat on a small table next to Blackstone's armchair. Jimmy quailed. His boss was a vindictive drunk.

'Did you bring back my ponies?' Blackstone demanded, his sour breath causing Jimmy to gag.

'Yes, Mr Blackstone. And not just the Dartmoor ponies. You'll never guess what else I've got in the back of the lorry!'

'Go on – surprise me,' the old man replied.

'You remember that pony you bought off Tory Wickens all them years ago?' Blackstone nodded. It still sent his blood pressure rocketing when-ever he thought about the money he'd wasted on that no-good Connemara.

'Well, it was caught in the drift and I've brought it back for you.'

It took a moment for the penny to drop but when it did an unpleasant leer spread across his face. Jimmy could almost see the pound signs light up in his rheumy eyes.

'Well, well, that's a turn up for the books,' he said, picking up his walking stick and pushing Jimmy roughly out of the way in his haste to see Cloud.

Together they went out into the yard. While Jimmy shut the gate Blackstone let the lorry's ramp down with a clatter. He peered into the dark interior of the lorry but all he could see were half a dozen terrified Dartmoor ponies staring back at him.

'Where is it then?' Blackstone howled. Jimmy rushed over to the lorry, tripping up the ramp in his hurry to herd the ponies out into the yard. Standing at the back of the lorry was Cloud, the whites of his eyes piercing the gloom. Blackstone laughed nastily and followed Jimmy up the ramp.

'Go and see to the others, boy. You can shut the ramp behind me. I need to teach this one a lesson. No-one gets the better of George Blackstone,' he said softly.

Jimmy suddenly felt sorry for the dappled grey pony. But his fear of Blackstone was far greater and he turned away from the lorry and did as he was told, flinching as he heard the desperate crack of wood meeting horseflesh.

~

AN HOUR later George Blackstone's Dartmoor ponies had been fed and watered and were huddled together in the far corner of a small paddock at the rear of the farmhouse. Jimmy had checked them over, paying special attention to the three yearlings he would be driving to the horse sale in Tavistock the next day. He fed the border collies and gave the yard a half-hearted sweep, but his gaze kept returning to the lorry, which stood in the glow cast by the security light above Blackstone's back door.

After the first sickening crunch of wood on horse everything had been silent. Jimmy had gone about his jobs methodically, trying to blot out images of splintered bones and dark weals on once white flanks. But he couldn't put it off any longer. Leaning the broom against the back wall of the farmhouse he walked over to the lorry, clearing his throat nervously as he went.

'Mr Blackstone?' His voice came out croakily and he tried again, louder this time. 'Mr Blackstone! Is everything alright in there?'

There was no reply. Jimmy released the ramp and crept up. He stood for a moment trying to see, but the back of the lorry was in complete darkness. He became aware of laboured breathing. 'Mr Blackstone, are you OK?'

He remembered the small pen torch on his key ring and grappled around in his trouser pocket until his fingers closed around it. The tiny beam of light was next to useless but Jimmy shone it into the depths of the lorry anyway, praying it would reveal nothing but a lame, bedraggled grey pony and that his boss had gone back into the farmhouse while he was out in the paddock tending to the ponies. His hand was shaking, causing the pinprick of light to dance like a firefly inside the lorry. Jimmy took a deep breath and tried to steady both his hand and his nerves.

But when the light came to rest on a prone body lying on the straw all coherent thoughts vanished. Jimmy opened his lungs and screamed.

ike McKeever's plane touched down at Heathrow the next day after an uneventful six and a half hour flight. As he and his fellow passengers on board the airbus sat waiting for the seatbelt lights to go off he thought about the last few weeks. It had been a good trip and the programme editor had been pleased with Mike's reports from the front line. He had a natural empathy with both the British soldiers and the local people, which always came across in his pieces. He loved being in the thick of the action and told friends he had the best job in the world. Yet recently he found he was missing Caroline and the children more and more and was beginning to wonder if a desk job back in London might be better for the whole family.

Leaving them for this trip, so soon after the move to Riverdale, had been a real wrench. Charlie was his father's son and took his dad's work trips in his stride but Caroline, normally so cheerful, had seemed unhappy when he'd left. And there was Poppy. With her pale, heart-shaped face and green eyes she looked so much like Isobel that sometimes it took Mike's breath away. She was skinny, shy and awkward but Mike knew that one day she would be as beautiful as her mother.

From the moment Mike and Isobel had met during a lecture in their first year at university they'd been inseparable and were married within three years of graduating.

They'd had their lives mapped out. They'd both wanted careers – Mike at the BBC and Isobel as a primary school teacher - a family home, four children and a golden retriever. Within a few years they'd had the jobs, the Victorian terrace in Twickenham and, most importantly, Poppy. Mike felt the luckiest man alive. Then life dealt him its worst possible hand.

His grief after Isobel's death had threatened to consume him, but somehow he'd managed to hold everything together for Poppy's sake. Overnight she'd morphed from a confident and carefree four-year-old to a withdrawn, clingy and painfully shy shadow of her former self. Father and daughter had clung to each other like the battered and bruised survivors of a shipwreck.

Slowly the pain had lessened. Mike still missed Isobel acutely but he began to enjoy work again, and sometimes hours went by when she didn't fill his thoughts. Then Caroline had started working in Mike's department and the two had become friends. They were both gregarious and shared the same quirky sense of humour. To the delight of their friends and families they'd fallen in love. The arrival of Charlie was the icing on the cake.

Mike felt so grateful he'd been given a second chance. He wished Poppy felt the same. But no matter how hard Caroline tried Poppy refused to let down her defences. Caroline never complained about Poppy's remoteness and Mike was away so often it was easy to pretend everything was OK. Deep down he knew it was anything but.

The seatbelt light finally went out. Mike stood up, stretched his legs and reached for his hand luggage in the overhead locker. He knew that once he was home he would have to sit down and talk to Poppy about Caroline. Mike had once found an old shoebox filled with photographs of a pony, schedules from long-forgotten gymkhanas and dog-eared rosettes at the bottom of Caroline's wardrobe. His wife had been as pony mad as Poppy was at her age. They had so much in common, if only Poppy was prepared to look.

His taxi driver was a taciturn type so Mike was spared the effort of making small talk on the long drive back to Riverdale. Instead he spent the journey deep in thought, wondering how he could bridge the gap between his wife and daughter.

As they neared Tavistock the traffic slowed to a crawl and Mike realised they were stuck behind several livestock lorries all heading in the same direction. The taxi driver drummed the steering wheel with his fingers and let out the occasional deep sigh.

'It's like Piccadilly bleedin' Circus around here today,' muttered the driver, throwing Mike an accusatory look through the rear view mirror, as if he was personally responsible for the traffic jam. Mike smiled inwardly while trying to look sympathetic. They trundled on for another couple of miles. When they reached the outskirts of the town he saw a sign with the words 'Horse Sale, first left' on the side of the road.

It must be the auction where the Dartmoor ponies were sold, Mike thought. Caroline had mentioned the annual event in an email. Apparently it was quite a spectacle. His mind was racing. He remembered Poppy, white with disappointment when she'd realised there was no pony waiting for her at their new home the day they'd moved to Riverdale. He thought about the emails she'd sent him since, brimming with news about Chester, her new friend Scarlett's two ponies and little else. He pictured Caroline's scruffy shoebox, buried at the bottom of her wardrobe, filled with memories of her own pony-filled childhood.

Mike made a split decision. He tapped the driver on the shoulder, dazzled him with his practised television news smile and, with just the right mix of persuasion and authority, said, 'Actually, could you just take a left here? There's somewhere I need to go.'

32

The Tavistock Pony Sale in the town's livestock centre was the first of the annual drift sales and drew people from far and wide. Everyone, from the farmers to the workers running the sale, seemed to know exactly what they were doing. Mike, still in the crumpled suit he was wearing when he left the Middle East, felt distinctly out of place. He picked up a sale catalogue and studied it carefully, trying to glean as much information as he could. The sale had started at ten o'clock and was due to finish at four. He looked at his watch. Three thirty. He was worried he'd left it too late. But ponies were still being sent into the ring one by one. Mike watched as the onlookers cast critical eyes over the fillies and colts, searching for good conformation and the potential to make a decent riding pony. Standing over them all, in a wooden construction that resembled a prison watchtower, was the auctioneer, whose sharp eyes roved keenly over the crowds, so as not to miss a single bid.

The ponies were being sold in guineas. Mike caught the eye of the woman standing to his right. She was wearing a quilted jacket and a headscarf and looked like she might know a thing or two about horses. 'Excuse me, I'm new to all this. How much is a guinea?'

'Well, in old money it would have been one pound and one shilling, but these days it's £1.05,' she answered, happy to share her knowledge. 'Until recently ponies were selling for as little as a couple of guineas. They were worth more dead than alive. So sad. Now there's a minimum price of 10 guineas on every pony.'

Mike smiled his thanks and turned back to the ring where a diminutive chestnut foal was trotting obligingly around the ring, its ears pricked and its head held high. The bidding had reached 42 guineas.

'Are you buying or selling?' the woman asked. Her greying brown hair, long face and large front teeth reminded Mike uncannily of Chester.

He shook the thought away and replied, 'To be honest, it was a spur of the moment thing. I happened to be passing, saw the sign and thought I'd pop in and have a look.'

'I've bought a bay colt for my grandson,' she informed him. 'Silly really – Matthew's still in nappies. But by the time he's ready to ride the pony will be rising five. He's a fine looking fellow and should make a terrific riding pony.'

'My daughter Poppy's horse mad,' said Mike conversationally. 'She'd love a pony more than anything else in the world, but I know as much about horses as I do about quantum physics.'

'Well, it would be a mistake to buy a foal. Putting two novices together is a recipe for disaster. Much better to buy her a ready-made riding pony, if that's what you were thinking,' said the woman.

'I don't really know what I was thinking, if I'm honest,' admitted Mike. 'But she's been through a tough time and I think it would be good for her.'

'I agree. I think pony mad girls deserve their own ponies. But then horses are my thing,' said the woman. 'I'm Bella, by the way. Bella Thompson.'

'Mike McKeever. Nice to meet you,' said Mike, extending his hand. 'We've not long moved to Devon. We live near Waterby.'

'I know the village well. My old friend Tory Wickens used to live there, though I hear she's moved to Tavistock now. Haven't seen her in yonks.'

Mike laughed. 'It's a small world – we bought Riverdale from Tory at the beginning of the summer. Poppy inherited Tory's old donkey Chester, although it's a pony she'd really like.'

'Well I never,' replied Bella, pumping Mike's hand vigorously. She had an extraordinarily firm handshake for a woman in her sixties.

They turned to watch another couple of foals take their turn in the ring. The crowd had started to thin out and bidding had slowed right down. Mike checked his watch again. Nearly ten to four and the sale was almost over. He remembered the grumpy taxi driver still sitting outside.

'It was lovely to meet you, Bella, but I'd better be off. You're right – it was a crazy idea to even think about buying a foal for Poppy – she's only eleven. If we're going to get her a pony we should do it properly. Get some proper advice, find something safe for her to ride.'

As he spoke the gate into the ring opened to reveal a much bigger pony, twice the size of the foals but with none of their bounce. Receiving a forcible shove from the man at the gate it limped painfully in. Bella, who had been about to give Mike's hand another hearty shake, turned back to the ring, her attention fixed on the pony now hobbling around the inside of the rails. It was what Mike would have called white and Poppy would have said was grey, though it was hard to tell – its hair was matted and streaked with what looked suspiciously like blood.

'Now that, if I'm not much mistaken, was once a top class riding pony, though it's hard to believe it looking at him now,' said Bella. 'In fact, if I'm right, and I'm pretty sure I am, you might be interested to know that that poor pony once belonged to Riverdale,' she continued, turning to Mike with a glint in her eye.

Mike had been about to leave but his interest was piqued. 'Belonged to Riverdale? What do you mean?'

'I'm pretty sure that's Cloud Nine, a Connemara pony Tory Wickens bought for her granddaughter Caitlin years ago. He was a beautiful pony and he and Caitlin made an unbeatable team, that is until the accident -'

Bella was interrupted by the auctioneer, whose ringing voice was met with jeers from the handful of people still lining the ring as he attempted to get the bidding started.

'I know we've only just met and you probably think I'm a mad old woman for saying so, but you should bid for that pony. Buy him for your daughter,' said Bella.

Mike looked at her, his eyebrows raised. The pony looked half dead as it plodded unevenly around the ring. He shrugged his shoulders. He was beginning to wonder if it was all too much hassle, and turned to go.

'Trust me. Just start bidding!' said Bella urgently, tugging his sleeve.

Mike looked at the pony again. Head nodding with every painful step as he limped around the sale ring, he looked as though he'd lost the will to live. Could this sorry excuse for a pony really be the answer he'd been looking for, a shared interest to bring Caroline and Poppy together? Deciding he had nothing to lose, Mike reluctantly raised his hand and tried to catch the auctioneer's eye. He remembered what Bella had told him about the minimum sale price and said in a loud voice, which sounded more confident than he felt, 'Ten guineas.'

A man wearing dirty blue overalls standing opposite them immediately bid eleven, and when Mike raised his hand again there was a ripple of laughter.

'You're bidding against the knackerman!' hissed Bella. 'Keep going!'

The next couple of minutes passed in a blur of bid and counter bid. Mike felt confident that he could outbid the man from the slaughterhouse, and he was starting to picture Poppy's delight when he brought the pony home to Riverdale. But just as he was about to raise his hand for what he was certain would be the winning bid a man with a weasel-like face standing to his left dropped a bombshell.

'I'd save your money if I were you, mate. Did you know that animal killed a girl?'

'*What?*' demanded Mike. He stopped bidding and turned his full attention to the man.

'It's a bad 'un, you mark my words. The knacker's yard is the best place for it, if you ask me.'

'I didn't ask you,' Mike replied icily and turned back to the ring.

But it was too late. The sale had been made. The grey pony had disappeared and the auctioneer had already moved on to the next lot.

33

Poppy was lying on her bed, her chin cupped in her hands and a riding magazine open on the duvet in front of her, trying to pass the time until her dad arrived home. She'd barely glanced at the magazine. When she wasn't staring morosely out of the window at the darkening sky, she was watching the minute hand of the old Mickey Mouse alarm clock on her bedside table. The harder she looked at the dial, the slower the hand seemed to move. Her dad had been due home at four o'clock. It was now half past, and there was still no sign of him.

Poppy looked down at the magazine. It was open on a feature about first aid for ponies. 'How to save your pony's life!' ran the headline. She scanned the top ten things to include in a first aid kit and she skim-read the tips on treating wounds and common causes of lameness. Everything she saw, read or heard made her think of Cloud. She knew in her heart that he would never have been able to outrun the drift and by now was almost certainly back at George Blackstone's farm. The thought chilled her to the core.

Twenty five to five and her dad was still a no-show. Poppy could make out the sound of Caroline singing along to a song on the radio in the kitchen. Knowing Caroline, she was probably dancing around the kitchen table, too, and the thought made Poppy smile. She and Caroline had had a heart to heart earlier, just the two of them. Poppy had been mucking out

Chester and Caroline had come to see if she needed any help. They chatted easily now and Poppy no longer felt awkward around her step-mother. For the first time she could remember they'd talked about Isobel, and it had been OK. Better than OK, in fact – it had been good. As she looked over to the clock again her eyes fell on the photo of her mum. Poppy still missed her deeply, but she no longer felt so alone.

The distant rumble of a lorry interrupted her thoughts. It was a welcome distraction and she flung the magazine on the floor. The rumble grew louder and was followed by the crunch of tyres on gravel.

'Dad's home!' yelled Charlie at the top of his voice, and Poppy could feel the walls of the old house tremble as he galloped along the landing and down the stairs. By the time she reached the hallway Charlie had already flung open the front door. She had been expecting a taxi but was flummoxed to see a sleek horsebox parked outside.

'That's weird,' she said, half to herself. The horsebox was steel grey with a berry red logo. Poppy could just make out the words Redhall Manor Equestrian Centre. It was probably trying to reach the farm but had taken the wrong track, she thought. Then the passenger door opened and her dad jumped out. Charlie whooped and ran into his outstretched arms. Poppy waited a heartbeat and followed. Her dad's suit was crumpled and there were shadows under his eyes but his face was tanned and he was grinning from ear to ear.

'Come here and give your tired old dad a hug, kids,' he commanded.

'Mike!' called Caroline from the front door. She stopped in her tracks when she saw the horsebox. 'What on earth -?'

'I cadged a lift with Ted in Tavistock,' Mike said, gesturing at the driver, who was also jumping down from the cab. 'We got delayed for one reason or another and my taxi driver had another airport run to do. I bumped into Ted and he said he was coming this way and would give me a lift in return for a cup of tea.'

They all filed into the house, congregating in the kitchen where Caroline made tea. Mike looked at his daughter, who was offering everyone a slice of coffee cake. She was growing up so fast. 'Be an angel and go and get my hand luggage out of the horsebox, Poppy. It's in the groom's compartment, through the door on the side. There's a light switch on the left, I think. There might be something for you both in there,' he added, winking at Charlie, who whooped again. As she crossed the gravel to the lorry she heard him yell after her. 'Poppy! I nearly forgot. Your present might be harder to spot. Just keep looking and I'm sure you'll find it.'

She walked around to the far side of the lorry and let herself in, feeling in the darkness for the light switch. After a couple of sweeps of the wall she found the switch, flicked it on and looked around curiously. She'd seen plenty of horseboxes in her pony magazines but had never been inside one. Scarlett just had a trailer on the farm, which her dad towed behind his old Land Rover. The groom's accommodation reminded her of the inside of a caravan. There was a small sink and draining board with cupboards and a tiny fridge underneath, a sleeping area over the cab and a long seat the length of the wall opposite the door.

On the seat was the battered, black suitcase her dad used as hand luggage. Next to it was a carrier bag with the barrel of the biggest Nerf gun Poppy had ever seen poking out of the top. Charlie would be beyond excited. She walked over, picked both bags up and put them by the door. Poppy looked around her again. Her dad's big suitcase was by the sink. She tried lifting it but it was so heavy she could barely haul it an inch off the ground. He'd have to come and get it later. There was no sign of any other bags but as Poppy turned to go she noticed the interior door that led to the horse area. She paused. Ted hadn't said if he had any horses in the back but it wouldn't do any harm to poke her nose through the door and have a look, would it?

'Of course it wouldn't!' she exclaimed, her voice sounding unnaturally loud in the empty space. There was a thump from the horse area and a low noise that sounded very much like a whicker. Poppy reached for the door handle.

The light from the groom's area revealed the first of three padded partitions which stood at an angle to the sides of the lorry. Peering around the partition she saw a Dartmoor foal, blinking nervously behind a haynet that was almost as big as he was. Poppy smiled and went to stroke his nose, but he shrank from her touch. 'Don't worry, little fellow. I'm not going to hurt you. I just wanted to say hello. Are you all on your own?'

At the sound of her voice there was another whicker from the stall next to the foal. Poppy felt the hairs on her neck stand up. She hardly dared to look at the foal's companion but when she did she gasped. Standing with his legs slightly splayed was a skeletal grey pony. He looked as insubstantial as a wraith, but when he turned his brown eyes to Poppy they burned with life. 'Cloud!' Poppy breathed. She flung her arms around his bony neck and he stood patiently while she sobbed noisily, snot mingling with the sweat and dried blood in his tangled mane.

Minutes passed as they stood locked together. Poppy's mind was reeling. Could Cloud be for her? But how had her dad known about him – she'd never mentioned him in any of her emails. And anyway, things like that only happened in stories, not to girls like her.

More likely Cloud was destined for the flash-sounding Redhall Manor Equestrian Centre where he would be used as a riding pony for spoilt rich kids. But at least he was safe from the brutal hands of George Blackstone. Poppy realised that was all that mattered.

She hugged him fiercely. 'I'll find out where you're going and I will always look out for you, Cloud,' she muttered into his mane.

'No need for that. He's staying right here,' said a cheerful voice. She looked up and saw Ted opening the ramp of the horsebox.

'But I don't understand –' she gulped, wiping her nose on the sleeve of her jumper.

'Your dad bought him at the pony sale in Tavistock this afternoon. My boss offered the lorry to bring him back to Riverdale. He's as thin as a stick and very nervy but you two seem to have made friends already!'

Mike and Caroline were standing at the bottom of the ramp, arms around each other, broad smiles on their faces.

'It's Cloud!' Poppy told her stepmother, the disbelief on her face giving way to joy.

Caroline's blue eyes were sparkling. 'I thought it might be from the way your dad described him.'

'But Daddy, how did you *know*?'

'I'd like to take the credit but I'm afraid it was all down to Ted's boss, Bella. We bumped into each other at the pony sale this afternoon. She's a force to be reckoned with, I tell you.' Ted chuckled at the accurate description of his boss as he undid the first two partitions of the horsebox.

'I was looking for a foal for you but Bella said no, two novices together would be a mistake. Then this one walked into the ring and Bella reckoned he would be perfect for you, Poppy. He looked like a mess to me but she sounded so sure I found myself bidding. It was me against the knack-erman,' said Mike succinctly. Poppy shuddered.

'Then a man standing next to us told me the pony had killed a girl. I didn't know whether to believe him or not. But before I had a chance to ask Bella if it was true the bidding was over. Someone had bought him.'

Poppy held her breath as her dad continued. 'It was Bella. She told me he belonged to Riverdale and that I could pay her back later. And suddenly I was the owner of a dappled grey bag of bones with a notorious reputation and not much else. I had no idea you two had already met,' Mike finished, looking at his tear-streaked daughter. She was leaning heavily against Cloud, while he rested his head on her slight shoulder. It gave the illusion that they were propping each other up.

'I don't understand how he ended up at the pony sale. I thought George Blackstone would have wanted to keep him,' said Poppy.

'I can answer that,' answered Ted. 'Apparently he came off the moor yesterday afternoon in the drift near Waterby.'

Poppy and Caroline nodded. They'd guessed that much.

'He was taken back to Blackstone's farm. Blackstone's a miserable old sod who lives on the other side of the village,' Ted explained to Mike. 'According to gossip, Blackstone went into the back of his lorry with the pony. Who knows what he intended to do but knowing Blackstone it wasn't to give the pony a titbit. His farmhand Jimmy found Blackstone a while later. He'd fallen and knocked himself out. He was out cold for quite a while, apparently. Jimmy had to slap his cheeks a few times before he came round. Other than a blinding headache he was as right as rain. Unfortunately.' Ted added with feeling.

Poppy looked at the streaks of dried blood that were caked to Cloud's flanks and wondered what had gone on in the back of that lorry. She laid her cheek gently against Cloud's as Ted continued. 'Blackstone decided last night to send the pony to the sales. He wasn't prepared to throw good money after bad, Jimmy said. Cloud here was one of the last lots of the afternoon. Bella recognised him as soon as he came into the ring. And the rest you know. Right, shall we unload him now?'

Poppy pulled the quick release knot and led Cloud slowly down the ramp and around the back of the house to the stables. As she passed the kitchen window she saw Charlie watching her, a huge grin on his face. Her heart was threatening to burst as she undid the bolts of Chester's stable. The donkey looked up and hee-hawed loudly when he saw his old friend. Cloud limped straight over and they nuzzled each other affectionately.

'It's a bit of a squeeze. Do you think they'll be OK in there together?' asked Caroline, who was watching over the stable door.

Poppy looked at them and smiled. 'I think so. He looks pretty settled already, I'd say.'

'We'll get the vet out to have a look at his leg. You do realise it's going to be a long journey, getting him back to full strength, Poppy? His leg might be so badly damaged you'll never be able to ride him. And if it does heal it's been years since Cloud has had anyone on his back. We'll be starting from scratch,' said Caroline.

Poppy was glad her stepmother was planning to help. It felt right.

'I know, Mum. All I care about is that he's safe and he's here. Anything else will be a bonus.'

Caroline smiled. Cloud Nine lay down, exhausted, in the thick straw, with Chester standing over him as if keeping guard.

They knew they had a long road ahead of them, but they would travel it together. All that really mattered was that Cloud had finally come home.

AGAINST ALL HOPE

1

Poppy McKeever held her breath and waited for the vet to speak. A dark cloud had followed her like a shadow all day. The suspense of not knowing was almost unbearable. Cloud's ears flicked anxiously back and forth and when Poppy looked down at her hands she realised she'd been clasping his lead rope so tightly that her knuckles had turned completely white. The vet lowered Cloud's leg to the ground and straightened her back. Poppy tried to read her expression but she was giving no clues. Her face was calm, composed, professional. In contrast, Poppy felt like screaming. Cloud's ribs jutted out like the furrows of a newly-ploughed field and his brown eyes were fixed on Chester. The donkey was watching the proceedings with interest from over the stable door while Poppy's brother, Charlie, was surreptitiously trying to listen to his own heartbeat with the vet's stethoscope. Her stepmother, Caroline, gave Poppy an encouraging smile, although she looked as pale and worried as Poppy did.

'Well,' said the vet, her tanned arms reaching for her medicine bag. 'Do you want the good news or the bad news?'

Poppy's heart sank. 'The good news?'

'For a pony that's spent the last five years living wild on the moor he's in remarkably good shape. He is underweight and his teeth definitely need a rasp, but his eyes look healthy and his chest is as clear as a bell.

There's nothing wrong with his general health, at least nothing that a bit of TLC won't sort out.'

Poppy gave Caroline a quick smile. 'But what about his leg?'

'Ah, that's the bad news, I'm afraid. As you know he's very lame on his near hind leg and we need to work out what's causing it. If it was a stone or an abscess in his foot or, say, a pulled tendon, it would be easy to spot. But I can't see or feel any obvious sign of injury.' The vet ran her hand along Cloud's leg from his hock to his hoof again, shaking her head. 'I think we'll have to get him to Tavistock and X-ray his foot. It may be a fractured pedal bone, which is a worry.'

'What's a pedal bone and why is it worried?' asked Charlie, who had dropped the stethoscope on the ground and was making a beeline for the vet's bag of instruments, some of which looked as if they belonged in a medieval torture chamber. Caroline deftly swept the stethoscope and the bag off the ground and into the hands of the vet, who took them with a grateful smile.

'A pedal bone is a bone in a horse's foot,' she told the three McKeevers. 'It runs roughly from here to here.' She drew a line with her index finger from the top to the bottom of Cloud's hoof. 'Occasionally a horse can fracture its pedal bone. It's an impact injury. You could fracture it by landing heavily on a rock for example, which this chap could easily have done while he was out on the moor.' She gave Cloud's bony rump a gentle pat and he shifted his weight to the other leg. 'The only way to tell is with an X-ray. We'll get that done and hopefully we can rule it out.'

'What happens if his pedal bone is fractured?' Poppy asked, her nails digging into the lead rope.

'Well, he would need to be fitted with a special shoe that immobilised his foot. A good farrier would be able to make that.'

'My friend Ed's dad is a farrier!' said Charlie.

'There you are then. And once the shoe was fitted Cloud would need complete stable rest for up to two months. We'd X-ray his foot again after a few weeks to see if there were any signs of the bone healing and then it's a waiting game I'm afraid. If it does heal he should make a full recovery but if it doesn't it's not good news. He'll never be completely sound.'

'You mean Poppy would never be able to ride him?' Caroline asked.

'No, I'm afraid not. Anyway, I'd better get going. I've two more calls to make before evening surgery. Phone in the morning to make an appointment for the X-ray and once that's done we can see where we stand. In the meantime keep him in his stable, just to be on the safe side.' The vet saw the lines crinkling Poppy's forehead. 'It's no use worrying about something that might not happen. You concentrate on fattening him up and leave his foot to me.'

Poppy nodded, her face a picture of gloom. She led Cloud into his stable while Caroline walked around the side of the house with the vet and watched as her mud-splattered Land Rover disappeared down the Riverdale drive. Chester whickered softly and gave the pony a nudge. Poppy slipped off his headcollar and gave them each a bucket of nuts.

The trauma of being rounded up in the annual drift and then sold at auction with the native Dartmoor ponies had taken its toll on Cloud. He'd been so exhausted the night before that he'd barely been able to stand up. As well as being as thin as a stick he shrank to the back of the stable if anyone except Poppy, Charlie or Caroline went near him. Poppy hoped his anxiety was something she could heal with time. But if his foot was broken would she even get the chance?

2

'There you are!' said a familiar voice. Poppy turned to see her best friend Scarlett's freckled face, framed by dark red hair, peering into the stable. 'Did Cloud have a good night? He's scoffing those nuts like there's no tomorrow but he still looks like an equine coat hanger, Poppy. I thought I heard a car on the drive. Was it the vet?'

Scarlett's chatter always cheered Poppy up and she felt more positive as she filled her friend in on the prognosis as they walked together into the kitchen.

Her dad was reading the paper at the kitchen table, his glasses perched on the end of his nose. Mike McKeever was a war correspondent for the BBC and when he wasn't on an assignment in one of the world's trouble spots he was based in London. It was unusual to find him at home. He smiled when he saw the girls.

'Hello Scarlett. How are your mum and dad?'

'Good thanks, though it's a busy time of year for them, what with the harvest and everything.'

Caroline was chopping tomatoes. 'Have you eaten?' she asked Scarlett, who shook her head. 'Fancy some dinner? It's only pizza and salad.'

'Sounds good to me,' said Scarlett, sitting down. 'Hey, have you heard the news?' The McKeevers looked at her blankly. 'You know those two old cottages on the edge of the Blackstone farm? Jimmy Flynn, George Blackstone's farm hand, lives in one with his mum and dad but the other one's been empty since old Mrs Deakins died three years ago. Anyway, Mum says new people are moving in next week. And guess where they're coming from?'

'Crikey, I've no idea,' said Caroline.

'London!' she announced. 'You might even know them.'

'Hardly likely, Scarlett. London is massive. Millions of people live there. It's not like Waterby where everyone's related,' laughed Poppy.

Scarlett waved her hands airily. 'Whatever. Anyway, it's a mum and her daughter, according to Jimmy's auntie's brother-in-law, who's married to one of my dad's second cousins.'

'See what I mean?' said Poppy, raising her eyebrows at her dad and Caroline.

'I'm not sure how old the girl is and I have no idea what's happened to her dad,' continued Scarlett. 'One thing I do know - the cottage is an absolute dump. I wouldn't move there if you paid me. I went inside once with Mum not long before Mrs Deakins was taken into hospital. She was a nice old dear, although sadly lacking in the dental department.'

'What?' asked Poppy's dad.

'She didn't have any teeth,' Scarlett grinned.

'You are funny Scar. People moved in and out of our old street in Twickenham all the time. It's not that big news,' Poppy said. But despite this her curiosity was stirred. It wasn't that long ago that the McKeevers had made the move from Twickenham to Devon in search of a quieter life.

'Once they're in we'll go and say hello,' suggested Scarlett. Poppy wasn't keen on meeting new people but Waterby was such a small village she had to concede that this was a major event.

'If we must,' she agreed reluctantly.

Cloud's X-ray was booked for the following Saturday. The week flew by. Poppy set her alarm for six every morning so she could spend an extra hour grooming the pony before school. She became familiar with the contours of his body and discovered that he loved being rubbed behind his ears but was ticklish under his stomach and stamped a back foot to remind her if she happened to forget. He leant on her when she picked up his feet and nibbled on his lead rope when he was bored. Poppy would sing her favourite hits to him as she trimmed his tail and combed his mane and she always went straight to his stable after school to spend another hour with him.

'He knows when you're on your way home,' Caroline told her over dinner one night. 'He starts banging on the stable door about ten minutes before the bus gets in. Anyone would think he's psychic.'

When the time came to take Cloud to the veterinary surgery in Tavistock Caroline enlisted the help of Scarlett's dad Bill. He arrived at Riverdale with his Land Rover and trailer and they loaded first Chester and then Cloud. Poppy had been adamant that Chester should come too – she knew he would have a calming influence on the Connemara. Poppy spent the journey craning her neck to watch Cloud and Chester through the open slats of the trailer. The minute Bill pulled into the yard behind the surgery she unclicked her seatbelt and scrambled out. Cloud was damp with sweat and his ears jerked back and forth. She could feel him trembling beneath her touch. Chester, on the other hand, looked completely at ease.

Charlie led the old donkey down the ramp and Poppy followed with Cloud close behind. The vet appeared from the open doors of a building at the far end of the yard. 'Follow me,' she said. 'The X-ray equipment is in the barn. We're all set up and ready to go. It shouldn't take too long.'

The concrete yard was flanked on one side by a line of kennels under a wide pitched roof. Each kennel housed a different dog. Some lay quietly, sleeping off the anaesthetic from earlier operations, others whined or barked as Poppy and Charlie led Cloud and Chester past.

'These are the dogs that are in for treatment. The cats are all inside. We also have a couple of stables, but they're empty today,' said the vet.

As Poppy turned to look at the stables Cloud stopped, raised his grey head and whinnied. She tugged his lead rope and clicked her tongue encouragingly. 'Come on, Cloud. It's just an X-ray to see what's wrong with your leg. No-one's going to hurt you, I promise.'

Chester's hairy rump was disappearing into the barn but Cloud refused to budge. He was staring at the last kennel before the double barn door, with feet planted firmly to the spot.

'What are you looking at, Cloud?' Poppy followed his gaze but all she could see was an empty kennel with what looked like a long-forgotten black and tan blanket crumpled in a heap in the corner. But as she stared the blanket stirred and a black head with a tan muzzle appeared. Cloud gave a whicker and the dog barked softly in response, its plumy tail thumping the ground.

'Oh! I thought it was an old blanket but it's a dog,' she said to Caroline, who had joined her by the cage.

The dog was emaciated and its shaggy hair was matted in places. It struggled to its haunches and offered them its paw, which was swaddled in a cast and bandage, as if to shake hands.

'What happened to her?' Poppy asked.

'She's a he, actually,' said the vet. 'The police brought him in yesterday. He was found dodging the traffic on the Okehampton road. His leg was broken so I think he'd probably been hit by a car, though he was lucky – there's no damage internally.'

'Who does he belong to?'

'I expect he was probably dumped. People do it all the time, I'm afraid. He'll stay with us for a few more days and then I'll ask Moorwings, the local animal sanctuary, to come and pick him up. They'll look after him until someone gives him a permanent home.'

Charlie joined them, with Chester following patiently behind. Charlie leant his forehead against the wire cage to get a closer look at the dog, which seemed bemused by all the attention. 'What's his name?'

'One of the veterinary nurses christened him Freddie after her first boyfriend. She said he had the same brown eyes and scruffy black hair, but much nicer manners apparently.'

Caroline sighed. She had a feeling she knew exactly what was coming next. Her instincts proved correct when Charlie fixed his bright blue eyes on her and wheedled, 'Can we give Freddie a home, Mum? You did promise we could have a dog when we moved to Riverdale because we were leaving all our friends behind. And it would stop me looking for the big cat.'

'Charlie and I will look after him and take him for walks,' said Poppy, giving her stepmother an imploring look. 'You needn't do a thing. Imagine how awful it would be if no-one else gave him a home? He'd have to spend the rest of his life in a cage.'

Caroline opened her mouth to speak but the vet joined the offensive before she could utter a word. 'I know he does look a bit of a state but other than that broken leg there's nothing wrong with him. And I think he's probably only about eighteen months old, so he would give you years of pleasure. I'd take him in myself if I didn't already have four at home.'

'Do we really need another waif and stray? What will your dad say? What will Magpie say?' asked Caroline. But she had to admit the dog really did have the softest brown eyes. Almost as if he could sense her wavering, Cloud gave her a nudge and she turned to the children and laughed.

'OK, OK. I know when I'm beaten. But I'll hold you to your promise. He can be your responsibility. And you two can break the news to your dad.'

Charlie flung his arms around his mum and Poppy gave her a quick kiss on the cheek. She still felt a little shy around her stepmother but things were so much better between them now. Caroline enveloped her in a hug, ruffled Charlie's blond hair and gave the vet an ironic smile. 'Come on you lot. We'd better say goodbye to Freddie for now and get this X-ray done, before we end up offering a home to any more lame ducks.'

3

Half an hour later Cloud and Chester were back in the trailer and Poppy and Caroline had joined the vet in one of the consulting rooms. She used a pencil to point at an X-ray, which glowed a ghostly white against the dark background.

'This is his pedal bone. And this is what I was worried about. Can you see the hairline crack? I'm afraid he has fractured the bone.' Poppy nodded mutely. A natural pessimist, she had spent the last week fearing the worst, but she took no pleasure in being proved right. Caroline squeezed her hand.

'But it could be a lot worse. There's no wound, which means there should be no danger of infection, and the fracture hasn't reached the coffin joint. That's the joint between Cloud's pedal bone and his short pastern.'

'So what happens now?' Caroline asked.

'Box rest is the most important part of the treatment for a fractured pedal bone, and you're already doing that. He'll need two to three months of total box rest. We need to completely immobilise that foot to give the bone the greatest chance of healing. He needs to be fitted with a bar shoe, and if that doesn't work we'll look at applying a cast to his hoof and pastern. With the right treatment the prognosis for a full recovery is very good.'

'Is there anything else I can do for him?' Poppy asked.

'No, you carry on exactly as you are. He's already looking so much better than when I saw him on Monday. We'll repeat the X-ray in four weeks' time to see if the bone is beginning to heal and go from there.'

When Caroline and Poppy stepped back out into the yard Charlie was leaning against Freddie's cage, stroking the dog's nose through the wire.

'The vet wants Freddie to stay here for a week so she can keep an eye on him. She said we could pick him up on Friday,' Caroline told him. 'That gives you precisely six days to win your father around.'

~

ON SUNDAY MORNING Poppy was woken by a bleep on her mobile phone. It was a text from Scarlett.

Hi Poppy, fancy a ride? Thought we could go and say hello to the new people. Be here for ten. C U later, Scar xx.

Poppy yawned and stretched. Magpie, the McKeevers' overweight black and white cat, was curled up in a ball on the end of her bed. He eyed her briefly before tucking his head under one paw and going back to sleep. Poppy jumped out of bed, opened the curtains and was greeted by a crisp autumn morning, the sun low in a bleached blue sky. She gazed down at the stables. Cloud's grey head looked out over the stable door, his warm breath like curls of smoke in the cold air. Poppy opened her window and called softly to him. He saw her and whickered. She calculated that she still had time to spend a couple of hours with him before meeting Scarlett. She threw on some clothes, ran down the stairs and grabbed a plate of toast from Caroline in the kitchen, grinning her thanks as she headed for the back door.

Chester had shouldered Cloud out of the way and it was the donkey she could see over the stable door as she pulled on her wellies. Cloud was at the back of the stable resting his bad leg. Poppy ran her hand over his neck and leant on his withers. His mane tickled her cheek and she sighed with contentment.

She let Chester out into the yard and Cloud watched her muck out the stable, change the water and re-fill the hayrack. 'I'm going to give you a groom and then you are going to test me on my German homework. I've got to learn the numbers from twenty to forty by tomorrow otherwise

Miss Maher will have my guts for garters,' she told him as he started tugging wisps of hay from the rack.

Poppy lost track of time and had to run most of the way to Ashworthy, where she and Scarlett spent half an hour brushing the worst of the mud from Scarlett's two Dartmoor ponies, Flynn and Blaze. Scarlett had talked her mum into having Blaze clipped but Flynn's winter coat was growing thicker by the day and his mane was bushier than ever. When Poppy bent down to pick out his feet he seized the chance to nibble her pockets. 'Do you ever think about anything other than your stomach?' she asked him, rubbing his ear with affection.

Scarlett grimaced as she hauled a rucksack over her shoulder. 'Mum's insisted on giving me some chocolate brownies to give to the new people as a moving in present. I told her they'd be broken into a million pieces by the time we get there but she still made me bring them.' Scarlett eyed Flynn's round belly, then looked down at her own sturdy legs and sighed. 'She thinks feeding people is the answer to everything.'

The two girls swung into their saddles and clip-clopped down the farm track to the lane. They turned left, passing the Riverdale drive and heading towards the Blackstone farm at the other side of the valley. The two semi-detached farm cottages were on the Waterby side of the ramshackle farm. Poppy had ridden past them a dozen times without paying much attention. The two white rendered houses, built in the 1950s, were at first glance mirror images of each other. But as they approached she realised the difference was enormous. The cottage on the left sat behind an immaculately manicured front garden whose symmetrical flowerbeds, filled with cyclamens and winter pansies, reminded her of a municipal park. A concrete Greek goddess gazed benignly at them from her plinth in the centre of this kaleidoscope of colour. The windows of the cottage gleamed and a row of white shirts danced in the breeze at the side of the house. Poppy could just make out the navy brass name plate by the front door. Rose Cottage.

The house to the right was more like something out of a Brothers Grimm fairy-tale than a Greek myth. A wooden gate, hanging precariously from rusty hinges, led to a concrete path that was breaking up in places. Brambles and nettles had long taken over the lawn and were now waist high. The wooden window frames were rotten and the windows themselves were opaque with years of grime. A wheelie bin to the side of the front door was painted with the words Flint Cottage. Poppy and Scarlett looked at each other dubiously.

'I'll go. You stay here and hold the ponies,' Scarlett offered, much to Poppy's relief. Scarlett was as outgoing as Poppy was shy and although Poppy knew she shouldn't depend on her friend to take charge it was sometimes easier to.

Scarlett edged her way past the nettles and brambles to the front door and pressed a doorbell at the side of the tarnished letterbox. The resulting chime was unexpectedly loud, making her jump. For a while nothing happened and Scarlett was about to press the buzzer a second time when the front door opened an inch.

'Hello?' Scarlett said. 'Is there anybody there?'

The safety chain was on and the door opened no further. Scarlett glanced uncertainly at Poppy. She turned back to the house and froze as she saw thin fingers curl around the door jamb. The hairs on the back of her neck stood to attention as a voice whispered, 'Who are you?'

4

Poppy, from her vantage point in the lane, only heard Scarlett's reply.

'My name's Scarlett and my best friend Poppy is just over there. We live next door to each other on the other side of the valley. We heard new people had moved in and wanted to say hello. Oh, and my mum made some brownies for you, though they look more like the broken bits of cake that go at the bottom of trifles now. I knew we shouldn't have had that canter. I tell you what, I'll leave them on the doorstep. We need to get going anyway. You can keep the box they're in – it's only an old biscuit tin. Well, welcome to Waterby. It was nice meeting you, er –'

Poppy caught a murmured answer. The fingers uncurled from the door and it closed with a creak inches from Scarlett's freckled nose. Poppy watched her friend place the tin of brownies on the doorstep and re-trace her steps down the concrete path. When she glanced up at the house again, curious to see what was behind the filthy windows, the face of the girl suddenly appeared. Her huge eyes stared at Poppy for a couple of seconds before she turned and vanished from view.

'Well, that was seriously creepy,' said Scarlett, taking Blaze's reins from Poppy. They mounted and turned the ponies for home. Scarlett filled her friend in on the short-lived conversation she'd had with the mysterious girl. 'She's called Hope. She said she couldn't let me in because her mum wasn't there. And did you see what a state the house was in? Trust George Blackstone to rent out such a dump. I wouldn't let my worst enemy stay there. But Mum always says he's as tight as they come. I doubt he's spent a penny doing it up for the new family.'

Poppy nodded. Blackstone was public enemy number one as far as she was concerned. Five years ago the belligerent farmer had bought Cloud, thinking he was going to make a packet selling the pony on, but when Cloud escaped onto the moor, the farmer had nursed a grudge against him. After the annual drift, the Connemara had been sent back to the Blackstone farm, albeit briefly. Poppy shivered as she pictured the dried blood caked to Cloud's flanks when he'd finally returned to Riverdale. She felt sorry for the newcomers.

As they trotted down the lane Poppy was haunted by the face at the window. The girl had stared at her with such intensity that she felt uncomfortable. Something else wasn't right, she was sure of it. But she had no idea what it was.

'Did you see the girl's face?' she asked Scarlett.

'No, just her arm. She had long, skinny fingers and a red mark on the inside of her wrist. Oh, and she bites her nails. I suppose she'd been told by her mum not to open the door to strangers. Though I hardly look like the Child Catcher from Chitty Chitty Bang Bang. My nose isn't half as long as his for a start...'

The two Dartmoor ponies walked towards home with an easy stride. Poppy let Scarlett chatter on as she mulled over the visit. Every now and then Flynn, sensing that Poppy's mind was elsewhere, seized the opportunity to snatch a mouthful from the hedge. His bay ears were pricked and she felt his pace quicken as they turned into the rutted farm track that led to Ashworthy.

'You're quiet,' Scarlett remarked.

'That's because you do enough talking for two, Scar. Only kidding. It's because I'm thinking. There's something about that house – about that girl – that's bothering me. But I can't think what it is.'

They untacked the ponies, gave them a brush down, put on their rugs and turned them out in their paddock. Then the realisation hit Poppy like a sledgehammer. She felt prickles of disquiet on the back of her neck. She put her hand on Scarlett's arm and said, 'I know what it is about that girl at the Blackstone cottage.'

'What?'

Poppy paused. Was it any of her business anyway? But she saw the curiosity on her friend's face and carried on regardless.

'She had no hair.'

5

———————

C harlie spent the week preparing the house for Freddie's arrival. He held impromptu counselling sessions for Magpie, showing him pictures he'd sketched of black and tan dogs and holding the protesting cat up to the television every time a dog appeared on the screen. They went to Baxters' Animal Feeds on the Tavistock road and bought a navy blue dog bed, a collar, lead and water and food bowls. With Poppy's help Charlie cleared the alcove under the stairs of its usual jumble of shoes, bags and coats.

'We can put his bed here. He'll be like Harry Potter at the Dursleys' – sleeping under the stairs. Though he won't be locked in like Harry was. I wonder what happened when Harry needed the loo in the middle of the night?' Charlie pondered.

Their dad watched the preparations with mild amusement. Charlie had been right about him – he loved dogs and was looking forward to Freddie's arrival as much as Poppy and Charlie. He also thought that having a dog in the house would offer extra security for Caroline and the children during his long work trips abroad.

'I don't think Freddie's necessarily guard dog material,' Caroline pointed out, remembering the dog's liquid brown eyes and his attempt to shake hands. 'He's a big softie.'

'Not once I've started his special forces training. I'm going to teach him to kill on command,' declared Charlie.

'Don't let Magpie hear you,' warned their dad. 'You've been telling him all week that dogs are really big friendly cats in disguise.'

Charlie grinned unashamedly and held his finger to his lips. 'Our little secret, Dad. I won't tell Magpie if you don't.' He paused. 'Poppy, do you think Freddie and Cloud have already met? They seemed to recognise each other at the vet's.'

Poppy thought back. Charlie was right. If Cloud hadn't whinnied she'd have walked straight past Freddie's kennel, assuming it was empty. 'I suppose they could have come across each other on the moor. I wonder how long ago Freddie was dumped.'

'Long enough for him to need some serious fattening up,' said Caroline. 'Which reminds me, we need to pop into Waterby after school tomorrow to get some dog food. It's the only chance we'll get before we pick Freddie up on Friday.'

∾

WATERBY POST OFFICE and Stores was the nerve centre not only of the village but also of the wider rural community. The nearest supermarket was almost ten miles away and the shop was a lifeline for many. It was owned and run by Barncy Broomfield, who the McKeevers had nick-named Father Christmas because of his white beard, twinkly blue eyes, rounded paunch and penchant for red sweaters. They felt it was no coincidence that the only day of the year the shop closed was Christmas Day.

Barney took an eccentric and eclectic approach to ordering stock.

'Oh look, some Big Ben money boxes. Cool!' said Charlie, who was wandering up and down the three aisles while Poppy and Caroline scrutinised the labels on different brands of dog food.

'They're for the grockles, lad,' boomed Barney's deep voice from the other side of the shop. 'Classy, aren't they? I've some T-shirts with the Queen's corgis printed on the front arriving next week.'

'Grockles?' whispered Poppy, looking at Caroline in bemusement.

'It's what people in the West Country call tourists,' Caroline whispered back. 'Though I'm not sure grockles visiting Dartmoor are going to want corgi T-shirts and Big Ben money boxes.' Poppy stifled a giggle.

Then from an aisle behind them she heard a girl's voice.

'But I don't want to do it anymore, Mum. You promised me I wouldn't have to when we moved here.' The voice was quiet, breathy. Poppy wondered if it was the girl from Flint Cottage.

'Yeah well, things change, don't they babe? Get over it.' There was an edge to the woman's voice that made Poppy uneasy. Caroline was busy scooping tins of dog food into the shopping basket one-handed and clearly wasn't listening.

Poppy picked up the basket and followed her stepmother towards the till where Barney stood waiting for them, his hands resting on his vast stomach.

As Caroline paid a woman with blonde highlighted hair scraped back in a ponytail stepped out from the furthest aisle, a small, thin girl scurrying in her wake. They queued behind Caroline. Poppy eyed them from under her long fringe. The woman was wearing leggings, satin ballet pumps and a denim jacket. Her daughter was clad in raspberry pink jeans, a navy parka coat and a dark grey knitted beanie hat that was pulled down low over her forehead. Most of Barney Broomfield's customers wore Barbours and wellies. The two looked out of place.

Caroline noticed the mother and daughter standing behind her and smiled. The woman stared back, her heavily kohled eyes looking Caroline up and down. Then she rearranged her features into a half-smile and gripped her daughter's hand. When she spoke it was with a nasal twang.

'Alright?'

'Have you met Shelley and Hope Taylor? They've moved into George Blackstone's farm cottage,' said Barney, as he scanned the tins of dog food. So this was the mysterious Hope, Poppy thought. She looked different wearing a hat.

'How are you settling in?' Caroline asked. 'We only moved down from London in the summer but we absolutely love it here, don't we, Poppy?'

Caroline turned to the girl, whose face was solemn as she watched the exchange. 'Have you started school here yet, Hope? Poppy goes to the high school in Tavistock and her brother Charlie, who's around here somewhere, goes to Waterby Primary.'

Shelley cut across her daughter before she had a chance to reply. 'Hope is home-schooled, aren't you, babe?' Hope bobbed her head obediently.

'She has a school at your home? Is it for everyone?' piped up Charlie, who had appeared beside them with a plastic chicken dog toy and a beseeching look in his eye. 'It squeaks when you squeeze it,' he said. 'It'll help with Freddie's special forces training.'

Caroline sighed. 'Alright then. Give the chicken to Barney. Home-schooled means your mum or dad teaches you at home,' she added, smiling at Shelley and Hope. 'Why don't you come over for coffee on Saturday?'

Poppy groaned inwardly. She had Cloud and Chester at home and Scarlett next door. She didn't need any more friends. Hope looked about as enthusiastic as Poppy felt. Shelley looked at her daughter's morose face and then at Poppy. 'OK, why not? We'll be there about eleven.'

~

ON FRIDAY MORNING Poppy sat with her form in the school hall for the annual harvest festival assembly. Four trestle tables had been placed centre stage behind the deputy head, who was rambling on about the season of mist and mellow fruitfulness while torrential rain hammered an angry beat against the floor to ceiling windows that looked out over the school playing fields. The legs of the tables were splayed under the weight of hundreds of tins of baked beans and packets of rice and pasta, all destined for local pensioners - whether they wanted them or not. Poppy kept looking at her watch but it wasn't making the time go any quicker. As the whole school shuffled to their feet to sing We Plough the Fields and Scatter, Scarlett nudged her. 'What time are you picking him up?' she whispered.

'Straight after school. I've got to walk to the vet's and Caroline and Charlie are meeting me there at four. Want to come? We can give you a lift home.'

'You bet! I'll text Mum at break and let her know I won't be on the bus.'

The rest of the day trickled by as slowly as treacle. When the last bell sounded Poppy and Scarlett couldn't get out of the school gates fast enough. As they walked into the surgery car park Caroline and Charlie appeared from reception, followed by the vet.

'How's that pony of yours doing? Are you fattening him up nicely?'

Poppy nodded. 'He's definitely put on a bit of weight and he's had his shoe fitted. I just hope his foot is getting better.'

'Give him time. When we X-ray him again we should get an idea whether it's healing or not. It's a waiting game, I'm afraid.'

They heard a woof. 'It's Freddie,' cried Charlie. 'He knows we're here.' He ran across the yard to Freddie's cage and poked his fingers through the wire. The dog gave him a friendly lick.

'We'll X-ray Freddie's foot when you bring Cloud over. With any luck they'll both get the all clear. In the meantime Freddie also needs lots of rest. No walks until we know his fracture has healed and you'll need to keep him on the lead when he goes outside to do his business.'

'Oh, it's OK,' said Charlie, his blue eyes earnest. 'We're going to pay for all his food and stuff. He won't need to go out to work.'

The vet looked nonplussed. Caroline laughed. 'She means when he goes to the toilet, Charlie. Right, shall we let him out?'

Freddie stood as the vet opened his cage. He tottered out on three legs, his feathery black tail swooping back and forth like a windscreen wiper on full speed.

'You were right, Poppy. He's lovely,' said Scarlett, giving the dog a pat. 'What breed do you think he is?'

'Oh, mainly German Shepherd with a smidgen of border collie, I should think,' said the vet.

'So he's a police dog and a sheep dog rolled into one. How cool is that, Charlie?' said Poppy.

'A police dog and a sheep dog. That's epic! He'll be able to track down and round up. We could go out onto the moor and…'

'Charlie! Don't even think about it,' warned Caroline. 'I'm not having you going after that wretched panther again, with or without Freddie,' she added, remembering the danger Poppy and Charlie had faced when Charlie decided to go hunting for big cats while she was in hospital with a broken wrist. Poppy had gone looking for him and the two children had become lost on the moor, sparking a massive rescue operation. 'I need to know that you're not going to be pulling any more stunts like that, Charlie.'

'It's OK, Mum. I promise I won't.'

Caroline produced Freddie's new collar and lead from her handbag. 'Here you are, Poppy. You do the honours.'

Poppy stroked Freddie's silky ears, eased the collar over his head and clicked on the lead, which she handed straight to Charlie. He whipped a dog treat out of his pocket. Freddie sniffed the treat and took it daintily from Charlie's flat palm, his tail thumping.

The vet watched with satisfaction. 'I think you're all going to get along just fine. I love it when a plan comes together.'

~

SATURDAY MORNING FOUND Poppy sitting cross-legged in the corner of Cloud's stable, her history homework on her lap. The pony listened intently as she read extracts from a school textbook on the Roman Empire.

'Did you know that Hadrian's Wall took at least five years to build? And that when Mount Vesuvius erupted the lava flew twenty kilometres into the air? A flock of six hundred sheep was swallowed into a huge crack in the ground. Imagine that! But I've got to write about the Roman army, so I suppose I'd better get on with it. What *is* the difference between a legion and a century?'

Poppy flicked open the textbook to the page on Roman soldiers. She was chewing the end of her fountain pen and contemplating how to begin the essay when a scrabble outside made her jump. She looked up in time to see Magpie heaving his swinging stomach over the stable door. He landed with a heavy thud, picked his way fussily over the straw to Poppy and curled up beside her. She stroked him absentmindedly and was about to begin writing when she was interrupted again, this time by her brother.

'Poppy, they're here!' Charlie announced. 'Mum says to come and say hello.'

'OK. I won't be a minute.' Poppy sighed, gave Magpie's chin a tickle and kissed Cloud goodbye. She followed the brick path around the side of the house and, as she reached the front garden, saw Caroline talking to Shelley while Charlie and Freddie waited by the front door. Hope was standing awkwardly to one side, chewing a nail. She was wearing the same green coat and beanie hat that she'd had on in the village shop. She was so slight she could have blown away in the wind. Poppy's natural shyness anchored her to the spot until Freddie noticed her loitering and woofed a greeting.

'Poppy, there you are! Come and say hello. Why don't you take Hope to see Cloud and Chester while I put the kettle on?' Caroline suggested, leading Shelley indoors.

'Who are Cloud and Chester?' asked Hope.

'Chester's a donkey. He belonged to the lady who used to own Riverdale, but she moved to a flat in Tavistock and couldn't take him with her. We kind of inherited him when we moved here. And Cloud's my pony.' Saying the words out loud still gave Poppy a thrill.

Hope's features lit up like a beacon. 'You have your own pony? No way! You're so lucky!'

'I still can't quite believe it myself,' Poppy admitted with a grin. 'Follow me, it's this way.'

As they walked around the house to the stables Poppy described how she'd found Cloud running wild on the moor and her desperate attempts to rescue him from the drift. 'To cut a very long story short, he ended up at the pony sales where my dad bought him.'

Cloud was standing at the back of his stable. 'He's nervous around people he doesn't know so don't be offended if he doesn't come and say hello,' she told Hope, who hesitated by the stable door.

'I don't think I've ever been this close to a real horse before. There aren't many in Croydon. Big, aren't they?'

Poppy slipped through the stable door and scratched Cloud's forehead fondly. 'He's broken a bone in his foot and needs to have complete box rest. That means he's not allowed out of his stable until it heals. He's due to have another X-ray in a fortnight,' she explained.

'I would love to learn to ride,' said Hope, watching Cloud nuzzle Poppy's pockets.

'I'm afraid no-one can ride Cloud until his foot heals and Chester's too old for riding, so I can't help you there. But I could have a word with Scarlett if you like. She might let you have a go on Flynn. He's a Dartmoor pony. She taught me to ride on him this summer.'

'Would you?' said Hope, her pale blue eyes shining. Then her face fell. 'I don't suppose my mum'll let me. She'll say it's too risky or something.'

'You don't know until you try. Let me speak to Scarlett first.'

'Thanks Poppy, you're really kind. But you don't understand what she's like.'

6

The fire in the lounge was crackling, sending sparks shooting up the chimney. Caroline and Shelley were perched either end of the sofa, sipping mugs of coffee. Charlie and Freddie sat on the rug in front of the fire, Freddie's bandaged paw in Charlie's lap. Magpie had retreated to the window ledge, where he eyed the dog with loathing. It was no surprise that Charlie's counselling sessions had not had the desired effect and Freddie's appearance had put Magpie's whiskered nose severely out of joint.

'I've lived in Croydon for most of my life,' Shelley was saying. She noticed the girls' arrival and patted the sofa beside her firmly, inviting her daughter to sit next to her. Hope, who had discarded her coat but was still wearing the dark grey beanie hat, sat down, leaving a noticeable gap between them.

'What brought you to Waterby? Caroline asked.

'It's just the two of us these days, isn't it, babe?' said Shelley. 'The last year hasn't been great and I thought we could both do with a change of scene.'

'Why? What happened?' asked Charlie, his curiosity piqued. Caroline shot him a look but Shelley shrugged her shoulders.

'It's OK, we don't mind people knowing, do we Hope? Last November Hope was diagnosed with leukaemia, weren't you, babe?' Hope nodded mutely. Poppy felt a swooping sensation in her stomach. Caroline looked shocked.

'What's luke…lukema?' Charlie asked.

'It's cancer of the blood. She'd been losing weight and had no energy. We found out after our doctor sent her for tests.'

'That's awful,' said Caroline.

'Tell me about it. She's spent the last ten months having chemotherapy. That's why she lost her hair.' Shelley reached over and pulled off Hope's hat. The way she did it, almost with a flourish, reminded Poppy of a waiter lifting the silver platter from a dish of food. A single tear trickled down the side of Hope's nose.

Her head was completely bald, her pink skin as soft and vulnerable as the snout of a mole. Hope gave her mother a dark look, snatched her hat back and tugged it down over her forehead.

'Alright Hope, don't get narky. I was just showing Caroline and Poppy your hair. Or should I say lack of it. I'm joking! Honestly, where's your sense of humour?'

'How is Hope now?' Caroline asked tentatively.

'Not so good. That's why she's not at school. Her immune system is so weak after all the chemo that she'd catch every infection going if she went to Waterby Primary. The oncologist has told us there's nothing more he can do. But there's a new treatment in America that's having amazing results with Hope's type of leukaemia. I just need to find a way of sending her there and paying for her treatment.'

'Crikey, I don't suppose that's going to be cheap,' Caroline said.

'I reckon it'll cost about ten grand, what with our flights to San Francisco, accommodation and the treatment itself. There's no way I can afford that. Actually I'm thinking about setting up a fund to raise the money. I might call it Hope for Hope, or something like that.'

'What a fantastic idea. We'd help, wouldn't we kids?'

Poppy was still reeling from the news of Hope's illness. She nodded vigorously. 'Yes, of course. Scarlett and I could hold a cake sale at school.'

'No offence babe, but it'll need more than a cake sale. I could do with a story in the local rag. That's what other families do and it always seems to do the trick.'

'What about Sniffer? He'd help,' said Charlie.

'He's a reporter on the Tavistock Herald. His real name's Stanley

Smith but everyone calls him Sniffer,' explained Caroline. 'He did a story on Poppy and Charlie when they saw the Beast of Dartmoor a while back. I'm sure he would be interested. I probably have his number here somewhere.'

Shelley clapped her hands. Poppy noticed she had a butterfly tattoo on the inside of her right wrist. 'I'll give him a call this afternoon. We might be able to go America after all, Hope. Wouldn't that be wicked?'

Hope looked as though it would be anything but. She looked...weary. There was no other word to describe it.

~

THE VILLAGE of Waterby was still slumbering on Friday morning when a white transit van pulled up outside the Post Office and Stores. Only Barney Broomfield was up, the lights in his shop cheerily bright in the murky half-light. The driver hopped out of the van and hauled out several bundles of newspapers, which he stacked in an untidy heap at Barney's feet. Barney hefted them one by one into the shop, sorting the national newspapers into one pile and the Tavistock Heralds into another, ready for his small band of paperboys and girls. It was a ritual he'd carried out at five o'clock every morning since he took over the shop over twenty years ago. The only lie-in he allowed himself was on Christmas Day.

After all the papers were sorted he made himself a cup of tea and picked up a copy of the Herald. He raised his eyebrows when he read the headline and saw the two faces staring solemnly back at him from the front page. 'She's a fast worker, that one,' he said to himself, as he took a slurp of tea and settled down to read.

~

POPPY DIDN'T SEE the paper until that evening. She let herself in the back door after school and ran upstairs to change out of her uniform. Her dad peered around her bedroom door.

'Hi Poppy, how was school?'

'Fine,' she replied.

He came in and sat down on the wicker chair by the window. 'Anything exciting happen?'

'Nope.'

'Are you settling in OK?'

'Yep.'

'Charlie is having tea at Ed's and Caroline has popped over to the farm to pick up some eggs. I'm in charge of dinner.'

'Oh, right,' said Poppy, impatient to see Cloud after a day apart. She pulled on a fleece top and eyed the door. Her dad sighed and stood up. He had been looking forward to a chat with Poppy. She had virtually moved into Cloud's stable and he couldn't remember the last time they had talked properly.

He tried again. 'How's Cloud doing?'

'Good, Dad. He's doing really well,' Poppy finally turned her attention to her father. He could feel the happiness radiating from her. He'd taken some convincing to buy the emaciated grey pony at the Tavistock Horse Sales but it had been the right thing to do, there was no doubt. The girl and pony belonged to each other.

'I'm glad. I've got to go to London for a couple of days tomorrow. The car's coming to pick me up at eight. We can drop you off at school on the way through if you like?'

'And Scarlett?'

'Yes, of course.' He smiled. 'Right, you'd better go and see that pony of yours. We can have a chat in the morning.'

'Thanks, Dad,' grinned Poppy. She kissed him briefly on the cheek before flying out of the room, her ponytail swinging. She paused on the landing as he called after her.

'Oh, I almost forgot. Caroline said you should have a look at the Herald. It's on the kitchen table.'

She grabbed the paper as she raced through the kitchen and out of the back door. Caroline had already brought Chester in from his paddock and the pony and donkey were both watching over the stable door for her.

'I'm sorry,' she said. 'I'll be two minutes, no longer. I promise.' In the tack room Poppy scooped pony nuts, chaff and soaked sugar beet into two buckets. She swung open the stable door, tossed the newspaper into the corner and held out the buckets. 'Here you go. Dig in.'

While they were eating she mucked out the stable. As she bent down to pick up the grooming kit she noticed the photograph on the front page of the Herald.

'That's Hope and Shelley!' The pair gazed out below an enormous headline, *Hope for Hope*. She picked up the paper and started reading.

A Waterby mum has launched a £10,000 appeal to send her daughter to America for life-saving cancer treatment.

Brave Hope Taylor was diagnosed with a rare and aggressive form of leukaemia almost a year ago and has spent the last 10 months having chemotherapy.

But the 10-year-old, who moved to Waterby with her mum Shelley earlier this month, faces an uncertain future as the chemotherapy was not successful.

'We've been told that there's nothing more doctors in the UK can do for her,' said single mum Shelley, 36.

Her only hope for Hope is a radical new treatment, which is being pioneered by a team of cancer specialists in California.

Shelley has launched a fund to raise money to pay for the treatment. She hopes people will throw their weight behind the appeal, which she has called Hope for Hope.

'We need to reach £10,000 and the sooner the better as Hope is getting weaker all the time,' she explained.

'I want people to imagine how they would feel if their only child had terminal cancer. I've set up a special Hope for Hope Facebook page where they can find out more about the treatment and how to make donations -'

Poppy stopped reading and studied the photo. Shelley's arm was draped protectively around her daughter's slight shoulders. Poppy could just make out the butterfly tattoo on her wrist. Hope wasn't wearing a hat and her eyes looked huge in her pale face. Poppy decided there and then that she would do whatever she could to help her new friend get the treatment she so badly needed.

7

When she'd settled Cloud and Chester for the night, Poppy found Caroline laying the kitchen table while her dad stirred a saucepan on the stove. Charlie was lying on his back waving his legs and arms in the air. Freddie was watching him, his head cocked, a bemused expression on his black and tan face.

'What on earth are you doing, Charlie?' asked Poppy, shaking off her boots and dropping the newspaper on the worktop.

'Teaching Freddie some tricks for the Waterby Dog Show. It's on the second Saturday of half term. Ed's mum told me about it,' he replied. 'If Freddie's foot's better we're going to enter one of the classes, aren't we Fred?' The dog thumped his tail.

'There's probably something about the dog show in the Herald. Did you see the story about Hope and Shelley?' asked Caroline, as she took four pasta bowls out of the cupboard.

Poppy nodded. Her dad started heaping spaghetti into the bowls, followed by spoonfuls of Bolognese sauce. He called it his speciality dish. In fact it was the only dish he knew how to make. Caroline was definitely the cook of the family.

'What are they like then?' he asked, as he grated parmesan cheese over the four steaming bowls.

Poppy gave her hands a cursory wash under the tap and sat down next to Caroline.

'Shelley is quite -' Caroline paused, searching for a word that wouldn't sound too judgemental. 'Single-minded, I suppose you could say. She must be, to go through all that and still come out fighting. Hope's very quiet, isn't she, Poppy?'

Poppy remembered the exchange she'd overheard in the village shop. 'Mmm,' she replied, through a forkful of spaghetti. 'She wants to learn to ride. I told her Scarlett might let her have a go on Flynn but she doesn't think her mum would let her. I suppose she thinks it'd be too dangerous, what with the cancer and everything. I also thought that Scarlett and I could have a go at baking some cakes and if they're any good we could ask Barney if we could sell them outside the shop one Saturday morning to make some money for the appeal.'

'That's a lovely idea, sweetheart. Shelley's got her work cut out, raising all that money. Perhaps we can make a donation?' Caroline asked her husband.

'Of course we should. It sounds as though Hope needs all the help she can get. Now I might sit down with the paper if that's OK with you lot? It's going to be the last chance I get to put my feet up for a couple of days.'

Poppy helped Caroline clear the table and they chatted about the weekend. Tory Wickens, the former owner of Riverdale, was coming for Sunday lunch. Since the McKeevers had bought the house she'd become a close family friend. Poppy tried to pop in to see the old woman in her sheltered flat in Tavistock every couple of weeks but it would be good to spend the day together and she was looking forward to showing her how well Cloud was looking.

'Blimey! Looks like Charlie's big cat has struck again,' said Poppy's dad from the lounge. He walked into the kitchen, the Herald in one hand, his reading glasses in the other. 'Listen to this,' he said, perching his glasses on the end of his nose.

'A big cat expert has claimed that the Beast of Dartmoor was responsible for the mutilated body of a sheep discovered near Waterby, the Herald can exclusively reveal.

'The ram's half-eaten body was found in a dense area of woodland on the outskirts of the village by two birdwatchers on Sunday morning.

'The twitchers called police and officers took the body to Tavistock Veterinary Surgery where a post mortem was carried out on Monday afternoon.

'Vet Sarah Brown told the Herald: "The ram's throat had been crushed, which is consistent with an attack by a large dog like a Rottweiler or German Shepherd."

'But when pressed by the Herald Mrs Brown said she could not rule out the possibility that an even larger animal – such as a panther – had attacked the sheep.'

Mike paused to check he still had everyone's attention. Poppy and Caroline were sitting at the kitchen table, listening avidly. Charlie was gaping at him, open-mouthed.

'Farmers fearing for the safety of their flocks urged dog owners to keep their animals under control and warned that any dog caught chasing sheep would be shot. But big cat enthusiast John Clancy, who has been tracking the fabled Beast of Dartmoor for the last five years, said he was certain that the ram had been killed by the large black cat seen by two local children near the Riverdale tor last month.

'"Although I have yet to see this majestic animal with my own eyes I am so convinced it exists that I and my fellow members of the Big Cat Society are spending every waking hour trying to track the panther down so we have proof that we have been right all along –"'

'Why can't they leave him alone!' howled Charlie, his arm around an anxious-looking Freddie.

'Don't they realise it's a wild animal, not an exhibit in a zoo?' Poppy added with feeling. When she and Charlie had glimpsed the panther on the tor she'd been in awe of its raw, untamed beauty. She hated the thought of big cat fanatics trying to track it down just to prove the cynics wrong.

'You must promise me you won't go looking for it again. Remember what happened last time,' said Caroline, concerned by the fervent expressions on the children's faces.

'Why would I? I'd be as bad as all those men chasing after him if I did. I want him to be free on the moor, not caught by the big cat men or shot by a farmer,' said Charlie, tears trickling down his cheeks.

'I know, sweetheart. Don't upset yourself. That big cat of yours knows how to stay out of everyone's way. You and Poppy are the only people to have ever seen him, don't forget. Come on, let's see if we can find anything in the paper about that dog show.' Caroline patted the chair beside her but Charlie, his thumb in his mouth, shook his head. He clung briefly to Freddie's warm neck before running out of the kitchen and upstairs to his room.

'Nice one, Mike,' Caroline said shortly, pushing back her chair and following Charlie out of the room. Poppy shot her dad a withering look.

He shrugged his shoulders. Sometimes he didn't understand his family at all. 'What did I say?'

8

By the time Mike's taxi drew up outside Riverdale the following morning all had been forgiven. After stowing his overnight bag in the boot he jumped in beside the driver and Poppy slid into the back seat. At the bottom of the Ashworthy drive they picked up Scarlett and the three of them chatted about school all the way to Tavistock. Outside the school gates he gave Poppy a hug. 'Be good for Caroline and keep Charlie out of trouble. I'll see you in a couple of days.'

She and Scarlett stood and waved as the taxi did a three point turn and accelerated off towards Plymouth. Scarlett linked arms with Poppy and they joined the stream of students walking through the school gates.

'Let's try out our baking skills tonight, shall we Poppy? I could come round to yours after tea. What d'you reckon?'

'Good idea. I keep thinking about Hope. What must it be like, having no hair? And imagine being told that all the chemotherapy was for nothing? But I have to warn you, I'm about as good at cooking as I am at algebra, and that's not saying much.'

~

POPPY SNORTED with laughter when Scarlett arrived at the back door that evening wearing a Superman apron.

'Yes, well, I didn't want to get my new top dirty. My brother bought it for Dad last Christmas, not that I've ever seen him cooking. It was the only one I could find. Anyway, it's not that funny,' Scarlett grumbled, as she unpacked eggs from a carrier bag. 'Mum sent these over in case we needed them. We've got a glut at the moment.'

Caroline poked her head around the door. 'Hello Scarlett! I've left the cupcake recipe on the dresser. Give me a shout if you need anything.'

Within a few minutes the kitchen looked like the set of MasterChef. Scarlett lined up bags of flour, caster sugar and chocolate chips from the cupboards while Poppy ferreted around in the fridge for the butter.

'I should have got it out earlier. It's as hard as a rock,' she said, giving the butter a hopeful squeeze.

'I'm sure it'll be fine,' said her friend breezily. Scarlett's mum Pat was renowned across Dartmoor for her baking skills and her creations usually won first prize in the village show. As a result Scarlett considered herself to be something of a cake connoisseur. Unfortunately she hadn't inherited Pat's light touch in the kitchen. She wiped her hands on the Superman apron. 'Right, let's get this show on the road.'

Fifteen minutes later Scarlett's freckles were covered by a light dusting of flour and Poppy's jumper was smeared with streaks of egg and butter. She tucked her hair behind her ears and looked dubiously at their cake mixture.

'It looks a bit...lumpy,' she said, picking out a shard of egg shell.

'Nah, it'll be fine once it's cooked. Let's spoon it into the cases and stick it in the oven. I think it says twenty five minutes, doesn't it?' asked Scarlett.

'Gives us just about enough time to clear up the kitchen a bit before Caroline sees it,' giggled Poppy. How they had managed to use quite so many bowls and utensils to make twenty cupcakes was beyond her.

Just as the timer on the oven started beeping Charlie ran into the kitchen, swaddled in his fleece dressing gown and his hair smelling of shampoo. Caroline followed him in.

'They smell lovely! Can I have one, Mum? I'll clean my teeth again,' he promised.

'You two can be our guinea pigs, although I'm sure they'll be delicious,' said Scarlett.

But when Poppy lifted the tray out of the oven she and Scarlett gasped.

Charlie was puzzled. 'I thought you were making chocolate chip cupcakes?' he said. 'Those look more like dog biscuits!'

'They do look slightly well done,' Caroline said. 'And are you sure you used self-raising flour?' She picked up the packet. There was silence as they all read the label. Plain flour.

'Oops,' said Scarlett, grinning. 'I was in charge of flour. My mistake. Shall we try again?'

But Poppy had a thought. She turned to Charlie. 'What did you say they looked like?' she asked him.

'Dog biscuits. I bet Freddie would love them,' he said. Freddie looked up from his basket and woofed softly. 'See?' he added.

'I don't think dogs are supposed to have chocolate, I remember reading it somewhere. But we could have a go at making proper dog biscuits. I'm sure we could find a recipe on the internet,' Poppy said.

'We could sell them at the Waterby Dog Show!' said Scarlett. 'We'd have a captive audience. We'd sell loads!'

'That's an excellent idea, you two. I'll have a look for some recipes later. Come on Charlie, let's get you to bed.' Caroline paused at the door. 'By the way, I love the apron, Scarlett. But I'm not sure you fully channelled Superman's powers tonight.'

9

As November approached the Riverdale wood had never looked more beautiful. The cold nights had quickened the transformation of the wood's acid green shades to vibrant autumnal hues. The horse chestnuts had been the first to turn gold and amber, closely followed by the ash and sycamore trees. But as the days raced by even the oaks and beech trees caught up, their leaves a stunning array of burnt orange, saffron and cinnamon.

Four enormous pumpkins in Caroline's vegetable garden were growing plumper by the day, as was Freddie, whose once matted black and tan coat now shone with good health. Charlie, who never let a brush near his own hair, was meticulous about grooming the dog every evening after school. Freddie sat patiently in front of the fire while the six-year-old brushed and combed, preened and primped. Charlie was still deciding which class to enter at the Waterby Dog Show. 'I don't think we're going to be able to go in for the agility ones this year,' he told his family over dinner on Friday night. 'Freddie's leg might not be better in time.'

Poppy reached for the Tavistock Herald and flicked through until she came to a report on the forthcoming show. 'You could try for the dog with the waggiest tail or the most appealing eyes,' she suggested. 'Or there's a class for the most handsome dog and another for the dog the judge would most like to take home.'

'I'm not entering that one - I don't want the judge taking him home!' cried Charlie, horrified.

'I don't think that's what it means, Charlie. But look, here's a perfect one for Freddie – the best rescue dog. He'd have a really good chance of winning that.'

The phone rang and Caroline disappeared into the lounge to answer it. She came back and sat down. 'That was Shelley. She's invited us over for coffee tomorrow morning.'

Charlie pulled a face. 'Do we have to? I'd much rather go and see Ed.'

'Yes,' she replied firmly. 'It won't do you any harm to keep poor Hope company for an hour or so.'

Privately Poppy agreed with Charlie. She'd much rather spend the morning with Cloud. And she had a ton of homework to do. But she had a fleeting image of Hope standing alone at the window of George Blackstone's ramshackle farm cottage and felt a tug of sympathy for the girl.

'I don't mind,' she told Caroline. 'We can tell Hope and her mum about the dog biscuits. They might even like to come to the dog show.'

'Thank-you, sweetheart,' Caroline said, flashing Poppy a grateful smile. It wasn't so long ago that Poppy had felt alienated by her step-mother, despite Caroline's best efforts to connect with her. These days she basked in Caroline's approval. What a lot of time she'd wasted. She smiled back, her heart as light as a feather. 'Anytime, Mum.'

FLINT COTTAGE LOOKED SLIGHTLY LESS DILAPIDATED than when she and Scarlett had last visited. Someone had hacked down the brambles and nettles in the front garden and the grimy windows had been treated to a perfunctory clean. Poppy and Charlie followed Caroline up the uneven path and watched as she rang the bell. This time Shelley flung open the door.

'Alright? Welcome to the madhouse. Hope's in the front room. Why don't you kids go and find her and I'll put the kettle on.'

The children slipped off their shoes. Charlie stopped in his tracks when he clocked the massive flat screen television on the wall in the lounge. It was about three times the size of the McKeevers' aging set.

'I wish we had a telly like that!' he said.

Poppy, meanwhile, had noticed the brown-haired girl sitting curled up on a scruffy armchair in the corner of the room. Her shiny conker-brown bob had fallen forward, hiding her face as she read a book. White wires trailed from her ears to an iPod on her lap. Her head was nodding in time to the music.

Was it Hope? But this girl had a glossy head of hair. She seemed oblivious to their presence.

'Hello?' said Poppy tentatively. The girl didn't react so Poppy tried again, louder. The girl still didn't look up.

'HOPE!' Charlie bellowed at the top of his voice, the sound reverberating around the small, square room. 'IS THAT YOU?'

The girl gave a start and looked up from her novel, her eyebrows raised in surprise. Underneath the heavy fringe was Hope's pale face. For the briefest second Poppy saw a look of apprehension – or was it fear – sweep across her features. She took her earphones out, wound the lead around her iPod and closed the book. Her actions were slow and deliberate, as if she needed time to compose herself. And when she looked up again the expression on her face was blank.

'Crikey, your hair grew back quickly,' remarked Charlie, heading for a closer look at the television.

'Charlie!' Poppy admonished.

'It's a wig,' Hope said in her breathy voice. 'My mum sent for it the other day and it arrived in the post this morning. It's made with human hair.'

Charlie turned from the television and stared at Hope in fascination. 'What, from a real live dead person?'

'Charlie!' cried Poppy again, her face flushing with embarrassment. Sometimes he had the sensitivity of a gnat.

'S'alright,' said Hope, with the barest hint of a smile. 'Some people donate their hair to charities that make wigs for people like me. It doesn't come from dead people.'

'I like it,' said Poppy firmly, trying to make amends for her brother's lack of tact. 'It suits you.'

Charlie opened his mouth to speak, but when he saw the expression on his sister's face he snapped it shut again.

'What was your hair like before?' Poppy asked, sitting down on the edge of the faded brown sofa opposite Hope.

The girl smiled. Her face was transformed. 'It was down to my waist and was as yellow as straw. My dad used to call me Rapunzel. This hair feels a bit weird, to be honest. But at least it makes a change from the hat.'

'Where is your dad? Is he dead?' asked Charlie, plonking himself on the sofa next to his sister. Poppy winced and elbowed him sharply in the ribs.

'Ow! What did you do that for! I was only asking!'

'No, he isn't dead. He moved out last summer,' said Hope, her voice low. 'He and Mum are getting a divorce.'

'Do you get to see him very often?' Poppy asked.

'I haven't seen him for over a year. He lives in Canada now with Kirstin, his new girlfriend. My mum won't let me -'

'Your mum won't let you *what?*'

Hope almost jumped out of her skin at the sound of Shelley's voice. No-one had noticed the lounge door open. Hope fell silent, leaving the sentence dangling like a spider on a silk thread, and stared at her mum warily.

'You won't let me go to school. Because of all the germs,' she finished lamely.

Shelley's face cleared. 'That's right, babe. I can teach you everything you need to know right here. Who needs school anyway? It didn't exactly do me any favours. Do you lot want a drink?'

She was back moments later with three glasses of orange squash which she set down on the coffee table. Hope went to stand up but caught her foot on the corner of a rug and lost her balance. As she put out a hand to steady herself she knocked the tray, which wobbled as dangerously as a ship on a stormy sea. Hope paled as the vivid orange liquid sloshed over the tops of the glasses.

Shelley seized Hope's wrist and pulled the girl towards her. 'Look what you've done now, you stupid girl!' she spat.

'I'm sorry, Mum. It was an accident. I'll clear it up.'

Shelley twisted Hope's wrist and pushed her towards the door. 'Too right you will. Go and get a cloth before it leaks onto the carpet,' she ordered.

Remembering that Poppy and Charlie were still in the room Shelley turned to them and forced a smile. But her eyes remained narrowed. 'I don't know, how clumsy can you get?' she asked. Poppy picked at a broken nail and said nothing. Even Charlie had been left speechless by the venom in Shelley's voice.

'Right. Well, I'll leave you to it.' With that Shelley swept out of the room. Poppy noticed Hope standing just outside the door, holding a cloth in one hand and twiddling nervously with a strand of her copper-coloured wig with the other as her mum passed. She slunk into the room and began dabbing ineffectually at the spilt squash.

'Here, let me do it,' said Poppy. She eased the cloth from Hope's thin fingers and wiped up the mess. 'There you go, all sorted.'

Hope murmured her thanks and folded herself into the armchair.

'Hope –' Poppy began. But the girl turned away. The shutters had come down. The atmosphere in the small lounge suddenly felt oppressive and Poppy was relieved for once when Charlie broke the silence.

'Can we turn on the telly?'

'If you like.' Hope stood up, crossed the room and switched on the television. She picked up the remote control and pressed a couple of buttons. Nothing happened. She waved the remote in the direction of the set and kept pressing. The screen remained stubbornly blank.

'Sorry, I haven't sussed out how to work it yet,' she admitted.

'Let me have a look,' offered Charlie. Hope passed him the remote control. 'It's the same as Ed's.' Charlie fiddled with the remote and the reassuring face of Sir David Attenborough filled the screen. 'Oh cool, a wildlife programme. Can we watch this?' he asked.

Poppy and Hope, each deep in their own thoughts, nodded. Neither girl knew quite what to say to the other so they watched TV without speaking until it was time to go home.

Tory Wickens eased the yellowing newspaper cutting into a clear plastic sleeve and placed it in her handbag, careful not to crease it. She had spent the last hour sifting through a box of papers and photos before finding the cutting buried at the bottom. She hadn't touched the box for years. It held too many memories, some of which were still raw. Tory could look at her wedding photographs with equanimity – it was fifteen years since her husband Douglas had died and in that time her grief had softened and blurred. But she could hardly bear to look at the photos of her daughter, Jo, and her granddaughter, Caitlyn. Since Caitlyn's death she and Jo had barely spoken. Tory ran a hand through her white hair and tried to drag her thoughts away from the hunter trial in Widecombe where Caitlyn and her pony had fallen. The chiming clock on the mantelpiece interrupted her thoughts. Ten o'clock. Her nephew was a stickler for punctuality and would be here any moment to drive her to Riverdale. Tory picked up her bag and her two walking sticks and shuffled to the front door to meet him.

POPPY PACED up and down the stable, her hands behind her back, with the air of a Brigadier inspecting his troops. She stopped to pick an errant piece of straw out of Chester's woolly forelock before straightening Cloud's rug for the second time.

'I think you pass muster. In fact you both look gorgeous, even though I say so myself,' she told them. She looked down at her fleece top and jeans, now covered in the dust and grime that she'd spent the last hour brushing off Chester and Cloud. 'Although I can't say the same for me – I'm filthy. I'd better go and change before Tory gets here. Now you two,' she added sternly. 'Remember to be on your best behaviour, please.'

When she heard a car pull up outside the front door, Poppy ran down the stairs, two at a time, and slid to a halt in the hallway, where Charlie was introducing Tory to Freddie. The dog offered his bandaged paw to Tory.

'It's nice to meet you too, Freddie,' she told him. 'What a handsome chap you are. I hear that you're going to be the star attraction at Waterby Dog Show this year.' The dog thumped his tail and Charlie grinned.

'We've been practising, haven't we, Freddie? I've been watching some of the dancing dogs on YouTube. It's given me lots of ideas.'

Caroline and Poppy groaned in unison. Caroline took Tory's coat. 'Would you like a cup of tea,' she asked.

Tory shook her head. 'Tea can wait. I'd much rather see Cloud and Chester first. Poppy can take me, can't you, pet?'

Poppy took Tory's arm and they made their way down the hallway, through the kitchen and out of the back door.

'Are they still sharing a stable?' Tory asked.

'I did try them on their own but Cloud made a terrible racket, calling and kicking the door. I was worried he was going to do himself some serious damage. As soon as I put Chester back in the stable he was OK.'

'They always did share, you know. Ever since that first day I brought Cloud home from the horse sales. Caitlyn and I didn't like to separate them.'

Tory's reminder that Cloud had been Caitlyn's long before he was Poppy's needled. For the last few weeks she hadn't given Caitlyn a second thought. Tory walked slowly over to Cloud, who was standing behind Chester at the back of the stable. Cloud stood motionless, his brown eyes never leaving Tory's lined face as she placed a hand on the Connemara's forehead. It was such a tender, affectionate gesture that Poppy felt as though she was intruding on an intensely private moment. She tried to concentrate on the back of Tory's hand, but the old woman's papery-white skin, dotted with liver spots, swam before her. Suddenly she saw Caitlyn, crouched low over Cloud's neck as he galloped across the moor, his silver mane and tail streaming behind him. She remembered Tory's words the day she'd told Poppy about the accident. How Cloud would do anything for Caitlyn. How they trusted each other completely. How the pony's heart had been broken the day she died. Poppy shook her head and the picture of Caitlyn and Cloud disappeared.

Tory returned to her side. 'Cloud is looking so well, Poppy. You really are doing a super job.'

'I don't know, Tory. I don't know anything about looking after a pony. Not compared to you. Or Caitlyn.'

'Well, it doesn't look like it to me. Chester's never looked better and it's hard to believe that Cloud has spent the last few years running wild on the moor. Don't do yourself down.'

Chester chose that moment to walk over and give his former owner a businesslike nudge. Tory laughed and produced a new packet of Polos from her coat pocket. 'Alright Chester, is this what you were looking for? You have the memory of an elephant, my old friend.'

～

AT THE KITCHEN TABLE, in front of mugs of tea, Tory ferreted around in her bag.

'I've brought something to show you, Poppy. It's an old newspaper report of Brambleton Horse Show in 2006. Caitlyn and Cloud came first in the open jumping class. You remember the photo I have of the two of them being presented with a red rosette? That was the day it was taken. I thought you might like to see it.'

Poppy scanned the article. Phrases like 'huge potential', 'winning streak' and 'unbeatable team' leapt out at her from the faded type. She felt Tory's eyes on her and forced a smile.

'It's excellent, Tory. You must have been so proud of them both,' she said, to the old woman's obvious pleasure.

Caroline, busy peeling potatoes at the sink, was the only one to notice the tiny catch in Poppy's voice, but said nothing.

Over lunch the McKeevers filled Tory in on the Hope for Hope Appeal and Poppy showed her the recipe for dog biscuits Caroline had found.

'That poor girl. Pass me my bag would you, Charlie dear? Please give this to Hope's mum with my best wishes the next time you see her, Caroline.' Poppy watched as Tory slid a cheque for five hundred pounds across the table.

'Are you sure, Tory? That's an awful lot of money,' said Caroline.

'I was going to treat myself to a new washing machine but it can wait. This is much more important. I'd like to do whatever I can to help,' the old woman said firmly.

Scarlett's dad, Bill, had once again offered to take Cloud to Tavistock for his next vet appointment. Poppy and Scarlett rode in the front of the Land Rover while Caroline and Charlie sat in the back with Freddie. Scarlett sang along to songs on the radio, making up the lyrics she didn't know, which gave Charlie the giggles. Poppy watched the moor race past the window, her thoughts, as always, dominated by Cloud.

'Do you remember Caitlyn, Bill?' she said in a gap between songs. He nodded.

'What was she like?'

'She was a lovely girl, always smiling. You remember her, don't you Scarlett? She used to babysit you and your brother occasionally when your mum and I were busy lambing.'

Scarlett was silent, trying to remember, then exclaimed, 'Yes, I think I do! Did she have long, blonde hair? Almost down to her waist? I used to love it when she babysat! She let us watch whatever we wanted on the telly.'

'That's her. It was such a tragedy when she died. The whole village was in shock. Why do you ask, Poppy?'

'Oh, no reason. I just wondered, that's all.' Poppy returned her gaze to the window. As they reached the outskirts of town, she felt a flutter of nerves. What if Cloud's fracture hadn't healed? What if it was worse? Caroline, watching from the back seat, read her mind.

'Don't worry, Poppy. I'm sure it'll be good news.'

~

CAROLINE WAS RIGHT to be optimistic.

'Let's start with Freddie's X-ray,' said the vet, as they joined her in the consulting room an hour later. 'See here? His bone has knitted together perfectly, just as I'd hoped. We can take his cast off today. I'm sure he'll be glad to see the back of it.'

'What about Cloud's?' asked Poppy, although she'd known as soon as the vet had pinned the X-ray to the light box. She could still see a faint crack running down the length of his hoof.

'I'm afraid he's not got the all clear yet. But look, here's the X-ray we took a month ago. There's definitely an improvement. The bone is healing, Poppy. It's just going to take time.'

Poppy gave the vet a wan smile.

'I'll see Cloud again in another month and hopefully his foot will be as good as new. Right, let's take off Freddie's plaster cast.'

Caroline looked at her watch. 'I promised Bill we'd be finished by now. I'd better go and tell him we're almost ready. Come and find me when you're done here, you two.'

Poppy held Freddie's lead as the vet rooted around in her bag for a pair of surgical scissors. Charlie noticed her silver name badge as she bent down to start snipping away at the grubby cast. 'Are you the vet who was in the paper talking about the black panther?' he asked suddenly.

'You've got a good memory. Why do you ask?'

'Do you really think that sheep was killed by a dog?'

The vet busied herself tidying away the pieces of plaster. Eventually she looked up. 'Look, the last thing I want to do is scaremonger,' she hedged.

'You can tell us. We won't tell anyone, I swear. We just want him to be safe. It was me and Poppy who saw the panther on the moor, you see.'

The vet was silent for a moment. She had worked for a spell at London Zoo when she'd first graduated and knew exactly what a carcass looked like when it had been mauled by big cats.

'It's OK,' said Poppy. 'We really won't tell.'

'Alright. But this has to remain between these four walls, otherwise the big cat fanatics will start causing mayhem. Yes, I am one hundred per cent certain that the ram was killed by a big cat. It probably was a panther, judging by the size of the teeth marks.'

'I knew it!' breathed Charlie. 'But why has no-one ever seen him apart from us?'

'I've been wondering about that,' admitted the vet. 'He might be old, he might be ill. Dartmoor is so vast only a desperate animal would come so close to Waterby to hunt.'

Poppy could see her brother was looking tearful and she squeezed his hand. 'He looked pretty healthy when we saw him. He'll be OK. Come on, Charlie. We'd better go and find Caroline.'

Poppy couldn't get the image of Cloud and Caitlyn out of her mind for the next couple of days. Looking after Cloud had been second nature but suddenly she felt clumsy and inept. As if he sensed her crisis of confidence, Cloud withdrew to the back of his stable. The harder she tried to get things right, whether it was tying a quick release knot or picking out his feet, the more ham-fisted she became. She found herself constantly apologising to the pony.

One evening after school Caroline found her in the kitchen, her head in her hands, staring morosely at a pile of schoolbooks that lay untouched in front of her.

'What's wrong, Poppy?'

'Oh, it's nothing. Not really,' she answered evasively.

'Is it school?'

'No. School's fine. Too much homework as usual, but no change there.'

'Have you and Scarlett had a falling out?'

Poppy looked at Caroline as though she was mad.

'Have I done something to upset you?'

Poppy shook her head.

'Is it Cloud?'

'Not really. Well, yes. Sort of.' Poppy hid behind her fringe so her stepmother couldn't see her face.

'Come on, sweetheart. You can tell me. What's bothering you?' Caroline smoothed her fringe away.

'It's Caitlyn,' she finally admitted.

'Caitlyn?'

'She was such a good rider. She and Cloud won loads of competitions together. Did you see that newspaper article Tory showed me? They were an 'unbeatable team'.' Poppy sketched apostrophe marks in the air. 'When – if – Cloud is ever sound again I'll never be as good as her. I know Scarlett's taught me the basics but I don't know how to do a collected canter, let alone a flying change. I'm worried I'll let him down.'

'Don't be so hard on yourself, Poppy. We all have to start somewhere. Don't forget you only began riding in the summer. Look how well you've come on since then.'

'But Flynn's a schoolmaster. He looks after me, not the other way around. Cloud hasn't been ridden for years. It'll be like backing a youngster and I don't have the experience to do that. I'll be next to useless.'

'Leave it with me,' Caroline said firmly, as an idea formed in her mind.

The next morning Poppy's dad came to find her as she swept the yard. He came straight to the point. 'Caroline says you're worried that you're not experienced enough to ride Cloud.'

Poppy leant the broom against the stable door and nodded mutely.

'I was going to mention this at Christmas, but it seems silly not to tell you now. When your mum died she left you a bit of money. Not much - a couple of thousand pounds. I was thinking, would you like to use some of it to have some proper riding lessons? While Cloud's stuck in his stable?'

'Dad, are you serious?'

'Absolutely.'

'I would love to! Not that Scarlett hasn't been a good teacher, she has. But there's so much I don't know.'

'I thought you might say yes. I've already rung Bella Thompson and explained the situation.'

'Who?'

'Bella's a friend of Tory's and owns Redhall Manor Equestrian Centre on the Okehampton road. She's the lady I met at the pony sales in Tavistock.'

Poppy cast her mind back to the day Cloud arrived at Riverdale. Bella had convinced her dad to buy the emaciated pony and for this Poppy would always be grateful.

'She's quite a character,' her dad continued, remembering Bella's hearty handshake and her striking resemblance to Chester. 'But she certainly knows her stuff. She says she would be delighted to give you some private lessons. I've booked your first one for Thursday at five.'

Poppy flung her arms around her dad and he ruffled her hair. 'It was Caroline's idea,' he said. 'And your mum would definitely have approved.'

12

Poppy spent the twenty minute journey to Redhall Manor trying to calm the butterflies in her stomach. She knew any nerves would be transmitted to the pony she would be riding.

'Don't worry, once you get started you'll be absolutely fine,' said Caroline, as they pulled into the yard.

As they climbed out of the car a woman's booming voice ricocheted off the walls of the stable blocks, which lined three sides of the yard.

'Sam! Why is Murphy still in his stable? He should have been turned out half an hour ago. And that hay still needs soaking!'

A boy not much older than Poppy appeared from an open door and scuttled across the yard, disappearing into a stable opposite. Hot on his heels strode a woman in jodhpurs and a quilted jacket, her grey hair covered by a headscarf. She stopped when she saw Poppy and Caroline.

'Hello! I'm Bella Thompson. Mike's told me all about you, Poppy, and of course I know Cloud of old,' she bellowed, pumping their hands vigorously.

'I wanted to thank you for everything you did at the pony sales. I don't know what would have happened if Dad hadn't met you there,' said Poppy.

'A beautiful pony with a long life ahead of him would have ended up as dog food. We were bidding against the knackerman, after all. It doesn't bear thinking about. Anyway, let's not dwell on such gloomy thoughts. Are you all set?'

Poppy nodded.

'You're going to ride Red Rose. Rosie for short. She's tacked up and waiting in her stable. At least I hope she is. Sam!' she yelled. 'Have you done Rosie yet?'

The boy poked his head over the stable door. 'Yes Gran, she's all ready. I'll bring her out.'

'My eldest grandson,' Bella explained. 'He's a good boy at heart but he's a terrible daydreamer. He's on another planet most of the time.'

The boy shot them a rueful look and led a pretty strawberry roan mare out of the stable. 'I'll hold her while you get on,' he said, pulling down the stirrup leathers.

Poppy grabbed her skull cap, placed her left foot in the stirrup and swung into the saddle. Rosie was at least a hand higher than Flynn and much narrower than the rotund Dartmoor pony. The butterflies re-appeared with a vengeance.

'We're in the indoor school today. This way,' said Bella. Rosie followed her owner obediently towards the door of the school before Poppy had a chance to try any of her aids.

'Rosie is a New Forest pony. They make great riding school ponies because they can turn their hand to anything, whether it's polo, gymkhanas, jumping or dressage. I bred Rosie myself. I still have her dam, although she's retired from the school now.'

By now they had arrived in the indoor school. The walls of the floodlit steel-framed building were whitewashed and Poppy noticed the dressage markers A, K, E, H, C, M, B and F painted in black at ground level.

'So, how much riding have you done?' Bella asked.

'I only started at the beginning of the summer. I've been riding my friend's Dartmoor pony. She gave me some lessons at the start and we've hacked out a lot but that's about it. I'm sorry, I don't feel that I know very much at all really,' Poppy trailed off.

'No, that's good. It's the riders who think they know it all that are the hardest to teach. By the time they come to me they've usually picked up so many bad habits it's almost impossible to re-educate them. Never apol-ogise for wanting to learn, Poppy. Right, I'd like you to walk Rosie around the school on the right rein please.'

Poppy gathered up her reins and squeezed her legs gently. Rosie responded immediately and started walking clockwise around the school. Her stride was much longer than Flynn's and Poppy tried to sit as deeply in the saddle as she could.

'A good rider has a feel for their horse. Good balance is vital,' said Bella, watching her appraisingly. 'Relax your arms, Poppy. They look like they're glued to your sides. You need to keep the contact with Rosie's mouth but I don't want you looking like a robot.'

Poppy tried to relax her arms, her eyes fixed on Rosie's roan ears.

'Look ahead, Poppy, not down at Rosie. That's better. I want you to sit tall in the saddle. Imagine someone's tied a balloon to your head and grow taller from the waist up. Right, change rein diagonally from M to K and at F I'd like you to ask Rosie to trot.'

Poppy had just passed H. Used to Flynn's strong mouth and laidback attitude to schooling she started tugging her right rein at M, aiming for the diagonal. Rosie gave a couple of shakes of her head and flicked her tail in displeasure.

'Don't yank at her reins, she has a soft mouth, Poppy. You should use each of your legs and hands when turning. Your inside leg creates impulsion and your outside leg controls the pony's hindquarters. Use your inside hand to ask her to bend and guide her direction and your outside hand to control the amount of bend and impulsion. Does that make sense?'

Poppy nodded.

'Right. Let's try again when you reach F. I want you to change rein from F to H. As you are preparing to turn you should look in the direction you want to go. Put a light pressure on your inside rein. This will warn Rosie that you are about to ask her to turn. Keep your inside leg on the girth and your outside leg just behind the girth and when you're ready ask her to turn with your inside hand and squeeze your legs. You want Rosie to bend with her whole body, not just her neck. That was much better. When you're ready ask her to trot.'

Poppy squeezed with her legs and Rosie started to trot.

'Sit for a few strides until you feel her rhythm change then you can start to rise. Keep your hands nice and still and keep a light contact with Rosie's mouth. Very good, Poppy. Slow to a walk at K and I'd like you to change rein on the diagonal again from H to F.'

As she walked around the school Bella kept talking. 'A transition from trot to walk needs to be ridden just as positively as walk to trot to keep the pony's impulsion. Maintain your contact on the reins and sit for a few strides before you ask her to walk. When you are ready apply pressure to the reins. Make it firm but don't tug. Sit up tall and deep in the saddle and squeeze your legs so her back end doesn't trail and you bring her quarters under. You can give her a slightly longer rein once she's walking but you must maintain contact and impulsion.'

For the rest of the hour Poppy practiced her transitions from walk to trot and back again under Bella's eagle eye. Once she started using her aids correctly Rosie proved herself a willing and responsive ride. At the end of the lesson Bella gave the pony a pat and smiled at Poppy.

'Well done. You've a lot to learn but you have a natural balance and, more importantly, you listen. Having the right attitude is what'll help you become an accomplished rider, Poppy. Same time next week?'

Poppy floated back to the car and on the journey home gave Caroline a minute by minute account of the last hour, forgetting that her stepmother had watched the whole lesson.

When she finally stopped talking Caroline said, 'I'm glad you enjoyed it so much. Listen, I've had an idea that I wanted to run past you.'

Poppy was silent as her stepmother outlined her suggestion. As far as Poppy was concerned it was a no-brainer.

'It's a great idea, Mum. I wish I'd thought of it myself,' she said.

The minute the car had crunched up the Riverdale drive she raced around the side of the house to see Cloud.

'I rode a mare called Rosie who's about as big as you. She's lovely, though not as perfect as you, obviously. I'm already learning loads, Cloud. We did transitions from walk to trot today and next week Bella said we might try a canter. You know all this stuff already, of course.' Poppy pictured Caitlyn and Cloud flying over a brightly-painted show jump but she pushed the thought aside. 'I'll keep going until I'm as good as Caitlyn,' she whispered into his mane.

13

A t the weekend, Caroline insisted on popping into Flint Cottage to see Shelley on their way home from the supermarket.

'I've got a bag of clothes Poppy's grown out of and I wondered if they'd be any good for Hope,' said Caroline to Shelley when she answered the door.

'Oh, thanks. Have you got time for a quick cuppa?'

Shelley was wearing her blonde hair loose around her shoulders and she'd swapped her trademark leggings and denim jacket for a pair of skinny jeans that looked brand new, shiny leather boots and a fitted checked jacket. Funny, thought Poppy. It was exactly the kind of outfit Caroline wore.

'You look great. New hairdo?' Caroline asked as she followed Shelley into the kitchen.

'Yeah. Thought I'd treat myself. Hope's moping in her room, Poppy. Honestly, she's as miserable as sin. Perhaps you can cheer her up.'

Hope's bedroom was little more than a box room at the back of the house, overlooking the overgrown back garden. The only furniture apart from the bed was a chipped white melamine bedside cabinet and a matching bookcase. The magnolia walls were bare apart from the occasional scuff mark and the faded red curtains clashed with the fuchsia pink duvet cover and the threadbare green carpet. Poppy pictured her own bedroom at Riverdale. Twinkling fairy lights over a wrought iron bedframe, walls covered in her favourite horse posters and a patchwork blanket, knitted by Caroline, on the end of her bed. Hope's room, by comparison, felt unloved. Much like Hope herself, Poppy thought.

'It's not as nice as your room,' said Hope, reading her mind.

'Don't be silly, it's a great room,' Poppy lied. 'And look at the view from your window. You can even see the moor.'

Hope sat on the end of her bed while Poppy investigated her collection of pony books. She was impressed. There were dozens of tattered Pullein-Thompson, Ruby Ferguson, Patricia Leitch, Elyne Mitchell and Monica Edwards novels as well as a stack of more modern books.

'Wow, you've got loads more than me.'

'My dad used to get them for me. He was always looking in charity shops and car boot sales and bought anything with a horse or pony on the cover because he knew I'd love it. He always said his best find was this one. It only cost him twenty pence at a boot fair.' Hope reached for a hardback book of short stories and gave it to Poppy.

As she flicked through the pages she yelped.

'What's wrong?' asked Hope.

'Nothing, just a paper cut.' They both watched as a drop of dark red blood oozed from the pad of Poppy's right index finger. 'I don't suppose you have any plasters?'

'Yes, there should be some in the bathroom cabinet. Help yourself.'

The bathroom was at the top of the stairs. Poppy could hear Shelley and Caroline chatting in the kitchen below. She wound a piece of toilet roll around her finger, holding it in place with her thumb while she opened the door of the bathroom cabinet. There was the usual jumble of lotions and potions: antiseptic cream, eyewash, indigestion tablets, cotton wool and a couple of packets of painkillers. Poppy found a small box of plasters tucked between a can of shaving foam and a packet of razors. She took one out, threw the now blood-stained piece of toilet roll in the overflowing bin and stuck the plaster on clumsily with her left hand.

At the top of the stairs Poppy paused to listen to Shelley and Caroline.

'I think country life must be agreeing with Hope. She looks so well,' Caroline was saying.

'Whaddya mean?' Shelley answered sharply.

'Oh, only that she has more colour and she's put on a bit of weight. She seems to be thriving.'

Shelley made a noise that was somewhere between a harrumph and a tsk. Poppy cocked her head so she could hear the reply. Shelley's tone was reproachful. 'The oncologist did say Hope would feel a lot better once the final dose of chemotherapy was out of her system. He told us to make the most of this time because it would be the calm before the storm.'

'Of course. How tactless of me. But actually, I wanted to talk to you about that. Poppy's started having riding lessons at Redhall Manor and we were wondering if Hope would like to join her.'

'Riding lessons? Why on earth would Hope want riding lessons?' Shelley scoffed. 'There's no way I'm forking out for that.'

'We thought that after all she's been through it would give her something positive to focus on. And there's no need to worry about the cost. I spoke to the woman who runs the riding school yesterday and explained about Hope. Bella's read all about the appeal in the Herald. She said she would waive the cost of Hope's lessons. In fact she insisted on it. She's brilliant with beginners. Poppy is having lessons every Thursday evening from five until six. I can pick Hope up and drop her off home afterwards. I told Poppy not to mention it to Hope just in case you thought it wasn't such a good idea. Have a think and let me know.'

'For free you say?' There was a pause as Shelley considered the offer. Poppy crossed her fingers. 'Oh OK, if it's not going to cost me anything, why not? Don't look a riding school gift horse in the mouth, that's what I say.'

Poppy could hear Shelley titter at her own joke as she turned and headed for Hope's room.

'All sorted,' she announced, holding up her finger to show Hope the plaster. 'And I know I should probably wait until your mum tells you but I can't. You know how desperate you are to learn to ride? I've got some news.'

14

The week dragged slowly as Poppy counted the days until her next riding lesson. They picked up Hope on the way. She was quiet on the drive to Redhall Manor, which Poppy put down to nerves. Dressed in Scarlett's hand-me-down jodhpurs and black jodhpur boots and an old quilted anorak of Poppy's, Hope stood awkwardly when they arrived at the riding school.

Sam was nowhere to be seen but Bella was tacking up a chestnut Dartmoor pony slightly smaller than Flynn but no less wide of girth.

'Hello Poppy! And Hope, I presume? I'm Bella. Pleased to meet you, dear. I'm so glad you could come. This is Buster. I thought he'd be perfect for you.'

Poppy noticed a dull flush creep up Hope's neck. It must be hard when everyone thought you were a charity case, she thought. But still, no-one in their right mind would turn down free riding lessons with the indomitable Bella Thompson.

'Rosie's in her stable, Poppy. I'd like you to have a go at tacking her up for me while I get Hope started. The tack room's the last door on the left.'

Once Bella had found Hope a skull cap that fitted she checked Buster's girth, pulled down his stirrups and showed Hope how to gather her reins in her left hand, place her left foot in the stirrup and swing into the saddle. While she talked Hope through the correct riding position Poppy walked the length of the yard to the tack room. It was a long, narrow room with a small window at the far end. One wall was covered with saddles on red racks. Hanging below each saddle was the corresponding bridle and above was a small wooden plaque showing each horse or pony's name. Poppy breathed in the heady mix of leather and saddle soap.

'Rosie's saddle is the last but one on the end,' said a voice, making her jump.

Sam was standing in the doorway, an empty bucket in one hand, a muddy headcollar in the other.

'Sorry, I didn't mean to startle you,' he added, dumping the bucket on the ground and lifting the lid off one of the metal feed bins.

'You didn't. I was miles away,' she said, watching him deposit a scoop of nuts into the bucket. 'Bella's asked me to tack up Rosie. I'm used to tacking up my friend's pony but I'm not sure how to do Rosie's martingale.'

Sam pushed his blond fringe out of his eyes and grinned. 'She does have high standards, does my Gran. I'll show you if you like. You make a start. I won't be a minute.'

Poppy found Rosie's saddle and bridle and let herself into her stable. The mare turned to watch her, her pretty roan head still as Poppy undid her headcollar. Poppy, determined to make a good impression, was suddenly all fingers and thumbs. How annoying, she thought crossly. She tried to ease the snaffle bit into Rosie's mouth but the pony, sensing her hesitation, clamped her teeth shut and refused to accept the bit.

'Come on Rosie, there's a good girl,' Poppy encouraged, clicking her tongue hopefully. But the pony's mouth remained stubbornly closed.

She became aware of Sam's head over the stable door. She wasn't sure how long he'd been watching her futile attempts.

'Rosie's a great pony but she can be a bit of a moody mare sometimes, especially when she's in season. Would you like me to try?'

'No, I'm alright thanks,' Poppy muttered. She took the bridle in her left hand again and held the bit to Rosie's mouth with her right hand. This time, as if sensing her resolve, Rosie opened her mouth obligingly and Poppy brought the headpiece over her ears before she had a chance to change her mind. 'There.'

Poppy watched as Sam placed the neckstrap of Rosie's running martingale over her head then slipped her girth through the loop on the other end. He unfastened the reins and fed each end through a ring of the martingale before buckling the reins back up. He worked quietly and efficiently and when he finished he gave the mare's forehead an affectionate rub.

'Have you ever heard the saying, 'You can tell a gelding, ask a mare, but you must discuss it with a stallion'? My Gran uses it all the time.'

Poppy shook her head.

'I prefer working with mares. They are more temperamental for sure, but when you find a mare you click with she'll go to the ends of the earth for you.'

'Do you have your own pony or do you just ride the ones in the school?' asked Poppy, suddenly curious.

'Yes, I have a black Connemara mare called Star.'

'I have a Connemara, too. He's dappled grey. He's got a fractured pedal bone and is on box rest at the moment. He hasn't been ridden for years. That's why I wanted lessons with your Gran. Talking of which, I'd better go. Thanks for the help.'

Poppy led Rosie out of the stable, checked her girth, pulled down the stirrups and swung into the saddle. Bella was leading Buster and Hope into the indoor school and she cast her eyes over Rosie's tack as Poppy joined them. 'Good job. Now are you both ready?'

Poppy grinned at Hope and they both nodded.

'I'm going to lunge Hope and Buster while you work on your transitions, Poppy. I want you to think about your impulsion and keeping those transitions smooth and balanced.'

Poppy was so absorbed in the lesson that the hour flew by. She sat tall in the saddle and tried to give Rosie clear instructions when she wanted to walk or trot.

'Rosie was going well for you today, Poppy. Well done,' said Bella. Poppy beamed with delight.

On the way home the girls chatted to Caroline about their lesson.

'I think Sam likes you, Poppy,' said Hope out of the blue.

'What?'

'He spent the whole hour watching you. He was standing by the door. Didn't you see him?'

Poppy had been so engrossed in her lesson that she hadn't noticed. She fidgeted uncomfortably in her seat and wound down the window.

'What's wrong, Poppy. Are you feeling car sick? Do you want me to pull over?' asked Caroline, looking at her in the rear view mirror.

'No, it's a bit stuffy in here, that's all. I'm fine.' Poppy could see her own reflection in the mirror. Her face was flushed. The car's heating must be on overdrive.

She turned to Hope and replied as nonchalantly as she could. 'Don't be ridiculous, he was watching Rosie, not me.'

Hope shrugged. 'If you say so.'

15

Poppy and Scarlett met several nights after school the following week to bake batches of dog biscuits for the Hope for Hope Appeal. Caroline had chanced upon a bone-shaped biscuit cutter nestling between a pile of Kendal mint cakes and boxes of fishing tackle in the village shop and the girls used it to cut dozens and dozens of dog-friendly treats. After a couple of burnt batches they had finally – with Caroline's help – got their biscuit-baking down to a fine art. It was torture for Freddie, whose gaze never wavered from the growing piles on the kitchen table.

The day of the dog show was dry and bright, the sun low in a powder blue sky. The show was being held south of the village in a field normally grazed by black-faced sheep. A show ring had been roped off and cars lined the perimeter. As the McKeevers' car bumped through the gate Charlie exclaimed, 'I've never seen so many dogs in all my life. They're everywhere!' He was right. Dogs of all sizes, from German Shepherds to miniature dachshunds, strained on leashes or sat patiently while their owners chatted. Poppy watched, fascinated, as an over-excited West Highland terrier raced three times around its middle-aged owner, its lead coiling around the man's tweed-clad legs like a boa constrictor. Blissfully unaware, the man turned to move. He would have fallen flat on his face if it hadn't been for a passing marshal, who shot out a steadying arm just in time.

The McKeevers were directed to their pitch and Caroline parked their estate car next to the dry stone wall that marked the edge of the field.

'Scarlett said she would meet us here. Her dad and Meg are giving a sheepdog demonstration later,' said Poppy, as she helped Caroline unload a trestle table and four folding camping chairs from the boot of the car. They had cut long trails of ivy from the hedge at the back of the stables to decorate their sage green table cloth which Poppy arranged with the cellophane bags of dog biscuits as artfully as she could. She had photo-copied and laminated the Tavistock Herald's story about Hope's fundraising appeal and was just taping it to the front of the table when Scarlett arrived.

'Hi Poppy! The table looks great. I love the ivy. What a good idea. And the biscuits look delicious. But we still haven't decided how much we are going to charge,' she said, without drawing breath.

'Why don't you ask people to make a donation to the appeal in return for a bag of biscuits instead of charging a fixed price? You might find that people will give more,' suggested Caroline.

'And we could chop a few biscuits up into little pieces to offer as samples. Just to get them interested,' said Poppy.

As a marketing strategy the free samples did the trick and soon a small knot of people, dogs in tow, had gathered around. Scarlett may have been a liability in the kitchen but she was a natural saleswoman.

'I can't think of a better cause. It's so important for Hope to get to America,' she told people, watching with satisfaction as they ferreted around in purses and wallets to find five and ten pound notes which they readily exchanged for a bag of home-made dog biscuits.

Poppy was serving a customer when Scarlett nudged her and said, 'Look, there's Hope and her mum.' She looked up and saw Shelley striding towards their table, Hope a couple of paces behind, her slight frame wrapped in a knee-length padded coat and her head bare.

'How's it going?' Shelley asked, her eyes roving over the table, taking in scattered crumbs and the remaining bags of biscuits. Poppy watched Shelley's eyes linger on the jar of money in front of Scarlett. It was stuffed full of notes. The last time they'd checked they'd counted more than two hundred and fifty pounds. Poppy had been staggered at people's generosity.

'I thought we could sit Hope behind the table to see if she can drum up a bit of extra business,' Shelley said.

Caroline looked appalled. 'Are you sure she wants to?' she asked faintly. But Shelley appeared not to have heard and prodded her daughter forcibly in the back. 'Well, go on then! Go and sit down next to Poppy. I'm going to get a cuppa.' With that she turned on her heels and disappeared in the direction of the refreshment tent.

'Why aren't you wearing your new wig, Hope? Your head must be freezing,' Charlie said.

'My mum told me not to. She said we'd make more money for our trip to America if people could see my bald head,' the girl answered. Poppy felt doubly sorry for her. Imagine having cancer and a mum like Shelley. Life really threw some people a curve ball.

But Shelley was right. People were now happily handing over twenty pound notes for one bag of dog biscuits with their faces full of concern, wishing Hope a speedy recovery. The girl's pale face was flushed with embarrassment as she mumbled her thanks. Poppy knew exactly how she felt – she would have hated the attention, too.

By ten to twelve the girls had completely sold out. A quick count up revealed that they had made just over four hundred pounds in less than three hours. Poppy and Scarlett high-fived each other, whooping with pleasure. Hope sat watching them, an unreadable expression on her face.

Caroline had walked Charlie and Freddie to the show ring as the best rescue dog class was due to start at noon. There was no sign of Shelley.

'Come on, let's go and watch Charlie and Freddie. He'd never forgive us if we missed their big moment. Do you want to come with us, Hope, or stay here and wait for your mum?' said Poppy.

'I'll come if that's OK?' Hope answered diffidently, her thin arms crossed and her shoulders stooped. Her whole demeanour appeared apologetic. Not for the first time Poppy thought how different she was from the brash Shelley.

Hope followed the two friends to where Caroline was watching Charlie and half a dozen other people walking their dogs around the show ring.

Charlie's face was the picture of concentration, his eyes fixed firmly ahead as he followed the elderly woman in front of him, Freddie trotting obediently by his side. After a couple more circuits of the ring the judge motioned everyone to line up with their dogs. He worked his way along the line, chatting to the owners and assessing their pets. Scarlett, who went to the Waterby Dog Show every year, was giving Caroline and Hope a running commentary.

'Look, he's checking that dog's conformation now,' she said, as the judge ran a practised hand over a shivering brindle and white whippet, its ears flat and its tail between its legs. Freddie, who was standing two dogs down, looked totally at ease, his pink tongue hanging out and his feathery tail wagging nineteen to the dozen.

Suddenly Poppy spied Shelley standing on the far side of the ring. She was about to tell Hope but something made her pause. Shelley was talking animatedly to a grey-haired man wearing corduroy trousers and a brown hacking jacket that had seen better days. He was in his early sixties, Poppy estimated. He had the sort of puffed out chest and arrogant expression that reminded her of a cockerel. Shelley pointed to the McKeevers' car. The old man looked over and broke into a wheezy laugh that soon turned into an almighty coughing fit that seized his whole body, the convulsions bending him double.

'Who's that man Shelley's talking to?' Poppy whispered to Scarlett.

Poppy watched her friend's face cloud with confusion.

'It's George Blackstone!' Scarlett exclaimed, her voice low. They watched as Shelley patted the spluttering old man gently between the shoulders. But when she saw the two girls watching her Shelley stepped smartly away from Blackstone, pretending to watch the dogs in the ring.

'Are you thinking what I'm thinking?' said Poppy.

'It's a bit strange,' admitted her friend. 'They look far too cosy for a landlord and his tenant.'

Poppy was still puzzling over the possibility that Shelley and George Blackstone knew each other of old when she heard a shriek and a volley of excited barking from the ring. She looked over to see the judge handing Charlie a small silver cup before bending down on one knee to fix a red rosette to Freddie's collar. Caroline, Hope and Scarlett were cheering and Poppy joined in as her brother and Freddie trotted around the ring together, both grinning from ear to ear.

'Did you hear what the judge said?' gabbled Charlie as he re-joined them. 'He said Freddie was the bestest rescue dog he'd ever seen and he was the winner by a mile. I can't believe it! We didn't even get a chance to show our latest trick.'

They watched as Charlie stood in front of Freddie and commanded, 'Roll over!' He smiled with satisfaction as the dog lay down, rolled over and sat up again, his tail wagging.

Poppy hadn't noticed Shelley return. She was talking with Caroline.

'We need to make a move. Things to do. People to see. You know how it is. I'll take the money now then, shall I?' she said.

'Oh, yes, I guess that makes sense, although I've got to go into Tavistock on Monday. I can easily pay it into the Hope for Hope Appeal account at the bank for you,' Caroline offered.

'No, you're alright. I'll have it now thanks.'

Caroline had locked the money in the car and Poppy watched as her stepmother and Shelley walked over to get it. As if she sensed Poppy's eyes on her retreating back Shelley turned and shot her a look. Her face was hostile and there was an expression in her eyes that Poppy couldn't place. It was only as she lay in bed that night, mulling over the day, that she realised what it was.

Defiance.

16

Poppy's dad flew out to Syria on the Monday of half-term. During the three week trip he would be responsible for sending daily reports back to London on the crisis in the Middle East. His taxi turned up after breakfast and Poppy, Caroline, Charlie and Freddie lined up outside the front of the house to wave him off. He shook the dog's paw and hugged Poppy and Charlie before wrapping his arms around Caroline, holding her close. Poppy looked down at her feet, not wanting to see Caroline's face. Her stepmother always looked a bit weepy when her dad left for an assignment and Poppy was worried it would set her off. She used to feel utterly desolate when he was away. These days, now she and Caroline were so much closer, she didn't feel as alone as she used to, but she still missed him deeply. It was hard when the only time she saw him was on the six o'clock news.

When the taxi had disappeared down the Riverdale drive Poppy scooted around the side of the house to the stables. Today was an important day. She had decided to try to tack Cloud up for the first time. She'd discovered his old saddle and bridle at the back of the tack room soon after they'd moved to Riverdale, but had assumed it had belonged to Tory's old mare, Hopscotch. Festooned with dusty spiderwebs, the leather was cracked and brittle with age.

'No, that's for Cloud,' Tory had said, when Poppy had shown her. 'I should have thrown it away. It's Caitlyn's saddle and bridle. We had them specially made for Cloud. I don't like to think of you using them, Poppy. What if they bring bad luck?'

But Poppy, who wasn't afraid to walk under ladders and never worried about spilling salt, dismissed Tory's fears as irrational. Caroline ordered a specialist leather cleaner and conditioner from the internet and Poppy spent hours working on the leather until it felt supple under her fingers.

Cloud was still finishing his breakfast. Poppy mucked out his stable and re-filled his water bucket while he ate. Despite wearing a stable rug his winter coat was thick and she spent the next half an hour giving him a brisk groom, chatting away to him all the while. She felt a flutter of nerves as she wondered how he would react to wearing tack. The last time he'd been ridden was at the hunter trial when Caitlyn was killed. Poppy held his head in her hands and gazed into his brown eyes.

'Do you remember that day, Cloud? The day you fell and Caitlyn died?' she said softly. He turned his head to look out of the stable door at the sound of Caitlyn's name, as if expecting her to stride in, her long, blonde hair swinging, and her skull cap under her arm. Poppy fought the usual feelings of jealousy and inadequacy and wondered if she would ever have enough self-confidence to believe she was equal to Caitlyn.

'I'm here, Cloud,' she whispered. 'I know you miss Caitlyn but you mean everything to me. You are my world.'

He turned and whickered and she felt her heart swell with love.

'Here goes. I promise I'll stop if you don't like it,' she said, reaching for the bridle. Cloud had never been head shy with Poppy and as she unfastened his headcollar she ran her hands over his head, giving his poll a scratch and kissing his nose. She held the bridle and eased open Cloud's mouth. Unlike Rosie he accepted the bit straight away and Poppy slid the headpiece over his ears as if she'd been doing it all her life. 'You clever, clever boy,' she told him.

Poppy lifted the saddle from the stable door. She showed it to Cloud and let him sniff it. She felt his muscles tense as she placed it gently on his back. She watched his face for a reaction. His ears twitched back and forth but he didn't move. She reached for the girth and buckled it up loosely. Cloud remained still. He looked different in his tack. Taller, more imposing somehow. All she wanted to do was jump on his back and gallop across the moor, just the two of them, Poppy and Cloud. Instead she flung her arms around his neck and buried her face deep in his mane. She felt certain that the day would come. She just had to be patient.

~

'SHELLEY'S ASKED us to have Hope for the day on Saturday. She's got to go to London to see Hope's oncologist,' said Caroline that afternoon.

'On a Saturday?' Poppy was sceptical.

'That's one of his clinic days, apparently. Shelley's going to drop her off early and then drive up to town. She's hoping to be back just after tea.'

An orange sun was peeping over the horizon when Shelley's car accelerated up the Riverdale drive, sending gravel flying. Shelley left the engine running as Hope let herself out. Poppy, watching from the lounge window, heard Shelley bark an instruction to her daughter. Hope nodded obediently, her shoulders hunched. Poppy waited until the car had disappeared down the drive before she opened the front door and let Hope in. She had no desire to see Shelley.

The temperature had plummeted overnight and the grass in the paddock was stiff with frost. Hope helped Poppy muck out and feed Cloud and Chester and Poppy showed her how to groom the old donkey before they turned him out.

'Shall we show Hope the Riverdale tor?' asked Charlie, when they finally went inside, their hands red with cold.

'That sounds fun. It's where you saw the big cat, isn't it?' said Hope.

She was wearing her wig and in the warmth of the kitchen her cheeks were rosy. No-one meeting her for the first time would ever have guessed she was in remission from cancer, thought Poppy.

'How's the appeal going, Hope?' asked Caroline. The Herald ran a story every week about the latest fundraising events. It seemed that the people of Waterby had taken the girl's plight to their hearts.

'OK, I think. But Mum deals with all that. I try not to think about it.' Hope looked far from pleased at the prospect of a life-saving trip to America. But then who would, thought Poppy. It would be nothing but tests, scans, treatments and more tests. Hardly what you'd call a holiday.

The three children let themselves out of the back gate and began the steep climb to the top of the tor. Conversation petered out as they negotiated rocks and tussocks, Freddie bounding along beside them. Hope was soon breathing heavily. She stopped, wincing as she clutched her side.

'Are you OK?' Poppy asked in alarm.

'It's a stitch. I'm fine. Just unfit I guess,' she replied.

Eventually they reached the rock where Poppy and Charlie had seen the panther months before. Charlie went down on hands and knees to show Hope exactly where the big cat had stood. Poppy sat on a wide, flat boulder and looked back at Riverdale. She could just make out Chester grazing in his paddock. From this distance he was the size of the toy donkey in Charlie's farm set. Hope sat down beside her, her knees drawn up under her chin, her wig slightly askew.

'The view from here's amazing. There's Riverdale and Ashworthy, and if you look over there you can just see the roof of the Blackstone farm. And I think that white building to the left of it is your house. Can you see it?'

Hope nodded. They watched Charlie scouting for rocks which he was using to build his own cairn, a scaled down version of the mound of rocks at the top of the Riverdale tor.

'Do you mind if I ask you something, Hope?' Poppy asked. With Shelley safely two hundred and fifty miles away in London it was the first time she'd felt able to tackle the subject. Hope didn't answer so Poppy ploughed on. 'The day we first met you and your mum in the village shop, I heard you telling her that you didn't want to do something anymore. What was it?'

Hope was silent.

'Is she forcing you to do something?' Poppy faltered. It sounded crazy even thinking it. But she was worried something was wrong. 'Is she... hurting you?' she finished lamely.

Hope shook her head vigorously, leaving her wig even more lopsided.

'No, it's not that,' she whispered.

So there was something, Poppy thought. But what?

Hope was quiet for a beat. When she spoke her voice was a monotone. 'I don't know what to do. After the last time she promised me it would never happen again. But she was lying.'

'Lying about what? I can't help unless you tell me, Hope,' said Poppy.

Hugging her knees to her chest Hope turned to face her friend. Tears were streaming down her face and there was a look of such despair in her eyes that Poppy was momentarily lost for words.

'You'll hate me if I tell you, Poppy. You all will.'

'Don't be silly, of course we won't. You can trust me. I promise.'

Hope took a deep breath, about to speak. But before she had a chance to form any words Charlie dropped a large rock on his big toe. Distracted by his howl of pain Hope fell silent. Charlie was hopping around on one foot. Poppy could quite cheerfully have dropped the biggest rock she could lift onto the other one.

'You were saying?' she said to Hope, trying her best to ignore her brother.

But Hope had wiped away her tears and her face was giving nothing away. Poppy knew she had missed her chance. The shutters had come down again and there was no way Hope was going to tell her what was wrong.

17

loud's third X-ray after two months of box rest finally brought some good news.

'He looks a different pony, Poppy. You're doing a brilliant job,' said the vet, casting an eye over the Connemara. It was true. Cloud's ribs had all but disappeared and the hollows in his flanks had filled out. Although he kept half an eye on Chester, who loved coming along to keep him company, he looked around with interest at the row of kennels and didn't flinch when the vet X-rayed his foot. Poppy felt immeasurably proud of him.

The hairline crack along his pedal bone was still visible – but only just.

'Another three or four weeks in his stable and I think we're there,' said the vet, to Poppy's delight. 'How's he coping with box rest?'

'He's bored out of his mind,' admitted Poppy. 'I spend as long as possible with him but I'm at school most of the time. He has Chester for company but hates it when Chester's in the paddock and he's left behind in the stable.'

'Try putting a carrot or apple on a string and hanging it from the roof. It'll give him something to nibble on. Or hide some Polos in his hay. Some people put shatterproof mirrors up in the stable so horses on box rest have something to look at. It sounds silly but it might do the trick. But the good news is I don't think he'll be stuck in there for too much longer.'

～

WHEN POPPY and Hope arrived at Redhall Manor for their lesson later that week Bella had some exciting news.

'You've both been doing so well with your flatwork that I thought we might try a bit of jumping. We'll start very slowly and see how it goes.'

Poppy flew into the tack room, nearing colliding with Sam, who was on his way out with Buster's tack.

'Sorry!' Poppy said breathlessly. 'I didn't see you.'

'You don't say,' he replied with a grin. For a moment Poppy forgot why she was there and gazed around blankly.

'Rosie's tack?' asked Sam helpfully. 'It's at the end on the left, where it always is.'

'Yes, alright thanks. No-one likes a smart Alec,' she muttered, brushing past him, her face an unflattering shade of puce. Honestly, why were boys so annoying?

Bella was waiting next to three evenly-spaced red and white painted poles in the centre of the indoor school as Poppy and Hope rode in on Rosie and Buster.

'First we need to shorten your stirrups a couple of notches. Then we're going to start with some trotting poles,' she said. 'Trotting over these will help you learn to keep a well-balanced position that will stand you in good stead when you learn to jump. Buster's a bit lazy so you're going to need a lot of impulsion, Hope. But Rosie loves jumping, Poppy. Your problem will be holding her back.'

After half an hour Bella, satisfied with their positions, put a low cross pole at the end. Poppy went first. Used to Flynn's lackadaisical approach to jumping she was unseated when Rosie flew over with a foot to spare.

'You're hanging onto the reins, Poppy. Your balance needs to come from your legs and your seat. Keep a good contact with Rosie but don't be heavy-handed.'

'Sorry,' mouthed Poppy, as she struggled to right herself and ease Rosie back into a balanced trot.

Hope proved a natural and was soon popping Buster over cross poles and cavalettis as though she'd been jumping for years. But Poppy struggled and by the end of the lesson her back ached and her arms felt as though they'd been pulled out of their sockets. Her face was the picture of dejection when she dismounted.

'Chin up, Poppy. I'm sure you'll get there in the end,' boomed Bella from the other side of the yard. It wasn't exactly a vote of confidence, Poppy thought miserably. Sam was filling water buckets from the tap outside Rosie's stable and she felt her face grow hot. Trust him to have heard how useless she was.

Poppy didn't see his sympathetic smile as she passed – she was too busy looking at her feet. She untacked Rosie as slowly as she could and by the time she let herself out of the mare's stable Sam was thankfully nowhere to be seen.

She fared no better the following week. She was unseated every time Rosie jumped. The harder she tried not to lose her balance the more tense she became and the more Rosie acted up.

'You're leaning too far forwards,' shouted Bella. 'Push your weight down into your heels so your lower legs don't tip back when Rosie jumps.' But Poppy's back felt wooden and any connection she'd had with the roan mare during flatwork was long forgotten.

'Poppy, watch the way Hope stays balanced and keeps her hands steady as Buster approaches the jump. See how supple she is. She is going with the pony, not working against him. Don't worry if you can't anticipate where Rosie is going to take off, that'll come with practice. At this stage I just want you to relax and go with her. Enjoy it!' Bella commanded.

Poppy sat deep in the saddle and squeezed Rosie into a canter. She was determined to show Bella that she was as good as Hope. As they approached the cavaletti she remembered not to hang onto Rosie's reins. But the sudden dropped contact in the last stride before the jump confounded the mare, who sloped her shoulders and stopped dead in her tracks. Poppy, on the other hand, flew over the jump and landed in a twisted heap on the floor. The impact knocked the wind out of her and for a few long moments she lay in a ball struggling for breath as Rosie careered delightedly around, throwing in a couple of bucks for good measure.

Caroline, watching the lesson from the small spectators' area, cried out in alarm and ran over to her stepdaughter, who was lying motionless on the ground. By the time she reached her Poppy's diaphragm had stopped going into spasm and she'd managed to gulp a few lungfuls of air.

'Only winded,' she groaned, as Caroline held out a hand and pulled her to her feet. Sam appeared from nowhere and called softly to Rosie, who slowed to a stop and stood meekly for him. He led the mare to Poppy and held out her reins.

'It's always best to get straight back on,' he advised.

Poppy dusted down her jodhpurs and grabbed the reins. 'I do know that,' she said ungraciously, putting her foot in the stirrup. Unfortunately as she sprang onto Rosie's back the mare's saddle slipped and, with a howl of frustration, she ended up on the floor again, her backside bruised and her pride well and truly dented.

18

By the next morning Poppy was beginning to see the funny side of it all and had Scarlett in stitches on the school bus as she described her riding lesson from hell.

'Honestly, Scar, I couldn't have been any worse if I'd tried. I was *terrible*,' she wailed.

'Wish I'd been there to see it,' Scarlett giggled.

'I'm glad you weren't,' said Poppy fervently. She paused. 'I suppose what I'm most fed up about is that Hope is a natural. She just seems to get it.'

'You'll get it too, don't worry,' consoled Scarlett. 'Forget about Rosie and jumping for a while. Why don't we take Blaze and Flynn up onto the moor for a picnic tomorrow? It'll be fun.'

They set off just after ten, saddle bags filled with sandwiches, sausages rolls and Pat's homemade flapjacks. The sun shone weakly in a cloud-studded sky the colour of faded denim. Black-faced sheep skittered out of their way as they skirted the Riverdale tor and headed deep onto the moor. Flynn felt round and reassuringly solid after Rosie and Poppy felt herself relax.

'Why do I let myself get so uptight?' she asked Scarlett when they finally stopped for lunch beside a narrow stream.

'You're a perfectionist,' answered Scarlett, passing Poppy a ham sandwich. 'The trouble is, if you set your standards too high you're setting yourself up for a fall. In this case both metaphorically and literally,' she giggled.

'Ha ha, very funny. I just want to be the best I can be for Cloud. Caitlyn was such a good rider I'm bound to be a disappointment to him,' Poppy replied.

Scarlett was quiet for a moment. She wished Poppy could see what everyone else could – that she was kind, loyal and brave. 'You mustn't compare yourself to other people, Poppy. If you want to be a better rider then do it for yourself, because it'll make you happier, not because you want to be better than Caitlyn or Hope.'

'Maybe,' said Poppy, unconvinced.

'I mean it. Everyone's different. You, for example, are rubbish at cooking, whereas I am a brilliant cake baker and probably should audition for the next series of the Great British Bake Off.'

'Hey, that's a bit harsh! You were the one who used plain flour remember,' Poppy grinned. But she thought about what Scarlett had said as they rode home. Perhaps her friend was right. Maybe she shouldn't be so hard on herself.

THEY WERE ten minutes early for their next lesson at Redhall Manor and while Caroline and Hope plied Buster with Polos Poppy went off in search of Bella. She started with the tack room but that was empty, so she crossed the yard to the indoor school. The doors were closed which suggested Bella was giving a lesson. Poppy let herself into the spectators' area and sat down to watch.

The indoor school had been transformed into a mini Hickstead with a course of brightly-painted show jumps. A mixture of uprights, spreads, a double and a wall were all at least 100cm high and to Poppy looked enormous. Bella stood in the middle as a boy on a black pony cantered around the edge.

'Right, assume you've had a clear round and have made it into the jump off,' boomed Bella. 'Let's see how fast she can fly.'

The pair approached the first jump, a rustic oxer. The pony's ears were pricked and the boy sat quietly as they cantered up to the jump, his hands light and his shoulders straight. It was only after they had cleared it with centimetres to spare that Poppy realised the boy was Sam, riding his Connemara mare, Star. She watched as they flew over a gate and swung around to jump the double. Sam turned the mare on a sixpence and she soared over a wall before turning to another oxer which they also cleared with ease. Sam whooped and lent down to pat the mare's neck as she slowed to a walk.

'Nice job, Sam. If you can do that at the weekend you'll make mince-meat of the competition,' said Bella. As she strode over to her grandson she saw Poppy watching. 'We're holding an affiliated jumping show here on Saturday,' she explained. 'People are coming from across the west of Devon to compete. Obviously as a riding instructor I should tell you that it's the taking part not the winning that matters. But it will be good if Sam can win a couple of ribbons for Redhall. It's a great advertisement for the riding school.'

'No pressure then Gran,' grinned Sam, as he dismounted. He ran up the stirrup leathers and loosened Star's girth a couple of notches. 'Although she's jumping out of her skin at the moment.'

Poppy, who had been wondering ruefully if she'd ever reach Sam's standard of riding, remembered Scarlett's words. Everyone was different. Some people were excellent at jumping, others were better at baking cakes. She, on the other hand, was pretty damn good at falling off. She smiled to herself and said graciously, 'Lovely round. Good luck for Saturday.'

'Thanks. Maybe you'll come along to watch?'

''Er, not sure. I'll have to ask Caroline. Shall I go and tack up Rosie?' she asked Bella.

'Yes please, Poppy. I'm going to put these fences right down to about a foot and we'll see how you both get on jumping a course shall we?'

Poppy made a conscious decision not to try too hard. She pretended that Rosie was solid, dependable Flynn and that they were jumping cavaletti in the field at Ashworthy with no-one watching them but a few sheep. The New Forest mare sensed that her rider was more relaxed and settled to the task without a quibble. Soon they were popping over the fences as easily as Hope and Buster. Poppy still found it hard to judge Rosie's strides but Bella reminded her that it would come with practice.

By the end of the lesson she felt immensely cheered. Perhaps she would be able to master this jumping lark one day after all.

∼

CAROLINE WAS happy to drive them all to Redhall Manor for the horse show. Scarlett had already agreed to go and Poppy couldn't wait to tell Hope. She cycled to Flint Cottage, leant her bike against the rickety fence at the front of the house and rang the bell. Hope answered the door and smiled when she saw Poppy on the doorstep.

'Is your mum out?' asked Poppy hopefully

'No, she's upstairs re-decorating her bedroom. She's bought some new furniture which is due to arrive next week. She wanted to get the room painted and the new carpet in before it arrives.'

'Is she going to decorate your room, too?' said Poppy, picturing the scuffed magnolia walls and chipped melamine furniture in Hope's cheerless bedroom.

'Oh, I don't think so. She hasn't mentioned it.'

What a surprise, thought Poppy.

'Anyway, the reason I came over is that Scarlett and I are going to Redhall Manor this afternoon to watch the jumping and we wondered if you'd like to come?'

'I'd love to. But I'd better ask Mum. Won't be a minute.'

Poppy waited awkwardly while Hope disappeared upstairs. She picked up a handful of letters from the doormat. Several were addressed to the Hope for Hope Appeal c/o Flint Cottage. A brown envelope at the bottom of the pile was for a Mrs M. Turner.

Hope bounded down the stairs, grinning. 'Mum says yes as long as Caroline doesn't mind picking me up and dropping me off.'

'No problem,' said Poppy, handing Hope the letters. 'Looks like that one's for the old lady who used to live here. I thought she died ages ago,' she observed.

The grin slid from Hope's face. She grabbed the envelopes and dropped them on the kitchen table as if they were hot to the touch.

'You alright?' Poppy asked, surprised at Hope's sudden change of mood.

'Of course! Why wouldn't I be?'

'Just asking. Anyway I promised I wouldn't be long. I'd better go. We'll pick you up at two.'

19

Poppy hadn't realised the size of the show until they drove up to the entrance of Redhall Manor and saw the number of horse lorries and trailers parked on the hardstanding next to the main yard. While Caroline found a place to park the girls gawped at the goings-on around them. Everywhere they looked there was something to see. A girl with a long blonde plait down her back was bending down to undo her chestnut pony's travel boots. A boy dressed in white breeches and a black jacket was leading a strikingly handsome skewbald cob down the ramp of a trailer. Elsewhere people were re-plaiting manes, tying stocks, grooming and tacking up.

'This brings it all back,' said Caroline, who had finally found a space to park. 'I used to love going to shows with Hamilton. We never went to one quite this big though.'

As they headed towards the indoor school a girl about their age rode past them, scowling. She hauled her grey pony to a halt outside a smart sky blue lorry, dismounted and flung the pony's reins at a harassed-looking woman who was grooming a dark bay mare tied to the side of the lorry. 'He totally misjudged his stride in the double and knocked down the spread,' the girl announced in a clipped voice.

'Never mind,' soothed the woman. 'Let's hope Barley can do better.'

'I sincerely hope so. Where is he?'

'In the back of the box. I've tacked him up so he's ready to go.'

Scarlett nudged Poppy. 'That's Georgia Canning. She went to my old school until her parents came into money and moved her to Beresford House.' Seeing Poppy and Hope's blank faces Scarlett explained, 'It's this really posh girls' boarding school on the other side of Okehampton.'

The friends watched Georgia stomp up the ramp of the deluxe horse lorry and appear two minutes later dragging a flashy palomino behind her.

'Mum!' she yelled. The woman tied the grey pony next to the bay mare, took the palomino's reins and gave her daughter a leg up. Georgia turned the pony and clattered off towards the outdoor ménage where riders were warming up over a couple of jumps.

'Good luck, Georgie,' the woman called to her daughter's retreating back. But her words were carried away with the wind. When she turned back to the bay mare her face was resigned.

Scarlett raised her eyebrows at Poppy, Hope and Caroline. Once they were out of earshot she said, 'Georgia's mum used to work in a supermarket and her dad was a builder. They lived in a three bedroomed semi and had a clapped out old hatchback. Now they live in this enormous mansion, her dad drives around in a Bentley and her mum has a Range Rover.'

Hope's eyes widened. 'Did they win the football pools or something?'

'Georgia's parents always claimed they inherited the money but Mum is convinced it was a lottery win. And a big one at that. Georgia used to beg me to let her have a ride on Blaze. Now she has a string of about five jumping ponies and her own personal riding instructor. Imagine that!'

'Were you friends at school then?' Poppy asked, surprised. She couldn't imagine Scarlett befriending the haughty Georgia Canning.

'Not really. She was in the year above me. But our mums were friendly. I think they used to take us to the same toddler group. You know what it's like around here, Poppy. Everyone knows each other,' Scarlett grimaced. Sometimes she found village life suffocating and longed to live in a place where no-one knew her name, let alone remembered her wearing a false beard to play the part of Joseph in the school nativity when she was five. 'Shall we go and watch them warming up before we go inside?'

They leant on the post and rail fence of the outdoor ménage. Poppy studied Georgia's face as she trotted the palomino around the ring. She had china blue eyes and hair as black as molasses. With her high cheek-bones and flawless English rose complexion she could have been a child model if it hadn't been for an imperfection Poppy only noticed when she cantered past. In profile Georgia had a hooked Roman nose that was at odds with her otherwise perfect features. It lent her face a superior expression that bordered on arrogance. She turned the pony towards a spread and jumped it easily, the palomino's tail swishing as it landed.

'She's a really good rider,' Poppy observed.

'We all would be if we had our own riding instructor and the best ponies money could buy. I'm going to outgrow Blaze any minute now and there's no way Mum and Dad can afford to buy me one new pony, let alone five. Not with the way things are with the farm at the moment. It's alright for some,' Scarlett said gloomily as Georgia cantered past.

'Cheer up,' said Poppy, linking arms with her friend. 'I think you're a brilliant rider, much better than Georgia Canning. Come on, let's go and watch the jumping.'

~

THEY FOUND their seats in the spectators' area and settled down to watch a BSJA affiliated open class for ponies up to 148cm.

'That's 14.2hh to you,' Poppy told Caroline kindly. 'They're jumping a 100cm course, which is three feet three inches high if you were born in the Dark Ages.'

'Yes, thank you for that Poppy,' her stepmum replied drily. 'I'm not that old, you know. It's just that when it comes to horses I'm conditioned to think in hands, feet and inches.' They watched a girl on a blue roan demolish the wall, sending bricks flying. 'I wonder how many clear rounds there have been.'

As she spoke the girl on the roan pony exited in tears and Georgia Canning entered the ring, her back ramrod straight and her jaw set. Her pony looked balanced and alert.

'She looks as though she means business,' Poppy said. She was right. The pair executed a textbook clear round, the palomino sailing over the jumps with ease. There was a faint ripple of applause and Georgia gave a superior smile. But she didn't pat her pony, Poppy noticed.

'Georgia's mum paid over ten thousand pounds for that pony apparently,' said Scarlett. 'He a JA, of course.'

'What does that mean?' asked Hope, who had been watching the round mesmerised.

'That he's won more than £700 in prize money. He's her top jumping pony. She competes all over the South West on him.'

'Look, Sam's next,' said Caroline.

'Who's Sam?' asked Scarlett.

'He's Bella Thompson's grandson and he works at Redhall Manor. We see him when we have our lessons every Thursday. His pony's a Connemara like Cloud, but she's a mare and she's called Star,' said Hope, pleased to be able to put Scarlett in the picture for a change.

'I've heard all about Bella, Rosie and Buster. You didn't mention Sam though, Poppy,' said Scarlett, an amused expression on her face.

'Oh, didn't I?' Poppy asked airily. 'Yes, anyway, that's him.'

Sam, who had been scanning the spectators as he cantered past, saw where they were sitting and waved. Star's black coat gleamed. Her mane and tail were plaited and Sam had brushed a checkerboard quarter mark on her rump. She looked stunning. The bell went, Sam ran his hand down Star's neck and cantered towards the first jump, a blue and white painted spread.

Poppy was so engrossed watching Sam and Star fly round the course that she didn't notice Bella sit down next to them and jumped when Bella boomed, 'Good job, Sam!' as her grandson cleared the last fence with inches to spare. Poppy grimaced at Bella's habit of talking at the same volume regardless of whether you were at the other end of the indoor school or sitting right next to her.

'That's six clear rounds, so he'll get a ribbon whatever,' she told them with satisfaction. 'With any luck he'll show that Canning girl a thing or two in the jump-off. I used to teach her, you know. Then she decided she wanted some fancy trainer from I don't know where and left Redhall.'

The stewards came in and raised some fences for the shortened jump-off course. A boy on a fleabitten grey was first to jump. The pony was totally over-excited and crabbed into the ring sideways. The bell went and the boy gave the pony his head. He raced towards the blue and white spread and took off far too early, jumping flat and knocking a pole out with his back legs. The boy struggled to regain control and notched up a cricket score by the time he finished the round.

The next rider fared no better. Attempting to turn too tightly into the gate the pony lost its impulsion and refused. The third rider, a girl on a diminutive Exmoor with characteristic mealy markings around its eyes and muzzle, jumped clear, to a loud round of applause, but at well over a minute her time was slow. The fourth rider was eliminated after taking the wrong course and then it was the turn of Georgia Canning, who cantered in on her flashy palomino as if she owned Redhall Manor.

'She's fast,' said Poppy, as Georgia and her pony galloped around the course. They were jumping clear until the last jump, a double. The palomino flew over the upright but flattened over the spread, giving the pole a hefty clout. It rattled in the cup and Poppy saw Georgia glance over her shoulder, her face like thunder. But luck was on her side. The pole didn't fall and the pair notched up their second clear round in a time of fifty six seconds.

'Sam and Star have their work cut out to beat that,' Caroline said.

'The fastest horses don't necessarily win,' Bella told her. 'In a jump-off it's often the balanced, accurate riders who take the shortest route who clinch it. And jump-offs are Star's speciality. She loves them.'

Sam trotted into the ring. He halted, nodded to the judge and squeezed Star into a canter. The black mare's ears were pricked as she approached the first jump. Poppy realised she was holding her breath. Sam might be irritating but Poppy had taken an instant dislike to the spoilt, sneering Georgia Canning. She knew whose side she was on, no question.

Sam and Star's round was a lesson in accomplished horsemanship. He sat quietly, perfectly balanced as the pony soared over the fences. They turned inside the wall, saving crucial seconds, but still managed to leap over the gate almost from a standstill. Poppy checked the clock. Forty five seconds with only the double to go. They cleared the first part but as Star took off for the second part of the combination Poppy gasped – one of the cups was dangling precariously where it had been knocked by Georgia Canning's palomino, leaving the back pole hanging on a thread. Star cleared the pole by an inch but the impact of her landing was enough to dislodge it and it crashed to the ground as the mare crossed the finish line in just fifty one seconds. Sam looked back ruefully, wrapped his arms around his pony's neck and cantered out of the ring.

'That's not fair!' cried Hope, who had been sitting on the edge of her seat, chewing her nails. 'Star didn't even touch the pole. It was Georgia who knocked it.'

'That's the luck of the draw, I'm afraid,' said Bella. 'I should have asked the stewards to check the fence. Still, he's got third place. And the satisfaction of knowing that he knocked five seconds off the Canning girl's time. On any other day he would have been first.'

20

---

eorgia Canning accepted her small silver cup with a supercilious smile and kicked her palomino into a canter to lead the lap of honour. But the biggest cheer went to Sam and Star as they cantered past the spectators.

'That's because everyone knows he should have won,' said Hope with feeling.

When they joined Sam outside the indoor school he was as sanguine as his grandmother. 'It's just one of those things. Luck'll be on my side next time,' he assured Hope.

Scarlett dug Poppy in the ribs. 'Aren't you going to introduce us then?'

Poppy sighed. 'Scarlett, this is Sam. Sam is Bella's grandson and works at Redhall. Sam, this is my best friend Scarlett. She talks a lot.'

'Charming,' said Scarlett. 'Hello Sam. I'd love to say I've heard all about you but it wouldn't be true. Anyway I thought you and Star were brilliant and -'.

Before Scarlett could finish Georgia rode up. 'Bad luck, Sam. It really wasn't your day, was it? Only managed to scrape a third on home turf? Not much of an advert for Redhall, is it?' she taunted.

Scarlett's auburn eyebrows shot up so high they almost touched her hairline and Poppy stared at Georgia in stunned silence, astonished at her audacity. Only Sam seemed unperturbed.

'Oh well, you can't win 'em all. Star was the fastest on the day, and I'm happy with that,' he said, patting his mare's coal-black neck and smiling at the three girls.

'Brought your fan club today, I see. Wait a minute, don't I know you?' she said to Scarlett.

'Never seen you before in my life,' said Scarlett, deadpan. Georgia frowned and was about to speak when her palomino shied at a passing lorry. She cursed under her breath, gathered her reins and turned her attention to Sam again.

'Our offer still stands, you know.'

'The answer's no. Again,' he told Georgia. His hand was clenched tightly around Star's reins and a muscle twitched in his jaw.

'You won't get a better offer,' she insisted.

'She's not for sale. And even if she was I wouldn't sell her to you if you were the last person on earth, Georgia Canning. Come on girl, let's get you back to your stable,' he told Star. He held up his hand in a mock salute to Poppy, Scarlett and Hope and turned his mare towards the yard. Georgia watched them go, her expression stony.

A PAINT-SPLATTERED Shelley opened the door of Flint Cottage when they dropped Hope off on their way home.

'Are you rushing off?' she asked Caroline. Poppy crossed her fingers inside her jacket pocket hoping Caroline would say no.

'Actually I could murder a cup of tea. But we can't stay too long. I promised I'd get Scarlett back before six,' she said.

They piled into the lounge. Scarlett had never been inside Flint Cottage and she looked around avidly. Her eyes widened when she noticed the flat screen television.

'Blimey Hope, your TV's as big as a cinema screen. It must have cost a fortune.'

'What? Oh, it's ex-display or something,' she muttered, sitting next to Poppy and chewing the nail of her index finger.

Shelley appeared from the kitchen carrying a teapot and mugs on an old metal tray. She swept a tabloid newspaper, a holiday brochure and some clothing catalogues off the coffee table and kicked them under the sofa before placing the tray on the table. 'Try not to knock it flying this time, you clumsy oaf,' she told Hope coldly.

'So, did you enjoy your first horse show, Hope?' Caroline asked.

Hope hadn't stopped talking about the show on the way home. As she'd chattered about the ponies they'd seen and the riders they'd met even Scarlett had struggled to get a word in edgeways, and that didn't happen very often. But suddenly Hope was monosyllabic.

'It was OK, thanks,' she said, her knuckles white as she clasped her mug of tea.

'She had a great time,' Scarlett told Shelley. 'Though we were all fed up when Georgia Canning won the open jumping. But it's easy to be the best if you throw enough money at it. Mum reckons they won the lottery a few years back, though no-one knows for sure. They're really cagey about it. But it must have been a massive win.'

Shelley's eyes lit up. 'What makes you think that?'

'They live in a huge mansion, drive flash cars and own loads of ponies. Georgia's an only child and she's spoilt rotten. The pony she won the open jumping on cost ten thousand pounds,' Scarlett continued.

'Ten grand? For one pony? You're kidding, right?' Shelley was incredulous.

'That's a drop in the ocean for the Cannings. Apparently their house is absolutely rammed full of antiques and works of art.'

'Have you been to their house? Where is it?'

'It's called Claydon Manor and it's on the outskirts of Tavistock. You know the kind of place. Wrought iron automatic gates, a long, sweeping drive and security cameras everywhere. I think they even have guard dogs. I suppose they're worried about being burgled.'

'Honestly, it makes me sick. Here I am, a single mum with next to nothing, doing everything I can to send my poor daughter to America for life-saving cancer treatment when people like that have so much money they could write a cheque for the whole trip tomorrow if they wanted to,' said Shelley.

Hope stood up abruptly, muttered something about needing the bathroom and disappeared out of the room. Caroline looked at her watch, taken aback by the seething resentment in Shelley's voice.

'Heavens, it's ten to six. We'd better make a move.'

Poppy stared at her reflection in the car window on the way home, half-listening to Caroline and Scarlett as they talked about Christmas while her mind drifted over the events of the day. She wondered what Georgia Canning, the girl who had everything, would be given for Christmas. Not Star, that was for sure. Apparently there were some things money couldn't buy after all. Poppy pictured Shelley's face, calculating and covetous. Scarlett had certainly touched a nerve when she'd described the Cannings' fortune. Yet for someone who was always pleading poverty Shelley always seemed to be spending money – on herself at least. And finally, Poppy thought about Hope. All she must want for Christmas was a chance to get better. But would she be given that chance?

Poppy couldn't shake a growing sense of unease that behind the shabby front door of Flint Cottage all was not as it should be. On the car journeys to Redhall Manor Hope opened up like a flower, talking about Buster and his idiosyncrasies and quizzing Poppy about Cloud and Chester. The minute they dropped her home she clammed up. Her face was guarded. Wary, even. The day they'd walked to the top of the Riverdale tor Poppy knew that Hope was a heartbeat away from confiding in her. But since then Hope changed the subject every time Poppy tried to raise it and she was no nearer to gleaning the truth.

One night, as she sat at the kitchen table struggling with her maths homework while Caroline tested Charlie on his spellings, a theory began to take shape. It was formed by a chance remark from Charlie, who hated homework more than he hated Brussels sprouts. And that was saying something.

'I bet Hope never has homework,' the six-year-old grumbled. 'She doesn't even go to school. I thought everyone had to go to school. So how come Hope doesn't?'

'You know why, Charlie. It's because she's got cancer. Her mum is giving her lessons at home because she has a weak immune system,' Caroline reminded him.

'She looks pretty healthy to me,' he said.

'Charlie!' Caroline admonished. 'She's in remission, that's all. She's still a very sick little girl.'

'Well, I'd like to be in remission if it meant I didn't have to do stupid spellings,' he announced, flinging down his pencil in disgust. 'It's not fair.'

'Come on now, there's no need to throw a strop. Homework is really important, isn't it Poppy?' Caroline looked to her stepdaughter for support, but Poppy's thoughts were far away in Flint Cottage. Random images that had seemed unrelated were gradually connecting in her mind.

'Poppy?' Caroline repeated.

'Sorry, I was miles away. Yes, Charlie, homework is really important. Speaking of which, I need the laptop to look up something for science. Is it OK to take it up to my room?'

Poppy spent the next hour on the internet hopping from one website to another, frowning to herself as pieces of the puzzle gradually fell into place. True, she had made a few assumptions and a lot of her 'evidence' was conjecture. But there were far too many coincidences for her liking. Just as Poppy knew it would never hold up in a court of law, she was also certain she was right.

WHEN SHE WOKE the next morning she had come to a decision.

'I'll be on the late bus tonight. I want to pop in and see Tory,' she said over breakfast.

'No problem. I'll see to Chester and Cloud so there's no rush. Give her our love.' Caroline's blonde head was bent over the dishwasher and her voice was muffled. She and Charlie were so lucky, Poppy thought. Caroline was such a kind, easy-going person. Perhaps her only fault was that sometimes she only saw the good in people. When her stepmum straightened up Poppy crossed the kitchen and gave her a quick hug.

'Hey, what's that for sweetheart? Everything OK?'

'Yes,' Poppy brushed her fringe out of her eyes. 'I'm just glad you're you, that's all.'

'Well, I'm glad you're you, too, angel. And I'm glad Charlie is Charlie. Most of the time anyway,' she laughed. 'Right, we'd better get ourselves into gear otherwise you'll both be late for school.'

Poppy kept her head down as she arrived at the block of sheltered flats in Tavistock. She was hoping to avoid the warden, an overbearing woman called Mrs Parker, who usually bent her ear for ten minutes berating the youth of today. But luck was on her side and there was no sign of the old battleaxe. Poppy sighed with relief as she scooted down the dimly-lit corridor, stopped outside Tory's front door and knocked. Tory's lined face creased into a smile when she saw Poppy.

'Hello pet, how lovely to see you. Come in. I'll put the kettle on.' Tory reached down for Poppy's rucksack. 'Lummy, what've you got in there – bricks? It's a wonder you haven't given yourself a hernia carting that around all day.'

'You get used to it after a while. And who on earth is Lummy?' said Poppy, taking the bag from Tory and hefting it over her shoulder.

'Oh, it's an expression my old mum used to use. I don't suppose anyone says it any more. One sugar, isn't it? Or would you prefer a hot chocolate? I've plenty of milk.'

'Hot chocolate please, Tory.' Poppy shrugged off her coat and blazer and sat down in the stiflingly hot sitting room while Tory pottered about in the kitchen. Poppy automatically reached for the framed photograph of Caitlyn and Cloud, taken at the Brambleton Horse Show more than five years before. Although she had consigned it to memory long ago she still scrutinised the photo every time she visited. It fed her obsessive need to find out everything she could about Caitlyn. Cloud's mane was plaited and his dappled grey coat gleamed. He looked muscled and fit, every inch the champion pony as the red rosette was hooked onto his browband. Caitlyn's black show jacket matched her polished black leather riding boots and her white breeches were spotless. She was grinning into the camera, her joy at winning the open jumping class pure and unadulterated. No-one looking at the golden pair could have predicted that a few months later Caitlyn would be dead and Cloud would be a broken shadow of himself, running wild on the moor with the Dartmoor ponies. Poppy knew it was crazy to be jealous of a dead girl. She placed the photo carefully back on Tory's oak side table and remembered why she had come.

'So how are you all? How are Cloud and Chester?' said the old woman as she settled herself in the other armchair.

'They're both fine. Cloud's still putting on weight and is much less nervy around people, especially Caroline. He'll even let her pick up his feet now. Dad's in Syria at the moment.'

'I know, pet. I saw him on the late news last night.'

Poppy took a deep breath. 'Tory, what would you do if you thought someone you knew had committed a crime?'

The old woman paused before she replied, her eyebrows knotted in concern.

'What kind of crime, Poppy?'

'I'm sorry, I can't tell you at the moment. But it's not murder or anything,' she added quickly.

'Well, I suppose I would tackle the person I thought was responsible and give them the chance to own up. And if they weren't prepared to do that I would tell the police myself. I don't think I could turn a blind eye. It wouldn't be right.'

'Mm. That's what I thought, too. I just wanted to run it past someone first. Thanks Tory.'

'You're not in any trouble are you?' asked her old friend.

'It's nothing to do with me. I've just discovered something that needs to be put right. I'll tell you as soon as I can.' Poppy was silent until a thought occurred to her. 'Does George Blackstone have any children?'

'Goodness me, no. Can you imagine anyone wanting to marry him?' Tory chuckled. 'He had a brother, Cyril, but he died thirty odd years ago. His widow was left to bring up their daughter all on her own.'

'Does she live in Waterby?'

'No, she moved away with the little one soon after Cyril died and hasn't been back since.'

'Can you remember what the daughter was called?'

'It was a long time ago. I'm afraid my memory isn't what it was. I can hardly remember what I had for breakfast these days.' As the smell of toast constantly pervaded Tory's small flat Poppy thought she could probably hazard a guess, but kept the thought to herself. Tory, meanwhile, was adding two and two together and getting pretty close to the mark.

'Is this anything to do with the secret you've uncovered,' she asked, her faded blue eyes suddenly flint sharp.

Poppy realised that she should have been more subtle in her line of questioning. 'I just wondered, that's all.' As she looked around for inspiration her eyes fell on the clock on Tory's mantelpiece.

'Crikey, is that the time? I'd better go or I'll miss the bus.'

2 2

For the next few weeks Poppy was swept up in the build up to Christmas. During their weekly riding lessons she watched Hope like a hawk. The Tavistock Herald continued to print updates on the Hope for Hope Appeal as villagers organised quiz nights, boot fairs and even a sponsored walk to raise money to send Hope to America. Poppy knew she would have to tackle her friend soon, but the days were so packed with school carol concerts, end of term productions and Christmas shopping expeditions that she didn't have time to stop and think.

The weekend before Christmas Caroline drove them to Bromley to stay with her sister Lizzie. Scarlett had offered to look after Cloud and Chester while they were away and was patiently responding to the text messages Poppy was sending hourly to check all was well.

On Saturday evening, after a frenetic trip into London to see the Christmas lights, Poppy sat curled up on the sofa in Lizzie's chaotic kitchen watching the two sisters prepare dinner. Charlie was on the rug by her feet playing with an old box of Lego that Lizzie had unearthed in the loft. Poppy was exhausted. She'd felt strangely out of place as they'd jostled with hordes of Christmas shoppers in Oxford Street. They'd only moved from Twickenham to Devon six months earlier but she already felt like a country mouse visiting her cousins in the city. She wasn't used to seeing so many people in one place at one time. She also missed Cloud with an ache that refused to go away. After texting Scarlett yet again she picked up a crumpled copy of the local paper from the arm of the sofa and began flicking through it. As she scanned story after story of police incidents, council intrigue and court cases she had a flash of inspiration.

'Auntie Lizzie, can I borrow your computer for a minute? I want to Skype Scarlett, just to check how things are at home.'

Lizzie stopped chopping vegetables. 'Of course you can, darling. You know where it is, don't you?'

Poppy nodded and made her way to the cellar, which had been converted into a den. She switched on the computer and within a couple of minutes the freckled face of her best friend was grinning at her as if she was in the same room, not two hundred and fifty miles away on the edge of Dartmoor.

'How's London? Did you get a chance to go to Harrods or Hamleys? What were the Christmas lights like? I bet they were a million times better than the ones at home. Honestly, Poppy, sometimes I feel like I live in the back of beyond.'

'You are funny, Scar. I can't wait to get home. London is so *busy*. Anyway, how are Cloud and Chester?'

'They're fine. We've just been over to check. Cloud was lying down in his stable and Chester was standing watching over him. They're so sweet together.'

'I know. It's almost as if Chester is Cloud's guardian angel. I miss them so much.'

'You're back tomorrow evening, aren't you? Only one more sleep,' teased Scarlett.

'Thank goodness. Have you seen Hope?' Poppy asked.

'No. We spent yesterday in Plymouth finishing off the Christmas shopping and drove over to see Great Aunt Lucy today.'

'Where does she live?' asked Poppy, homesick for Devon.

'Near Holsworthy. She's my dad's spinster auntie and used to be the head teacher of an all-girls boarding school. She's totally terrifying. But she makes a lovely fruit cake.'

'While we're on the subject of old ladies, what was the name of the woman who lived at Flint Cottage before Hope and Shelley?'

'Mrs Deakins. She died ages ago.'

'So why would someone be sending letters to Flint Cottage addressed to a Mrs M. Turner?'

'Search me.'

'Scar, I've been thinking about Hope and her mum, about the appeal and everything.'

'And?'

Scarlett listened intently as Poppy voiced her suspicions. Even to her own ears they sounded implausible. And yet…

'Are you sure?' Scarlett was scandalised.

'Not one hundred per cent,' Poppy admitted. 'Maybe my imagination's running away with me. But there are too many coincidences. I just need to find a way of proving I'm right. What would the name Shelley be short for?'

'Michelle?' Scarlett hazarded.

'That's what I thought. Look, there's something I want to try. In the meantime promise me you'll keep it to yourself? It would be awful if I was wrong.'

'Of course I promise, you twit. As long as you promise to keep me posted.'

They ended the connection and Poppy sat twiddling a strand of hair that had come loose from her ponytail. She began typing furiously into a search engine and at last found a website that confirmed her suspicions. The reason for Hope's secrecy was there in black and white. But Poppy felt no sense of triumph. She switched off the computer with a heavy heart.

23

P oppy carried the weight of her untold secret heavily until Monday morning, the first day of the Christmas holidays. After mucking out and feeding Cloud and Chester she ran virtually all the way to Ashworthy. By the time she reached Scarlett's back door she was panting heavily. Scarlett led her up to her bedroom, where Poppy collapsed on the floor in a sweaty heap.

'Well?' demanded Scarlett.

'I was right. Look, it's all here,' said Poppy, waving a printout from Lizzie's computer in Scarlett's face. She grabbed it and Poppy watched her eyes widen as she started reading.

'Poor Hope,' Scarlett whispered. 'What are we going to do?'

'Nothing. At least not for a few days.' Poppy had made the decision in the early hours. 'Let's all enjoy Christmas first. Then we can come up with a plan of action.'

MIKE MCKEEVER'S plane was due to land at Heathrow early on Christmas Eve and he'd promised to be home just after lunch. Poppy spent the morning sweeping out the tack room, wrestling with spider webs and re-arranging the grooming kit, tack, rugs and feed bins into some semblance of order before giving Caroline a hand indoors.

'Just as well your dad's back today,' Caroline remarked as she and Poppy wrapped streaky bacon around cocktail sausages and rolled sage, onion and chestnut stuffing into balls. 'Snow's forecast tonight.'

'A white Christmas! Seriously?' said Charlie. 'That would be epic!'

Poppy had purloined the McKeevers' old artificial tree for her bedroom and had adorned it with the leftover tinsel, baubles and home-made creations she had found at the bottom of their enormous cardboard box of Christmas decorations. Some, including the toilet roll fairy for the top of the tree, had been made when Poppy was at pre-school and her mum was still alive. Right at the bottom of the box were a couple of red felt stocking decorations that Poppy still remembered embellishing with buttons and ribbon. She pictured her four-year-old self, her brown hair falling forward and her tongue between her teeth as she concentrated on getting glue on the buttons and ribbons and not her fingers, her mum helping with the tricky bits. The memory made her smile.

Just after two o'clock she heard car doors slam and by the time she had run downstairs her dad was already in the hallway, hanging his jacket on the bottom of the bannister. Poppy flung her arms around him.

'Hello, my gorgeous girl. How's Cloud? Is his leg better yet?' he asked.

'You're hopeless, Dad. It's his foot, not his leg. And no, not yet. His next X-ray is due in a fortnight.'

'Foot, leg, it's all the same to me. How are the riding lessons going?'

'Brilliant. We've moved on from flatwork to pole work and a bit of jumping now. I'm working on my contact and impulsion and getting Rosie into a nice outline.'

Her dad ruffled her hair. 'I've got absolutely no idea what you're talking about but it all sounds very impressive.'

They spent the afternoon catching up and, after an early tea, settled down in front of the fire to watch a Christmas film.

'I love Christmas Eve better than Christmas Day, if I'm honest,' said Caroline. 'I remember when I was your age Poppy, I used to creep down-stairs in the middle of the night to go and see Hamilton.' Poppy pictured a young Caroline tiptoeing down the stairs to see the fleabitten grey pony she'd owned as a girl. 'I'd read about this legend that claimed that animals were able to talk at the stroke of midnight on Christmas Eve,' her stepmum continued. 'I tried it two years running but no luck. He was pleased to see me and I think I got a whicker but he never said a word. I gave up after that.'

That night Poppy set the alarm on her mobile phone for a quarter to midnight, making sure it was on vibrate mode before shoving it under her pillow. When the pillow started shuddering a couple of hours later it took her several minutes to come to but when she did she dressed quickly. She tugged the duvet from her bed, dragging it silently behind her like a bride's train, down the stairs, through the hallway and into the kitchen. Stuck on the back door was a note, written in Caroline's familiar handwriting.

I thought you might be heading for the stables. Give Cloud and Chester my love and don't forget to tell me if the magic works for you!

Poppy was grinning as she pulled on her coat and wellies and let herself out of the back door.

It was a cloudy night and bitingly cold. She could almost taste the ice in the air. She lent on the stable door and peered in. It took a few moments for her eyes to adjust to the inky blackness inside but as she stared the outlines of Cloud and Chester slowly began to take shape. They were standing nose to tail, their heads drooping as they slept.

Poppy checked her watch. Ten to midnight. Almost Christmas. The day was always bittersweet. It was the day more than any other that she missed her mum. Poppy often wondered if the gash in her heart left by Isobel's death would ever fully heal. Her mum had adored Christmas and had always gone completely over the top, throwing decorations at their Twickenham home until it resembled Santa's grotto in Hamleys. She'd insisted on inviting more relatives than could comfortably squeeze into their terraced home, and the party usually lasted for several days. Caroline's approach was more measured. They'd still had a six foot tree in the bay window of their front room but until this year they had always spent the day itself at Lizzie's in Bromley.

Poppy gazed at Cloud, his face now so familiar to her that she could have drawn it from memory. Something cold landed on her nose, making her start. It was a flake of snow, sparkling in the beam cast by the security light over the stable door. She squinted into the dark. More flakes were coming, falling from the sky like tiny parachutes, dancing in the gusts. It was going to be a white Christmas. Charlie would be so excited. For the first time since Isobel's death, Poppy felt her mother's presence so keenly it was as if she was standing beside her, her arm wrapped around Poppy's shoulders.

She eased open the bolt on the door and crept into the stable. Cloud, who had only been dozing, woke and turned towards her. When he realised it was Poppy he gave the softest whicker. Chester jerked his head up, opened his liquid brown eyes and hee-hawed loudly.

'Shh! It's only me,' whispered Poppy. 'I wanted to wish you both a happy Christmas.' And see if you would talk to me at midnight, she thought, even though she knew it was as unlikely as finding snow in the Sahara. Chester shook his woolly head, dismissing such nonsense, walked over and started nibbling her pockets. Cloud gave her a friendly nudge.

'OK, OK, be patient,' Poppy told them, fishing around for a packet of Polos. She gave them one each and popped a third into her mouth before settling in the corner of the stable, the duvet wrapped around her. As all three crunched companionably Poppy smiled contentedly. She checked her watch. A couple of minutes to go.

'If someone had told me a year ago that I'd be spending the next Christmas Eve with my own pony and donkey I'd have thought they were crackers,' she said. Right now Dartmoor seemed light years away from leafy Twickenham. 'I thought I was the unluckiest girl in the world when my mum died. I thought so for years. But not anymore. It's like my luck changed the moment we moved to Riverdale. Perhaps there is magic here.'

Cloud locked eyes with her and she crossed her fingers, willing him to speak. 'It's midnight, Cloud. It's now or never,' she whispered.

The stable was so quiet a field mouse could have dropped a miniature pin and no-one would have heard it fall. Poppy held her breath.

Cloud, her perfect pony, her beautiful boy, lifted his silver tail and broke wind noisily. The sound reverberated around the stable's four walls like a rumble of thunder. Poppy felt bubbles of laughter rising from deep inside her belly and was soon bent double, cackling like a hyena. 'So much for Christmas Eve magic,' she spluttered. 'Wait until Caroline hears about this!'

24

'Poppy! Wake up!' The command was whispered in her ear, dispatched on a wave of warm breath that tickled her earlobe. Poppy pulled the duvet over her face. 'Go away. I'm asleep,' she muttered, rolling over to face the wall. But Charlie was not deterred that easily. He tried a different tack.

'Poppy?' he wheedled through the duck down duvet. 'Poppy, please wake up. It's Christmas! Santa's been. My stocking's full of presents!'

'What time is it?' she growled.

'I don't know. It's still dark outside but it must be nearly morning. I've been awake for *hours*.'

Poppy turned over and grabbed her alarm clock. Twenty to five. Charlie had been given strict instructions the night before not to wake Caroline and their dad before half past six. Poppy sighed. 'We've got ages before we can open any presents. You must be freezing. Come on, hop into bed and I'll warm you up.'

Charlie's feet were like blocks of ice. She shuddered as he wound them around her legs. He put his thumb in his mouth and mumbled, 'Will you tell me a story while we wait?'

Poppy knew she had no chance of getting back to sleep. 'Oh alright then, seeing as it's Christmas,' she said. 'What kind of story?'

'One about how Freddie and Cloud used to live together on the moor and how they became friends with the panther. Please,' he added as an afterthought.

Poppy paused. She never minded talking about Cloud. 'Once upon a time there was a beautiful Connemara pony called Cloud. His dappled grey coat was the colour of slate and snow and his mane and tail rippled like molten silver as he galloped across the moor. He was wild and untamed yet had the kindest, biggest heart. His best friend in all the world was a dog called Freddie, who was loyal and brave. Freddie was the best companion any pony could hope to have by their side. One day, as Cloud and Freddie walked together through the Riverdale wood -' As Poppy's story of adventure and derring-do unfolded she felt Charlie grow heavy beside her, his breathing slowing. She felt tiredness seep through her body and soon she, too, was sound asleep.

BY A QUARTER past seven Charlie was awake again. By half past he had ripped open all the presents in his stocking and was sitting on the end of his parents' bed surrounded by wrapping paper, his hair sticking up and his eyes shining. Poppy took her time, examining every present before opening the next. A new hoof pick and mane comb, Polos for Cloud and Chester, the latest pony book by her favourite author. Her dad and Caroline sipped tea and watched them indulgently. Once the stockings were opened the McKeevers moved downstairs to the lounge. Charlie shrieked with joy when he saw another pile of presents under the tree. Her dad lit the fire and Poppy and Charlie distributed the presents. Poppy was delighted with a pair of cream jodhpurs, black leather jodhpur boots and a smart blue New Zealand rug for Cloud.

'I thought that he'd be needing a rug soon. It won't be long before his foot is better and you'll be able to turn him out. And you'll be riding him before you know it. You'll need your own jodhpurs and boots then. You can't borrow Scarlett's brother's old ones forever,' Caroline said.

Poppy had thought long and hard about what to give Caroline. The answer had come to her as she'd rootled through her jewellery box looking for a silver bangle a couple of weeks earlier. She'd checked with her dad and although he'd looked a bit choked he'd said he thought it was a brilliant idea.

'I hope you like it,' she said as she handed the brightly-wrapped present to Caroline. She watched her stepmum's face as she untied the ribbon and prised open the wrapping paper. Inside a layer of white tissue paper was a small silver locket on a simple silver chain. Caroline gasped. 'But Poppy, wasn't this your mum's?' she asked, her brows furrowed.

'It was. But it's yours now. I wanted you to have it. Have a look inside.'

In one window of the locket was a tiny photo of her dad, taken on holiday the year before. His face was tanned and his hair windswept. He looked every inch the famous BBC news correspondent. In the other window was a picture of Poppy and Charlie, both laughing. Charlie had set the timer on his camera to take the photo, but had taken so many attempts before he'd managed to get the settings right that they'd had a fit of the giggles. Caroline was silent as she studied the photos. Poppy held her breath. What if it had been a terrible mistake and her stepmum hated the thought of wearing Isobel's old locket? But when she looked at Poppy her eyes were bright with tears. 'Oh Poppy,' she said. 'Will you help me put it on?'

Poppy swept her stepmum's blonde hair over one shoulder and fiddled with the two ends of the chain. The clasp closed safely around the final link like two circles on a Venn diagram, indelibly entwined. She hoped the locket would in some small way make up for the years she'd spent giving Caroline the cold shoulder, subconsciously blaming her for her mum's death. There was a wistful look in her dad's eyes. Christmas must be tough for him too, she realised.

'Your mum would have been so proud of you, Poppy,' he said, a catch in his voice. 'So very proud.'

~

THE SNOW CONTINUED TO FALL, silently and steadily. By the time the McKeevers had demolished a small mountain of bacon sandwiches Riverdale had been blanketed in white. Caroline put the turkey in the oven, wiped her hands on a tea-towel and checked the clock.

'It's half past nine. We've got plenty of time for a walk before I need to put the potatoes on. Though we'd better make sure we have lots of layers on,' she said.

A bracing walk on Christmas morning was a McKeever family tradition that went ahead whatever the weather. Poppy could remember Charlie as a baby, bundled up in a white snowsuit, riding in a baby back-pack on their dad's shoulders like a Maharaja atop an elephant, as they strolled along the Thames to Richmond and back. When Charlie was older they'd driven up to Richmond Park and watched herds of red and fallow deer grazing below old English oak trees, their branches stark against the pale December sky.

Poppy grabbed a couple of carrots on her way out and called softly to Cloud and Chester from the back door. Their heads appeared over the stable door. 'I think I'll turn you out for a couple of hours this morning, Chester.' Cloud stamped his foot impatiently and whinnied. 'I'm sorry Cloud. I know how desperate you are to go out with him. But it won't be much longer, I promise.'

'Look at Freddie! He's gone crazy!' cried Charlie. The McKeevers watched as the dog raced around in circles, flicking sprays of snow into the air with his nose, barking with delight. His joy was contagious and Charlie, his cheeks pink, ran behind him laughing loudly. Poppy lay down and waved her arms and legs in the snow. She sprang up and pointed at the marks she'd made. 'Look, a snow angel!'

'So which way are we going to go?' asked her dad.

'Let's walk through Riverdale wood. The stream will look so pretty in all this snow,' suggested Caroline, and they set off across the field to the right of the house until they reached the post and rail perimeter fence. Poppy remembered the first time she and Charlie had explored the wood, the day after they'd moved to Riverdale. Then the trees had been heavy with bright green leaves and the air had been warm and still. Now snow flurries swirled around them as they climbed the fence and the bare branches were covered with a layer of white. Charlie led the way, Poppy close behind him. Freddie bounced back and forth, snapping at snowflakes and weaving between them as swiftly as a Prince Philip Cup pony in a bending race.

The McKeevers followed the stream until the trees started to peter out and they emerged onto the open moorland at the base of the tor. A herd of woolly Dartmoor ponies were grazing on the horizon. Just seeing them made Poppy shiver and she wondered if Cloud would have survived the harsh winter had he not been caught in the drift. She fell behind as they skirted the tor and began heading for home. She had the beginnings of a headache and her legs felt leaden. Caroline waited for her to catch up.

'Are you OK Poppy? You look very pale.'

'I am a bit tired,' Poppy admitted. 'The early start must be catching up with me. I don't know how Charlie does it.' They watched the six-year-old as he streaked towards them, his red coat as bright as a holly berry against the snow-covered moor. Freddie raced after him, a black and tan shadow at his heels. Charlie slid to a halt a few feet in front of them and clutched his sides dramatically.

'I'm *so* hungry. Can we *please* have Christmas lunch now?'

25

Before long the McKeevers were pulling crackers and laughing at the terrible cracker jokes.

'What's the best Christmas present in the world?' asked their dad. Everyone shrugged and Charlie, by now completely over-excited, yelled, 'I don't know! What *is* the best Christmas present in the world?'

'A broken drum – you just can't beat it,' he replied, to a chorus of groans. Caroline and Poppy had decorated the dining room with armfuls of holly and ivy. Candles flickered on the mantelpiece and the table was laden with enough food to feed at least a dozen people. Poppy was sure the roast turkey must smell delicious but she suddenly had no appetite.

'How are you feeling, sweetheart?' asked Caroline, watching her push the food about on her plate.

'Actually, I don't feel too good. Sort of hot and cold at the same time.' It was true. One minute she was shivery and the next she was boiling. The thought of eating even a mouthful of turkey made her queasy.

'Sounds like you might be coming down with something. I'll do Cloud and Chester tonight. You stay beside the fire and we'll find a nice film to watch,' said Caroline firmly.

By six o'clock Poppy's head was throbbing and she felt overwhelmed with tiredness. Caroline felt her forehead. 'You've got a temperature. Come on, let's get you to bed.' Once she'd changed into her pyjamas

white coat reached his elbows and the plastic stethoscope bounced jauntily on his chest. In his hand he carried a small red case with a white cross.

'Where's the patient?' he asked, walking over to Poppy and feeling her wrist for a pulse. 'Yes, she's definitely still alive,' he announced with a grin.

'We thought it might make you laugh,' said Caroline. 'How are you feeling?'

'The same. Is Cloud OK?' she croaked.

'Yes, he's fine. I've just brought Chester in. We're completely snowed in. I haven't even seen a snowplough go past. And there's more snow forecast tonight. Good job we've got plenty of food in. I think it's going to be a few days before we can get the cars out.'

'I made an awesome snowman, Poppy,' said Charlie. 'I wish you were well enough to come and play.'

'I'm sorry, Charlie. Maybe I'll be better tomorrow,' she said, her head sinking back into the pillows.

'It's OK, you can't help it. Mum says I can feed Cloud and Chester tonight, can't I Mum?'

Caroline smiled. 'Yes, you can.' She turned to Poppy. 'He's desperate to help. I've told him how much they both have.'

Poppy nodded. She felt an overwhelming desire to sleep. Noticing her eyelids flutter, Caroline chivvied Charlie out of the room and closed the door gently behind them.

That night Poppy's dreams were vivid. Hope was sitting in a tiny round room at the top of a stone tower, carefully plaiting her long blonde hair as she whispered and giggled with Caitlyn. Caitlyn handed Hope a pretty turquoise box and said to her, 'Inside is the key to Cloud's heart. Use it well'. The image became fuzzy and suddenly Hope was galloping Cloud around the indoor school at Redhall Manor, egged on by Shelley, who was standing in the middle of the school, cracking a lunging whip. Cloud galloped faster and faster, his flared nostrils and the whites of his eyes showing his terror. Poppy, watching from the side, tried to run towards them but it was as if her arms and legs were caught in treacle. She shouted and when Shelley turned around Poppy's blood ran cold. The face staring back at her wasn't Shelley at all. It was George Blackstone. He roared with anger when he saw Poppy and bellowed, 'You thief! You stole my pony!' Poppy tried to run but her legs refused to move. Cloud slowed to a standstill, his flanks heaving. Poppy watched helplessly as his legs buckled beneath him and he fell to the floor with a loud crash.

She woke with a start, her heart thudding. It's a dream, she told herself. But she could still hear crashing and banging. She sat up in bed and tried to identify where the noise was coming from. Apart from the usual creaks and sighs the house was quiet. It seemed to be coming from the stables.

Poppy looked at her clock. Half past four. She slid out of bed and tried standing up. Her legs felt wobbly but at least they worked. She reached for her clothes, dressed quickly and crept downstairs. In the kitchen she grabbed a torch and flung on her hat, gloves and coat. She unlocked the back door and slipped out of the house like a sprite, heading for the stables.

The security light at the back of the house came on as Poppy crunched through the snow to the stables as quickly as she could. As she neared the old stone building she heard a strange grunting noise. Her heart in her mouth, she looked over the stable door. Cloud was standing in the middle of the stable, his head low, breathing rapidly. Chester, standing at the back, hee-hawed loudly when he saw Poppy's frightened face.

'Oh no!' she cried, reaching for the bolts on the door. Cloud sank to the ground and started rolling, his legs thrashing wildly in the air inches from the old donkey, who shrank back into the far corner. Poppy stopped, her head still woozy. I don't know what to do, she thought help-lessly. What should I do?

As if sensing her panic Chester hee-hawed again. The sound spurred Poppy into action. She ran into the tack room and grabbed Cloud's head-collar. Within seconds she was edging around the stable trying to avoid his flailing hooves. Once she was behind his head she knelt down and tried to put the headcollar on. But her hands were shaking and every time she got near he jerked his head away.

'Cloud, you must stay still. Just for a minute,' she pleaded. For a beat he stopped moving and she grabbed her chance. The headcollar finally on, she stood up and pulled on the lead rope. 'Up you get. Come on Cloud, stand up.'

Cloud rolled on his back, kicking his stomach, and Poppy tugged again, no thought for her own safety. 'You can do this Cloud! Stand up!' He grunted, gathered his legs together and stood up shakily. There was blood on his cheek and his neck was dark with sweat.

Colic. It must be colic, Poppy thought frantically. But what to do? They were completely snowed in – there was no way the vet would get here, even in a Land Rover. She racked her brain, trying to remember what her pony books said. Walking every half an hour, that was it.

'We need to walk, Cloud. To stop you getting a twisted gut.' She looked at his foot, encased in its special shoe. 'Your foot will have to take its chance. This is more important.' He seemed calmed by her voice and she kept talking as she led him slowly out of the stable. Although the back of the house was banked in snow the old stone building had protected the yard from the worst of the drifts and Poppy coaxed the pony up and down the length of it.

'Five minutes' walking every half an hour. I think that's what we need to do,' she said, trying to inject some confidence into her voice. Cloud walked slowly, stopping every so often to kick or bite at his stomach. 'No, my beautiful boy. You mustn't do that. Keep walking. Please,' she begged.

After five freezing minutes she returned him to the stable and investigated the blood on his face. He'd grazed his cheekbone thrashing around in the stable and flinched when Poppy tried to touch it. He was restless and pawed at the ground. He tried to roll again but Poppy held his lead rope firmly and managed to stop him lying down. She checked her watch every couple of minutes and when twenty five minutes had passed she led him back out of the stable for another five minutes of walking. She'd lost all feeling in her feet long ago and her fingers felt icy despite the gloves. Every time Cloud stopped and arched his neck or made the strange grunting noise Poppy felt panic rise up. Horses died of colic. What if Cloud had already twisted his gut? An image of an obscenely pink intestine curling around itself like a giant worm inside her pony's stomach danced in front of her eyes. She shook her head, casting the mirage aside, and concentrated on putting one foot in front of the other. She wondered if she should go for help, wake up Caroline and her dad, call the vet. But the vet would never make it through the snow and there was nothing her dad or Caroline could do. Anyway, she couldn't bear the thought of leaving Cloud, not even for a minute.

The snow kept falling, covering their footprints almost as soon as they had made them. It was as if they were ghosts, already dead, Poppy thought with a shudder. The five minutes were up and she led the pony back into the stable.

How could he have suddenly developed colic? She hadn't changed his food or bedding. He'd seemed perfectly fine on Christmas Day. A bit bored maybe, but that was it. She cursed herself for not checking him on Boxing Day. But she wasn't sure she'd have been able to drag herself out of bed. And then she remembered Charlie in his doctor's outfit, taking her pulse, offering to feed Cloud and Chester. She pictured him in the tack room, lifting the lid on the feed bin nearest the door, not realising that Poppy had re-arranged everything when she'd had her big clear out. Not noticing that the pony nuts were in fact unsoaked cubes of sugar beet…

Poppy thought she was hallucinating again when Cloud curled his lip up at her as if he was laughing, as if he thought it was all a massive joke. But she remembered it was another symptom of colic, and stroked his neck gently, murmuring to him softly. Chester watched them from the corner of the stable, his brown eyes sadder than she'd ever seen them. He knew, she thought wildly. He knew that Cloud was going to die. She checked her watch. Half past five. Another fifteen minutes and she'd take him out again. Cloud's legs started buckling as he prepared to sink down and roll.

'Cloud, no!' she shouted in alarm. 'Stand up, you must stand!' She grabbed the cheek straps of his headcollar and, with a superhuman effort, hauled him to a standing position. He gave an almighty shake, the lead rope rattling in her hands. Poppy felt waves of desolation and exhaustion wash over her.

'Don't die, Cloud. Please don't die,' she sobbed. But the pony looked defeated, his head low and his eyes dull.

She wrapped her arms around his neck and howled.

27

'**P**oppy! What on earth -?'

Caroline's anxious voice roused Poppy from her torpor. She looked up and saw her stepmother's white face over the stable door.

'It's Cloud,' she said flatly. 'He's got colic. He's dying.'

'*What?*'

'I heard him crashing about in his stable last night. He was in agony. I walked him up and down like you're supposed to but it was no good. I couldn't save him. Just like I couldn't save him from the drift.' Poppy's voice was hoarse, her face wet with tears.

'But Poppy -' Caroline began.

'It's my fault. If I hadn't moved the feed bins around Charlie wouldn't have got the sugar beet mixed up with the pony nuts and everything would have been alright. It's all my fault,' she repeated, her voice a monotone.

'I'll call the vet. Maybe there's a chance she can get here.'

'There's no point. He's twisted his gut, you see,' Poppy continued, looking at her stepmother with puffy eyes. 'He can't have long left.' She swallowed a sob.

Caroline took in the scene before her. Poppy, purple shadows under her eyes and her face drawn, propped against Cloud. The grey pony stood as still as a statue, his eyes on Caroline. At the back of the stable Chester's head was drooping as he dozed. The straw bedding looked as if it had been whipped up and flung around by a band of whirling dervishes. A pile of fresh droppings on the stable floor steamed in the cold.

'Are you sure?' Caroline pressed.

'Of course I'm sure. I'm staying with him until the end. I promised him I'd never leave him.'

Caroline suddenly found it difficult to speak. In that moment she knew she loved her shy, complicated stepdaughter as if she were her own. Poppy could be insecure and stubborn, but her courage and loyalty took Caroline's breath away. She let herself into the stable and touched Poppy lightly on the shoulder. The girl looked up, her face anguished. She took two shaky steps towards Caroline and buried herself in her stepmother's arms, her body racked with sobs.

'Oh sweetheart, don't upset yourself. It breaks my heart to see you like this,' she whispered.

'I'm going to lose him. I can't bear it.'

But something was niggling Caroline. As her gaze swept over the stable for a second time her face cleared.

'Poppy, Cloud's been to the toilet. Look!'

Poppy shrugged, broke away from Caroline's embrace and wiped her tear-streaked cheeks. 'So?'

'Don't you see? The blockage in his gut must have shifted. It means the worst of the colic has passed. Quickly, see if he wants a drink.'

Poppy still looked dazed so Caroline picked up the closest water bucket and held it under Cloud's nose. He sniffed it cautiously then drank thirstily. He finished half the bucket and snorted loudly, spraying Caroline with droplets of water. She laughed. 'See? You did exactly the right thing, Poppy. You saved him!'

They stood together and watched Cloud. After ten minutes or so he edged over to the hayrack and pulled out a couple of wisps of hay. When he lifted his tail and deposited another mound of steaming manure by their welly-clad feet they clutched each other in joy.

'I'll call the vet anyway, just to be on the safe side. Even if she can't make it out here she can give us some advice on the phone. But I think he's going to be fine, Poppy. Thanks to you.'

Poppy was just about to reply when the ground shifted beneath her feet and her head felt so light she thought it might float away. The last thing she noticed before she lost consciousness were black spots dancing in front of her eyes and a ringing in her ears.

~

WHEN SHE WOKE up she was back in bed, the worried faces of her dad, Caroline and Charlie looming over her.

'You fainted. Not surprising really. You're recovering from the flu, you've been up half the night and you haven't eaten for forty eight hours,' said Caroline. She offered Poppy a mug of tea. 'It's got plenty of sugar in it. Please try to have some.'

Poppy sat up in a panic, almost sending the mug flying.

'Cloud? Is he OK?'

'Yes, he's fine. I've phoned the vet and explained everything. She's happy. We've just got to keep an eye on him over the next day or so.'

Relieved, Poppy took the tea and sipped. Caroline and her dad left the room but Charlie stayed. He hovered by the door, red-eyed. When he eventually spoke his voice was small.

'I'm sorry I gave Cloud the wrong nuts, Poppy. I didn't mean to give him tummy ache.'

'It wasn't your fault. You were only trying to help. I should have told you I'd moved the bins about. You weren't to know. And he's alright, so there's nothing to be sorry about.'

Charlie didn't look convinced.

'Honestly Charlie, it's OK. Want to come for a cuddle?'

He stuck his thumb in his mouth and nodded. Poppy patted the bed and he sidled over.

'What would cheer you up?' she said, as she wriggled up the bed and put her arm around his shoulders.

Charlie thought for a moment. 'A snowball fight?' he said hopefully. 'I think that would probably do it.'

Poppy laughed. He really was incorrigible.

'It's a deal. But first I must have breakfast. I'm so hungry I could eat -'

'A horse?' her brother suggested.

'No!' Poppy pretended to be outraged and was glad to see Charlie giggle.

'A full English breakfast, is what I was going to say. Sausages, bacon, tomatoes, mushrooms, a fried egg,' she listed, ticking each off on her fingers. 'Oh, and toast. Loads and loads of toast.'

~

ONLY ONCE POPPY had seen for herself that Cloud was settled and eating normally again did she agree to sit down and have breakfast, by which time her stomach was growling ominously.

'I hope I haven't made his fracture worse,' she said, as she demolished an enormous plateful of food.

'You did exactly the right thing,' replied Caroline firmly. 'OK, so even if he has damaged his foot the worst case scenario is more box rest. But the vet didn't seem to think walking up and down in the snow every half an hour would have made a huge difference. In fact she said he was more likely to have made it worse thrashing and banging about in the stable. So stop worrying. And that's an order,' she added, waving a spatula at Poppy.

Poppy knew her stepmother was probably right and for once she let herself feel optimistic. Her phone bleeped.

'It's Scarlett. She wants to know if we'd like to go tobogganing at Ashworthy. Can we go?' Poppy asked.

'Only if I can come, too. I used to love tobogganing when I was your age. There weren't many chances to do it in London. I might even try to drag your dad along. He could do with the exercise,' her stepmother answered.

The family spent the next couple of hours climbing up and whizzing down Ashworthy's top sheep field on plastic fertiliser sacks filled with snow, shrieking with glee as they sped feet first down the hill and laughing wildly as they collided in a heap at the bottom.

Pat invited them to stay for lunch and as they squeezed around the pine table in the kitchen they regaled her and Bill with stories of hotly-contested races and spectacular tumbles. Pat had made two vast dishes of cauliflower cheese which they mopped up with chunky slices of granary bread. Despite her massive breakfast Poppy was ravenous and was soon having second helpings.

Conversation drifted from sledging to her dad's trip to Syria. The room was silent as he described his life as a war correspondent.

'It must be difficult not to get too emotionally involved,' observed Bill from the head of the table.

'It is, sometimes,' her dad admitted. 'I'm supposed to be objective, to be an observer, but it is hard, especially when children are involved.'

'Speaking of which, how's young Hope Taylor?' asked Pat.

'Oh, she's still in remission, isn't she Poppy?' said Caroline. Poppy shot a glance at Scarlett, who was listening intently.

'I save all my two pound coins and give them to a different charity every year. Last year we gave more than £300 to the RSPCA. I thought I'd like to donate them to the Hope for Hope Appeal this year,' said Pat.

Across the table Scarlett made a strange gurgling noise as she choked on a piece of cauliflower. Her dad patted her on the back. 'That's a nice idea, love,' he told his wife.

Poppy looked at the kind, open faces of Pat and Bill. Farming was a tough business and she knew they sometimes struggled to make ends meet. She thought about the piles of dog biscuits she and Scarlett had spent hours baking and Tory's £500 cheque, all the quiz nights and raffles. It was no good. This had to stop.

28

O ver the next 24 hours the snow disappeared almost as quickly as it had arrived. Mild westerly winds coaxed the temperatures above freezing and soon the countryside had shed its white winter coat and was green once more. Poppy checked Cloud obsessively but he seemed to have made a full recovery and if anything was more impatient than ever to escape the confines of his stable. Letting Chester out each morning had become a two person job – one to lead out the old donkey and the other to police the stable door to stop Cloud barging his way out behind him. When Poppy laid a palm on Cloud's dappled grey flank she fancied she could actually feel the pent-up energy pulsing through his veins in time to her own heartbeat. Poppy, back to full strength, was also restless, although she couldn't say why. The only time she felt settled was in Cloud's company. He, too, was less edgy when they were together so she spent hours in his stable, grooming him, tacking him up and dreaming of the day she could jump on his back and they could ride off into the sunset together, as if they were the stars in their own cheesy film.

The start of term was looming when Shelley called Caroline asking if she could look after Hope while she went to London for the day.

'Off to see the cancer specialist again is she?' asked Poppy cynically.

'Funny, isn't it, how she always comes back from seeing Hope's *oncologist*,' Poppy emphasised the word heavily, 'with a new outfit and hairdo.'

'Poppy!' said Caroline, shocked. 'The appeal's nearly reached its £10,000 target, apparently, so she's going up to finalise details of their trip to America.'

'I bet she is,' muttered Poppy under her breath, remembering the holiday brochure Shelley had kicked under the sofa at Flint Cottage.

Either Caroline hadn't heard or she had chosen to ignore Poppy's remark. 'I can't believe how quickly they've raised the money. People have been so generous. But then it is such a great cause. Think how wonderful it would be for Hope and Shelley if the treatment works this time.'

'What time is she dropping Hope off?' Poppy asked, knowing she must seize this chance to tackle her friend while Shelley was well out of the way.

Caroline looked at her watch. 'In about half an hour. I've got to go to the supermarket later so you can have an hour in Tavistock together if you like. You don't mind, do you?'

'No, it'll be good to catch up. I haven't had a proper chat with Hope for ages,' she said.

~

POPPY WAS in the stable grooming Cloud when she heard Shelley's engine revving and a car door slamming. She let herself out and met Hope as she appeared around the corner of the house.

'Poppy! Your mum told me about the colic. It must have been terrifying. How is he?'

'Better now, thanks.'

The concern in Hope's pale blue eyes appeared genuine and Poppy wondered yet again if she'd got it all wrong. It was all so far-fetched.

'Can I give you a hand?' Hope asked, interrupting her thoughts.

'Uh, yes, sure. You brush his tail while I do his mane. He's still a bit head shy with people he doesn't know so well.' Poppy picked up the comb and began running it through Cloud's silver mane, teasing out the knots and tangles as gently as she could. As she combed she wished life was as easy to untangle.

They worked in silence for a few minutes before Poppy cleared her throat and took the plunge. 'So, how are you feeling?'

'I'm OK. Same as usual,' Hope answered, uncertainly.

'Yes, you're looking well. The picture of health, some might say.'

'Poppy, you're being a bit weird. Is something wrong?'

'You tell me, Hope. I don't want to sound unsympathetic but you don't seem very ill to me.'

Hope didn't reply but her face was flustered.

'I was thinking this morning how generous everyone has been towards you and your appeal,' Poppy continued, her jaw tight. 'Tory gave her washing machine money, Dad and Caroline gave a couple of hundred pounds, Pat and Bill are donating their coin collection and Scarlett and I spent hours baking dog biscuits to raise money. That's just the people I know about. Hundreds of others have been raising money. Sponsored walks, boot fairs, quiz nights, you name it, they've organised it. Remind me, what's it all been for?'

'Mum's appeal,' Hope whispered so quietly that Poppy had to strain to hear.

'Yes, the appeal. That's right. But what's the appeal actually paying for? Specialist cancer treatment in California, or a holiday in Florida? And let's not forget the flash telly and the spanking new outfits your mum seems to be wearing every time I see her. What's really going on, Hope?'

'You already know this, Poppy. I have an aggressive form of leukaemia. It's a cancer of the blood. Doctors here say it's terminal but there's a new treatment in America that's going to cure me,' Hope intoned. It was as if she'd learnt the script by rote.

'So you say. But I'm afraid I don't believe you.' Poppy slipped a hand in her pocket and fingered the folded sheet of A4 paper she'd printed out at Lizzie's house in Bromley.

'This is your last chance to come clean, Hope. I want you to tell me the truth.'

'I don't know what you mean,' Hope blustered.

Poppy pulled out the printout, unfolded it with exaggerated care and held it out to Hope. 'Take it,' she ordered, her voice grim. 'It's from the Croydon News four years ago. I want you to read it. Although I have a feeling you already know what it says.'

She watched Hope's face for a reaction. If she'd needed any convincing that her theory was right the evidence was there in front of her. Guilt was written all over Hope's thin face.

29

Hope shrank back against the wall of the stable, her eyes glistening with tears. She glanced at the printout and shook her head.

'Please, no,' she whispered.

'Have it your way,' said Poppy. 'I'll tell you what it says, shall I?'

Poppy had read the newspaper report so many times she could have probably recited it from memory.

'A Croydon woman who shaved a girl's head in an elaborate cancer scam has been told she was lucky to escape jail.

'Michelle Turner pretended the six-year-old had leukaemia and set up a £5,000 appeal to raise money to send her to America for life-saving treatment.

'But the 32-year-old's story was nothing more than a web of lies, prosecutor Daniel Watkins told Croydon Magistrates' Court on Thursday.

'Turner admitted fraud and was given a six month suspended prison sentence. Magistrates also ordered her to pay more than £5,000 in compensation. The money will be returned to everyone who donated to her bogus appeal.

'The deception began almost a year ago when Turner took the girl, who cannot be named for legal reasons, out of school for a month. Turner claimed the six-year-old was in hospital having aggressive chemotherapy and when she returned to school she had lost all her hair.

'But the court heard that Turner had shaved the girl's head to give her story credibility and had pocketed all the cash donated by concerned well-wishers.

"It was a particularly cynical scam that took advantage of people's generosity,' Mr Watkins told the court.'

Poppy paused for breath. Hope had slid down the wall and was sitting on the straw in a ball, her hands covering her ears. Poppy felt anger bubbling inside her.

'Michelle Turner and Shelley Taylor are the same person, aren't they? And you were that girl, weren't you Hope? How could you do it to us all? Deep down I've known something was wrong for weeks. It just took me a while to realise what it was. I still can't believe anyone could be so deceitful.'

A tear rolled down Hope's cheek.

'It was something Charlie said that made me start to realise what was going on. He said you didn't look very ill to him. But you'd lost your hair because of the chemo so this cancer business must be true. So why have you still got eyebrows?'

Hope reached up involuntarily and felt one eyebrow with her index finger. Her face filled with horror.

'Then I remembered the shaving cream and razors in your bathroom cabinet. I don't think you lost your hair through chemotherapy at all, did you Hope? I've been checking, you see. According to the cancer websites you'd have lost your eyebrows, too. And someone's hair almost always grows back when they've finished their chemo, and yours has had plenty of time to grow back. I started thinking your mum might have been shaving your head to make it look as though you were having chemo-therapy, but she's so dense she forgot to shave your eyebrows. I was beginning to wonder if you even had cancer at all.'

Hope lifted her head and tried to speak, but Poppy was on a roll. She was pacing up and down like a detective in a daytime television crime drama. 'Then Scarlett and I saw your mum with George Blackstone at the Waterby Dog Show. You remember, when we were selling all those biscuits we made to raise money for your fund?'

Hope flinched.

'Shelley and George were as thick as thieves. Which is pretty apt in the circumstances, I think you'll agree. They definitely looked far too cosy to be landlord and tenant. So that also got me thinking. And then Tory told me that George Blackstone had a niece who'd moved away from Waterby when she was a child and never came back. But what if she had, thirty years later, and she turned out to be as scheming as her uncle?'

'Poppy-' Hope began, her voice a strangulated whisper. But Poppy ignored her.

'I remembered the envelope addressed to Mrs M. Turner that turned up at your house. I'd assumed it must have been for the old lady who used to live there, but I checked. She was Mrs Deakins. I tried Googling Mrs M. Turner but there were thousands of hits. Then I remembered Shelley can be short for Michelle. So I tapped in Michelle Turner and Croydon and bingo. The top hit was the Croydon News report. And then I knew I was one hundred per cent right.'

∾

THE WALLS of the stable felt as though they were closing in and Poppy reached for Cloud's solid bulk seeking reassurance, but he turned away from her and headed for his hayrack. She had a horrible feeling she'd gone too far. Hope was sobbing uncontrollably now and Poppy felt something inside her shift. The anger dissipated as quickly as it had come and there was a catch in her voice when she finally spoke again. 'I thought you were my friend.'

Hope wiped her tear-stained cheeks. 'You don't understand,' she stammered. 'Mum made me do it. I had no choice.'

'How do I know you're telling the truth now when everything else you've told me has been a pack of lies?' Poppy demanded.

'I wanted to tell you, Poppy, I really did. But Mum said if we got caught she'd be sent to prison and I'd end up in care.'

'What about your dad?'

'He left when she was arrested last time. He said he couldn't put up with her anymore. I begged him to take me with him but he couldn't. He was living in a bedsit and there wasn't enough room for me. Then he emigrated to Canada. He promised me that once he was settled I could go and live with him but Mum told me he'd changed his mind once he met Kirstin and didn't want me. I've been so happy here, making friends with you and Scarlett, learning to ride and everything. The last thing I wanted to do was pretend I had cancer again.'

Poppy remembered the conversation she'd overheard in the shop. Perhaps Hope hadn't wanted to go along with Shelley's plans. But she still wasn't satisfied.

'You could have told me. I would have helped, you know.'

'I didn't want to do it, Poppy. You have to believe me. We got chucked out of our flat in Croydon because Mum was behind on the rent. She was always talking about her Uncle George and how he was rolling in money. I heard her on the phone to him one night and the next morning she told me we were moving into one of his farm cottages. I was so happy. I've always wanted to live in the country. I thought it might be a fresh start for me and Mum. Then when we arrived she said we needed some cash while she tried to find a job and I'd have to pretend I had cancer again. I pleaded with her not to but she refused to listen.'

Poppy had to admit it made sense. 'OK, maybe I do believe you. But we have to do something. Your mum can't go on conning people out of money. We need to report her to the police.'

'We can't! She'll go to prison and I'll end up in care! She promised she would stop as soon as she reached ten thousand pounds. We were going to go to America and when we came back she was going to let my hair grow back and tell everyone the treatment had worked.'

Hope cradled her head in her hands and rocked on her heels. Poppy knelt down in the straw beside her and put an arm around her shoulder. 'It's OK, Hope. We'll do it together. Your mum won't be able to force you to do anything ever again.'

'No Poppy, I won't.' She lifted her head and sniffed loudly. 'I *can't*.'

30

Hope looked Poppy straight in the eye. 'I'm frightened of her, Poppy. I'm frightened of what she might do if she finds out I've told someone again. That's why I'm not allowed to go to school. I told my teacher last time, you see. I let it slip that my mum shaved my head. School told the police and Mum was arrested. She went absolutely ballistic.'

Poppy remembered the conversation they'd almost had on the Riverdale tor.

'Has she ever hurt you, Hope?'

'She sometimes yanks my arm when she loses her temper but it's only when I've done something wrong, dropped something or made a mess, you know?'

Poppy shook her head in disbelief. She couldn't even begin to imagine the tightrope Hope must walk every day.

'She's never actually hit me. And it's my fault she gets cross.'

'Normal people don't behave like that, Hope. No mum should take out their anger on their child, or force them to do something they don't want to do. I'm sorry but people like your mum never change. How can you be sure that one day she won't lose her temper and lash out at you?'

Hope had no answer.

'You can't let her get away with it. We need to tell the police.' Poppy thought for a moment. How could she convince Hope to do the right thing?

'What would your dad tell you to do if he was here?'

Hope sniffed. 'Go to the police,' she whispered.

'Then that's what we must do. We'll do it together. It'll all be OK, you'll see.'

'Do you promise?'

Poppy gave her a squeeze. 'Yes. I promise.'

THEY HEARD the back door slam and Charlie's head appeared over the stable door seconds later.

'What do you want?' Poppy sighed.

'Mum sent me to tell you…hold on, why are Hope's eyes so red?'

'Hayfever,' supplied Poppy, hoping the six-year-old wouldn't remember it was mid-winter.

'Oh. It looks like she's been crying, that's all. Anyway, Mum says she's going into town in half an hour so you need to come and get ready.'

Once he'd gone Poppy handed Hope a tissue and she blew her nose noisily.

'We'll go to the police station while Caroline's in the supermarket. We'll ask to see whoever's in charge and explain everything. They'll know what to do,' said Poppy, more confidently than she felt.

Hope sat silently chewing her nails during the drive to Tavistock. Poppy tried valiantly to keep the conversation going. It was at times like these that you really needed Scarlett's easy chatter, she thought. Caroline glanced at Hope in the rear-view mirror.

'Everything OK, sweetheart?' she asked. Hope, who had been staring at the passing countryside, gave a start.

'Oh, yes. I'm fine thank you,' she answered quietly. Caroline seemed satisfied. Poppy fidgeted in her seat and wondered if they should have told Caroline first. But what if her stepmum decided to tackle Shelley herself? Poppy was convinced that Shelley would vanish, taking Hope with her, at the merest hint of trouble. And she had given Hope her word that everything would be alright.

'I'll be at least an hour. Shall I meet you back at the car at about four?' asked Caroline, as they turned into the supermarket car park.

'Yes. We're going to go and have a look around the Pannier Market, aren't we Hope?' said Poppy. She gave Hope a nudge.

'What? Oh yes, the Pannier Market,' she said.

'And don't forget –' Caroline began.

'Yes, I know Mum. Be careful crossing the roads, stick together and text if we're running late,' Poppy finished.

Caroline smiled and disappeared in search of a trolley leaving the two girls in the car park, their faces grave.

'I know it probably doesn't feel like it but the sooner we get this over with the better. Come on, let's go,' said Poppy and she started marching towards the police station, Hope following reluctantly behind.

THEY HADN'T EXPECTED to queue but when they pushed open the heavy door an elderly man in a tweed jacket was leaning against the counter in the small reception area. He was talking loudly to a female police officer. Poppy could see a hearing aid in his right ear.

'So when did you last see your wallet, Mr Bristow?' asked the PC, enunciating carefully.

The old man spluttered, 'If I knew that I wouldn't be here, would I? It's lost, that's the point. Has anyone handed it in?'

The PC glanced up at the newcomers and flashed them a smile. She looked kind and capable. Suddenly Poppy knew it was going to be OK. She and Hope stood patiently while the PC took down the pensioner's details and Poppy opened the door for him as he left. He gave her a curt nod and was gone.

'Mr Bristow loses his wallet at least once a month but it always turns up, usually in the most unexpected places. Last time he found it in his potting shed. The time before that it was in his freezer,' said the PC. She looked at Poppy closely. 'I know you, don't I? You're the girl from Waterby who got lost on the moor. Poppy something. McKendrick, wasn't it?'

'McKeever,' said Poppy. 'That's right. I was looking for my brother Charlie.'

The PC looked pleased with herself. 'I never forget a face. I was with your mum at the hospital while the search and rescue teams were looking for you. She was so relieved when they found you both. I'm PC Claire Bodiam. What can I do for you two?'

Poppy looked at Hope's pale face and took a deep breath. 'Is there somewhere we can talk in private? We want to report a crime.'

~

PC BODIAM LED them into an interview room behind the front counter.

'I want you to take your time and tell me what's happened,' she said, sitting down opposite them, her pocket notebook open. She listened silently as Poppy began talking. When Poppy produced the newspaper printout from her pocket she held up her hand.

'I think my guvnor needs to hear this. He's in a meeting upstairs. I'll see if I can interrupt it.' As she left the room Poppy noticed Hope was on the verge of tears.

'I don't think I can do this. Mum'll never forgive me, I know she won't.'

'It'll be alright,' soothed Poppy. 'I trust PC Bodiam. She'll know what to do for the best.'

When the PC returned she was with an older police officer who introduced himself as Inspector Bill Pearson. His ruddy face was cheerful and his shirt strained over his large stomach. He looked more like a farmer than a police inspector, thought Poppy.

'Right, what about a cup of tea before we start,' he said. 'There's a new packet of biscuits in the rest room. Bring them down won't you, Claire?' He patted his belly. 'I really shouldn't but I can't resist a couple of digestives with my tea. My wife keeps trying to put me on a diet but I think it's a bit late for all that, don't you? Now what's all this about the Hope for Hope Appeal?'

Half an hour later Poppy had explained everything. Inspector Pearson had listened intently and PC Bodiam had taken copious notes.

'So when is your mum due home?' the inspector asked Hope.

'About six o'clock I think. Caroline – that's Poppy's stepmum – was going to drop me back after tea at about half past.'

'Now Hope, I want to assure you that you aren't in any trouble. You've done absolutely the right thing coming here to tell us what's happened and I don't want you to be in any doubt about that,' said Inspector Pearson, helping himself to his third digestive.

'What will happen to my mum?'

'You leave that to us. Do you have any other family apart from your mum who could look after you for a short while?'

'There's Great Uncle George, but please don't make me stay there. My dad lives in Canada. I've got his mobile number if you want it.'

PC Bodiam nodded. 'Yes, let me have the number and I'll contact him now.'

'Hope can stay with us while everything's sorted out,' said Poppy. She looked at the clock over the door. It was five to four. 'We're supposed to be meeting my stepmum at the supermarket at four. I'd better text her to let her know where we are.'

Poppy tapped out a quick message. *We're at the police station. Can you meet us there? NOTHING TO WORRY ABOUT! Xxx*

Caroline arrived less than five minutes later, bursting through the front door, her face anxious. Her expression turned from disbelief to indignation as Inspector Pearson filled her in on Shelley's exploits.

'To think I convinced Tory to give £500 to the appeal! I can't believe I was so naïve,' she said.

'Don't worry, you're not the only one. Hundreds of others have been taken in. Unfortunately individuals like Ms Taylor rely on people's generosity for their scams to work. She isn't the first person to take good, honest people for a ride, and I'm afraid she won't be the last,' the inspector told her.

Hope hugged herself tightly, her head bowed, as she listened to the exchange. Caroline lifted her chin gently. 'You poor love. No-one's going to blame you. And you can stay with us for as long as you need to.' She was rewarded with a weak smile.

Inspector Pearson stood up, signalling that the interview was over. 'There are things I need to be seeing to. PC Bodiam will see you out. And keep Mrs McKeever informed of events, won't you, Claire?'

'Yes, boss.'

31

After that things happened quickly. Inspector Pearson briefed a small team of detectives who spoke to their counterparts in Croydon. They confirmed that Shelley Taylor and Michelle Turner were indeed one and the same. The Hope for Hope Appeal bank account was frozen and an arrest warrant issued. When Shelley arrived at Flint Cottage just before six o'clock, clutching several designer carrier bags, she was greeted by two detectives, who drove her to Plymouth for questioning. PC Bodiam called Riverdale just after eight to say Shelley was being held in custody overnight and was due to appear before magistrates in the morning charged with fraud offences.

'She's made a full and frank admission,' PC Bodiam told Caroline. 'Maybe she's seen the error of her ways, maybe she's hoping the magistrates will be lenient if she pleads guilty at the first opportunity, who knows? She's a slippery customer. But she's almost certainly going to get a prison term because of her previous conviction. I'd say she was looking at three years inside, minimum. And can you let Hope know that I've spoken to her dad? He's catching the first available flight out of Toronto and is hoping to be in the country by tomorrow evening.'

'That's fantastic news, I'll let her know. Will Hope have to give evidence in court?' asked Caroline.

'I would imagine the court would be happy with a written statement from her, especially as Shelley is pleading guilty. And Hope's anonymity will be protected because she's a minor.'

Caroline ended the call and updated Poppy and Hope. Hope had discarded her wig and she looked younger than ever. Her eyes shone when she heard that her dad was on his way.

'See?' Poppy said. 'I told you everything would be OK.'

While Caroline made up the camp bed in Poppy's room and found Hope some of her old pyjamas, Poppy slipped out of the back door to see Cloud. She had the sense that he'd understood exactly what was going on in the stable that afternoon and hadn't approved of the way Poppy had tackled Hope. He was lying down in the straw, his legs tucked under him, his eyelids heavy. Chester was rootling around by their buckets hunting for any stray pony nuts. Poppy sat down and draped her arm around Cloud's neck.

'I know you think I was too hard on Hope, Cloud, but I was so angry she'd lied to me. You were right though, I should have realised it was all Shelley's idea and Hope wasn't to blame. But I've apologised to her and we're friends again.' She stroked Cloud's nose absentmindedly and he blew gently into her hand, his warm breath tickling her fingers. She felt forgiven.

∼

HOPE'S DAD arrived at Riverdale the following evening, dishevelled after a night flight from Toronto. Hope tore through the house like a mini-hurricane when she heard his taxi and hurled herself into his arms.

He introduced himself to the McKeevers. 'Matt Taylor. Pleased to meet you. Sorry it's not under better circumstances. Hope, I wish you'd told me what was happening.'

'I couldn't, Dad. Mum said she'd be put in prison and I'd end up in a children's home if anyone found out. She said you didn't want me anymore, not now you had Kirstin and your new life in Canada.' Hope buried her face in his jumper.

'Your mum said a lot of things that weren't true, Hope. But things are going to change. Kirstin and I want you to come and live with us.'

'In Canada?'

'Yes. No-one will know about your mum and what she's done there. It'll be a new start. Would you like that?'

'More than anything. Though I'll miss everyone here. Especially Buster. He's the pony I've been having riding lessons on,' she explained.

'There are riding schools in Canada, you know,' laughed her dad. I'm sure we can sort something out.'

∽

ONCE AGAIN SHELLEY TAYLOR was front page news in the Tavistock Herald. But this time it was for all the wrong reasons. Her court case was heard quickly and, despite her guilty plea, magistrates jailed her for three-and-a-half years. Fortunately Hope wasn't around to see the story. The day before the paper came out she flew to Canada with her dad. Away from Shelley's clutches she had morphed into the bright, fun-loving girl Poppy had seen glimpses of during their time together.

'I'm going to miss you all so much,' she told the McKeevers. 'Especially you, Poppy. You will keep in touch, won't you? I want to know how Cloud and Chester are doing. And Buster and Rosie. Can you thank Bella for me? I feel bad that she gave me those lessons because she thought I had cancer.'

'It wasn't your fault, Hope. Bella will understand. And everyone who gave to the appeal will get their money back. So stop apologising!' Poppy ordered with a grin.

It felt strange saying goodbye to Hope for the last time. 'We've only known her for a few months but it seems much longer than that,' Poppy said to Caroline as they watched the Taylors' taxi disappear down the drive.

'I know what you mean. She feels like part of the family. I wonder how Shelley's coping in prison. It's terrible that she's going to miss out on so many years of Hope's childhood.'

Poppy raised her eyebrows. Her dad spoke firmly. 'Spare your sympathy for someone who deserves it, Caroline. Shelley was quite happy to con little old ladies out of their hard-earned savings. She had it coming to her.'

Perfectly put, thought Poppy, watching her dad link arms with Caroline and walk back into the house. Although she wasn't sure Tory would have appreciated being called a little old lady.

~

THE LAST FEW days of the Christmas holidays flew by and before she knew it Poppy was sitting on the school bus next to Scarlett on the first day of term. After being given the first few months to find their feet, Poppy, Scarlett and the rest of the Year Sevens were suddenly disappearing under a mountain of homework. Her dad had managed to secure a temporary secondment to the BBC's foreign desk in London and left Riverdale at four every Monday morning, returning home late every Friday night. Poppy's riding lessons at Redhall Manor were still a highlight of her week. Under Bella's expert tutelage she was learning how to slow Rosie to a collected trot and canter and then lengthen her strides into extended paces. With Hope gone, Poppy had Bella's full attention and the riding school owner didn't miss a trick. If Poppy wasn't being chided for rounding her shoulders Bella was castigating her for not maintaining contact with Rosie's mouth. Sometimes Poppy wondered if she was making any progress at all. She treasured any nuggets of praise, however small, and the day Bella told her she was a tidy little rider she virtually floated home.

The first snowdrops were flowering in time for Poppy's twelfth birthday. It fell on a Sunday and Caroline woke early to pick Poppy a small bunch of the waxy white flowers from where they grew in drifts in the border next to her vegetable garden. Delicate in appearance yet tough enough to push their way through frozen soil, the snowdrops reminded Caroline of her stepdaughter. She arranged them in a small vase on a tray with some croissants and honey. Treating Poppy to breakfast in bed was not something she would have felt able to do a year ago. Poppy would have rejected the attempt to reach out to her. It still gladdened her heart that they had moved on so far since then.

As she approached Poppy's bedroom, Charlie bounded out, his hair tousled.

'She's still asleep,' he told his mum in a stage whisper.

'I was,' came Poppy's voice from behind her door, 'Until you sneaked in and trod on Magpie's tail and he squealed and woke me up.'

Charlie grinned at Caroline. 'Oops,' he said. 'Is Dad awake?'

Soon they were all sitting on the end of Poppy's bed watching the birthday girl eat her croissants. When she'd finished Charlie ran out again only to reappear with a pile of presents in his arms, which he deposited on his sister's lap.

'Open mine first,' he demanded, waving a rectangular parcel under her nose.

'OK, OK!' she laughed. Charlie had used so much sticky tape it took Poppy a good five minutes to peel open the wrapping paper. She pulled off the last strip to reveal two wooden name plates.

'I remembered we saw some in Baxters' but I didn't have enough pocket money to buy them so I made my own. There's one for Cloud and one for Chester. I painted their names and they've both got their pictures on. Mum did the outlines and I coloured them in,' Charlie said proudly.

With Charlie's spidery handwriting and inexpertly coloured heads that were only vaguely equine-shaped, they were a far cry from the professionally painted and varnished name plates in Baxters' Animal Feeds. But Poppy didn't mind.

'They're brilliant! Thank you Charlie. I'll hang them on the stable door later.'

Her dad handed her a large, flat present. 'I hope you like it. We didn't really know what to get you, what with your birthday so close to Christmas.'

Poppy tore off the paper. Inside a layer of bubble wrap was a framed watercolour of Cloud and Chester in the shadow of the Riverdale tor. The pony and donkey stood looking straight at her, perfectly captured in time. She traced her finger across Cloud's neck and smiled. It was a beautiful painting.

'Caroline heard about a local artist who specialises in horses and commissioned him to paint it,' said her dad.

'It's amazing. How did he get such a good likeness?' Poppy wondered.

'I took dozens of photos and emailed them to him,' said Caroline. 'Then one day while you were at school he drove over and did some sketches. Do you like it?'

'I *love* it. Thank you so much,' she said, flinging her arms around her stepmum and blowing her dad a kiss.

'So what does twelve feel like?' he asked her.

'Absolutely ancient,' groaned Poppy.

~

IT WAS a wonderful start to a perfect day. When Poppy went down to feed and muck out Cloud and Chester she found another present hidden in their hayrack. The label read, *To Poppy, our favourite human in the whole world. With all our love, Cloud and Chester xx*. Inside were a body protector and a pair of leather riding gloves.

While she was sweeping the yard Scarlett turned up riding Blaze and leading Flynn.

'Happy birthday, Poppy. It's time to down tools and come for a ride. Here's your mount for the day,' she said, handing Flynn's reins to Poppy. 'I think you'll agree he's been beautifully groomed for the occasion.'

Once Poppy had raced inside to change the two girls headed onto the moor for their favourite hack, a two hour ride that followed the valley towards the Blackstone farm before skirting a copse and returning along quiet country lanes. Scarlett craned her neck as they passed Flint Cottage but there was nothing to see. The curtains were drawn and the house had a desolate, forsaken look about it. But it had never been a happy place, thought Poppy.

'I wonder how Hope's getting on,' said Scarlett, reading her mind.

'I had a birthday email from her this morning. She's due to start school in the next couple of days and said she's really looking forward to it. Her dad's already found a riding school near them and she's going to have lessons once a week. Oh, and she really likes Kirstin, that's her dad's girlfriend.'

'So it all worked out for the best in the end.'

'Shelley might not agree. She's in prison in Gloucestershire, according to a story in the Herald this week.'

'She deserved everything she got,' said Scarlett firmly, kicking Blaze into a trot.

~

THAT EVENING, just before seven o'clock, Scarlett sent Poppy a text. *Dad says would you and Charlie like to see a lamb being born? He's got a ewe due to deliver in the next hour xxx.*

Caroline walked with them across the field to Ashworthy. All the ewes were in a large barn at the far side of the farmyard. Scarlett was already there watching her dad checking over a black-faced ewe that was pawing the ground and panting. Charlie was clutching his digital camera in one hand and his binoculars in the other.

'This is so exciting. It's like a real life nature documentary,' he whispered.

'Aye, all we need now is David Attenborough and a camera crew to appear,' chuckled Bill.

'Don't worry, Bill. My camera does short films as well. How long will we have to wait before the lamb is born? I'll need to get in position.'

'I don't think she'll be long now, lad,' Bill told the six-year-old. He was right. The ewe lay down in the straw and a few minutes later her lamb was born head first, its front feet tucked neatly under its chin. Once the head and shoulders were out the rest of the lamb's body soon slithered to the ground. Charlie, who had filmed the birth through the bars of the gate, gave them the thumbs up.

'A nice healthy ewe,' said Bill with satisfaction as he cleared the mucus membranes from the lamb's mouth and head and placed her in front of her mother.

'I think we should call this one Poppy, as they share a birthday,' said Scarlett.

They watched transfixed as the ewe began licking her lamb. After a while Poppy's tiny namesake struggled to her feet, her legs wobbly as she searched for milk. Just twenty minutes after being born she was suckling contentedly.

'This little one's lucky – she has a good mum. Some of them aren't so fortunate and the ewes reject them at birth. That's why they end up as sock lambs,' said Bill.

Poppy leant on the gate of the pen, thinking about mothers and daughters. Hope and Shelley. Scarlett and Pat. Isobel, Caroline. Who could tell whether or not you'd end up with a good mum, like the spindly-legged lamb in front of them? Perhaps it was all a giant lottery, down to the luck of the draw.

In which case, Poppy felt very lucky indeed.

3 2

The date of Cloud's X-ray loomed ever closer and Poppy was counting down the days with a mixture of trepidation and excitement that gave her permanent butterflies. No matter how hard she tried not to show it, she knew Cloud sensed her tension. He radiated nervous energy and was almost bouncing off the walls of his stable after being cooped up for so long.

Finally the day arrived and once more Bill pulled up outside Riverdale with his Land Rover and trailer ready to transport Cloud to the vet centre in Tavistock. Caroline loaded Chester first and Cloud dragged Poppy up the ramp behind the donkey as if he knew it was his ticket to freedom.

'He was a nervous wreck that first time, do you remember?' said Caroline. 'He's come a long way these last few months, Poppy.'

'I know. It's easy to forget when you see him every day. I think he'd still be lost without Chester though.'

The vet was waiting for them in the yard. The moment Bill parked Poppy was out, undoing the bolts on the trailer. The vet watched closely as she backed Cloud slowly down the ramp and led him across the yard to the barn at the end.

'He certainly looks sound. Let's see if the proof's in the pudding, shall we?'

Poppy jiggled from one foot to the other as the vet fiddled with the X-ray equipment. Within a few minutes it was over and she was leading Cloud back to the trailer, her heart in her mouth. She followed the vet and Caroline into the consulting room where they'd first heard the news that Cloud's pedal bone was fractured and it was uncertain if he would ever fully recover.

The vet was smiling as she placed a new X-ray on a light box alongside the original.

'Well Poppy, tell me what you think,' she said.

The hairline fracture that ran the length of Cloud's foot in the first X-ray had disappeared in the latest ghostly picture.

'It looks better than it was,' offered Poppy, the natural born pessimist.

'I should say so. The bone has completely healed. You'd never know he'd broken it, looking at this. I'd say the box rest has done the trick. I can take the bar shoe off him today if you like,' said the vet.

Poppy's heart soared. Cloud was finally, indisputably, undeniably sound. There was only one question on her lips.

'Will I be able to ride him now?'

~

SCARLETT WAS WAITING for them as they turned into the Riverdale drive.

'I got your text Poppy! That's fantastic news, you must be so excited. Clever Cloud. When are you going to have your first ride? Shall we go out for a hack this afternoon?' she chattered breathlessly.

'Slow down, Scarlett,' laughed Caroline. 'Poppy needs to take things steadily. Cloud hasn't had anyone on his back for five years, remember. I'll speak to Bella on Thursday and see what her advice is.'

Privately Poppy thought there was no way she was waiting until Thursday. But she also didn't want everyone making a fuss. Since the summer she'd spent hours, days, imagining the moment she rode Cloud for the first time. But in all those daydreams it had been just the two of them. The last thing she needed was an audience. She knew everyone had her best interests at heart. But she wished they would back off.

'The first thing I'm going to do is turn him out. He's been going crazy cooped up in the stable for so long,' she said firmly.

Caroline nodded her approval. 'Good idea. It's so mild he won't need a rug. It'll do him good to feel the sun on his back.'

Bill parked and they all piled out. Cloud whinnied and they laughed.

'He knows he's home,' said Poppy. She let down the ramp of the trailer and backed him out. 'I think we should put Chester in the field first, then Cloud can join him.'

'How did you get on?' her dad asked, appearing from the side of the house, closely followed by Charlie and Freddie.

'As sound as a bell,' grinned Poppy. 'I'm just turning him out for the first time.' Cloud, realising they weren't heading straight for the stables as usual, was standing stock still, his head high, sniffing the wind. Caroline undid his travel boots and unfastened his day rug and slipped it off. Poppy laid a hand on his shoulder. He trembled beneath her touch. He whinnied again and Chester answered with a deep hee haw. Poppy clicked her tongue. 'Come on then. Let's go.' She pulled gently on his lead rope. Cloud gave a toss of his head, his mane silver in the sun, and started dancing on the spot. Poppy could feel the pent up energy flowing through him and she tightened her hold. She clicked her tongue again and he crabbed sideways after her, through the gate and into the paddock.

'I'd better leave his headcollar on. I don't know how easy he's going to be to catch,' she muttered to herself. She realised there was a side to him that she didn't know at all. This hot-headed, powerful pony who was pawing the ground in excitement was very different to the Cloud she'd spent the last few months getting to know within the safe confines of his stable. She felt everyone watching her as she stroked his mane and unclipped the lead rope. 'Stay safe,' she whispered.

But Cloud didn't hear. He was off, galloping around the field, his tail high and his mane streaming. He twisted his body and gave a series of almighty bucks. Chester lifted his head to watch as he thundered past, his hooves cutting into the turf. Cloud slid to a halt in the mud by the water trough and, with a loud grunt, sank to his knees and rolled. His hooves waved wildly in the air and he rubbed his head to and fro joyfully. By the time he stood up and shook he was covered from head to toe in mud. He snorted with satisfaction and crossed the field to join Chester. Soon the pony and donkey were grazing contentedly side by side.

Bill made noises about checking his ewes and left, taking Scarlett with him. Her dad and Charlie disappeared inside to resume their game of table football, Freddie following them like a shadow. Caroline headed in the direction of her kitchen garden to dig up some leeks for dinner. But

Poppy wasn't going anywhere. She sat on the post and rail fence and gazed at Cloud and Chester, her face beaming and her heart bursting with love.

33

Darkness wrapped itself around the old stone cottage at the foot of the Riverdale tor like a velvet blanket. Inside Riverdale's solid stone walls the McKeevers slept deeply. All except Poppy, who had never felt more awake, more alive, in her life. Once she was sure everyone was asleep she leapt out of bed and flicked on her bedside light. The noise of the switch woke Magpie, who was curled up on the patch-work blanket at the end of her bed. He stared at her, his green eyes unim-pressed.

'Sorry,' she mouthed, grabbing something to wear from the untidy tangle of clothes on the floor at her feet. Within seconds she was dressed and creeping down the landing, tiptoeing to avoid the creaky floorboard outside her dad and Caroline's room. In the kitchen Freddie lifted his head and watched her pass. 'I can't take you tonight Freddie, I'm sorry,' she told him. He thumped his tail against the floor anyway.

Letting herself out of the back door, she saw with satisfaction that the weather forecast had been right. The low cloud cover had lifted to reveal a full moon and a sky bright with stars. She crossed the yard to the tack room and shone her torch inside. She could hear Cloud moving restlessly in the stable next door and her heart fluttered. The beam of light picked out his saddle and bridle and she scooped both up and closed the door behind her.

Cloud had been easy to catch that afternoon, after all. She'd stood at the field gate and given a low whistle and he'd cantered straight over to her.

His head appeared over the stable door now and he whickered softly. 'Shh,' whispered Poppy, her finger to her lips. 'We mustn't wake anyone.'

She'd practised tacking him up so many times over the last few weeks that she could have done it in the dark. But tonight she didn't have to. The moon cast a silvery glow over them as she fastened buckles and pulled down stirrup leathers. Cloud stood perfectly still while she worked. By the time she was ready to lead him out of the stable she felt calm and composed. His unshod hooves made only a muffled sound as she walked him to the gate that led to the moor.

Poppy knew she was taking a risk. Her natural inclination was always to play safe, to do everything by the book. Tomorrow she would. She'd listen to Bella's advice, start slowly, take baby steps. But not tonight. Tonight was for the two of them. Poppy and Cloud. For once in her life she wanted to throw caution to the wind.

Together they stood quietly at the very edge of the moonlit moor, gazing at the Riverdale tor, Poppy's hand resting on Cloud's flank, their breathing in time. She took a deep breath, checked his girth, gathered the reins, edged a toe into the stirrup and, with a single fluid movement, swung into the saddle.

As Poppy lent down to whisper in Cloud's ear, he lifted his head, a ghost horse in the moonlight. She squeezed her legs and he danced on the spot. She laughed wildly and gave him his head. As they galloped towards the tor she crouched low over his neck, urging him faster. But Cloud needed no encouragement. The ground sped by as he stretched out his neck and lengthened his stride. Poppy felt his energy course through her. She felt elated, fearless.

But most of all, she felt complete.

INTO THE STORM

1

The sun was already peeping over the horizon when Poppy McKeever tugged open her curtains, her heart as heavy as a millstone. Vapour trails criss-crossed the tangerine orange sky and the flute-like warbles of song thrushes and blackbirds rang around the old stone cottage on the edge of the moor. There wasn't a breath of wind. It was going to be another beautiful day. But Poppy felt numb.

She opened her window, looked down at the stable below and whistled softly. A loud heehaw drowned out the birdsong and two noses appeared over the wooden door. The first was brown and hairy, the colour of milk chocolate. It belonged to Chester, the donkey she'd inherited when they'd moved to Riverdale. The second was silver grey. Cloud pushed his handsome head over the stable door and looked up. He saw Poppy's pale face framed in the window and whickered. She blinked back tears, rubbed an impatient hand across her eyes and eased the window closed.

A muffled buzz made her jump. She'd forgotten she'd set her alarm for the crack of dawn and had shoved the clock under her pillows so the ringing didn't wake everyone. It had been a complete waste of time. She'd barely slept. She'd spent most of the night staring, hollow-eyed, at the ceiling.

Silence restored, Poppy headed for the landing, trying her best to ignore the packed holdall in front of the wardrobe. She'd gone to bed in her jodhpurs and a long-sleeved tee-shirt so she didn't have to squander even a few minutes of the precious time she had left getting dressed.

Chester had pushed Cloud out of the way by the time she reached their stable. Poppy scratched the donkey's wide forehead and he nibbled the zip of her fleece. She darted into the tack room, returning with Cloud's saddle and bridle. The leather gleamed in the early morning sun. Poppy had spent hours the night before cleaning his tack when she should have been packing. But she had wanted everything to be perfect for their last ride.

Cloud stood calmly as she ran a body brush over his dappled grey summer coat. The Connemara was muscled and fit, a far cry from the skeletal, blood-stained pony he had been the previous autumn. She sniffed loudly. As if sensing her distress Cloud turned his head and nuzzled her hair.

'We'll ride up to the top of the tor and watch the sunrise,' Poppy told him. Chester watched with solemn eyes as she sprang into the saddle and turned her pony towards the gate that led to the moor.

Excited by the prospect of an early morning ride, Cloud danced through the gateposts and up the stony track that meandered lazily around the base of the tor. Poppy squeezed the reins, coaxing him into a walk.

'Soon,' she promised him.

They skirted the Riverdale wood, passing a small herd of Dartmoor ponies. A chestnut mare with a skewbald foal at foot looked up and whinnied. Cloud arched his neck and snorted back. Soon the olive-green slope of the tor lay before them, as inviting as a racetrack. Poppy gathered her reins and clicked her tongue. Cloud picked up a canter, his neat grey ears pricked. Poppy urged him faster and he lengthened his stride into a gallop. She didn't need to guide him. After living wild on the moor for so long Cloud was as sure-footed as the native ponies and he raced nimbly past boulders and tussocks, never putting a foot wrong.

By the time they reached the top of the tor there was colour in Poppy's cheeks and a light sheen of sweat on Cloud's neck. She slid off him, flung her arms around his neck and finally let the tears fall.

'Oh Cloud, I'm going to miss you so much,' she gulped. He regarded her calmly with his beautiful brown eyes. Poppy buried her face in his mane and sobbed noisily as the sun rose in the forget-me-not blue sky behind her.

~

CHARLIE WAS SWINGING on the stable door by the time they arrived back at the cottage. He took one look at Poppy's tear-stained face and his eyes widened.

'What's happened?'

'Nothing.' Poppy felt drained. The last thing she needed was an interrogation from her seven-year-old brother. She jumped down and led Cloud towards his stable.

'Shall I get Mum?'

'No!' she snapped. 'I'm fine. Cloud's fine. We're. Both. Fine.'

'Well, you look like you've been crying to me,' he pressed.

Poppy glared at Charlie. She knew she'd get no peace until she told him what was wrong. 'I was upset because I don't want to say goodbye to Cloud, if you must know.'

'Upset? Why?'

'Why do you think? I don't want to leave him.'

Charlie was quiet as he watched Poppy untack her pony. You'd have thought from the tragic look on her face that someone had died. He couldn't understand it. She'd been so excited when she'd found out.

'Poppy -' he ventured.

'What now?' She spun around and shot him a look that would have sent a lesser soul scurrying for cover. Their dad had always advised him against reasoning with emotional women, but Charlie was nothing if not tenacious. He took a deep breath.

'I don't understand what all the fuss is about. You're only going for *five days*.'

~

OK, so she probably was over-reacting, Poppy reflected as she flung her holdall into the boot of their car and waved goodbye to Charlie and her stepmum Caroline. But she was going to miss Cloud like crazy. She caught her dad's eye in the rear-view mirror as they bumped down the Riverdale drive.

'All set?' he asked.

'I guess so.'

'I thought you were looking forward to this holiday?'

Poppy had been, but now she wasn't so sure. 'Look, there's Scarlett,' she said, changing the subject.

Her best friend was waiting at the bottom of the drive, perched on a tan leather suitcase that looked like a relic from the turn of the century.

'Great case, Scarlett. Is it vintage?' asked Poppy's dad, as he heaved it into the boot.

Scarlett cackled. 'No, just ancient! We never go on holiday and it was the only case Mum could find. It smells of lavender and mothballs, so I think it must have been my granny's. I'm so excited. I didn't sleep a wink last night,' Scarlett grinned as she slid into the seat beside Poppy.

'Me neither,' said Poppy, her grey mood lifted marginally by the sight of Scarlett's freckled face and her best friend's infectious enthusiasm.

'I wonder what the ponies will be like. I hope I get something a bit fizzy.' Scarlett's Dartmoor pony Blaze was a safe, steady ride and no amount of oats made a difference to her even temperament.

'I wish I could have brought Cloud. What if he forgets all about me?' Poppy brooded. She felt anchorless and unsettled knowing her pony would be so far away. He wouldn't be the first thing she saw every morning when she looked out of her bedroom window. She couldn't slip out of the back door after breakfast and give him her last triangle of toast. The days would seem empty and meaningless without the routine of mucking out, making up feeds, changing water and grooming. Most of all she would miss riding him. Poppy always felt as if she'd come home when she was on Cloud's back. They were a perfect fit.

She rested her forehead against the window and watched mile after endless mile speed by. It was early summer and the motorway verges were lush with new growth. Scarlett hadn't stopped talking since the minute they'd left and Poppy had tuned out long ago. She rolled up her fleece jacket into a makeshift pillow and had just drifted off to sleep when she was woken by the tinny American drawl of the McKeevers' sat nav.

'In one mile take the next right,' it instructed.

Scarlett clutched Poppy's thigh. 'We're nearly there, Poppy! What's the place called again?'

'Oaklands Trekking Centre,' Poppy said, batting her friend's hand away. She was suddenly plagued by worry. What if all the other riders were better than her? Scarlett had learnt to ride before she could walk, but Poppy had been riding for less than a year and was still inexperienced. What if everyone else was way older than them and too cool to make friends? But that wouldn't matter, she told herself. She still had Scarlett.

'What an idiot,' Poppy's dad tutted, frowning into the rear-view mirror.

A silver saloon with its headlights flashing was a hair's breadth from their bumper.

'Why doesn't he overtake us if he's in that much of a hurry?' asked Poppy.

'Good question,' said her dad. 'Some people shouldn't be on the road.'

He eased his foot off the accelerator and pulled over. As the other car passed they stared at the driver, a man in his fifties wearing dark glasses and leather gloves.

'Old enough to know better,' Poppy's dad muttered.

'And he's on the phone!' shrieked Scarlett. Sure enough, a slim black mobile was tucked between his neck and shoulder.

The car accelerated hard past them with a throaty growl and kicked out a plume of black smoke from its exhaust. Poppy wrinkled her nose as her dad pulled back onto the road.

'In two hundred metres take the next right,' the sat nav commanded.

Scarlett was on the edge of her seat. 'Look, there's the turning!' she cried.

Poppy felt a flutter of nerves. She looked ahead and froze. Through the dazzling early summer sunshine she could see a blur of black and white. A large animal had bolted from their left and was heading at full pelt for the opposite side of the road.

'No!' Poppy screamed. The silver car was still accelerating, heading straight for the careering animal.

Scarlett's hand flew to her mouth. 'He hasn't seen it. He's going to hit it!'

Just when a collision seemed inevitable there was a screech of brakes and the silver saloon slewed to a halt with centimetres to spare.

Poppy exhaled loudly. 'That was close.'

'What on earth was it?' said her dad.

'A cow, I think. I'll go and shoo it out of the way.' Poppy unclipped her seatbelt and scrambled out, squinting into the sun. Before she'd taken more than a couple of steps up the road the silver car had roared off and the animal had disappeared. All that was left of the near disaster were some black skid marks on the tarmac and the smell of burning rubber.

Poppy was looking around in bewilderment when Scarlett joined her.

'Did you see which way it went?' she asked her friend.

Scarlett pointed at a blue and white sign, on which the words Oaklands Trekking Centre were painted in large letters. She looked up the long, potholed track behind them. 'I think it went up there. But I'm not sure it was a cow, Poppy.'

2

'FRANK!' A woman's voice sliced through the warm air. 'If you do that ONE MORE TIME there'll be trouble. And that's not a threat, it's a promise!'

Poppy and Scarlett paused at the five bar gate at the end of the driveway and looked at each other uncertainly. Poppy fumbled with the latch and as the gate swung open she saw a woman heading towards them, reading glasses on her forehead and a pencil stuck behind one ear. Following closely behind her was a black Shetland pony with a mischievous glint in his eye. The woman looked flustered but smiled as she held out her hand in greeting.

'You must be our competition winner. Poppy, isn't it? And Scarlett? I'm Nina Goddard, the owner of Oaklands. Nice to meet you.'

As Poppy shook the woman's hand she noticed a red-brick chalet bungalow opposite an immaculately-swept concrete yard, which was lined with two large weather-boarded barns standing at right angles to each other. Towering over the barns was a massive oak tree, at least twenty metres tall and in full leaf.

Nina set off towards the bungalow, calling over her shoulder, 'Follow me, girls. Everyone else is already here. We're just about to have lunch then I'll show you your ponies for the week.'

Poppy gave her dad a quick hug.

'See you both in a few days. Have fun,' he told them.

'Oh, we will,' said Scarlett, still grinning. She grabbed Poppy's arm and began dragging her after Nina. 'Come on, let's go and meet everyone.'

POPPY'S PULSE quickened as Nina opened the door to a large lounge and ushered them in. The buzz of conversation petered out and she felt several pairs of eyes swivel in her direction. Her palms felt sticky. She wiped them on her jeans, hoping no-one would notice. She knew she sometimes came across as distant, even aloof. She usually relied on Scarlett to chat enough for them both, but for once her best friend was silent.

'Hi everyone. This is Scarlett and Poppy, our final two trekkers. I'll let you say hello while I finish off in the kitchen.' Nina checked her watch. 'Lunch will be in about ten minutes.'

Poppy gazed around the lounge, registering two large squashy sofas, a scattering of beanbags in bright, primary colours and a widescreen television fixed to the wall. And faces. Lots of faces.

She remembered the advice her stepmum Caroline had given her when she'd admitted she was worried about meeting the other trekkers.

'People love talking about themselves, Poppy. Ask them where they live, what their hobbies are and look like you're interested in their answers, even if you're not. Try not to hide behind your fringe. And remember to smile,' she had advised. 'It works every time, I promise.'

Poppy licked her lips, pasted on a smile and took a step forward.

'Hello, I'm Poppy, and this is Scarlett. We've just driven up from Devon. What about you?' Her eyes swept around the room again, looking for a friendly face. Her gaze settled on a stunningly pretty girl, who was lounging on an orange beanbag. A couple of years older than Poppy and Scarlett, she was enviably tall and slim.

'I'm California. Cally for short.' Cally gestured airily to the girl sitting next to her. 'This is Chloe. And that's Jack and his little sister Jess.' The others murmured hellos but Poppy was too overwhelmed to take in either their names or faces.

Cally flicked her long blonde fringe away from her face. She had clear, glowing skin, perfectly straight teeth and eyes that were neither blue nor grey but a blend of both. It was the kind of face that graced the covers of teen magazines. Poppy thought back to that morning, when she'd gazed critically at her own reflection in the bathroom mirror as she'd brushed her teeth. Sludge green eyes, pale skin that flushed at all the wrong moments, a heart-shaped face and shoulder-length brown hair that Poppy called mousey but Caroline assured her was caramel. Oh, and a globule of toothpaste on her chin. She rubbed the spot self-consciously and made herself speak.

'California. That's an unusual name.'

Cally looked bored. Poppy realised she must get told this all the time and felt her cheeks redden.

'You could say. I've got my dippy mother to thank. It's because she's always wanted to go there. Fat chance.'

Scarlett, still speechless, was looking at the older girl with something approaching awe. Poppy elbowed her in the ribs. She shook her head as if she was coming out of a trance.

'I think it's an amazing name. So unusual. I've never been to America. In fact I've never been anywhere. The only time we ever leave the farm is to visit all our ancient relatives, which is *so* boring. That's why I was so excited when Poppy won the riding holiday.'

'You *won* the holiday?' said a stocky boy. He pointed the television remote control at her accusingly. 'How?'

To her horror Poppy found she was the centre of attention again. 'It was a short story competition,' she said. 'I've never won anything before. It was a complete surprise,' she added, remembering to smile.

'Lucky you,' drawled Cally. 'I've spent the last six months working my backside off to pay for this holiday.'

Poppy squirmed and examined her toes. She'd been over the moon when she'd arrived home from school a couple of months before and found a letter with a smudged London postmark propped against the fruit bowl. She'd ripped open the envelope and studied the single sheet of typewritten paper inside, her face wreathed in smiles. She'd read it so many times since that she knew it off by heart.

Dear Poppy,

Congratulations! I am delighted to inform you that your entry, Connemara Comes Home, has won first prize in Young Rider Magazine's short story competition. Your prize is a week-long riding holiday for two at Oaklands

Trekking Centre in the Forest of Dean. Please contact our editorial assistant, Jane Gray, on the above number so we can make the necessary arrangements.

In the meantime, thank you for taking part in this year's competition.

Yours sincerely,

Marie Chidders, Editor-in-Chief

Poppy glanced at Cally and was dismayed to see the older girl looking her up and down with ill-disguised contempt. All the pride she'd felt at winning the competition trickled away, leaving her hollow. She suddenly wished she'd spent the last six months working her backside off to pay for the holiday, too. It seemed much more real, more grown-up than writing a silly story. Scarlett, completely oblivious to Poppy's discomfort, pulled up a beanbag beside Cally and sat down.

'I'd love to have a part-time job but Mum says I'm not old enough. I've thought about getting a paper round but I'd really like to work in a tea shop. Imagine how many cakes you'd get to try. Where do you work, Cally?'

Cally turned her attention to Scarlett. Shorter than Poppy by half a head and sturdy where Poppy was slight, Scarlett hated her freckles and auburn hair with a passion. Poppy thought she was mad. Her hazel eyes were the colour of a tiger's and her hair was the russet red of beech trees in autumn. Poppy would have chosen auburn over mousey any day.

Scarlett was as outgoing as Poppy was shy and her non-stop chatter never failed to put people at their ease. Poppy watched glumly as her best friend worked her magic. Within minutes the sneering look had been wiped from Cally's perfect face and she was smiling, her voice warm as she described the riding school where she worked all hours for paltry wages. Poppy couldn't shake the feeling that Cally had put them both through some kind of invisible test. A test that Scarlett had obviously passed with flying colours and Poppy had failed miserably.

She shuffled over to the nearest sofa and sat beside a girl wearing a red polo shirt and navy jodhpurs. The girl smiled at her.

'Have you brought your story with you? I'd love to read it,' she said.

As Poppy nodded she caught a whiff of honeysuckle from the open window. She was transported home to Riverdale, where the climber's greeny-grey leaves and light yellow flowers, tinged with the barest hint of pink, trailed over a trellis archway that led to Caroline's vegetable garden.

She pictured her stepmother carefully weeding between rows of tiny lettuce and pea plants, her blonde hair scraped off her face in an untidy updo, her brow furrowed in concentration. Charlie would probably be sat astride the old stone wall that protected the vegetable garden from the worst of the westerly winds, pretending he was a cowboy. Her dad would be sitting on the old wooden bench that had been turned silver by the sun, reading the Sunday papers. She saw Cloud and Chester in her mind's eye, grazing side by side in their paddock to the side of the house. Watching over them all was the Riverdale tor, dominating the huge Dartmoor skyline. Poppy knew the tor so well she could have marched straight to the cairn at the top blindfolded.

She looked over at her best friend, seeking reassurance. But Scarlett's head was bent towards Cally, her voice suffused with laughter as she regaled the older girl with stories of her pony Blaze. Poppy felt a snag of homesickness, as sharp as barbed wire, pierce her insides.

3

- -

Poppy had no appetite by the time she took a seat next to Scarlett at the long pine table in Nina's scruffy kitchen. Sitting at the head of the table was a girl with the face of a cherub, who was noisily demolishing a plate of sausages and baked beans. Most of the sauce was smeared around her rosy cheeks. She smiled, pointed her fork at the older children as they piled in and shouted, 'Mum! New people!'

'This is my daughter Lydia. She's four,' said Nina.

'Nearly five,' grumbled Lydia through a mouthful of beans.

Nina plucked a wet wipe from a packet on the kitchen worktop and wiped it across Lydia's outraged face before she had time to duck. The resulting howls of protest made the girl in the red polo shirt giggle nervously.

'Take a seat everyone. Your mum said you're a vegan, Cally. I've cooked your vegetarian sausages in a separate pan.'

Cally looked even more incensed than Lydia. 'Mum may be a vegan. She is also an old hippy. I, on the other hand, am neither. I'll have the same sausages as everyone else, please.'

Nina passed around plates of sausages, beans and chips. Poppy pushed the food around her plate and tried not to think about home. Instead she took the opportunity to scrutinize their fellow pony trekkers.

Sitting directly opposite and tucking into his lunch with gusto was the stocky boy. He looked about twelve or thirteen. Poppy fished around in her memory for his name. James or Josh? No, Jack. That was it. He had a bullish, square jaw and thick black eyebrows that almost met in the middle. From the snippets of conversation Poppy could catch he was telling the girl to his left about his current fantasy football team. Sitting opposite Scarlett was the girl in the red polo shirt. She must be Jack's younger sister. She had the same determined chin. Jess, Poppy remembered. She guessed she was probably about ten.

The girl to Jack's left was stifling a yawn as he blathered on about penalty shoot outs and goal differentials. She was about the same age as Jess and was small and slight with direct brown eyes. She caught Poppy watching her and grimaced theatrically. Poppy suppressed a smile and turned to Scarlett, but her best friend was still talking to Cally. All Poppy could see was the back of her head.

Nina banged the table with her fork, halting the wave of chat. 'I'd like to take this opportunity to welcome you to Oaklands. I hope you will all fall in love with the place as deeply as I did. I can still remember how excited I was when I saw photos of the house and yard in an estate agents' window two years ago. I grew up in the Forest of Dean and always wanted to move back. I loved the fact that the house was miles from its nearest neighbours yet the forest was right on the doorstep.

'I thought the place was beyond our means but I must have caught my bank manager on a good day.' Nina gave the ghost of a smile. 'We started running our trekking holidays last summer and we're now in our second season. We love it here, don't we, Lyd?' Lydia nodded vigorously. Poppy was surprised to see Nina's eyes cloudy with tears. She wondered if anyone else had noticed, but they were all still ploughing their way through their lunch. Nina tucked a kiss-curl behind Lydia's ear and continued.

'The Forest of Dean is fantastic for hacking. We often see deer in the forest and if we're really lucky we might see a wild boar.'

'A wild boar?' repeated Jess, her eyes wide. 'Aren't they dangerous?'

'Well, yes, they can be, especially if they have young to protect. But they are very secretive and largely nocturnal so the chances of coming across one are pretty slim,' Nina assured her.

'But what if we do? Won't they charge at the ponies?' Jess persisted.

'Who cares if they do,' said her brother scornfully. 'We could out-gallop them, no problem.'

'They're faster than you think,' said Nina. 'The trick is not to antago-nise them in the first place. They usually hide in the undergrowth, so if we stick to the paths we'll be fine.' She noticed the lines creasing the girl's brow. 'Don't worry, Jess. I ride in the forest every day and I've only seen wild boar twice, and that was from a distance. We'll be fine.'

Nina smiled at them all. 'I've got some lovely routes planned for the week. We'll set off straight after breakfast each morning and we'll cover about twelve miles each day, stopping halfway for a picnic lunch. All the horses have saddle bags and I'll pack your lunches in them.' She pointed to an untidy heap of leather saddle bags next to a pile of unopened brown envelopes on the kitchen worktop. 'We'll be back at about four each after-noon and once you've finished your yard duties your time is your own.'

The girl next to Jack stuck her hand in the air.

'Yes, Chloe?' Nina asked.

'How many horses do you have?'

'Eight. My thoroughbred, McFly, Lydia's Shetland, Frank, and our six trekking ponies. I'll show you your ponies after lunch and we'll go for a gentle hack this afternoon so you can get a feel for them.'

'Will we be having a canter today?' Jack asked.

'We'll see how we go. You've all done quite a bit of riding, which is great. The group I had last week was a nightmare. One girl had never sat on a horse before. At least if you're all about the same level we can have some decent rides.'

There was a jangle of cutlery on plates. Nina stood up. 'All finished? Leave your plates and glasses on the draining board and I'll give you a tour of the house and stables.'

～

THERE WERE FOUR SMALL BEDROOMS, each with bunk beds, at the back of the house. Poppy and Scarlett's room looked out over the yard.

'Leave the unpacking, Poppy. We'll do it later,' Scarlett said impatiently as they changed into their jodhpurs. 'Let's go and meet the ponies.'

They caught up with the others outside the first of the two bitumen-black barns. It had been divided into loose boxes, three each down the two long sides and one at either end. Nina stopped at the first box. A bay horse appeared over the door and nibbled her hair. 'This is McFly. He's ten. I bought him as a yearling and produced him myself. We used to event but we don't get the opportunity to compete these days.'

McFly towered above them. 'How big is he?' wondered Scarlett.

'He's 17.2. Frank can actually walk under him. But he's a gentle giant. Just costs me a fortune in hay and feed. And his rugs are the size of small marquees. Now this is Blue. She's your ride for the week, Cally. She is sharp but I remember when you booked you said you were an experienced rider so she shouldn't be anything you can't handle. I think you'll have a lot of fun on her.'

Poppy stood on tiptoes to peer over Cally's shoulder. Standing in the corner of her box, delicately nibbling on some hay, was a rose grey Arab mare, whose dished head, silky mane and tail and wide-spaced, intelligent eyes exuded elegance.

Cally was delighted. Scarlett looked impressed. Poppy felt a twinge of envy.

'Chloe, you're next.' Chloe looked as if she was about to burst with excitement as Nina showed her a chestnut gelding called Rusty who had a white star in the centre of his forehead and two white socks. 'He's a real schoolmaster, as honest as they come,' Nina said.

Chloe's eyes were dancing. 'He's beautiful,' she breathed.

Jack's sister, Jess, was given Willow, a dun mare with soot black points. She was a Welsh Section B who was great for trekking and never put a foot wrong, Nina told her.

Jack's pony was a sturdy liver chestnut lightweight cob called Rocky. 'Cool,' he said, nodding his approval. They left him in Rocky's box as they crossed the barn to the last two loose boxes. Poppy could sense Scarlett's excitement. 'Scarlett, you'll be riding Topaz. She's a New Forest cross.' Poppy and Scarlett looked over the door and saw a pretty palomino mare with her head buried in a hayrack.

Scarlett's freckled face split into a grin. 'Oo, I've always wanted a palomino!'

'Topaz is the name of a golden gemstone. It suits her, don't you think? I'm glad you like her,' said Nina.

Poppy felt a frisson of anticipation as she followed Nina to the end of the barn. She'd been impressed by all the trekking ponies. Nina obviously had an eye for real quality. And as the competition winner, surely she'd be given the best of the lot? She crossed her fingers, wishing for a flashy Arab like Blue, preferably jet black, although she wasn't fussy, any colour would do.

A metal anti-weaving grill was attached to the door of the last loose box.

'Here's Beau,' Nina announced with a flourish, 'He's all yours, Poppy.'

Poppy stepped forward. She realised she was holding her breath. She held onto two of the metal bars and peered through them. A jolt of shock hit her in the stomach with the velocity of a high speed train. Nina had to be kidding, right?

'Very funny,' she said. 'So where is he really?'

Nina looked puzzled. 'That's him. That's Beau.'

Poppy looked into the loose box again and back at Nina's face. No tell-tale smirk or giveaway crinkling of the eyes. She was deadly serious.

Realising Nina was waiting for her reaction she forced a smile and said in a strangulated voice, 'Hello Beau.'

At the sound of his name a piebald cob with a long, tangled mane and a wall eye stuck his head over the loose box door. He yawned, flashing a set of yellowing teeth.

A feeling of bitter disappointment crept from Poppy's head to her toes, along with the uncanny suspicion that she had seen this horse before, although for the life of her she couldn't think where.

Then she remembered the silver saloon car's squealing brakes and her heart sank even further. Poppy looked desperately at Scarlett, and was disconcerted to see her best friend's mouth twitching, as if she was biting back a bubble of laughter.

And finally Scarlett confirmed her worst fears. 'Hey Poppy, I think we may have found the amazing disappearing cow.'

4

'S omeone was having a laugh when they called him Beau,' said Cally drily, looking over from Blue's loose box. 'He's no oil painting, is he?'

'Beauty is as beauty does,' said Nina tartly. 'Don't be too quick to judge him.' She smiled at Poppy. 'Beau is one in a million. He may not be the prettiest horse on the yard but he has the heart of a lion and if he decides he likes you he'll do absolutely anything for you.'

An image of Cloud's handsome grey head swam in front of Poppy's eyes. She'd only been gone a matter of hours but it felt like she hadn't seen him for months. She looked again at the piebald cob. His large head was black with a wide white blaze running down his face. His forehead was flat and broad. The eye that wasn't blue was as dark as mahogany. Under his long, straggly mane Poppy could see a crested neck set in a deep, broad chest. All four legs were white from the knee down and he had thick, muddy feathers. Other than his pink nose and his blue wall eye he was completely monochrome. Poppy held out a hand for him to sniff but he ignored her and turned back to his hay.

'The only one you haven't met is Frank. He must be around here somewhere.' Nina stepped into the yard, put two fingers in her mouth and whistled. The black Shetland pony Poppy and Scarlett had seen earlier appeared from the open door of the second barn, covered in hay.

'Frank! Not again! I can't afford for you to be helping yourself to hay whenever you feel like it! Come here, you monster.' The pony waddled over to Nina and she scratched his poll. 'This is Frank. What he lacks in height he makes up for in mischief. His speciality is untying knots and unbolting doors so you all need to keep an extra eye on him. He and Beau came together as a job lot at auction. They're inseparable.' As she spoke the Shetland bustled over to Beau's door. The piebald whickered and started eating the hay stuck in Frank's bushy mane. Everyone except Poppy laughed. She seemed to have lost her sense of humour.

'Right, let's get tacked up,' Nina said. 'Lydia's coming with us today but during the week she'll be with her childminder so we'll be able to up the pace.'

Poppy followed Scarlett into the tack room. Her friend took one look at her miserable face and frowned.

'What's wrong, Poppy?'

'What's wrong? What do you think's wrong? Nina must be out of her mind to think that old clodhopper is any good as a trekking pony. He should be pulling a cart! No wonder I thought he was a cow.'

'He looks sweet.' As Scarlett reached for Topaz's bridle Poppy saw a flash of annoyance cross her face. It cleared so quickly she wondered if she'd imagined it.

'You might find he's a lovely ride,' Scarlett said, her tone placatory. 'At least give him a chance.'

'And do I have a choice?' she growled.

She balanced Beau's saddle on her hip, swung his bridle over her shoulder and, with some trepidation, walked over to the cob's loose box. He had finished the hay in Frank's mane and had turned back to his hayrack. She patted his neck hesitantly and he gave her a baleful stare. It was as if his blue wall eye could see straight through her with X-ray vision - and was singularly unimpressed by what he saw. He took a step sideways and stood on her left foot, sending bolts of pain shooting up her calf.

'Ow!' she cried, leaning on his shoulder to make him move. But it was like pushing a brick wall. He wasn't going anywhere. 'Please move, Beau!' she gasped, her foot still pinned to the ground by an iron-clad hoof the size of a dinner plate. Beau ignored her and began chomping on his hay. Poppy looked around her helplessly. At this rate she'd be here all day, her foot being squashed thinner and thinner until it was as flat as filo pastry. She tried again but Beau didn't move. Outside the barn she could hear the others' chatter as they tacked up and mounted. Feeling increasingly desperate she remembered the Polos in her pocket and waved the packet under Beau's nose. He immediately lifted his foot off her jodhpur boot, gave her a hefty nudge and nearly bit her little finger off in his haste to snaffle the mint she offered him.

Nina's face appeared over the loose box door. She frowned when she saw that Beau still wasn't tacked up. 'Do you need a hand?'

Poppy felt her cheeks flush. 'No, thanks. I won't be a minute.'

Nina disappeared and Poppy eyed the cob with dislike. 'I don't want any more nonsense,' she told him firmly. 'And if you're good you can have another Polo. Alright?'

If horses could have shrugged with indifference Poppy would have bet money that's what Beau was doing right now. But at least he stood still as she whizzed around him, putting on his saddle and bridle, tightening his girth and pulling down his stirrup leathers. Soon she was leading him out of his box into the yard, where everyone else was standing waiting for her.

'Good, you're ready. The mounting block is over there,' said Nina, pointing to the opposite side of the yard. Poppy felt everyone's eyes on her as she led Beau over, checked the girth again and pulled herself gingerly into the saddle. At fifteen hands, Beau was slightly taller than Cloud, and felt enormous compared to her fine-boned Connemara. Poppy cringed with embarrassment when Lydia shouted, 'She's finally ready! Can we go now?'

'OK everyone. Just a few house rules,' said Nina. 'I'll ride up front with Frank and Lydia on a leading rein, then Topaz and Blue, Willow and Rusty and finally Rocky and Beau bringing up the rear. We'll be riding along country lanes for a mile or so before we reach the forest so please be polite to drivers, and once we're on the bridleways keep to the tracks and stay in line. Right, follow me.'

Nina turned McFly out of the yard. Poppy gathered up her reins and squeezed with her heels but Beau stood stubbornly still as the others filed in behind the bay thoroughbred and began walking down the track to the road. When Rocky's liver chestnut rump had disappeared through the gates and Beau was still refusing to budge Poppy kicked as hard as she could. The cob grunted and set off at a snail's pace behind him.

Beau's rolling gait was nothing like Cloud's graceful stride. Poppy wondered if this was what camels felt like to ride. Rocky was already twenty metres ahead and Poppy kicked again. Beau reluctantly broke into a trot and Poppy bumped up and down for a few strides until she found a rhythm and started to rise. She could feel a sheen of sweat across her forehead and her hands were clammy. Up ahead Scarlett was riding alongside Cally, who sat gracefully astride the elegant Blue. Scarlett's face was animated and she paused every now and again to run her hand along Topaz's golden neck. She was clearly having the time of her life. Poppy looked down gloomily at Beau's tangled mane and feathered feet. Why didn't Nina give her an old carthorse and be done with it, she fumed.

Some holiday this was turning out to be.

THE OTHERS HAD DISAPPEARED into one of the wide forest tracks that fed into the road like tributaries into a river when Poppy heard a car behind her. She heaved Beau to a halt and waited for the car to pass. Beau took the opportunity to grab a mouthful of cow parsley and she was leaning forward so she could pull it out of his mouth when she became aware of a silver bonnet drawing alongside them. Straightening her back she stared at the man who had almost ploughed into Beau just a few hours before. But he obviously hadn't made the connection, and to her surprise opened his electric window.

'Excuse me, I seem to be lost. I'm looking for Oaklands.'

Poppy fixed her eyes on Beau's ears and said nothing.

'Oaklands,' he repeated. 'Nina Goddard's place. According to the map it's down here somewhere. Do you know where it is?'

Poppy could see a map, a clipboard and the man's mobile phone on the passenger seat beside him. Oaklands was in all likelihood on the map anyway, she supposed.

'It's about a mile back that way,' she said finally, pointing behind her.

'Are you her daughter? Lydia, isn't it?'

Poppy shook her head.

'Do you happen to know if Mrs Goddard is in?'

'She won't be back for at least a couple of hours.' Beau stuck his head through the window and sneezed, spraying the man's shiny suit with droplets of snot. Poppy pulled his head back hastily.

'Beau! Sorry about that. Can I give her a message?'

Wiping his trousers fastidiously, the man looked up in irritation. 'What? No, don't bother. I'll track her down soon enough.' The window slid shut and the car pulled away. Poppy shrugged, kicked Beau on and they trotted down the lane. Nina and McFly met them as they crossed the road and joined the forest track.

'There you are!' said Nina. 'I thought I'd better come and find you. Everything OK?'

'There was a man looking for you,' said Poppy.

Nina's forehead creased. 'A man?'

'Yes, in a silver car. I saw him earlier as well. He overtook us on the way here and almost caused an accident.' Poppy wasn't sure if Nina knew Beau had been out on the road and felt it best not to worry her.

'What did he say?' Nina asked.

'He asked for directions so I told him where you lived. But when I asked him if he wanted me to give you a message he said no, he'd track you down himself.'

The colour sapped from Nina's face. 'Track me down?'

'Yes, that's what he said. He asked me if I was Lydia.'

'He knew Lydia's name?' she asked faintly.

'He didn't seem very friendly, actually.' Poppy considered the encounter. 'Did I do the right thing?'

'I should have known it was only a matter of time,' Nina said, half to herself. She looked at Poppy, her eyes anxious. 'Please don't mention this to anyone. With any luck we'll make it to the end of the week.' McFly pawed the ground impatiently and Nina gathered her reins. 'Come on, we'd better get back to the others.'

5

Poppy didn't have a chance to wonder what the man wanted and why Nina had seemed so troubled. All her energies were concentrated on keeping up with the rest of the riders. Never before had she had to work so hard in the saddle. Even Flynn, the stout Dartmoor pony she'd learnt to ride on, was more bouncy than Beau. No matter how much she kicked his piebald sides the cob refused to alter his pace from the leisurely rolling walk that she swore was making her seasick.

As they ambled along a grassy forest track that cut a swathe through lofty pine trees Beau snatched at his bit and stretched his neck down. Assuming he had an itch, Poppy let the reins slide through her fingers. But the cob had other things on his mind, and began snatching up mouthfuls of grass. 'Oh no, you don't,' she told him, hauling at his reins. But he ignored her and carried on grazing. It took Nina to re-appear alongside them and reach over to grab his right rein before he lifted his head.

'You need to be firmer with him, Poppy,' Nina said. 'I'm afraid he does try it on with new riders. You have to earn his respect.' She looked at her watch. 'Goodness, look at the time! We really need to get going. Do you think you can try to keep up?'

'I'll do my best,' Poppy said through gritted teeth. 'Although if you'd given me a half-decent horse to ride it wouldn't be an issue,' she muttered as Nina took Frank's lead rein from Cally and re-joined the front of the group.

Poppy spent the rest of the ride lagging behind the others, like a dawdling toddler trailing behind her parents. Only when they turned back down the grassy track towards home did Beau seem to wake up, and when the others broke into a canter he grabbed the bit and set off behind them like a racehorse out of its stall when the starter's pistol was fired. Poppy, thrown back in the saddle by the force of his acceleration, clutched the reins and a handful of his long mane for good measure as he thundered along the track, his feathers flying. The breeze felt cool on her pink cheeks and she began to relax into his long, loping gait. He must be the closest thing on earth to a rocking horse, she thought, as they gained ground on Rocky and Jack.

Poppy stood up in her stirrups as Beau's stride lengthened and the beginnings of a smile crept across her face. She realised with surprise that she was actually enjoying herself. But her pleasure was short-lived. The cob spooked at a clump of oxeye daisies growing in the long grass to the side of the track, slamming on his brakes and dropping his shoulder like an actor taking a bow. Poppy, her weight already forward, was thrown out of the saddle and landed heavily on a clump of thistles. Still holding Beau's reins, she heaved herself upright. He watched innocently as she plucked a couple of thorny spikes from her backside. She shot him a filthy look and gathered her reins, hoping she could jump back on before anyone noticed. But it was too late. Jack had slowed Rocky to a walk and was calling to Nina. Poppy just caught his words as they were carried away by the wind.

'It's Poppy again. She's fallen off this time.'

THE SUN WAS low in the sky by the time they began evening stables. As Poppy mucked out Beau's loosebox, scrubbed out and re-filled his water bucket and re-stocked his hayrack she thought about the man in the silver saloon car. He'd looked harmless enough so why had Nina been so worried when she'd found out he was looking for her? She'd seemed particularly upset when Poppy had told her he'd mistaken her for Lydia. And what did she mean about making it to the end of the week?

Poppy was dying to tell Scarlett about the mystery man and seized her chance when they changed for dinner.

'He seemed a bit...strange,' said Poppy. Scarlett was facing the small mirror over the chest of drawers, her back to Poppy. 'Hey, wait a minute. Since when did you start wearing make-up?'

Scarlett eyed her in the mirror. 'Cally lent me some. I thought I'd give it a try. Is that a problem?'

'No, of course not. I was only asking. Don't be so defensive. Anyway, he looked really angry when Beau sneezed all over his shiny suit.'

'I'm not surprised. Wouldn't you be?'

'But what do you think he wanted? And why did Nina look so worried?' Poppy said. But she could tell that Scarlett wasn't really listening. She was too busy striking poses in front of the mirror, her newly pearlescent lips catching the light as she pouted like a catwalk model. Finally satisfied with her appearance, she turned to face Poppy and gave a little twirl.

'How do I look?'

Poppy considered her best friend. Scarlett had swept pale pink blusher over her cheekbones and had smudged black eyeliner along her eye-lids before applying several layers of mascara. The smoky look accentuated her hazel eyes. She looked much older than her twelve years. Poppy wasn't sure she liked it. Scarlett tousled her hair, letting her fringe fall over one eye.

'Well?' she demanded, her hands on her hips.

'It's OK I suppose, but I prefer the natural look. Come on, we're going to be late for our tea.'

THE TOPIC of conversation over the dinner table revolved around the Oaklands horses. Everyone else was delighted with their rides, which made Poppy feel doubly short-changed to have been given Beau. That night, as they lay in their bunk beds, Poppy railed against Nina for giving her the ungainly cob.

'Honestly Scarlett, it's like riding a socking great elephant,' she moaned. 'He's about as responsive as a dodo.'

But if she was hoping to elicit any sympathy from her best friend she was out of luck.

'Did you know Cally went to a John Whittaker showjumping clinic last year? It was a fourteenth birthday present from her granny, lucky thing.'

'Really?' said Poppy. 'But I mean, Scarlett, you're alright. Topaz is great. Beau is an absolute nightmare. Do you think Nina would swap him for one of the other horses if I asked? After all, I did win the short story competition.'

'Cally says I've got a really nice seat, much better than the girls my age who go to her riding school,' Scarlett continued.

'Her riding school now, is it? I thought she just mucked out in return for the occasional ride,' said Poppy grumpily.

'She's got a proper job as a groom and she's going to train to be an instructor. I think she'd be really good, don't you?'

'Scarlett! Do you think Nina would give me another horse if I complained about Beau?'

Scarlett finally turned her attention to her friend. 'Nina has a soft spot for him, that's what Cally reckons anyway. I think you should give him another chance.'

Poppy stuck her tongue out at the dark shadow of Scarlett's mattress above her and pulled her duvet over her head. 'Why not give me Blue and let the wonderful California have Beau? See how she gets on with the great clodhopper,' she grumbled into her pillow.

Scarlett, who was having the time of her life, either didn't hear or chose not to answer. She turned over and promptly fell asleep while Poppy seethed quietly in the bunk bed below.

6

The early morning dew had turned cobwebs on the grass into glistening panels of lace that reminded Poppy of the delicate antimacassars on the two floral-patterned armchairs in her old friend Tory's small flat. Her jodhpur boots were quickly soaked through as she marched across the paddock Beau shared with Frank and Rocky, Beau's cob-sized headcollar on her shoulder and a Polo going sticky in her right palm. The piebald was tearing up tussocks of the dewy grass as if he'd been without food for a week. Poppy clicked her tongue and opened her hand.

'Look, I've brought you a Polo,' she told him. 'And if you behave yourself I've plenty more where they came from. But I don't want any more bad behaviour.'

She had woken in a peevish mood. Her body felt as though it'd been pulled on a rack, her left foot was a livid shade of purple and she swore she still had a thorn in her right buttock. Added to that, Scarlett's incessant chirpiness was starting to wear thin and she wasn't relishing the prospect of another day spent doing battle with the ill-mannered cob.

Beau lifted his shaggy head and Poppy slipped the headcollar over his muzzle, buckled up the strap and gave him the mint. 'Try not to bite my hand off this time.' Beau whickered. 'Was that for me?' she asked him in surprise. But he was looking over her shoulder at Frank, who had appeared from the other side of the field. 'Of course it wasn't. You like me about as much as I like you. Come on, I don't want to be the last one ready today.'

Topaz and Blue had been tied up next to each other. Poppy tugged on Beau's lead rope and he followed her unenthusiastically to the other side of the yard, depositing a large dropping on the concrete the minute she'd finished tying a quick release knot. She cleared it up before scooting over to the tack room in search of some grooming kit and spent the next fifteen minutes trying to brush the mud from Beau's thick coat. Frank was wandering around the yard stealing brushes and hoofpicks to the amusement of the others, who had already started tacking up.

Poppy mouth was gritty with dust and she had a horrible feeling that she was covered in a fine film of the mud she'd just brushed from Beau. Sighing loudly, she walked over to fetch his tack, stopping to listen to Scarlett and Cally on her way. The older girl was telling Scarlett about the riding school where she worked.

'The horses I ride are all thoroughbreds that used to race on the flat. Rose - she's the owner - buys up ex-racehorses and I help her re-train them before she sells them on.'

'Really? Ex-racehorses? That's amazing.'

Cally acknowledged Scarlett's admiration with a careless dip of her head. She had the kind of easy confidence that Poppy found incredibly intimidating and usually left her tongue-tied. But she remembered her stepmum Caroline's advice, edged over and said, 'Scarlett says you want to train as a riding instructor when you leave school, Cally.'

The older girl gave her a lofty look and nodded. 'Yes, but my ultimate ambition is to be picked for the British showjumping team.'

'Wow, that's impressive. Do you do much jumping now?'

'I started affiliated classes this spring. The trouble with training the ex-racers is that the minute they're jumping well Rose sells them and I have to start all over again. I need to find a way of getting my own horse, but Mum's always broke and I don't even earn a fraction of the minimum wage at the stables.'

Scarlett had disappeared into the tack room. Poppy tried to look sympathetic. 'These things have a habit of working out. That's what my stepmum always says, anyway.'

'Easy for you to say. Scarlett told me your dad works for the BBC and is always on the television. You must be rolling in it,' Cally said bitterly. She untied Blue, pulled her stirrup leathers down roughly and sprang into the saddle, shooting Poppy a scathing look as she did.

Poppy coloured and disappeared into the tack room in search of Scarlett, who was humming to herself as she pulled on her hat.

'I wish you hadn't told Cally what my dad did. She's just accused me of being loaded. Chance would be a fine thing,' she grumbled.

'You are, compared with Cally,' said Scarlett bluntly. 'Her dad left when she was a baby. Her mum is a part-time carer and they live in a council flat. Cally says they don't have two pennies to rub together.'

'Well, it's no reason for her to have a go at me. It's not my fault her mum can't get a decent job.'

'Poppy! That's a terrible thing to say. You know nothing about Cally or her mum. Sometimes you should try thinking before you speak.' Scarlett brushed past Poppy as she stomped out of the tack room. Poppy felt a stab of hurt and went to follow her friend, but was deterred by the set of Scarlett's shoulders. Instead she sat on a feed bin and watched a pair of swallows swooping in and out of their mud nest high on one of the rafters. Hearing the clatter of hooves she heaved Beau's saddle from its rack, picked up his bridle and headed back out into the yard. The sun was bright after the gloom of the tack room and she paused for a moment to rub her eyes.

Nina stepped in front of her, obscuring the sun. 'Where's Beau, Poppy?'

'He's over -' she began, but the words dried up as she looked across the yard in dismay. The loop of string she'd tied Beau to was flapping gently in the wind and the piebald cob was nowhere to be seen.

Poppy looked around her wildly. 'I left him tied up outside the barn while I popped in to get his tack. He must be here somewhere.' She became aware that the others had stopped what they were doing to listen.

'Are you sure you tied him up properly?' Nina said, running her hand through her hair.

'Yes!' cried Poppy, already doubting herself. She felt everyone's eyes on her and thought longingly of Riverdale, where it was just her, Cloud and Chester and no-one questioned her every move.

'He can't have gone far. The gate to the track's closed,' Chloe pointed out.

'Wait a minute - Frank's gone, too!' said Jess.

'I might have known,' said Nina grimly. 'Follow me,' she told Poppy, heading for the hay barn. She threw open the double doors to reveal Frank and Beau, who were happily working their way through a bale of hay.

'I did warn you that Frank was a little Houdini,' Nina said. 'Next time pass the end of the lead rope through the loop of the quick release knot. Frank can still undo that if he's got long enough to figure it out, but at least it buys you some extra time.' She smiled briefly at Poppy, who was willing the earth to swallow her up. 'It's OK, no harm done, and you'll know for next time. She glanced at her watch. 'Come on everyone, let's see if we can be ready in five minutes.'

Soon they were clip-clopping down the lane. Or, if Poppy was being accurate, the others were clip-clopping down the lane and Beau was trundling along in his own little world, helping himself to mouthfuls of cow parsley and taking no notice of his rider and her efforts to chivvy him up. She doubted the cob even remembered she was still on board. She was so used to seeing Cloud's small grey pricked ears in front of her that she kept doing a double take when she saw Beau's enormous black ears flicking back and forth. Cloud's silver mane was neatly pulled and lay smoothly to his off-side. Despite her best efforts to tame it, Beau's thick mane was flopping over on both sides and was already starting to tangle. Poppy had spent the last few weeks counting the days until the riding holiday. Now she was counting the hours until she returned home. She gathered up the reins and attempted to kick Beau into a trot.

'Come on, you lazy toad,' she said, clicking her tongue. Beau gave a shake of his large head and broke into an unenthusiastic jog. She caught up with Scarlet and Cally, who were riding two abreast down the quiet country lane. Blue flicked her grey tail in displeasure and snaked her head at Beau, her ears back and her teeth bared.

'Oh, Nina says Blue doesn't like Beau,' said Cally. 'It might be better if you don't ride next to us.'

'Oh, right,' Poppy said, flustered.

'Come and ride next to me and Chloe,' said Jess. 'Willow and Rusty won't mind.'

Grateful not to be lagging behind on her own yet again Poppy manoeuvred Beau alongside the two girls.

'Do you have your own pony at home, Poppy?' asked Chloe.

'Yes, I have a dappled grey Connemara called Cloud. And a donkey called Chester. What about you two?'

Chloe shook her head. 'I wish I did. I have riding lessons every Saturday, and I know I'm lucky to have that, but it's not the same, is it?'

Poppy smiled sympathetically. 'No, it's not. I know exactly how you feel. When we lived in London all I ever wanted was my own pony. I didn't even have riding lessons until we moved to Devon.'

'That's why my mum and dad gave me the riding holiday for my tenth birthday. They said it would be cheaper than buying me my own pony. I've been looking forward to it for *months*,' said Chloe, hugging Rusty's neck.

'What about you, Jess?' Poppy asked. She was pretty sure the answer was yes. Although Chloe sat in the correct riding position and kept her back straight, her heels down and her hands steady, her body was rigid and her grip on Rusty's reins was tight. It betrayed the fact that she was a novice, only used to riding once a week. Jess, on the other hand, had the relaxed, easy seat of someone who'd been riding all her life. She had Willow on a long rein and her body moved in rhythm with the dun mare's swinging walk.

'Jack and I share our sister Lucy's old pony, Magic,' said Jess, confirming Poppy's hunch. 'Lucy's at university and hardly rides these days. Jack's only really interested in bombing around at our pony club with his friends, so I get to ride Magic most. He's a bit old and creaky, but I love him.'

Poppy smiled and began to relax. As they wound their way along forest tracks behind the others she found herself telling the girls about Cloud.

'Last summer we moved from London to a cottage on the edge of Dartmoor. It's next to Scarlett's farm,' she added, glancing ahead to her friend, who was still deep in conversation with Cally. Poppy's smile faded and she turned back to the two girls.

'The cottage is called Riverdale and it used to belong to an old lady called Tory Wickens, who bought Cloud for her grand-daughter Caitlyn. But Caitlyn was killed when they fell during a hunter trial.'

'Killed!' said Chloe, aghast. 'What happened?'

Poppy remembered the rainy day the previous autumn when Tory, her weathered old face streaked with tears, had described the events of that terrible day. Caitlyn, a talented young rider with masses of potential, had been flying around the course on her beloved Connemara when he had lost his footing in the mud as the pair jumped a drop fence.

'He somersaulted over, throwing Caitlyn underneath him. Tory said she died instantly.'

'That's awful!' said Jess, her eyes wide.

'How old was she?' asked Chloe.

'Thirteen. A year older than me and Scarlett.'

The two girls fell silent. Poppy knew they would be imagining the sirens, the ambulance lurching over the uneven, muddy course, the screens being erected around the young rider as the paramedics shielded her lifeless body from the spectators. Poppy knew, because she had imagined the scene countless times herself.

'Poor Caitlyn,' whispered Jess.

'I know. Tory never really got over it.'

'What happened to Cloud?' asked Chloe.

'He was bought by a local famer, a man called George Blackstone. He's as nasty as they come. People say he beats the ponies he buys and sells and I can quite believe it.

'Cloud managed to escape from the Blackstone farm and spent the next few years living wild on Dartmoor. I saw him from a distance the day we moved to Riverdale and spent weeks trying to catch him. In the end he was rounded up with the Dartmoor ponies and Blackstone sold him at auction, but my dad was there and bought him for me.'

'Wow, it's like a fairy-tale. Why do things like that never happen to me?' said Chloe wistfully.

'Ah, but it wasn't quite as simple as it sounds. He'd broken a bone in his foot so there was a chance I might never be able to ride him. He had to have months of box rest. And then last Christmas, while I was in bed with the flu, my brother Charlie accidentally fed him unsoaked sugarbeet and he was so ill with colic that I thought he was going to die.'

After being virtually ignored and then admonished by Scarlett, Poppy was gratified by the rapt expressions on the two girls' faces. 'We were completely snowed in so the vet couldn't get to us,' she told them.

'What did you do?' Chloe asked, open-mouthed.

'I kept walking him every half an hour. I'd remembered reading that was what you're supposed to do. Luckily it did the trick and the colic passed. His fracture healed earlier this year and I finally started riding him this spring.'

'You saved his life,' breathed Jess.

'Yes, I suppose I did,' Poppy replied. She sat taller in the saddle and smiled modestly at Chloe and Jess. Unfortunately Beau chose that precise moment to sidestep into the trees to avoid a puddle and Poppy was almost knocked out of the saddle by the low-hanging bough of a sweet chestnut tree. She cursed under her breath as the whippy branch struck her cheek painfully.

'Are you alright?' Chloe asked in concern.

'Yes, I'm fine,' she answered, rubbing her cheek. Beau swung back onto the path, completely unaware that he'd almost knocked her flying.

Or did he know exactly what he'd done? Poppy couldn't be sure. All she knew for certain was that she missed Cloud with all her heart and would have given anything to have swapped the bumbling Beau for her beautiful Connemara.

7

Poppy's cheek was still smarting as she untacked Beau and brushed him down after their ride.

'What happened to you? It looks like you've been slapped in the face by a wet fish,' smirked Cally as she walked past the cob on her way to the tack room. Jack, who was untacking Rocky nearby, sniggered.

'No, Beau just chose to go the scenic route through the trees. But I'm glad you both find it so amusing,' Poppy muttered, bending down to pick up one of Beau's feet so they couldn't see her face. Beau turned his head and nipped her backside.

'Ow! What did you do that for?' she cried, dropping both his foot and the hoofpick, which skittered onto the concrete. She heard Cally stifling a snort of laughter as she crossed the yard to Blue. Poppy glared at her retreating back and then looked daggers at Beau, who was nibbling his lead rope unperturbed.

'You could show me some loyalty. As if I haven't got enough to put up with,' she told him, tugging at the quick release knot and dragging him towards the field gate. Nina joined them as they passed the hay barn. She gave Beau's ear an affectionate rub and smiled at Poppy.

'How are you finding Beau?'

Poppy scratched around for something positive to say and failed. 'He's certainly like nothing I've ever ridden before.'

'Good, I'm so glad you like him.' They passed under the old oak. 'Have I told you about our oak trees here in the Forest of Dean?'

Poppy was glad to have something to take her mind off Cally, Scarlett and Beau, and shook her head.

'Have you heard of Lord Nelson?' Nina asked.

'Yes. There was a pub near our old house in London that was named after him. He was a famous soldier, wasn't he?'

'Not a soldier, no. Nelson was a British naval commander during the Napoleonic wars. He visited the Forest of Dean in 1802 looking for timber to build warships. He was so shocked at how few trees there were that he urged the Admiralty, which was in charge of the Navy, to plant more oaks. Thirty million acorns were planted, but by the time the trees had grown it was too late and ships were being built out of iron and steel.'

'So that was a complete and utter waste of time.'

'Oh no, I wouldn't say that,' said Nina. 'If they hadn't planted those millions of acorns we wouldn't have our beautiful forest today. I'm glad they didn't think too far ahead.'

Poppy looked at the old oak. Its girth was so wide she doubted that three people could have linked arms around it. 'So is this one of the trees Nelson's lot planted?'

'Who knows? But it's certainly hundreds of years old. And it gave the house its name, of course.'

Poppy thought for a minute. Something was nagging her. 'Aren't acorns poisonous to horses?' she said.

Nina looked impressed. 'Yes, they are. So are the leaves. I spend most of the autumn sweeping the yard to make sure there aren't any for the horses to eat. It's hard work. But the tree is so much a part of Oaklands that I don't really mind.'

They reached the gate and Nina opened it so Poppy could lead Beau through.

'You must really love this place,' Poppy said.

Nina tightened her grip on the gate and Poppy was alarmed to see a look of anguish cross her face.

'Yes,' Nina said quietly. 'I do.'

POPPY DECIDED NOT to join the others in front of the television after dinner that evening, and instead disappeared into the bedroom to read. She had half hoped that Scarlett would persuade her to stay but instead her friend, who was sitting on the sofa with Cally, had barely thrown her a backward glance. She felt both irritated and dismayed at the way Cally had so effortlessly hijacked her best friend. It was as if Scarlett had been dazzled by the older girl's personality and had forgotten Poppy even existed. Poppy rubbed her aching shoulders and found the latest issue of Young Rider Magazine, which she'd stuffed inside her bag when she'd packed. Her winning story had been published in full along with those of the two runners up. The editor had asked her to email in a photo of her and Cloud, and Poppy had picked her favourite picture, taken by Charlie on his little digital camera a few weeks before. Cloud's silver mane was blowing in the wind and Poppy was laughing as she held a carrot for him in the palm of her hand. *'Great photo!'* the editor had emailed back, and they'd used it above her story. Poppy studied the picture and wondered yet again if Cloud was missing her. There was no mobile phone signal at the house, otherwise she'd have been ringing or texting Caroline several times a day to check he was alright. She didn't like to ask to use the phone at Oaklands unless it was an emergency.

She remembered the last email she'd had from the editor, letting her know when her story would be published. *'Perhaps you'd consider writing a small report on your holiday for us to publish in a future edition,'* she had added.

'Hmph,' said Poppy as she switched on the bedside light and settled down to read. 'I don't suppose Young Rider Magazine is interested in horror stories about pig-headed carthorses.'

She tried to concentrate on an in-depth article about dressage but it was no good. Her attention kept wandering. Flinging the magazine down beside the bed she went in search of a glass of water. As she passed the door to the lounge she glanced in and saw Scarlett and the others laughing uproariously at a sitcom. It was one of Poppy's favourite programmes but she felt too left out of things to join them. Instead she carried on towards the kitchen, trying to ignore the loneliness that had been her constant companion since they'd arrived at Oaklands.

The kitchen was in darkness, the only light coming from the digital clock on the oven and the red flashing light of the answerphone. Not bothering to turn on the light Poppy headed for the larder, where Nina kept the glasses, mugs and plates. She opened the old wooden door and was reaching up for a tumbler when she heard footsteps. Suddenly the room was flooded with light. Poppy froze. Nina had told them they should help themselves to drinks but she felt awkward skulking around in the dark. She realised it was Nina, humming to herself as she filled the kettle. Poppy was about to breeze out with a glass in her hand when she heard the click of the answerphone and a man's voice filled the air.

To sidle out now would seem suspicious so Poppy crept to the furthest corner of the larder, squeezing between a sack of potatoes and a shelf stacked with saucepans and baking tins.

'This is a message for Nina Goddard of Oaklands Trekking Centre,' the man announced in an officious tone.

Nina stopped humming. Even from the depths of the larder Poppy could sense the tension in the air.

'My name is Graham Deakins and I am a financial asset investigation specialist,' he continued. Poppy caught Nina's sharp intake of breath.

'I need to talk to you urgently about monies due. Please phone me at your earliest convenience on -' Nina cut the man off mid-sentence. When Poppy heard a small sob she wished she was anywhere but there, witnessing Nina's distress. She breathed as quietly as she could, her heart thudding, until the kitchen light went out and she heard the door close. She didn't know who the man was, or what he wanted. But she knew one thing for certain. It wasn't good news.

THE NEXT MORNING Nina seemed her usual cheerful self and Poppy wondered if she'd misunderstood the answerphone message. To her surprise she managed to catch Beau, groom him and tack him up without being bitten, knocked flying or having her feet stamped on, and felt as though she was making real progress. It was a glorious early summer day and the hedgerows were brimming with frothy-white cow parsley and magenta red campion. The sun was warm on her back and she whistled quietly to herself as she and Beau ambled down the lane behind the others.

They stopped for lunch in a grassy clearing deep in the forest,

surrounded by oaks and electric green bracken. They took their sandwiches and drinks from their saddle bags and looped their reins over
their horses' heads so they could hold them while they ate. Poppy's
stomach was rumbling and she wolfed down her squashed cheese and
pickle sandwich in seconds. Beau's head fell, his eyes closed and before
long he was fast asleep, his bottom lip drooping unattractively. Poppy
took a swig of her water and listened to the conversations going on
around her. Chloe and Jess were debating the merits of cross country
over showjumping and Jack was telling Nina about his latest computer
game. Although she was giving a good impression of being interested,
there was a vacant look in her eyes and her mind was obviously elsewhere. Scarlett was quizzing Cally about the latest ex-racehorse she was
re-training.

'We think she has great potential as an eventer. I'm working on her
dressage at the moment then Rose says I can enter her in her first one day
event. They fetch more money if they've started competing.'

'That's so cool,' Scarlett said. 'Maybe I could come and watch.'

Poppy tutted to herself and yawned. Rays of sunlight piercing the
heavy oak leaves lit yellow celandines and waxy white wood anemones on
the forest floor like tiny spotlights illuminating characters on a theatre
stage. She leant against the bough of a tree and watched Beau dozing until
her own eyelids felt heavy. Before long she, too, was asleep.

SHE WAS WOKEN by a gentle nudge on her shoulder and opened her eyes to
see Beau's hairy face centimetres from her own. His warm breath smelt of
spring grass and his whiskers tickled her cheek. The others were gathering up their lunch things and Poppy jumped to her feet and pulled on
her hat. She found a tree stump to use as a mounting block and sprang
into the saddle. Steering Beau over to Topaz and Scarlett she said lightly,
'Hello stranger. How's things?'

'Great, I'm having a fantastic time. Topaz's brilliant. I'm going to miss
her so much,' said Scarlett passionately. Poppy pictured Blaze, her friend's
loyal Dartmoor pony, grazing in her field back home.

Scarlett guessed what she was thinking. 'I love Blaze, of course I do,
but I've almost outgrown her, Poppy, you know that. You've got Cloud

waiting for you at home. Imagine how ridiculous I'll look on Blaze when we ride out together. I wish Mum and Dad would buy Topaz.'

'But she's not for sale, Scar. Nina needs her for the riding holidays. She'll be someone else's pony next week.' When Poppy saw the hurt on her best friend's face she could have kicked herself for being so tactless, but it was too late to take the words back. She wasn't surprised when Scarlett resumed her place beside Cally, leaving her on her own behind Jack, staring at Rocky's chestnut hindquarters yet again.

They passed a farm. 'That's where my nearest neighbours, Bert and Eileen, live,' Nina told them. 'I have permission to ride on their land. We'll be going through the farmyard and then we'll cross the river and follow the line of trees back home.'

'Are we going to ride through the river?' asked Jess, her eyes wide.

'Heavens, no,' laughed Nina, as they reached the gate to the yard. 'There's an old stone clapper bridge. We'll ride over that. I'll open the gate. Who's going to close it for me?'

'I will,' said Poppy, and they all looked around in surprise, as if they'd forgotten she was there.

'If you're sure,' said Nina.

'Of course,' replied Poppy. She'd never actually opened a gate while riding - Scarlett always did that - but, honestly, how hard could it be? Poppy kicked Beau through the gate after the others and hauled him to a halt. He stood perfectly still. The only trouble was, they were just out of reach of the gate. She squeezed her legs. He ignored her. She exhaled loudly and booted him in the sides. The cob took a step sideways. Poppy leant over his shoulder, puffing as she strained to reach the latch. Her hand tightened around the iron post and she kicked again. Beau took another reluctant step forward. She was millimetres away from setting the latch in its keeper. She leant even further out of the saddle, her arms stretched taut as she lunged for the gatepost.

Beau, bored of waiting, took a step backwards. And then another. Poppy teetered for a nano-second but it was no good. With the inevitability of night following day, she slid to the ground and landed, backside first, into a freshly-laid cow pat.

8

T hings went from bad to worse when they arrived back at the yard and Nina announced that they were going to spend the rest of the afternoon playing gymkhana games.

'I'll split you into two teams of three and we'll have our own Prince Philip Cup competition,' she said. Jack whooped and Chloe and Jess high-fived each other. Scarlett was also smiling. Poppy pictured the back of Scarlett's bedroom door, which was plastered with the many rosettes she and Blaze had won at local gymkhanas. Cally looked unimpressed, her mouth turned down in disdain. At fourteen and about to compete in her first one day event on a former racehorse, she was obviously way too cool for gymkhana games. Poppy looked at Beau in despair. How on earth was she supposed to navigate the great oaf around bending poles at high speed when she could barely get him to break into a trot down a straight country lane? It would be yet another opportunity for some ritual humiliation.

Nina untacked McFly and turned him out with Frank in the top field and then opened the gate into the smaller paddock behind the hay barn. It was a flat, square field surrounded by hedges and in the middle were two sets of five evenly-spaced poles set in rows in the ground. Traffic cones marked the start. The children followed Nina in.

'Jack and Scarlett, you can be my two captains, and I'll let you take it in turns to pick your teams,' said Nina. Brilliant, thought Poppy with relief. At least Scarlett would pick her.

'Ladies first,' said Jack, and Scarlett nodded her thanks. She glanced at Poppy, her face inscrutable. Poppy had a horrible feeling she knew what was coming next.

'Cally,' Scarlett said, and Poppy squirmed. It was obviously payback time for being so thoughtless. Cally smiled sweetly at Poppy and rode over to Scarlett's side.

'Jess,' Jack said.

'Thanks Jack!' said Jess, surprised and delighted to be her brother's first choice.

Scarlett looked from Chloe to Poppy and back again. Poppy's heart sank. She didn't need to be Einstein to work out who Scarlett was going to pick.

'Chloe, please,' said her best friend, avoiding Poppy's gaze.

'I suppose I'd better have Poppy, then,' said Jack. Poppy's face was expressionless as she kicked Beau into a trot and joined Jess and Willow.

'Jack's brilliant at gymkhana games,' Jess whispered. 'He and Magic were picked for our pony club's mounted games team a couple of years ago. He's really competitive.'

'Great,' Poppy replied, forcing a smile.

'We'll start with a bending race,' Nina called. 'Captains can decide who races who. I'll give you two points for every win and one point for second place. We'll add all the points up at the end and the winning team gets to have a free evening. The losing team must do evening stables. All clear? Right, who's first?'

Scarlett and Jack both rode up to the starting line beside Nina.

'On your marks, get set, go!' she shouted and Rocky and Topaz set off at a canter. Jack was all arms and legs as he spurred Rocky on, reminding Poppy of a human windmill. The liver chestnut cob valiantly thundered around the poles as fast as he could but couldn't keep up with Topaz. The palomino darted around the poles like a minnow through seaweed and won by a couple of lengths. Scarlett punched the air, her face flushed, and Cally and Chloe cheered.

Jess and Cally were next. Blue was totally over-excited and crabbed over to the starting line, her rose grey neck arched and her tail carriage high. Cally sat quietly in the saddle as the Arab mare danced beneath her.

Poppy could hear her murmuring to Blue. Willow stood placidly, her dun ears pricked. Jess looked distinctly green.

Nina started the race and the two girls set off. Although Blue was by far the faster horse she overshot the turns and Cally struggled to keep her balance. In contrast Willow cantered steadily around the poles and turned tightly at the top and by the time they both crossed the finish line they were neck and neck.

'Photo finish!' yelled Jack.

Nina, who had been scrutinising the finish as closely as a line judge at Wimbledon, straightened her back. 'Sorry Jack, the budget doesn't run to cameras. I'm going to call it a dead heat and give both teams two points. So Scarlett's team are still in the lead by a point. Chloe and Poppy, you're next.'

Poppy pushed her hat firmly down over her forehead and gathered her reins. Beau's head was hanging low and she had the horrible feeling he'd fallen asleep again.

'Come on, Beau,' she said firmly and gave him a none-too-gentle kick. The piebald cob's head shot up in surprise and he trotted obediently over to the start line. Poppy was cheered. Maybe they wouldn't make a show of themselves. Maybe Beau was an old pro at this kind of thing. But as she lined up beside Chloe and Rusty, Nina gave her a sympathetic smile. 'I'm afraid gymkhana games aren't really Beau's thing, Poppy. Do the best you can.'

'Great,' Poppy muttered again, glancing over at Scarlett and Cally. The amused expression on Cally's face hardened her heart and she whispered in Beau's hairy ear, 'Let's show them we mean business, eh?'

'Ready?' asked Nina. Both girls nodded. 'On your marks, get set, GO!'

Beau gave a giant cat leap forward, almost unseating Poppy, and she grabbed the pommel of the saddle as he cantered towards the first pole. Rusty and Chloe were streaking ahead and she crouched low over Beau's neck and hauled him around the first pole with brute strength. She could hear his hooves as they cantered around the next two poles, but her eyes were fixed on the furthest pole. She knew the race could be won by a close turn at the top. Miraculously, Beau executed a perfect flying change as they turned for the final pole and suddenly they were half a length in front of Chloe and Rusty. As they headed back towards the finish line at a gallop, Poppy looked over her shoulder to reassure herself they really were winning. But as she did she dropped the reins a fraction and Beau thundered straight past a pole. Poppy tried to slow him down so they could turn back and go around it but it was no good. Beau's blood was up and he was unstoppable. He gained even more ground on Chloe and Rusty and by the time they crossed the finish line he was three lengths ahead. He slowed down to a walk and snorted in pleasure, thinking he'd won. Poppy stroked his black and white neck automatically and kept her head down to avoid Jack's furious stare.

'Sorry Poppy, I'll have to disqualify you. Beau missed three of the poles,' Nina told her.

'I know. But it wasn't Beau's fault. It was mine.' Poppy could have kicked herself for losing concentration.

'Cheer up,' Nina said. 'It's not all bad. Beau turned on a sixpence at the top and I've never seen him do a flying change before. Maybe you'll have more luck in the walk, trot, canter and run.'

As it was Nina's optimism was misguided and Poppy didn't win a single race. Cally and Blue notched up a victory in the walk, trot, canter and run, the fourteen-year-old covering the ground on the final leg in easy strides. Scarlett and Jack fought hard for first place in the flag race, but the hours Jack had spent training with his pony club's mounted games team paid dividends and he won by a head. Jess proved to have a steady hand and was a demon in the egg and spoon race. Poppy tripped over her feet and landed face down in the grass in the sack race. Her temper was frayed and her nerves frazzled by the time Nina announced the last game.

'We'll finish with a relay race. Scarlett, your team is only one point ahead, so if you win this you have the evening off. If you don't you'll tie and you'll do evening stables together. I don't have batons so just high-five each other instead. Best of luck everyone.'

Jack beckoned Jess and Poppy over for a team talk. 'Jess, you're going to go first. Push Willow as fast as she'll go but don't overshoot. You need to make your turn as tight as possible. Poppy, you go next. Just try not to get disqualified, OK? I'll try to make up the time you've lost. Got that? Come on, let's give it our best shot.'

Poppy scowled and turned Beau for the start line. Jess and Chloe set off at a gallop, their ponies' manes streaming behind them as they disappeared towards the far pole. Willow was the fastest around the pole and Jess was grinning as she galloped back down towards Poppy. Poppy gathered her reins in her left hand and high-fived Jess with her right. Beau sprang into action, his ears back and his head stretched forward as he charged for the far pole. Poppy turned him tightly and headed for home. She didn't dare look around to see where Cally was. Rocky, standing at the start line, registered Beau's great bulk bowling towards him like a black and white tornado and recoiled backwards. Jack kicked him on, his right arm held aloft ready to high-five her, but the chestnut cob refused to move.

Catching a glimpse of Cally and Scarlett high-fiving, Poppy pointed Beau towards Rocky and kicked.

'Hold him still, you twit!' she shouted to Jack, as Beau motored on like an equine steamroller. She stood up in her stirrups, leant over and slapped Jack's palm as hard as she could. He winced in pain and Rocky sprang away from Beau and towards the far pole. Poppy swung around in the saddle in time to see Scarlett cantering sedately over the finish line, Jack miles behind her.

'Well done, Poppy. You really showed them how it's done,' said Jack, as he and Rocky passed her on their way back to the stables.

'Hold on a minute,' Poppy replied furiously. 'You were the one who couldn't keep your horse still. It wasn't my fault.'

'Yes it was. You and Beau are as useless as each other. And now I've got to spend all evening mucking out. Thanks for nothing.'

POPPY'S RESENTMENT simmered as she, Jess and Jack silently worked their way through evening stables. It started to bubble during dinner and by the time they all sat down to watch television it had reached boiling point. She had made up her mind. She was going to find Nina and ask her to swap Beau for another horse. She would point out that she was a competition winner, after all, so should expect a decent ride. In fact, she had a good mind to email the editor of Young Rider Magazine to complain about the fact that she'd been given the worst horse in the yard.

Poppy had no intention of kicking Scarlett off Topaz. Her best friend was barely talking to her as it was. Anyway, there was no need. Cally the expert rider was apparently so experienced in tackling problem horses that it made sense for her to take Beau on and give Blue to Poppy. It was a no brainer.

Nina had disappeared after putting Lydia to bed. Poppy followed the hallway in the opposite direction to the guest rooms and lounge. The first door she came to was slightly ajar. Light seeped through into the hall and she could hear the murmur of a television. Through the crack between the door and its frame she saw Nina sitting at a paper-strewn desk, her back to the door and her head in her hands. Poppy knocked gently.

There was a pause. Poppy stood awkwardly, unsure whether to knock again.

'Come in,' Nina said eventually. Poppy pushed open the door and Nina swivelled her chair around. 'Oh Poppy, it's you.'

When Poppy saw Nina's blotchy face all thoughts of Beau disappeared. 'Are you OK?' she asked in alarm.

'Not really, no. But it's nothing for you to worry about.' Nina's voice was wobbly.

'What's happened? Is it Lydia?'

'No, thank goodness. Lydia is fine.' Nina ran a hand across her forehead in an effort to compose herself and pointed to the well-worn armchair next to her desk. 'Have a seat. What did you want to talk to me about?'

'Something's wrong, I know it is,' Poppy said. But Nina didn't answer. She was staring blankly at the portable television in the corner of the room. The ten o'clock news had started and the newsreader was talking about the latest Government re-shuffle. Poppy glanced at the reproduction mahogany desk. There were four drawers on each side and a green leather inlaid top, which was almost completely hidden by credit card and bank statements, brown envelopes and bills.

'Nina -' Poppy persisted.

Jolted back into the present Nina scooped the paperwork into one untidy pile and attempted to straighten it into some kind of order. She stood up and pulled the heavy damask curtains closed. Poppy took the opportunity to scan the top statement. There was a jumble of numbers set out in columns. By stretching her neck she could just make out the outstanding balance of four hundred and ninety two pounds. Stamped in red over the top of the statement were two unforgiving words. FINAL REMINDER.

9

Nina saw Poppy looking at the bills piled in front of her and her face sagged. She looked ten years older.

'Is there a problem?' Poppy asked, gesturing at the paperwork.

'I've just been going through my accounts, that's all.'

Poppy pictured the man in the shiny suit who had been so keen to track Nina down. She replayed the answerphone message she'd overheard the night before in her head and everything fell into place.

'It's something to do with that man who was looking for you the other day, isn't it?'

'It's nothing for you to worry about,' Nina repeated, sitting down heavily.

Poppy wasn't about to be fobbed off. 'Nina, I heard the answerphone message last night. That man who was talking about monies due. I was in the larder getting a glass,' she explained, feeling shifty. 'I didn't mean to eavesdrop.'

Nina was beaten and Poppy saw her chance. 'Please tell me what's going on. I might even be able to help.'

'No-one can help. It's too late for that.' Nina finally met Poppy's eyes. 'You really want to know what's wrong?'

Poppy nodded.

'I've fallen behind with the mortgage payments. My credit cards are maxed to the limit. The horses are due to be shod but the farrier is refusing to come because I still haven't paid him for his last visit. And the next feed bill is due any minute. That man who left a message is a debt collector, Poppy. The irony is, I don't even know who he's working for, I owe so many people money.'

'Oh, I see.'

'I mortgaged myself to the hilt to buy this place, you see. Lydia's dad and I split up when she was a baby. I was so determined to give her an idyllic childhood, growing up around horses, that when I saw this place I had to have it. Perhaps I was overcompensating. Who knows? But I thought it would work. I did all the research and the bank liked my business plan. I've had so much bad luck, Poppy, you wouldn't believe.' Nina ran her hand through her hair. She had kept everything bottled up for so long that now the floodgates were open there was no stopping her.

'Early on I discovered that the house had dry rot and both barns needed re-roofing. Then one of the trekking ponies developed navicular and ran up massive vet's bills. Bookings were much slower than I'd predicted and everything has been so much more expensive. I took out credit cards to keep things ticking over but the interest they've been charging me is crippling. The final straw came last week when the bank warned me that it's going to foreclose on my loan if I can't make this month's payment.'

Nina buried her head in her hands again. Her fingers were trembling. When she finally spoke, her voice was muffled with tears.

'I'm going to lose it all, Poppy. Everything.'

Poppy looked around her helplessly. It was at times like these that she wished she had Scarlett's easy manner, Caroline's natural empathy or her old friend Tory's old-fashioned common sense. She had no idea how to comfort Nina. She stood up and laid a hand gingerly on the woman's shoulders. But Nina had wrapped herself so tightly in her own misery that she didn't even notice.

Poppy nearly jumped out of her skin when she heard her dad's voice behind her. She spun around to see his face staring out from Nina's portable television. She'd forgotten that her dad, a war correspondent for the BBC, had been sent to northern France to cover the anniversary of the D-Day landings. He was interviewing a veteran whose lined face was wet with tears as he remembered the events of June 1944. She could hear the compassion in her dad's voice and wished with all her heart that he was here with her. She glanced at Nina. What would he do, in her shoes? He'd stay level-headed and practical, that's what he'd do. Poppy spied a box of tissues on the window ledge and offered them to Nina, who finally lifted her head, gave her a watery smile and blew her nose noisily.

'Thank-you, Poppy. I shouldn't have burdened you with all this. I was hoping we'd make it to the end of the week before I had to close down the yard, but I've ruined your holiday now anyway.'

'No, you haven't,' said Poppy, offering Nina another tissue. 'Anyway, it's not your fault. You've just been unlucky. Isn't there anything else you could do? Sell off some land or a couple of the ponies, to give you a bit more time?'

'No, it would be too little, too late. Unless I come up with two thousand pounds by the end of the week the house and land will be repossessed by the bank and I'll probably be declared bankrupt. It'll be down to the bailiffs to sell the horses, and they're not going to care whether they go to good homes or not. How will I tell Lydia that we're moving, let alone that she's going to lose Frank? He and Beau were the first horses I bought for the business, that's why I'm so fond of them both. They've been my talismans from day one, although they don't seem to have brought me much luck recently.'

Poppy remembered why she had sought Nina out and felt immensely relieved that she hadn't added to her troubles by complaining about the piebald cob. She could kick herself for being so petty and self-centred. She gave Nina the box of tissues. 'I'm going to make you a cup of tea. You sit and watch the end of the news. I won't be long.'

Nina was watching the weather when Poppy let herself back into the study, a mug of tea in each hand. The map of the UK was awash with black clouds and lightning symbols.

'Uh oh. Are we in for a storm?' she asked.

Nina had used the short time while Poppy was in the kitchen to collect herself and her voice was almost back to normal.

'Yes, I'm afraid so. The Met Office has issued severe weather warnings for tomorrow night. We're getting the tail-end of a hurricane that hit the Caribbean last week, apparently.'

'So our last night might go out with a bang, then?' said Poppy, attempting to raise a smile. Nina nodded bleakly.

~

SCARLETT WAS ALREADY in the top bunk when Poppy let herself into their bedroom.

'Scar, are you awake?' she whispered. Scarlett's shoulders were stiff and her shallow breathing wasn't the rhythmic inhale, exhale of someone fast asleep. But she didn't reply.

Poppy sighed. She would have liked to have talked to her best friend about Nina's revelations. As Poppy had left the study Nina had asked her not to say anything about her money troubles to the others. But Poppy always shared everything with Scarlett.

At least she always had.

Scarlett was nowhere to be seen when Poppy arrived for breakfast. Everyone else was sat around the table, plates of toast in front of them. Nina hadn't touched hers and her face was pale but she gave Poppy a wide smile.

'Has anyone seen Scarlett?' Poppy asked.

'She said she didn't feel like breakfast. I think she's in the yard,' said Chloe.

Poppy bolted down two slices of toast. 'Thanks Nina. I'm going to go and find her if that's OK? What time are we setting off?'

'Ten o'clock. I've got an extra special route planned for today.'

Frank met Poppy at the back door and followed her across the yard to Topaz's loose box. She hesitated outside. Scarlett was talking to Topaz as she groomed the palomino mare. Poppy knew eavesdropping only led to trouble but she couldn't help herself.

' - I'm going to miss you so much. I've had such a great holiday. I wish Mum and Dad had the money to buy you. You'd love it at Ashworthy.' Poppy heard a sob. She reached into her pocket for a tissue and let herself into Topaz's box. Scarlett was standing with her arms around the mare, her shoulders shuddering. Poppy had never seen her friend cry.

'Have this,' she said, handing Scarlett the tissue.

'Oh, it's you.' Scarlett looked far from pleased to see her.

Poppy took a deep breath. 'I'm sorry I was so thoughtless yesterday, I really am. I didn't realise how much Topaz meant to you.'

Scarlett was silent. Poppy persisted. 'I know I haven't been much fun to be around and I don't blame you for hanging out with Cally. But I've missed you, Scar. Please forgive me so we can be friends again.'

Scarlett sniffed and wiped her face on the sleeve of her sweatshirt. She ran her hand down Topaz's neck and looked at Poppy coolly.

'You're doing it again. Me, me, me. You have to remember that it's not all about you, Poppy. At least Cally is interested in what I think and how I feel. She doesn't just go on about herself all the time.'

Poppy was stung. 'Yes she does!' she said indignantly. 'If she's not boring the pants off us with stories about what a good rider she is she's going on about how popular she is at school. She never stops talking about herself. And you encourage her by hanging onto her every word like some kind of saddo.'

'How dare you! At least I'm not always feeling sorry for myself. Some people would give their eye teeth to be given a horse like Beau for a week and all you've done is whinge and moan since the minute we arrived.'

'You ought to try riding the lumbering great brute before being so quick to judge. My legs are killing me, and as for my back -'

'There you go again!' Scarlett exploded. 'You just can't see it, can you?'

Poppy bit her bottom lip as Scarlett turned her back to her, picked up a body brush and started sweeping it over Topaz's golden flank.

'I'm going then, seeing as you obviously can't stand my company anymore,' she said, hoping Scarlett would dissolve into giggles and tell her that she was only kidding and that Poppy would always be her best friend.

But she didn't.

Instead she said tonelessly, 'Suit yourself.'

Poppy, shaken by the indifference in Scarlett's voice, let herself out of the loose box, almost colliding with Beau, who was making a beeline for the hay barn.

'How on earth did you get out?' she cried, grabbing his headcollar. As she did she saw a car pull up the track. It was the silver saloon. Poppy stood and watched as the driver's door swung open and the man in the shiny suit emerged. He saw her and beckoned her over. Poppy glanced at the back door of the bungalow. Nina must still be clearing up their breakfast things. She strode purposefully towards him, dragging Beau behind her.

'Oh, it's you,' he said, echoing Scarlett. No-one seemed pleased to see her today. Poppy nodded, noticing with satisfaction that his suit was still peppered with flecks of dried snot.

'Before you ask, Nina's not here,' she told him, her voice hostile.

The man looked pained. 'Do you know when she'll be back?'

Poppy shrugged. 'No idea.'

He reached inside his jacket. 'Here's my card. Give it to her and tell her to call me, will you? It's vital that I speak to her and the sooner the better. Do you understand?'

Poppy grunted, stuffed the card deep into her pocket and pulled Beau back towards the barn. She sneaked a look over her shoulder as she tied him up but the car had disappeared down the long, bumpy track.

F or once Poppy was glad of Beau's snail's pace, which put a welcome distance between her and the others as they headed down the lane towards the forest. It gave her head space to analyse the row with Scarlett. Poppy wasn't blind to her own faults. She knew she'd been thoughtless. And maybe she had gone on a bit about Beau. But she also felt aggrieved. Scarlett had virtually ignored her ever since they'd arrived at Oaklands. When Poppy had said sorry her best friend had thrown the apology back in her face. And then she'd had the nerve to say it was Poppy's fault for being self-obsessed. She wished Caroline was with her so she could talk it over, but as there was no mobile phone signal at the house she couldn't even give her stepmum a call.

She looked down at Beau's tufty black ears, which were pointing resolutely ahead as he followed the others down a narrow bridleway that wound its way through beech trees. As Nina had handed them their sandwiches she'd told them they were heading deep into the forest for their last ride of the holiday, and that they were to keep their eyes peeled for fallow deer and wild boar.

'What do you think about it all, Beau?' The piebald cob flicked back an ear at the sound of her voice. She talked all the time to Cloud, she realised guiltily. There was no reason she shouldn't talk to Beau, too. 'Is it my fault, or Scarlett's fault? Or is it six to one and half a dozen to the other? I wish I knew.'

The path opened out into a plantation of imposing pine trees whose gnarly trunks soared high into the sky. The air was warm and still and there was no sign of the storm the weather forecaster had predicted the night before. A grey squirrel darted down one of the trees head first and paused at the bottom where it eyed Poppy and Beau warily. Scarlett temporarily forgotten, Poppy tugged at Beau's reins and they stopped to watch the squirrel streak across the path in front of them and up a tree on the opposite side. It settled on a branch above their heads and began nibbling on a pine cone, its whiskers twitching and its tail wrapped around its back like an inverted question mark. Tired of the pine cone the squirrel discarded it and it fell to the forest floor like a stone. Beau, who had been nibbling on a patch of grass, walked over to the cone and snorted loudly, making Poppy laugh. The squirrel froze at the sound and vanished through the leaf-laden branches. Poppy picked up her reins and looked along the path for Rocky's chestnut rump. But it had disappeared from sight.

'Great, they've gone without us.' They picked up a trot until they reached a fork in the path and Poppy pulled Beau up. 'Left or right?' she pondered. Beau took a step towards the left-hand fork, which climbed steadily through the conifers. 'No Beau, I think it's this way,' she told him, turning him down the path to their right.

When twenty minutes had passed and there was no sign of the others Poppy began to doubt her wisdom. She should have trusted Beau. He'd probably been on this ride dozens of times. She'd just decided to cut her losses and turn back the way they'd come when she heard hooves pounding behind them. Cally was cantering up on Blue, her face like thunder.

'There you are!' the older girl said in exasperation. 'Nina sent me to find you. The others are way ahead. How on earth did you end up here?'

'We must have taken a wrong turn,' said Poppy. 'Sorry.'

Cally exhaled loudly. 'We'd better cut the corner to catch them up, otherwise we'll be here all day.'

She steered Blue off the path and Beau and Poppy followed them into bracken so tall it skimmed their stirrups. Under the canopy of green fronds the ground was broken and uneven. Almost as though it had been turned by a rotavator like the one Caroline had hired to dig over her vegetable patch when they'd first moved to Riverdale. Although why someone would want to plant vegetables in the middle of the forest was beyond Poppy. Beau tripped over a mound of freshly-turned earth, forcing Poppy forwards as his nose almost touched the ground.

'Steady on, Beau,' she said, pulling his head back up. Cally shot her a disparaging look. Even Blue flicked her silky tail with derision. Poppy pulled a face at them and patted the cob's neck. 'I'd ignore them if I were you,' she said to him under her breath.

The bracken was by now virtually impenetrable and Poppy was about to question Cally on the wisdom of her short cut when she heard a rustle to their left. Beau stopped and stared intently into the undergrowth, his ears flicking back and forth. Poppy clicked her tongue and squeezed firmly with her legs.

'Come on Beau, it's just a rabbit or something. Walk on,' she instructed. But the cob was deaf to her aids and stood rooted to the spot, his nostrils flared.

Cally spun Blue around. Her face was a mask of irritation. 'What's wrong now?'

As she spoke, the bracken rippled and the russet head of a tiny animal poked out. It had a black snout and vertical dark stripes ran along the length of its body.

Poppy couldn't believe her luck. A wild boar piglet! Beau was stock still beneath her and she stroked his neck to calm him. She watched, enthralled, as three more piglets joined the first and began snouting around in the long grass a few metres from where they stood.

Blue began backing out of the bracken, snorting with fear.

'They won't hurt you, you silly horse, they're tiny,' Cally said, kicking her on. 'Come on, Poppy, we really need to go.'

But the highly-strung Arab was trembling with fear. She had seen something far more dangerous than a litter of wild boar piglets thrusting its way through the undergrowth. Poppy gasped as an enormous sow, ready to defend her young, burst through the bracken with an angry squeal.

In the split second before the wild boar charged Poppy registered her bright black eyes and thick, bristly black coat. The boar had short, stocky legs and a powerful body with a ridge of coarse long hair along her spine, like a raven-haired punk with a Mohican. Her head low, she hurled herself towards them, scattering the piglets in her wake. Poppy gripped her reins and prepared to turn and gallop. But Beau stood his ground. She felt his strength beneath her, so solid and utterly dependable, and suddenly knew what they had to do. Kicking Beau into a canter she took a deep breath and began yelling at the top of her voice. She stood up in her stirrups and waved her arms in the air as they thundered towards the sow.

After ten years' living wild in the forest the boar knew which fights to pick and when to give in gracefully. The sight of a black and white, blue-eyed beast with a screaming banshee on board galloping hell for leather towards her was enough to stop her in her tracks. She slid to a halt, her snout quivering, and turned and fled back through the wall of bracken.

Poppy whooped, her adrenalin levels sky high, and swivelled around to Cally. The older girl was struggling to control Blue. The sight of the boar had sent the mare into a blind panic. Her ears were flattened and Poppy could see the whites of her eyes. She was spinning around like a pirouetting ballerina. Cally tugged at Blue's reins in an attempt to steady her but it only seemed to terrify her more. The mare's head shot up and her muscles tensed as her instinct for flight took hold.

Poppy saw Blue shift her weight onto her hindquarters and knew with dread what was going to happen before the mare's front feet left the ground.

'Lean forward! She's going to rear!' she shouted. Cally shot a frightened glance in her direction as Blue stood on her back legs, waving her forelegs wildly in the air.

'Wrap your arms around her neck! She's losing her balance!'

Time slowed down as the panic-stricken mare thrashed about in the bracken. Cally had lost a stirrup and was fighting to keep her own balance. Poppy pushed Beau forwards. Maybe if they got close enough she could grab Blue's reins and stop her rearing. They were within a few tantalising feet when Blue stumbled on an old tree trunk on the forest floor that was so green with lichen it was almost invisible. The last thing Poppy heard as Blue somersaulted backwards was Cally's scream as she landed with a sickening crash in the bracken.

1 2

Blue picked herself up, tossed her dished head and galloped away through the pine trees, her reins and mane flying. Poppy dithered for a few seconds, unsure whether to follow the mare or stay with Cally. The sound of the older girl groaning spurred her into action. She scrambled off Beau and ran towards the noise. Cally was sitting on her haunches at the base of a tree, cradling her head in her hands.

'Are you OK?' Poppy asked urgently.

'What?' Cally looked dazed.

'Did you hit your head when you fell?' Poppy said, crouching down next to her.

'How do I know? Anyway, I'm not worried about that. Where's Blue?'

'She's gone, Cally.'

'You're joking. Why didn't you catch her?' Cally stood up shakily and glared at Poppy. When she started swaying Poppy grabbed her elbow and pushed her firmly back down.

'Sit down, for goodness sake. You hold Beau and I'll see if I can find her.'

Cally was about to argue when she saw the determined set of Poppy's jaw. She sank back against the tree and took Beau's reins without a quibble. 'I can't believe I fell off. What an idiot. And why didn't I hang on to the reins? How on earth am I going to tell Nina I've lost her best trekking pony?' she muttered.

Poppy felt an unwelcome twinge of sympathy. 'You won't have to. I don't suppose she's gone far.' She ran her hand down Beau's neck and gave Cally a brief smile. 'I'll find her, I promise.'

~

SHAFTS OF LIGHT played on the acid green bracken as Poppy fought her way through the undergrowth in the direction Blue had disappeared. The smell of earth and decomposing leaf mulch all at once reminded her of the Riverdale wood. Only this time she was looking for Blue and not Cloud and she didn't have Charlie at her side, his face streaked with camouflage paint and a pair of binoculars around his neck as he inspected the ground for big cat paw prints. The seven-year-old would be gutted when he heard he'd missed a close encounter with a whole family of wild boar.

Poppy scanned the trees for any sign of the mare. Cally had looked defeated and much younger than her fourteen years as she'd leant against the trunk of the enormous pine tree. Her bravado, the over-confidence Poppy had found so intimidating from their very first encounter, had completely evaporated. Perhaps it had all been bluster and deep down she was as insecure as Poppy. How ironic that would be.

Broken fronds of bracken brushed Poppy's jodhpurs. When she looked down she realised the vegetation had been trampled and she was following a distinct path through the undergrowth. Her senses on full alert, she heard the mare before she saw her.

'Blue,' she called softly. 'It's OK, I'm here.' Blue was pawing the ground by a fallen tree, her reins entangled in the branches, her neck dark with sweat. Poppy knew that if she startled the mare she could pull back in panic, snap the leather and career off again, her reins dragging danger-ously by her feet. She lowered her eyes and inched towards her, talking in a low murmur, just as she had when she'd approached Cloud in the Riverdale wood. She stole a glance at Blue and saw with relief that she had stopped pawing the ground and was watching her curiously, her velvety brown eyes fixed on Poppy. When she was a couple of paces away Poppy reached in her pocket for a Polo and held out her palm. Blue lowered her head and sniffed suspiciously, her muscles tensed. But it gave Poppy enough time to take hold of her reins and untangle them from the branch.

'Come on, girl. Let's get you back to Cally. I think she's going to be pretty pleased to see you.'

Poppy considered jumping onto the mare and cantering back to Cally and Beau. But the prospect of riding the horse she'd hankered after all week had lost its appeal. Suddenly all she wanted was her level-headed cob.

~

CALLY WAS STILL SITTING with her head in her hands at the base of the pine tree, Beau by her side.

'We're back,' Poppy called. 'I've checked her over and she looks fine. She hasn't even broken her reins. I'd say you've both had a lucky escape.' She pretended not to notice Cally's tear-stained cheeks as she handed Blue's reins back to the older girl. 'I'll hold her for you while you get on,' she offered.

Cally nodded her thanks and mounted Blue. She looked down at Poppy, her blue-grey eyes appraising.

'That was a really brave thing to do. That wild boar could have attacked you both.'

'Oh, I knew Beau would look after me,' Poppy replied lightly. 'Although I think I may have permanently damaged my vocal chords with all the screaming,' she grinned.

Cally was quiet for a while as they headed back through the bracken to the path.

'I think I may have been wrong about you,' she said eventually.

'What do you mean?'

'I thought you were stuck-up and standoffish. Poppy the Ice Maiden.'

Poppy giggled. 'That's funny, because I thought you were a massive show off with an ego the size of Texas.'

'Why Texas?' Cally asked, her mouth twitching.

'Oh, I don't know. It was the first place I thought of. And Texas is pretty big.' Poppy paused. 'Anyway, I'm not stuck-up, Cally. It's shyness. People always think I'm being unfriendly but I'm really not. I just find meeting new people terrifying. And before I know it they've made up their minds about me. Like you obviously did.'

'Maybe you're right,' Cally conceded. 'Mum's always telling me not to be so quick to judge. Scarlett's so open and friendly. She's the complete opposite of you. I couldn't for the life of me work out how you ended up best friends.'

'That's because she didn't give me a chance to be shy.' Poppy recalled the day Scarlett had first turned up at Riverdale, her bubbly personality cancelling out Poppy's natural diffidence. Then she remembered that she and Scarlett weren't speaking and looked down at Beau's unruly mane in despair.

'I thought you'd made friends with Scarlett just to annoy me.'

'That's so not true,' Cally retorted. 'I made friends with Scarlett because she's good company and we have a laugh together.'

'I see that now. And you've got a good taste in friends. Scarlett's the best,' Poppy replied, a catch in her throat.

Cally smiled sympathetically. 'You two'll make up, don't worry. If it's any consolation, Scarlett has spent the whole holiday trying to convince me what an amazing person you are.'

Poppy found that hard to believe, but it was kind of Cally to say so. 'Anyway, now we've decided that I'm not a stuck up ice maiden and you're not a big fat show off, shall we start again? Friends?' she asked.

'Friends,' Cally confirmed.

They continued without talking until they saw the others on the brow of a hill. Poppy broke the silence.

'I don't think we should tell Nina what happened back there. Just tell her I'd gone further than you thought.'

'Are you sure?'

'Definitely. There's no point worrying her. She's got enough on her plate at the moment.'

Cally smiled gratefully. 'Thanks, Poppy.'

Nina held her finger to her lips as they caught up with the others. They were all staring into the valley below. Poppy and Cally followed their gaze and saw a small herd of fallow deer grazing in front of the next band of woodland. Above them a large bird of prey glided over the clearing, its white body flecked with black.

'A goshawk. Probably a female, judging by the size,' whispered Nina.

'The females are much bigger than the males. This time of year she'll be hunting for her young. She probably has a nest somewhere nearby.'

'What's she hunting for?' asked Poppy.

'She'll catch anything from rabbits and squirrels to crows and pigeons. She's even powerful enough to kill a pheasant.'

They watched the deer grazing and the goshawk soaring high above until the horses started fidgeting.

'Come on, I know the perfect place for our picnic,' said Nina, gathering McFly's reins. 'We've probably had our wildlife fix for today.'

'I wanted to see a wild boar,' Jack grumbled to his sister as they followed Nina and McFly back into the trees. 'Deer and hawks are alright, but that would have been awesome.'

Scarlett, riding beside Cally, was puzzled to see the older girl giving Poppy a conspiratorial smile. She arched her eyebrows in surprise.

'What were you and Poppy grinning about? I thought you couldn't stand each other,' she quizzed.

'Oh, it turns out we were wrong and you were right,' Cally replied. 'I'll tell you all about it over lunch.'

13

All too soon their last ride had come to an end and they were clip-clopping down the lane towards the yard. Although the others were being picked up by their parents before dinner, Poppy's dad had arranged with Nina for her and Scarlett to stay an extra night so he could collect the two girls the following morning on his way back from London.

The yard was a picture of activity as they all dismounted and tied up their horses. Lydia's childminder dropped the four-year-old off and Lydia led Frank around the yard saying goodbye to everyone. Poppy broke away from sponging Beau's sweaty saddle marks to watch people untack and brush down their horses. Chloe looked tearful as she smothered Rusty with kisses. Poppy knew she would be going back to her weekly riding lessons, her yearning for a pony of her own stronger than ever. Jess's arms were flung around Willow's neck, her face buried in the mare's black mane. Even Jack looked subdued as he said goodbye to Rocky. At least the brother and sister had the elderly Magic waiting for them at home. Cally and Scarlett were swapping mobile phone numbers and email addresses.

'Are you going to miss us, Poppy?' said a high-pitched voice, and she looked around to see Lydia and Frank behind her. The Shetland walked straight up to Beau and started nibbling Poppy's quick release knot.

'Come here, you monster!' commanded Lydia, echoing her mum the day they'd arrived and Frank had been caught in the hay barn. Poppy smiled. Time was so elastic, she thought, as she dipped the sponge in a bucket of water and ran it over Beau's back. In some ways it felt as though they'd only arrived that morning, yet she was already so deeply embedded in the Oaklands routine that she felt as though she'd been there for months.

'Are you?' Lydia repeated.

'Well, I can't wait to see my own pony. And it'll be nice to be home. But do you know what? I will miss you,' she said, watching Beau nuzzle Frank's bushy mane. 'All of you.'

Jess and Jack's mum drove up in a people carrier, and the brother and sister were sent indoors to pack. Chloe's dad was next to arrive. He virtually had to prise the ten-year-old away from Rusty with promises of new jodhpurs and a trip to Olympia. Poppy was saying goodbye to Jess and Chloe when a rusty VW camper van lurched up the track and stopped at the gate. Spray-painted a lurid purple, the van had been so completely plastered in daisy car transfers it looked as though it was suffering from a bad attack of the measles.

A slim blonde woman who could have passed for Cally's older sister sprang out of the driver's side. Her hair was tied in two long plaits and she wore a baggy, hand-knitted jumper in rainbow stripes, a long, faded denim skirt and scuffed brown boots. Poppy remembered Scarlett telling her that Cally's mum was a part-time carer and that they struggled to make ends meet. Cally must have worked hard for months to save up for the few days at Oaklands. Poppy realised how galling it must have been for the older girl when she found out Poppy had won the holiday just for writing a story.

Poppy slipped into the barn and stuck her head over the door of Blue's loose box. Cally was brushing tendrils of bracken from the mare's tail.

'Cally, your mum's here.'

Cally looked up, dismayed. 'Already?'

''Fraid so. She's talking to Nina.'

Poppy stroked Blue's dished head. 'I'm glad we sorted everything out this afternoon.'

Cally dropped the dandy brush she'd been using into the box of grooming kit and joined Poppy by the loose box door.

'It's just as well. Scarlett has invited me down to the farm for a week in the summer holidays. You two can show me around.'

'That's if Scarlett is still speaking to me,' Poppy said gloomily.

'Don't worry. Apparently these things have a habit of working out. That's the old cliché you trotted out the other day, anyway,' Cally grinned.

'Very funny, I'm sure.'

Cally handed Poppy the grooming kit, her face suddenly solemn. 'Tell my mum I'll be over in a minute. I want to say goodbye to Blue.'

~

SCARLETT'S HAZEL eyes were downcast as they said their farewells.

'I'll be down before you know it. You can show me all the best rides on Dartmoor,' said Cally, giving her a hug.

Poppy caught the older girl's eye. 'Good luck. I hope you find your prizewinning showjumper.'

'Yeah, well, you never know.' Cally turned to her mum. 'I'm going to miss Blue so much. I thought I'd ask Rose for some extra hours so I can start saving for a holiday next year.'

Poppy's buoyant mood plummeted. In all the drama she'd forgotten about the debt collector. If Nina was right, Oaklands wouldn't be in business next week, let alone next year. Blue would be sold, along with Topaz, McFly, Rusty, Rocky and the others. She realised with a pang that Frank and Beau would be split up, and she wondered how Beau would cope without his pint-sized alter ego. She glanced at Nina. She was smiling and making small talk with Cally's mum but she looked strained, as though she was carrying the weight of the world on her shoulders. Poppy was full of admiration for her. Despite the fact that her world was about to fall apart, she was holding it all together.

But only just.

14

Scarlett and Nina were both silent over dinner, wrapped up in their own thoughts. Poppy struggled to keep the conversation going and, once they'd cleared the plates away and stacked the dishwasher, offered to do the final check on the horses so she could escape the oppressive atmosphere.

'That would be great, thanks Poppy. I need to watch the weather forecast,' said Nina. Scarlett left the kitchen wordlessly, heading in the direction of the lounge, and Poppy let herself out of the back door. The air was still and silent and the sweet smell of honeysuckle hung heavily. All the horses were in the barn except Frank, who was grazing in the small paddock at the far end of the yard. Poppy could just make out his dark outline under the old oak tree. She pulled open the double doors of the barn, breathing in the familiar smell of warm horse, and walked the length of the barn, running her eyes over each horse and pony until she was satisfied they were all well. The last loose box she reached was Beau's. He was lying in the straw, his feathered legs tucked neatly beneath him and his whiskered chin resting on his knee as he dozed.

Poppy leant on his door, watching his flanks gently rise and fall. As if he sensed her presence, the cob opened his wall eye and whickered. Poppy swung around, assuming Frank must have let himself out of his paddock and followed her in, but the Shetland was nowhere to be seen. A gust of wind blew through the half-open double doors, banging them against the inside wall of the barn. McFly whinnied in alarm and Poppy backtracked to his loose box. The thoroughbred looked fretfully over his door.

'It's OK,' she soothed, stroking his nose. 'It's just the wind picking up. There's going to be a storm tonight, but you'll be safe in here.'

Slate grey clouds had appeared on the horizon by the time Poppy pulled the barn doors closed and as she crossed the yard to the back door of the bungalow a few fat raindrops began to fall. She found Nina in her study, glued to the weather, her face anxious.

'They've upped the severe weather warnings from amber to red,' she told Poppy. 'Were the horses alright?'

'All present and correct,' said Poppy. 'The barn doors were rattling in the wind so I've bolted them shut.' She stifled a yawn. 'I think I might head off to bed. It's been a long day.'

'Thank-you, Poppy. I'm going to turn in soon, too. Lydia's bound to have me up in the night. She hates thunder.'

Poppy poked her head around the door of the lounge on her way to the bedroom. Scarlett was sitting slouched on one end of the sofa, her feet on the oak coffee table, apparently engrossed in a quiz show. Poppy dithered by the door for a minute, her stomach in knots. Then she came to a decision and marched into the room. Perching on the coffee table, she grabbed the remote control and turned off the television.

'Can we *please* stop fighting now?' she asked. 'I'll promise to stop whinging if you promise to stop sulking. Call it quits?'

Scarlett dragged her eyes away from the screen. She was frowning.

'There's something I need to say first,' she said.

'Oh, right.' Poppy wondered what she'd done wrong now. 'What is it?'

'I'm sorry. I'm sorry I've spent so much of the holiday with Cally, especially as I wouldn't even be here if you hadn't invited me. I'm sorry I was so touchy about Topaz. Most of all I'm sorry I didn't accept your apology. I've been a terrible friend and I wouldn't blame you for hating me.'

Poppy felt the knots vanish and she grinned. 'Scar, you idiot! Of course I don't hate you. I know I've been a pain, too. Let's forget all about it.'

'Cally told me what happened this morning. You were really brave, Poppy.'

'It wasn't me, it was Beau. When he stood up to the wild boar she realised she'd met her match and scarpered. It wasn't as dangerous as it sounds.'

'And Cally says you two have finally made friends.'

Poppy smiled sheepishly and sat next to Scarlett. 'Yes. It turns out you were right about us both, if you must know. How annoying you must find it, being right all the time.'

Scarlett smirked. 'You get used to it.'

Poppy turned the television back on and soon they were convulsed in giggles, shouting out inane answers to the questions fired at contestants by the heavily spray-tanned quiz show host.

As the credits rolled at the end of the programme Poppy groaned, clutching her sides theatrically. 'That was fun, but I suppose we ought to get to bed.'

The rain was lashing against their bedroom window by the time they climbed into their bunks. Poppy shivered. It felt more like January than the beginning of June.

'I'm glad we're friends again,' said Scarlett.

Poppy pulled her duvet under her chin. 'Me too.'

'Bet you can't wait to see Cloud.'

She wriggled her toes in anticipation. 'No, I can't. Let's go out for a ride the minute we get back.'

'Good plan. I've enjoyed riding in the forest but do you know what? It's not a patch on Dartmoor,' said Scarlett.

'I agree.' Poppy pictured Cloud's pricked grey ears in front of her as they cantered across the moor, past rocky tors and black-faced sheep. She wondered if he'd missed her as much as she'd missed him. The wind battered the walls of the bungalow and she could hear the oak tree creaking. She yawned into the darkness.

"Night Scarlett.'

"Night Poppy, see you in the morning.'

As FATE and the weather would have it, they didn't have to wait that long. A rumble of thunder, followed by the sound of Lydia wailing, dragged both girls from their dreams.

Poppy sat up groggily and checked her alarm clock. Ten to two in the morning.

'Did you hear that? It sounded like it was right over our heads,' exclaimed Scarlett, swinging her legs over the side of the bunk bed.

Suddenly their room was lit by a flash of lightning which illuminated Scarlett's bare feet as they dangled in front of Poppy's face. Scarlett climbed out of bed and raced to the window.

'Quick, count how many seconds before it thunders. See how far away the storm is,' she said.

Together they counted to ten before a long, loud rumble reverberated around the room. 'Ten miles,' said Scarlett.

'Dad says that's an old wives' tale,' Poppy told her. 'He says you need to divide the number of seconds by five.'

'Two miles then,' said Scarlett impatiently. 'I *love* thunderstorms.'

'Me too. I'm not sure Lydia would agree with us, though.' The four-year-old had ratcheted up her wailing by several decibels and was now howling at the top of her voice. They could hear Nina murmuring as she tried in vain to settle her.

Another flash of lightning rent the inky sky, followed a few seconds later by a clap of thunder.

'It's getting closer!' exclaimed Scarlett. As she spoke they heard a click and the light in the hallway went out. 'Uh oh. Power cut.'

'I'll ask Nina if she has any candles.' Poppy turned to go but before she reached the door the room was lit by a third strobe of lightning, followed immediately by a deafening crack of thunder. There was a flash of yellow and an ominous creak. Scarlett, her forehead pressed against the window, gasped. When she turned to Poppy her face had drained of all colour.

'The lightning's hit the oak tree!' she cried. Poppy ran to the window. They watched, horrified, as flames shot out of the old tree as though someone had fixed a giant Catherine wheel to its trunk. With a terrifying groan the tree sliced in two and toppled into the yard with a thunderous boom. Then everything went quiet.

Poppy and Scarlett clutched each other, their thoughts in sync.

'The horses!' they cried.

15

Never had Poppy dressed so quickly. Within seconds she was running out of their room, Scarlett on her heels.

'Go and tell Nina what's happened and meet me in the yard,' she panted. Scarlett nodded and they sprinted in opposite directions, Poppy heading for the back door, Scarlett towards Lydia's bedroom. Poppy grabbed a heavy duty torch from the hook by the door and pulled on her jodhpur boots and coat, her stomach liquid with fear. She cursed as she fumbled with the lock which stubbornly refused to open. 'Come on!' she muttered, forcing herself to pause and take a couple of deep breaths before tackling it again. This time the key turned smoothly. She yanked the door open and stared into the dark. Driving rain was coming down in sheets, soaking her to the skin in seconds. Remembering the torch, she flicked it on and followed the beam towards the yard.

The scene that greeted her was like the set of a disaster movie abandoned halfway through filming. The lightning strike had cut the oak in two with a surgeon's precision. One half of the tree had crashed into the hay barn, taking the electricity and phone lines with it. The other half had sheared off and fallen in front of the barn where the horses were stabled, blocking the barn doors and the gate to the drive.

Poppy could hear a horse's frantic neighing over the sound of the rain bouncing off the concrete. She ran over to the doors but a huge branch barred her way. She lowered her shoulder to it and pushed with all her strength, but it was immovable.

'Poppy!'

She looked up at the sound of Nina's voice. She was holding a hysterical Lydia in her arms, Scarlett beside her. All three were drenched. Poppy ducked under the branches and made her way over to them.

'The tree's blocking the barn door. I've tried moving it but it's stuck fast,' she told them.

'The horses'll be safe in there though, won't they?' asked Scarlett.

'They should be. The roof's fine, although the same can't be said for the hay barn,' said Poppy.

Lydia lifted her head from her mum's shoulder and stared at the roof of the hay barn. 'More lightning!' she howled, burying her face in Nina's neck.

They spun around. Poppy felt her blood run cold. The electricity cable severed by the tree was arcing wildly like a demented serpent, the end of it glowing as blindingly white as a magnesium flame in a school science lab. They watched, horrified, as it hissed and fizzed, metres away from the barn full of tinderbox dry hay.

'We need to call the fire brigade!' Scarlett shouted to Nina over the wind and rain.

'We can't! The phone line's down and there's no mobile signal here. And I can't get the jeep out - the tree's blocking the gate.' Nina's voice was shaky.

'There must be something we can do. How far is the nearest house?' shouted Poppy.

'Three miles away. It's the farm we rode past the other day,' Nina reminded them. It seemed like a lifetime ago. 'It'll take almost an hour to walk there, especially in this weather.'

Poppy looked helplessly at Scarlett and then back at the electricity cable twitching and jumping on the roof of the hay barn. Lydia lifted her tear-streaked face again and peered over her mum's shoulder. 'Frank!' she sobbed.

'He'll be OK, he's in the paddock,' Nina soothed, stroking her sodden hair.

'No, Mum! He's here!' she cried, pointing into the dark. The Shetland stepped into the beam of the torch and Lydia wriggled out of her mum's arms and ran to him.

'Wait - who's that behind him?' said Poppy. She raised the torch and her heart gave a funny little skip. A hairy face with a forelock like rats' tails, a pink nose and a blue eye staring dolefully at them emerged before their eyes like a mirage.

'Beau! How on earth -' Nina spluttered.

'Frank must have escaped from the paddock and let Beau out of the barn before the tree came down,' said Scarlett.

Poppy found herself taking two steps forward. The cob whickered and she flung her arms around his neck. She became aware of Nina talking.

' - and I think it should be you, Poppy.'

'What should be me?'

'You need to ride Beau to the farm to get help. I can't leave Lydia, not when she's in this state.'

'What about his tack?' Poppy knew without looking that they couldn't get into the tack room - a branch the size of a small tree pinned the door shut. 'He hasn't even got a headcollar on.'

'I've got a spare headcollar in the house. It's a bit small but it'll do. Scarlett, it's hanging on the coat stand in the hallway. Will you run and get it?'

Scarlett nodded and raced towards the house.

Poppy still wasn't sure. 'I've never ridden bareback before. What if I can't stay on?'

'You'll be fine. Beau'll look after you. Head for the far end of the top field, turn left after you've gone through the gate and follow the line of trees for a couple of miles until you get to the clapper bridge. The farm's straight ahead. Tell Bert and Eileen what's happened and get them to call the fire brigade. Even if their phone line's down I think they get a mobile signal there.'

Scarlett appeared beside them and thrust the headcollar and a frayed lead rope into Poppy's hands. She tried to unfasten the buckle on the headpiece but her fingers were so cold they wouldn't work properly. Scarlett grabbed the headcollar back, slipped it on and fastened the buckle. She clipped the lead rope to the ring on one side, tied the end to the ring on the other and handed the makeshift reins to Poppy, who took them reluctantly.

'I think Scarlett should go. She's a much better rider than me,' she stalled.

'Beau trusts you, Poppy. Just look at him,' said Scarlett. Poppy realised the cob had edged towards her and was nuzzling her hand, his breath warming her freezing fingers, his pink nose as soft as velvet.

Nina broke the silence. 'Listen, we haven't got time to argue. I'll give you a leg up.'

Still Poppy was rooted to the spot.

Scarlett bellowed in her ear. 'Hurry up Poppy! I couldn't bear it if something happened to Topaz.'

The thought of the horses trapped in the barn while the deadly electricity cable was writhing unrestrained a few feet away finally brought her to her senses. She ran around to Beau's near side, put her knee in Nina's cupped hands and grabbed a handful of Beau's mane.

'On the count of three,' Nina shouted. 'One...two...three!' Nina pushed Poppy skywards and she flung her right leg over Beau's back, landing with a jolt. Nina passed her the makeshift reins and she took a hank of mane in each hand and wound it around her fingers.

Nina took a step back. 'So you know where you're going?'

Poppy nodded. 'I think so.'

'You'll have to ride around the back of the barn and over the muck heap. It's the only way out. Good luck. And stay safe.'

Poppy gave the ghost of a smile and clicked her tongue.

'Come on Beau. Let's go.'

16

They trotted out of the yard towards the muck heap, a horseshoe-shaped construction with old railway sleepers stacked five feet high on three sides and piled high with manure. Beau paused at the bottom and Poppy squeezed her legs. 'Come on boy, up you go.' With a grunt he sprang from his hindquarters to the top of the heap. Poppy gasped as she felt herself sliding backwards. She baulked at the sheer drop down the other side of the sleepers to the field but Beau had no such hesitation. He leapt over the edge, landing heavily on the saturated ground. The impact threw Poppy forwards and she clutched his neck, clinging on like ivy. Beau lifted his head, tipping her upright again, and she tightened her grip on the lead rope.

The rain pelted down, gluing her eyelashes together, and she leant forwards and wiped her face on her arm. She knew she had to cross the field diagonally to the gate at the far end but in the dark it was impossible to see where it was. She just had to guess. She kicked Beau into a canter and within seconds he was loping along, his long, rocking-horse strides eating up the ground. She urged him faster and he extended his stride into a gallop. Without thinking Poppy adopted a jockey's position, crouching low over the cob's outstretched neck, her hair plastered to her face.

After a while Beau slowed to a canter and then broke into a trot.

Poppy could just make out the shadow of the post and rail fence that marked the end of Nina's land. She guided Beau along the length of the fence until they reached the gate. Beau stood like a rock as she leant down and groped for the latch. Her hands closed around the cold, hard links of a metal chain and she groaned. She pictured them riding through the gate two days before. It had been padlocked and Nina had had to jump off McFly and open the lock with a key she'd taken from the pocket of her riding jacket. In her panic she'd forgotten to give the key to Poppy.

'What do we do now?' Poppy cried to Beau. 'There's no other way out!' She looked over her shoulder in the direction of the yard, wondering if the electricity cable was already burning through the roof of the hay barn like the glowing tip of a soldering iron scorching through metal. She looked back at the gate. There was no other option.

'We're going to have to jump it, Beau,' she told the cob, swinging him around so they could get a decent approach. She had no idea whether Beau was capable of jumping a five bar gate, let alone whether or not she'd be able to stay on bareback. Would he even be able to see the gate in the dark? But they had to try. She kicked him back into a canter and whispered, 'Come on boy, you can do this.'

Beau's ears were pricked as he cantered towards the gate. Poppy sat quietly, trying to keep her centre of balance in line with Beau's. The cob pushed off from his hind legs and suddenly they were soaring over the gate with centimetres to spare. Both terrified and exhilarated, Poppy leaned forwards, her hands tangled in his long mane. All too soon Beau was landing on the wet ground. Adrenalin was pumping through Poppy's veins and she found herself punching the air. Beau shook his big head and picked up a canter.

'You clever, clever boy,' Poppy told him. 'Now we need to follow the trees.' She squeezed with her right leg and Beau veered left. They thundered on, galloping parallel to the wood. Poppy tried to picture the layout of the land. But she'd been in such a strop the day they'd ridden back through the farm that she'd paid hardly any attention. She had no idea where the bridge was in relation to the trees.

'I'm such an idiot, Beau,' she muttered.

They galloped on. Poppy almost lost her balance when Beau swerved to avoid a deer which bounded out of the trees a few feet in front of them.

'Hello dear!' she shouted, laughing slightly manically. The deer stopped and watched the girl and horse as they flew past.

There was a maelstrom of noise pulsing through her head. The pounding of the unrelenting rain was melding with the beat of Beau's hooves as he galloped through the mud. On top of this Poppy became aware of another sound. If she was not mistaken it was the roar of rushing water. They must be approaching the river.

'Whoa, Beau. Steady now,' she said softly, and the piebald cob slowed his pace to a walk. He was blowing hard and Poppy untangled her right hand from his mane and stroked his neck. The whoosh of the river was getting louder and soon they were standing on its bank. Squinting into the dark, Poppy could just make out the torrent of water as it surged past.

'We need to follow the river to the bridge,' she told Beau, and they turned right and continued until they reached the clapper bridge. Built from large slabs of stone resting on a single stone pillar in the middle of the water, the bridge was around two metres wide and six metres long. Poppy remembered Nina telling them as they rode across that it was almost four hundred years old. Beau stopped at the edge of the bridge. Poppy squeezed her legs. He took a step forward, his hoof making a brittle chime as his metal shoe hit the stone slab. He hesitated, his head high as he sniffed the air. Poppy could feel his muscles tense and she squeezed again.

'Just across the bridge and we're almost there!' she shouted over the wind and rain. But Beau stepped backwards, almost unseating Poppy. She clicked her tongue and pushed him on with her heels. 'We're running out of time! Come *on* Beau!' she urged.

For a fraction of a second the cob wavered. Poppy seized her chance and kicked again. He pitched forwards onto the bridge.

Beau felt the stone slab move a beat before Poppy did and he tried frantically to backtrack onto solid ground. But the rain-sodden field was too wet, too slippery, for his hooves to gain any purchase. Time stood still as the old stone bridge wobbled for a few terrifying seconds. And then Poppy and Beau were plunging headfirst into the swirling water below.

17

Nina had watched Poppy and Beau disappear out of the yard hoping she hadn't sent them on a fool's errand. Scarlett stood next to her, gazing into the darkness.

'Do you think they'll be alright? It's pitch black out there. There aren't even any stars. How on earth will they know where they're going?' she fretted.

'Horses can see better in the dark than we can. And Beau knows the way. I trust him with my life. Don't worry, Scarlett. He'll look after her.'

Scarlett was unconvinced but said nothing. Nina looked around the yard, assessing the damage. The electricity cable was still convulsing sporadically but there was no sign of fire. She was more worried about the horses. The crashing and banging from their barn could easily be heard over the sound of the wind and rain. Every now and then one would whinny, setting the others off. At least Lydia had calmed down now the thunder had stopped and was crouched beside Frank, her face buried in his tufty mane.

'There must be a way I can get into the barn. I need to settle the horses before they do themselves any damage,' Nina said.

But the huge branch blocking the barn door was an impenetrable mass of solid oak wood that was strong enough to build warships from.

'Do you have a chainsaw?' Scarlett asked. 'I've watched Dad use ours hundreds of times. It looks easy enough.'

Nina shook her head. 'There's an old handsaw in the garage. I'll go and find it.'

The blade of the saw was riddled with rust. The rain had made the branch slippery and it was almost impossible to get a rhythm going. They worked silently, taking it in turns when the muscles in their arms started burning but after half an hour, when they'd failed to cut even a couple of centimetres through the oak, Scarlett flung the saw on the ground.

'This is pointless,' she shouted to Nina over the rain. 'Let's hope Poppy's having more luck.'

THE WATER WAS SO cold it took Poppy's breath away. She gasped for air, choking as she sucked in a mouthful of muddy river water. The sound of rushing water filled her ears and she fought for breath, her chest heaving. Her hands felt as if they were lashed together by rope and she tried to pull them free from their bindings, panic rising. It was seconds before she realised groggily that the ties were strands of Beau's mane, which were wound around her fingers like seaweed. By some miracle she was still on his back. She gripped tighter as the cob kicked for the riverbank, his head raised above the raging river. Completely disorientated, she had no idea which side they should be heading for. But Beau seemed to know. She could feel his legs moving under the water as the river flowed past. Poppy pictured a duck gliding on a mirror-flat pond, its face serene as its yellow webbed feet paddled furiously below the surface. Nice weather for ducks.

'Get a grip,' she muttered. They were drifting downstream and Poppy sensed that Beau was tiring. 'You can do it, Beau!' she shouted. 'Come on boy, we're nearly there.' Beau quickened his kicking. At last, with a herculean effort, he lunged for the riverbank and she cried out with relief as she felt his feet dig into the solid riverbed. He heaved himself out of the water, Poppy still clinging on, and gave an almighty shake that made her teeth rattle.

Beau was trembling beneath her. She ran her hand down his neck. 'You brave, brave boy,' she whispered. Nina was right. He had the heart of a lion. How had she been so blind? She stared through the gloom in the direction of the farm. A faint light glowed in the distance.

'We're almost there, Beau. Not far now.' She squeezed her legs and the cob broke into a steady canter. Poppy's saturated clothes clung to her body and she could still taste the gritty river water. Soon they reached the gate where Poppy had fallen off. For the first time that night luck was on their side. The gate was swinging open and they cantered through. The clatter of Beau's shoes on the concrete farmyard floor was a welcome sound. But the knot of fear had returned to her stomach with a vengeance. What if they were too late? Was fire already sweeping through the barn, obliterating everything in its path?

THE LIGHT she'd seen from the riverbank was coming from a single over-head lamp in the corrugated steel farm building to her left. The building was full of Friesian cows.

'Hello!' called Poppy. But her voice was drowned out by the plaintive mooing of the cattle. She cleared her throat and tried again. 'Hello!' she yelled. 'Is there anybody there?'

There was a volley of barking and an elderly man appeared from around the side of the barn, a border collie skulking behind him.

'Are you Bert?' Poppy asked.

'Aye, that's me,' said the man, who was ninety if he was a day. He motioned the dog to lie down and slowly crossed the yard to Poppy. 'What's up, lass?'

'Nina sent me. You need to call the police. I mean the fire brigade. The oak tree's been struck by lightning and it's fallen down. The horses are trapped in the barn. And the tree's brought the electricity and phone lines down, too,' Poppy gabbled.

'The oak tree, you say?' said Bert, his face ponderous.

'Yes, the oak. The horses are trapped.' Poppy repeated. 'And the electricity cable is sparking. It's about to set fire to the hay barn. We need to phone the fire brigade.'

'There's a problem there, lass. Our phone line is down, too.'

'Nina said you get a mobile signal here. Do you have a mobile phone?'

Poppy asked, realising she'd forgotten to bring one with her. She slid off Beau, hugged him briefly and went to stand in front of Bert.

'Aye, we do. Our Stuart bought it for us in case of emergencies. I expect Eileen will know where it is,' he said.

'This *is* an emergency!' shrieked Poppy, finally losing her patience. 'Please, we need to be quick!'

'Calm down, lass, I hear you. You'd better follow me,' Bert said, heading for the back door of the farmhouse. He let himself in and called up the stairs, 'Eileen! Where do you keep the mobile telephone?'

Poppy jiggled from one foot to the other as she waited by the back door. After an age a white-haired woman in a long, cotton nightie and a coral pink polyester dressing gown appeared. Her faded grey eyes widened when she saw Poppy standing on the doorstep.

'What's happened, love?' she asked.

'Nina's oak has been struck by lightning. We need to call the fire brigade on your mobile phone,' Poppy told her. Eileen nodded and disappeared into the kitchen. She re-appeared a moment later with an ancient mobile the size of a brick. She peered at the keypad myopically. 'I haven't got my glasses on. Can you see the numbers?'

Poppy grabbed the phone and checked for a signal. Three bars. She dialled 999, her index finger jabbing the keypad frantically, her heart pounding. She held the phone to her ear and listened to the dial tone. There was a click and a woman's voice.

'Which emergency service do you require?'

Poppy took a deep breath and spoke as calmly as she could.

'Fire. We need the fire brigade.'

18

The phone call seemed to galvanise Bert. He found Poppy an empty stable for Beau and they gave the bedraggled cob some hay and water. Eileen joined them in the yard, wearing a worn waterproof jacket over her dressing gown, and the three of them climbed into the front of Bert's Land Rover.

'We'll go across the fields. It'll be quicker,' said Bert, turning the ignition.

'We can't,' remembered Poppy. 'The bridge has been washed away.'

'Well I never. They said it would be a bad storm but I can't remember anything like it.' He flicked on the windscreen washers, rammed the gearstick into first and the Land Rover bunny-hopped out of the yard. Poppy realised she was shivering. Eileen reached behind her for a blanket.

'Here, wrap this around you. You must be frozen.'

'I hope we're not too late,' Poppy mumbled, picturing the writhing power cable. 'What if the barn has caught fire?'

'Everything will be fine, don't you worry,' Eileen reassured her.

Bert saw the fire engine's blue flashing lights in his rear-view mirror before they heard its ear-blasting sirens. He pulled into a layby to let it pass. Moments later a second engine hurtled down the flooded lane towards Oaklands. Bert followed the V-shaped wake pattern left by the truck's huge wheels. Relieved that the fire brigade had taken her seriously,

Poppy drummed her fingers on the dashboard as they chugged slowly down the lane. When at last Bert pulled up behind the second fire engine she unclipped her seatbelt and let herself out of the door before the old farmer had even pulled up the handbrake.

Poppy ran past the two fire engines to the gate. It had finally stopped raining and the first blush of dawn was creeping over the horizon, enabling her to see just how much devastation the old oak had caused. One huge bough had splintered the gate like matchwood and the fire crews were forcing their way through the branches to reach the yard. Poppy followed, her eyes on the barn roof. She could see the power cable twitching and jerking but to her relief there was no sign of fire and the barn was still intact. On the other side of the yard Nina and Scarlett had seen the fire engines arrive and were scrambling over branches to reach them, Lydia close behind.

A firefighter in a white helmet strode up to them. After more than twenty years in the fire service, watch manager Mick Goodwin had dealt with the whole gamut of incidents, from motorway pile-ups to house fires. Poppy was immediately reassured by his air of calm competence.

'Is anyone trapped in either of the barns?' he asked Nina.

She shook her head. 'No, just the horses. They're in this one,' she pointed to the barn behind her. 'The other one is filled with hay.'

'What about the house? Is anyone inside?'

'No, it's just Lydia, Scarlett and me. We've been outside trying to keep the horses calm. Poppy went to call you.'

'Control said the tree brought down a power cable,' Mick said, his eyes scanning the yard.

'It's over there, on top of the hay barn. We were terrified it would set the barn on fire,' said Nina.

'Not if we can help it,' Mick replied cheerfully. 'Right, I need you three to stand well clear of the yard. And you,' he added, as Poppy joined them, scratches from the oak's branches vivid on her pale face.

The firefighter beckoned one of his crew over and, heads bent, they discussed their plan of attack. Nina ushered the three girls towards the bungalow. Scarlett was holding Lydia's hand, her freckled face serious. 'The horses have been terrified. Can you hear McFly crashing about? I'm surprised he hasn't kicked the barn down. Nina found an old handsaw in the garage and we've been trying to cut through the branches so we could let them out but it was so blunt it was next to useless.' She looked around her. 'Where's Beau?'

'I left him at the farm. Bert and Eileen drove me here once we'd called the fire brigade. They're here somewhere.' Poppy desperately wanted to tell her friend about the ride to the farm but now wasn't the time. Mick came over and spoke to Nina.

'We've put a call into control to ask the power company to isolate the electrical supply. Our priority now is to rescue the horses. We'll use chainsaws to clear the branches from the barn door and then we'll need your help to lead them to safety. Is there a field we can use?'

Nina nodded. 'We'll put them in the top field. They'll be safe there.'

'Once the horses are out of the way we'll need to use the jets to damp down the hay barn in case there are any hot spots. The smallest ember can smoulder for days before igniting and the last thing we want is for fire to break out once we've gone,' said Mick. He saw the worry on Nina's face. 'I'm afraid the hay'll be water-damaged but at least the barn will be safe, and your insurance will cover the loss.'

Poppy wondered when Nina had last been able to afford to pay her insurance premiums. Not recently, judging by her resigned expression. 'At least the horses are OK,' she whispered and Nina gave her a wan smile. 'You're right, Poppy. At least the horses are OK.'

Soon the sound of neighing was drowned out by the roar of three chainsaws. The firefighters worked quickly and efficiently, cutting through the wide branches like butter and stacking them on a growing pile by the muck heap. Eileen appeared clutching mugs of tea, which Nina and the girls took gratefully. 'Look at you, you're all soaked to the skin. Go and change into dry clothes,' she scolded, batting away Nina's protests with an impatient wave of her hand. 'You'll be no use to anyone with hyperthermia. And look at Lydia, the poor lamb. She's shivering.'

By the time they returned in dry clothes the firefighters had cleared enough of a gap for them to open the barn doors and lead the horses to the top field.

'We'll take McFly, Blue and Rusty first, then we'll come back for Willow, Rocky and Topaz. Lydia, you stay here with Eileen,' instructed Nina. The firefighters turned off the chainsaws and Poppy, Scarlett and Nina each grabbed a headcollar from the row of hooks inside the barn door. Topaz whinnied when she saw Scarlett. McFly was drenched in sweat, his brown eyes anxious as he paced restlessly around his loose box. Poppy let herself into Blue's box. The Arab mare was jumpy and she talked to her quietly as she put on her headcollar. She pictured Cloud, safe with Chester in the stable they shared at Riverdale, oblivious to the drama at Oaklands. It was impossible to believe she'd be back with him in a few hours. Nina was struggling to put McFly's headcollar on. Every time she reached up to pass the strap over his ears he shot his head high in the air and wheeled around in a panic. Blue seemed calmer and Poppy tied her up and crossed the barn to McFly's loose box.

'What can I do to help?' she asked Nina, who was dwarfed by the big bay thoroughbred. He was trembling with fear and reminded Poppy of a coiled spring ready to explode. Nina, on the other hand, was totally unfazed. Coping with more than half a ton of panicking horse was second nature to her and Poppy was in awe of her composure.

'Bring Blue over. She might calm him down,' Nina replied with a quick smile.

Poppy untied Blue and led her over to McFly. The grey mare whickered quietly, the sound soft, low and reassuring in the high-ceilinged barn. The gelding stopped his pacing and took two cautious steps forwards, extending his neck so he could blow into Blue's nose. Nina stroked his neck, working her way up to his withers, which she kneaded gently, talking to him all the while. McFly's breathing slowed and he dropped his head and took a couple more steps forwards. Nina slipped the headcollar over his head and fastened the strap.

'Good lad,' she said, patting his neck. 'Let's get you out of here.'

Once they'd turned the three horses out in the field they returned for Willow, Rocky and Topaz. Poppy took Willow, marvelling at how calm she was, despite the commotion. Scarlett looked tearful as she smothered Topaz with kisses and Poppy knew her friend would be dreading the moment she had to say goodbye. As she led Willow past Beau's empty box she hoped he didn't think she'd abandoned him. That was too terrible to contemplate, especially after he'd risked his life for her. Then again, she thought fondly, picturing the unconventional piebald cob working his way through half a bale of hay in Bert's stable, as long as he had plenty to eat he'd be absolutely fine. All of a sudden she realised what a big Beau-sized hole he was going to leave in her life and her throat constricted.

'Your Beau is a hero,' she told Willow thickly. The little dun mare cocked an ear back to listen. 'I spent the entire holiday moaning about him, and tonight he saved my life. I would have drowned if it hadn't been for Beau.' The mare gave her a friendly nudge and Poppy sniffed loudly. Nina had already reached the field gate with Rocky and was looking back to see where they were. Poppy rubbed her eyes and led Willow towards them.

'I've been a prize idiot, Willow. An absolute, utter idiot.'

The top of an unashamedly gilded sun had appeared over the horizon, turning the dawn sky the same shade of coral pink as Eileen's dressing gown. Four of the firefighters were using their jet hoses to damp down the hay barn while three had picked up their chainsaws again and had started clearing the branches from the five bar gate.

Mick Goodwin looked at his watch. 'It's six o'clock. We shouldn't be here much longer.'

'Thank you so much for everything.' Nina looked shattered. 'I don't know what we would have done without you.'

'Just doing our job,' smiled Mick. 'An engineer from the power company is on his way so hopefully you won't be without electricity for too long.'

Soon the firefighters were loading their equipment back into their fire engines. They waved at Nina and the girls as they drove away.

'We'll be on our way, too, Nina love,' said Eileen.

'Can I come with you and bring Beau home?' asked Poppy. She knew by rights she should be exhausted but adrenalin was still buzzing around her system and she wasn't ready to crash just yet.

'Are you sure, Poppy?' said Nina. 'At least you can take his tack with you this time.'

'Actually, I'll just take his bridle, thanks. I loved riding him bareback. He was as comfy as an armchair,' Poppy grinned. 'But we might be a while. The clapper bridge has collapsed into the river so we'll have to go along the lanes.'

'The clapper bridge? How on earth did you manage to reach the farm?' said Nina, her eyebrows raised.

'We swam, of course,' called Poppy over her shoulder as she headed for the Land Rover, Beau's bridle on her shoulder and her ponytail swinging jauntily.

∽

BEAU HAD DEMOLISHED the small mountain of hay they'd given him and was dozing in his borrowed stable, his whiskery bottom lip drooping. Poppy rested her elbows on the stable door and watched him sleep. He twitched every now and then and she wondered if he was dreaming about their adventure. She wished with all her heart that she could turn the clock back and start the week over. What would her wise old friend Tory have said?

'Never judge a book by its cover,' she whispered. Beau opened his wall eye at the sound of her voice and whickered softly. Poppy smiled, let herself into his stable and wrapped her arms around his neck.

'I'm going to miss you, Beautiful Beau,' she said. He nibbled her pocket and she laughed.

'OK, OK, I'll see if I've got any.' She reached into her pocket for a packet of Polos but instead found the card the man in the silver saloon had given her the day before. She pulled it out and read the black print.

Dunster and Deakins
Financial Asset Investigation Specialists
'Always happy to help'

'Always happy to help!' cried Poppy, outraged. 'Happy to help ruin people's lives, more like. Poor Nina.' Poppy tore the card into tiny pieces and shoved them back in her pocket. Beau sighed loudly as he realised that the Polos he'd been hoping for were unlikely to be forthcoming anytime soon. He stood patiently while Poppy slipped on his bridle and led him out of the stable to an old wooden picnic table, which she used as an improvised mounting block.

The dawn chorus was in full voice as Poppy and Beau ambled down the lane towards Oaklands. Poppy wondered whether she ought to tell Nina about the man's visit but decided against it. It was the last thing Nina needed after the night she'd had. Before long they were turning up the track towards the bungalow. Nina and Scarlett had been busy clearing the pieces of smashed gate and had fashioned a make-do barrier with three jumping poles tied in place with baler twine. Poppy slid off Beau and led him through the narrow gate at the end of Nina's front garden. She found Scarlett sitting on a bale of hay, her face glum.

'What's up?' Poppy said, sitting down beside her. Beau began pulling wisps of hay from the end of the bale.

'Nina's just told me about the business going belly-up. It's awful, Poppy. What's going to happen to the horses?'

'I don't know. But I'm sure they'll all go to good homes,' she said, not believing it for a minute.

'Imagine how hard it's going to be for Nina. She hasn't even told Lydia yet. I know I moan about Mum and Dad not having much money, but at least we own the farm. No-one can ever take that away from us. And it's not like it's Nina's fault. She's just been really unlucky. Why does every-thing have to be so unfair?'

They watched silently as Frank crossed the yard to Beau, greeting him like a long lost brother.

'Where is Nina?' asked Poppy.

'Putting Lydia to bed. She was going to try and have a nap, too. What time's your dad picking us up?'

'Mid-morning, I think. So that gives us a couple of hours at least.' Poppy surveyed the yard. The firemen had cleared the biggest branches but the concrete was covered in leaves and twigs, the untidy detritus of the storm. 'Shall we have a tidy up?'

'That's a great idea. It'll take my mind off saying goodbye to Topaz. You put Beau and Frank in the field and I'll find a couple of brooms.'

They spent the next two hours sweeping the yard and mucking out the loose boxes. They filled hayracks and water buckets and mixed the evening feeds following the list Nina had pinned to the door of the tack room. By the time they'd finished Poppy was light-headed with exhaustion but she smiled with satisfaction as she emptied the wheelbarrow on the muck heap for the last time.

'It'll do Nina good to have a day off. It must be such hard work looking after this place and Lydia all on her own,' she said, picking up a broom that she'd left leaning against the wall of the barn.

'It's not going to be for much longer though, is it?' Scarlett replied despondently. 'Come on, let's go and find something to eat. I'm starving.'

They were halfway across the yard when they heard a car turn into the track.

'Must be my dad,' said Poppy, checking her watch. It was almost noon. They walked over to the makeshift gate, expecting to see her dad's blue estate car. Poppy's face fell when she saw the bonnet of a silver saloon bumping down the track towards them. The sun was glinting off the windscreen so she couldn't see the driver's face, but she didn't need to. She knew exactly who he was.

And she had a feeling there was no avoiding him this time.

20

Poppy fingered the tiny scraps of card in her pocket. 'Scarlett, can you go and wake Nina? Tell her the man's come back.'

'What man? Poppy, what's going on?'

'It's the debt collector, Scar. I managed to fob him off the other day but this time I don't think he's going to go until he's seen her.'

Appalled, Scarlett looked over to the car. The man in the shiny suit let himself out of the driver's side and stretched his back. There was a loud clunk as he swung the door shut. Clipboard in hand, he made his way over to the two girls. Scarlett melted away towards the bungalow and Poppy took a deep breath and greeted him, her hand on the broom handle, her face impassive.

'Mr Dunster? Or is it Mr Deakins? Or perhaps it's neither. Perhaps you're just a gofer sent by the bosses to ruin people's lives?'

Completely wrong-footed, the man gazed around uneasily. Poppy found his discomfort empowering. Suddenly she was enjoying herself.

'So Mr D - you don't mind me calling you that, do you?' she smiled sweetly. 'How can I help? I'm *always* happy to help, but then so are you, aren't you?'

'Erm, is Mrs Goddard available?' he asked, clutching his clipboard in front of him like a shield.

'I'm sure she'll be along in a moment. So, tell me, is there much job satisfaction in your line of work?'

'Well, yes, there is. I find it very rewarding, as a matter of fact,' he said, looking towards the bungalow nervously.

'Rewarding! You find turning people's lives upside down *rewarding*? I've heard it all now,' Poppy fumed.

'Look, I haven't got time to stand here and discuss this with you, young lady. I'll go and see if I can find her myself,' the man said, ducking under the top pole. Unfortunately, Scarlett had been distracted when she'd looped the baler twine around the jumping pole and gate post. As he crouched down his back jarred the pole and the knot slipped undone. The heavy pole fell, clouting his head on the way down. Poppy watched, open-mouthed, as the man in the shiny suit collapsed on the floor, knocked out cold.

∾

SHE WAS WONDERING what to do when Nina ran over to them, Scarlett close behind. Scarlett took in shiny suit man lying prostrate on the ground and Poppy standing over him, clutching the broom handle tightly, and her face went white.

'Oh my God, Poppy, have you killed him?' she squawked.

Poppy shot her a bemused look, then realised how it might look. 'No, you twit!' she said. 'He banged his head on your pole, actually. Anyway, he's not dead. I can see his chest moving.'

Nina was kneeling down, checking his airway and feeling his pulse. She rolled him expertly into the recovery position and gave his shoulder a gentle shake. He groaned, opened his eyes and looked around him in a daze.

'You've had a bump to the head,' Nina told him. 'Up you get.' She held out a hand and he grasped it gratefully. He struggled to his feet, his hand holding the back of his head gingerly. She handed him his clipboard and said in a resigned voice, 'We'd better go inside. I'd rather get this over and done with as quickly as possible.'

Shiny suit man looked surprised. 'You know why I'm here?'

'Of course I do. I don't know who's sent you, but I know what you want. The problem is, I haven't got any left.'

The man looked even more bewildered and consulted his clipboard in an effort to hide his confusion. 'Any what left?' he asked.

'Money. I haven't got any money left. You'll have to declare me bankrupt to stand a chance of getting a penny.'

'I'm sorry Mrs Goddard, but I think you may have confused me with someone else. I don't want your money. I'm from Dunster and Deakins. We're financial asset investigation specialists. I work for the probate research side of the business. My job is to trace living descendants of people who have died intestate.'

Nina looked as nonplussed as Poppy felt. What on earth was he talking about? But Scarlett was jumping from one foot to the other, a huge grin spreading across her face as his words sank in.

'I don't believe it,' she shouted. 'You're an heir hunter, aren't you? Nina, you know what this means, don't you?'

Nina looked from Scarlett to shiny suit man and back again and shook her head. 'No, I don't. Will somebody *please* tell me what's going on?'

'Of course. But first, is there somewhere we can sit down? I'm still feeling rather faint,' said the man.

Nina nodded. 'Follow me.'

～

SOON THEY WERE SITTING around the kitchen table, mugs of tea in front of them.

'First, let me introduce myself properly. My name is Graham Deakins and I'm a partner in Dunster and Deakins. My particular area of expertise is genealogy, that is the study of family history. Most genealogists trace people's ancestors, but I specialise in tracing people's descendants.'

He paused, checking he had everyone's attention. Poppy couldn't work out why Scarlett was still grinning like an idiot. He took a quick sip of tea and continued.

'Every year thousands of people in the UK die without making a will. It's called dying intestate. Often these people leave large amounts of cash or property which, if not claimed by living relatives, goes to the Government.

'Probate detectives - or heir hunters as some people call us - seek out the families of people who have died without leaving a will. Most of the people I trace don't even realise their relatives existed. And it's a double shock when they find out they are entitled to some - or even all - of a long-lost relative's estate.'

Graham Deakins took a stripy handkerchief from the top pocket of his jacket and ran it across his brow. 'Was your mother's maiden name Winterbottom?' he asked Nina.

Poppy could see that the sudden change of tack had flummoxed her.

'Yes,' she replied faintly. 'Her name was Margaret Anne Winterbottom. Why?'

'And you're an only child?' he pressed.

'Yes, that's right. So was my mum. But I don't see what that's got to do with anything.'

'Your mum wasn't an only child, Mrs Goddard. Before the war your maternal grandmother, that's Margaret's mother, gave birth to twin boys. One boy, Kenneth, died during the Blitz. He was only two. Six months later his brother Harold was given up for adoption. It seems your grandmother was hospitalised for some kind of breakdown, which isn't surprising after losing a child in such tragic circumstances.'

Nina looked numb. 'Mum never told me.'

'I don't suppose she ever knew. Harold was adopted by a Scottish couple and grew up in Edinburgh. His adoptive father was an engineer who ran a small steelworks on the outskirts of the city. Harold took over the factory when his adoptive father died in the 1970s. It seems he had a head for business and the steelworks made a tidy profit. Harold's adoptive mother died ten years ago at the grand old age of ninety. The couple had no other children and she left everything to her son. Harold - your uncle - never married.'

'My uncle?' wondered Nina. 'I had no idea. I'd love to meet him.'

Graham Deakins' voice was grave. 'I'm afraid that's not possible, Mrs Goddard. Harold died last year. He was seventy five. He'd sold the business and had moved to the coast. He spent his retirement playing golf, according to his neighbours. I drove up there two weeks ago to do a bit of fishing about. I looked out his birth certificate, which named your maternal grandparents as his parents. As you know, your grandparents died many years ago and you lost your mother last spring. I could trace no other living relative.'

Scarlett had spent the last five minutes jigging around on her chair like a cat on hot bricks. 'You do understand what this means, don't you Nina?' she burst out.

But Nina, devastated to have found and lost an uncle in an instant, shook her head dully. Poppy was also none the wiser and looked blankly at her friend.

Scarlett leapt out of her chair and exploded in frustration. 'Good grief, you two. Don't you *ever* watch daytime TV?'

21

S carlett's auburn hair bobbed vigorously as she talked. 'Have you never seen Heir Hunters? It's my mum's favourite programme. I watch it with her if I'm off sick from school. We're always hoping someone will knock on our door one day and tell us we've inherited a fortune from some dotty old great auntie we never knew we had. We're still waiting.' Scarlett sat down again, her face beaming. 'Don't you see? Unless your Uncle Harold spent all his money on golf clubs, you'll inherit his estate. It'll mean you don't have to sell up after all.'

Nina looked to Graham Deakins for confirmation. He nodded, smiling for the first time that day.

'Your young friend is right. I don't want to get your hopes up too high. The estate's not massive, but there's a four bedroomed house to sell plus various stocks and shares. By my calculations the estate is worth at least half a million, after inheritance tax and our fees of course.'

'Half a million,' Poppy marvelled. 'That would be enough to save Oaklands, wouldn't it, Nina?'

Nina looked shell-shocked but her mind was whirring. 'Yes, it would. I could pay off the mortgage and all my debts, and have enough of a cushion in the bank to tide me over. Are you absolutely sure about all this?' she asked.

Graham Deakins appeared ruffled at the suggestion that he might be mistaken. 'My dear, my research into Harold's family tree has been meticulous. You are indeed the one and only heir, I can assure you of that.'

Tears were sliding slowly down Nina's cheeks and she flapped her hands impatiently.

'Happy tears,' she assured them, smiling. 'I'll be able to buy new hay, repair the damage to the barn, maybe even get a couple more ponies. But the best bit will be phoning the bank to tell them their money's on its way. Lydia will be able to grow up here after all. I can't believe how lucky I've been, all thanks to Harold, an uncle I didn't even know I had.'

～

AFTER A CELEBRATORY CUP of tea Graham Deakins gathered his clipboard and was on his way.

'To think I had him down as a debt collector,' said Nina, as they watched the silver saloon disappear down the track.

'Never judge a book by its cover. Appearances can be deceptive,' said Poppy sagely. An image of Beau, hairy and ungainly, but phenomenally brave and loyal to the last, popped into her head and she swallowed. Her dad would be here any minute and she would have to say goodbye to the cob who had driven her demented and then risked his life for her.

'You said Beau and Frank were your talismans but that they hadn't brought you much luck recently. If Frank hadn't let Beau out of his loose box last night and if Beau hadn't been so brave we'd never have been able to get help so quickly. The barns could easily have burned down, the horses with them,' Poppy told Nina as they walked back to the house. 'They did bring you luck after all.'

～

THE TWO GIRLS were packing away the last of their things when the doorbell chimed.

'It'll probably be Dad,' said Poppy, who didn't know whether to be glad or sorry to see him. She couldn't wait to get home and see Cloud and Chester. She was looking forward to filling Caroline in on the dramas of the last few days. She even missed Charlie, although she'd never admit it to her seven-year-old brother. But she knew she would be leaving a tiny piece of her heart in the Forest of Dean.

'Will I have time to say goodbye to Topaz?' asked Scarlett, her voice wobbly.

Poppy zipped up her suitcase and gave her friend a feeble smile. 'Let's go now. I'm sure Dad won't mind.'

Scarlett followed her down the hallway and out of the back door. They crossed the yard to the far gate and stopped in front of the jagged trunk of the oak tree.

'It looks brighter out here now, don't you think?' said Scarlett. She was right, thought Poppy. Nina may have loved the towering oak, but the long, low branches of the ancient tree had cast an oppressive shadow over the yard. They leant on the gate and watched the horses grazing. Topaz and Blue stood nose to tail grooming each other. Beau, who had a couple of burrs in his tail and mud stains on his white bits, was dozing in the sun, Frank by his side.

'I'm so glad everything worked out for Nina. It would have been awful if she'd been forced to sell up,' Scarlett said.

'It's funny how things usually work out for the best,' agreed Poppy, remembering the highs and lows of the past week. 'Come on, let's go and say goodbye.' She climbed over the gate and stooped to pick a handful of grass.

'Beau,' she called softly, and the cob opened his wall eye. When he saw Poppy he whinnied and walked towards her. Poppy held out her hand and he wolfed the grass down greedily before rubbing his face on her jumper, leaving it covered in white hairs. She brushed his long forelock out of his eyes and kissed his hairy nose. He whickered and she laid her face against his.

'I'm sorry I was so wrong about you, Beau,' she told him. 'You were the best last night, you really were.' Poppy realised she hadn't told anyone how close they'd both been to drowning. She decided then and there that she probably never would. There was no need to worry her dad or Caroline. It was between her and Beau. Realising she didn't have any more treats the cob lost interest and ambled back towards Frank. Smiling, Poppy patted his rump and joined Scarlett at the gate. Her friend's eyes were red.

'OK?' Poppy asked. Scarlett nodded.

Poppy linked arms with her. 'Come on, Scar. It's time to go home.'

NINA and her dad were loading their bags into the boot of the McKeevers' car when they arrived back in the yard.

'Dad!' shouted Poppy. He swept her into a hug.

'There you are! Nina's been filling me in on everything. It sounds as if it's been quite a week.'

'You could say that,' grinned Poppy. 'I'm going home for a rest!'

But Nina was frowning. 'I'm sorry your riding holiday didn't turn out to be much of a prize, Poppy.'

'That's OK, Nina. It wasn't your fault. I'll certainly have lots to write about when I do my report on the holiday for Young Rider Magazine.'

'You won't mention Mr Deakins and Uncle Harold's inheritance, will you? I don't want Lydia to know we nearly lost Oaklands, so I'd rather we kept that to ourselves.'

'Of course not,' said Poppy. 'It'll be a glowing review of the trekking centre. Hopefully it'll boost bookings.'

'Thank-you, Poppy. I really do feel my luck has finally changed. I know it'll always be hard work, but with a bit of money in the bank to tide me over when things are quiet I really think I can make a go of the business.' Nina paused, then clapped her hands. 'I've had an idea! I'd like to invite you both back for another week at Oaklands in the summer, as a thank you for everything you did last night. Hopefully it won't be quite so action-packed.'

'That would be amazing,' said Scarlett, suddenly looking more cheerful.

'Are you sure?' Poppy asked.

Nina nodded. 'Yes, I'm sure. And you can have the pick of the horses. I'll even let one of you ride McFly if you like.'

Scarlett's eyebrows shot skywards as she considered the offer. Poppy didn't have to think twice. Her mind was already made up.

'I'll ride Beau, please Nina,' she said, her heart soaring.

Scarlett looked at Poppy in disbelief. Poppy smiled serenely back.

'Lift your chin off the ground, Scarlett,' she said briskly. 'Why on earth would I want to ride anyone else?'

THREE HOURS later they had dropped Scarlett home and were turning into the Riverdale drive. Cloud and Chester were grazing in their paddock and they lifted their heads and watched the car as it passed.

'I won't be a minute,' Poppy told her dad. She let herself out of the passenger door, ran over to the fence and called. Cloud whinnied and cantered over. Poppy was beaming as she climbed over the post and rail fence, threw her arms around his neck and buried her face in his silver mane.

'Oh Cloud, you wouldn't believe how much I've missed you,' she said, breathing in his familiar smell. 'It seems as though I've been away for *months*. It's been an amazing week, it really has. But I tell you something,' Poppy paused to kiss his nose. 'It's good to be home.'

REDHALL RIDERS

1

---

oppy McKeever knew that the haunting cry of the curlew would forever remind her of the accident. *Coor-lee, coor-lee, coor-lee* called the bird into the vast Dartmoor sky as Cloud thundered across the moor towards the isolated farm they had passed an hour earlier. Poppy crouched low over the saddle, urging her pony faster. Cloud, his ears flat and his nostrils flared, responded by lengthening his stride until they were galloping flat out. Poppy wound her hands through his silver mane and chanced a look back, but the others were already tiny specks on the horizon. An old stone wall loomed ahead and she eased Cloud back into a canter. Seeing a stride she squeezed her calves and he soared over the wall with a foot to spare, landing nimbly on the spongey grass on the far side. They turned right, following the steam as it dipped and curved towards the farm, Poppy's heart crashing in time with Cloud's pounding hooves.

Coor-lee, coor-lee, coor-lee cried the curlew from the marshland between the stream and a belt of emerald green conifers. A dark stain of sweat was seeping across Cloud's grey flanks and Poppy could feel him beginning to tire.

'Not far now,' she whispered, running a hand across his neck. He flicked an ear back at the sound of her voice. 'Look, I can see the farm.'

With every stride the farmhouse grew bigger. Poppy remembered the rosy-cheeked woman in a red and white checked shirt who'd been picking runner beans as they'd ridden past earlier. Balancing a trug on her hip she'd called a cheery greeting and they'd waved back. Poppy hoped with all her heart that she was still at home.

They clattered up a stony track to the farmyard. Poppy slithered to the ground and looped her pony's reins over a fence post. Bella would be horrified but there was no time to waste. Cloud watched her, his ears pricked, as she ran into the farmyard, scattering a handful of chickens pecking about in the dirt. Their indignant squawking woke an elderly collie curled up on a rug by the back door. He raised his head and gave a low woof before settling back to sleep.

'Please be in,' Poppy muttered, tugging at the brass door knocker. She almost wept with relief when the door swung open and the woman in the checked shirt stepped out, brushing flour from her hands.

'There's been an accident. I need to use your phone,' Poppy croaked, her mouth dry.

The woman glanced briefly at Cloud standing patiently by the fence and ushered Poppy into a shabby hallway that smelt of freshly-baked scones.

'Whatever's happened? Are you hurt?'

'Not me. One of the other riders. Her pony fell.' Poppy pictured Niamh lying motionless on the ground and Merry standing next to her, the bay mare's hind leg hanging uselessly from her hock. She felt the prickle of tears. 'There was no phone signal. I need to call an ambulance.'

The woman handed her a phone and a tissue and watched as Poppy dialled 999. As she waited for the call to connect Poppy looked wildly around. 'I don't know where we are!'

'Tell them to head for Pegworthy Farm and we can take them from here. I'll write down the postcode.'

Poppy took the scrap of paper and gave the woman a grateful smile. 'Thank-you.'

'That's alright.' She laid a hand on Poppy's arm, leaving a faint floury imprint. 'Don't worry. I expect they'll send the air ambulance. Everything will be OK.'

Poppy nodded. But inside her heart she knew the woman was wrong. Everything was not going to be OK.

~

THE DAY HAD STARTED SO WELL. When Poppy's battered Mickey Mouse alarm clock pulled her out of a deep slumber with a persistent ringing that had bordered on impolite, she groaned, pulled the duvet over her head and almost went back to sleep. Until she remembered with a delicious jolt that it was the first day of the summer holidays. No school, no homework, no interminable talk of coursework and options for a whole six glorious weeks. And as if that wasn't exciting enough, the day she and Scarlett had been looking forward to for weeks had finally arrived.

Poppy jumped out of bed and crossed her room in a couple of strides, picking up a pair of jodhpurs from the end of her bed on the way. She flung open her bedroom window and whistled. Cloud looked up from where he was grazing in the paddock and whinnied. Chester gave an echoing heehaw. Poppy narrowed her eyes and scrutinised her pony. The Connemara had a grass stain on his dappled grey rump, a patch of mud running down his shoulder and a tangled mane. She glanced at the alarm clock. Seven o'clock. Two hours before Scarlett's dad Bill was due to arrive with the trailer to take Cloud and Scarlett's Dartmoor pony Blaze to Redhall Manor Equestrian Centre. Two hours to transform the muddy vision in front of her into a beautifully turned out pony. She knew she was lucky to be invited to Redhall for the week. The least she could do was to meet the exacting standards of Bella Thompson, Redhall's owner.

A bucket of warm water in one hand and a carrot in the other, Poppy headed out of the back door. Wisps of mist that had settled in dips and hollows the night before were already evaporating under the strong midsummer sun. Cloud and Chester stood at the gate flicking flies away with their tails. Poppy measured out their breakfasts and let them into the small area of crumbling concrete in front of the stables and barn that she ambitiously called the yard. While they ate she squirted horse shampoo into the bucket and set to work on Cloud, using a sponge to rub the shampoo into his coat and her fingers to work suds into his mane and tail. She gently hosed him down and used a sweat scraper to squeeze out the excess water. Chester nudged her, as if to remind her it was his turn. Poppy kissed his nose.

'I'm sorry, Chester. You're staying at home with Caroline and Dad.'

At five past nine Bill's Land Rover bounced up the Riverdale drive, the trailer swaying gently behind it. Scarlett leapt out and slammed the door.

'Poppy! We're here!'

'I heard you,' grinned Poppy, emerging from the tack room with Cloud's saddle on one arm and his grooming kit in the other.

'I'll take that. You load Cloud. I've done a haynet for him.' Scarlett opened the door of the Land Rover, propped the saddle alongside her own and squeezed the grooming kit into a space between a sack of sheep pellets and a metal feeding trough. 'I'll get your bridle. Where's your bag?'

'Here,' said Caroline, appearing from the house with Poppy's battered holdall. 'The place is going to feel a bit empty with you off for the week and Charlie at Cub camp.'

'Least Dad's at home,' said Poppy.

Caroline nodded. 'I've got a list of jobs for him, starting with clearing the guttering. He's going to wish he was at work.'

Cloud safely loaded, they said goodbye and Bill nosed the Land Rover back down the drive. Soon they were on the Okehampton road heading towards Redhall Manor.

'So you're going to be guinea pigs for the week?' said Bill.

'That's right. Bella wants to start offering pony camps in the holidays. She's put together an itinerary but wanted to have a trial run before she starts,' said Poppy.

'So we're getting a whole week at Redhall absolutely free.' Scarlett jiggled in her seat. 'I can't wait.'

Once they'd pulled into Redhall's immaculately-swept yard Poppy and Scarlett unclipped their seatbelts and went in search of Bella. They found her in the office, staring in exasperation at Harvey Smith, the tabby stable cat named after the famous showjumper, who was stretched across the keyboard of her laptop purring loudly.

'Damn cat. How am I supposed to finish the accounts?' Bella tutted. 'Let's get these ponies settled and I'll tell you my plans.'

Half an hour later Cloud and Blaze were happily munching hay in their borrowed stables and Poppy and Scarlett had joined their fellow guinea pigs around Bella's large kitchen table.

'I think you all know each other,' Bella said, looking at the five expectant faces before her.

The children nodded. Joining Poppy and Scarlett for the week were

Bella's grandson, Sam, and two girls from Poppy and Scarlett's school, who also had weekly lessons at Redhall Manor. Tia had brought along her own pony, a chestnut gelding with a white blaze called Rufus, and Niamh would be riding one of the Redhall ponies, a bay mare called Merry. Sam would ride his black Connemara mare Star.

'As you know, some of the children on the pony camps we'll be running will be bringing their own ponies and some will be using ours, so it's a good mix. We'll be hacking out on the moor every morning and having group lessons in the afternoons, tackling a different theme each day, from pole work and jumping to dressage. I'll also be giving lessons on stable management in the evenings. With me so far?'

The children nodded. Bella looked at her watch.

'Today's hack is a six mile circular ride around the base of Barrow Tor. We'll leave at half past ten.'

A WARM WESTERLY breeze ruffled the ponies' manes and tails as they clip-clopped out of the yard, crossed the road and set off down a rutted track onto the moor. Bella led the way on her liver chestnut Welsh cob Floyd. Tia and Niamh rode two abreast behind her and Poppy, Scarlett and Sam brought up the rear. Cloud jogged down the track, his neck arched and his tail high.

'He's full of beans,' said Bella, looking back. 'A blast on the moor will do him good.'

Poppy nodded. She could feel excitement zipping through her pony like an electric current. She relaxed into the saddle and kept the lightest touch on his reins until he took her cue and broke into a walk. Bella nodded approvingly.

They followed the track as it climbed steadily, Dartmoor ponies and black-faced sheep watching as they passed. Falling into single file they crossed through a gate onto a rough lane which led past a remote farm-house, waving to a woman picking runner beans in the garden. Eventually they came to a wide grassy ribbon of a track. Bella pulled Floyd up.

'All OK for a canter?'

'You bet,' said Scarlett. Cloud danced on the spot and Poppy tightened her reins.

Bella kicked Floyd on and the cob broke into a canter. Tia and Niamh followed.

'You two go next. I'll bring up the rear,' said Sam. Poppy squeezed her legs and Cloud sprang forwards into an easy canter, Blaze following close behind.

'Yee-hah!' shouted Scarlett, waving an imaginary lasso. She was getting so tall she joked that she would soon need roller skates to ride Blaze. This would probably be her last summer riding the big-hearted Dartmoor pony that she'd had since she was five and she was planning to make the most of it. Poppy felt giddy with exhilaration as they sped on.

'Pony camp rocks!' she cried, pushing Cloud faster. She was so focused on Cloud's grey pricked ears that she didn't see the rabbit hole ahead. Neither did Merry. The bay pony's near hind leg shot down the hole and she pitched forwards. There was a gut-wrenching crack and Merry span into a somersault, throwing Niamh into the path of Tia's pony Rufus. Poppy watched with horror as Tia yanked the reins to the right. But it was too late. There was nothing the chestnut gelding could do to avoid Niamh and his hoof landed squarely on the small of her back as she lay face down in the grass.

In the seconds before Scarlett screamed Poppy heard the plaintiff cry of a curlew echo across the moor. *Coor-lee, coor-lee, coor-lee.* And then there was silence.

2

P oppy, Scarlett and Sam sat on upturned bales of straw outside the tack room listening to Bella's one-sided phone call with growing horror.

'Injured her spine? Are they sure?'

A pause.

'And there's nothing they can do? She could be in a wheelchair for life?'

Scarlett clutched Poppy's hand. They could hear an angry buzz from the other end of the phone.

'Yes, I understand that. But it was an accident. The pony fell down a rabbit hole. There was nothing anyone could have done.'

More enraged buzzing, like a mosquito was trapped in the handset.

'I'm so very sorry.' Poppy was sure she could detect a catch in Bella's voice. She gripped Scarlett's hand back.

'If there's anything I can do please let me -' Before Bella could finish there was a click. Conversation over, she tramped out of the office, her normally ramrod-straight shoulders stooped, muttering about it being the final straw.

When she saw the three children she cocked her head towards the office. 'I expect you heard all that.'

They nodded.

'Who was it, Gran?' Sam asked.

'Gordon Cooper.'

They looked at her blankly.

'Niamh's dad,' Bella said. 'He's threatening to sue. Says it should never have happened. I tried to explain it was an accident but he wasn't having any of it. Apparently I should have inspected the route and carried out a risk assessment.'

'That's ridiculous!' exploded Scarlett. 'Perhaps he'd like to sue the rabbit, too.'

'Poor Niamh,' said Poppy. 'Will she be in hospital for long?'

'A few weeks. And then she'll be transferred to a specialist spinal unit, according to her father. Rufus's hoof damaged her spinal cord. It's unlikely she'll ever walk again.'

Scarlett stifled a sob and Poppy put her arm around her shoulders. 'We should keep busy. Keep our minds off it. We'll do evening stables tonight, Bella.'

Bella rubbed a hand across her face. 'That would be a real help, Poppy. There's a million and one things I need to do. Sam'll show you where everything is.'

'Do you think your gran'll be alright?' Poppy asked Sam, trying not to look at Merry's empty stable. The police had radioed for a vet once the air ambulance had taken off, its whirring propellers flattening the wiry moorland grasses. The vet slammed the door of his 4x4, strode over to Merry, took one look at her broken leg and shook his head.

'There's nothing I can do. I'm sorry,' he told Bella.

She nodded. 'Just make it as comfortable for her as possible.'

Poppy couldn't bear to watch as the vet sedated the pony.

'Take the horses to the farm. It'll only upset them. I'll come as soon as we're done,' Bella said.

Sam took Floyd's reins from his grandmother and they started walking. Poppy glanced back to see Bella rubbing the bay mare's ears, talking to her in a low murmur as the vet reached inside his bag. They were half a mile away when a single gunshot rang out over the moor. Poppy gasped and clung to Cloud's neck. She could hear Scarlett sobbing. Sam's face was like granite.

'She'll be OK. She's as tough as they come,' he said now, handing Poppy a pitchfork.

'What did she mean about it being the final straw?'

'A new livery yard opened at Claydon Manor a couple of months ago. State-of-the-art facilities. The horses are stabled in luxury loose boxes and they've got indoor and outdoor schools, a cross country course and a horse walker. They've even got a horse solarium. Gran's already lost two of her best liveries to Claydon and she's worried they won't be the last. That's why she wanted to start the pony camps. She needed the extra income.'

'Did you say Claydon Manor?' said Scarlett, poking her head over Floyd's stable door.

Sam nodded.

'But that's -'

'Georgia Canning's home,' he said. 'According to Gran, they've spent their way through their lottery win and are now having to make the place pay. Georgia's trainer has been promoted to livery yard manager and Georgia's had to sell most of her jumping string to make way for liveries.'

'Ouch. I don't suppose that went down too well,' said Poppy, remembering Georgia's supercilious smile as she'd beaten Sam and Star in the open class at Redhall's affiliated show the previous autumn.

'And Angela Snell seems intent on poaching Gran's liveries.' Sam kicked the bale of hay outside Floyd's stable.

'Who's Angela Snell?' asked Poppy.

'Georgia's trainer. She's a nasty piece of work. She knows she'll be out of a job if the yard isn't a success. And knowing Angela she won't let anything or anybody stand in her way.'

THAT EVENING, as Poppy cleared the kitchen table and Scarlett began attacking their dirty plates with a soapy washing up brush, Bella asked them if they wanted to leave.

'I've decided to postpone the launch of the pony camps in light of

Niamh's accident,' she said heavily. 'Tia's gone home. I quite understand if you want to go too.'

'Are you kidding? We've been looking forward to our week at Redhall for ages,' said Scarlett.

'We don't mind that the camp is cancelled. But we'd like to stay and help. That's if you want us to,' said Poppy shyly.

Bella looked at Sam, who was flicking through a tattered copy of Horse and Hound.

'It's fine by me. What do you think, Sam?'

He looked up from the magazine and glanced at Poppy. She found her cheeks growing hot.

'Makes sense, now they're here,' he said. 'We could probably use the help.'

'That's settled then.' Bella smiled briefly. 'You ought to be making a move, Sam. Otherwise your mum'll be moaning about child labour again.'

Sam nodded, plucked his cycling helmet from the detritus on the Welsh dresser and headed out of the back door with a casual 'See you in the morning'. Poppy picked up a tea towel and started drying up, trying to ignore the knowing smile on Scarlett's face.

The phone rang.

'That'll be my insurance broker. I've been trying to reach him all afternoon.' Bella picked up the phone, listened for a moment and replaced the handset.

'No luck?' said Poppy.

Bella shook her head. 'Wrong number. It's the second one this evening. Leave the rest of the washing up. I'll show you where you're sleeping.'

Bella led the two girls to a double bedroom at the front of the house, overlooking the drive. The walls were painted the colour of ripe corn and a reproduction Munnings had been given pride of place above the fireplace. The room was simply furnished - two single beds, a large pine chest of drawers and an old pine door in the wall, which Poppy presumed led to a built-in cupboard - but Bella had added brightly coloured patchwork quilts, scatter cushions and a pile of pony magazines on the chest of drawers.

'What a lovely room,' Poppy said.

'The other bedroom is along the landing. I've painted that moss green and there's a Stubbs over the fireplace. That's where Tia and Niamh should have been staying.' A look of anguish crossed Bella's face and she sat down on one of the beds. 'I can't stop thinking about poor Niamh. If only we'd gone a different way.'

Poppy looked at Scarlett helplessly. Bella was usually so indomitable, although Poppy knew her brusque exterior was misleading. She cared deeply about her ponies and riders.

'You mustn't blame yourself. It was an accident,' she said. 'Niamh's dad'll realise that once he's had a chance to think.'

Bella shook her head. 'You didn't hear him, Poppy. He was incandescent. And he holds me wholly responsible.' She cocked her ear. 'And the blasted phone is ringing again. I suppose I'd better get it.'

Once Poppy and Scarlett had unpacked they went down to find Bella. She was sitting at the kitchen table with her head in her hands.

'What's the matter?' said Scarlett.

Bella exhaled slowly. 'And there I was thinking that today couldn't get any worse. My Auntie Margaret's had a fall and broken her hip. I need to go and see her.'

'That's alright,' said Poppy. 'You can go in the morning. We'll look after everything here, won't we Scar? Sam can help us.'

Scarlett nodded. 'Where's she in hospital? Plymouth?'

Bella shook her head. 'Inverness.'

~

POPPY AND SCARLETT were watching an old episode of *Friends* when Bella found them half an hour later.

'It's all sorted,' she said. 'My godson Scott is going to come and stay for a few days. He's a working pupil at a showjumping yard in Exeter. He used to have a Saturday job here when he was younger and knows the place inside out. I'd cancelled all lessons anyway because of the pony camp, so it's just a matter of looking after the liveries and the riding school ponies. My daughter Sarah - Sam's mum - is also going to move in until I'm back. She's hopeless with horses but she's a wonderful cook and she'll look after you all.' Bella paused. 'Do you think you'll be able to cope?'

The two friends nodded.

Bella smiled. 'Thank you, girls. I know Redhall will be in good hands.'

411

❧

THE NEXT MORNING Bella lifted her suitcase into the boot of her car, slammed it shut and turned to face Poppy, Scarlett and Sam.

'I've phoned around the liveries and told them what's happening. A couple of them weren't too happy but there's not much I can do about that. The only one I couldn't get hold of is Vivienne. She'll probably be up this afternoon anyway. You'll have to tell her then. Sarah's on her way and Scott said he'd be here by eleven. You've got my number, haven't you Sam?'

He patted the mobile phone in his pocket.

They watched Bella's car disappear down the drive. Poppy was puzzled. Sam had gone quiet the minute Bella had mentioned her godson.

'What's Scott like,' she asked.

'He's OK. If you like that sort of thing,' he muttered, sweeping his blond fringe out of his eyes.

Scarlett's ears pricked. 'And you don't, by the sound of it.'

'Let's just say we don't always see eye to eye. But other people seem to like him. Especially girls,' he said darkly.

Scarlett raised her eyebrows and winked at Poppy. 'He sounds interesting.'

3

Poppy unfolded the list of instructions Bella had pressed into her hand before she'd left. 'What should we do first?'

Sam peered over her shoulder. 'I'll start on poo-picking if you two can muck out. Do the liveries first, just in case they turn up.'

Poppy nodded. Bella's five liveries were all stabled in the newest loose boxes on the south facing side of the yard. She and Scarlett had helped Bella turn them out before breakfast. Two nervy thoroughbreds, one chestnut, one bay. A skewbald, a palomino and a showy Danish warmblood.

Poppy followed Scarlett over to the wheelbarrows, which were propped along the side of the barn, and picked up a pitchfork and broom. They worked together, forking out the muck and wet straw and banking the clean, dry straw around the sides of the stable. While the floors dried they filled the hayracks and water buckets and emptied the wheelbarrows onto Bella's towering muckheap. Poppy was balancing two bales of straw precariously on the wheelbarrow when she heard a car turn into the yard and the sound of a door slamming. As she looked up to see who it was the top bale toppled over and knocked over a bucket of water.

A tall, thin woman wearing pristine white jodhpurs and black leather riding boots strode over and looked down her aquiline nose at Poppy.

'Where's Bella?' she asked in clipped tones.

'I'm sorry, she's not here. Can I help?'

The woman eyed Poppy with disdain. 'I don't suppose so for a minute.'

'Bella's had to go away for a couple of days,' said Scarlett, emerging from the stable behind them.

'Who's running the yard?'

'We are,' said Poppy. 'With help from Sam and Bella's godson Scott. He works in a showjumping yard in Exeter. He'll be here soon.'

The woman's lips grew thin. 'I see.' She tapped her thigh impatiently. 'I wanted to check the farrier's coming this afternoon.'

Poppy consulted Bella's instructions.

'John the farrier is due at three o'clock to shoe three of the liveries,' she read. 'Cherry, Otto and Ariel.'

'Make sure he does Ariel first. We have the National Dressage Championships qualifier tomorrow and if my horse hasn't been shod in time there'll be consequences.' She looked from Poppy to Scarlett and back again, her eyes narrowed. 'Understood?'

Poppy and Scarlett watched the woman stalk back to her car.

'What an old bag,' whispered Scarlett, sticking her tongue out at the woman's bony back. Poppy stifled a snort of laughter, quickly disguising it as a cough when she stopped in her tracks and turned back to face them.

'And leave him in the stable in the morning. We've got an early start and the last thing I need is to be traipsing halfway across the paddocks to catch him,' she said.

'It'll be a pleasure,' Poppy said, hoping the woman didn't detect the irony in her voice.

'That must be Vile Vivienne. Sam warned me about her earlier. He said she orders him about like he's her personal slave,' said Scarlett as the woman drove off.

'Which one's Ariel?' Poppy asked.

'The black Danish warmblood that shares a paddock with Paint the skewbald. He's a real sweetie apparently.'

'Nothing like his owner then.' Poppy blew her fringe out of her eyes. 'Let's get this straw down and we'll see how Sam's getting on.'

Scarlett produced a penknife from her pocket and cut open the first bale of straw. 'What time is Scott supposed to be here?'

Poppy checked her watch.

'Half an hour ago,' she said drily.

~

POPPY AND SCARLETT were shaking out the last of the straw when a second car pulled into the yard.

'Perhaps that's Scott,' said Scarlett hopefully.

But a pretty woman in shorts and a vest top was emerging from the car. Judging by her honey blonde hair she was Sam's mum, Sarah. She saw the two girls and smiled.

'Are you ready for some lunch?'

'Am I ever,' said Scarlett.

'Good. I've made a mountain of sandwiches. Mum made me promise to keep you both fed and watered, like you were two of her riding school ponies.'

'I'll fetch Sam,' Poppy said, heading for the top paddock where she could see the quad bike and trailer Bella used for poo-picking. Sam was in the far corner.

'Your mum's here,' she said.

'That's good timing. I've just finished. Want a ride back?' he said. 'I'm as safe as houses, honest.'

'I guess,' said Poppy, looking at the seat of the quad bike dubiously. It didn't look very big.

Sam climbed on and looked around to see where she was. 'C'mon then, I'm famished,' he said, patting the padded seat behind him.

Poppy gave a tiny shrug and climbed behind him. He turned on the ignition.

'Hold on then,' he said, revving the engine. Poppy held on as loosely as she could and soon they were off, bumping along the field towards the yard. The quad bike hit a rut and lurched sideways. Poppy shrieked, her arms instinctively tightening around Sam. She could feel the muscles in his back flexing as he steered the bike onto more even ground.

'I'll just get rid of this lot on the muck-heap,' Sam shouted over his shoulder. He stopped at the gate to the yard and Poppy leapt off like a scalded cat. But not before Scarlett had seen them and had given her a knowing wink.

'Don't,' Poppy said. 'It was quicker than walking, that's all.'

Scarlett smirked. 'I'll take your word for it.'

~

THEY WERE FINISHING the last of Sarah's homemade chocolate brownies when the throaty growl of a motorbike cut through the warm afternoon air. Sam checked the time on his phone.

'Only an hour late,' he said.

Scarlett rammed the last piece of brownie into her mouth, stood up and ran her hands through her hair. She was already halfway across the yard when a black and silver motorbike roared in. The rider turned off the engine, kicked down the side stand and pulled off his helmet.

'Are you Scott?' said Scarlett, holding out a hand. Instead of shaking it the visitor handed her his helmet.

'I certainly am. And which one of my lovely helpers are you, Poppy or Scarlett?'

'I'm Scarlett,' Scarlett said breathlessly. 'We've already mucked out and done the liveries' hay and water and we'll do the riding school ponies after lunch so the only thing you need to do is make sure the farrier does Ariel first because Vile Vivienne's got a dressage qualifier in the morning and she said if he isn't shod there'll be consequences and Bella's had enough consequences this week to last her all year, so we really don't want any more.'

Scott threw his head back and laughed loudly. One of his front teeth was chipped, the only flaw in an otherwise perfect smile. 'Slow down Scarlett. I have absolutely no idea what you're talking about. Let me have a cup of tea first, eh?'

'Sorry Scott,' Scarlett said, bobbing her head. 'I'll go and stick the kettle on.'

'White, strong and sweet please,' he called after her. He gave Sarah a hug and pinched the half-eaten brownie on the paper plate on her lap. She smiled indulgently and batted him on the arm. Sam returned his high-five with about as much enthusiasm as a turkey invited to be guest of honour at lunch on December the twenty-fifth. Poppy allowed herself a small smile. Assuming it was meant for him Scott grinned back.

'And you must be Poppy,' he said, his muddy brown eyes assessing her.

She nodded and fled to the kitchen. Scarlett was stirring a mug of builder's tea, a dreamy expression on her face.

'He's so hot,' she said. 'He looks like Benedict Cumberbatch.'

Poppy raised her eyebrows. 'D'you think?'

'No, you're right. He's even better looking.' Scarlett picked up the mug and headed for the yard. Poppy sighed and followed her.

Scott was lounging against the door to Ariel's stable. Curls of damp hair were stuck to his head and tickled the collar of his battered black leather jacket. When he pulled off his leather gloves to take the tea from Scarlett Poppy noticed his nails were bitten to the quick.

Harvey Smith, woken from his cat bed in the tack room by the roar of the motorbike, padded out, saw Scott and made a beeline for him, rubbing his tabby cheek against Scott's skinny jeans. Scott took a slurp and looked around him.

'It's good to be back,' he said.

~

SCOTT DISAPPEARED INSIDE to unpack and Sarah began tidying away lunch.

'We'd better make a start on the other stables before the farrier gets here,' said Sam. 'I'll muck out if you two do the hay and water.'

Sam worked sparingly and methodically down the line of stables while Poppy and Scarlett emptied wheelbarrows, scrubbed out and filled water buckets and replenished hayracks. Soon the eight stables used by the riding school ponies were finished and it was time to catch the three liveries.

'You bring Ariel and Scarlett and I'll get Cherry and Otto,' Sam said, handing Poppy a brand-new leather headcollar. 'Just mind Paint because he has a habit of following Ariel out of the gate if you're not careful.'

Poppy and Scarlett followed Sam down the dusty track that led to the paddocks. Halfway along he stopped and pointed to a bay mare and a chestnut gelding who were standing nose to tail under an apple tree.

'That's Cherry and Otto,' he said. 'They've only been with us a few months. They're owned by a husband and wife, Debbie and Tim. They're both a bit highly-strung.'

'Cherry and Otto, or Debbie and Tim?' Poppy asked, admiring the two thoroughbreds' fine build and handsome heads.

'They all are actually,' said Sam. 'Not a good combination. Debbie and Tim are both over-horsed really. They'd only been having lessons for a few months when they bought these two from a yard in Yorkshire that produces top competition horses. They have lessons with Gran but they're both a bit neurotic and worry about absolutely every little thing. They treat Cherry and Otto like their children. There's Ariel, over there.'

The big Danish warmblood was watching them from the next paddock. He was a glossy jet black apart from four white socks.

'He's beautiful,' Poppy said.

'Much too nice for Vile Vivienne,' agreed Scarlett.

Grazing in the far corner of the paddock with his rump towards them was a hogged skewbald cob. Poppy's heart lurched. Paint was a dead ringer for Beau, the horse she'd fallen in love with during her trekking holiday in the Forest of Dean. She opened the gate and walked over to Ariel, offering him a Polo. He lowered his head and took the mint from her palm. She was standing on tiptoes buckling his head strap when she felt a nudge and warm breath on her back. Paint was standing behind her, eying her expectantly.

'Where did you spring from?' she laughed, peeling off a mint for him. He snatched it greedily and nibbled her pocket. 'Alright then, just one more. I was saving these for Cloud,' she told him.

Poppy clicked her tongue and started leading Ariel towards the gate. Paint pricked his ears and followed. They reached the gate and Poppy looked back. The skewbald cob was so close to Ariel that there was no way she would be able to lead him out without Paint following. She looked around for help but Cherry and Otto's rumps were already disappearing around the corner into the yard. She pushed Paint gently on the shoulder but the sturdy cob simply leant his bulk towards her.

'You're more like Beau than I thought,' she told him. 'Luckily I know something you won't be able to resist.' She peeled off the remaining Polos and dropped the first onto the grass under Paint's nose. Ariel followed her patiently while, one by one, she laid a trail of mints leading away from the gate. As the cob sniffed his way along the trail, snaffling the mints up, Poppy opened the gate and led Ariel through.

'Job done!' she said, patting the black gelding's muscular neck.

By ten to three all three liveries were in their stables ready for the farrier. Poppy picked up a broom and began sweeping the yard. Three o'clock came and went with no sign of John. By a quarter past Sam was anxiously checking the time.

'It's not like him to be late,' he said.

'He's probably been held up at his last job. He's not even half an hour late yet,' reasoned Poppy.

By half past three Sam's forehead was creased with worry. 'It wouldn't normally matter, but if Ariel's not shod today Vivienne will have a nervous breakdown,' he said. 'Gran must have John's number somewhere. I'll phone him.'

As Sam disappeared into Bella's office the phone started ringing.

'That'll be John, letting us know he's running late,' said Scarlett.

'What's up?' Poppy asked, as Sam came out shaking his head.

'It was another wrong number. So I tried phoning John, and he said he had a call from Gran cancelling his visit this morning. He's on the other side of Okehampton and won't make it today.'

'Why would Bella have cancelled him and not told us? It doesn't make sense,' said Scarlett.

'Maybe she forgot about tomorrow's dressage test and thought the farrier would be one less thing for us to worry about,' Sam shrugged.

'But he's on the list,' said Poppy, pulling it out of her back pocket. 'John the farrier at three o'clock to shoe Cherry, Otto and Ariel. Was it definitely Bella who called?'

'That's what John says and he wouldn't have any reason to lie. He's usually really reliable. That's why Gran always has him.'

Ariel leant over his stable door and nibbled at Poppy's pony tail. Her face paled.

'Oh God. Who's going to break the news to Vile Vivienne?'

4

S cott drew the short straw.

'On account of him not being here,' said Poppy. 'Come on Scar, let's go and tell him the good news.'

They found Sarah peeling potatoes in the kitchen.

'Have you seen Scott?' Scarlett asked.

'I've made a bed up for him in Sam's room. He went upstairs to unpack,' she said.

As they climbed the stairs they became aware of a soft whistling sound coming from the back of the house.

'Someone's snoring,' said Poppy.

'It sounds as if it's coming from Sam's room,' whispered Scarlett. 'What should we do?'

They stood outside the room and looked at each other uncertainly. The door was ajar. Poppy pushed it open with her index finger and peered around it. There was Scott, fast asleep on top of the duvet in the bed furthest from the door, his shoes still on and his rucksack beside him.

'Dead to the world while we've been hard at it. I thought he was supposed to be here to help,' fumed Poppy.

'But we can't wake him. He looks so peaceful,' protested Scarlett.

'Too right we can,' said Poppy. She coughed loudly. Scott didn't stir. She shoved open the door, letting it hit the wall with a satisfying bang.

They watched as Scott opened first one eye, then the other, before yawning so widely they were given an unrivalled view of his tonsils. Puppy pulled a face.

'Sorry to wake you, Scott, but we've got some bad news,' said Scarlett.

He sat up, ran a hand through his hair and eyed them blearily.

'Must have just nodded off. Had a late one last night,' he said. 'What's happened?'

'I'll leave you to fill Scott in,' Poppy told Scarlett. 'I'm going to see if I can find Vile Vivienne's number. It must be in Bella's office somewhere.'

Sam was sitting in Bella's swivel chair with his head in his hands. Poppy stood at the door watching him for a moment. He looked as though he was carrying the weight of the world on his shoulders.

She cleared her throat. Sam looked up and gave her a fleeting smile.

'I'm after Vivienne's phone number. Perhaps Scott can go on a charm offensive and smooth things over,' she said brightly.

Sam reached for a blue ledger buried under a pile of Horse and Hound magazines. He flicked through to the back page, copied a phone number on an old envelope and handed it to Poppy.

The phone rang. Sam stared at it as if it was contagious.

'Aren't you going to answer it?' said Poppy.

'What if it's Vile Vivienne? I don't know what to say to her,' he said.

Poppy crossed the room and picked up the handset, bracing herself for Vivienne's clipped tones.

'Redhall Manor Equestrian Centre. Can I help?'

But there was nothing but silence on the other end of the line.

'Can I help you?' she repeated.

Poppy held her breath and listened really carefully. Was that static on the line or the sound of someone breathing? A shiver ran down her spine and she stabbed the end call button with her finger. She realised Sam was watching her.

'Wrong number again?' he asked.

'I guess. They didn't actually have the courtesy to say,' said Poppy.

'We've had a few this weekend. I'll have to get Gran to call out the engineers when she gets back. She's obviously got a crossed line.'

Scott appeared with Scarlett at his heels. Poppy handed him the phone and Vivienne's number.

'Just explain there's been a misunderstanding and that the farrier has promised to come out first thing tomorrow,' said Sam.

Scott nodded at the door. 'Clear off you lot. I don't want an audience. There must be plenty of jobs that need doing.'

Sam shot Scott a filthy look and Poppy rolled her eyes. Only Scarlett seemed happy to do his bidding.

'I'll go and make you another cup of tea,' she said, virtually skipping across the yard. Sam shut the door and beckoned Poppy to follow him down the side of the office to an old window at the end.

'I've got to hear this,' he said.

They crouched down under the window and listened as Scott dialled.

'Hello, can I speak to Vivienne Montague? It's Scott from Redhall. I'm afraid I have some bad news. No, Ariel's absolutely fine. It's the farrier. He crashed his van on the way here and won't make it tonight.'

Sam shook his head at the bare-faced lie.

'He says he's really sorry and he'll be here at seven tomorrow to shoe Ariel. Will that be in time for your dressage test?'

Poppy held her breath as Vivienne squawked down the line.

'No, there's no point you phoning him. He said he won't be able to get here any earlier. I'll make sure Ariel's groomed and plaited before the farrier arrives if that's any -'

There was a thud. Poppy presumed it was the phone being flung onto the desk. It was followed by the sound of the swivel chair scraping along the flagstone floor and Scott muttering under his breath. Poppy strained to hear. She thought she caught the words 'Bloody woman.'

Scott threw open the door. Scarlett scampered across the yard and handed him his tea.

'How did it go?' she asked.

'As well as can be expected,' he said. 'Are you any good at plaiting?'

~

POPPY CHECKED HER WATCH. Half past four. The stables were mucked out and the hay and water had all been done. The horses had been groomed and were grazing peacefully in their paddocks. There was a natural lull before evening stables. Sam was schooling Star in the indoor school. Scarlett had offered to help Sarah with a supermarket shop and Scott had zoomed off on his motorbike, muttering about needing some down time. Poppy found a sunny corner of the yard and sat down, Harvey Smith purring beside her.

She was texting Caroline when a lorry with a postbox-red cab turned into the Redhall drive, easing its way through the gateposts into the yard with millimetres to spare. The ruddy-faced driver climbed down from the cab, a clipboard in his hands. Poppy slipped her phone into her pocket, hauled herself to her feet and walked over.

'I've got Mrs T's delivery,' he said.

Poppy noticed the embroidered logo above the pocket of his red overalls. *Baxters' Country Store*. Bella hadn't mentioned a delivery on her list.

'Oh, we didn't know you were coming today. I'm not sure where it's supposed to go.'

'It's OK, I usually unload it outside the tack room,' said the driver. He walked around to the back of the lorry, slid open the doors and reached for a mustard-yellow sack barrow.

'The old girl's really pushed the boat out this week, hasn't she? Enough food to feed the flippin' cavalry and all them fancy supplements. They cost a bleedin' bomb. Has she won the lottery or summat?'

'Er, no.' Poppy joined the driver at the back of the lorry and peered inside. 'Crikey, is that all for Redhall?'

'Yup.'

'Are you sure there hasn't been a mistake?'

The driver whipped a stubby pencil from behind his ear and tapped his clipboard. 'It's all on the order form. Just sign here.'

Poppy scrawled her signature and the driver began pulling sacks of expensive-looking horse feed onto the sack barrow and wheeling it over to the tack room. Poppy picked up a couple of cartons of liquid probiotics and followed him. For the next ten minutes she helped him unload the lorry. Supplements for healthy bones and joints, strong hooves and glossy coats. Antioxidants and draughts to aid gastric health and digestion. Herbal tinctures promising vitality. Who knew all this stuff even existed? And since when had Bella, an old-school equestrian, had her head turned by all the marketing hype?

Once they had finished unloading the lorry Poppy sat on a tub of herbs for hormonal mares and watched it reverse slowly out of the drive.

She was just finishing her text to Caroline when Sam led Star out of the indoor school and did a double take.

'What on earth's all that?'

'It's Bella's delivery from Baxters'. The driver said he usually leaves it outside the tack room.'

'It can't be. This is way too much. Gran has about a fifth of this. And none of this expensive stuff.' He picked up a tub and read the label. "Electrolyte supplement for the performance horse.' I don't even know what it is. And look at the price - nearly twenty quid! Gran hasn't ordered this.'

Poppy felt the colour drain from her face. 'But it was all on the order form, Sam. The man from Baxters' showed me before I signed for it. Bella must have changed the order.'

'You signed for it?' Sam's eyebrows shot up. 'This is going to cost hundreds of pounds. There's no way Gran can afford it, especially at the moment.'

'I'm sorry,' Poppy said in a small voice. 'I thought I was doing the right thing. I should have come and found you.'

'It's not your fault. I'll phone Baxters' now. Explain there's been some sort of a mix-up. I'm sure they'll sort it out.'

'I'll do Star,' she offered.

Sam handed her Star's reins and Poppy led the mare over to the tie ring outside her stable.

'I feel terrible,' she whispered as she untacked Star and ran a body brush over her gleaming coat. The mare whickered as Sam tramped over from Bella's office.

'Any luck?' Poppy asked.

He shook his head. 'They have an exchange policy on tack and rugs, but not on food.' He rested his head on Star's flank and stared at the mountainous pile of feed and supplements. 'Looks like we're stuck with it.'

AFTER DINNER POPPY took a mug of hot chocolate and a carrot out to the yard, her eyes on Cloud's borrowed stable. She whistled softly and his head appeared over the stable door. He watched her cross the yard, his silver grey ears pricked. She offered him the carrot and he crunched it noisily while she opened the stable door and settled in the straw to drink her hot chocolate.

She still felt bad about the Baxters' order, although Sam had told her not to blame herself. If only she had checked with him before she'd signed the order form. She had offered to use her savings to buy half a dozen of the tubs of supplements, joking that she would have the shiniest, calmest, least hormonal gelding with the healthiest digestive system and hooves ever seen. But Sam had told her not to be silly and that Bella would sort it all out when she was back.

'And I haven't spent any time with you today, have I Cloud?' she said, kissing his nose. 'It's just been manic.' It was true. She had hardly stopped. Her back and shoulders ached from hefting bales of straw and wheelbarrows of muck and despite five minutes spent scrubbing with a nail brush until the tips of her fingers were pink her nails were still black with grime. And tomorrow it would start all over again.

'Whoever says that working with horses is easy should give it a try for a few days. It's like painting the Forth Bridge.' Cloud nuzzled Poppy's hand, which still smelt enticingly of carrots. She scratched his forehead. 'It takes so long that by the time you've finished you have to start all over again.'

Realising Poppy didn't have any more titbits, Cloud sank to the floor and lay down in the straw. Poppy snuggled up close and sighed contentedly.

'We'll try and get out for a ride tomorrow,' she promised him. 'Just you and me.'

～

POPPY WAS LETTING herself in the back door when the phone started ringing. When no-one answered she picked up the extension in the kitchen, expecting another wrong number. She almost jumped out of her skin when Vile Vivienne began screeching down the phone.

'I phoned the farrier and there was no crash! He said Bella cancelled his visit. Well, she had no right. I have been working towards tomorrow's qualifier for the last six months. Six months! And she's ruined my chances. But worse than that, I have been lied to. I will put up with a lot, but I will not tolerate lying. I shall be removing Ariel from the yard.'

'But -' began Poppy.

'And in the light of what's happened I consider my contract with Redhall to be null and void. I will not be giving one month's notice. Please have him ready at ten o'clock in the morning.'

The line went dead. With a sinking heart Poppy headed for the lounge to break the bad news.

oppy woke early to the chatter of magpies. She squinted at her watch. Ten to five. She closed her eyes and tried to empty her brain so she could drift back into unconsciousness. But a shaft of sunlight that had slunk through a crack in the curtains like a cat burglar flitting through a heavily-alarmed art gallery played on her eyelids, banishing any chance of sleep.

Sighing, Poppy threw off her duvet and grabbed a clean teeshirt and pair of jodhpurs from her case. As she did she glanced at Scarlett. Her best friend's auburn hair was fanned around her face, her duvet was tucked under her chin and she was breathing deeply. She didn't look like she would be waking up anytime soon.

Poppy picked an apple from the fruit bowl and scribbled a note on an old envelope. *Gone for a ride. Will be back by seven.* She found her jodhpur boots in the tangle of wellies and riding boots by the back door and went in search of her pony.

Cloud must have had a sixth sense. When Poppy burst out of the back door, the apple between her teeth, he was watching over his stable door as if he'd been expecting her. He whickered and she scratched behind his ear, took a last bite of apple and gave him the rest.

Poppy reached under the flowerpot brimming with pale pink geraniums for the key to the tack room, plonked her hat on her head and carried Cloud's saddle and bridle to his stable. He shook his head impatiently as she tacked him up. Blaze, Star, the riding school ponies and the liveries all watched with interest as she led the Connemara over to the mounting block, tightened his girth, pulled down his stirrups and swung into the saddle. Soon they were turning out of the yard towards the moor.

They crossed the road outside the riding school and followed the rutted track they'd ridden along on Bella's first fateful trek to Barrow Tor. So much had happened since the accident it seemed like another life, yet it was only two days ago. An unwelcome memory of Merry pitching forwards as her hind leg disappeared down the rabbit hole swam in front of Poppy's eyes and she shook it away. The last thing she wanted to do was re-live that terrible morning. Instead she fixed her eyes on Cloud's pricked grey ears and tried to forget.

Ahead an orange sun smouldered behind the purple and grey horizon. Behind her the moon was fading in the early morning sky like a footprint in wet sand. The air smelt fresh, cold and clean and Poppy breathed deeply. Gradually she felt the tension of the last forty-eight hours ease from her shoulders. Her thoughts turned to Scott. Scarlett seemed in awe of Bella's godson but Poppy had been relieved to discover within minutes of meeting him that she was totally immune to his charms. He was way too smooth for her liking. And his laidback attitude to his new responsibilities irritated her. He was supposed to be helping, yet he'd barely lifted a finger while the rest of them worked their socks off to keep the yard running like clockwork. And she hated the way he belittled Sam.

Sam had got his own back the night before. As they'd sat down to eat Sarah's legendary fish pie, Scarlett had asked Scott how he'd chipped his front tooth.

Scott had run his tongue along the offending tooth and given them a rueful smile.

'An argument with a feisty gelding,' he said mysteriously.

'At the showjumping yard in Exeter?' Scarlett asked, impressed.

Sam snorted with laughter and Scott shot him a filthy look.

'Not exactly. He fell off Treacle,' Sam smirked.

'Our Treacle?' said Poppy. She couldn't imagine Scott atop the diminutive Welsh pony that Bella used for Redhall's beginners, despite his uncanny knack of dumping most of them in the nearest puddle while they were out on a hack. With a stomach the size of a barrel and an evil glint in his eye, the chestnut Section A gelding shared more than a passing resemblance to a Thelwell pony and was definitely not as sweet as his name suggested. It was a wonder the beginners came back for more.

'I was eight at the time,' Scott clarified. 'I learnt to ride on him. And he can buck like a bronco when he's in the mood, you know.'

'That's funny, I never had a problem with him,' said Sam, looking more cheerful than he had all day.

Cloud reached the gate at the top of the track. Ahead was the lane that led to the farmhouse where Poppy had called for help. A bridleway to the right led back down to the riding school. Poppy's stomach rumbled and she checked her watch. Half past six. She turned him right.

'Come on Cloud, let's go and get some breakfast.'

POPPY FED Cloud and Blaze and followed the smell of bacon that was wafting from the open kitchen window. As she heeled off her jodhpur boots by the back door a white van pulled into the yard. A woman wearing a royal blue apron let herself out of the driver's side and went around to the back of the van. Poppy pulled her boots back on and wandered over. Painted on the side in a curly script decorated with denim blue forget-me-nots were the words *Fern's Flowers*

The woman in the apron appeared holding a huge bouquet of white lilies.

'These are for Bella Thompson,' she said.

'They're beautiful,' said Poppy. 'She's not here at the moment but I can take them.'

The woman handed Poppy the bouquet. The scent they gave was cloying and Poppy rubbed her nose with the back of her hand to head off a sneeze.

'There's a card in with them,' said the woman, pointing to a small white envelope tucked between the stalks. She smiled sympathetically. 'I'm sorry for your loss.'

What a strange thing to say, Poppy thought, as she carried the flowers into the kitchen. Sarah was standing by Bella's massive range cooker frying bacon.

'Flowers?' she asked, surprised.

'They're for Bella,' Poppy said. She fished around for the envelope and handed it to Sarah.

'Perhaps Mum's got an admirer,' Sarah joked. 'I'm sure she won't mind me having a look to see who they're from.'

She used the bread knife to open the envelope and took out a card with a dove on the front. The knife slipped through her fingers and clattered to the floor. Her hand flew to her mouth.

'What's wrong?'

'It can't be right. They must have delivered them to the wrong address,' she said.

'The *Ferns Flowers* woman definitely said it was for Bella. Why, what does the card say?'

'RIP,' said Sarah faintly.

Poppy's mind went blank. 'What does that stand for?'

'Rest in Peace,' said Sarah with a shiver.

~

'THAT'S what people say when someone's died, isn't it?' said Scarlett, as they waited for Vile Vivienne to arrive to take Ariel to his new home.

Poppy nodded. 'Sarah was a bit freaked out at first, and then she wondered if someone in the village had heard about her Great Auntie Margaret's fall and jumped to the wrong conclusion.'

Scarlett looked sceptical. 'What, like Chinese whispers? Sounds unlikely to me.'

'That's what I thought, too,' said Poppy.

At ten o'clock on the dot a familiar-looking smart sky blue lorry pulled into the yard.

Poppy watched glumly from Paint's stable as Vile Vivienne jumped out of the passenger door and strode over to the office, her lips pursed. Another woman let herself out of the driver's side and began letting down the ramp. Poppy wracked her brains, trying to remember where she'd seen the lorry before. And then she noticed a small navy logo on the passenger door and groaned.

Vivienne emerged from the office with Scott trailing behind her.

'Are you sure I can't persuade you to stay?' he said half-heartedly.

Vivienne waved him away with her hand. 'My mind is made up. I've been considering a move to Claydon Manor for a while. The facilities there put this place to shame. I only stayed out of misguided loyalty to Bella. But I will not be lied to. Fortunately Angela was more than happy to offer me a place.'

I bet she was, thought Poppy, watching Georgia Canning's former instructor fix partitions in the horse lorry. She walked down the ramp and looked around, unimpressed. She had cold grey eyes and a contemptuous look on her face, as if she had a permanent bad smell under her nose.

'Where's the horse?' she asked, looking around disdainfully.

Vile Vivienne pointed to Ariel's stable. His noble head appeared over the stable door and Vivienne's normally arch expression softened. She may be an old dragon but she does love him, Poppy realised.

Sam appeared with Ariel's tack and grooming kit while Scarlett ran into the tack room to find his rugs. Soon the big black gelding had been loaded onto the lorry and it had pulled onto the Okehampton road bound for Tavistock.

'Good riddance,' said Scott. 'That woman was as mad as a box of frogs if you ask me.'

'She also paid through the nose for Gran's deluxe bespoke livery package. And now she's gone. And to Claydon Manor of all places,' said Sam.

'Chill out Samantha,' mocked Scott.

'Vivienne may have been vile, but she and Ariel have been here for years. Perhaps you'd like to phone Gran and let her know her oldest livery has gone.' He shoved his hands into his pockets. 'Actually don't bother. I'd rather break the news to her myself when she gets back from Great Auntie Margaret's. Just try not to lose us any more liveries will you?'

'I don't know why he's so uptight,' said Scott as Sam stomped over to the trailer, hooked it onto the quad bike and roared off towards the top paddocks.

Poppy stared at him in disbelief. 'Because he's worried about Redhall's future!' she spluttered. 'Angela Snell has poached so many of Bella's liveries she's struggling to keep the place afloat. That's why she decided to start trekking holidays. But that's on hold after Niamh's accident. No wonder Sam's upset.'

Was that a glimmer of uncertainty flickering across Scott's face? Poppy wasn't convinced. But as she pushed the wheelbarrow towards the hay barn she hoped he might have finally got the message that all was not well at Redhall.

6

P oppy and Scarlett were fluffing up the straw bed in Paint's stable when Sam appeared with three headcollars.

'Where's Scott?' he asked.

'He went in to make us a cup of tea,' said Scarlett.

'Really? I don't think I've ever known him to make a drink for anyone other than himself,' said Sam.

'Yes, but he did disappear about half an hour ago. He's probably fast asleep on the sofa by now,' said Poppy.

'It's hardly surprising. He must work so hard at that showjumping yard,' said Scarlett.

Poppy and Sam exchanged a look.

'I could do with some help exercising the liveries. Fancy coming with me?'

Scarlett's eyes lit up. 'You get to ride the liveries?'

Sam nodded. 'Debbie and Tim pay extra for Cherry and Otto to be exercised a couple of times a week. So does Kim, Ellie's owner. Some-times Gran lunges them, sometimes I school them, but I reckon we deserve an hour off to go for a hack, don't you?'

'Bags I ride Cherry,' said Scarlett.

'I'd better take Otto. He can be a bit unpredictable.' Sam held out a navy headcollar for Poppy. 'Are you OK with Ellie?'

Poppy nodded. Ellie was a showy palomino mare with four white socks and an extravagantly long mane and forelock. At 15.2hh she was a hand taller than Cloud but more finely-built.

'Her name's actually Elidi, which means gift of the sun in Greek,' said Sam as Poppy tied Ellie up next to Otto. 'She's not a novice ride, but I reckon you can handle her.'

The mare fidgeted while Poppy set to work brushing the dust from her butterscotch-coloured coat. She tossed her head as Poppy combed her mane and pawed the ground impatiently when Poppy appeared with her tack.

Poppy placed the saddle on the mare's back, buckled the girth loosely, looped the headcollar around Ellie's neck and put the bridle on. As she fastened the noseband Harvey Smith darted out of the tack room door and flashed across the yard with his tabby tail as bushy as a fox's, sending an empty bucket flying. Ellie leapt about a foot in the air, her hooves jangling on the concrete yard.

'Easy girl,' Poppy murmured, running her hand along Ellie's neck. She felt a flutter in her stomach at the thought of riding the flighty mare.

Scarlett was already leading Cherry over to the mounting block. Poppy re-tied her ponytail, put on her hat, unfastened Ellie's headcollar and waited while Scarlett mounted the towering thoroughbred.

'It's about two degrees cooler up here,' Scarlett grinned. 'Blaze is going to feel like a Shetland pony after Cherry.'

Poppy tightened Ellie's girth, adjusted the stirrup leathers and led her over to the mounting block. She climbed the steps, gathered the reins in her left hand and was just about to put her left foot in the stirrup when the mare swung her quarters away, leaving a yawning gap between them. Poppy got back down, circled the mare and led her back to the mounting block. But she did exactly the same again, swinging away just as Poppy was about to get on.

'Having a spot of bother?' said a voice. Poppy turned to see Scott lounging against the post and rail fence around the school, his hands curled around a mug of tea.

Poppy felt her face grow hot. 'Third time lucky,' she muttered, circling Ellie again. This time the mare backed away from the mounting block before Poppy had even climbed onto it.

'I'll hold her for you if you like,' Scott said, not waiting for an answer.

He took Ellie's reins and pushed her rump firmly towards the mounting block. He scratched the mare's poll and she lowered her head demurely and stood perfectly still while Poppy jumped on and gathered her reins.

Ellie nibbled Scott's pockets and sniffed at the dregs of his tea. Poppy wouldn't have been surprised if she'd fluttered her long eyelashes at him. The palomino mare had obviously fallen for his charms, too.

'Thanks,' she said.

'Anytime. Enjoy your ride.'

'The buckets and water troughs need filling,' Sam said as they rode out of the yard. Scott pulled a face and disappeared into Bella's office.

'If they're done by the time we get back I'll eat my hat,' Sam sighed.

~

ELLIE JOGGED up the road behind Otto and Cherry, her nostrils flared as she spooked at the tattered remains of a plastic carrier bag caught on a barbed wire fence. Poppy grabbed a handful of her long mane and held on tight.

'It's alright, you silly horse. It's a bag, not a bogeyman. It won't hurt you.'

In the year since she'd learnt to ride on Flynn, Scarlett's brother Alex's rotund Dartmoor pony, Poppy had only ever ridden four other horses. Cloud, Bella's New Forest mare Rosie, Sam's Connemara Star and Beau, the big, hairy piebald cob she'd fallen in love with during their week at Oaklands Trekking Centre in the Forest of Dean. Ellie was nothing like any of them. She felt like an active volcano, ready to erupt at any minute.

Sam pulled Otto alongside her.

'Alright?' he asked.

Poppy licked her lips. The roof of her mouth was sandpaper dry. 'She's quite, er, lively,' she said, as Ellie shied at a sheep, cannoning into Otto before Poppy could stop her.

'She's always a bit spooky when she hasn't been out for a few days. She'll settle down in a minute,' he said.

'I'll take your word for it,' Poppy muttered, tightening her reins.

Instead of turning onto the track Poppy and Cloud had followed that morning, Sam took a right into a narrow lane that ran parallel to a stream. A clutch of fluffy yellow mallard ducklings glided gracefully after their parents. Poppy imagined their tiny feet paddling furiously under the water and smiled.

'OK for a trot?' Sam called.

'You bet!' cried Scarlett.

Ellie needed no encouragement either and sprang into the floatiest trot Poppy had ever experienced. It felt as though they were trotting on air.

They reached a T-junction and turned right over an old stone bridge. Ellie spooked, boggle-eyed, at a yellow salt bin, but this time Poppy was ready for her and sat relaxed in the saddle.

'We usually have a canter through the woods,' said Sam, turning Otto down a bridleway. Ellie snatched at her bit and crabbed sideways down the track, but Poppy was unperturbed. She'd realised that nothing the mare did was malicious, she was just fresh. And Poppy had to admit her canter was as amazing as her trot. They cantered through the woods, one after the other, the horses' pounding hooves sending pheasants scurrying for cover.

Too soon they'd reached the end of the bridleway and turned for home.

'This road brings us out at the back of Gran's. We can ride through the fields back to the yard,' said Sam.

Ten minutes later they came to a five bar gate.

Ellie gawked at a puddle of water.

'That's funny,' Poppy said.

'What is?' asked Scarlett.

'Look at that massive puddle. But I can't remember the last time it rained, can you?'

Scarlett shrugged. 'Perhaps it rained last night.'

They rode past the field Cloud was sharing with Blaze and Treacle. Poppy held her hand over her face.

'What on earth are you doing?' said Sam.

'Hiding from Cloud. I don't want him to see me riding another horse,' Poppy whispered. At that moment Cloud lifted his grey head and whinnied. 'Oh no, he's seen me!' she cried.

Scarlett howled with laughter. 'What, are you worried he'll be jealous? He's a *horse!*'

~

SCOTT WAS SITTING on a bale of hay texting on his phone when they arrived back in the yard, a row of empty water buckets at his feet.

'I might have known,' muttered Sam, jumping off Otto.

Scott shoved his phone in his back pocket. 'Good ride?'

'It was great. Cherry's just brilliant. I've decided I want my next pony to be a 16.2hh thoroughbred. I'm going to skip the 14.2hh stage,' said Scarlett.

Scott noticed Sam scowling at the empty water buckets. 'Before you say anything, Samantha, I did try and fill them, but there's no water.'

'What do you mean?'

Scott sauntered across to the tap outside the tack room and turned the handle. The tap coughed, gurgled and spluttered out a few paltry drops of water.

'See? I've told your mum. She doesn't know where the stopcock is so she's trying to get through to Bella, but it's just going straight to answerphone at the moment.'

Poppy tied Ellie up and began untacking her. 'It might be a leak. Remember that puddle we passed on the way in? I could phone the water board. They might send someone out to have a look.'

'In the meantime where on earth are we going to get water for the horses?' said Scarlett.

She had a point, thought Poppy. The nearest neighbour was probably a quarter of a mile away. She remembered the family of mallards.

'What about the stream? It's a bit of a trek but if we do it together it shouldn't be too bad. At least the water is clean and fresh.'

'Sounds like our only option,' said Sam. 'I'll turn Ellie out if you phone the water board, Poppy. There should be a number in the office somewhere.'

Harvey Smith was sprawled over Bella's dog-eared phone book. Poppy tickled his chin and deposited him on the floor. He immediately jumped onto her lap and began kneading her thighs, purring loudly. Poppy flicked through the phone book to W and there was the number she was looking for in Bella's precise handwriting.

She was just about to pick up the phone and dial when it rang, making her jump. Harvey Smith mewed crossly and sprang off her lap.

'Hello?'

Poppy listened for an answer but all she could hear was static.

'Can I help you?'

Still no answer. Poppy felt irritation rise. This wasn't crossed lines. Someone was deliberately phoning Redhall and giving them the silent treatment, she was sure of it.

'Look, if you're the person who keeps calling, I think you've got the wrong number. You need to check it and stop phoning this one. It's getting really annoying,' she said.

She nearly jumped out of her skin when a bark of bitter laughter rang in her ear.

'Who *is* this?' she said.

But the laughter had been replaced by the drone of the ring tone. Whoever it was had hung up.

～

POPPY FOUND the others stacking buckets ready to carry them down to the stream.

'The water board is going to send someone out in the morning. They say if no-one has turned off the stopcock it's probably a leak. And since none of us know where the stopcock is, they're probably right,' she said. 'Oh, and there was another nuisance call, though this time I heard someone laughing. And when I dialled 1471 it was number withheld.'

'I took one before breakfast,' said Scarlett. 'It's a bit creepy, isn't it? Do you think someone's trying to freak us out?'

Scott's face was scornful. 'They'll have to try harder than that.'

7

Poppy collapsed in an exhausted heap in the shade of an apple tree. Opposite her a pink-faced Scarlett was grimacing as she stretched out her back.

'I'm so sweaty,' she moaned.

'Horses sweat,' Poppy corrected her. 'Men perspire and ladies *glow*.'

'Well, I'm glowing like a lightbulb at the moment. I'm shattered.'

It had taken the four of them a solid two hours of back-breaking work to fill all the water troughs and buckets. The stream had seemed a lot closer when they'd ridden past it. In fact it was a ten minute walk there and even longer on the way back with heavy buckets bumping against their shins and water sloshing all over their feet.

While Poppy had hefted buckets she'd mulled over the last couple of days and she had come to the conclusion that the series of unfortunate events to befall Redhall was no coincidence.

'Scar, I think someone's trying to sabotage the riding school,' she blurted out.

'What do you mean?'

'I know it sounds far-fetched but think about it. The nuisance calls. The delivery from Baxters' that no-one ordered. The lilies. Someone called the farrier to tell him not to come and it wasn't Bella.'

'I think your imagination's gone into overdrive. Who on earth would want to harm the riding school?'

'It's obvious isn't it? Who's in direct competition with Redhall? Who's going to benefit if Bella goes out of business?'

Scarlett gawped at her. 'You don't mean -?'

'Yes, I do,' said Poppy. 'Angela Snell.'

They heard the click of a gate. Sam was walking towards them with a couple of cans of lemonade.

'Don't say anything yet,' Poppy whispered to Scarlett. 'We need to get some hard evidence before we accuse her of anything.'

'How on earth are we going to do that?'

Poppy grinned. 'Fancy a trip to Claydon Manor?'

'But how will we get there?'

'There are a couple of old bikes at the back of the hay barn. We'll ask Sarah if we can borrow them. And we'll go this evening.'

Poppy found Sarah in the kitchen stirring a huge saucepan of bolognese sauce. She glanced at the clock above the sink. 'It'll only be another twenty minutes,' she said.

'It smells yummy. Sarah, you know those two old bikes in the barn?'

Sarah smiled. 'I certainly do. They were mine and my brother's. Why?'

'Scarlett and I wondered if we could go on a bike ride on them after dinner.'

Sarah dipped a teaspoon into the sauce, tasted it and added a pinch of oregano. 'You don't have any cycling helmets.'

'We could wear our riding hats,' Poppy said.

'Alright. As long as you promise to stick to the lanes and be back before it gets dark.'

'I KNEW I shouldn't have had seconds, but Sarah's such a good cook. Her spaghetti was to die for. And now I'm absolutely stuffed,' groaned Scarlett.

They pushed the two mountain bikes out of the barn. Poppy wheeled hers past Cloud's stable and peered in. He was pulling wisps of hay from his hayrack.

'Hey baby,' she called softly. He abandoned the hay and came over to say hello. She breathed in his familiar scent and sighed.

'I wish I could stay here with you all evening, Cloud, but I've got to go. Things to do, people to see,' she told him, kissing his nose. He nudged her and returned to his hay.

'I used to pretend my first bike was a pony,' she told Scarlett. 'I used to practice my rising trot as I cycled round and round the park near our house. And when we got home I would poke handfuls of grass into the handlebars and offer it a bucket of water.'

Scarlett hooted with laughter. She looked down at Sarah's rusted pink Raleigh. 'Let's pretend these are famous horses. It'll make the ride much more fun. Bags mine is Red Rum.'

'Hello Black Beauty,' Poppy said, patting the coal black frame of her bike. She clicked her tongue and pedalled off, Scarlett in close pursuit.

'Trot on,' Poppy shouted in her best riding instructor's voice. 'On the left diagonal please, Scarlett. That's it. Up down, up down.'

The two friends circled the yard, their bikes wobbling dangerously as they bobbed up and down. Horses heads appeared over stable doors as they careered past. Poppy was giggling so hard her insides ached.

'Come on Beauty,' she cried, pedalling as fast as she could. 'Let's race Red Rum to Claydon Manor!'

~

TWENTY MINUTES later the two girls pulled onto the verge opposite a pair of grand wrought iron gates set in an imposing stone wall. To the right was a keypad on a metal post and set into the stone was a slate sign saying *Claydon Manor*.

'Electronic gates,' said Scarlett.

'And CCTV,' said Poppy, nodding towards a small camera on top of one of the huge gate posts.

'How are we going to get in?'

Poppy reached into her backpack and pulled out a royal blue book.

'I found Ariel's equine passport in Bella's office. I'm amazed Angela Snell didn't ask for it when they picked him up. Perhaps she's not quite as efficient as we think. We'll say Sam sent us over with it.'

Scarlett looked impressed. 'Ingenious. Perhaps I'd better let you do the talking.'

'There's a first time for everything,' Poppy teased. 'C'mon, let's press the buzzer.'

They wheeled their bikes across the road and Poppy studied the keypad. 'I guess it's the one with the bell on,' she said, jabbing it with her index finger.

A tinny voice made them jump. 'Who is this?'

Poppy cleared her throat. 'It's, um, Poppy and Scarlett from Redhall. Sam sent us over. We've got Ariel's passport.'

An exasperated sigh emanated from the keypad and the gates clicked and began to swing open.

'You'd better come in,' said the voice.

Poppy and Scarlett pushed their bikes towards a beautiful grey stone Georgian manor house. Poppy's eyes were on stalks as she took in the sleek thoroughbreds grazing in immaculate paddocks on either side of the sweeping gravelled drive.

'Wow,' she said. 'This is some place.'

'Don't forget it was all down to a winning lottery ticket,' said Scarlett, waving her hand dismissively. 'They didn't earn it. They just got lucky.'

A figure was beckoning them from a stable block to the right of the house. Even from this distance Poppy recognised the prickly demeanour of Angela Snell.

'So what are we looking for?' Scarlett asked.

Poppy shrugged. 'I'm not really sure. Anything that might link Snell or the Cannings to what's been happening at Redhall, I suppose.'

They set their bikes against a granite wall and walked over to Angela Snell. The livery yard manager held her hand out. Poppy gave her the passport.

'Thanks,' said Angela curtly. 'I thought Vivienne had it.'

A whinny rang out across the cobbled yard.

'It's Ariel,' said Poppy. 'Can we say a quick hello?'

Angela Snell sighed. 'Just a quick one. I have work to do.'

The black gelding seemed pleased to see them and delicately ate the Polo Scarlett offered him.

'Nice loose box,' said Poppy, noticing the rubber matting, automatic water drinker and thick bed of shavings. 'There's even a smoke alarm. No wonder Vile Vivienne wanted to move him here.'

Angela strode across the yard, checking her watch. 'All done?'

'Is Georgia around?' asked Scarlett.

'Why, are you friends?' said Angela, surprised. Her eyes travelled over Scarlett's dishevelled appearance with barely disguised contempt.

'Not friends exactly,' said Scarlett, unperturbed. 'We used to go to the same school. When Georgia and her mum and dad still lived in a three bedroomed semi in Tavistock and the family car was a clapped out hatchback.'

Poppy's eyes were drawn to the pristine white Range Rover parked in the furthest corner of the yard next to a silver Bentley. It was impossible to imagine the family who owned all this ever having to make do with a clapped out hatchback.

'She's schooling Barley in the indoor arena,' Angela said.

'I'm sure she won't mind us watching,' said Scarlett, dragging Poppy towards the huge wooden-slatted building behind the row of loose boxes before Angela could stop her.

'Trust Georgia to have an indoor *arena*,' she muttered.

Poppy recognised the palomino gelding Georgia was cantering in perfect twenty metre circles at the far end of the arena.

'He's the one Georgia beat Sam on, isn't he?' she said.

Scarlett nodded. 'He's her top jumping pony. Her mum paid over ten thousand pounds for him. He's a demon against the clock.'

'Not as fast as Star though,' said Poppy, remembering how Sam had only lost to Georgia because Barley had rattled a pole which had fallen during Sam's round.

Georgia changed reins and the palomino executed a flawless flying change. As she cantered towards them she noticed them watching and eased Barley into a trot. She stared at them with china blue eyes.

'I recognise you. You were at the Redhall affiliated show last summer. You're Sam's fan club. What are you doing here?' she said.

Scarlett scowled and was about to say something but Poppy cut across her. 'Angela told us to come and say hello. We've just dropped off Ariel's passport.'

Georgia patted her pony's neck and slid off. She was wearing a crimson polo shirt, cream jodhpurs and expensive-looking leather boots the same shade of bitumen black as her plaited hair. Her high cheekbones and English rose complexion made Poppy think of Snow White. Without the seven dwarfs of course. Although Angela would make a convincing Evil Queen.

'Nice place you've got here, Georgia. It puts Redhall to shame,' Poppy said.

Scarlett's eyes widened but Poppy winked at her and she took the hint.

'It's amazing,' she agreed. 'We'd love a guided tour. If you've got time.'

Georgia looked at them warily. Poppy held her breath. They needed evidence that Angela Snell was trying to sabotage Redhall and if being nice to stuck-up Georgia Canning was the only way they were going to get it, it was a price worth paying. She smiled at Georgia hopefully.

'OK,' Georgia shrugged. 'I'll just put Barley away first.' She led the palomino gelding to a row of looseboxes opposite Ariel's.

'How many liveries do you have?' asked Poppy.

'Ten with Ariel. Plus my ponies, Barley and Fizz.'

'You used to have way more than two didn't you?' said Scarlett.

Georgia gave a brief nod and began untacking Barley. Poppy studied the girl's expression for clues but her face gave nothing away. Yet something about her was different. Poppy thought back to the day of the Redhall show. When Georgia had ridden past Poppy had been struck by her hooked Roman nose, the only imperfection in an otherwise flawless face. But as she watched Georgia undo Barley's girth and run up the stirrup leathers she realised the Roman nose had gone, smoothed away by a surgeon's knife.

Georgia led them to the largest tack room Poppy had seen in her life. It looked like a high-end tack shop, with rows of gleaming saddles and bridles and piles of neatly-folded day rugs, night rugs and New Zealand rugs. The room smelt of saddle soap and hoof oil.

'Each livery has their own storage trunk where they keep their grooming kits. Every horse has a daily groom as part of the service,' said Georgia. 'And this is the feed room.'

Poppy and Scarlett followed her into an adjoining room which contained huge bins of food.

'You must get through tons of feed with twelve horses. Where do you get it from,' asked Scarlett conversationally.

'Baxters,' said Georgia. 'They do a monthly delivery.'

Poppy gasped as Scarlett elbowed her sharply in the ribs. Fortunately Georgia had already turned away.

'This is the solarium,' she said, opening the double doors of a high-ceilinged barn. 'We have two heat lamps so two horses can use it at once.'

Poppy cricked her neck to examine the space-age bulbs set in curved units above two empty stalls. 'What do they do that the sun can't?' she asked, genuinely curious.

'The lamps have infra-red rays that help increase blood circulation and muscle elasticity, which can help reduce healing time for injuries. We also use them for drying horses after a bath, especially in the winter.' Georgia sounded as if she was reading from a brochure. She flicked a switch on the wall and the lamps in the solarium nearest to them glowed orange. 'And they're nice and warm to sit under when you're cleaning your tack.'

'You clean your own tack?' asked Scarlett in disbelief.

Georgia shot her a scornful look. 'Who else do you think does it?'

She switched off the solarium and stalked over to a huge metal contraption which reminded Poppy of an industrial-sized rotary washing line.

'This is the horse walker. All the horses have weekly solariums and are exercised daily, either by Angela or me or on the horse walker.'

'Wouldn't they prefer to go out for a hack?' said Scarlett. Poppy gave her a warning look. They were supposed to be keeping Georgia on side after all.

Georgia shrugged. 'Probably. But owners expect us to have one for the price they're paying.'

'Do you have any vacancies at the moment?' asked Poppy.

'Why? Think you can afford it here?'

Poppy shook her head and kept her face neutral, although inside she was seething. 'I prefer to keep my pony at home, thanks. I just wondered.'

'Whatever,' said Georgia. 'We have two at the moment. The two loose-boxes next to Ariel. Though Angela is confident they'll be filled very shortly.'

They walked back to the yard. Behind the palatial Georgian mansion the sun was setting.

'Thanks for showing us around. It was very *interesting*, although I don't think my pony Blaze would like it here,' said Scarlett.

Georgia stared at her. 'I used to know a pony called Blaze. She was the first pony I ever rode. She was owned by the daughter of a friend of my mother's. They lived on a ramshackle farm in Waterby.'

'We still do,' Scarlett said quietly.

'I *thought* I recognised you at the Redhall show but you said we'd never met before.' Georgia's cut-glass accent sounded unnecessarily loud.

'We used to go to the same school a long time ago. Before you had all *this*,' Scarlett said, with a sweep of her arm.

There was an awkward silence. Poppy could feel Scarlett bristling beside her and gave her a nudge.

'Come on Scar, we'd better make a move. There aren't any lights on the bikes and we promised Sarah we'd be home before it gets dark.'

Scarlett nodded, turned on her heels and headed for the bikes without a word. Poppy gave Georgia an apologetic look and went to follow her but stopped when the older girl started speaking.

'Your friend Scarlett won't believe me but I was insanely jealous of her and her brother, growing up on a farm like Ashworthy. I know it was tatty and tumbledown, but I used to love spending time there. It seemed like the perfect life to me.'

'And this isn't?' said Poppy, perplexed, thinking of the solariums, the horse walker and the huge indoor arena.

Georgia looked at her feet. 'Some things are more important than money.'

8

'That's easy enough to say when you've got millions in the bank,' said Scarlett scathingly as they pedalled back to Redhall.

'Sam says they've spent all their money, remember. That's why they had to sell most of Georgia's ponies and take on all the liveries.' Poppy swerved to avoid a pothole, almost colliding with Scarlett. 'Sorry Red Rum.'

But Scarlett wasn't in the mood for make believe any more and they rode the rest of the way in silence. It was only that night as they lay in bed that Poppy decided to tackle the subject again.

'So do you think Angela and Georgia are behind all this?'

Scarlett looked at Poppy as though she was mad. 'You bet I do! Look at the evidence. They use Baxters'. They have vacancies. And, most importantly, they have a motive.'

'Do they,' asked Poppy faintly. It all seemed a bit circumstantial to her.

'Money!' Scarlett declared triumphantly. 'Isn't that what everything comes down to in the end?'

~

A MAN in a white van pulled into the yard as Poppy was grooming Cloud

447

the next morning. He showed her an identity card on a lanyard around his neck.

'I'm from the water board. I've come to see what the problem is with your supply,' he said.

Poppy jogged across to the house and called Sarah, who showed him the stopcock. He scratched his head.

'There's no problem this end. It must be further down the line.'

'There's a water leak in one of the fields. I can show you if you like. I was just about to turn Cloud out anyway,' said Poppy.

He grabbed a tool kit from the back of his van and followed her to the paddock they'd ridden through the day before. The puddle was even bigger.

'Hmm, this looks serious,' he said, pulling out a mobile phone and calling for reinforcements.

Poppy, Scarlett and Sam had finished morning stables and were about to start the weary trudge to the river for water when the engineer reappeared, a satisfied smile on his face. He walked over to the outside tap and turned it on. The three children cheered when a jet of water gushed out.

'Well, I've solved the mystery,' he said, showing them two short lengths of blue plastic pipe. 'But I can't explain why it happened.'

'What do you mean?' asked Poppy.

'Pipes like this are buried about a foot underground and should last for decades,' he told them. 'But someone had dug down and cut this one clean through.'

～

Poppy, Scarlett and Sam watched in silence as the van disappeared down the Redhall drive.

'I don't understand. Why would anyone want to cut our pipe?' said Sam.

Poppy looked at Scarlett, who nodded and mouthed, 'Tell him.'

'We think someone's got it in for Redhall, Sam,' Poppy said. 'That all the stuff that's been happening - the mixed-up order from Baxters', the nuisance calls, the flowers, the water leak - is being done deliberately to sabotage Bella's business.'

'That's ludicrous,' said Sam. 'Why would anyone want to do that?'

'Why do you think?' cried Scarlett. 'Use your brain for goodness' sake. They want to steal her liveries.'

'But who would want to do that?' he said with a frown.

'Angela Snell and Georgia La-Di-Da Canning, that's who,' hissed Scarlett.

'Well, we're not one hundred per cent sure,' said Poppy. 'But it's certainly looking like it might be.'

Sam looked at each of them in turn. Scarlett glared back and Poppy held her hands up helplessly. 'We can't think who else it might be,' she said.

'I suppose I ought to tell Scott,' he said. 'Any idea where he is?'

'He's popped into Tavistock. He said he'd be back before lunch,' said Scarlett.

'That's another morning stables he's conveniently missed. I don't know why Gran bothered to ask him to come. He's been about as much use as a chocolate teapot.'

Poppy silently agreed but Scarlett leapt to his defence. 'He did help get the water yesterday. And I'm sure he'll help with evening stables.'

'There's a first time for everything,' Sam grumbled.

Hoping to head off an argument, Poppy clapped her hands.

'Hey you two, I've had a brilliant idea! Now we don't have to spend an hour fetching water let's take the ponies out for a ride.'

THAT NIGHT POPPY lay in bed mulling everything over. Should they phone Bella and tell her what was happening? Poppy didn't think so. Not yet. She had enough on her plate looking after her Auntie Margaret. Should they call the police? Poppy pictured portly Inspector Bill Pearson and his penchant for digestive biscuits. When Poppy and her friend Hope Taylor had turned up at Tavistock Police Station with what must have seemed a dubious account of deceit and duplicity he had listened to everything they had to say - and had believed them. But all Poppy would be able to report this time was a series of events that could be linked but could also be totally unrelated.

Poppy tried to see it through Inspector Pearson's eyes. John the farrier could have misunderstood a call from Bella confirming his visit to shoe

Ariel. All it needed was a crackly line and, after all, the phone reception out here was patchy at best. Sarah's theory about someone in the village hearing about Margaret's fall and jumping to the wrong conclusions might be right after all. Perhaps Baxters' had made a genuine mistake and accidentally mixed their order up with someone else's. No matter how hard she tried Poppy couldn't explain away the nuisance calls and the damaged water pipe, but she could see they didn't exactly amount to a vendetta.

And if it was some kind of hate campaign, who was behind it all, anyway? Scarlett was convinced that it was Georgia Canning and her hard-nosed livery yard manager. Poppy wasn't about to rule the pair out either. But they hadn't exactly found any incriminating evidence during their visit to Claydon Manor. And there had been something about Georgia Canning that evening that didn't fit with the win-at-all-costs spoilt little rich girl Poppy had always assumed she was. Although there had been flashes of her trademark snootiness she'd also seemed subdued. If Poppy had been pushed to describe her she'd have said she was lonely.

Poppy checked the time on her phone. Half past twelve. She was physically exhausted yet sleep seemed tantalisingly out of reach. The room was uncomfortably hot. She threw off her covers, padded across the room to the window and pulled open the curtains. The moon was large and low, almost but not quite a full moon. Poppy opened the catches of the Victorian sash window and was just about to heave it open when a movement on the driveway caught her eye.

A hooded figure was creeping along the side of the hedge towards the road. For a moment Poppy was rooted to the spot, paralysed by indecision. The figure stopped and glanced back towards the house. It must have seen her pale face at the window because it turned, crouched down and ran towards a vehicle parked haphazardly on the verge on the other side of the road. The sight of the fleeing intruder galvanised Poppy into action. She tugged at the sash window, but years of neglect had left it stuck fast. Instead she banged on the glass with her fist as hard as she dared. But it was too late. The car was disappearing down the road. Poppy watched with resignation until the tail lights were tiny red pinpricks in the dark and then disappeared altogether.

Her nerves were so taut that when she heard a sound behind her she almost jumped out of her skin.

'Wha's goin' on?' her best friend mumbled. Scarlett sat up and rubbed her eyes. She saw Poppy at the window. 'What on earth are you *doing?*'

Poppy started pulling on jeans and a jumper. 'I've just seen an intruder. We need to go and check everything's OK. You get dressed and I'll go and wake Sam and Scott. I'll meet you in the kitchen.'

Before Scarlett had a chance to answer Poppy legged it out of their room and turned down the hallway towards the bedroom Sam and Scott were sharing. She tapped on the door and let herself in. Sam was asleep in the nearest bed, the frown he'd worn since Scott's arrival softened by sleep. Poppy shook his shoulder. His eyes snapped open.

'What's wrong?'

Poppy told him about the intruder. 'We need to check on the horses. I'll wake Scott.'

But Scott's bed was empty.

'He's still not back?' Poppy said in exasperation.

Sam shook his head. 'I'll text him.'

They met in the kitchen. Poppy handed them each a torch and unlocked the back door. They looked at each other, their faces grave.

'I'll check the stables and barn if you two look over the paddocks,' said Sam. 'Stick together, just in case. And shout if you need me.'

Poppy and Scarlett nodded and let themselves out. But when Poppy headed for the yard instead of the fields Scarlett grabbed her arm.

'Where are you going?'

'I have to check on Cloud first, Scar.'

She ran across to her pony's stable and slid open the bolt. Training the torch on the straw bed so she didn't blind him with its powerful beam she whispered his name. Cloud opened an eye and whickered. Poppy balanced the torch on the narrow window ledge and threw her arms around his neck in relief.

Scarlett's tousled head appeared over the stable door.

'All OK?'

Poppy nodded.

'Blaze too. Come on, let's go and check on the riding school ponies.'

Poppy kissed Cloud's nose and joined her friend. On the other side of the yard they could see the beam of Sam's torch as he looked in each stable.

'How many are out?' Poppy asked. Her brain felt scrambled and she couldn't remember who was stabled and who wasn't.

'Rosie and Buster are in the first paddock,' said Scarlett, counting on her fingers. 'Salt and Pepper are in the next and Treacle's in the top paddock on his own.'

Poppy exhaled with relief when her torch picked out Rosie. The strawberry roan mare was standing in a field shelter with Buster, the chestnut Dartmoor pony Poppy's friend Hope had learnt to ride on.

'We should check them over,' said Poppy. The two girls climbed the gate and crossed the field to the shelter. The ponies watched them sleepily as they ran their hands along them and lifted their feet.

'They're fine,' said Scarlett. 'Let's check on Salt and Pepper.'

The two fleabitten grey New Forest geldings were brothers, bred by Bella out of Rosie's dam, an elderly mare called Conker who was stabled overnight. Salt and Pepper had inherited their dam's easy-going nature and none of Rosie's occasional stroppiness and were the most popular ponies with the more experienced riders at Redhall.

Woken by the sound of voices, the two geldings stood by the gate watching them, their grey ears pricked. Their breath was warm in the chill of the night and they nibbled at the girls' pockets for treats as they were checked over.

'They're OK, too,' said Scarlett. She paused. 'Are you sure it was a man you saw Poppy?'

'Yes!' Poppy replied hotly, though she was actually beginning to doubt herself. Her eyes couldn't have been playing tricks on her in the moonlight, could they? But no, she had definitely seen the figure and heard the car engine splutter into life.

'Don't get your knickers in a twist, I was only asking,' said Scarlett mildly.

'I know it sounds far-fetched. But I definitely saw someone, Scar.'

In the distance they heard the rumble of a motorbike.

'Sounds like Scott's back at last,' said Poppy. She climbed the gate into Treacle's paddock and shone the torch in front of her, zigzagging the beam to and fro as though she was waving a sparkler on Bonfire night.

'I can't see him, can you?' said Scarlett, who was searching the other side of the paddock.

'Perhaps he's in his field shelter,' Poppy said. She directed the torch into the wooden shelter. It was empty. 'Perhaps not,' she said, half to herself.

'I've checked the rest of the field. He's not here,' said Scarlett, her voice rising a level. 'Do you think he could have got out?'

Poppy pictured the solid post and rail fences that bordered the Redhall paddocks. Bella was meticulous about maintenance and they were kept in perfect condition. She doubted that even the wayward Treacle could stage an escape. Even so, it was worth checking.

'You check the fences and I'll look behind the shelter. Poppy remembered there was a gap of about a metre between the back wall of the weather-boarded shelter and the fence. Bella used it to store wheelbarrows and the skip and rake for poo-picking. She shone her torch down the gap. The light settled on a perfectly round chestnut rump.

'There you are, you little monkey.'

'Any luck?' Scarlett called.

'I've found him!' Poppy shouted. She walked over to him. 'Come on little man, let's get you back in the field.' She gave him a gentle push. Treacle took a step forward and squealed in pain. 'What's wrong?' Poppy cried, shining the torch down. Her blood began pounding in her ears. Rusty barbed wire clung to the pony's back legs like ivy strangling a sapling.

9

P oppy could see beads of blood where the barbs had pierced Treacle's skin. He tried to free his legs but as he struggled the wire twisted tighter.

'Steady boy,' Poppy murmured. 'You're making it worse.'

Another beam of light appeared around the far end of the shelter. Behind it was Scarlett's familiar silhouette.

'He's caught in barbed wire, Scar. You need to get Sam to call the vet. And see if Bella has any wire cutters. I'll stay with Treacle.'

Scarlett shone her torch at the little chestnut gelding's back legs and gasped. 'How did it happen?'

'That's not important right now. We need the vet Scar. Just go!'

Scarlett turned on her heels and began running towards the house. Poppy moved carefully up to Treacle's head and stroked his neck, talking to him quietly. Every now and then the gelding tugged at the wires and Poppy pictured the barbs sinking their rusty teeth even deeper into the thin skin around his cannon bones.

'Hurry up,' she whispered into the dark, willing Scarlett to arrive with help. What seemed like hours later she heard voices crossing the field.

'Where is he?' Scott asked urgently. Poppy was sure she could detect a catch in his voice.

'Behind the shelter,' panted Scarlett.

Scott appeared with Sam at his shoulder. When he saw Treacle he dropped to his knees and ran his hand along the gelding's back. Poppy could sense Treacle relaxing to his touch.

'Shine your torch on his back legs Poppy,' Scott said.

Poppy did as she was told. Scott swore under his breath as he took in the torn skin on Treacle's poor legs. He looked up at Sam, his face ashen. 'Pass me the wire cutters. We need to cut the wire before it does any more damage.'

Sam handed the solid metal wire cutters to Scott and joined Scarlett and Poppy. He slipped a headcollar onto the gelding. Treacle offered no resistance. His head was low and his normally mischievous eyes were dull with exhaustion. Poppy kept her torch trained on Treacle and they talked in low whispers as Scott snipped away at the barbed wire.

'The vet's on his way. Mum'll bring him straight over the minute he gets here. It's the same one who came out to put Merry down.'

Scarlett gave a small cry. Poppy put her arm around her.

'He'll be OK Scar. Though he's going to need a lot of stitches.'

'Good job Gran keeps up to date with all their injections,' said Sam, looking at the lengths of rusty wire.

Scott stood up and stretched his back. 'That's the wire cut,' he said.

'Should we walk him back to the yard?' asked Poppy.

'Let's see what the vet says,' said Scott.

They all breathed a sigh of relief when they saw the beams of two torches approaching from the direction of the house. Sarah had pulled on some leggings and a fleecy jumper, though she hadn't realised in her haste that she was wearing it back to front. The vet also looked bleary-eyed and his dark auburn hair was dishevelled. But he'd probably been dragged from his bed by the emergency call too, Poppy realised.

'Bella's not having a very good week, is she?' he said, dropping his medicine bag on the floor and stooping to look at Treacle's legs. They watched in silence as he examined the cuts, one by one, under the beam of Poppy's torch.

'He's going to need a few stitches, but it's not as bad as it looks,' he said finally, sitting back on his heels. 'I'll wash out the wounds with a saline solution and give him a course of antibiotics to prevent an infection. I'll also give him something to ease the pain. But I think he's probably had a lucky escape. If those cuts had been deep enough to damage his joints or tendons it could have been a whole different story.'

Poppy felt a wave of relief wash over her.

'Let's get him back to the yard. It'll be easier to do the stitches there.' The vet closed his medicine bag and set off with Sarah towards the stables. Scott took Treacle's lead rope from Sam and the gelding hobbled slowly back.

'Let's pick up those bits of barbed wire. The last thing we need is for another of the horses to cut themselves,' Poppy said.

They picked up as many pieces as they could see.

'That'll do for now. We'll have another look in the morning,' said Sam.

By the time they reached the yard the vet had washed out Treacle's cuts and was stitching the flaps of torn skin back together, a look of deep concentration on his face. After half an hour Treacle's two white socks resembled a jagged patchwork of black stiches. The vet peeled off his pair of blue surgical gloves and ran a hand through his rumpled hair.

'That's him done. He's had a shot of antibiotics and I'll give you some painkillers to add to his feed for the next couple of days. Keep him stabled and I'll pop by in a couple of days' time to see how he's doing.'

'We'll put him in Ariel's stable,' said Scott, handing Treacle's leadrope to Scarlett. 'I'll make it ready for him.' He shook the vet's hand. 'Thanks for coming so quickly. We really appreciate it.'

The vet nodded, climbed into his Land Rover and gave them a brief wave as he drove away into the night. Scott disappeared into the barn, emerging with a bale of straw. He filled the hayrack with a couple of sections of meadow hay and filled two water buckets. Soon Treacle was settled in Ariel's stable, pulling wisps of hay from the rack. Satisfied the pony was comfortable Scott bolted the door and kicked over the bottom door latch.

'Come on, let's go,' he said.

Poppy followed the others into the kitchen and accepted a mug of hot chocolate from Sarah with a grateful smile. They sat at the kitchen table cradling the mugs in their hands, deep in their own thoughts.

Sarah broke the silence. 'I'll phone Mum in the morning to tell her what's happened.' She glanced at the clock above the range cooker. It was a quarter to three. 'Well, later this morning,' she corrected herself. She drained the rest of her hot chocolate and stood up. 'I'm going up. Don't be too late.'

They shook their heads. Once they heard Sarah's footsteps on the landing Scott turned to Poppy and said, 'Sam told me you saw someone driving away. Tell me what happened.'

Poppy described the shadowy figure, dredging up any details she could think of that might help identify their intruder.

'He was wearing a coat with the hood up rather than a hoodie. It was dark grey or black. And he was wearing dark navy jeans,' she said.

'He?' asked Scarlett sharply.

Poppy shrugged. 'I wouldn't swear on it. But I just got the feeling it was a man by the way he walked.'

'And you checked the other horses and the rest of the yard?'

'Everything else was OK,' said Sam.

Scott pushed his mug away, as if he suddenly didn't have the appetite for it. 'And you think this was deliberate?'

Sam nodded. 'Gran hates barbed wire. That's why all the fences are post and rail. You know how careful she is, Scott. I bet there wasn't a single strand of barbed wire in the whole place.'

'And yet Treacle was trapped in coils of the stuff. Why would someone want to hurt him? It doesn't make sense.'

'They weren't trying to hurt Treacle,' said Poppy. 'They were targeting Redhall. They want to hurt Bella.'

oppy felt as though she'd been asleep for a nanosecond when the unwelcome buzz of the alarm on her mobile phone dragged her from her dreams. They'd agreed to put morning stables back until half past seven, an hour later than usual, because they'd been so late the night before. Scarlett groaned and pulled her duvet over her head but Poppy climbed stiffly out of bed, picked up her towel and headed for the bathroom.

By the time she'd showered Scarlett had at least got out of bed and was staring out of the window.

'It's too dry for footprints and tyre marks,' she said glumly.

'Who are you, Sherlock Holmes?' Poppy teased.

'I wonder what car Angela Snell drives,' said Scarlett, ignoring her.

Poppy raised her eyes to the ceiling and headed downstairs. To her surprise Scott was already at the table, working his way through a mountain of scrambled eggs on toast.

'Scrambled or poached?' said Sarah, waving a wooden spoon at Poppy. She realised she was starving.

'Poached please,' she said, pouring a glass of orange juice. 'Did you manage to get through to Bella?'

Sarah shook her head. 'I couldn't work out why her mobile wasn't working. And then I found this.' She pulled a mobile phone charger from a kitchen drawer. 'She's only forgotten to take her charger.'

'If her phone's dead, how did she phone the farrier?' Poppy pondered.

'Have you tried Great Auntie Margaret's home phone?' asked Sam from the doorway.

'Yes. It just rings and rings and there's no answerphone so I can't leave a message. I suppose Mum's spending each day at the hospital with her. I'll try again tonight.'

Scott wiped his last piece of toast around his plate.

'I'll change Treacle's dressings and then give you a hand with the liveries,' he said.

He must have caught the look of surprise that flashed across Poppy's face because he added sheepishly, 'I know I haven't been much help since I arrived, but that's going to change, I promise.'

Scott was as good as his word and once he'd seen to Treacle he began mucking out Cherry and Otto's stables. Poppy had to hand it to him, once he'd made up his mind to help he worked like a demon, finishing both stables before Poppy was even halfway through Paint's. Little beads of perspiration dotted his forehead like raindrops on a car windscreen. He wiped them off with the back of his hand and grinned at Scarlett, who had wandered across the yard with a broom, still looking half asleep.

'Afternoon,' he teased. Scarlett yawned and grinned back.

'I just can't wake up,' she said. 'I reckon we only had about three hours' sleep last night.' She glanced over to the drive. 'Oh, I wonder who that is.'

Poppy pushed the laden wheelbarrow out of Paint's stable and joined her. A red people carrier was crawling up the drive. The sun was glinting off the windscreen making it impossible to see who was driving. The car came to a stop and a slight figure in jeans and a teeshirt flung open the door and jumped out.

'Tia!' cried Scarlett, dropping the broom she was carrying and running over to give her a hug. 'It's great to see you, but what are you doing here? There aren't any lessons this week.'

'I know. I was going mad at home on my own. I persuaded Mum to give me a lift up,' she said. She looked over to the car. Her mum wound down the window, tapped her watch and called out, 'I'll see you in an hour.'

Tia nodded and turned back to Poppy and Scarlett, her face suddenly serious. 'I just wanted to be with people who were there when it happened. Mum and Dad have been trying to talk to me about it but they don't really understand.'

Poppy knew exactly what she meant. No matter how hard she tried not to think about it during the day, at night, when she finally succumbed to sleep, her dreams were filled with images of the accident. Merry somersaulting forwards. Rufus landing on Niamh's back. Scarlett's eyes wide with shock as she screamed. Sometimes Poppy wondered if her dreams would be haunted forever.

Poppy stuck her head over Cherry's stable door. 'Is it OK if we finish the stables after lunch, Scott?'

He nodded. 'Sure.'

'Sam's in the barn,' said Scarlett, linking arms with Tia. 'Let's go and find him.'

Poppy loved Bella's hay barn. From the outside the timber-framed weather-boarded building was nondescript, but inside the feeling of space and timelessness reminded her of a cathedral. Shafts of light danced from floor to ceiling like swirling sprites and although the intense smell of newly-cut hay made her sneeze, Poppy swore it captured the very essence of summer.

As they walked through the big double doors there was a shout - 'TIMBEERRR!!' - and a bale of hay bounced down from the top of the stack and landed at their feet. They looked up to see Sam grinning at them from the small space between the tightly-stacked hay and the roof.

Scarlett, who had been playing in hay barns since she could walk, scaled the bales as nimbly as a mountain goat. Tia and Poppy looked at the near vertical wall of hay and then at each other.

'You go first,' Tia said.

'Thanks.' Poppy stuck a toe between two bales as if she were mounting a horse and pulled herself up. Bale by bale she clambered up the hay, eventually reaching the top. She heaved herself over the last bale and sat down with relief. Seconds later Tia joined her.

Poppy studied Tia's face as she caught her breath. A year older than her and Scarlett, Tia wasn't textbook pretty, but she had thick, wavy dark blonde hair which framed delicate features. Today her eyes were puffy, as if she'd been crying. Which, Poppy imagined, she probably had.

Scarlett was the first to speak. 'So, how's Niamh?'

Tia shook her head and bit her bottom lip. 'Not good. Mum spoke to her mum last night. She's bruised her spine. She can't move from the waist down.'

'Bruised, not broken?' said Poppy, hope flooding through her.

Tia nodded. 'At first they thought she might have fractured it but she had another scan yesterday morning and it's just bruised.'

'So she'll be able to walk again, once the bruise has healed?' said Scarlett.

'That's the million dollar question, Mum says. She might, she might not.' Tia took a deep breath. 'It depends how much damage the swelling has done to her spinal cord and they might not know that for weeks. Even months.'

'Poor Niamh,' said Sam.

A single tear ran down Tia's cheek. 'And it's all my fault.'

'No it isn't,' cried Poppy.

'Yes it is! If I'd reacted quicker I could have stopped Roof in time. If I'd pulled him left and not right he would have missed Niamh altogether. If I hadn't been there, she would have been fine. Maybe a bit winded, but that's all. Don't you see, I was to blame!'

'You can't think like that, otherwise you'd spend your whole life thinking what if,' said Poppy. 'Anyway, what if we hadn't cantered? Merry would probably have missed the rabbit hole altogether. What if I'd been riding behind Niamh instead of you? It would have been Cloud's hoof in her back, not Rufus's.'

'What if Claydon Manor had never opened a livery yard?' spat Scarlett. 'Bella wouldn't have lost any liveries, she wouldn't have had to start holding riding camps, we wouldn't have been her guinea pigs and Merry and Niamh would never have even been on that ride, that's what. I blame Angela Snell.'

Tia looked at Scarlett in confusion. 'Who's Angela Snell?'

'Doesn't matter,' said Sam.

Poppy felt the beginnings of a sneeze fizzing up her nostrils. She pinched the bridge of her nose. 'Do you know if Niamh's dad is still planning to sue Bella?'

Tia looked shocked. 'I didn't know he was going to. Mum didn't mention that. Anyway, he thinks it's my fault, too.'

'What do you mean?' said Sam.

'I wanted to go and see Niamh in hospital to say sorry. Her mum didn't mind but her dad said over his dead body. Mum said she could hear him yelling at Niamh's mum while they were on the phone. She reckons he's probably having some kind of breakdown.'

11

Tia left just before lunch.

'Let us know if you hear any news about Niamh,' said Scarlett.

Tia nodded. 'And tell Bella to give me a ring once everything is back to normal.'

They waved as the red people carrier drove off.

'I don't think it ever will be,' said Poppy.

'Will be what?' said Scott, appearing from the barn with a bale of hay in each hand.

'Normal,' said Poppy. 'I don't think it'll ever be normal again.'

Scott dropped the bales, sat down on one and motioned Poppy, Scarlett and Sam to do the same.

'We need to talk about that,' he said. 'After I mucked out I searched the fields for barbed wire. I checked every fence and hedge. And do you know what?'

'There isn't any,' said Sam.

'That's right, Samantha. There isn't any. So how did Treacle end up with barbed wire wrapped around his legs?'

The other three were silent.

'Anyway,' said Scott, 'it got me thinking about everything else that's been happening since Bella went up to Inverness. And I reckon it's too much of a fluke for it not to be connected.' He paused for effect. 'I think someone has a vendetta against Redhall.'

Poppy exhaled loudly. Sam raised his eyes to the sky. Even Scarlett, for whom Scott could do no wrong, tutted loudly. He looked at them all in turn, confusion in his muddy brown eyes.

'What is it?'

Sam jumped to his feet. 'We worked that out ages ago, super sleuth. The question is, what are we going to do about it?'

'We need to put some simple security measures in place. I want to chain and padlock the field gates, make sure the office, tack room and barn are locked at all times - even if we're around - and I want us to take it in turns to check on the horses every couple of hours during the night.'

Scarlett groaned. 'You're kidding. I'm already shattered! Look at the size of the bags under my eyes! You could do a weekly supermarket shop with them, and I'm not joking.'

'Sam and I'll do checks at midnight and two o'clock, and you two can do the four o'clock one. We're all up at six anyway.'

Before Scarlett could reply the phone in Bella's office began ringing.

'I'm not getting it,' she said. 'It'll be another one of those nuisance calls and they freak me out.'

Poppy was about to get up and answer it when Scott jumped to his feet and headed for the office. But before he was halfway across the yard the ringing stopped. Seconds later Sarah appeared with a bag of carrots in one hand and the phone in the other.

'It's a man called Stanley Smith from the Tavistock Herald,' she said. 'He wants to talk to someone about the riding school, so I suggested he speak to you, Scott.' She held out the carrots.

'I don't think that's going to work,' he said.

Sarah looked down and laughed. 'Sorry. Try the phone.'

Scott sat back down on the bale of hay and held the handset close to his ear. Poppy nudged Scarlett, who was grumbling about another broken night's sleep, pointed at Scott and held a finger to her lips. Stanley Smith, nicknamed Sniffer because of his nose for a good story, had once interviewed Poppy and her brother Charlie when they'd seen a big cat on the moor. Sniffer loved a bad news story above all else. Why did he want to speak to someone at Redhall? It didn't bode well.

Scott chewed on a nail as he listened to Sniffer, his expression turning from curiosity to disbelief and then to outrage.

'You've heard *what*? Who on earth told you that? No, it's not true! Yes, the vet was here, but that was to see one of the riding school ponies. No, he hasn't got strangles! He was cut by barbed wire. You need to get your facts straight before you start throwing around accusations like that, mate.'

Scott shot up and began pacing across the yard. 'What d'you think I mean? Someone's been feeding you a pack of lies. The yard isn't on shut down. We don't have strangles. And if you publish anything to suggest we have I will sue you. And that's not a threat, it's a promise.'

Scott ended the call with an angry jab of his index finger and turned to face them. 'Someone emailed the Herald this morning to say the yard was on shutdown after two of the ponies were diagnosed with strangles.'

He sat down heavily on the hay bale and ran his hands through his hair.

Sarah looked puzzled. 'What's strangles?'

'It's a super-contagious disease that affects horses' upper respiratory tracts, Mum,' said Sam. 'It can cause these really nasty pus-filled abscesses on the sides of their heads and their throats.'

Sarah pulled a face. 'Not sure I needed quite that much detail, thank you Sam. But none of the horses have strangles, do they?'

Scott shook his head.

'So what's the problem?'

'Don't you see? All it needs is for a rumour to get out that there's a confirmed case and Redhall's future is on the line. The liveries Bella does have left will be out of here like a shot. People will be worried about coming here for shows. The place will be stigmatised. I know a livery yard that had an actual outbreak. The horses were quarantined and eventually all recovered. But the yard never did. It went out of business shortly after,' said Scott.

'Did Sniffer say who told him?' Poppy asked.

'An anonymous email was sent to the newsroom from a Hotmail account.'

'No way of tracing it, I suppose,' said Sam. 'Is there anything we can do?'

Poppy thought hard. They needed to be upfront and quash any

rumours before they reached the liveries. 'We should phone everyone and tell them what's happened before they hear anything themselves. If they need reassuring they can phone the vet. He'll be able to tell them why he was here last night.'

Scott spent the next half an hour on the phone talking to Bella's few remaining liveries.

'How did it go?' asked Scarlett when he finally finished.

'Debbie virtually had a meltdown and was threatening to pull Cherry and Otto from the yard. I did point out that if the rumour was true no other yard would touch her horses with a bargepole until we were clear of strangles anyway. And if it wasn't true there was no reason not to stay. She's going to phone the vet to check, but I think she'll probably stay. Ellie and Paint's owners were both fine. They've kept horses here for years and were more worried about who could be starting the rumour.'

'Join the club,' said Sam morosely.

Poppy looked around at their worried faces. 'Come on, let's go for a ride. Otherwise we'll end up going stir crazy, staying here and worrying about everything.'

Scarlett's face brightened. 'Can I ride Cherry?'

SCARLETT WAS ALREADY SITTING on Cherry by the time Poppy led Cloud over to the mounting block. Scott was riding Otto and Sam was on Star. The two Connemaras, one as black as night, the other dappled grey, followed the bay and chestnut thoroughbreds out of the yard.

Scarlett swung around in the saddle. 'Let's head over towards Claydon Manor,' she called.

'She's obsessed,' Poppy muttered to Sam.

'There is a nice ride that goes past the manor house. It takes a couple of hours but we've got time,' he said.

'Perfect,' said Scarlett. Soon she was chatting to Scott about his job at the showjumping yard. He was a great rider, Poppy had to admit. He sat tall and deeply in the saddle and had the lightest contact on Otto's reins. The big chestnut gelding's long, loping gait was relaxed as he strode out next to his stablemate.

They turned off the road onto the moor and followed a dusty farm track. Cloud felt fresh and full of energy and every so often he snatched at his bit and broke into a jog. Cherry swished her black tail irritably whenever he came too close for comfort. They clattered along the track until they reached a farmyard. Cloud spooked at a rusty plough half buried by brambles and almost collided with Star.

'Sorry,' said Poppy. 'He's a bit full of himself today.'

'There's a great place for a gallop in a minute,' said Sam. The track cut through two fields of barley, which shimmered silver green in the sun. Scott looked back.

'Ready?' he asked.

'Yes,' said Sam, tightening his reins. Even the perfectly-schooled Star was now jogging sideways up the path. Poppy nodded.

The two thoroughbreds broke into a canter, Cloud and Star hot on their heels. Soon Cherry and Otto were galloping, their hooves thundering like racehorses in the Derby. Cloud lengthened his stride and Poppy crouched low over his neck as he raced to catch up with them. Star matched him stride for stride, their necks outstretched and their manes rippling in the wind. Cloud was strong and surefooted and Poppy felt a bolt of total euphoria that pasted a grin to her face and cancelled out all the worry of the last few days.

The track cut through the barley and climbed the side of the valley. The four horses galloped up the hill, their tails flying.

'Horse ahead!' called Scott. He pulled Otto back into a canter and the others followed suit. Poppy looked up to see a palomino pony standing as still as a sentry on the brow of the hill. A girl in a candy pink teeshirt with matching silk was watching them intently, a hand to her forehead to shield the sun from her eyes. The four Redhall horses slowed to a walk. The girl spun her pony around and shrieked, 'Stay away from us!'

Poppy would have recognised that voice anywhere. 'It's Georgia Canning!'

'Why's she screaming at us?' said Scarlett.

Georgia and her pony were now only metres away. 'I said stay away! You shouldn't even be out. It's totally irresponsible!'

'What do you mean?' said Scott.

Suddenly Poppy realised. 'She thinks we've got strangles!'

Scarlett was shocked. 'But how can she? Only the person who emailed the Herald and that reporter know. Unless -'

'-she or Angela were the ones who sent that email,' finished Poppy.

Georgia was still screeching at Scott, who was trying to get close enough to tell her that there was no strangles at Redhall.

'I've had enough of this,' said Scarlett. She cleared her throat and bellowed, 'There's no strangles at Redhall!' Cherry leapt about three feet into the air. Scarlett didn't bat an eyelid. Poppy wished yet again that she was half as good a rider as her best friend.

Georgia narrowed her eyes and looked Scarlett up and down. 'Why should I believe you?'

'Do you really think we'd be mad enough to take the horses out if the yard was on shut down?' Sam said scathingly.

Georgia looked uncertain. Her pony stepped forward and whickered softly to Cloud. She caught Poppy's eye.

'It really is true,' said Poppy quietly. 'The horses are all fine. But who told you?'

Georgia shrugged. 'I can't remember.'

Scarlett tutted loudly.

'Please tell us, Georgia. It's really important we find out who's spreading these rumours,' Poppy said.

Georgia stared down the valley towards Redhall. Something tugged at Poppy's memory. Something Bella had said about Georgia the day of the affiliated show, when Georgia had beaten Sam to second place.

'Hey, I remember. You used to ride at Redhall, didn't you?'

Georgia glanced at Poppy and gave a faint nod.

'Gran taught you to ride, didn't she Georgia?' said Sam. 'Before your family came into all that money. She was always singing your praises. She loved that you were so single-minded and ambitious. In fact she didn't charge your mum for your lessons half the time, did she?'

Poppy saw indecision behind Georgia's eyes and took advantage.

'Redhall's in serious trouble. Someone's trying to put Bella out of business and we need to stop them before it's too late. Who told you about the strangles, Georgia?'

'Angela,' said Georgia finally. 'She told me while I was tacking up Barley. She sounded -'

'What did she sound?' said Scarlett sharply.

'She sounded *pleased*.'

12

'I knew it!' said Scarlett. 'We need to ride straight to Claydon and have it out with her, right now.'

'There's no point,' said Georgia.

Scarlett's eyes narrowed. 'What do you mean?'

'She isn't there. It's her day off. She always drives down to Cornwall to see her parents. She passed me as I rode down the drive. She won't be back until late tonight.'

The horses were growing impatient.

'Which way are you going?' Sam asked Georgia.

'Home,' she said, pointing to the track in front of them. 'Mum helps me do the horses on Angela's day off but she needs me there to tell her what to do.'

'Mind if we join you for a bit?' Sam said.

'I suppose not.'

Poppy rode Cloud alongside Barley and began telling Georgia about all the things that had happened at Redhall since Bella had left for Inverness. Her china blue eyes widened when she heard about the wire around Treacle's legs.

'I remember Treacle! He bucked me off into a puddle once. Is he OK?'

'He'll be fine, but it could easily have been much worse. That's why we need to find out who's behind all this, so we can stop anything else happening.' Poppy paused. 'What's she like?'

'Who, Angela?'

Poppy nodded.

'Driven, strict, demanding and really competitive. She's a perfectionist and she hates failure.'

'So she would hate it if Claydon's livery yard wasn't a success?'

Georgia nodded. 'But there's one thing wrong with your theory. She may play to win, but she loves horses. She would never have hurt Treacle.'

'Perhaps she didn't mean to. Perhaps she just left the barbed wire in the field as a warning? Perhaps the wire was already there and what happened to Treacle was a genuine accident and we've just assumed it was part of the vendetta.'

'Perhaps,' agreed Georgia. 'But you won't be able to ask her until the morning.'

They rode on in silence until they reached the far boundary of Claydon Manor's huge estate.

'Please don't say anything to Angela. We'll come over in the morning,' said Poppy.

Georgia nodded briefly and turned Barley for home.

'You two seem to have hit it off,' said Scarlett. Poppy thought she could detect a touch of resentment in her best friend's voice, though Scarlett had tried to disguise it.

'Not really. I was just pumping her for information,' she said. She didn't add that she thought Georgia's haughty exterior was probably shielding a less confident person underneath and that the older girl had looked genuinely shocked when she'd told her about all the things happening at Redhall. If Angela Snell was behind the plot to bring down Bella's yard, Poppy was convinced Georgia Canning knew nothing about it.

THE YARD WAS quiet when they finally arrived back an hour later.

'All OK?' Scott asked Sarah as she ladled spoonfuls of tomato soup into bowls and passed them around the kitchen table.

'Not a hint of trouble,' she confirmed.

'Well, there wouldn't be, would there?' said Scarlett. 'That Snell woman's in Cornwall.'

'We'll still padlock the gates and do the checks tonight, just to be on the safe side,' said Scott.

As Poppy did afternoon stables she could feel wave after wave of exhaustion sweeping over her. Her eyes felt gritty with tiredness and her limbs were sluggish. She longed to find a quiet corner in the hay barn and sleep for a week. When they sat down to eat Sarah's homemade cottage pie she couldn't stop yawning and after she'd helped Scarlett wash and dry up she announced that she was heading up to bed.

'There's no point me staying to watch TV. I'll only fall asleep. I'll set the alarm on my phone for four o'clock, Scar.'

'It doesn't need to take long,' said Scott. 'Just a quick check on the paddocks and stables to make sure everyone's where they should be and that the gates are locked and then you can go back to bed.'

~

POPPY SANK GRATEFULLY into bed and pulled the duvet under her chin. She had never felt so bone-tired in her life. She switched off her bedside lamp, curled up in a ball and was just drifting off to sleep when she realised with a start that she'd forgotten to set her alarm. She sat up abruptly, grabbed her phone from the bedside table and stared blearily at the screen.

'Is it even light at four o'clock?' she muttered to herself, tapping the tiny alarm clock icon and scrolling down until she'd reached 0400 hours. She turned the volume up as high as it would go and set the snooze button just in case. Satisfied the alarm was set, she placed her phone back on the bedside table and snuggled back down under the duvet. Seconds later she was asleep.

~

THAT NIGHT POPPY dreamt she was riding Cloud bareback and without a headcollar across the moonlit moor. She wound her fingers around his mane, gripped with her knees and crouched low as he galloped through valleys and past tors towards Claydon Manor. As they grew close to the boundary of the manor house Poppy saw a huge yew hedge looming in front of her. Cloud lengthened his stride.

'You can't jump it, it's too high!' she cried, tugging his mane, terrified he was going to attempt to hurl himself over. At the last minute she saw a narrow opening the size of a doorway in the wall of yew. Cloud galloped through it without hesitating. They were flanked each side by walls of dark green foliage so high they blocked out the moonlight. Cloud slowed to a trot, and then to a walk. Poppy stared around wildly and shivered as the green walls seemed to close in around her.

In a moment of clarity she realised they were in a giant maze. 'We need to head for the centre,' Poppy said. She knew it was vital they found the heart of the maze, although she had no idea why.

She used her heels to guide Cloud left and right. They twisted and turned, hitting dead end after dead end. Soon they were completely lost and Poppy could feel panic rising.

Just when she thought she couldn't stand any more Cloud stood stock still, sniffed the air and neighed. An answering whinny echoed around the walls of the maze. Poppy felt a shiver run down her spine. Cloud walked forwards purposefully and she sat quietly, letting him choose his route. Poppy became aware of a pearly glow ahead, like moonlight reflected on water. As they came closer the light became stronger, until it glowed as bright as magnesium. Poppy shielded her eyes. She knew they had almost reached the centre of the maze.

Cloud turned the final corner and whickered. Poppy gasped. Standing in front of them, lit by the ghostly glow, was Merry, with Niamh sat astride her. The bay mare whickered and Cloud stepped forward and blew softly into her nostrils.

Niamh jumped down from Merry and smiled.

'We've been waiting for you, haven't we, Merry?' she said.

Poppy could feel tears welling behind her eyes. 'We just kept hitting dead end after dead end.'

'But you found us in the end.'

Poppy nodded. She slid off Cloud's back and tried to peer around Niamh and Merry. 'What's in the centre of the maze?'

Niamh stepped forward, obscuring the source of the light. 'The truth,' she said simply.

'I need to see it!' cried Poppy. 'I need answers!'

'The answers are there, Poppy. You just need to know where to look.'

As Poppy leant forward Niamh grabbed her shoulder and started shaking it. 'No, Poppy, no!'

'Get off!' Poppy cried. But the shaking wouldn't stop. Poppy felt herself swim back to consciousness. She opened her eyes groggily. Scarlett was standing over her, shaking her shoulder.

'Oh no, Poppy! No! We've slept through the alarm!'

The image of the dream was still so powerful it took a moment for Poppy to register what Scarlett was saying.

'Wake *up*, Poppy!' Scarlett flung Poppy's jeans and sweatshirt at her. 'We need to check on the horses!'

Poppy sat up slowly. Scarlett was already dressed and had pulled the curtains. The bedroom was flooded with light. Poppy checked the time on her phone. Twenty five past six.

'But I don't understand,' she gabbled. 'I set the alarm last night. I remember doing it.'

'You set it for two o'clock this afternoon,' said Scarlett, pointing. 'Look.'

Poppy scanned the screen. Scarlett was right. The alarm was due to go off at 1400 not 0400. She must have accidentally pressed one instead of nought. What an idiot. She grabbed her jeans and pulled them on, trying to ignore the knot of fear tightening in her stomach.

'They'll be OK. It's all padlocked,' she said, more to convince herself than Scarlett.

They had reached the bottom of the stairs when Sam bowled in like a tornado. He skidded to a halt on Bella's oak floor when he saw them and looked at Poppy. His face was leached of all colour.

Poppy knew then that something had happened to Cloud. It was her punishment for not setting the alarm properly. She felt light-headed with fear and grabbed hold of the newel post to steady herself.

'What is it? What's happened to him?' she whispered.

Sam shot a desperate look at Scarlett, who put her arm around Poppy's trembling shoulders.

'I'm so sorry, Poppy. He's gone.'

oppy's legs buckled under her and she sat down on the bottom
stair with a thump.

'Gone? What do you mean, gone?'

'He was there when we checked at two o'clock. I woke up at six and
thought I might as well check on them. Someone had cut through the
chain around the gate and it was swinging open.'

'Are any of the others missing?' Scarlett asked, her face pale.

Sam shook his head. 'Cloud's stable door was the only one that was
open. I've spent the last half an hour checking all the fields but I can't find
him anywhere. I'm sorry Poppy. He's gone.'

'This is all my fault!' Poppy wailed.

'What do you mean?' Sam asked, frowning.

'I set the wrong time on the alarm. We didn't do the four o'clock
check. Oh Scarlett, what am I going to do?'

Scarlett sat down beside Poppy. 'It's alright. We'll find him, I promise.'

'He lived wild on the moor for *five years*, Scar. I couldn't catch him last
time. What makes you think this time'll be any different?'

'We don't know he's on the moor,' Scarlett reasoned.

Poppy jumped to her feet. 'You're right. I need to check the fields
again.' She marched over to the back door and pulled on her jodhpur
boots, Scarlett and Sam trailing behind her.

'Did you check behind the shelter in Treacle's field?' she asked Sam.

He shook his head.

'Well then, that's where we'll start.' Poppy set off at a jog towards Treacle's paddock. She scanned the fields for any sign of Cloud, but the only grey ponies in sight were Salt and Pepper, who lifted their heads and watched as she ran past.

Poppy paused at the open gate to Treacle's paddock. Her heart was thudding painfully in her chest. She puffed out her cheeks and blew. Her mouth was so dry it took three attempts before she could muster a half-decent whistle. Poppy held her breath. Normally there would be an answering whinny and Cloud would appear in search of a titbit and a welcome scratch behind his ear. But today all she could hear was the blood pounding in her head.

She raced across the field to the shelter, trying not to think about poor Treacle's shredded skin. She crossed her fingers and peered around the back wall. But the only thing there was a green wheelbarrow.

She became aware of Scarlett and Sam behind her and spun around.

'I'm going to double-check the other fields too,' she panted. She knew she sounded slightly hysterical but she didn't care. If Cloud felt even a fraction of the love for Poppy that she felt for him he wouldn't have run away, would he?

She spent the next half an hour checking and re-checking the paddocks, running to and fro like a kid with a sugar rush. Eventually Sam grabbed her arm and pulled her to a stop.

'He's not here, Poppy,' he said.

Poppy knew in her heart that he was right. She looked at him, her face streaked with tears.

'Come on,' said Scarlett gently. 'Let's go back to the house.'

Scott was by the gate inspecting the chain when they tramped back. He beckoned them over.

'Whoever did this must have had a really heavy duty set of bolt croppers,' he said, showing them where the metal had been cut cleanly through.

'But why was Cloud's the only stable he opened?' wailed Poppy.

'It's the closest one to the drive. Perhaps he was intending to let all the horses out but got spooked and legged it,' said Sam.

Poppy knew he was probably right but it didn't make it any easier to bear. If only she'd put Cloud in Merry's stable. If only she'd set her alarm properly. If only they hadn't come to Redhall in the first place none of this would have happened. Cloud would be safely tucked up in his stable with Chester, waiting for his breakfast. As it was, he could be miles away, frightened and alone.

Scarlett guessed what she was thinking. 'Remember what you told Tia, Poppy. You've got to forget the what ifs. What we need to do is decide what we're going to do next.'

'I'll do morning stables so you three can look for Cloud,' said Scott.

Poppy ran her hands through her hair. 'But where do we start?'

'We'll phone the police and all the local vets and animal sanctuaries,' said Sam. 'Have you got a photo of Cloud we can send them?'

Poppy thought of her phone, lying on her bedside table. 'Hundreds,' she said.

'Good. Mum can start phoning around while we go up onto the moor.'

ONE OF THE things Poppy loved most about Dartmoor was the vastness of it. She loved the sense of freedom and adventure the huge landscapes and sweeping panoramas promised. But this morning, as she trudged down the Redhall drive with Cloud's headcollar on her shoulder and a bucket of pony nuts in her hand, the sheer size of the moor only served to remind her of the enormity of the task ahead. Sometimes, when they hacked out alone on the moor, Cloud would stand stock still, lift his head, sniff the air and Poppy would feel him quivering with excitement. She often wondered if he pined for the freedom he'd once taken for granted. Poppy knew that by bringing him home to Riverdale she'd taken his freedom away and replaced it with a life of captivity and routine, dependence and predictability. What if he hated her for it and longed to be free?

Where would he go? Would he head for Riverdale, pulled by an unconscious force back to the safety of home, the companionship of his stablemate Chester and the promise of a bucketful of breakfast? Or would his flight instinct take over, send him galloping for the horizon, the lure of rediscovered freedom erasing Poppy and Riverdale from his memory?

'We'll check the routes we've ridden on first,' said Sam, interrupting Poppy's spiralling thoughts.

She automatically glanced left and right as they reached the road. An image of mangled metal and Cloud's lifeless body pushed its way into her mind's eye like a mirage.

'What if he's been hit by a car?' she cried. Her mum Isobel was killed in a car crash when Poppy was four. Surely fate wouldn't be so cruel?

Scarlett shook her head. 'He'll be fine, Poppy. I know he will.'

They set off down the rutted track onto the moor, their shoulders hunched and their heads bowed as the track climbed steadily. Soon they were passing the farmhouse where Poppy had called for help. The woman in the red-checked shirt was pegging out a line of washing. She waved when she saw them.

Scarlett waved back. 'You haven't seen a grey pony, have you?' she called.

The woman dropped her bag of pegs into the basket of wet washing and walked over.

'A Dartmoor pony?'

'No, he's a dappled grey Connemara, about so high,' Scarlett said, holding her hand above her shoulder. 'He escaped from Redhall last night.'

The woman shook her head. 'Sorry, I haven't.' She noticed Poppy, who was standing behind Scarlett. 'You're the girl who asked to use the phone after the riding accident the other day.'

Poppy nodded.

'How is your friend? I've been thinking about her.'

'Not good. And her pony had to be put to sleep,' said Scarlett.

'I did wonder when I saw the vet's Land Rover. What an awful thing to have happened. And now you've lost a pony, too.' She turned to Poppy. 'Is it the one you were riding when you came for help?'

'Yes.' Poppy swallowed the lump in her throat. 'If you see him, please will you phone me?'

'Of course. I'll get a pen and paper and you can write your number down. I'll tell my husband to keep a look out while he's checking on the sheep. And I can pass the word to our neighbours, too, if you like.'

'Thank you, that's really kind,' Poppy said, smiling feebly.

They asked everyone they passed that morning but no-one had seen Cloud. Poppy's hopes were raised when a couple walking their chocolate Labrador said they'd seen a grey pony drinking from a nearby stream. She raced over, her heart in her mouth, only to find the pony was an iron grey Dartmoor mare with a bay filly foal at foot. She could have wept.

At one o'clock, when there was still no sign of the Connemara, Sam suggested they went back to Redhall.

'We can ride out this afternoon. We'll be able to cover much more ground than we can on foot. We'll head over to Claydon Manor to see if he went that way,' he said.

'OK,' said Poppy dully, though she knew it was a waste of time. Cloud was gone. And he was never coming back.

~

SARAH WAS WAITING by the back door and ushered them in.

'I've phoned the three nearest vets, two local animal sanctuaries and the police. There haven't been any accidents and no injured ponies have been brought in. So that's good, isn't it?' she said brightly.

'But no-one's seen him,' Poppy said flatly.

The smile slipped from Sarah's face. 'No, they haven't. But I've left our number with everyone. He's bound to show up sooner or later.'

Poppy's nerves, already stretched to breaking point, suddenly snapped. 'Horses aren't like homing pigeons, Sarah. He's not going to suddenly turn up on the doorstep.'

Sarah flushed. 'I'm sorry. I didn't mean to upset you.'

Poppy hadn't thought it possible she could feel any worse. But when she saw the hurt on Sarah's face she knew she was wrong.

'No, I'm sorry. I shouldn't have snapped. It's not your fault. And I do appreciate your help, I really do.'

Scarlett banged her forehead with the heel of her hand. 'Talk about homing pigeons, you have phoned Caroline to check he hasn't gone home, haven't you?'

Poppy shook her head numbly. In all the panic she had completely forgotten. How stupid. If Cloud was going to go anywhere, surely it would be Riverdale?

Sam passed her the phone and as Poppy dialled she felt a tiny glimmer of hope flare in her heart. Caroline answered on the fourth ring.

'It's me,' Poppy gabbled. 'Is Cloud with you?'

The glimmer of hope was snuffed out like a candle the second she heard Caroline's sharp intake of breath.

'What do you mean is Cloud here? He's with you, isn't he? What's happened, Poppy?'

Poppy looked at Scarlett, Sam and Sarah's expectant faces and shook her head. She held the phone close to her ear.

'It's a long story.'

THEY SET OFF AFTER LUNCH, Poppy on Rosie, Scarlett riding Blaze and Sam on Star. Poppy rode ahead, her eyes swivelling left and right as she scanned the horizon for Cloud. Rosie, who was infamous at Redhall for being highly temperamental, had picked up on her mood and she walked meekly as they rode up the dusty track, through the farmyard and into the field of barley.

Poppy's thoughts slipped back to the day Cloud had arrived at Riverdale in Bella's horsebox, his coat matted with blood and his ribs standing out like the wooden bars of a xylophone. She had promised him then that she would always look out for him. And she had broken that promise. It was unforgivable.

The tight ball of fear in Poppy's stomach was morphing into a knot of anger, directed solely at the shadowy figure who'd let her beloved pony out of his stable and in doing so had broken her heart. Life without Cloud didn't bear thinking about. She kicked Rosie into a canter without even telling the others and soon she was crouched over the roan mare's neck as they thundered through the barley.

By the time Scarlett and Sam caught up with her at the top of the hill Poppy had made up her mind.

'I'm going to go and have it out with Angela Snell,' she said.

Sam looked at her in consternation. 'We don't know she's behind all this.'

Scarlett gave him a scathing look. 'She has the motive, the means and the know-how. And anyway, who else could it be?'

'She knew about the strangles,' Poppy reminded Sam.

'I know, but -'

But Poppy didn't hear any more. She had already turned Rosie towards Claydon Manor.

~

ANGELA SNELL WAS STRAPPING a big chestnut thoroughbred when they clattered into the yard. She greeted them with a steely gaze.

'I hope for all your sakes that Georgia was right when she said there's no strangles at Redhall. Otherwise you'll be hearing from our solicitors.'

Poppy jumped off Rosie and marched over to Angela. 'Our horses are perfectly healthy. Who told you the yard was on shutdown?'

Angela frowned. 'I had an email.'

'I need you to show me,' Poppy said, handing Rosie's reins to Scarlett. She eyed Angela defiantly, challenging her to refuse. Angela nodded slightly.

'Follow me.'

She beckoned Poppy inside the airy office next to the tack room, flipped open an expensive-looking laptop and opened her email account.

'It was sent the day before yesterday,' Angela said, pointing to the screen. 'There's no name on it.'

Poppy read the brief email over her shoulder:

WARNING: A case of highly-infectious strangles has been diagnosed at Redhall Manor Equestrian Centre. Please help everyone keep their horses safe and spread the word. Redhall is a no-go area.'

Poppy checked the sender's address. It was a Hotmail account she didn't recognise.

'Probably the same account used to email the Herald.' She glared at Angela Snell. 'And you didn't bother checking this was true before you started telling people Redhall was on shutdown? What if someone was spreading lies about Claydon Manor? How would you feel?'

'Alright, you've made your point. Anyway, I only mentioned it to Georgia. I've been down in Cornwall with my parents. I didn't get back until nine.'

'Nine last night?' Poppy said sharply, thinking of Cloud.

480

Angela gave her a black look. 'No, nine this morning. I decided to stay the night. Why?'

Poppy felt her throat constrict. 'Someone let my pony out of his stable at Redhall last night. He escaped onto the moor. We've been looking for him all day.'

Angela studied Poppy's face. 'That's tough, and I'm very sorry. But if you think I'd stoop so low you are very wrong. Redhall might be in competition with Claydon but I never play dirty. It's not my style.'

14

Poppy lay in bed staring at the ceiling. In the bed beside her Scarlett's breathing grew slow and regular. Once she knew her best friend was definitely asleep she flung back the duvet, pulled on thick socks, jeans and a fleece and slipped out of the room. After less than a week at Redhall she was already familiar with the creaky floorboards and she stepped over them lightly and headed down the stairs, her hand trailing down the polished mahogany banister. In the kitchen she made herself a cup of tea and carried it carefully out into the yard. The moon was full and heavy and it gleamed in the sky like an illustration in a children's storybook. Blaze's chestnut head appeared over her stable door and she whinnied when she saw Poppy.

'Shush, you'll wake the others,' Poppy said. She found a couple of pony nuts in the pocket of her jeans and held out her palm. Blaze whickered her thanks and Poppy laid her head against the mare's soft head. 'Oh Blaze, do you think he'll be OK?'

Blaze regarded Poppy with limpid eyes. Poppy gave her one last stroke and headed for Cloud's empty stable. She leant on the door, her chin resting on her folded arms. Scott had mucked out while they'd been on the moor. He'd even filled the hayrack and water buckets. She slid the bolt across and tugged the door open. Moonlight flooded into the empty stable. Poppy left the door open wide and sat down in the straw, her hands clasped around her mug of tea. She wondered where Cloud was, what he was doing. Closing her eyes, she pictured his face, as familiar to her as her own. She literally could not bear the thought that she would never see him again.

Perhaps she could try sending him a telepathic message. Poppy didn't believe in that type of thing but surely anything was worth a try?

'Come back to me, Cloud,' she whispered, willing her thoughts to span the wide expanse of Dartmoor between her and her beloved Connemara. She sent message after message, pleading with him to hear.

But there was no clatter of hooves on the concrete, no whicker of recognition. She knew she was wasting her time. Cloud had gone and he wasn't coming back.

She thought about their visit to Claydon Manor that afternoon. Poppy felt bad that she'd ever blamed Angela Snell for the vendetta against Redhall. As they'd left Claydon they'd bumped into Georgia, who confirmed that the livery yard manager had arrived home just after nine o'clock. The pair were either telling the truth or they deserved Oscars for their performances. Poppy believed them, anyway. That hadn't stopped Scarlett's lips curling in disbelief when she'd told Scarlett and Sam as they'd ridden home. Scarlett was still convinced of their guilt.

Poppy took a sip of her tea and listened to the sounds of the yard. Horses shifting in their stables, the rustle of straw, the steady breathing of Blaze next door as the mare settled down to sleep. The sounds were soporific and Poppy felt her own eyelids grow heavy. Before long she had nodded off.

～

POPPY AWOKE to the oddest sensation that someone was in the stable with her. She froze. What if it was the intruder, come to finish what he'd started? What if he was towering over her right now, his bulk obscuring the shafts of moonlight that had cast a friendly glow over Cloud's stable? Poppy realised her best option was to pretend to still be asleep. At least she would have the element of surprise. She kept her eyes squeezed tight and tried to marshal her groggy thoughts. Stupidly she'd left her phone on her bedside table and the nearest pitchfork was in the barn, which was no use at all. She inched her hand towards the mug in the straw beside her. It was the only thing she had at her disposal. She decided to throw it at the intruder and make a run for it.

Poppy was so focused on her escape plan that at first she didn't notice the draught of warm breath on her cold cheek. She didn't register the feather-like tickle of whiskers against her earlobe. Her fingers curled around the handle of the mug and she drew it close to her chest. And then, in the silence of the stable, a pony whickered softly. Her eyes snapped open.

There, standing in front of her, his face centimetres from her own, was Cloud. Poppy wondered if he was an apparition, an image conjured up by her deep longing for him. She reached out to touch him, half-convinced he would disappear, wraith-like, in a puff of smoke. But the tips of her fingers met warm horse. He stepped forward and gave her the gentlest of nudges. Finally allowing herself to believe he really was there, Poppy jumped to her feet and threw her arms around his neck as tears streamed down her face.

'Oh Cloud, I thought I was never going to see you again. But you came back.'

He nibbled the pocket of her fleece and Poppy rested her face against his, delighting in the feel of his soft coat against her skin. She realised she should never have questioned the bond between them. Cloud must love her as much as she loved him.

She gazed into his deep brown eyes. 'You could have gone back to Riverdale. But you didn't. You came back to me.'

❀

THE NEXT MORNING Poppy and Scarlett free-wheeled into the Baxters' car park and propped their bikes against a green bottle bank. Normally Poppy loved wasting half an hour in the cavernous shop, drinking in the smell of new leather and inspecting the displays of riding gear and equipment, but today her stomach was churning.

'What's the plan? Shall I cause a diversion while you try and slip behind the counter?' whispered Scarlett.

Poppy shrugged helplessly. 'I guess. Although I'm not sure what I'm supposed to be looking for.'

'All Dad's invoices from Baxters' have his contact phone number on.

See if you can log into the computer, open Redhall's account and find Monday's invoice.'

Poppy swallowed. 'You make it sound easy, Scar. What if I get caught?'

'Look,' she said, waving her arm. 'The car park's deserted. They only ever have one member of staff on at this time of the afternoon. If it's Tanya we'll be fine. She can talk for England. I'll keep her busy while you do the business. And if anyone sees you behind the counter just pretend you dropped your phone or something.'

Poppy frowned. It didn't sound like much of a plan. But, she realised, it was the only one they had.

'Alright, here goes.'

She pushed open the double doors and stepped in. Scarlett nodded towards the dark-haired girl sitting behind the counter and gave Poppy a surreptitious thumbs up.

'Tanya!' she cried. 'Haven't seen you for ages. How's things?'

'Hi Scarlett. What brings you here?'

'Mum and Dad sent me over to choose a new hat for my birthday. Dad said to stick it on his account.'

Poppy raised her eyebrows. Scarlett's birthday was in May, a cool ten months away.

'Sure,' said Tanya. 'Let me just finish this and I'll come over and measure you up.'

Tanya tapped away at the computer keyboard in front of her and, with a couple of clicks of the mouse, the printer chugged into life, spewing out an invoice. She tore it off and opened the middle drawer of a metal filing cabinet behind her. Poppy watched as Tanya's fingers walked along the files until she found the one she was looking for. She pulled the cardboard folder out, slid the invoice inside, replaced the folder and pushed the drawer closed with her backside.

'Right,' said Tanya, lifting the hinged counter open. 'The hats are over there.' She pointed to the far corner of the shop, where a couple of dozen hats were on display on wooden shelving units.

'I'm just going to have a look for a card for Caroline's birthday,' said Poppy, edging over to a wire carousel beside the counter.

'Help yourself,' smiled Tanya. 'So Scarlett, do you want a hat for hacking or are you going to be using it for competitions as well?'

Poppy pretended to scan the arty horse cards and Thelwell cartoons while Tanya and Scarlett disappeared to the back of the shop. After a couple of minutes she glanced up. Tanya was standing with her back to Poppy, holding a tape measure around Scarlett's head. Scarlett caught Poppy watching and winked.

Poppy realised this could be her only chance. She darted behind the counter and stared at the computer screen. It was on the Baxters' home page. Poppy pressed enter and groaned inwardly when she was asked for a password. She tried 1234 and 4321 and then Baxters1234 and Baxters4321, but the computer stubbornly refused her entry. She could hear Tanya murmuring about the new regulations governing riding hats. Poppy abandoned the computer and turned to the filing cabinet. Four drawers, the first marked A-G, the second H-M. Poppy eased open the third, marked N-S, and looked wildly for Redhall. But there was no folder for the riding school. Sure she must have missed it, Poppy checked again. Still nothing.

She thought hard. Maybe the invoices were kept under Bella's name. She slid the third drawer closed and opened the bottom one, marked T-Z. There were five files marked Thompson and Poppy cursed Bella for having such a popular name. Adrenalin coursed through her veins as she pulled out each file and checked inside.

As Poppy pulled out the second to last file she risked a look over her shoulder. Tanya and Scarlett were still deep in conversation, Tanya holding a mirror as Scarlett modelled a skullcap with an emerald green silk. Poppy opened the file.

Bella Thompson
Redhall Manor Equestrian Centre

Bingo.

'So you found the latest invoice?' Scarlett whispered as they pushed their bikes across the car park.

Poppy nodded.

'And there was a mobile number on it?'

Poppy waved her hand in Scarlett's face. 'I couldn't find a piece of paper so I wrote it on my hand. It's definitely not Bella's number. I've just checked.'

'Don't forget it's there and go and wash your hands,' Scarlett cautioned.

'Do I look stupid?' said Poppy hotly. The adrenalin that had helped her through her spying mission was now threatening to bubble into ill temper.

'No need to bite my head off.'

'Sorry.' Poppy gave her best friend a brief smile. 'What did you tell Tanya?'

'That I couldn't make my mind up and that I would come back next time Dad's over. She seemed to buy it. Shall we try the number now?'

Poppy checked her phone. 'No signal.'

They jumped on their bikes and began pedalling slowly towards Redhall. At the top of a particularly steep climb Poppy called Scarlett to stop.

'I've got two bars. Shall we give it a go?'

They collapsed on the verge and Scarlett grabbed Poppy's hand.

'I'll read you the number.' She screwed up her face. 'Is that a seven or a nine?'

Poppy squinted at the smudged biro scrawl on the back of her hand. She'd scribbled it down so quickly it was almost illegible.

'Um, a nine I think.'

Poppy dialled as Scarlett read out the number. She felt a flutter of nerves as she waited for the call to connect.

'Put it on speakerphone,' Scarlett said urgently. Poppy nodded and pressed the speakerphone icon.

A woman's robotic voice cut through the summer afternoon. *'Your call cannot be completed as dialled. Please check the number and try again.'*

Poppy groaned. 'I must have written the number down wrong.'

'Try a seven instead,' Scarlett said.

Poppy re-dialled.

This time the call connected. Time slowed down as the phone rang. Poppy realised she was clutching Scarlett's arm in a vice-like grip. On the fourth ring, just as she was beginning to lose hope, someone picked up.

A gruff voice. 'Hello?'

The two girls were silent.

'Who is this?' The voice sounded irritated. 'I said, who's calling?'

Poppy panicked. 'Er, sorry. Wrong number,' she cried, and ended the call.

～

BACK AT REDHALL they found Sam mucking out Treacle's stable. He listened in silence as they relayed what had happened.

'So we're no nearer to finding out who phoned in that order,' Poppy said glumly.

Sam stared into the middle distance. 'I've had an idea. It might not work, but it's worth a try. Follow me.'

He crossed the yard to Bella's office, tipped Harvey Smith gently off the office chair and booted up the laptop.

'What was the number?' he said.

Poppy checked her call log and read out the eleven digit number. 'What are you going to do,' she asked.

'Put it into Google and see if it comes up with anything. You never know.'

They watched as Sam tapped in the number and pressed search. He hit the top result. A website for a building firm slowly opened.

'Another dead end,' sighed Scarlett.

Sam's hand hovered over the mouse, ready to click away from the page.

But Poppy had seen something the other two had missed. She pointed to the bottom right hand corner of the screen.

'Of course,' she muttered, replaying the events of the past week in her mind's eye. 'It's completely obvious. How can we have been so blind?'

15

The door to the office swung open and the silhouette of a man appeared. Poppy jumped out of her skin and Scarlett smothered a small scream.

'Three guilty faces if ever I saw some,' said Scott, perching on Bella's desk. 'What's up?'

'You wouldn't believe us if we told you,' said Poppy.

'Try me.' Scott yawned widely, showing his chipped tooth. 'But you'd better be quick. I was going to sneak forty winks before evening stables.'

'Some things never change,' said Sam drily. 'Poppy and Scarlett went over to Baxters' this afternoon and managed to get the mobile number of the person who made that massive order. And it's him.'

Scott studied the computer screen and looked back at them.

'Am I missing something here?'

'It's a building company. Owned by Gordon Cooper,' said Scarlett.

Scott shook his head. 'Er, still none the wiser.'

'Gordon Cooper,' said Poppy patiently. 'Owner of Cooper Construction.'

Scott shrugged.

'Never heard of him.'

'He's Niamh's dad.'

Scott grabbed his helmet and was threatening to race over to the offices of Cooper Construction to confront Gordon Cooper.

'We know that he made that order, but we can't prove he did anything else, Scott. Not yet, anyway,' said Poppy.

'You were sure the intruder you saw was a man, weren't you?' said Scarlett. 'Even though I didn't want to believe you at the time.'

'And cutting through the water pipe wouldn't be a problem for a builder, would it?' said Sam.

'All circumstantial though, isn't it?' said Poppy. 'We need proof.'

'But how are we going to get that?' Scarlett asked.

Poppy gave a helpless shrug of her shoulders. 'I don't know.'

THE DINNER TABLE was quiet that night, everyone lost in their own thoughts. They'd decided not to tell Sarah about their discovery - not until they had some concrete proof that Gordon Cooper was behind the vendetta. When the phone rang half way through Sarah's mouth-watering apple pie they held their breath as Sarah picked up the phone in the lounge, wondering if it was yet another nuisance call. Poppy felt her shoulders relax when Sarah walked in, a smile on her face.

'That was Mum. Great Auntie Margaret's settled in a nursing home for some respite care until she's back on her feet and Mum's decided to come home. She's setting off shortly and is going to drive through the night. I told her to wait until tomorrow but she insisted. She should be home just after breakfast.'

'Did you tell her about all the things that have been happening?' said Sam.

Sarah shook her head. 'I decided there was no point worrying her. We'll fill her in when she's back. Anyone for seconds?'

Later, when Sarah had gone to bed, they discussed what to do.

'I vote we do hourly checks tonight. I'll pair up with Scarlett and you two can go together,' said Scott.

Scarlett's face flushed with pleasure. 'That's a great idea.'

But Poppy wasn't going to rely on hourly checks while Gordon

Cooper was still at large. 'There's no way I'm leaving Cloud tonight, after everything that's happened. I'm sleeping in his stable,' she announced.

Sam nodded. 'I'm with Poppy on this. I'll bring my duvet down and sleep in Star's stable.'

Scott looked at them both in amusement. 'You are more than welcome to hunker down with your horses. I, however, need my beauty sleep so I'm afraid I won't be joining you. And if you two are spending the night in the yard you won't need me and Scarlett to do our rounds, will you?' He rubbed his hands together in satisfaction.

Poppy could see the indecision in her best friend's hazel eyes. Scarlett loved her sleep and she idolised Scott but would she risk anything happening to Blaze? Poppy didn't think so.

She was proved right when Scarlett finally stood up and said: 'Looks like it's a night in the stable then.'

～

THE HORSES LOOKED on with curiosity as Poppy, Scarlett and Sam dragged their duvets and pillows across the yard and into the three stables. Cloud was the only one who wasn't surprised - at home Poppy often slipped down to his stable in the early hours if she'd been woken by a nightmare and couldn't get back to sleep.

They inspected each other's makeshift beds.

'Looks cosy,' said Sam. 'So, have you both got torches and your mobile phones?'

'Yes sir!' said Poppy, saluting. Scarlett giggled.

Sam sighed. 'I'm just trying to be practical. And we'll text each other if we hear or see anything?'

The girls nodded.

'Is there anything else we should do?' said Poppy.

Scarlett clapped her hands. 'I know! We could set some booby traps.'

Sam looked at her as if she was mad, but Poppy's mind was whirring.

'You're right. You know that roll of electric fence wire in the hay barn?' The other two nodded. 'Why don't we lay it along the front gate so when he goes to open it he gets an electric shock?'

Scarlett grinned evilly. 'Oh yes, I'm loving that idea. And we could arrange those bits of barbed wire he so kindly left on the driveway so he gets a puncture.'

'Neat,' Poppy said. 'What about tying together baler twine to make a trip wire? We could fix it just inside the gate.'

Scarlett nodded vigorously. 'And I could do the old Tom and Jerry classic and leave a couple of rakes on the ground. With any luck he'll stand on one and whack himself on the head.'

Sam's eyebrows were raised as he looked from one girl to the other. 'Remind me never to get on the wrong side of you two. You're reprobates.'

'He won't be getting anything more than he deserves,' said Poppy grimly.

~

HALF AN HOUR later their traps were laid. After Sam had positioned the strands of barbed wire Scott had cut from Treacle's legs across the drive like a police stinger device, he'd wrapped the electric wire tightly around the latch and top bar of the five bar gate and plugged it in. Poppy had tied together a dozen lengths of baler twine and fixed them between two fence posts a few paces into the yard. When she gave the taut orange twine a tug it gave a satisfying twang. Scarlett spent ages arranging and re-arranging the three rusty rakes she'd found languishing in the back of the hay barn.

The last glimmer of dusk was fading into blackness as they inspected their work.

'Good job,' said Scarlett, shining her torch at the electrified gate and Poppy's tripwire. 'He's going to wish he never picked on Redhall.'

'We'd better make sure we get up early enough to take it all down before Gran gets home,' said Sam.

Scarlett chuckled. 'Good point. We should all set the alarms on our phones for five o'clock.'

Poppy yawned, wondering if she would ever enjoy a lie-in again. 'Let's try and get some sleep while we can. It could be a long night.'

Cloud blew in her hair as she let herself into his stable and she kissed his nose. She wrapped herself in her duvet and wriggled around in the straw until she was comfortable. She closed her eyes and listened to her pony chewing hay. Scarlett was murmuring to Blaze in the stable next door.

"Night Scar," Poppy called, her voice already drowsy.

"Night Poppy."

Poppy's limbs grew heavy and her breathing deepened. Soon she was asleep.

~

POPPY WOKE with a start and she sat up, looking around her groggily. It was dark. Too dark to see her hand in front of her face. She felt a fizz of fear pulse down her spine. Cloud stirred beside her and she relaxed. He was safe. And then she heard someone tapping gently on the stable wall.

'Scar, is that you?' she whispered.

'I thought I heard a car,' Scarlett whispered back. 'It's either driven off or stopped, I can't tell which.'

Poppy cocked her head and listened. 'I can't hear anything.'

'Nor can I now. But I'm telling you, I'm sure I heard a car's engine a minute ago.'

'I'll text Sam,' whispered Poppy, groping in the straw for her mobile. She tapped out a text.

This is a Code Red. I repeat, this is a Code Red. Stand by your stations.

A few seconds later her phone vibrated.

Copy that. I am standing by. Over and out.

Poppy slipped her phone into the back pocket of her jeans, picked up her torch and edged out of the duvet, trying to make as little noise as possible, but every time she moved the rustle of straw seemed to reverberate around the walls. Cloud was staring out of the stable, his nostrils flared as he sniffed the wind. Suddenly he gave a snort and wheeled around, almost knocking Poppy off her feet. She ran her hand along his flank, trying to calm him, even though her own heart was thudding.

'It's OK baby. I won't let him hurt you,' she whispered.

She stiffened as she heard the unmistakable sound of a car door clunking shut. She crept over to the stable door and peered into the yard. But the moon was veiled by thick cloud and she couldn't see a thing.

Was that the crunch of gravel? Poppy strained her ears to hear but it was impossible to tell. She jumped out of her skin when one of the thoroughbreds whinnied loudly, the sound slicing through the still night air like a speedboat through water.

Her phone vibrated in her pocket. She was just reaching for it when a guttural cry and a string of expletives rang out. Scarlett gasped in the stable next door and Poppy's fingers tightened around her torch. She stared into the dark, willing her eyes to distinguish between shadow and shade. As she stared the outline of a hunched figure began to take shape, like a drawing in one of Charlie's dot-to-dot picture books.

It was the same man Poppy had seen the night Treacle was hurt, Poppy would have bet her life on it. And he was heading straight for them.

16

Poppy narrowed her eyes and watched the hooded figure stumble over the tripwire and curse again. She braced herself for a confrontation as he approached Cloud's stable. But he strode straight past, heading for the padlocked barn. As he walked by Poppy noticed he was carrying a pair of bolt croppers and a red plastic petrol can. It took her a moment to grasp the significance of the can but when she did white-hot anger began bubbling up inside her, giving her courage.

'Oh my God, he's going to burn down the barn!' she cried, sotto voce.

'What do we do?' Scarlett hissed through the wall.

'Call the police. Tell them there's an intruder and they'll send out a patrol car. I need to stop him.'

She laid her face against Cloud's cheek as if to draw strength and let herself out of the stable. As she did she saw Star's stable door swing slowly open and Sam appeared, his finger on his lips. He pointed his thumb towards the intruder. Poppy joined him and they crossed the yard in silence. The man had reached the barn doors and had lifted the bolt croppers to the heavy-duty padlock when Sam whispered.

'Ready? On the count of three. One, two, THREE!'

Sam yelled, 'Stop right there!' And they simultaneously switched on both their torches. The man dropped the bolt croppers and his hand shot to his forehead as he tried to shield his eyes from the glare of the two torch beams.

'What the -?' he roared, lunging towards Sam.

'Not so fast! The police are on their way,' shrieked Poppy, hoping with all her heart that they were.

'You've called the police?' he asked in such a menacing voice that Poppy's blood froze. 'Now why would you want to be doing that?'

Poppy watched in horror as he turned his back on them and began unscrewing the top of the plastic can. The noxious smell of petrol filled her nostrils.

'In an ideal world I'd have got inside the barn. But needs must,' he muttered to himself, splashing petrol up the huge double doors of the barn.

'What are you doing?' Poppy cried. 'You'll destroy everything!'

He turned to Poppy. She kept the torch trained on his face, though the dancing beam gave away her trembling fingers. She lifted her chin and met his gaze. Under a deeply-lined forehead his eyes were emotionless.

'Bella Thompson deserves to lose everything.'

He turned back to the barn, reached into his pocket and pulled out a box of matches. 'Why don't you children run along and leave me to it?'

Poppy heard Sam move away but her feet were rooted to the ground. She had to keep him talking to stop him setting fire to the barn.

'It wasn't Bella's fault Niamh fell off. I was there. I saw what happened. It was an accident!'

He turned to face her again. 'So you know who I am?'

'Gordon Cooper,' she whispered. 'Niamh's dad.'

'My beautiful Niamh is lying in a hospital bed unable to walk because of Bella Thompson,' he spat. 'She's ruined my daughter's life. And I'm going to make her pay.'

Gordon Cooper's mouth stretched into a rictus grin and he pulled a match out of the box, his dead eyes never leaving Poppy's face. He struck the match against the box once, twice. On the third attempt the match splintered in two and he flung it on the floor at his feet. He took out another and struck it viciously.

For a split second the smell of burning sulphur dioxide as the match ignited masked the petrol fumes. And then there was a whoosh as the sleeve of Gordon Cooper's coat caught fire. Poppy screamed as flames darted up his arm and set his coat alight. Within seconds he was engulfed in flames.

Suddenly Sam was at her side, pointing the yard hose at the human fireball in front of them.

'Scarlett, bring one of the duvets!'

Poppy ran to Cloud's stable and grabbed his two buckets of water. As she ran back Scarlett joined her, holding the duvet in her outstretched arms.

'Hold the hose,' Sam shouted to Poppy. She took it from him and spurted it at Niamh's dad. Sam took the duvet from Scarlett and threw it over him.

'Now roll on the floor!' he yelled.

Gordon Cooper's dead eyes were now filled with panic. He dropped to the floor and began rolling around on the ground by their feet.

'The police are on their way,' Scarlett said, just as the back door slammed and Sarah and Scott came running out.

'What on earth's going on?' Sarah shouted.

Scott took one look at Cooper. The duvet had smothered the flames but he was still writhing around on the concrete, his soot-blackened face twisted in fear.

'Is this him?' Scott asked.

The children nodded.

Scott hauled Cooper to his feet.

'Are you burnt?' he said.

Cooper rubbed his arms gingerly and shook his head. Scott marched him across the yard, flung him in Merry's empty stable and bolted both doors.

'You can stay in there until the police arrive,' he said.

The adrenalin that had given Poppy the courage to confront Cooper was seeping away and her legs had turned to jelly. She stumbled over to Cloud's stable, sank to the floor and listened as Sam and Scarlett told Sarah and Scott what had happened.

'Some of the petrol must have splashed back onto him when he was dousing the barn doors,' said Sam.

'He's lucky he was wearing such a thick coat,' Sarah said.

'And that Sam knew what to do,' Scarlett added.

Sam shook his head. 'I can't take credit for the booby traps.'

'Booby traps?' said Sarah faintly.

'Speaking of which, I'd better switch off the electric fence and move the barbed wire before the police arrive, otherwise they'll be arresting me as well as Niamh's dad.' Scarlett headed for the gate, reappearing a few minutes later with a wide grin on her face and lengths of barbed wire, like a deadly bouquet, in her hand.

'Our homemade stinger worked like a dream,' she told them with satisfaction. 'He had three punctures. Three! He'd never have got away in a million years.'

～

THE REASSURING SOUND of sirens grew louder and soon a police patrol car, its blue lights flashing, pulled up behind Gordon Cooper's old van. Poppy hauled herself to her feet and joined the others by the gate. A female police officer emerged from the driver's side, followed shortly by an older male colleague who was talking into his radio. Poppy recognised the female officer immediately. It was PC Claire Bodiam, the kind and capable officer she and her friend Hope Taylor had met at Tavistock Police Station the previous year.

PC Bodiam recognised her, too. 'Hello Poppy! What on earth are you doing here?'

'It's a long story,' Poppy said.

PC Bodiam took in the petrol can, the abandoned duvet and the strong reek of petrol. 'So, who would like to tell me what's been going on?'

She listened in silence as between them Poppy, Scarlett and Sam explained the events of the last week, Scott interjecting every so often.

Soon the two police officers were leading Gordon Cooper away in handcuffs. His head was bowed and he looked utterly defeated, as if all the fight in him had gone. Perhaps he had finally realised Niamh's accident wasn't Bella's fault. Poppy hoped so, for Redhall's sake.

Once he was safely in the car PC Bodiam walked back over.

'He's been arrested on suspicion of criminal damage and attempted arson, although there may well be other offences. We'll know more when we've taken statements from you all,' she said. 'In the meantime I've just called out our crime scene investigators who'll be here first thing to take photos of the petrol can, matches and bolt croppers, and to examine the barn doors, so please don't touch anything until they've been.'

'OK,' Sarah nodded. 'Thank you.'

'No problem,' said PC Bodiam. She smiled at Poppy, Scarlett and Sam. 'You did exactly the right thing back there. If you hadn't stopped the fire Mr Cooper could easily have died. And Niamh would have lost her dad, just when she needed him most.'

'I don't suppose he's going to see it like that,' said Sam bitterly. 'He hates Gran's guts.'

'Oh, I don't know. I think some time down at the station will give him a chance to reflect. I don't think he'll be giving your gran any more trouble. And if he does, you're to let us know immediately,' she said.

'What shall we do about his van?' Sarah asked.

'We'll push it out of the way for now and let his wife know she needs to arrange a recovery truck to come and collect it,' said PC Bodiam's colleague.

They watched the patrol car accelerate away towards Tavistock. Although the sky was still inky blue a lone blackbird had begun a fluty warble from the hawthorn hedge that bordered the Redhall drive, sounding the first mellow notes of the dawn chorus.

'I can't believe Niamh's dad hates Mum so much that he was prepared to burn down the yard,' said Sarah.

'Tia did say she thought he was having some sort of a breakdown,' said Sam.

Scott scowled. 'That's no excuse for putting the horses' lives in danger.'

'I was wrong, wasn't I?' said Scarlett. 'I blamed Georgia Canning and Angela Snell. I thought the motive was money. But it wasn't. Gordon Cooper's motivation was revenge, pure and simple.'

17

E veryone was bleary-eyed but cheerful at breakfast. The nameless threat that had cast its menacing shadow over the riding school for the past week had evaporated the minute Gordon Cooper had been led away in handcuffs. Sun streamed through the kitchen windows as Sarah made pancakes drizzled with maple syrup and freshly-squeezed lemon juice. Poppy wolfed hers down, suddenly ravenously hungry. She was going to miss Sarah's cooking.

They whizzed through morning stables in record time and the horses had all been groomed and turned out by the time the crime scene investigator sent by PC Bodiam arrived in her white van and started dusting for fingerprints.

They showed her the barbed wire and the two pieces of cut water pipe and she photographed the abandoned petrol can, the bolt croppers, the box of matches and the petrol stains on the door of the barn. Poppy carefully undid the dressings on Treacle's legs and held the Welsh pony so she could take pictures of the wounds. The thin skin around Treacle's cannon bones was beginning to heal and there were no signs of an infection but Poppy knew that he would always bear the scars of the barbed wire.

The crime scene investigator was reversing out of the drive when Bella pulled up in her dusty estate car. Poppy ran over and opened the gate so she could park in the yard.

Bella yanked the handbrake up and wound down the window.

'What was a police crime scene investigation van doing here?' she asked, mystified.

'How was the journey?' Poppy asked brightly, hoping to deflect the questions until Sarah arrived. She didn't think Bella was the type to shoot the messenger, but you never knew. She could be a formidable character at times.

Bella heaved herself out of the driver's side and slammed the door so firmly the whole car shuddered. She scanned the yard, her razor-sharp eyes falling on the petrol can. Treacle chose that moment to poke his head over the stable door and give a high-pitched whinny.

'Never mind the journey. Why's Treacle in? Why is there a can of petrol by the barn doors?' She fixed Poppy with a penetrating gaze. 'And what was that crime scene investigation van doing here?'

Poppy held up her hands in surrender. 'The important thing is, everything is fine now.' She lifted Bella's case out of the boot and gave her what she hoped was a beatific smile. 'Why don't we go and find Sarah and she can fill you in.'

~

ONCE POPPY HAD DELIVERED Bella to the kitchen she wandered over to the paddock Cloud shared with Blaze. She leant on the gate for a while and watched the two ponies grazing side by side. Vaulting the gate, she gave the ponies a Polo each and sat down with her back against the knotty stump of an apple tree and turned her face to the sun. An introvert by nature, Poppy was beginning to crave some time on her own, so she could recharge her batteries. She let her mind drift aimlessly through the events of the past week. She couldn't believe the morning they'd turned up as Bella's pony camp guinea pigs was only seven days ago. It didn't seem possible. This was their last day at Redhall and Bill was due to pick them up at six o'clock. Poppy knew she would be sad to leave after everything that had happened, but she was looking forward to going home. And she and Scarlett still had five whole weeks of the summer holidays left to enjoy. It wasn't so bad.

Scarlett found her in the paddock half an hour later. She waved her mobile phone in Poppy's face.

'Tia's just called. She'd heard about Niamh's dad being arrested and wanted all the gory details. She said it's the talk of their village. But she also had some good news about Niamh. She wiggled her toes this morning.' Scarlett collapsed in a heap beside Poppy.

'Does that mean she'll be able to walk again?'

'Not sure, but it's a good sign, isn't it?'

Poppy picked a daisy and began pulling the petals off, one by one. 'Pity her dad didn't wait a week before he completely lost it. He might have thought twice about waging war on Bella if he'd known Niamh was on the mend.'

'Tia said that according to village gossip his marriage is on the rocks and his building company is about to go bust. There was a fire in his warehouse a couple of weeks ago and the police hauled him in for questioning. Apparently they suspect he started it because he wanted to claim the insurance money. Niamh's mum packed his bags and chucked him out. He's been living in his van ever since. Sounds like Niamh's accident tipped him over the edge.'

'That would make sense,' Poppy said. 'How did Bella take it?'

'I think she's just relieved he's been caught and everyone is alright.'

'Is she cross about losing Vile Vivienne?'

Scarlett grinned. 'Nope. She said she and Angela Snell deserved each other.'

Poppy giggled. 'It's a match made in heaven.'

The two girls watched their ponies companionably. Poppy twirled the petal-less daisy between her thumb and forefinger.

'We should go for a ride this afternoon. All of us. And we should go on the Barrow Tor ride. Finish what we started.'

'Blimey, that's a bit deep.' Scarlett picked a blade of grass and chewed it thoughtfully. 'But it's an excellent idea. Let's go and tell the others.'

~

ONCE AGAIN BELLA led the way on Floyd. Sam and Scott, on Star and Otto, rode two abreast behind her. Scott was winding Sam up as usual, but they were both laughing - these days Sam gave as good as he got. Poppy and Scarlett rode side-by-side behind them on Cloud and Blaze.

The track onto the moor was bone dry and the horses' hooves sparked little puffs of dust every time they hit the ground. They passed a herd of solemn-faced black and white belted Galloway cattle.

'They always remind me of zebra crossings,' Poppy said inconsequentially.

'If you say so,' said Scarlett.

Soon they reached the gate to the lane which led past the farmhouse where Poppy had called the ambulance. The farmer's wife must have heard them coming, because an upstairs window was thrown open and she leant out.

'You found him then?' she called.

Poppy ran her hand along Cloud's neck and smiled back.

'Actually, he found me.'

They reached the wide grassy ribbon of a track where it had all gone wrong. Bella pulled Floyd up.

'I don't think we'd better canter today,' she said.

'I do,' said Sam.

'But what about the rabbit hole?'

'It's not there any more. I brought the quad bike up the day after the accident and filled it in.'

'Nice work, Samantha,' Scott said.

Sam rolled his eyes and tightened his reins. Star tossed her ebony head and crabbed sideways but he sat easily in the saddle.

'So are we going to lay those ghosts to rest or not?' he asked.

'Yep,' said Scarlett. Poppy nodded.

'If you're sure,' said Bella, kicking Floyd into a canter. Sam and Scott followed suit, still riding side by side. Poppy clicked her tongue but Cloud needed no encouragement. He cantered behind the others, his neck arched proudly and his mane rippling. She crouched low over the saddle as Cloud lengthened his stride and soon they were galloping as one across the moor towards the distant horizon.

Poppy glanced over to Scarlett and was shocked to see a single tear sliding down her best friend's cheek.

'You OK?' she called.

Scarlett nodded. 'Just thinking about Niamh.'

'Niamh's going to be OK, Scar. I know she is,' Poppy said.

And in that moment, as she and her friends galloped across their beloved Dartmoor, the wind in their ears and their horses' hooves thrumming on the springy grass like a beating heart, Poppy knew with absolute certainty that she was right.

THE SECRET OF WITCH COTTAGE

1

P oppy McKeever squinted into the sun, her eyes never leaving her best friend Scarlett as she cantered off towards the horizon. Scarlett's shoulders were stiff and unyielding, in contrast to her loose ponytail of auburn curls, which bounced jauntily on her back with every stride. Her Dartmoor pony Blaze was growing smaller by the minute. Which was ironic, Poppy thought wryly, as that had been the catalyst for their row. Cloud stamped an impatient foot, desperate to gallop after them, but she ran a hand down his neck and shook her head.

'Let them go. She'll come round once she's had a chance to cool off. Drama queen,' she added under her breath.

Cloud gave a tremulous whinny.

'She'll be fine. All I did was tell her that she looked like a drum on a pea when she rode Blaze these days. It was meant to be a joke and she totally over-reacted. Ridiculous.'

Poppy sighed. On reflection, it had sounded pretty mean. And she felt a small sliver of remorse as she remembered Scarlett's last words before she'd taken flight.

'I know I'm too big for Blaze, Poppy. You don't have to rub it in. It's alright for you. You've got Cloud. Mum and Dad have already told me they can't afford another pony. It's Blaze or nothing.'

Poppy had tried to backtrack but Scarlett, her eyes shining with unshed tears, had held her hand up to silence her.

'Save your breath. I'm not interested. I'm going home.' And she had wheeled Blaze around and kicked her into a canter, leaving Poppy gaping at her retreating back, completely lost for words. It was only when Blaze had disappeared that Poppy realised she didn't know the way home. Bored with their usual rides, Scarlett had taken them on a new route across the high, open moorland towards Princetown. Poppy loved the bleak, windswept panoramas they had crossed, but landmarks were few and far between and one craggy tor looked much like another. She patted the pocket in which she kept her mobile but pride stopped her from phoning Scarlett.

'We can find our way home, can't we Cloud?' The Connemara flicked an ear back and stamped his foot again. Poppy gathered his reins and clicked her tongue. 'Come on, let's go.'

~

BEFORE LONG THE WIDE, stony path split in two. The first track was deeply rutted and lined with a gorse hedge and veered off sharply to the left. The second path was narrower and less well trodden and led in arrow-like precision towards a cluster of conifers straight ahead.

Poppy glanced over her shoulder. She could just make out the high granite walls of HMP Dartmoor. The impenetrable building, constructed two centuries before to hold prisoners of the Napoleonic Wars, dominated the skyline on this part of the moor. Her brother Charlie was fixated with the prison and had a ghoulish fascination for stories about the many convicts who'd escaped over the years.

'If Princetown is behind us, we must be facing east, so I think we need to follow the farm track,' Poppy said. Cloud was sniffing the wind, his nostrils flared and his eyes fixed on the conifers. He whinnied again, the tremors shuddering along his dappled grey body like a mini earthquake. Perhaps he'd caught the faintest scent of Blaze and the chestnut mare was ahead, hidden from sight in the trees. Poppy trusted her pony implicitly. After all, he had roamed wild on the moor for years. If he couldn't lead her home to Riverdale, no-one could.

She gave him his head and he stepped onto the narrow path. It was a gloriously sunny afternoon in the middle of August yet the ground was still boggy in places. Poppy admired the way Cloud instinctively avoided the squelching peat by sticking to the grassy tussocks. At the edge of the band of trees the grass gave way to a carpet of rust-coloured pine needles and pine cones and when the path petered out Cloud kept walking, his ears pricked and his eyes still fixed ahead.

The deeper they walked into the trees the more the light leached away like sand in an hourglass. It was as if someone had pressed fast-forward to dusk. Charlie would say the shadowy forest was a perfect place for escaped prisoners to hide. Poppy shivered in her thin cotton tee-shirt.

They skirted a fallen tree and a clump of acid-green forest ferns. Poppy twiddled with a length of Cloud's silver mane.

'Are you *sure* this is the right way?' she said. But Cloud ploughed on through the towering conifers. Scratchy branches grazed Poppy's bare arms and the scent of pine needles filled her nostrils.

'Scarlett!' she yelled. 'Are you there?' Poppy cocked her head to listen for an answering shout, but the only sound was the static-like crackle of Cloud's hooves hitting the forest floor. 'Ridiculous!' she muttered again, as a branch caught her cheek. She was sure Scarlett would never have ridden this way home. But they had come so far she was curious to see what lay beyond the trees, and why Cloud was so intent on leading her there.

Gradually the gaps between the conifers widened and the sunlight streamed through the green canopy once again. Cloud stepped out onto open moorland, sniffed the wind and whickered softly. Poppy gazed around in astonishment.

'This is *beautiful*,' she breathed.

The small forest of evergreens concealed a teardrop-shaped tarn, on the banks of which stood a tumbledown cottage. A dry stone wall circled the cottage like a granite necklace. Poppy slithered to the ground and laced her fingers in Cloud's mane. He whickered again and began walking resolutely ahead.

'Wait! We don't know who lives here,' she whispered, tugging his reins. She stared at the cottage, looking for signs of life, aware they could be trespassing on private property. What if it was the home of a terse old hill farmer, with a distrust of strangers and a shotgun under the bed? Poppy's eyes travelled over the building, taking in the gaping hole in the catslide roof, the front door hanging off its ancient hinges and the rotting wooden window frames. She realised that the cottage must have been abandoned decades ago. Cloud strained forwards and Poppy finally relented.

'You win,' she told him. 'We'll go and explore.'

~

THE COTTAGE WAS TINY, as small as a shepherd's croft. A battalion of nettles, heavy with tiny white flowers, guarded the front door. Poppy looped Cloud's reins over an old fence post, edged past the nettles and gave the door a tentative push. It swung inwards, hitting the wall with a clatter. She took a deep breath and stepped over the threshold.

The front door led straight into a small, empty square room that Poppy supposed must once have been the parlour. The air smelt fusty, as if it hadn't been disturbed in years, and when she ran her fingers along the windowsill they picked up a layer of fine, sooty dust. Blackened beams intersected the low ceiling and the uneven floor was laid with cracked and stained quarry tiles in shades of sienna and ochre. On the outside wall was a fireplace with a granite hearth and a simple wooden mantelpiece. Opposite the fireplace was another door. Poppy tugged at the tarnished brass handle.

The kitchen was even smaller than the parlour and was also empty apart from a stone sink under the window and a rusty range. A creaky narrow staircase led to two tiny rooms in the eaves. Poppy inched her way across the woodworm-ridden floorboards in the larger of the two bedrooms to the window to check Cloud was still happy nibbling grass where she'd left him. A movement in the corner of her eye made her jump, but it was only a swallow, swooping out of a gap in the roof towards the still waters of the tarn. Hearing high-pitched cheeping, Poppy craned her neck and saw four baby swallows peeking out of their mud nest tucked under the eaves.

An old hessian sack had been tossed into one corner and two wooden crates were arranged in the middle of the floor facing the window. Almost like chairs, it occurred to Poppy. The silence in the old cottage was absolute. She wondered what kind of person would choose to live such a remote and lonely life so high on the moor. She gazed at the sloping ceilings and uneven walls, but the cottage wasn't giving away any of its secrets.

Feeling a sneeze looming, Poppy tramped back down the stairs. Cloud lifted his head as she emerged into the sunlight and she unhooked his reins and led him to the water's edge. He grazed while she threw stones into the dark water of the tarn, enjoying the ripples they made as they sank out of sight. Cloud seemed so at ease Poppy was sure it wasn't the first time he had been to the cottage.

'This place is so cool. Charlie and Scarlett will love it,' she said, before remembering that Scarlett wasn't talking to her. Poppy's earlier irritation had waned, to be replaced by an anxious knot in her stomach. She hated conflict and usually avoided it at all costs. She knew Scarlett was devastated that she had almost outgrown her beloved Blaze and was gutted that her parents couldn't afford another pony. It was hardly surprising she'd had a serious sense of humour failure. Poppy wished she could turn back the clock. Falling out with her best friend in the middle of the summer holidays was the last thing she wanted to do. She reached for her mobile and tapped out a quick text.

Sorry Scar, didn't mean to upset you. Still BFF???

But the screen remained stubbornly blank. After half an hour of checking and re-checking her phone she admitted defeat, dragged herself to her feet and swung back into the saddle. She and Cloud re-traced their steps back through the conifers.

'This time we'll go my way,' she said, turning him down the gorse-lined farm track to their right. 'These tractor tracks must lead somewhere.'

The track climbed steadily until Poppy could see over the band of conifers to the cottage and lake below. After a couple of miles the track became even more rutted. The gorse bushes were replaced by an old stone wall, which they followed for another mile or so to a farm tucked in the hollow between two tors. The farmyard was deserted, save for a couple of bantams scratching around in the dirt. When the track merged with a tarmac lane Poppy squeezed Cloud into a trot. Eventually they reached a staggered crossroads and a lichen-covered sign. *Waterby four miles.*

Poppy wondered if Scarlett was still seething at her thoughtless jibe. She could kick herself for being so insensitive. As she turned Cloud towards home one thing dominated her thoughts. How could she make amends?

2

The next morning Poppy found Charlie helping Caroline stick labels onto dozens of jars of homemade raspberry and strawberry jam.

'You haven't forgotten it's the fete today?' Caroline mumbled, a pen between her teeth.

Poppy groaned. 'Do I have to come?'

'You promised to do pony rides, remember? Cloud's one of the star attractions. You can't let all those children down,' her stepmother said.

Poppy pulled a face. 'He's not a novice ride. Some awful screaming toddler is bound to fall off and end up with concussion. And then I'll be sued. I don't think I should go.'

'No-one is going to fall off. Cloud will be on the lead rope and the children will be wearing hats. You never know, you might even enjoy it,' Caroline said.

Charlie licked a label and smoothed it onto a jar of strawberry jam.

'Charlie, that's disgusting!' Poppy shrieked.

'Someone got out of bed the wrong side this morning,' said Charlie, smoothing out the air bubbles with his thumbs.

Poppy shot him a filthy look and slammed two pieces of bread in the toaster. She had woken up grumpy and her mood hadn't improved when there was still no text or missed call from Scarlett. At least her best friend had agreed to help with the pony rides, giving Poppy a chance to apologise face to face.

The phone rang. Caroline stuck the pen behind her ear and answered it.

'Hello Pat! Yes, the tombola's done and we've almost finished the jam. We just need to load the car and we're ready. Poppy will ride Cloud over and meet us there.' There was a pause. Caroline frowned. 'Oh, that's a shame. I hope she feels better soon. Give her our love, won't you?'

'What's happened?' Poppy demanded.

'Scarlett's not feeling too well. She's decided not to come.'

Poppy gouged a piece of butter from the tub and began attacking her toast. 'Just brilliant,' she grumbled.

'Why *are* you in such a bad mood?' said Charlie, who had finished packing the jam into cardboard boxes and was counting the float.

'I. Am. Not. In. A. Bad. Mood,' Poppy growled. But Charlie wasn't listening. His eyes had taken on a faraway look and a smile was tugging at the corners of his mouth.

'Mum, do we have any brown wool?'

'I expect so. Have a look in the dresser.'

Charlie scrabbled around in a drawer and pulled out a ball of soft, mocha-brown wool.

'Perfect,' he said.

Despite herself, Poppy was curious. 'What do you want it for?'

'You know I'm doing pin a tail on the donkey for the Canvas Challenge?'

Poppy nodded. Charlie's Cub pack had launched an appeal to raise money to buy new camping equipment to replace its leaky tents. Charlie had spent the last week tracing out and colouring in a huge, lop-sided donkey which he'd pinned to a cork board and planned to set up on an old easel Caroline had found in the loft. Blindfolded fete-goers would be invited to try their hand at pinning the tail on the donkey for fifty pence a go, and anyone who managed to pin the tail anywhere near its backside would win a plastic cup of sweets.

'I'm going to do a 3D version,' he announced.

Now Charlie was a dab hand with Lego but Poppy sincerely doubted that even he could knock up a donkey in the hour they had before they had to set off for the fete.

'I just need to make a tail out of this,' he said, waving the wool in Poppy's face, 'and check Chester's nice and clean and we're in business.'

Poppy almost choked on a mouthful of toast.

'You are *not* using Chester for pin the tail on the donkey!' she screeched. 'Are you *mad*?'

'Why not? Chester loves children and he's too old for donkey rides.'

'You can't have people sticking drawing pins into him. It's animal cruelty!'

Charlie gave her a withering look. 'I wouldn't use drawing pins, grumpy-pants. I'm not that stupid. We've got some double-sided sticky tape in the craft box. I'll use that instead.'

Caroline held up her hands. 'That's enough, you two. How about a compromise? We bring Chester along to the fete so children can make a fuss of him, but we use Charlie's lovely picture to pin the tail on. I can still make you a wool tail if you want, Charlie?'

Appeased, Charlie nodded.

'We'll leave at nine. That'll give us plenty of time to set the stall up before the fete opens at ten,' said Caroline.

THE ANNUAL WATERBY SUMMER FETE, held on the third Saturday in August, was one of the highlights of the village's social calendar, eclipsed only by the Christmas Eve nativity service, which drew people from far and wide. The nativity boasted real animals in a lovingly re-created Bethlehem stable at the front of the church. More impressive still, the youngest babe-in-arms in the parish was always given the honour of playing Jesus. One especially memorable year, when there had been a shortage of babies, the job had been given to a wilful eighteen-month-old toddler called Isaac, who had thrown his swaddling cloth off just as the Three Kings arrived, climbed out of the manger, pointed at Mary and bawled, 'That's not my mummy!' It had made headlines in the Tavistock Herald.

Every group in the village ran a stall at the summer fete to raise funds for their own organisation and the competition to outdo each other was fierce. Caroline had been roped into running the tombola for Charlie's school's PTA, and had, through a combination of cajoling and coercion, amassed a vast array of prizes, from cans of fizzy drink and bottles of bubble bath to food hampers and, the star prize, a digital camera.

When Caroline had first asked Poppy if she and Scarlett would like to organise the pony rides it had seemed like a good idea. Poppy had been obsessed with horses all her life and it wasn't so long ago that she would have happily traded the clothes on her back for five minutes on someone else's pony. It would be good to let other pony-mad kids have a ride on Cloud. She and Scarlett would have a laugh. But running the pony rides on her own wasn't going to be half as much fun.

She tied Cloud and Chester to the fence behind their car and gave them the haynets she'd filled earlier. Satisfied they were happy chomping away, she helped Caroline put the finishing touches to their stall.

'Have you decided who you're raising money for yet?' Caroline asked.

'Either the PTA or Charlie's tent fund, I suppose,' she said, although she had little interest in either. She'd never attended Waterby Primary as they'd moved to Dartmoor when she was eleven. Her old primary school was miles away in Twickenham. And she would rather pull out her own fingernails one by one than join Charlie and his fellow Cubs for a night under canvas, even if the tent didn't leak.

She gave the handle of the tombola drum a hefty crank, imagining all the folded raffle tickets somersaulting inside like popcorn in a microwave. Her gaze wandered to the empty space next to their stall.

'Who's supposed to be there?'

'Some animal rescue charity, according to Pat.' Caroline checked her watch. 'But they need to get a shift on. The fete opens in fifteen minutes.'

As she spoke an ancient Land Rover came flying into the field. It narrowly missed the Methodist ladies' cake stand and drove straight over a couple of the guy ropes on the bunting-clad tea tent. It finally came to an abrupt halt in front of the McKeevers' stall. A blonde girl in her early twenties in cut-off denim shorts and a red tee-shirt leapt out and slammed the door shut behind her.

'Is that for me?' she said without preamble, pointing to the space beside them.

Caroline stepped forward, a smile on her face. 'Yes. Do you need a hand setting up? Poppy and I can help, can't we Poppy?'

Poppy, who had picked up a box of after dinner mints and was pretending to read the list of ingredients, shot her stepmother a mutinous look. 'I need to go and get ready.'

'Nonsense. You can spare ten minutes.'

Inside the back of the Land Rover was a long trestle table and several tall display panels.

'Pat said you're from an animal rescue charity,' said Caroline.

'Nethercote Horse Rescue,' corrected the girl, pointing at the logo on her tee-shirt.

'We'll help you unload,' Caroline told her. But the girl shook her head.

'I can manage.'

Ignoring her, Caroline nodded to Poppy to take one end of the top display panel. As they opened it up Poppy almost dropped it in shock. A huge photograph pinned to the royal blue panel showed a skeletal skewbald mare. She was so thin Poppy could count every rib. Her sunken flanks were covered in angry red sores, her head drooped listlessly and her eyes were dull. She looked hours away from death.

'That's Kirsty. She was skin and bone when she came to us. She was riddled with worms and had infections in both her eyes. Our vet said she'd never pull through.' The blonde girl's voice was matter-of-fact. She opened another fold of the display panel. 'That photo was taken last week.'

Poppy shook her head. She couldn't believe the plump mare standing proudly in a field, her skewbald coat glossy and her eyes bright with life, was the same horse.

'That's incredible.'

The girl dipped her head in acknowledgement. 'I think so.'

Charlie appeared, his face painted like a Ninja warrior, the woollen donkey tail clutched in his hand. He looked the blonde girl up and down. 'Who are you?'

'Jodie Morgan. Who are you?'

'Charlie McKeever. And that's my sister Poppy. But be very careful. She got out of bed the wrong side this morning.'

Poppy glared at Charlie, who raced back out of their gazebo holding the tail in the air like a pennant. Sometimes he was so embarrassing.

She helped Jodie unload the rest of the panels. Before and after photos of horses and ponies were pinned to each section, with handwritten stories alongside each one. In one of the pictures a horse had overgrown hooves so long they curled up like Aladdin's slippers. Others had matted coats, hollow necks and bony rumps. Poppy had a sick feeling in the pit of her stomach. How could anyone treat an animal so badly? It was beyond belief.

'Some people complain our photos are too graphic and say we shouldn't use them because they upset people.' Jodie gave a derisory snort. 'I don't care. You can't sweep cruelty and neglect under the carpet. These pictures need to be seen. What do you think?'

Taken aback by her directness, Poppy glanced towards Caroline. But her stepmum was deep in conversation with the woman running the face-painting stand.

'They are shocking,' she said. 'But I agree with you. People should know it goes on. And maybe it'll help with donations.'

Jodie's lips thinned. 'If only. People have absolutely no idea how much it costs to run Nethercote. They seem to think I can feed the horses on thin air.'

Charlie re-appeared. 'It's one minute to ten, Poppy!' he cried. 'You need to start the pony rides.'

'Pony rides?' Jodie asked.

'My pony Cloud is over there with our donkey Chester.'

Chester's long brown ears had flopped forward as he dozed but Cloud was looking around with interest as fete-goers began streaming into the field.

'Did you say Cloud?' Jodie said.

Poppy nodded, wondering why the older girl was staring at the Connemara as if she'd seen a ghost. Then she had an idea. 'I was going to raise money for new tents but I'd much rather give the money to help your horses. It might not be much, but anything is better than nothing, right?'

Jodie dragged her eyes away from Cloud. 'Yes,' she echoed faintly. 'Anything is better than nothing.'

THE NEXT TWO hours passed in a blur of shortening and lengthening stirrup leathers, giving leg-ups and leading young riders up and down the length of the field as proud parents snapped away on their mobile phones.

Poppy had been worried how Cloud would react to the swarms of people but he was basking in all the attention, standing patiently as he was stroked and petted, taking the Polos and tufts of grass proffered on countless sticky palms so gently that Poppy's heart swelled with love. Chester was an old hand at village events and when Poppy hit on the idea of charging fifty pence for the privilege of having a selfie with the donkey an orderly queue quickly formed.

Halfway through the morning Jodie appeared with a plastic cup of lukewarm orange squash.

'Your mum sent me over with a drink. And you can put this on if you like,' Jodie said, handing Poppy a red tee-shirt that matched her own.

Poppy pulled the tee-shirt over her head and smiled. 'I reckon I've made about fifty pounds already.'

'Wish I could say the same. People are so tight they won't even fork out the price of a cup of coffee.' Jodie rubbed Cloud's forehead and he snuffled at the pocket of her shorts. She looked as if she was about to say something else, then thought better of it. She patted him on the neck and smiled briefly at Poppy. 'Anyway, gotta go.'

By two o'clock the queue of children waiting for a ride had dwindled to nothing. Poppy left Cloud tied up next to Chester and went in search of Caroline. Charlie charged through the crowd towards her, shaking an old biscuit tin heavy with loose change.

'I've made millions!' he said. 'Enough to buy ten tents, I reckon.'

'I've made lots, too. I was going to have a count up and give the money to Jodie before I take Cloud and Chester home.'

'She's gone.'

'You're joking.'

'Nope. She told us it was a waste of time and she'd have been better off staying at home.'

Poppy jiggled the coins in her pocket. 'How am I supposed to get all this money to her?'

Charlie shrugged. 'Ask Mum.'

Poppy found Caroline at their stall wrestling with the trestle table.

'I was just about to come and find you. Are you all done?'

'Done in, more like. I'm shattered. You have no idea how tiring giving pony rides is.' Poppy collapsed on the ground. 'And Charlie said Jodie's already gone.'

'She had to get back for the horses. I said we'd drive over tomorrow. There's a map on the back of the leaflet she was giving out.' Caroline pulled a crumpled piece of paper from the pocket of her jeans. On the front was a picture of Kirsty the pretty skewbald mare looking inquisitively over her stable door. Inside were some of the before and after photos Jodie had used on her display board and on the back of the leaflet was a map.

'It's really close,' Poppy said, surprised. Nethercote was half way between Waterby and Princetown. In fact she and Cloud must have ridden pretty close the day before. And yet until today she'd had no idea the horse rescue sanctuary even existed.

3

The sanctuary was at the end of a long and windy track flanked by fields of black-faced sheep. Nethercote itself was a squat stone farmhouse with a slate roof and incongruously tall chimneys. Ivy crept up the walls and net curtains blocked the view into every window, giving the house a shuttered look. As Caroline parked the car Poppy noticed a small sign pointing around the side of the house.

'It says the rescue centre is this way.'

Poppy led Caroline and Charlie through a gate and into a wide strip of concrete sandwiched between two long rows of whitewashed stables that looked as if they had once been cow byres. On the wall by a door to what Poppy presumed was the feed room was a bell with a sign above, *Please ring for attention.* She gave the bell pull a tentative tug and jumped a foot in the air when Jodie appeared over the nearest stable door and barked, 'Who is it?'

'Only us,' Caroline said.

The scowl on the older girl's face lifted fractionally. 'Sorry,' she said, pushing the stable door open. 'People think that because we're an animal sanctuary they have the right to just turn up on the doorstep any time they like.'

Poppy fingered the small brown envelope in her pocket. 'We've brought the money we raised yesterday,' she said.

Jodie wiped her hands on her shorts. 'Thanks.'

Charlie, who had been walking up the line of empty stables peering into each one, fixed his cerulean blue eyes on Jodie and said, 'Can we have a tour?'

Caroline smiled apologetically. 'I'm sorry about my son. He has no manners. We can see you're busy. Perhaps we'll pop by another day.'

Jodie checked her watch. 'No, you're OK. I've got time to give you a quick tour. Show you where your money will go.'

'I'd love to meet Kirsty,' Poppy said shyly.

'Kirsty's gone, I'm afraid,' Jodie said.

'Oh, no! What happened to her?'

'Not *gone* gone. I mean gone from here. She was put up for adoption in the spring. She's gone to live with a family near Taunton. She's settled in really well.'

'That's good,' Poppy said, relieved that the skewbald mare was still enjoying life after the cruelty and neglect she'd endured.

'We run an adoption scheme, otherwise we'd never be able to take on any more horses,' Jodie said.

'How does that work?' Charlie asked, looking around with interest.

Caroline sighed. 'Don't get any ideas, Charlie. We haven't got room for any more animals.'

'I was just asking,' Charlie said indignantly, then flashed a grin at Jodie. 'We've already rescued our dog Freddie. We gave Chester a home when Tory couldn't look after him any more. And I suppose we sort of rescued Cloud. Dad says Riverdale's turning into a home for waifs and strays.'

Jodie finally smiled. 'Good for you. Why buy an animal when so many desperately need new homes?' She beckoned them to follow her to the fields at the end of the two rows of stables, where more than a dozen horses and ponies grazed, dozed in the sun or stood head to tail, swishing flies.

'Once a horse or pony has fully recovered they go up for adoption and I put their details on our website. New homes are vetted and if everything is OK they have the horse on permanent loan, with the understanding that should the horse need to come back for any reason, they'll always have a place at Nethercote.'

Poppy gazed at the horses. An idea was forming in her mind. 'Who's up for adoption at the moment,' she asked.

'Percy. He's the Welsh Section A over there,' said Jodie, pointing to a cheeky-looking grey gelding with a bushy mane and a pink nose. 'He's available as a companion. And Mr Darcy. I called him that because he's tall, dark and handsome.' They followed Jodie's gaze to a dark bay thoroughbred gelding who was grazing next to a swaybacked chestnut mare. 'He has a touch of arthritis so can only do light work.'

'You haven't got any between fourteen and fifteen hands?' Poppy said hopefully.

Charlie gaped at her. 'You don't need another pony. You've got Cloud!'

'Not for me, you twit. I was thinking of Scarlett. She's my best friend,' Poppy explained, ignoring the fact that Scarlett hadn't spoken to her for a whole forty eight hours, the longest time they'd ever fallen out. 'She lives on the farm next door to us. She's almost outgrown her pony but her parents can't afford to buy her a new one. I was wondering if you had anything that she could adopt.'

Jodie leant on the fence and stared at her disparate herd of horses and ponies. 'Is she a good rider?'

'Really good. She's been riding since she was two.'

'She lives on a farm, you say?'

Poppy nodded. 'They've got loads of lovely grazing and a spare stable and whoever came would have two Dartmoor ponies for company.'

'There is someone who might fit the bill.'

Jodie whistled and a rangy chestnut gelding lifted his head and trotted over. He gave Jodie a gentle butt and she scratched his ear affectionately.

'This is Red. He was born at Nethercote. We didn't realise his dam was in foal at first. Unfortunately we lost her the night he was born and I had to hand rear him. I started breaking him this spring. He's coming on well but he needs to go to a really experienced home.'

Poppy knew Scarlett would fall in love with the chestnut gelding the minute she saw him. He was a couple of inches bigger than Cloud and had a flaxen mane and tail, four white socks, an extra daub of white on his nose and kind eyes. Poppy imagined Red and Cloud cantering along a moorland track together, matching each other stride for stride. He was absolutely perfect.

'She would have to come and see him first,' said Jodie. 'I only let horses go if I'm satisfied they are a good match with their new guardian.'

'That won't be a problem,' Poppy said. 'I'll speak to her when I get home.'

'Do you get upset when the horses go to their new homes?' Charlie asked.

'Can't afford to. A job like this toughens you up.'

'He's sweet,' said Caroline, pointing to an appaloosa pony who was lying down in the sun.

'He looks like he's been out in a snowstorm,' said Charlie.

He was right, Poppy thought. The white spots on the pony's chestnut back looked like snowflakes.

'That's Biscuit. All the horses here have a story to tell, but his is probably the most incredible. If you read about it in a book you wouldn't believe it,' said Jodie. 'He was found by the RSPCA tethered to railings on top of a tower block of flats in the Midlands.'

'I remember that!' Caroline said. 'I saw it on the news. They had to airlift him down by helicopter, didn't they?'

'That's right. The lift was broken and they thought it would be less traumatic for him to be winched down by helicopter than to be carried down the twenty seven flights of stairs.'

Charlie was staring at Biscuit with his mouth open. 'He lived on top of the building?'

Jodie nodded. 'No-one knows for sure how long he'd been up there. And no-one was ever prosecuted. Neither the RSPCA nor the police could prove who he belonged to. He'd been kept alive on vegetable peelings, scraps of bread and rainwater. He was pretty thin and had terrible rain scald when he came to us.'

Poppy couldn't imagine what life must have been like for Biscuit, living on his own on top of a tower block, with sheer drops in every direction, at the mercy of the elements.

'That's awful. How was he found?'

'A new tenant moved in and tipped off the RSPCA. The inspector told me their call centre didn't believe him at first and they almost dismissed it as a prank call. Luckily for Biscuit someone decided to check it out.'

'He looks pretty content now,' said Caroline. Biscuit yawned, showing a row of yellow teeth, and collapsed, asleep, in the daisies.

Jodie smiled. 'He is the most chilled out pony I have ever known. Sometimes, when things get on top of me and I fantasise about walking away from it all, I look at Biscuit and remember what all the blood, sweat and tears are for. He keeps me going.'

'Do you run the centre on your own?' Poppy asked.

Jodie gazed at Biscuit's snowflake-splotched flanks gently rising and falling. Poppy was shocked to see a look of bitterness darken her features, but the expression was so fleeting she wondered if she'd imagined it.

'This is my dad's dream, not mine,' Jodie said eventually.

'So he helps you with the horses?'

'He would if he could,' Jodie conceded. 'But he's away at the moment.'

'Our dad's always away, too. He works for the BBC,' said Charlie. 'What does your dad do?'

Jodie bent down to pick a handful of grass for a bay mare who had wandered over to say hello. 'He runs a small import business. Mobile phones, mainly.'

Caroline looked impressed. 'Mobiles are big business. He must be doing well.'

'Not really. It's a very confined market where he is. In more ways than one,' she muttered.

Poppy remembered the envelope in her pocket.

'Here's the money we made yesterday. I hope it helps a little bit.'

The older girl gave the ghost of a smile. 'It'll keep the wolf from the door for a few days.'

4

———————

Caroline had barely pulled up the handbrake before Poppy had unclipped her seatbelt and jumped out of the passenger door.

'I'm going to tell Scarlett about Red,' Poppy said.

She'd taken a dozen photos of the chestnut gelding on her phone and scrolled through them as she crossed the field of sheep that separated Riverdale and Ashworthy, the farm where Scarlett lived with her older brother Alex and their parents Bill and Pat. Red was the same shade of burnt umber as both Blaze and Scarlett's own auburn hair. It was fate, Poppy told herself, as she climbed over the gate onto the roughshod Ashworthy drive. All she had to do was convince Scarlett to see her.

Pat was kneading a huge ball of dough in the farm's shabby but cosy kitchen when Poppy poked her head around the door.

'I wondered if Scarlett wanted some company.'

Pat pushed the dough down and out with the heel of her hand, pulled it back into a ball and sprinkled it with flour. She nodded in the direction of the lounge. 'Your guess is as good as mine. She's been moping around the house since Friday. I don't know what's up with her.'

'Caroline said she wasn't very well and that's why she didn't come to the fete yesterday.'

Pat dropped the dough into a bowl to prove on top of the Rayburn. 'That's what she says, but I'm not convinced. She hasn't got a temperature.

She hasn't been sick. She just seems to be down in the dumps. Perhaps you can cheer her up.'

'I'll do my best. But before I do, can I talk to you about something?'

~

POPPY TOOK a deep breath and pushed open the door to the lounge. Scarlett, wearing faded My Little Pony pyjamas and a glowering expression, was curled up on the sofa with Meg, the family's border collie. The dog gave a welcoming woof and jumped down to see Poppy, her tail wagging.

'At least someone's pleased to see me,' joked Poppy. She stroked Meg's silky ears and chanced another look at Scarlett. On closer inspection she realised her best friend was clutching a tissue and her eyes were red-rimmed.

'Hey, are you OK?'

Scarlett waved the remote control at the television. They watched together as a beautiful bay gelding galloped in blind panic through No Man's Land, shells exploding all around him and barbed wire tearing his chest. War Horse was one of Poppy's all-time favourite films - it was right up there with International Velvet - but it was so sad it was enough to make a statue weep. No wonder Scarlett was crying.

'Turn it off before Joey gets caught in the barbed wire. I can't stand that bit,' Poppy said, plonking herself down on the sofa beside Scarlett. 'I know you're really cross with me, and I don't blame you, but I've got some really exciting news I promise you'll want to hear.'

Scarlett blew her noise noisily and glared at Poppy, who ignored her and reached in her back pocket for her phone.

'This is Red. He's fifteen hands and four years old. Gorgeous, isn't he?'

Scarlett glanced at the screen and looked away. 'Are you getting another horse?' she said dully.

'No, you idiot, he's for you!'

A damson-dark flush was inching its way up Scarlett's neck. 'How many times do I have to spell it out, Poppy? Mum and Dad can't afford another horse.'

'Red's not for sale.'

'So why are you showing me his picture?' Scarlett uncurled her legs and swung her feet to the floor. 'I'm going upstairs.'

'Blimey, Scarlett, you can be a stroppy mare sometimes. Just listen for a minute, will you? Red is a rescue horse. He lives at Nethercote Horse Rescue. He's about to go up for adoption. I've had a word with the girl who runs the place. He's as good as yours if you pass the home visit and you and he get on.'

Eyes wide, Scarlett gawped at Poppy. 'Are you serious?'

'Absolutely. We met Jodie, the girl who runs the rescue centre, at the fete yesterday. She's -'

But Scarlett wasn't listening. She was two steps ahead and her voice was resigned. 'It won't work. Mum and Dad are bound to say no. It's another mouth to feed, isn't it? Another horse to shoe. More vet's bills. Tack we can't afford.'

The door opened and Pat appeared with two mugs of tea. 'What can't we afford?' she asked, winking at Poppy.

'Nothing,' said Scarlett, sliding Poppy's phone down the side of the sofa.

'Poppy's just been showing me the photos of Red. He's a handsome lad, isn't he?' Pat set the mugs on the coffee table. 'Are you going to go and see him?'

'There's no point, is there? We can't afford to keep him.'

Pat smiled at her daughter. 'Barney was only asking me the other day if you might be interested in a Saturday job at the shop. If you take him up on his offer and use your wages towards Red's keep, I'll make sure we find the rest. It's been a good year for lambing and the pigs are doing really well. You'll have to make do with second-hand tack, but you're used to hand-me-downs, aren't you?'

Scarlett nodded, a smile creeping across her freckled face at last. She sprang up from the sofa and threw her arms around her mum.

'You have Poppy to thank. It was all her idea,' Pat said.

Poppy caught Scarlett's eye. 'Am I forgiven?'

Scarlett's forehead creased in a frown and she tilted her head to one side and rubbed her chin thoughtfully. Poppy's heart sank. If finding Scarlett a new horse wasn't enough to win her over she didn't know what was. Then Scarlett broke free from her mum and hugged Poppy.

'Of course you are, you twit! I had already forgiven you really. I should know by now that tact isn't one of your strong points. I was just feeling sorry for myself. And now I feel like Christmas has come early and Santa has promised me the best present ever!'

Friends again, the two girls decided to celebrate with a ride. Feeling magnanimous, Poppy asked Charlie if he wanted to tag along on his bike. 'As long as you only speak when spoken to and promise not to be annoying,' she told him sternly.

Charlie smiled his sweetest smile. 'I'm *never* annoying.'

'Ha! That's open for debate.'

Back at Ashworthy Scarlett was zinging with excitement. 'Mum's phoned Jodie. We're going to see Red in the morning. Want to come, too?'

'You bet.'

'Never mind tomorrow. Where are we going today?' Charlie asked.

'Follow me,' Poppy said mysteriously. 'I know exactly where I want to go.'

~

CLOUD'S EARS were pricked as they approached the band of conifers that cloaked the tumbledown cottage. The ground was so squelchy Charlie had to push his mountain bike. 'My feet are soaking,' he grumbled. 'Where exactly are we supposed to be going?'

'Stop whingeing and keep walking, little brother. It's worth the wait, I promise.'

They plunged into the conifers. Poppy grinned at the other two. 'Almost there.'

Scarlett gasped when she saw the dilapidated building and the dark waters of the tarn.

'It's Witch Cottage! We can't go there!'

Poppy jumped off Cloud and gave Scarlett a puzzled look.

'It's fine. Cloud and I explored it the other day. No-one lives there any more. I reckon it's been empty for years.'

'You don't understand! It's haunted!'

Charlie propped his bike against a tree and stared at Scarlett agog.

'The pool's in the shape of a tear, isn't it?' Scarlett said.

Poppy nodded. 'Why?'

'My Granny Martha used to say the pool came from a single teardrop wept by an old woman whose only son was killed in a tin mining accident like about five hundred years ago. Granny said it's bottomless, and anyone who gazes into the waters at midnight on Midsummer's Eve will see a reflection of the next person in the parish to die.'

Scarlett's voice had taken on a low, chilling tone. 'People thought the old crone was a witch and one full moon a group of villagers crept into her cottage, dragged her from her bed and burnt her and her familiar at the stake.'

Charlie frowned. 'Her familiar what?'

'A familiar is another name for a witch's animal companion, Charlie. In this case it was a cat.'

Poppy tutted. What a cliché. 'Was it black, by any chance?'

'No, it was ginger, actually. He was called Marmaduke. That's what the legend says, anyway. And now the witch can be seen gliding around the banks of the pool on the night of every full moon, with Marmaduke riding on her withered old shoulders and the ends of her tattered cloak on fire.'

By this time they had reached the stone wall surrounding the cottage and tarn.

'And,' said Scarlett, pointing to a small wooden cross Poppy hadn't noticed before. 'About five years ago a group of wild swimmers were crossing the pool when one of them got into difficulties and drowned. And do you know what?'

'What?' breathed Charlie, who was hanging onto her every word.

'The swimmer who died was *exactly* the same age as the old woman's son when he was killed in the tin mine.' Scarlett drew her hand across her neck in a cut-throat gesture. Poppy rolled her eyes.

'But that's not all,' Scarlett said dramatically. 'Sometimes at night lights can be seen in the windows of the cottage. Some people say it's the old crone lighting candles in memory of her son.'

'Some people talk a load of absolute rubbish,' said Poppy. 'Are you going to come and have a look around or what?'

Scarlett was aghast. 'Haven't you heard a word of what I've been saying? There's no way you're dragging me into that house of horrors. I'll stay and look after the ponies, thanks.'

Charlie had no such reservations. He sprinted to the crooked front door and heaved it open, beckoning Poppy to follow. She handed Cloud's reins to Scarlett and ran after him.

Charlie was already disappearing up the creaky staircase.

'Be careful, some of the floorboards are a bit rotten,' she called.

'No need to worry, sis. I can look after myself,' he shouted back.

'Famous last words,' Poppy muttered, inspecting the decrepit remains of the kitchen. Someone must have lived in the cottage since the old crone in Scarlett's dubious legend, although Poppy guessed the house must have been empty for at least half a century. A corroded black kettle sat atop the rusty range. A couple of tarnished knives and forks gathered dust on some woodworm-infested shelves. Poppy pulled open a couple of cupboards, but there was nothing inside apart from ancient cobwebs and a couple of dead bluebottles. Upstairs she could hear Charlie exclaiming with delight as he thundered between the two bedrooms like a baby elephant with a sugar rush.

She was prising open the door of the range when there was a shout and the ceiling above her head shook ominously, sprinkling her with a layer of dust as fine as icing sugar. She raced up the stairs, two at a time. Charlie was sitting with his back to her, hugging his right knee.

'What on earth's happened?'

Charlie looked over his shoulder. 'My foot's stuck,' he said sheepishly.

'In one of those rotten floorboards I warned you about?' Poppy knelt down next to him. Charlie's foot had broken clean-through the crumbling plank and was wedged between two joists. She slipped her hand into the gap and felt for his shoe. 'I think it's your trainer that's stuck. If I undo your laces you should be able to wiggle your foot out. We'll give it a try.'

Poppy began picking at the double knot but the gap was so small that every time she moved her hand she grazed her knuckles on the rough underside of the floorboards. Eventually she felt the laces slither undone. She sat back on her haunches and Charlie wiggled out his foot.

'You're lucky you didn't break your ankle,' Poppy told him, reaching back into the gap for his trainer. As she did her fingers brushed against a hard edge. It didn't feel like a joist. It was more like the cover of a book. Poppy leant on her elbows and slid her hand further in. It was definitely a book. But who would hide a book beneath the floorboards of an abandoned croft where an old woman who may or may not have been a witch had once lived? The hairs on the back of her neck stood up.

'Have you got my shoe yet?' Charlie asked. He had a cobweb in his hair and his knees were filthy.

'No, it's caught on something' she lied, keen to keep this discovery to herself. 'Go over to the window. There's a swallow's nest under the eaves. See if you can see the babies.'

Once Poppy was sure his attention was diverted she swivelled around on her heels so her back was facing him and pulled out the book. It was long and slim with a black cover and the year embossed in silver leaf on the front. A diary. Poppy flicked through it, as furtive as a pickpocket stealing a wallet. Pages and pages were crammed with tiny writing. Her heart was hammering in her ribcage as she tried to decipher the loops and curls.

'What are you doing?' Charlie asked.

'Nothing,' said Poppy, tucking the diary in her waistband and reaching back into the hole in the floorboards. 'Here's your shoe,' she said, tossing him the white and navy trainer. She checked her watch. 'We'd better go or Scarlett will have a fit. She hates it here.'

'I think it's awesome. It could be our secret den where we plan all our adventures.'

'Maybe we'll come over on the next full moon. See if Scarlett's right about the place being haunted,' said Poppy, half-joking.

But if she thought her brother would be fazed by any ghostly goings-on she was wrong. His eyes were sparkling.

'Cool idea!' he said, grinning at Poppy. 'Why didn't I think of that?'

THE DIARY PRESSED UNCOMFORTABLY into Poppy's back all the way home. As they cantered across the moor, Charlie pedalling furiously to keep up, she wondered why she hadn't shared her discovery with Scarlett. Perhaps it was because her best friend had showed no desire to have anything to do with the tumbledown cottage. She'd flung Cloud's reins at Poppy and jumped on Blaze the second they'd re-appeared, muttering about bad vibes and negative energy. Scarlett was one of the most superstitious people Poppy knew. She shrieked with horror if Poppy spilled salt and forgot to hurl a pinch of it over her left shoulder, and if Poppy dared dice with death by walking under a ladder she virtually went into meltdown. Poppy didn't hold any truck with superstitions - she supposed it was having a cynical journalist as a dad. As far as she was concerned Scarlett's tale of supernatural happenings was utter nonsense.

'We're leaving at ten tomorrow,' Scarlett said, as they clip-clopped down the Ashworthy drive.

'I'll be there,' Poppy said, grimacing as she surreptitiously shifted the diary further down her jodhpurs.

'Why are you pulling a face? Don't you want to come?'

''Course I do. I'm just trying to scratch a mosquito bite,' Poppy lied.

Back home, once she'd turned Cloud out with Chester, Poppy raced upstairs to her bedroom, closed the door, and propped her old wicker chair under the door handle. It wouldn't stop Charlie coming in, but it would buy her enough time to hide her find. She sat cross-legged on her bed and opened the diary with trembling fingers.

5

The first two pages were covered in doodles. Circles and spirals, squares and triangles, stars and flowers. So many squiggles and scribbles that at first Poppy didn't see the three words in the middle of the facing page. When she did, she blinked and looked again, in case the loopy, slanting script somehow untangled itself and snaked into three completely different words. It didn't. The words were there in black and white. *Caitlyn Jones's Diary.*

Poppy realised she was gripping the book so tightly she was in danger of breaking the spine. She closed it, drummed her fingers on the black leather cover and wondered what to do. Caitlyn Jones had always been a complete enigma to Poppy. Someone she had obsessed about and felt inferior to ever since the McKeevers had moved to Riverdale. Someone who, if ghosts did actually exist, came as close to haunting Poppy's subconscious as anyone ever would.

Caitlyn was the other girl in Cloud's life. Poppy corrected herself. *Had been* the other girl in his life. Not any more.

There was a photo of Caitlyn and Cloud in Tory's flat, taken at the Brambleton Horse Show the same year Poppy's mum Isobel died. Poppy scrutinised it every time she visited, battling the jealousy and inadequacy it inevitably stirred, feelings that were as invasive as goosegrass, no matter how hard she tried to suppress them.

Poppy loved Cloud with all her heart. She would walk over burning coals for him, no question. And she knew her pony loved her. After all, he'd found her when he'd been let loose on the moor during their stay at Redhall Manor Equestrian Centre, hadn't he? But did he love her as much as he'd loved Caitlyn? Poppy had no answer to that.

And yet here, in her hands, was the key to unlock Caitlyn's innermost thoughts. A window to her dreams and fears. A chance for Poppy to see the world through Cait's eyes.

Poppy gazed at the diary almost reverently, her fingers flicking through the pages as if it was a kids' flip book. She itched to read it. And yet the diary held secrets and thoughts Caitlyn had scribbled down never imagining that anyone else would ever see them. It was private property. Poppy had kept a diary ever since Caroline had bought her one for Christmas the previous year. She hated the thought of anyone reading it. It would be so embarrassing. More than that, it would make her feel exposed, vulnerable. Poppy slammed the book shut. If she felt like that about her own diary, it would be hypocritical for her to read someone else's, wouldn't it?

Poppy shoved the diary under her pillow and stood up. She was halfway across her room when she stopped, as if glued to the floor. The desire to read the diary was overwhelming. Caitlyn was dead, killed seven years ago when Cloud fell at a fence during a hunter trial. What harm could reading it do? Poppy would never divulge what she'd read. It would be their secret, a bond between them as strong as the one they each shared with Cloud. With a certainty she couldn't explain, Poppy knew Caitlyn wouldn't mind. She spun on her heels, jumped back on her bed and pulled out the diary before she could change her mind.

A slip of folded paper fluttered out of the pages and settled between her crossed legs like a sycamore seed on a blustery autumn day. It was an old newspaper cutting, brittle and flaking. Poppy smoothed it out, tucked a strand of hair behind her ear and began to read.

Friends and rivals compete for showjumping glory

Best friends Jodie Morgan and Caitlyn Jones were the only two young riders to make it through to the jump-off in the final class at the South Devon Open Showjumping Competition on Saturday.

Fourteen-year-old Jodie and her pony Nethercote Nero jumped first, giving a textbook performance with a fast, clean round, piling on the pressure for her thirteen-year-old friend and fellow Pony Club showjumping team member Caitlyn.

Caitlyn and her pony Cloud Nine looked like they were in with a chance, but knocked a pole in the double to collect four faults and second place.

Earlier this year Jodie, a rising showjumping talent, was selected to represent Great Britain in the British Showjumping Pony European Championships squad.

'Both Nero and Cloud have been jumping out of their skin all season so winning the open jumping class against such stiff competition was pretty special,' said Jodie.

'Hopefully we can keep up the momentum for the European Championships in Malmo, Sweden, in August.'

Jodie and Caitlyn had been best friends! Poppy studied the photo next to the story, the diary forgotten. Cloud stood proudly, his neck arched and his mane neatly plaited, an enormous blue rosette fixed to his brow-band. Caitlyn sat gracefully astride him, holding the reins with one hand, her head turned towards the girl next to her, who was riding an eye-catching light bay gelding, her hand clasped around the stem of a silver trophy. Jodie was winking at Caitlyn and laughing. She looked younger, more carefree, less spiky, but it was definitely her. Poppy checked the date. Seven years ago. She squinted at Nero, trying to remember if she'd seen him when they'd visited Nethercote. She didn't think so. She was sure she'd have remembered him.

Poppy supposed it was no fluke that the two girls had known each other. They must have been in the same school year and they were both talented riders. They had a lot in common. It was inevitable they'd been friends. Suddenly Jodie's reaction to Cloud made sense. Poppy shivered. Poor Jodie. Coming face to face with her old friend's pony must have been a shock.

A thump, thump, thump on the stairs caught her attention and the handle on her bedroom door turned. Poppy shoved the newspaper cutting back in the diary and slipped it under her mattress. She streaked across the room and whipped the wicker chair away as the door creaked and swung open.

Charlie eyed her suspiciously. 'Why are you holding your chair?'

'Just re-arranging my room. Felt like a change,' Poppy said airily.

Charlie raised his eyebrows. 'Mum sent me up. Dinner's nearly ready. You need to come down and lay the table.'

~

POPPY DIDN'T GET another chance to look at the diary until she'd gone to bed. Her lamp cast a pool of sallow light over the crackly pages as she scoured the tiny loopy handwriting, looking for mentions of Cloud. She found the first on the fifth of January.

> *Mum finally agreed to drive me up to Gran's this morning. I was getting desperate. I hadn't seen Cloud since New Year's Eve. That's five whole days ago! I think he was pleased to see me. But not as pleased as I was to see him! It was freezing, but we managed a quick ride around the lanes. I'm never going to get his fitness up for competing if I can only ride a couple of times a week. Gran said she would've lunged him but the fields were too waterlogged. But I shouldn't have to rely on her to exercise my pony. Mum just doesn't get it. I wish, wish, wish she was into horses like Jodie's dad is. She doesn't know how lucky she is.*

Poppy realised she was lucky, too. Imagine only seeing Cloud a couple of times a week! It would be torture. She could see him first thing every morning and last thing at night. She could ride him whenever she wanted. She could even watch him from her bedroom window. They spent every spare second together. For the first time in her life Poppy felt stirrings of sympathy for Caitlyn.

She scanned through the weekday entries, which seemed to consist mainly of Caitlyn moaning about school and the amount of homework she'd been given. The bits that fascinated her were the references to Cloud and Jodie. One entry on the twentieth of May caught her attention.

> *What a fantastic weekend! The Annoying Parents had some boring wedding to go to in Somerset. They were going to take me until I suggested I stayed at Gran's. So they dropped me off at eight yesterday morning and didn't pick me up until six tonight. It was brilliant, having a whole two days with Cloud. And Chester and Gran of course. Jodie's dad brought Nero over in their box yesterday and we went on this amazingly long ride. We were gone for hours. Mum would have been panicking, thinking we'd been kidnapped by aliens or something, but Gran's so*

chilled. She always says she trusts Cloud to look after me. Anyway, we found this awesome place. It's an old abandoned cottage over towards Princetown way. You have to ride through a forest to reach it. There's even a small lake for the ponies to drink from. We decided we'd hang out there whenever we can. It's so cool.

And then a couple of weeks later:

No shows this weekend so Jodie and I rode over to the cottage. We took a picnic this time, which we ate on the banks of the lake. I brought along an article I'd printed from the internet about how to teach your horse tricks. It was so funny. Honestly, we were in stitches. Cloud was a quick learner, and by the end of the afternoon he was giving me a kiss for a pony nut. Nero was hopeless. But secretly I didn't mind. It was nice to be better at something than Jodie for once!

Poppy yawned and checked the time. Five to eleven. She closed the diary, slid it back under her mattress and turned off her bedside lamp. It's funny, she thought sleepily, as she wiggled under the duvet trying to get comfortable. She'd spent two years feeling inferior to Caitlyn. But, as she'd flicked through pages and pages peppered with the insights and insecurities of any teenage girl, she realised they were not so very different after all.

6

A fine drizzle as soft as a whisper had settled on the moor overnight and, despite promises by the weathermen that the afternoon would be hot and sunny, the mizzle seemed as stubborn to linger as an unwelcome houseguest reluctant to pack their bags and go home. Poppy's hair had frizzed by the time she had fed Cloud and Chester, cleaned and re-filled their water trough and poo-picked their field.

She was changing into a pair of marginally-cleaner jodhpurs when she heard the toot of a horn and saw Bill's Land Rover bump to a halt outside the front door. Scarlett slid across the bench seat to make room for her.

'Excited?' Poppy said, fixing her seatbelt.

'I feel a bit sick, actually.'

Poppy was surprised. Scarlett usually took everything in her stride. Things that would make Poppy's knees knock with fear, like meeting new people or talking to the whole school during assembly, never fazed her. She was normally so confident and laid-back, everything Poppy wasn't.

'What's up?'

Scarlett hugged herself. 'What if Jodie takes one look at me and decides she hates me? What if Red and I don't click? What if we fail the home check? So many things could go wrong.'

'It'll all be fine,' Poppy soothed.

Scarlett stared glumly ahead as the windscreen wipers whisked to and fro, and remained unusually quiet as they trundled through the lanes to Nethercote. Poppy chatted to Bill about the fete, although her mind was elsewhere. She hadn't made up her mind whether or not to tell Jodie that she knew she and Caitlyn had been friends. She wanted to know if Jodie had ever made the European Championships in Sweden. According to the newspaper cutting she was a promising young rider. So why was she working her fingers to the bone at a small, local horse rescue centre in the middle of Dartmoor and not competing for glory on the national showjumping circuit? Poppy remembered a throwaway remark Jodie had made during their visit. She'd said the horse sanctuary was her dad's dream, not hers. Had her dream been to be a professional showjumper? If so, why had she thrown it all away to look after the rescue horses? And where was her dad in all of this? It didn't make sense.

Bill turned off the main road and the Land Rover lurched along the long and windy track to Nethercote. Poppy jumped out and pointed to the side of the house. 'It's this way.'

Scarlett and Bill followed her to the two long rows of whitewashed stables. A familiar spotted head appeared over the door of the nearest stable.

'Hello Biscuit.' Poppy felt in her pocket for some pony nuts and offered them to the appaloosa. 'He was rescued from a high rise block of flats,' she told Scarlett, who was looking decidedly green.

But Scarlett wasn't listening. Her eyes were tracking back and forth across the yard. 'Is there a loo?'

Poppy spied Jodie leading Red out of the paddock. The chestnut gelding walked obediently by her side. It wasn't until the pair reached them that Poppy realised he wasn't wearing a headcollar.

Jodie read her mind. 'I don't bother with one. He's always followed me around like a shadow. It's because I hand-reared him.'

Scarlett gazed at Red, her expression a jumble of longing and fear. She held out her hand tentatively and the gelding stretched his neck and blew gently into her palm. Scarlett scratched his poll and beamed at them. 'He's the most beautiful horse I have ever seen in my life.'

'I wouldn't go that far, but yes, he's not a bad sort,' said Jodie.

Jodie tacked Red up and led him to the mounting block.

'He was only backed in the spring and is still very green, but he's a fast learner,' she said, holding the gelding while Scarlett swung deftly into the saddle. Her hazel eyes were sparkling as she followed Jodie into a small, empty paddock.

'Have a walk and trot and see how he feels.'

Poppy, Bill and Jodie leant on the post and rail fence and watched Scarlett and Red as they walked around the field.

'You're right, she's a nice little rider,' Jodie said.

'Aye,' said Bill. 'She learnt as soon as she could walk and hasn't stopped since. It's broken her heart that she's almost outgrown Blaze, especially as we couldn't afford to buy her another horse, but she's never once complained. She's a good girl, is our Scarlett, and she'll look after your Red, I promise you that.'

There was a catch in Bill's normally gruff voice. Poppy caught Jodie's eye and was surprised to see her face darken.

'She's lucky to have a dad like you.'

Red trotted past, his chestnut ears pricked. Jodie gave a brief smile. 'I'll need to do a home visit of course, but I think we can safely say these two were a match made in heaven. The adoption forms are in the house. I'll go and find one.'

Scarlett jumped off Red and smothered him with kisses. 'I'm in love,' she declared, and then clutched Poppy's arm. 'Do you think I did OK?'

'More than OK. Jodie said you two were a match made in heaven. She's just gone to get the paperwork.'

Scarlett flung her arms around the chestnut gelding's neck. Red seemed to be enjoying the attention. Poppy loosened his girth and ran up his stirrup leathers.

Bill checked his watch. 'We'd better make a move. Baxters' are delivering the pig feed in half an hour.'

'Do you think we should turn Red out?' Scarlett asked.

'I don't know. I'll go and find Jodie.' Poppy ran past the stables to the house. As she drew near to the open back door the sound of raised voices and the angry clatter of saucepans stopped her in her tracks.

A woman's voice, high-pitched, verging on hysterical, rang out. 'I don't care what your father says. I don't want you to do it!'

'But it's not about what you or I want, is it? It never has been,' Jodie hissed back.

'We'll manage somehow. I'll ask for some more shifts at the pub.'

'A few extra hours' pulling pints won't feed this lot, Mum. You know that. I can make more in one night than you earn in a year.'

'I'll sell my wedding ring. That'll give us a bit of breathing space while we work something out.'

'Don't be ridiculous. It's the only piece of jewellery you have left.'

'Do you think I care more about a band of gold than I care about you?' The woman's voice softened, and Poppy had to strain to hear her. 'I worry, Jodie love. What happens if you get caught?'

Jodie laughed mirthlessly. 'We'll end up with two black sheep in the family, won't we? But don't worry, it'll be fine. I've gone over it a million times. Nothing can go wrong.'

Poppy darted back into the stable yard. She was scratching Biscuit's ear in what she hoped was a nonchalant manner when Jodie stalked out of the house, the adoption papers in one hand and a biro in the other.

'I see you've found a friend,' Jodie remarked, pausing to stroke the appaloosa's speckled forehead.

Poppy reddened, even though there was no way Jodie could have known she'd eavesdropped. 'We weren't sure what you wanted us to do with Red,' she mumbled.

'We'll put him back in the field.'

Poppy stole a look at the older girl as they walked across to Scarlett and Bill. There was a fierce expression on her face and a resolute set to her shoulders. Jodie caught her staring and raised her eyebrows.

'Anything wrong?' she asked.

I should be the one asking that, Poppy thought. Why was Jodie's mum so worried? What was it she didn't want Jodie to do? Instead she shook her head and smiled brightly.

'No. Everything is absolutely fine.'

7

T he hands of Poppy's battered Mickey Mouse alarm clock had
barely crawled around to seven o'clock the next morning when
Charlie bounded into her bedroom.

'Don't forget our picnic! I've already planned our route and made
some sandwiches. I just need to do drinks and some cake. It's going to be
epic.' Charlie bounced back out of the room. Poppy groaned. She'd
planned to spend the day helping Scarlett clear out the old stable Bill had
earmarked for Red. She'd forgotten she'd promised her brother that they'd
spend the day on the moor. She couldn't pull out. She'd never hear the
end of it. Sighing, she threw back the duvet, waking Magpie, the McKeevers' cat, who had been snoring softly at the end of her bed. He narrowed
his emerald green eyes at her before tucking his head between his paws
and going back to sleep. Poppy reached for her mobile and texted Scarlett
to say she would try and pop round before dinner.

Downstairs, Charlie was carefully cutting squares of lemon drizzle
cake and wrapping them in cling film.

'I've cut up some carrots for Cloud. I even peeled them for him,' he
said. Caroline had only recently let Charlie start using the sharp kitchen
knives. Personally Poppy thought it was asking for trouble and quite
expected to find pieces of chopped finger in her food, but by some small
miracle he had so far managed to keep all his digits intact.

'Where d'you want to go?' she asked.

'I thought we'd try somewhere new.'

Poppy was surprised. Usually they picnicked in the Riverdale wood, on the small sandy strip of beach where they'd first seen Cloud. And then the penny dropped.

'Are we going to the old cottage by any chance?'

'What old cottage?' said Caroline, walking into the kitchen with a basket of dirty laundry balanced on her hip.

Charlie held his finger to his lips and Poppy nodded. She was as keen to go back to the old croft as her brother but knew that Caroline would worry if she knew. Deep water and derelict buildings seemed to freak adults out.

'Charlie wants to head down the bridleway that goes past the thatched cottage by the church,' Poppy said, crossing her fingers behind her back.

'Sounds lovely. I wish I could come too, but I must do some gardening. Make sure you've got your phone with you, and be back by four at the latest. Otherwise I'll send out a search party.'

'And we don't want that happening again, do we?' said Poppy, remembering the day she and Charlie had had to be rescued from the moor the first summer they'd moved to Riverdale.

'We certainly don't!' Caroline said, giving her a hug.

∽

POPPY SPLIT their picnic into the two small saddle bags resting on Cloud's dappled grey flanks and tightened his girth. Smelling the carrots, the Connemara nibbled the hem of her checked shirt. She blew into his nose and he blew softly back.

'Ready?' she called to Charlie, who was wheeling his bike out of the barn. He was wearing a cycling helmet, a pair of their dad's old aviator sunglasses and his school rucksack.

'You bet!'

Poppy jumped into the saddle. 'Come on then, let's have ourselves an adventure!'

The August sun was high in the sky as they let themselves out of the gate that led to the moor. Puffs of candyfloss cloud wafted by and in the distance three crows shamelessly mobbed a buzzard. Soon they had left

Waterby behind and were climbing steadily towards Princetown. The wind ruffled Cloud's mane as he tossed his head and snatched at the bit.

'OK for a canter?' she asked. Charlie nodded. He crouched low over the handlebars and started pedalling furiously, his elbows jutting out like chicken wings. Poppy kicked Cloud on, keeping pace with her brother until she could see he was beginning to tire.

Before long the dark green belt of conifers appeared on the horizon.

'Those trees are the perfect camouflage, hiding Witch Cottage from prying eyes and nosy parkers,' Charlie said.

'I'd never have found it if it wasn't for Cloud,' Poppy agreed.

'Do you think he'd been there before?'

Poppy pictured Caitlyn's diary, hidden in the bottom of her sock drawer. 'Maybe,' she hedged, as they wound their way through the evergreens.

Charlie flung his bike and rucksack on the grass and raced over to the tumbledown building. Poppy watched him pull open the front door and disappear inside. Seconds later a startled pigeon flew out of the hole in the roof in a blur of feathers and affront. Poppy jumped off Cloud and led him over to the banks of the tarn. She stared at their reflections as he drank, remembering Scarlett's ghost stories about the old woman and her son and the superstition that claimed anyone gazing into the still waters on Midsummer's Eve would see a reflection of the next person in the parish to die.

'Utter rubbish,' Poppy told her undulating reflection. A second face appeared at her side and she shrieked.

'Charlie! Don't creep up on me like that! You nearly gave me a heart attack!'

'Thought you didn't believe in ghosts,' he grinned.

'I don't, you twit. You made me jump, that's all.'

'If you say so,' Charlie said, undoing the saddle bags. Poppy ran up her stirrups and loosened Cloud's girth. Looping his reins over the crook of her arm she sat cross-legged at the water's edge and caught the crumpled bag of crisps Charlie lobbed her way.

'Chocolate spread and cheese?' he asked, holding out a squashed-looking sandwich.

'Don't you mean chocolate spread or cheese?'

Charlie shook his head. 'Nope. Chocolate spread and cheese. I was going to make jam and ham, it had a nice ring to it, but I thought it might be a bit *out there* for you.' He gave her a faintly patronising look, as if she was an aged auntie.

'So you thought you'd go for the more traditional chocolate spread and cheese option,' Poppy grimaced, taking the sandwich, which was wrapped in enough cling film to keep the entire contents of their fridge fresh.

'You can be very narrow-minded sometimes, Poppy. You really need to broaden your horizons.'

She gave him a withering smile. 'Thanks for the advice, little brother.' Peeling back the sandwich, she sniffed it cautiously. 'Gross,' she grumbled, nibbling a corner. It was surprisingly tasty. Who knew?

'It's not as bad as it sounds,' she conceded, taking a huge bite.

Charlie smirked. 'Told you so.'

~

AFTER THEIR PICNIC Poppy followed Charlie into the cottage. She left him poking around in the kitchen and headed up the rickety staircase. She was keen to see if Caitlyn had left anything else under the floorboards. Ducking her head, she entered the larger of the two bedrooms. She paused. Was it her imagination or did the room feel different somehow? She narrowed her eyes and tried to remember how it had looked on their last visit. The old hessian sack was still in the corner next to the broken floorboard Charlie had put his foot through. He had piled the two wooden crates on top of each other in front of the window. Poppy checked to see if the baby swallows were still in their nest in the eaves and smiled as she counted four orange beaks.

'Should have saved you some of Charlie's sandwiches,' she told them.

She kneeled on the floor, carefully prised open the broken floorboard and peered inside. A black beetle scuttled away, its antennae waving furiously. As it disappeared under a joist Poppy noticed a glint of metal. She reached in and pulled out a silver trophy. The silver had tarnished in places, but it was easy enough to read the inscription. *South Devon Open Showjumping Competition. 1st place: Jodie Morgan and Nethercote Nero.*

~

CHARLIE WAS OUTSIDE with Cloud by the time Poppy had hidden the trophy under the floorboards and gone back downstairs. She tightened Cloud's girth, ran down his stirrups and swung into the saddle. She stared at the grimy bedroom window. Something about the room was niggling her.

'Why did you move the crates?' she asked Charlie finally.

He looked at her in confusion. 'I didn't. I thought you must have.'

'How could I? I went up after you.' Poppy gave an involuntary shiver. 'If I didn't move them, and you didn't move them, who did?'

8

_____

P oppy and Charlie had emerged from the dark canopy of conifers when Charlie stopped pedalling and pointed straight ahead.
'Someone's coming.'

Poppy halted Cloud and squinted into the sun. She could just about make out a chestnut-coloured blob in the distance. 'It's only a Dartmoor pony.'

'You need to get your eyes tested.' Charlie reached in his pocket for his small birdwatching binoculars. 'It's someone riding. Look.'

He handed the binoculars to Poppy. Charlie was right. A horse and rider were cantering towards them. The horse had four white socks and a flaxen mane and tail.

'It's Red!' Poppy exclaimed.

'I thought you horsey people called it chestnut, like white is always grey?' said Charlie.

'No, you twit. It's Red. Scarlett's new horse. But what's he doing here?' She trained the binoculars on the slim girl riding the chestnut gelding. She would have recognised the determined set of her shoulders a mile off. 'And Jodie,' she said, handing the binoculars back to Charlie.

'Let's go and say hello.'

'OK. But don't mention we've been to Witch Cottage,' Poppy told him.

'Er, why would I? It's our secret place.'

Red's flanks were dark with sweat as Jodie pulled him up a few metres from them.

'What are you two doing here?' she said warily.

'Just out for a hack,' said Poppy. 'We took a picnic,' she said, pointing to the saddlebags.

Jodie's face cleared. 'It's a lovely day for it. I decided to make time for one last ride before Red goes to Scarlett's in the morning.'

'She's beyond excited. She's spent hours getting everything ready for him. He's going to be treated like royalty,' Poppy told her.

Jodie ran her hand down the gelding's neck. 'King Red. It suits him.'

'Are you heading back? We could ride with you some of the way.'

Red stretched his neck towards Cloud and gave a low whinny. The Connemara pricked his ears and whickered back. Jodie glanced briefly towards the belt of conifers and checked her watch.

'Sure. Why not? I've got to get back for evening stables anyway. It'll give the boys a chance to get to know each other.'

Poppy smiled as Cloud and Red's noses touched. 'I think they're going to get along just fine.'

~

THAT EVENING, after checking her dad, Caroline and Charlie were safely downstairs engrossed in an episode of Dr Who, Poppy closed her bedroom door, reached in her sock drawer and pulled out Caitlyn's diary. She sat on her wicker chair with a cushion on her lap and turned to the last entry.

I am sitting on the banks of the tarn as I write this, dangling my feet in the icy water. Cloud keeps trying to nibble my pen. Nero is dozing next to him and Jodie is watching the swallows feeding their babies in the nest in the eaves.

So now I've set the scene.

I feel both happy and sad. Is that even possible? Happy because Jodie and I have had a brilliant summer, riding, competing and just hanging out here at 'our' cottage together with the ponies away from the Annoying Parents. Sad because it's the last day of the summer holidays and this time on Monday I won't be daydreaming here by the tarn, I'll be sitting in a stuffy classroom bored out of my mind. Riding will have to fit in around school and homework and when I can persuade Mum to give me a lift up to Gran's. It sucks. The only thing I've got to look forward to is the hunter trial at Widecombe. Jodie's not doing it - it's showjumping or nothing for her - but she's promised to come and be my groom for the day.

Back to today. Jodie and I wanted to mark the cottage as our territory. Tigers wee or scratch the bark of trees. Not us! We decided to each leave something of ours here, to lay claim to it. So I'm going to leave my diary and Jodie's going to leave the trophy she won at the South Devon show. We've found a loose floorboard in the big bedroom and we're going to hide them under it. I wonder if anyone will ever find them??

So I'm signing off now. I was getting too old for diaries anyway. If I need to offload I tell Cloud. He's the official Keeper of my Secrets. LOVE that pony!!

It's so long from me. See ya on the other side! :)

Poppy stared at the smiley face until her vision blurred with tears. Caitlyn had been so excited about the hunter trial at Widecombe. She'd had no idea that catastrophic disaster lay around the corner. All it took was a slippery drop fence and a moment's loss of concentration and her fate was sealed. What if Cloud hadn't been spooked by the crowds? What if she hadn't decided to compete? What if it hadn't rained?

Poppy knew that worrying about the what ifs got you precisely nowhere, but even so. Caitlyn would be the same age as Jodie now, and Cloud would still be hers, not Poppy's. She hid the diary back in her sock drawer and peered out of the window. Cloud and Chester were standing nose to tail by the gate, their tails swishing lazily. As if he had a sixth sense, Cloud lifted his head, saw her watching and whickered. Poppy brushed the tears from her cheeks. Did it matter that he'd been Caitlyn's first? For the first time in her life she realised she hadn't felt the usual dart of jealousy at the thought of Caitlyn and Cloud together. All she felt was intense sadness that Cait's future had been wrenched from her so cruelly.

Had Jodie acted as Caitlyn's groom that fateful day? Poppy pictured the brusque blonde girl standing with Tory and Cait's mum Jo on the sidelines, her hands full of grooming kit and bandages as she cheered horse and rider on as they'd galloped up to the drop fence, her eyes widening in horror as Cloud twisted in mid-air, lost his footing and somersaulted over, throwing Cait underneath him.

Poppy tried to imagine how she would feel if it was Scarlett tumbling to the muddy ground in a tangle of flailing limbs. It didn't bear thinking about. The image was so vivid she could almost hear the gasps of shock and the wail of sirens. She shivered. Poor Jodie. And poor Caitlyn.

Thoughts of the accident consumed Poppy's thoughts for the rest of the evening. It wasn't until she was lying in bed, staring at the ceiling, that she remembered the wooden crates. Caitlyn and Jodie may have marked the cottage as their territory. But someone else had now muscled in.

9

'So, what d'you think?' Scarlett asked, chewing her bottom lip. 'Is it good enough?'

Poppy surveyed the stable next to Blaze's. Up until a couple of days ago it had been used to store farm machinery and spare feed troughs. Every inch had been scrubbed and swept. Scarlett had laid a thick bed of straw and filled the hay rack with new hay. Two water-filled buckets stood in old rubber tyres. There was even a mineral lick attached to the ring by the door. Scarlett was hopping from one foot to the other. Poppy had never seen her look so nervous.

'It looks awesome!' she said. 'You've done a brilliant job. Jodie's going to be super impressed and Red's going to love it.'

'Are you sure?'

"Course I'm sure. What time are they due?'

'Ten o'clock. What time is it now?'

Poppy checked her watch. 'Quarter to.'

Scarlett groaned. 'Fifteen whole minutes! That's *ages*.'

'Come on, let's groom Blaze and Flynn. It'll pass the time.'

At ten past ten they heard the rattle of Jodie's Land Rover and trailer as it negotiated the potholed farm drive. Scarlett dropped the body brush and curry comb she'd been holding and clutched Blaze's neck in excitement.

'Oh my God, they're here! I must go and tell Mum.'

Poppy smiled indulgently as her best friend sprinted towards the back door. Jodie parked the Land Rover and jumped out.

'All ready for King Red?' she asked.

Poppy grinned, curtseyed and gestured to the immaculate stable. 'His palace awaits, ma'am. I'm surprised Scarlett didn't manage to find a roll of red carpet for his majesty.'

Jodie glanced inside and raised her eyebrows. 'I see what you mean. I think we can safely say Scarlett's passed the home visit. It puts Nethercote to shame. Red won't know he's born.'

Scarlett appeared, followed closely by Pat, who was carrying a tray laden with mugs of tea and a chocolate cake.

'Hello Jodie love. I thought I'd bake a cake to celebrate Red's arrival,' Pat said, setting the tray on the bonnet of the Land Rover. Jodie pulled down the ramp of the trailer, unloaded Red and handed Scarlett his lead rope.

The chestnut gelding's head was high and his nostrils flared as he took in his new surroundings.

'Red, I'd like to introduce you to Flynn,' said Scarlett. Flynn turned his head briefly and returned to his haynet, unimpressed by the new arrival. 'And this is Blaze.' Blaze and Red blew into each other's nostrils, their ears pricked. Blaze squealed loudly, throwing one hoof in the air. 'Be nice!' Scarlett scolded her.

'It's probably a good idea not to turn them out together for a couple of days. Let them get used to each other,' said Jodie.

She and Scarlett settled Red into his pristine stable while Pat cut generous slices of cake.

Jodie poked her head over the stable door. 'Poppy, can you get the adoption certificate? It's on the passenger seat.'

Poppy heaved open the heavy door of the Land Rover. The seat was covered in sweet wrappers, loops of baler twine, empty wormer packets and unopened envelopes that looked suspiciously like bills. She rummaged through the detritus, finding what she was looking for at the bottom. As she tugged on the sheet of white card bearing the Nethercote logo and the words *Certificate of Adoption* she dislodged Jodie's iPhone and it slid into a gap between the seat and the gearstick.

Sighing, Poppy stretched her arm into the gap and grabbed the phone. It beeped. She dropped it in surprise and it slithered right under the seat.

'Damn,' she muttered, tucking her hair behind her ears and feeling for the phone again. This time she pulled it out and without thinking scanned the text on the home screen.

Delivery tonight. Leave cash as agreed. Used notes or deal's off. You have been warned.

A voice behind Poppy made her start.

'Did you find it?'

Poppy shoved the phone back under the envelopes and sweet wrappers and smiled brightly at Jodie.

'Here it is!'

'Great. Let's celebrate with a slice of cake and then I must be off. There's somewhere I need to be.'

~

CHARLIE WAS SMACKING a golf ball around the garden with one of their dad's old five irons when Poppy arrived home.

'Guess what?' he said, his tongue between his teeth as he flexed his knees and lined up for a shot.

'Tiger Woods has asked you to take his place in next year's Open Championship?'

'Ha ha, very funny.' Charlie lifted the club and swung at the ball. Shielding his eyes, he scanned the sky. 'Where did it go?' he asked, puzzled.

'It's still there.' Poppy pointed at his feet.

He stared at the pitted white ball nestling in the grass. 'Oh.' He took another swipe. They both watched as the ball sailed in a graceful arc, smashing the glass on one of Caroline's cold frames. Charlie's face paled.

'You are going to be in *so* much trouble,' Poppy told him.

He thought for a moment, worry lines creasing his forehead. Then his face cleared. 'I know! I'll mend it with Dad's Super Glue.'

'I'm not sure that's going to work. Anyway, what were you going to tell me?'

Charlie pointed the club at the sky.

Poppy sighed. 'What exactly am I supposed to be looking at?'

'The moon,' said Charlie. 'The *full* moon,' he added dramatically.

Poppy looked again. There, peeping behind a cloud almost apologetically, as if it had turned up to a party uninvited, was the muted, perfectly spherical face of the moon.

'And?' said Poppy, bemused.

Charlie looked left and right to check no-one was in earshot, then whispered furtively, 'We can go to Witch Cottage and see if the legend is true.'

'What, Scarlett's supernatural claptrap about the old crone and Marmalade and the burning cloak?' Poppy scoffed. 'Of course it's not true!'

'It's Marmaduke actually, and how can you be so sure?'

'Because there are no such things as ghosts or witches, Charlie. It's an old wives' tale, I promise you.'

Charlie nodded to himself. 'I might have known.'

'Might have known what?' she said sharply.

'That you'd claim it was rubbish because really you were too frightened to go.'

Poppy bristled. 'I am not! Alright then, if it means that much to you we'll go. We'll wait until Dad and Caroline are asleep and ride Cloud over together. Happy now?'

Charlie whooped and sprinted towards the house, the golf club and shattered cold frame forgotten. As she watched him go, Poppy had the distinct impression she had been played like the proverbial fiddle by a master manipulator.

10

The sky was a deep indigo as Poppy and Charlie crept out of the house and headed for the stables. After waiting so patiently the moon had taken centre stage and was glowing with pearlescent luminosity, encircled by a smattering of glittering stars.

Cloud was dozing at the back of the stable he shared with Chester, but lifted his head and whickered when he heard the bolt slide open. Poppy offered them a handful of pony nuts, slipped on Cloud's bridle and led him into the yard. Charlie handed Poppy her riding hat and fastened up the straps of his cycling helmet.

'You'll be fine as long as you hold on tight,' she whispered, leading Cloud over to the low stone wall she used as a mounting block. 'I'll get on first.'

Once she was satisfied Charlie was safely on and his arms were wrapped around her waist, she clicked her tongue and turned Cloud towards the moor.

The Connemara was as excited as Charlie about their night-time adventure and jogged up the track towards the Riverdale tor. Poppy could feel her brother's warm breath on the back of her neck as she eased her pony back into a walk.

'You OK?' she asked.

'You bet!' he cried. 'This is awesome!'

Charlie had brought his digital camera, convinced he was going to snap a shot of the old witch as she glided around the banks of the tarn. Poppy had slipped her mobile in her back pocket, just in case. Adventures with her brother often ended up with a trip to accident and emergency. She wanted to be prepared.

Cloud's mane was burnished silver in the moonlight and his neck was arched. All he needed were wings and he could be Pegasus.

'Do you think you'll be alright to go a bit faster, if we take it steady?' Poppy called.

'Uh huh,' Charlie said, tightening his grip.

Poppy squeezed her legs and Cloud broke into a canter. He was as surefooted as the black-faced sheep that every so often loomed out of the darkness, the glow of their eyes just visible in the inky light. It was exhilarating, racing across the wide, open moor in the dead of night, and a smile crept across Poppy's face. Charlie clung on like a limpet.

'I thought riding was for girls and sissies but this is brilliant! When we get home can you teach me?'

"Course I can. We'll ask Scarlett to lend us Flynn.'

Ahead Poppy could just make out the shadowy strip of conifers that hid Witch Cottage from view. 'Nearly there,' she whispered.

Cloud slowed to a walk. The squelch of his hooves as he crossed the peaty ground sounded unnaturally loud in the still night air. He plunged into the darkness of the trees without hesitation. The conifers towered over them, their branches like twisted limbs, and Poppy felt her pulse quicken. She checked the luminous hands of her watch. Five to midnight. Ghosts or no ghosts, this was seriously spooky.

Cloud shifted and swerved through the trees. Eventually they reached the edge of the narrow forest. Poppy asked the Connemara to halt and he stood quietly as she peered into the gloom. The silhouette of Witch Cottage was as elusive and unformed as the first strokes of a watercolour painting.

'Now what?' she whispered.

'We should stay hidden in the trees, just in case,' said Charlie, slithering to the ground.

'In case of what?' Poppy jumped off, too, and held Cloud's reins tightly.

'Old crones and ginger cats, of course.' Charlie's grinning teeth gleamed in the moonlight.

They stood in silence either side of Cloud. Charlie fiddled with his camera. Poppy scuffed the ground with the toe of her jodhpur boot. She felt as conspicuous as an angel perched atop a Christmas tree, and not a little foolish. She stifled a yawn. Why on earth had she agreed to let Charlie drag her into the middle of nowhere in the middle of the night on such a crazy adventure?

After ten minutes in the dank shadows Poppy was starting to feel the cold. She turned to her brother. 'Come on, Charlie. Let's go home. There's patently no-one here. Not even a ghost is silly enough to be out at this time of night.'

'Five more minutes?' he pleaded.

Poppy hugged herself and exhaled loudly. 'Alright then. But I am never, ever coming on one of your stupid adventures again. Got it?'

'Thanks, sis.' Charlie ducked under Cloud's neck. Soon he was twiddling with his camera again, pointing it at the cottage and zooming the lens in and out.

Poppy was stifling another yawn when he clutched her arm and whispered urgently, 'There's a light in the cottage.'

'Absolutely Hilarious with a capital H,' Poppy whispered back, rolling her eyes.

'No, really Poppy, there is. Look!'

The tremor in his voice made Poppy grab the camera. She pointed it at the cottage. At first she thought the glow in the upstairs bedroom was moonlight reflecting off the window.

'Is it the old crone's burning cloak?' stammered Charlie. 'I knew Scarlett was telling the truth.'

Poppy shook her head. The beam of light was moving, as if a powerful torch was being waved around. Cloud had stiffened, his head high as he stared intently ahead. Charlie gripped her arm even tighter.

'Look at that!'

Poppy followed his gaze and gasped. A pick-up truck was rolling silently down the hill towards the cottage. They watched, transfixed, as two burly-looking men let themselves out, pulled an old tarpaulin off the back of the beaten-up truck and started unloading wooden crates.

'What are they *doing*?' breathed Charlie.

Poppy held her finger to her lips. The men were talking to each other in low voices, pointing to the light in the window. One took a mobile out of his pocket and started tapping furiously. The other picked up a crate, ducked under the low door frame and disappeared into the cottage.

Cloud shifted uneasily. Poppy rubbed his forehead and willed him to stay quiet. The man with the phone hefted a crate onto his hip. Once he was inside the cottage Poppy turned to her brother. 'I don't like this. We should go.'

'But -'

'No buts, Charlie. I don't know what those men are up to, but I don't think we should hang around to find out. They don't look the type to be messed with.'

Not giving him the chance to argue, she led Cloud over to a fallen tree and vaulted on, holding her hand out for Charlie to follow suit. He clambered on, looking wistfully over his shoulder as she turned Cloud for home.

Once clear of the conifers Poppy pushed Cloud into a canter, keen to put as much distance as she could between them and the two shadowy men.

11

'You look washed out. Are you feeling OK?' Caroline looked at Poppy in concern as she nibbled on a piece of toast the next morning.

'I'm fine.' Poppy smiled briefly at her stepmother and took a slurp of orange juice. The truth was she was shattered. After they'd slunk back into the house she'd been so wired sleep had been impossible. She'd lain in bed, her imagination working overtime as she'd wondered about the men at Witch Cottage and, more importantly, the crates they'd been carrying.

A text from Scarlett was a welcome distraction.

Are we riding this morning or what??!! I have a new pony to try out you know!!

Poppy took a final swig of juice and tapped a message back.

'Course we're riding :) I'll be over in 20 mins x

◌

RED'S CHESTNUT coat shone and his four socks were dazzlingly white. Scarlett had even pulled his mane and oiled his hooves.

'Blimey, you must have been up at the crack of dawn,' said Poppy.

Cloud, who had grass stains on his hocks and a tangled mane and tail, looked positively scruffy in comparison.

'I woke up at four I was so excited,' Scarlett said. 'I've been getting him ready since six. He's even had a bath. With warm water, of course.'

'Of course,' said Poppy. Scarlett used the hose on Blaze and Flynn.

'Where shall we go?' said Scarlett.

'I want to head over towards Witch Cottage.'

'Not *again*. You and Charlie are obsessed with that place.'

'Ah, but wait until you hear this.' Poppy told her best friend about their nocturnal visit and the men they'd seen. Scarlett's jaw hit the floor.

'I can't believe I missed it. I wish you'd told me you were going.'

'You won't even go near the place in the middle of the day. Would you have really wanted to come on Charlie's ghost hunt at midnight?'

'Probably not,' Scarlett admitted. 'Do you think you should call the police?'

'What would I tell them? It was too dark to get proper descriptions or see their number plate. I don't even know if they were doing anything illegal. That's why I want to see what's in those crates they delivered.'

～

'I'D FORGOTTEN how close it is to the prison,' said Poppy, gazing at the granite walls of HMP Dartmoor, the two ponies walking side-by-side.

'We went to the museum there last summer,' said Scarlett.

Poppy raised her eyebrows. 'There's a museum at the prison?'

Scarlett nodded. 'You should go. Charlie would love it. They've got all the weapons the warders used to use on the prisoners, like straitjackets, manacles and cat o'nine tails, and the knuckledusters and other weapons the convicts made. It's really interesting.'

Poppy pictured the two thickset men she and Charlie had seen the night before and her heart missed a beat. 'Do prisoners still escape?'

'They used to, in the olden days,' said Scarlett. 'It's only a Category C prison now. The prisoners are low risk. They make gnomes and toad-stools to sell as garden ornaments, can you believe? Mum bought one for her rose garden.'

Poppy couldn't imagine the two men they'd seen the night before painting red hats and impish grins onto stone gnomes. The fact that

Witch Cottage was so close to the prison was a coincidence, she told herself.

Scarlett elected to hold the ponies while Poppy scooted across to the dilapidated stone building. The minute she walked through the door it felt different. The air, which had smelt so fusty the first time she'd explored the cottage, was alive with static. She ran lightly up the stairs to the first bedroom, expecting to find it piled high with crates. But the room was empty apart from the two wooden boxes still stacked by the window. Were they the same as the ones the men had unloaded from the pick-up? Poppy inspected the room, her eyes narrowed, searching for any clue. There were marks on the floor. Had they been there before? And had the doorframe always been cracked? She couldn't remember.

Frustrated, she walked around the room a second time, examining every inch. Her attention was caught by the hum of a mosquito. She watched it as it spiralled up towards the ceiling and landed on the loft hatch.

'Poppy!' Everything OK?'

Poppy yanked open the ancient window and stuck her head out. Scarlett was sitting on the old stone wall with Cloud and Red grazing next to her.

'Just coming,' Poppy shouted back.

Halfway down the stairs she stopped, shook her head at her own foolishness, and sprinted back up. The ceiling was so low in the tiny bedroom that she could almost touch it if she stood on her toes. She pulled one of the boxes into the centre of the room, climbed onto it and gave the loft hatch a tentative shove. It lifted easily. Poppy poked her head into the roof space. Expecting darkness she was surprised to see a patch of blue sky in the corner, then remembered the hole in the catslide roof.

She jumped off the box, carried the second one over and stacked them on top of each other. Now the ceiling was level with her shoulders and Poppy was sure she would be able to climb in. Testing her weight on the frame of the hatch, she looked around, taking in the shafts of sunlight, the swirling particles of decades-old dust, long-abandoned swallows' nests and the smell of dead mouse.

In the middle of the attic was the brick chimney breast. Behind it flapped the corner of a green tarpaulin. Her heart hammering, Poppy hauled herself through the hatch. A rusty nail caught her shin and she yelped in pain. The roof of the attic was so low she had to bend double. She crabbed sideways along one of the worm-ridden beams and peered around the chimney breast.

Hidden under the green tarpaulin were around a dozen wooden crates. Poppy pulled the closest one towards her and prised open the lid.

~

'MOBILE PHONES?' said Scarlett, her face perplexed.

Poppy nodded. 'Dozens of smartphones of all different makes. They were still in their boxes with the Cellophane on and everything.'

'And nothing else?'

'Nope.'

Scarlett looked around her fearfully, as if she was being watched. 'I knew this place was cursed. It was a mistake to come back.' She swung into the saddle and turned Red for home.

The chestnut gelding disappeared into the trees and Poppy had to trot to catch up. 'What are they doing there, that's what I want to know.'

'I don't know and I don't care. We should let the police deal with it, Poppy. Go and see that inspector you saw before.'

Poppy thought of the wide-girthed Inspector Bill Pearson and his penchant for digestive biscuits. Perhaps she should phone the police but a niggling voice in the back of her head told her she'd be wasting their time. 'Maybe.'

Seeing the worry on Scarlett's face she changed the subject. 'How's Red? Are you pleased with your new pony?'

'Pleased?' Scarlett reached down and patted the chestnut gelding's neck. 'I am beyond happy. He is the most gorgeous, lovely, brilliant horse in the world.'

'Apart from Cloud,' Poppy corrected her.

Scarlett laughed, the mobile phones pushed to the back of her mind, and she spent the rest of the ride home extolling Red's countless virtues. Poppy smiled and agreed in all the right places, but her thoughts were in a tiny attic under a catslide roof, where dust motes danced and faceless men stashed their ill-gotten gains under slippery green tarpaulins.

12

At breakfast the following morning Caroline announced a shopping trip to Plymouth. Poppy's shoulders slumped.

'Torture,' muttered Charlie into his Shreddies.

'You've grown so much this summer your trousers could pass as shorts. We'll have to either stop feeding you or start balancing books on your head,' Caroline told him. 'Poppy, you need a new blazer and school skirt. And you both need new school shoes. It's not long until the start of term.'

'Don't remind us,' grumbled Poppy. Although she couldn't say she actually hated school, she had so many more interesting things she could be doing than learning about poems and probability. And the prospect of standing in a manically busy shoe shop holding a ticket in her hand waiting to have her feet measured on a sweaty measuring machine while dozens of out-of-control toddlers weaved around her legs did not appeal.

'We'll pop into Baxters' on the way home if you like?'

Slightly mollified, Poppy nodded. She never passed up an opportunity to spend half an hour looking around the leather-scented tack and feed store on the Tavistock road.

Their shopping expedition was as torturous as Charlie had predicted, the only highlight being a bowl of pasta in a little Italian restaurant on the Barbican. Poppy drooled over the black leather jumping saddles and matching bridles in Baxters' and treated Cloud and Chester to a new lead rope each. On their way home Caroline remembered they needed eggs and pulled in outside Waterby Post Office and Stores.

'Hey, isn't that Scarlett?' Charlie said.

Through the glass window, which was pebble-dashed with posters advertising choral events, coffee mornings and rams for sale, Poppy saw her best friend ringing up someone's shopping on the till, watched by the twinkly-eyed shopkeeper Barney Broomfield.

'I'd forgotten it was her first shift at the shop this afternoon.'

Poppy waited until Scarlett had rung up an elderly lady's copy of the Radio Times and a tin of pitted prunes and asked, 'How's it going?'

'OK, I think,' said Scarlett, looking slightly flustered. 'Barney says it'll be brilliant for my mental arithmetic but I'm not so sure.' She sniffed her fingers and pulled a face. 'And my hands smell of money.'

Charlie jiggled coins in his shorts pocket. 'Can I have forty five pence worth of rhubarb and custards, please Scarlett.'

'Sure.' As Scarlett lifted the jar of sweets from a shelf she mouthed to Poppy, 'Look at the front page of the Herald!'

There was a pile of Tavistock Heralds by the front door. Poppy sidled over. The headline was like a punch in the solar plexus.

Exclusive: Police launch investigation after daring theft of mobile phones
By Stanley Smith

Blood pounding in her ears, Poppy picked up the top copy and scanned the article.

Police have launched an investigation after mobile phones worth £20,000 were stolen during a daring raid on a Plymouth warehouse.

The thieves disabled CCTV cameras and locked the security guard in his office before helping themselves to dozens of top-of-the-range Apple, Samsung and Sony smartphones.

'The phones were taken overnight on 15 August, and we are appealing for anyone who has information about the burglary to contact us,' said a police spokesman.

'Do you want to know a secret?' whispered a voice in her ear. Poppy jumped like a scalded cat, but it was only Charlie, brandishing a small paper bag of rhubarb and custards. 'Scarlett gave me an extra one for luck! You can have it if you like.'

~

POPPY CHANGED into jodhpurs and a tee-shirt the minute they arrived home. Hoping a ride on the moor might clear her head, she caught Cloud, gave him a cursory groom and tacked him up. Soon they were cantering towards the Riverdale tor. At the top Poppy slid to the ground, sat cross-legged on a flat granite boulder and shared an apple with her pony as she gazed at the sweeping panorama. Directly ahead, sandwiched between their two paddocks, was the slate roof of Riverdale. Poppy could just make out a Chester-shaped brown blob by the water trough. The McKeevers' gravel drive ran parallel to the track to Ashworthy. Scarlett's home was an archetypical working farm. An old, slightly shabby farm-house surrounded by a jumble of barns, stables and outhouses. Scarlett loved houses with clean modern lines, all glass and steel, but Poppy adored Ashworthy's low ceilings and mullioned windows.

She couldn't see Witch Cottage from here. Even the chimneys of Dart-moor Prison were hidden behind a distant tor.

'What should I do, Cloud?'

The Connemara rubbed his head on her tee-shirt, leaving a layer of short, white hairs on the navy brushed cotton.

'Tell the police, tell Dad and Caroline, or try to find out who stole the mobiles myself?'

Telling the police or her parents was the obvious, sensible thing to do, Poppy knew that. But that would mean admitting she had lied *and* that she had dragged Charlie to a crime scene in the middle of the night. She had a feeling they wouldn't be impressed.

'I wonder what Caitlyn would have done if she were me,' she pondered. Cloud pricked his ears at the sound of Cait's name, as he always did. But Poppy no longer felt resentful. She wished Cait was still alive. She felt sure they'd have been friends if things had been different.

Cait wasn't around to ask, but Jodie was. Jodie knew Witch Cottage. She was both smart and tough. Poppy had a feeling Jodie wouldn't judge her for not phoning the police. She made up her mind.

Tomorrow she would cycle over to Nethercote.
Jodie would know what to do.

13

Nethercote's tall chimneys cast shadows at her feet as Poppy pushed her bike up the drive. It was late afternoon and the sun burned orange in the sky. She'd told Caroline she was cycling to Scarlett's, but instead she'd turned in the opposite direction and had followed the narrow lanes to the horse rescue sanctuary.

Poppy walked past the ivy-clad farmhouse to the stables. The yard was quiet save for the reassuringly familiar sound of horses chomping their suppers, and they lifted their heads to watch her from their stable doors as she passed.

There was no sign of Jodie.

Poppy rang the bell outside the feed room but it failed to summon the older girl. Poppy dithered, not wanting to knock on the door of the house. She sidled over to Biscuit's stable and stroked the appaloosa's spotted face.

'Where's Jodie?' she asked the rescue pony. 'I need to talk to her.'

'I'm here.'

Poppy spun around. Jodie was behind her, a water bucket in each hand.

'What did you want to talk to me about?'

Poppy didn't know where to start. 'It's a long story. Is there somewhere we can sit down?'

'Sure. Follow me.' Jodie set the buckets down, splashing water over her boots. She led Poppy through the feed room to a tack room beyond. One wall was lined with saddle racks. Bridles hung from hooks on another. The only light came from a tiny, grimy window on the back wall. The old stone walls had leached any warmth from the room. Poppy shivered.

Jodie flicked a switch. A strip light flickered and died. 'Bloody light. Yet another thing that needs fixing.' She waved Poppy to a shabby tub chair in front of an ancient electric fire. 'What's up? It's not Red, is it?'

'Red's fine. He seems to have settled in and Scarlett's still treating him like royalty. We hacked out yesterday and he was as good as gold. Nothing to worry about there.' Poppy realised she was gabbling.

Jodie raised her eyebrows. 'So what's the problem?'

'You and Caitlyn were best friends, weren't you?'

Jodie fiddled with a loose strand of cotton on the arm of her chair. Her fingers were trembling. 'Did Tory tell you?'

'I haven't seen Tory for ages. I found an old newspaper clipping. You competed in the South Devon Open Showjumping Competition together. You won it.'

'And Caitlyn was second. Boy was she sore about that.'

'Why didn't you say anything when you recognised Cloud at the fete?'

'Seeing him brought it all back. I've spent the last seven years trying to forget what happened,' said Jodie.

'I'm sorry.'

'Why should you be? It wasn't your fault. It wasn't anyone's fault. It was one of those things. He's a lovely pony. I'm glad he's found a good home.'

'Do you still have Nero?' Poppy asked.

Jodie's features darkened. 'He went when Dad went...*away*. If that's it I'd better get on. There are a hundred and one things I should be doing.'

'There was something else,' Poppy said. 'It's about Witch Cottage.'

Jodie was still for a second, then shrugged. 'Never heard of it.'

'The old cottage on the moor towards Princetown that's supposed to be haunted. Where the wild swimmer drowned.'

Jodie shook her head. 'Sorry, I don't know what you're talking about.'

'But you do!' Poppy cried. 'I know you and Cait used to hang out there. I found her diary and your trophy under the floorboards. Exactly where you'd left them.' Poppy took Jodie's silence as an invitation to continue.

'I've found something else in the cottage. Something that shouldn't be there. And I don't know what to do.'

'What have you found?' Jodie asked sharply.

The palms of Poppy's hands felt sticky. She wiped them on her jodhpurs. 'Mobile phones. Dozens of them. All brand new. They're hidden under a tarpaulin in the attic.'

'What's that got to do with me?'

'I don't know what to do about them,' said Poppy.

'Have you told anyone else?'

'Only Scarlett. She says I should call the police.'

Jodie wound the cotton around her index finger and gave it a sharp tug. The thread snapped. She met Poppy's eyes. 'And will you?'

'Will I what?'

'Call the police?'

'I don't know. That's why I wanted to talk to you.'

'I'm all ears,' said Jodie, flicking the cotton onto the floor.

'I think the phones are the ones that were stolen from the warehouse in Plymouth. There was a story about it in this week's Herald.'

Jodie stared at the tack room's pitted ceiling. 'So what if they were? I still don't get what this has got to do with me.'

'You know what I'm talking about,' said Poppy.

Jodie stiffened. 'What did you say?'

'I don't mean you know about the phones. You know about the cottage. I wanted to talk it through with someone who understood.'

Jodie exhaled slowly. 'I understand alright.'

'So you'll help?' Poppy felt giddy with relief.

Jodie jumped to her feet and grabbed the Land Rover keys from a hook by the door. Her mouth had tightened into a hard, thin line. 'I think you'd better show me.'

JODIE WAS silent as the Land Rover bumped along the stony track towards the cottage. Poppy stared out of the window. There were a hundred questions she wanted to ask. Top of the list was why Jodie was claiming to have never heard of the cottage when she and Cait had practically spent their last summer together there. But one glance at Jodie's granite-like profile was enough to make her bite her tongue.

They rounded a bend and the cottage came into view. From this distance you couldn't see the hole in the roof and the rotting windows. Poppy imagined smoke curling from the chimney and a white-haired man with stooped shoulders tending a vegetable patch, watched by an elderly border collie.

Jodie pulled in alongside the tarn, braking so sharply that Poppy's seatbelt bit into her shoulder. The older girl sat for a while, her hands clutching the steering wheel. Somewhere in the Land Rover a mobile phone pinged with a new text message, but Jodie continued staring blankly ahead. Poppy found her stillness unnerving. Surreptitiously she felt her back pocket for her own mobile. It wasn't there. She'd meant to pick it up from the worktop in the kitchen where she'd left it charging but had been in such a hurry to leave that she'd clean forgotten.

When Jodie turned to face Poppy, her face was expressionless. 'Let's go.'

'The mobiles are in the attic. I can show you, if you like. There are a couple of wooden boxes you can stand on so you're high enough to see. There's a hole in the roof but there's a tarpaulin over them to keep them dry. Whoever hid them here planned it properly,' Poppy said, climbing the stairs. She knew she was babbling again but she couldn't help herself.

'Oh, it was planned alright,' Jodie said, following Poppy into the biggest bedroom. She pointed to the two boxes. 'Sit down.'

'Don't you want me to show you where they are?'

Jodie shook her head. 'Sit down,' she repeated.

Poppy did as she was told. Jodie walked to the window. She glanced over her shoulder at Poppy. 'I already know where they are.'

'I don't understand.'

'I know where they are because I put them there.'

14

Poppy gaped at Jodie. Sunlight streamed through the window but the older girl's profile was in shadow.

'What do you mean, you put them there?'

'I told you my dad deals in mobile phones.'

Poppy cast her mind back to the day they'd first visited Nethercote and Jodie had mentioned her dad ran an import business. But this was all wrong. Questions bubbled up inside her.

'But why is he storing them in a tumbledown cottage in the middle of nowhere? Is it because they were stolen from the warehouse in Plymouth? Where exactly *is* your dad, Jodie?'

'He's precisely two and a half miles north of here, staying full board at Her Majesty's pleasure.'

'What do you mean?'

Jodie gave an impatient shake of her head, as if she couldn't believe Poppy's naivety.

'He's in the slammer. The clink. He's a guest of HMP Dartmoor. He's in *prison*, Poppy. My dad the convict is serving time.'

Poppy swallowed. 'What did he do?'

'He didn't kill anyone or anything like that. He fiddled the books at the building company he worked for.'

'Fiddled the books? What do you mean?'

'It's easy for finance directors to steal a little bit here and there without anyone noticing, apparently. Only he got greedy. And careless. The other directors were suspicious and called in the police. Dad was convicted five years ago.'

'When you were still at school?'

Jodie laughed hollowly. 'He was sent to prison a week before my GCSEs. I bombed the lot.'

'I'm sorry.'

'You keep apologising, don't you Poppy? Even when it's not your fault. You need to toughen up, kid. Else people will trample all over you.'

Poppy recoiled at the bitterness in Jodie's voice. 'I'm... I mean, why did he do it?'

'He set up the sanctuary with the money my grandparents left him when they died, figuring that he'd be able to raise enough money to pay for the running costs. Of course he couldn't. Any idiot could have told him that. But then Dad's a dreamer, always has been.'

'So he used the money he'd stolen to pay for the horses?' Poppy said.

Jodie nodded. 'He wanted me to follow my dream, too, so he bought Nero and a top-of-the range horsebox so we could compete all over the South West. Mum turned a blind eye to his thieving and I never knew until the morning the police turned up at the house and arrested him.'

'What happened to Nero?'

'The police took everything of value because they said it was proceeds of crime, including Nero. I'll never forgive Dad for that.'

'So you had to give it all up?'

'He left me with twenty four rescue horses to look after. I couldn't ride professionally any more.'

'But you've managed to keep Nethercote going while he's been in prison,' Poppy said.

'Only just. And now the money's all gone.' Jodie stared out of the window. The silence in the tiny attic bedroom was stifling. Suddenly everything fell into place. The mysterious text message on Jodie's phone. Her dad's import business. The hidden mobiles. The towering granite walls of Dartmoor prison just a couple of miles away.

'You're going to try to smuggle those phones into the prison,' Poppy whispered.

Jodie balled her hands into fists and Poppy felt her stomach clench. But the older girl didn't move.

'It was his idea. He can sell a mobile phone for a flippin' fortune inside.'

'But how are you planning to -'

'Get them in? The wing Dad's in is nearest the perimeter wall. Two cells have windows looking out onto the moor. One on the fourth floor and the other directly above it. Dad's cell.'

Jodie left the window and sat on the box next to Poppy.

'The prison's a listed building so his window hasn't got a grating over it. He's spent the last couple of days making a rope from bedding and is going to lower it out of the window and over the wall. I'll be at the bottom, waiting.' She smiled mirthlessly. 'I'll tie the bag of phones to his rope and he'll haul them up. We'll make enough money in one night to keep the horses fed for a year.'

'Did you steal the phones from the warehouse?' Poppy asked.

Jodie bristled. 'I am not a thief. Not like *him*. He organised it all. I just met the men when they delivered the phones and hid them in the attic.'

Without thinking Poppy said, 'We didn't see you.'

Jodie looked at her in astonishment. '*What?*'

Poppy glanced out of the window towards the conifers. 'Charlie and I were watching from the trees.'

'What the hell were you doing here?'

Poppy rubbed her hand across her forehead. It was all too much to take in. 'Charlie wanted to see if the place was really haunted. We rode over on Cloud,' she muttered.

'What if they'd seen you? Those men aren't the kind of people to mess with,' Jodie said roughly.

Poppy had been through a whole gamut of emotions in the last half an hour. Shock. Anxiety. Fear. Incredulity. Suddenly anger superseded it all. 'What if *we'd* been seen? What about you? If you get caught you'll go to jail! Who'll look after the rescue horses then?' she cried.

'Don't you understand? I have to do this. I have no choice.'

Poppy shook her head in disbelief. 'So why've you told me all this?'

Jodie stood up and stalked over to the window again. 'I couldn't tell you at home because if my mum even gets a whiff that someone is onto us she'll go straight to the prison governor and incriminate Dad. She's already terrified I'll get caught. I couldn't risk you going to the police and reporting the phones. I had to stop you.'

'Of course I've got to tell the police! Have you gone crazy?'

Jodie feigned surprise. 'Well, well. Mild-mannered, quiet little Poppy actually has a backbone. Who'd have thought it?'

It was Poppy's turn to bristle. 'I'm phoning them as soon as I get home.'

Jodie's lips thinned again. 'You can't. I'll be sent to jail and you're right, there is no-one else to look after the horses. They'll have to be put down and it'll be your fault. Percy, Mr Darcy. Even Biscuit. Can you live with that on your conscience?'

Jodie was bluffing, Poppy was sure of it. 'Nethercote isn't the only horse rescue centre in Devon. There are dozens of them! Someone else will take them in.'

'Are you willing to risk it? Anyway, you're implicated now. You lifted the tarpaulin to have a look at the phones, right?'

Poppy nodded, unsure where this was heading.

'Your prints will be all over it. All over the cottage, in fact. I'll tell the police I recruited you and your brother to act as scouts.'

Poppy felt the blood drain from her face. 'You wouldn't!'

'Needs must,' Jodie said grimly. 'It'll be your word against mine. And let me warn you, I'm a very good liar. I'll take you down with me, for the sake of the horses. For the sake of Nethercote.'

15

Poppy slumped onto the box again, her head in her hands. What if Jodie was telling the truth, that she really was prepared to incriminate her? She couldn't believe the police would actually think she'd been involved, but you read about miscarriages of justice in the papers all the time. And if they heard that the son and daughter of a BBC war correspondent had been questioned about a prison smuggling ring the tabloids would have a field day. Her dad would probably lose his job and they'd have to move. Suddenly she was struck by a thought so terrible it pierced her heart. Without Riverdale she'd have to sell Cloud and Chester. That's if she wasn't already doing time in a Young Offender's Institute.

'It's not nice, being forced into something you don't want to do because you have no choice, is it?' said Jodie. 'Now you know how I feel. I don't want to break the law, but Dad gave me no alternative.'

'When are you doing it?' Poppy asked dully.

'Tonight at eleven. The sooner the better as far as I'm concerned.'

'He'll make you do it again, you know that, don't you?'

For the first time Poppy saw a flicker of doubt cross Jodie's face. The older girl shook her head.

'I've told him it's a one-off.'

'And you believe him, do you?'

Jodie gave an imperceptible nod.

'He probably even believes it himself,' Poppy said. 'When he decided to steal money from his company he probably told himself it would be the first and last time. But people get greedy. You said it yourself.'

Jodie exhaled loudly and stalked out of the room. 'It's happening tonight. End of.'

~

THEY DROVE BACK to Nethercote in silence. As Jodie pulled into the drive Poppy made a last ditch attempt to change her mind.

'There must be other ways to raise the money. Scarlett and I will help you.'

Jodie gave a short bark of laughter. 'Two gormless thirteen-year-olds? I don't think so. It costs thousands of pounds a year to run this place. Where are you going to find that kind of money? In your piggy banks? Down the back of the sofa? I promise you, this is the only way.'

'At least let us try.'

Jodie grabbed her arm. 'Haven't you been listening to anything I've said?' Her voice was thick with menace. Or was it unshed tears? Poppy couldn't be sure.

A door slammed. 'There you are! I made bacon butties for tea but you'd disappeared,' said Jodie's mum, appearing from the house.

Jodie let go of Poppy's arm, leaving a red hand-shaped imprint.

'I had a call about a mare that had been left tethered to a tree on the Tavistock road without food or water. Poppy and I drove over to have a look but we couldn't find her, could we, Poppy?'

Shocked at how smoothly Jodie had lied, Poppy said nothing.

Jodie's mum seemed oblivious to the undercurrents and smiled brightly. 'Would you like a bacon butty, love? There's plenty to go around.'

Poppy shook her head. 'No thanks. I've lost my appetite. Anyway, I need to get going. My stepmum will be wondering where I am.'

Poppy retrieved her bike but as she was about to pedal off, Jodie blocked her way.

'I'm not doing this for me or my dad. I'm doing it for the horses. So please, *please* don't tell anyone. You'll ruin everything.'

Poppy rushed past, too appalled to reply. Unshed tears burned her throat and anxiety knotted her stomach. Jodie went to grab her handlebar but Poppy swerved out of the way. The bike almost lost traction on the gravel but Poppy stamped on the pedals and brought it back under control. Once on the main road she put her head down and cycled as fast as she could towards Riverdale, relishing the burning pain in her thigh muscles as she attacked each hill because it took her mind off everything else. She wished she could turn back the clock. She wished she'd never asked Jodie for advice, never found the mobile phones, never let Charlie talk her into going looking for his stupid ghosts. She longed for blissful ignorance. But deep in her heart she knew it was too late for that.

The question was, what could she do to make things right?

POPPY FLUNG her bike on the grass and vaulted the gate to Cloud and Chester's paddock. The Connemara was dozing by the far hedge but opened his eyes and whickered with pleasure when Poppy called him. She threw her arms around him, breathing in lungfuls of his pure, horsey smell, imagining how awful it would be if they had to sell up and move away. She felt a sob rising in her throat at the thought of him being driven away in someone else's horsebox to a yard who knew where. The prospect was too terrible to bear and she collapsed onto the ground, tears streaming down her cheeks. When Cloud nuzzled her neck and blew softly into her ear she wailed even harder. She stayed like that, hugging her knees, with Cloud watching over her, until she was all cried out.

It was Chester who dragged her from her misery. The old donkey wandered over and gave her a determined nudge. As she gazed into his chocolate brown eyes she felt her resolve strengthen.

'I know, I'm being wet and pathetic,' she said in a quavering voice. 'What would Tory say? That every problem has a solution, that's what.'

She wiped her nose on the bottom of her tee-shirt and climbed stiffly to her feet. 'I just need to work out what it is.'

Her dad was in the lounge watching cricket, with Magpie on his lap looking daggers at Freddie, who was lying at his feet, his raspberry-pink tongue lolling.

'Hello, daughter of mine.' Mike McKeever patted the seat beside him.

Poppy sat down and tickled Magpie's chin. The cat gave Freddie a supercilious look and began purring loudly.

'Why the sad face?' her dad asked.

Poppy shrugged.

'You never have time to talk to me these days,' he said. 'You're always too busy with the other men in your life.'

Poppy looked quizzically at him until the penny dropped. 'You mean Cloud and Chester?'

Mike McKeever stuck out his bottom lip and nodded sorrowfully. He looked so like Charlie that she had to giggle.

'You twit,' she said fondly. 'It's because I love them more.'

'Fair enough. I know when I'm beaten. So I'm presuming that you've come to find me because you want something. A new Australian rug or some of those padded socks Cloud wears when he goes in Bill's trailer?'

'You mean a New Zealand rug, Dad. And they're not padded socks, they're travel boots. No, I don't want anything like that. I need some advice.'

Her dad muted the TV. 'Fire away.'

'If you had to raise a huge amount of money for a horse sanctuary, what would you do?'

'How much are we talking?'

'Thousands. And it needs to be raised quickly.'

'Is this for that place Scarlett got her new pony from?'

Poppy nodded. 'Nethercote'll have to close if Jodie can't find a way to raise enough money. She's getting desperate.' That was the understatement of the year, Poppy thought to herself.

Her dad rested his chin on steepled fingers. 'Britain is a country of animal lovers. If people knew her horses were under threat they'd dig deep into their pockets, I'm sure.'

'That's the problem. People don't know.'

'Well then, she must find a way to tell them.'

'But how?'

'She needs publicity and she must think big. She needs to tell her story to the TV and newspapers. The money'll come rolling in, I guarantee it.'

'But no-one's going to be interested in a tiny horse rescue place in Devon, Dad.'

'That's where you've got to think smart. Jodie needs a hook to draw the journalists in. An animal with a tragic back story that'll grab the headlines.'

Poppy pictured the real-life magazines her old friend Tory enjoyed with a cup of tea and a slice of Battenberg. There was no doubt Jodie could make a few quid selling her story. *How I smuggled stolen phones into prison to save my horses.* But Poppy didn't think any public relations guru worth their salt would recommend resorting to that particular course of action.

'Every horse at Nethercote has a tragic back story, Dad. That's why they're there.'

'Point taken. A tragic *out-of-the-ordinary* back story. You'll think of something, Poppy. You've lived with your old dad long enough to know what makes the news.'

It was true, Poppy thought. But her dad was a war correspondent. He covered conflicts in the Middle East. Proper weighty crises and catastrophes in which lives were lost and worlds turned upside down. Stories that newsreaders read with solemn voices, not the light and fluffy news items which ended the bulletins, leaving viewers with a happy heart, their faith in humankind restored.

'So if I do find a tragic, *out-of-the-ordinary* back story, can you help me?'

Her dad ruffled her hair. "Course I can, sweetheart. I went to journalism college with the producer of Spotlight. I'm sure I can pull in a favour or two. But the story needs to stand up.'

Poppy gave Magpie a last chuck under his chin. 'Fair enough. Better get started then, hadn't I?'

16

Hunched over the laptop at the kitchen table with a notepad and pen beside her, Poppy called up the Nethercote Horse Rescue website and clicked on a tab that said *Our horses*. Jodie had reproduced the photos that she'd used on the display panels at the fete. Kirsty, Mr Darcy and Percy were all there. Poppy even spotted the four white socks and white-splodged nose of Red as a foal, being bottle-fed by a much younger-looking Jodie. Poppy skim-read their stories, looking for a hook that would entice the local television station to send a camera crew to Nethercote. Each one was a litany of human cruelty, neglect and ignorance. But although they made Poppy feel sick to the stomach she knew such back stories were universal the world over. Nothing out of the ordinary there.

Sighing, Poppy flipped the laptop closed and stared out of the window, hoping for an epiphany. But the harder she tried to think, the emptier her mind became. Caroline came in from the garden and began washing lettuce for their dinner. Her dad wandered by in search of his reading glasses. Magpie rubbed against her legs before settling into Freddie's bed by the range, the feline equivalent of a self-satisfied smirk on his whiskered face. Still Poppy's mind remained stubbornly blank.

Her reverie was broken when Charlie bowled in like a mini hurricane.

'Can I have a biscuit, Mum?' he called, his hand already in the tin.

'Just one. Dinner won't be long,' said Caroline, taking a quiche out of the oven.

Biscuit. The word reverberated around Poppy's head like one of those tiny silver orbs in a pinball machine. Charlie rammed a ginger biscuit in his mouth and crunched noisily. Biscuit. Poppy clapped her hand to her head and Charlie and Caroline looked at her inquiringly.

'I'm so stupid! The answer's been there all along!' Poppy flung her chair back and hugged her brother. 'You're a genius, Charlie. An absolute, utter genius!'

Charlie's eyes widened in surprise. 'Usually you think I'm an annoying idiot.'

'Not today, little brother. Today you are the cleverest person I know. A proper mastermind. Right, I need to see Dad.'

He was in the lounge reading the paper. He peered over his glasses as she plonked herself on the sofa.

'I've found an *out-of-the-ordinary* back story,' she announced. 'What if there was a pony at Nethercote who'd been airlifted by helicopter from the top of a tower block where he'd been kept alive on vegetable peelings, scraps of bread and rainwater?'

Her dad folded the newspaper. 'I'd say that was pretty *out-of-the-ordinary*.'

'Caroline said this pony had even been on the news when he was rescued. So if his new home was under threat because of a lack of money, that might make headlines, right?'

'I'd say so,' said her dad. 'And this pony actually exists, does it?'

Poppy pictured Biscuit, the white spots on his chestnut coat like snowflakes as he snoozed in the daisies. His story wasn't on the Nethercote website, and in her desperation she'd completely forgotten him. 'Yes, he definitely exists. So will you phone your friend at Spotlight?'

Her dad was already reaching for his mobile. Poppy chewed a nail as she listened to the one-sided conversation. After what seemed like an age he hung up.

'You're lucky - it's the silly season and they're scratching around for news. They're sending a crew around first thing in the morning. Unless something else breaks it'll be top item on tomorrow's programme. With a fair wind and a bit of luck it'll be picked up by the nationals and those donations will come flooding in.'

Poppy hugged her dad. 'Thank you, thank you, thank you,' she gabbled into his lambswool sweater. 'You don't know how much this means.'

'No problem, sweetheart. You'd better go and tell Jodie the good news.'

∽

POPPY GRABBED a slice of quiche and went to catch Cloud. If she cut across the moor it was only about three miles to Nethercote. The Spotlight reporter was due at half nine the following morning. She had to convince Jodie that the interview was the right thing to do. That the publicity it would attract would raise enough money to keep the rescue centre afloat. But, most importantly, Poppy had to talk Jodie out of her plan to smuggle the mobile phones into the prison. Poppy had a feeling that would be the hardest task.

Cloud cantered across the moor, jumping a low stone wall with ease and flying over a small stream. Emotions churned in Poppy's stomach like a witch's potion in a steaming cauldron. Love for her pony. Terror she could lose him. Anxiety about the conversation that lay ahead. And a glimmer of hope that if she could change Jodie's mind, she stood a chance of making everything alright.

Cloud looked around with interest as they walked up the Nethercote drive.

'This is where your new buddy Red used to live,' Poppy told him, trying to keep her tone light and her breathing steady. But the waver in her voice gave away her nerves.

Jodie's Land Rover wasn't parked in its usual place. Poppy rang the bell by the tack room but no-one came. Perhaps Jodie was in one of the paddocks. Poppy led Cloud past the stables. His eyes rolled and his nostrils flared in mock horror as the rescue horses watched them walk by.

'It's alright, silly,' Poppy said, stroking his neck. 'They won't hurt you.'

Jodie wasn't in the paddocks either. Poppy checked her watch. Half past six. Time was running out. She knocked at the back door. Inside a radio was playing pop music. She knocked again, harder this time. A door slammed and heels clicked on a stone floor. Jodie's mum appeared, a lipstick in one hand and a handbag in the other. Bracelets jangled on her wrists and her hair had been newly blow dried.

Poppy took a deep breath. 'Sorry to bother you but is Jodie in?'

'She isn't, I'm afraid. Disappeared about an hour ago. Didn't even stay for her dinner, the little minx.' Her voice was indignant.

'Do you know where she's gone? I really need to speak to her.'

Jodie's mum looked cagey. 'No idea.'

'When will she be back?'

'I don't know, love. I'm not her keeper. Look, I'm late for work. Can I leave her a message?'

Poppy dithered. Could she confide in Jodie's mum? Cloud shifted his weight and nudged Poppy in the back. Jodie's mum looked at her watch and frowned.

Poppy made a snap decision she hoped she wouldn't live to regret.

17

The air was close and alive with the hum of a million biting insects and the sun was disappearing over the horizon as they arrived home. Poppy untacked Cloud and sponged the sweaty patch under his saddle. Once she'd turned him out with Chester she mindlessly swept the yard until her back ached and sweat trickled down her forehead and between her shoulder blades.

When she could sweep no more she leant on the gate and watched the pony and donkey doze. Every now and then one of them would twitch and shift their weight. Poppy was always dreaming about them. Did they ever dream of her? More likely their dreams were filled with newly-cut hay, sweet spring grass and carrots. Lots of carrots.

She blew them a kiss and headed indoors, where her dad and Caroline were in the lounge watching television. Poppy slumped on the sofa.

'OK sweetheart? Was Jodie pleased?' said Caroline.

'Yes,' Poppy said. She kept her eyes glued to the screen so Caroline couldn't read her face.

'Where's Charlie?'

'Just gone up to bed. He's desperate to come over to Nethercote and watch the filming tomorrow. He's hoping they'll interview him as a concerned animal lover. D'you think Jodie would mind?'

Poppy shrugged. 'Probably not.'

Her mobile beeped. She checked the message.

I've made the call. It's over to you.

'Scarlett?' Caroline asked.

Poppy nodded. Did it count as a lie if she didn't actually articulate it? 'She wants me to go over and watch a film. Is that OK?'

'As long as you're back by ten. And make sure you take your phone.'

Poppy tapped out a reply and shoved the phone back in her pocket. For better or worse, the first part of her hastily-devised plan was in place.

~

POPPY'S BIKE was leaning up against the old stone wall around Caroline's vegetable garden, but she walked straight past it and headed for the tack room. Pedal power was no match for horse power in situations like this. She fixed her dad's head torch to her hat and grabbed Cloud's saddle and bridle.

The Connemara showed no surprise when she let herself into the paddock, as if night-time hacks were an everyday occurrence. Poppy glanced nervously towards the house as the gate clicked shut behind her, but the blind in the kitchen was drawn. As long as she was back by ten her parents would be none the wiser.

Something dark swooped in front of her face and she flinched, but it was only one of the bats that had made a home in the rafters of the barn. She led Cloud through the gate and jumped into the saddle.

The setting sun had turned the rippled mass of altocumulus cloud such a vivid shade of fiery orange that it resembled molten lava. Beneath the sky the moss-green moor stretched before them unremittingly, the vast expanse broken only by rocky granite outcrops and the occasional sheep.

Behind her, Riverdale was bathed in tangerine light. Poppy pictured her brother, tucked up in bed, his thumb in his mouth and Magpie curled in a ball by his feet, snoring gently; the television turned down low as her dad and Caroline chatted about their day; Freddie, fast asleep in his basket by the range, his beetle-black nose twitching as he dreamed his doggy dreams. The urge to turn back and join them was so strong Poppy almost succumbed to it. This was Jodie's mess. Why should it be up to her to sort it out? Jodie had made her bed. Let her lie in it.

But Poppy knew it was too late. She'd set off a chain of events and had no choice but to see it through. She had to do right by the Nethercote horses. She just hoped her plan worked. And if it didn't....

Anxiety gnawing at her insides, Poppy clicked her tongue and asked for a canter. Cloud needed no encouragement and sprang forwards. He was fizzing with nervous energy, his neck arched and his tail high. Poppy licked her lips and tried to slow her racing heartbeat. The last thing she wanted was for her pony to pick up on her tension. The Connemara lengthened his stride until he was galloping flat out. She sighed. It seemed he already had.

'Hey boy, not so fast. There's a long way to go,' she soothed. She tried checking him but the reins slipped through her clammy fingers. A dark stain of sweat was spreading across his neck and shoulders and his head was tucked into his chest. Poppy sat down in the saddle, kept her legs firmly against Cloud's sides and gave a firm, even pull with both reins.

'Whoa,' she murmured. Cloud flicked back his ears and finally slowed his stride. Poppy checked him again and he broke into a fast, unbalanced trot.

'Steady,' she said, sitting for a few uncomfortable strides until she was able to ease him into a walk. She bent down and stroked his neck.

Poppy loosened the reins, relieved to have brought him back under control. He had never taken off like that before. She kept up a stream of chatter as they crossed the moor, hoping her voice would keep him calm. The sun was sinking below the horizon and the sky had darkened to the grey of a stormy sea. By Poppy's reckoning they were over halfway. With any luck they'd reach the cottage before darkness fell. She'd hoped for a clear night but no such luck. She'd have to rely on her pony's instinct and the beam of the head torch to guide them home.

They passed a small herd of Dartmoor ponies grazing by the side of a stream. A roan mare with a bay foal at foot lifted her head and whinnied. Cloud skittered to the left and Poppy clamped her legs to his sides and tightened her reins.

After a mile or so Cloud finally began to settle. Poppy let the reins slip through her fingers so he could stretch his neck. As she relaxed into his long, loping walk her mind began to wander. Humming tunelessly, she scratched a mosquito bite on her arm and played with a hank of the Connemara's mane. She was so preoccupied she didn't see the flash of iridescent green until too late. As they approached a clump of gorse bushes a male pheasant squawked in alarm and swooped in front of them, its speckled conker and black wings outstretched. Cloud boggled and leapt about three feet into the air, throwing Poppy out of the saddle. For a split second, as she teetered on the brink, she thought she might save herself. But the saddle slipped and with it went her balance. The ground rushed towards her as fast as a fairground helter-skelter and Poppy landed heavily, her right leg buckling underneath her. She gasped as she felt her ankle pop. Intense pain shot up her leg. And then everything went black.

oused from semi-consciousness by a draught of warm air, Poppy reached for the alarm clock on her bedside table. When her hand came into contact with wiry grass and a small slab of cold granite her eyes snapped open. Cloud's nose was a few inches from her own. He blew softly into her face, as if he was trying to wake her. That explained the warm air at least.

Totally disorientated, Poppy looked around her, wondering if she'd fallen asleep in the paddock again. She sat up groggily and winced at the stabbing pain in her leg. Cloud whickered and nuzzled her neck, his liquid brown eyes dark with concern. She tried to piece together what had happened. Bit by bit she remembered: the text, the made-up visit to see Scarlett, the dash across the moor to the tumbledown cottage, the pheasant...

'Pesky pheasant!' Poppy muttered, attempting to stand. But the searing pain took her breath away and she collapsed on the grass again. Gingerly, she peeled down her sock. Her ankle had ballooned in size, the skin around it stretched and puffy. Her heart sank. How was she ever going to reach Witch Cottage now?

As if sensing her thoughts Cloud gave her a gentle nudge. Poppy swallowed back tears. 'I can't ride you, Cloud. There's no way I can stand to get on. And I can't walk a single step. I'll have to call Caroline and Dad. I have no other choice.'

She slid her phone out of her back pocket and groaned. No signal. Not even one measly bar. She threw it onto the grass in frustration. Cloud sniffed it cautiously, his nostrils flared, and took a step back.

'Don't leave me!' Poppy cried, the gravity of her situation beginning to sink in. It was almost nine o'clock at night, she was in the middle of the moor with a useless leg and an equally useless phone. Jodie was about to throw her life away and there was nothing Poppy could do to stop her. Her shoulders sagged in defeat.

Cloud must have registered the desperation in her voice, because he walked forward and rubbed his head against her, as if to say *Don't worry, I'll stick around*. She pressed her face against his warm cheek.

'I can do this,' she told him. Heaving herself upright she gathered Cloud's reins, rested her left hand on his withers and grabbed the stirrup. But her right ankle was too feeble and she crumpled to the ground. 'Oh Cloud, what am I going to do?'

The Connemara pawed the ground and sank to his knees with a grunt.

'Don't roll, you'll squash your saddle!'

But Cloud didn't roll. He lay down beside her and nudged her hip.

Was he lying down in sympathy? Poppy knew horses were empathetic but this was ridiculous. Maybe he'd twisted his leg when he'd spooked, too.

'Have you hurt yourself?' she cried.

Cloud nudged her again. Poppy leant against him, reassured by his solid bulk. She often lay down with him in the stable. She'd once read that if a horse even let someone near them while they were lying down it was a sign of trust. It had made her feel slightly superior that Cloud was so relaxed with her that he sometimes dozed off with his head in her lap. She'd watched videos on YouTube of horses who'd been trained to lie down on command. Some even lay down so their riders could mount them from their wheelchairs.

Suddenly a thought popped into her head. She knew from Caitlyn's diary that she'd started teaching Cloud tricks. Had she taught him to lie down so she could get on from the ground? It seemed unbelievable but it was worth a try. There were no other options.

Poppy shuffled on her bottom to Cloud's saddle, gathered the reins again and grabbed a handful of mane.

'Are you OK with this?' she asked him. He looked completely at ease. She took a deep breath, put her weight on her left knee and hauled her right leg over. Once she was sitting in the saddle she touched his withers and held on tightly as he scrambled to his feet.

Poppy threw her arms around his neck. 'You clever, clever boy!'

Leaving her swollen foot dangling she crossed the right stirrup over the saddle so it didn't bump against his side and clicked her tongue, her optimism restored.

'Come on Cloud. We have a disaster to avert!'

POPPY SAW the headlights of Jodie's Land Rover before they left the inky blackness of the conifers. It looked as though they had arrived in the nick of time. Jodie, wearing a dark baseball cap and riding gloves, was cramming dozens of phones into a large black holdall.

'Jodie! It's me, Poppy.'

Jodie spun around. Her face, caught in the beam of Poppy's head torch, was twisted with fury and fear.

'What the hell are you doing here?'

'I've come to stop you.'

'Too late.'

'It isn't! You don't have to do this!'

'I do,' Jodie said grimly.

'But I've found another way to raise the money!'

'Yeah, right.'

'I really have. The BBC is sending a camera crew to Nethercote in the morning.'

'What?'

'They're going to do a story on your appeal.'

'There is no appeal.'

'There will be by the morning,' Poppy said. 'You're going to set one up on your website tonight.'

Jodie turned back to the holdall. 'It'd be a complete waste of time.

There are too many animal sanctuaries out there asking for money. I've already told you that.'

'None of the others will be top item on tomorrow's news. My dad's had a word with the producer. She loves Biscuit's story. She's going to use old footage of him being carried down by the helicopter, and they're going to interview you about him and the appeal. Once people see the great work you're doing the donations will come flooding in!'

Jodie tucked a loose strand of hair behind her ear. Poppy noticed the slightest tremor in her fingers.

'Didn't it occur to you to ask me first?' Jodie said coldly.

Poppy was silent.

'No, I didn't think so. I'm not doing it. I don't need to. By this time tomorrow I'll have enough in the bank to keep Nethercote running for a year.'

'But it's all organised!'

Jodie shoved the last few phones into the bag and yanked the zip closed. 'Well, you've wasted your time. Now beggar off and leave me to it.'

'You'll get caught,' Poppy said.

'You sound like my mother. How many times do I have to say it? I will not get caught. Everything is planned. So if you'll excuse me, there's somewhere I need to be.'

'Your dad won't be there.'

Jodie flung the holdall in the back of the Land Rover and slammed the door. 'What are you wittering about?'

Poppy took a deep breath. 'He won't be lowering the rope. He's in solitary confinement.'

'*What?*' Jodie said again.

'The Governor knows what your dad's planning. He had a tip off. There are four prison officers in his cell and police on the ground waiting for the phones to arrive.'

'You've grassed us up?' Jodie hissed.

'Not me. It was your mum. But no-one knows it's you bringing the phones. She told them it was some lowlife your dad met in prison.'

'And that makes it alright does it?'

'She reckons he'll end up serving extra time. But that it's a small price to pay in the circumstances.'

Poppy thought it wise not repeat Jodie's mum's actual words, that he could go to hell for all she cared. Instead she said, 'Your mum said he'd be happy as long as you and the horses were OK.'

Jodie leant against the Land Rover, her head bowed. 'If that's true, what am I going to do with the phones?'

Poppy glanced at the cottage. 'Put them back in the attic. I'll call the police in a couple of days and say I've found them. It won't matter if my fingerprints are all over them. There'll be nothing to link them to you.'

'What about the gang who stole them. They know who I am,' Jodie said.

'But they're hardly going to hand themselves in, are they?'

Sensing Jodie waver Poppy pressed home her advantage. 'What would Cait tell you to do, if she was here? Would she want her best friend to break the law and risk going to prison? It's the last thing she'd want.'

Jodie was silent. After what seemed like an eternity she edged over to Cloud and stroked his head. Poppy felt a pounding in her chest and realised she'd stopped breathing.

'She'd tell me I was nuts to even consider it,' said Jodie finally.

Poppy sent a silent missive of thanks to Caitlyn.

'So you'll do it? The interview and everything?'

'You really think it'll work?'

The beam of the head torch bobbed like a yo-yo as Poppy nodded. 'It'll work. I promise.'

19

'So, are you going to give me a hand with these phones or what?' said Jodie.

Poppy reddened. 'I can't get off. I fell off Cloud and busted my ankle on the way over.'

Jodie raised her eyebrows. 'Is it broken?'

'I don't think so. I can still wiggle my toes, although it really hurts. I think it's just a sprain.'

'How did you get back on?'

'Well, that's the funny thing,' said Poppy. 'Did you and Caitlyn teach Cloud and Nero tricks that last summer?'

Jodie hooted with laughter. 'I tried to. Nero was hopeless. But Cloud was a quick learner, weren't you boy? Cait taught him to give her a kiss and take a bow, that kind of thing.'

'Did she teach him to lie down?'

Jodie's forehead creased. 'Not that I remember. But it was so long ago. D'you want me to go home and get the trailer?'

'No, we'll take it easy. We'll be fine. But will you be OK to put the phones back in the attic?'

'Do I have an option?' Jodie's tone was sardonic, but she dragged the hold-all out of the back of the Land Rover and hefted it onto her shoulder.

'I'll see you tomorrow,' Poppy said.

Jodie held her hand in a mock salute. As Cloud plunged back into the conifers Poppy glanced back. In the beam of the Land Rover's headlights she could just make out the older girl disappearing through the door of the cottage. Poppy ran her hand along Cloud's neck and allowed herself a smile.

'D'you know, Cloud? I think it's going to be alright.'

It was only when they were almost home that she realised she had overlooked one small but crucial problem. How on earth was she going to explain her sprained ankle to her parents?

'SO YOU DECIDED to ride Cloud to Scarlett's - even though it was pitch dark - and fell off on the way home when he shied at a sheep?' Caroline asked, her eyebrows raised.

'Er, yes. That's right.' Poppy hopped over to the gate and rested her bad ankle on the bottom bar. Her nose would be as long as Pinocchio's if she carried on lying like this.

'We'd better take you to minor injuries first thing to check it's not a fracture,' said her dad.

'I can't miss the filming!' Poppy cried. 'I've promised Jodie I'll be there. Honestly, I'm fine. The swelling's gone down already.' She rotated her ankle, hiding her grimace behind her long fringe. 'See?'

Caroline sighed. 'Alright. But you won't be able to ride. I'll drive you.'

Poppy hopped over to her stepmum and gave her a hug. Caroline ruffled her hair.

'Come on, Hopalong Cassidy. It's getting late and you should be in bed.'

Poppy screwed up her face. 'What did you call me?'

'Hopalong Cassidy. He was a cowboy in the old Western films my grandad used to love. Hopalong had a grey horse, too, though he was called Topper, if my memory serves me right.'

Lying in bed, her ankle resting on two pillows and Magpie nestled in the crook of her arm, Poppy Googled Hopalong Cassidy.

'Wikipedia says he was often called upon to intercede when dishonest characters took advantage of honest citizens,' she told the cat, who yawned widely, showing two rows of tiny incisors.

Poppy turned off the iPad and tickled Magpie's chin. 'We've more in common than a gammy leg.'

~

OVER BREAKFAST POPPY checked Nethercote's website. Jodie had been busy. On the home page was a huge banner urging people to support the rescue centre's new appeal. Under a photo of Jodie with her arm around Biscuit's neck was an open letter. Poppy's toast grew cold on her plate as she read:

'Hi, I'm Jodie Morgan, and I run Nethercote Horse Rescue.

I want to take this opportunity to tell you a little bit about us and the work we do.

Nethercote was founded by my dad, Alan Morgan, ten years ago. Dad always loved horses and opening a rescue centre was his life's dream.

Dad never once turned a horse away. He gave them all a second chance.

Horses like Biscuit, our most famous resident here at Nethercote, who was rescued by helicopter from the roof of a high rise block of flats. We try and rehome as many horses as possible, but I have promised Biscuit that he has a home here for the rest of his days.

Five years ago Dad left the running of Nethercote to me. I was fifteen and still at school. Running a rescue centre wasn't my dream - I wanted to be a famous showjumper - but I owed it to the horses to carry on.

A job like this is a vocation. Seeing a pony that arrived skinny and terrified go off to his new home sleek and confident makes all the hard work worthwhile.

But the last few years have been tough. Really tough. Money has been tight and fundraising takes up precious time better spent rescuing, rehabilitating and rehoming our horses and ponies.

This summer we reached crisis point at Nethercote. Costs for hay and feed have soared and donations have plummeted. Without financial help we won't be able to pay the winter feed bill, let alone meet ongoing veterinary and farrier costs. What will happen to the horses, you may well ask. The truth is, I don't know.

So we have launched Biscuit's Appeal, to raise enough money to enable us to *carry on caring for the horses other people have forgotten. If you are able to help, please donate using the link below.*

Every penny counts: £5 will buy a bale of hay, £10 will buy a sack of food, £20 will pay for the farrier to trim a pony's feet and £80 will buy him a new set of shoes.

So, you see, your help really can make all the difference to Biscuit and his friends here at Nethercote. Thank you for listening in our hour of need.

Yours, Jodie

Poppy swallowed. Jodie's letter was heartfelt and emotive and, as if that wasn't enough to get people reaching for their chequebooks, there was a blurry photo in the bottom right hand corner of Biscuit being winched to safety from the tower block in the Midlands. The appaloosa was a bag of skin and bones, a far cry from the plump, contented pony he was now.

Charlie bounded in, his hair as tousled as a bird's nest, Freddie hot on his heels. He skidded to a halt when he saw Poppy.

'No tablets at the breakfast table!'

'I'm not playing games, I'm reading. The BBC film crew is coming today and I need to check the website so I can give Jodie some advice on handling the media, if you must know,' Poppy told him officiously.

'Doesn't look like she needs it,' said Caroline, reading over Poppy's shoulder. 'I'd say she was pretty much on message already.'

'Yes, well, I did brief her last night. I mean, yesterday afternoon.' Poppy felt her cheeks redden. Hoping Caroline hadn't noticed, she picked up her plate and hobbled over to the sink. The swelling in her ankle had gone down overnight but it was still too tender to take her full weight.

'What time do we need to go?' Caroline asked.

'They're coming at half past nine so if we leave at eight thirty I can make sure Jodie's ready.'

'Can me and Freddie come? They might want to do a vod pod,' said Charlie.

Poppy gazed at him in exasperation. 'A *what?*'

'You know, when they ask members of the public what they think about something. They might do a vod pod about how important it is to save the ponies.'

Caroline laughed. 'He means vox pop. I suppose it wouldn't do any harm. As long as you promise not to get under everybody's feet. You don't mind, do you Poppy?'

'I won't be annoying, I promise.' Charlie smiled beseechingly at his sister.

'Oh alright, if you must. But if you ruin everything by messing up a shot or something I will have no option but to kill you.'

'I understand,' he nodded earnestly, before giving a fist pump and bowling back out of the kitchen, Freddie still at his feet.

Poppy sighed. Brothers!

2 0

J odie looked as if she'd only managed to snatch a couple of hours' sleep. Purple shadows darkened her eyes like shading on a pencil portrait and her face was pale. But she greeted the McKeevers with a cheerful smile and made a great fuss of Freddie, who promptly rolled on the ground with his legs in the air offering his belly to be tickled.

'Is there anything we can do?' Caroline asked.

'I've just got the yard to sweep and Biscuit to groom. I wanted him looking his best,' said Jodie.

'Poppy can take care of Biscuit and I'll sweep the yard. You go and get yourself ready.'

Jodie smiled gratefully and disappeared inside. Poppy tied Biscuit outside his stable and set to work with a body brush. The appaloosa was already beginning to lose his summer coat and Poppy sneezed violently as she was enveloped in a cloud of horse hair. Catching a whiff of the Polos in her back pocket, Biscuit nibbled at her jeans until Poppy relented. He wolfed two from her open palm as if he hadn't been fed for a week, which, Poppy reflected, had probably been the case when he'd been tethered at the top of the high rise. It was little wonder he was a guzzle guts when a decent meal back then would have been a pile of potato scrapings and a couple of slices of mouldy bread. Poppy shuddered, then peeled another couple of mints from the pack.

She was brushing out the tangles in the appaloosa's tail when Jodie's mum tottered across the yard in the highest wedge shoes Poppy had ever seen. She laid a hand on Poppy's arm.

'Thank you for everything you did yesterday, Poppy. You don't know how grateful I am. I've got my old Jodie back.'

'I was glad to help. I don't think deep down she wanted to do it, she just felt she had no option.'

Jodie's mum's lips thinned. 'Her father should never have put her in that position. What was he thinking?'

Poppy considered this. She would lay down her life for Cloud. She could understand why Alan Morgan had been prepared to take such a risk. But it didn't make it right.

The back door banged shut and Jodie appeared, wearing a clean, if a little creased, red Nethercote tee-shirt, navy jodhpurs and black riding boots. Despite her wan face she looked upbeat, as though a great weight had been lifted from her shoulders.

'Are you ready for your moment of fame?' Caroline asked.

Jodie grimaced. 'My stomach's churning, my mouth is as dry as sandpaper and I've absolutely no idea what I'm going to say. But otherwise, yes, bring it on.'

'We can have a run-through if you like,' Poppy said shyly. 'I can pretend I'm the reporter and ask you some questions.'

'And I'll be the cameraman,' said Charlie, sticking an imaginary camera in Jodie's face.

'Anything that'll help.'

Poppy and Charlie had watched their dad on the news enough times to know how to conduct a television interview and they spent the next ten minutes grilling Jodie until she was word perfect. They had hardly drawn breath when a spotless black BMW pulled up at the gate.

'Oh God, they're here!' Jodie cried, smoothing her hair self-consciously.

'You'll be fine,' Caroline told her. 'Forget the camera's there and just be yourself.'

A man in his thirties dressed in a cream linen suit and reeking of a spicy, pungent aftershave introduced himself as reporter Ben Byrne. He shook everyone's hand and gave Biscuit a tentative pat while his camera-man, a smiley girl called Pippa, fiddled with her camera.

'We'll do the interview first, then Pippa will get some general shots of the yard and we'll finish with a piece to camera,' Ben told them.

Biscuit watched with interest as Ben held out a microphone and said, 'Can you give us your name for the level?'

Jodie cleared her throat. 'Um. Jodie Morgan.'

'Great. And can you spell your name for the tape?'

'J-O-I-D. Sorry,' she said, shaking her head and shooting a desperate look at the others. Poppy gave her an encouraging smile and Caroline mouthed, 'You'll be fine.'

'J-O-D-I-E-M-O-R-G-A-N.'

'Wonderful. Let's get started.'

After the first couple of questions Jodie's nerves vanished and she talked animatedly about the rescue horses. Ben asked her about Biscuit and his condition when he'd arrived at Nethercote.

'The vet said he'd never make it. But Biscuit's a fighter. In fact he's as stubborn as I am. He refused to give up.' Jodie scratched the pony's fore-head and he gave her an affectionate nudge. 'I promised him that if he pulled through he would never have to leave. And now I'm not sure I'll be able to keep that promise,' she said, her voice thick with emotion.

Poppy, who was standing behind the camera, could see that Pippa had zoomed in on Jodie's face, catching the single tear that slid down her cheek.

Interview over, they took Pippa on a tour of the rescue centre so she could get shots of horses grazing contentedly in the paddocks and looking over their stable doors.

'Jodie can send you some of the before pictures,' said Poppy, thinking of the photos of horses with matted coats, hollow necks, overgrown hooves and bony rumps that had had such an impact on her at the summer fete.

When Pippa had finished they returned to the yard.

'We don't need you for this bit, Jodie. I'm going to do a piece to camera telling everyone about the appeal,' said Ben.

'Why don't you hold Biscuit while you're doing it?' Pippa suggested.

Poppy untied the appaloosa and handed his lead rope to Ben, who took it gingerly.

'It's alright. He won't bite,' Jodie laughed.

Poppy darted forwards and brushed the reporter's linen jacket. He looked at her in bemusement.

'Just a bit of fluff,' she said, retreating to where Caroline, Charlie and Freddie were watching the proceedings.

Ben smoothed down his hair, glanced at his notebook and switched on his mike. Pippa squinted through the eyepiece of her camera and gave him the thumbs up. He gripped Biscuit's lead rope tightly and gave the camera a dazzling smile.

'Biscuit and his equine friends here at Nethercote Horse Rescue have been given a second chance by Jodie Morgan. But unless the rescue centre can raise more funds their future is uncertain...'

While everyone else was watching the reporter, Poppy's eyes were trained on Biscuit. *Come on*, she willed him silently. *You can do it.*

Ben was wrapping up his piece to camera when the gelding suddenly raised his head and sniffed the wind. He gave a comedy snort and turned towards the reporter. There was a glint in his eye as he gave Ben a purposeful nudge and started nibbling at his jacket. Momentarily thrown, Ben raised his eyebrows and shrugged theatrically. Biscuit, still picking at Ben's jacket, breathed in a lungful of the reporter's tangy aftershave, turned to face the camera and curled his top lip as if he was laughing his speckled head off.

Poppy held her breath as she watched Pippa focus on the appaloosa's yellow teeth. Beside her Charlie stifled a giggle. Poppy elbowed him in the ribs and held her finger to her lips. This was television gold. They'd never re-create it if they had to do a second take.

Ben had thrown his head back and was also roaring with laughter. 'And with that, it's back to you in the studio,' he spluttered, as Biscuit rolled his eyes at the camera and sneezed explosively all over the reporter's cream linen suit.

'THAT HORSE IS A COMIC GENIUS. You ought to get him an agent,' said Ben, as he helped Pippa heft the camera into the boot of the BMW.

'Comic genius? A total delinquent more like. I'm sorry about your jacket,' Jodie said for the umpteenth time.

'No worries. I'll get it dry cleaned on expenses.'

'What time will Jodie be on the news?' asked Charlie.

Ben checked his watch. 'Half past one and again at six thirty.'

'And you'll include the link so people can donate if they want to?' Poppy checked.

He nodded. 'I think people will be falling over themselves to help once they see Biscuit in action. He's a star in the making. I was well and truly upstaged,' he said ruefully.

~

'I BET I look like a complete and utter loser,' grumbled Jodie, as they settled in Nethercote's living room to watch the lunchtime bulletin.

'You don't need to worry. People'll be more interested in Biscuit than you,' said Charlie kindly.

'Thanks - I think.'

Poppy felt a flutter of nerves as the titles came up and the familiar soundtrack began to play. She was the one who had convinced Jodie this would work. What if it didn't? If no-one supported Biscuit's Appeal Jodie would be right back at square one. Actually worse than that. Poppy had already scuppered her money-making plan to smuggle phones into Dartmoor prison.

A willowy presenter with an improbably unlined forehead and immaculately coiffured hair swept into a chignon was sitting on a red sofa. She shuffled some papers on her lap and looked up as the titles ended. Poppy's mind wandered as the presenter read the headlines with a practised smile.

'- but first we go to a Devon horse sanctuary that needs your help. Ben Byrne reports.'

The camera cut to the main paddock where the plump, sleek Nethercote horses grazed serenely under a canopy of ancient oak trees, and then cut again to Ben's interview with Jodie, which was peppered with some of the less graphic photographs of the rescue horses. Jodie scowled when the camera zoomed in on the tear rolling down her cheek.

'Why did they have to show that?'

'It makes great television,' said Caroline.

Poppy's phone buzzed with a text from Scarlett.

OMG Poppy, you need to turn on the telly like NOW!! Jodie's on Spotlight!

I know, Poppy tapped back. *I fixed it.*

I'm recording it so I can show Red later.

You're nuts. He's not a human you know.

Yes he is!! Hey wait a minute, what d'you mean you fixed it?

Poppy grinned to herself. *It's a long story,* she tapped back. *Tell you later.*

Ben was now with Biscuit, doing his piece to camera.

'What I don't get is why he started eating Ben's jacket,' said Jodie.

Poppy absentmindedly fingered the packet of Polos in her jeans. She'd slipped one into the reporter's pocket when she'd pretended to dust off the piece of fluff, hoping that Biscuit would sniff it out. What she hadn't bargained for was the potency of Ben's aftershave, which had prompted the gelding to flash his teeth to the world.

'I never knew horses could laugh until Biscuit did that,' said Charlie.

'He's not laughing. It's called the flehmen response. I read it in my pony magazine,' Poppy said. 'When horses smell something they're not sure about they curl back their upper lips and breathe in with their nostrils closed. It must have been Ben's aftershave.'

'I'm not surprised Biscuit didn't like it. It was totally yuck,' Charlie said.

The appaloosa's reaction to the reporter looked even funnier on television. Even the presenter was hooting with laughter by the time Ben handed back to the studio.

'And they've remembered to include the link to the website,' said Caroline. 'I'd say that was a job well done.'

S livers of sunlight stole through a gap in Poppy's curtains and danced on her closed eyelids with dogged determination, willing her to wake up. She yawned, stretched her arms above her head and rotated her bad ankle. Relieved to discover it was well and truly on the mend, she reached for her phone and tried to open the Nethercote website.

Large red letters told her the server application was unavailable. She hit refresh but the page failed to load. Poppy stabbed at the refresh button a couple more times before texting Jodie.

What's happened to the website? It won't load.

Her phone beeped within seconds.

Damn thing's crashed. No idea why.

A smile crept across Poppy's face. She had a sneaking suspicion. And if she was right it could only be good news for Nethercote. She Googled the rescue centre and half a dozen stories appeared. Biscuit had made headlines in the Daily Mail, the Daily Mirror and even a couple of the broadsheets. A clip of Spotlight's news item on YouTube had been viewed just over nine thousand times. Poppy checked the Daily Mail's Facebook page. The story had been shared by almost three hundred people. She typed #Biscuit into Google. Dozens more tweets, posts and Instagram tags popped up. She sighed with satisfaction. Her plan had worked. She was a public relations genius. Biscuit the Laughing Horse had gone viral.

～

POPPY CANTERED Cloud across the field to Ashworthy, humming happily to herself. Caroline had taken a bit of convincing that her ankle was OK to ride but had finally relented when Poppy had promised she'd hack out with Scarlett and Red. Soon the two girls were heading out across the moor.

'The YouTube views went up by almost fifteen hundred in the time it took me to eat my breakfast,' Poppy told Scarlett.

'That's amazing. But no-one will be able to donate if the website's crashed.'

'It's back up and running now. Jodie said donations have already reached twenty eight thousand but they're still pouring in. Channel 5 is sending a reporter over this afternoon and ITN is doing an outside broadcast from Nethercote this evening.'

'Better tell Jodie to wear lots of perfume,' Scarlett said.

'I can't imagine her smothering herself in Christian Dior, can you? She's more like us. Prefers Eau de Horse,' Poppy giggled.

Scarlett ran her hand along Red's neck. The gelding's chestnut coat gleamed.

'Did you give him another bath this morning?'

'Just a quick one to get rid of his stable stains. It's quite exhausting, keeping him spotless,' Scarlett admitted.

Poppy looked down at the grass stains on Cloud's front legs. 'Why don't you chill out? A few stable stains aren't going to kill him.'

'I know.' Scarlett was silent for a while. Then, as they skirted the base of the Riverdale tor, she said, 'Where are we going to go?'

'We need to ride to Witch Cottage. There's something I need to do.'

Scarlett groaned. 'But I hate it there, you know that.'

'It's just a derelict old cottage, Scar. Stones and mortar. There are no ghosts.'

'So why are we going?'

Poppy wondered where to start. She had a feeling that, in her excitement over Red, Scarlett had all but forgotten the existence of the phones

Poppy had discovered hidden under the green tarpaulin in the croft's tiny attic. She may have realised that they were the ones stolen from the warehouse in Plymouth. But Poppy knew for certain that she had no clue they had been destined for the prison, and that Jodie had been pivotal in the whole shady enterprise.

Poppy and Scarlett now had to accidentally stumble across the cache of phones, paste on innocent faces and report their find to the police, as Poppy had promised Jodie she would.

'Poppy,' Scarlett repeated. 'Why do we need to go to Witch Cottage?'

'I'll tell you when we get there.'

The warm summer breeze tickled Cloud's silver mane and he snatched at the bit. His excitement was infectious. Poppy felt giddy with relief. As though it was seven o'clock on Christmas morning. Or the first day of the summer holidays. Everything had worked out just fine. Better than fine. Absolutely gobsmackingly brilliantly. And who could have guessed, a week ago, that Nethercote would be saved by an amazing, courageous, laughing horse?

The wiry moorland grass felt springy and perfect for a canter. Poppy kicked Cloud on. Red caught up with the Connemara in a couple of strides and soon the two ponies, one dappled grey, the other the colour of butterscotch, were galloping neck and neck towards Witch Cottage.

As they raced across the moor, their ponies' tails streaming like banners behind them, Poppy imagined Caitlyn and Jodie making the same journey on a warm summer's morning just like this one, their destination a tumbledown cottage with a teardrop-shaped tarn, a catslide roof and secrets woven into its granite walls.

Poppy glanced at her best friend. Scarlett must have sensed her gaze as she turned her head. Her hazel eyes sparkled.

'It feels like we're off on an adventure!' she cried.

Poppy, who was crouching low over Cloud's neck as he covered the ground in long, easy strides, couldn't help but agree. One adventure was over, but she was pretty sure there was another waiting for them, just beyond the vast Dartmoor horizon. And she couldn't wait.

MISSING ON THE MOOR

1

———————————

P oppy McKeever stared into the bathroom mirror and a ghost girl
stared back. A ghost girl with an ashen face and hollow eyes,
tinged with pink, like an albino rat in an animal testing labora-
tory. She grimaced as she registered the dark purple shadows under her
bloodshot eyes and her straggly, dull brown hair, scraped back into an
untidy ponytail. A wave of nausea rolled over her and she clung onto the
rim of the basin until it passed.

'You look *terrible*,' piped a voice behind her.

Poppy turned to see her brother on the landing.

'I love you, too,' Poppy said, but her sarcasm was lost on eight-year-old
Charlie, who was staring at her in fascination. She ran a flannel under the
cold tap and pressed it to her face.

'You look like a zombie. One of those scary undead people who go
around terrifying everyone. But Halloween was ages ago. Oh, wait, it's not
a getup, it's really you,' he smirked.

Poppy shook the flannel in Charlie's direction but he ducked out of
the way.

'Only joking, sis. You don't really look like a zombie. Shall I get Mum?'

The queasiness returned and Poppy held her hand over her mouth.
Charlie, who despite his daredevil attitude to life was as squeamish as a

sissy, backed down the landing with a look of horror on his face. Soon he was crashing down the stairs three at a time, yelling for Caroline.

Her stepmum ran upstairs with a roll of kitchen towel, an orange bucket and a concerned expression on her face.

'Are you poorly, today of all days? What bad luck.'

Poppy nodded mutely. Caroline felt her forehead and frowned. 'You don't have a temperature. Come and sit down and tell me your symptoms.'

She led Poppy into her room and they perched together on the bed, the bucket on the floor between them.

'I couldn't sleep last night. I was awake for hours just staring at the ceiling. And then when I got up my heart was racing and my hands were shaking. Look!' Poppy held out her hands to show Caroline her trembling fingers. 'Charlie says I look like the walking dead. And I feel really sick. My tummy's turning somersaults. I think I've got gastric flu.'

A look of understanding flitted across Caroline's face. She took Poppy's hands in hers. 'Have a shower and get dressed. You'll be absolutely fine once you get going.'

'Are you mad? I can't go to Claydon Manor like this. I'm on death's door!' Poppy shrieked.

Caroline patted Poppy's thigh and stood up.

'I was exactly the same on the morning of my first show. It's not gastric flu, sweetheart. It's nerves.'

∼

POPPY PULLED on her thickest fleece, filled a bucket with warm water and let herself out of the back door. A blast of cold air hit her in the face and she breathed deeply, as Caroline had instructed her to do whenever she felt anxiety begin to worm its way back into her stomach. She felt a bit sheepish that she'd let her nerves get such a grip and she marched over to the stables, determined not to let them ruin her big day.

Cloud and Chester watched from their stable as she set the bucket down and kissed them both on their peachy-soft muzzles. Cloud blew warm air into her face and Chester banged his leg against the door, impatient for his breakfast.

Poppy gave the donkey's ear an affectionate tug and disappeared into the tack room to mix their feeds. While they ate she filled two haynets and studied the list she'd written the evening before.

'Feed by seven at the latest,' she read, checking her watch. It was five to. She was on schedule. 'Fill haynets. Groom and plait. Pack grooming kit and tack. Don't forget water bucket. Put on travel rug and boots.'

'I don't think they'll fit you,' said an amused voice, making her jump.

'Tory!' cried Poppy.

Her old friend was in the doorway, leaning on her crutches. Poppy hugged her. Tory smelt of lavender and toast, as she always did.

'You said you were meeting us there!'

'I thought you might like some moral support. How are the nerves?'

Poppy gave the glimmer of a smile. 'The nerves are doing just great. It's me I'm worried about.'

'You'll be fine,' said Tory, making herself comfortable on an old wooden bench. 'Which class have you entered?'

'The novice jumping. It's two foot three!' Poppy felt another flutter of anxiety and took two deep breaths.

'You've been jumping courses much bigger than that with Bella, haven't you?' said Tory.

Poppy nodded.

'Well then, it'll be an absolute breeze, won't it Cloud?'

Hearing his name the Connemara poked his handsome head over the stable door and whickered. Poppy put his headcollar on and led him out of the stable. She'd groomed him until he'd shone the evening before but wanted to rinse off the stable stains on his legs and give him one final brush over before she tackled his mane.

'What time's Bill due?' Tory asked.

'Eight o'clock. I expect Scarlett's been up for hours getting Red ready.' Poppy knew her best friend wanted the former rescue pony looking his absolute best for their first show together. 'She texted me this morning in a panic because Jodie's announced she's coming to watch.'

Jodie Morgan owned Nethercote Horse Rescue, Red's old home. Forthright and not one to suffer fools gladly, Jodie had turned her back on her own showjumping dreams to run the horse sanctuary single-handedly. No wonder Scarlett was nervous at the prospect of jumping in front of her.

Poppy divided Cloud's mane into sections and secured them with elastic bands. She tapped each one, counting them in her head. 'Thirteen!' she cried.

'I thought Scarlett was the superstitious one,' said Tory.

'You're right, she is,' Poppy admitted. 'I'm being an idiot. It's only a number.' She began plaiting the sections as neatly as she could.

Charlie appeared with two mugs of tea and sat down next to Tory.

'I've got some news for you both,' Tory announced. 'You know the Christmas Eve Nativity service at St Mary's?'

The two children nodded. A team of volunteers worked for days creating a Bethlehem-like stable at the front of the church and real animals were drafted in to make the Nativity scene as authentic as possible.

'Rusty, the old donkey who's been appearing since before I can remember, has officially retired, so Reverend Kirton has decided to hold open auditions to find a new star for this year's service.'

Charlie leant forward, his eyes shining. 'Donkey auditions?'

'That's right,' said Tory. 'They're being held at the church after the service next Sunday. I thought you might want to take Chester.'

'You bet we would!' said Charlie. 'He'd be perfect. He's always really calm and he loves attention. And he wouldn't go to the toilet just when the Wise Men arrived like Rusty did last year.'

Tory took a sip of her tea. 'Good. I told Annette you'd bring him. She was delighted.'

Charlie screwed his face up. 'Wait a minute. Did you say Reverend Kirton's name was Annette?'

'Yes, why?'

A grin spread across his face. 'Annette Kirton,' he sniggered.

Tory and Poppy looked at him blankly.

Charlie was laughing hard. 'Come on, you two. Don't you get it? Annette *Kirton.*'

'Yes, very funny. But don't go taking the mickey out of her name at the audition. You'll ruin Chester's chances,' said Poppy.

'You're no fun,' he said, heading back indoors humming *Away in a Manger.*

Poppy curled up the final plait and wound the last elastic band around it several times to secure it. After oiling Cloud's hooves she gave him a quick blast of shine spray and stood back to admire her handiwork.

'You've done a beautiful job,' said Tory. 'Seeing him all plaited and gleaming takes me right back.'

Poppy thought she could detect a catch in Tory's voice. Small wonder. It must have been a morning just like this that had ended in disaster when Cloud had fallen at a drop fence during a hunter trial in Widecombe, throwing Tory's granddaughter Caitlyn beneath him.

An unwelcome thought occurred to her. 'This is his first proper competition since Widecombe, isn't it?'

'I suppose it is,' said Tory.

Poppy licked her lips. 'D'you think he'll be OK?'

Tory patted the seat beside her. 'I'm sure he will. He used to love competing. They both did.'

Poppy leant against Tory and gazed at her pony, trying to see him through a stranger's eyes. Cloud's dappled grey coat shone and he was muscled and fit. He looked every inch the superstar pony he was. They'd purposefully picked a novice class even though Cloud could have jumped it in his sleep. And she knew he'd look after her - he always did.

Poppy stretched out her fingers. They weren't trembling any more. And the butterflies had disappeared. Her phone beeped with a text from Scarlett.

'They're on their way,' she said.

Tory heaved herself to her feet. 'All set?' she asked.

Poppy felt a flutter in her stomach. But it was excitement, not nerves. She grinned.

'You bet. We can do this, can't we Cloud? Today Claydon Manor, tomorrow the world!'

2

Poppy felt her nerves resurface as Scarlett's dad steered the Land Rover through Claydon Manor's imposing wrought iron gates.

'I suppose Georgia will be lording it over everyone as usual,' grumbled Scarlett, who was studying the schedule. 'How come they're holding unaffiliated and affiliated classes at the same show, anyway?'

'It's a trial, to see if it works. That's what Bella said.'

'And why's she not holding it at Redhall?'

'Because she's got builders in repairing the roof of the indoor school,' Poppy reminded her.

Scarlett tutted. 'I'm surprised the Cannings are letting the hoi polloi in, what with all the security there usually is around here.'

Poppy glanced at the beautiful grey stone Georgian manor house in the distance and the immaculate paddocks on either side of its sweeping gravelled drive.

'How on earth do they manage to keep their fields looking so perfect?' she wondered. 'Ours are a quagmire. I lost my welly in the mud yesterday.'

'It's because they have the money to throw at it, of course,' said Scarlett darkly.

Poppy sighed inwardly. She loved her best friend to bits, but there was no stopping her once she got started on the unfairness of the fact that Georgia Canning's parents had won the lottery and hers hadn't.

'What time's Sam's class?' Poppy asked her, hoping to change the subject.

'Eleven o'clock.' Scarlett gave Poppy a sidelong look. 'Why, d'you want to stay and watch?'

Poppy felt her face grow hot. She shrugged. 'I guess we might as well, as we're here.'

'Georgia'll be jumping in his class on her ten thousand pound pony, no doubt,' said Scarlett.

'Give it a rest, Scar,' said Poppy, winding down the window and fanning the cool air into her face.

But Scarlett was still bellyaching about the Cannings when they pulled in next to a compact red horsebox on an expanse of hardstanding beside Claydon's huge wooden-slatted indoor arena.

Poppy had only been to one horse show before, and that was at Redhall Manor Equestrian Centre, where she and Scarlett had their weekly lessons with Redhall's indomitable owner, Bella Thompson. She'd only gone to watch and she still remembered how in awe she'd felt of the competitors as they'd stalked around in their bone white jodhpurs and midnight blue show jackets, laughing and chatting to each other like they were members of some exclusive club the rest of the population could only dream of joining. Poppy had stood on the sidelines, drinking it all in and wondering if she'd ever be included.

Now she had her own navy jacket, which was in the back of the Land Rover with her new white jodhpurs. OK, so they were both second-hand - Poppy preferred to call them *pre-loved* - but every time she'd tried them on in front of the mirror with her polished jodhpur boots she'd felt a step closer to joining the select few.

She surreptitiously practised the graceful smile she'd give as she bowed and accepted a red rosette from the judge before kicking Cloud into a canter and flying around the ring. There would be cheers from the spectators and approving nods from her fellow competitors. With a win at her first ever show she might finally stop feeling inferior to Caitlyn.

Scarlett elbowed her in the ribs, bringing her back to earth with a bump.

'Stop daydreaming, Poppy. We need to get the ponies sorted and go and walk the course.'

~

CLAYDON MANOR WAS BUZZING. Everywhere Poppy looked riders were giving their ponies a final brush, tacking up or pinning numbers to their jackets. The place was ringing with noisy chatter and the occasional whinny. Poppy caught a whiff of hot dogs and fried onions and her stomach rumbled loudly.

Cloud stopped halfway down the ramp of the trailer, his head high and his nostrils flared. Poppy gave the lead rope a gentle tug and clicked her tongue. 'Come on baby, it's just a show. There's nothing to worry about.'

He lowered his head and gave her a nudge.

'I know. I should take my own advice,' Poppy said, tying him up next to Red.

Satisfied their ponies were happy munching their haynets the two girls headed for the indoor arena. They were just passing the outdoor school, which was being used as the warm-up area, when they almost walked into Georgia Canning.

Already in her white jodhpurs and show jacket and staring disdainfully at the anaemic-looking hot dog she was holding, Georgia looked them up and down.

'I thought you might be here,' she said, addressing Poppy. 'Are you jumping in the novice class?'

Poppy, who could feel Scarlett bristling beside her, nodded. She smiled, feeling the need to overcompensate for her best friend's obvious hostility. The show would have been cancelled if the Cannings hadn't offered the use of their yard, after all. 'It's my first show. Do you have any insider information?'

'I certainly do. Don't go near the hot dog stand. I swear this thing's raw.' Georgia held the sad-looking sausage and its doughy coffin at arm's length. 'The couple running it were completely clueless. I shall probably go down with food poisoning.'

'She meant insider information about the *course*, not the *food*,' Scarlett said scathingly.

Georgia fixed her cornflower-blue eyes on Scarlett, looked over her shoulder and leaned in conspiratorially. 'Ah, you want insider information on the *course*. Silly me. Well, it's about so high,' she held out the hot dog just below waist height. 'It starts with the first fence and ends with the last and there are a few more in between.'

With that she tossed her hot dog over her shoulder and stalked off towards the stables.

'Flippin' hilarious,' growled Scarlett. 'Who the hell does she think she is?'

Poppy tugged her best friend's arm. 'Ignore her, she was just winding you up. Come on, let's go and walk this course.'

～

POPPY TOOK one look at the brightly painted showjumps in Claydon Manor's imposing indoor arena and froze.

'I can't do it!' she hissed. 'They're enormous!'

Scarlett peered into the arena. 'They're two foot three,' she said patiently. 'You've been jumping three foot three in our lessons. You'll be fine. Just take a deep breath, put on your game face and come and walk the course. You'll see they're not so bad.'

'It's alright for you. You've done loads of shows.'

'I might have, but this is Red's first time, remember. I know it's your first show, but Cloud is an old pro. That makes us even.'

'But -'

'Poppy, you've been working towards this for weeks. You can't wimp out now,' Scarlett said firmly. She looked over Poppy's shoulder and began waving frantically. 'Thank goodness. Bella's here. She might be able to talk some sense into you.'

Poppy turned to see her riding instructor bearing down on them. Bella was in her trademark wax jacket, tweed skirt and wellies, topped off with a headscarf. This one, Poppy noticed, was decorated with eggbutt snaffles.

'How does the course look?' Bella bellowed.

'I wouldn't know. Poppy's refusing to walk it,' said Scarlett.

Bella raised her eyebrows. 'What do you mean?'

Poppy looked beseechingly at her. 'I don't think I can do it.'

'Nonsense! Of course you can. Come on, I'll walk it with you,' she said, steering Poppy into the arena before she had a chance to protest.

Poppy practised her deep breathing as she followed Bella and Scarlett around the course. The first jump was a red and white upright. Poppy had to admit that it looked straightforward enough. A right turn to another upright followed by a small oxer, then right again to a set of planks and a brush and rails.

Jump six was the first double. Poppy followed Scarlett and Bella's lead and counted the strides between the two fences. Eight of her strides. Was that one or two of Cloud's? She racked her brain but for the life of her couldn't remember. It was as if her head had been tipped on one side and every single brain cell had fallen out of her ear.

Fortunately Scarlett saved her. 'That's good. It's a perfect single stride for our boys,' she said.

They turned left to a wall followed by an upright. Two girls with ringing public school voices and an air of self-assurance Poppy could only dream of breezed past them to jump nine, a parallel bar painted in sky blue and primrose yellow. They were exactly the kind of girls Poppy had felt so in awe of at the Redhall show. Girls who had been given their first ponies before they were two and had probably hunted before they started at their expensive prep schools. She knew she shouldn't feel inferior. She just couldn't help herself.

Distracted by their casual confidence, she stopped looking where she was going and cannoned into the wing of the blue and yellow jump, knocking it flying.

'Sorry sorry sorry,' she gabbled as an irritable-looking show steward bustled over and began replacing the fallen poles. Poppy blushed at her ineptitude. But if she was worried what the two girls might think she needn't have bothered - they were so deep in conversation they didn't even look in her direction.

'Come on, clumsy,' said Scarlett, linking arms with her and leading her to the next jump, a frighteningly solid-looking gate. Poppy was about to give it a rattle in its cups but stopped herself just in time. Knowing her luck she'd send it flying, too.

'You need to change reins for the last three,' said Bella, marching over to a blue and white upright that was followed by the second double of the course. Poppy counted her strides. 'Eight for me, one for Cloud,' she muttered.

'Don't forget to wait for the starting bell otherwise you'll be eliminated,' Bella continued. 'And remember to go through the finish line. So, have you any questions?'

'Can I go home now, please?' said Poppy, worried she'd already forgotten the course.

Bella tutted. 'There's no need to be nervous. Angela has done a good job. It's a lovely inviting course with nice easy turns. Just remember not to rush the planks and keep nice and balanced for the two combinations. Why don't you girls go and find your ponies? I'll ask Sam to put up a couple of practice jumps for you if you like.'

The ritual of tacking up, putting on her hat, tightening Cloud's girth and running the stirrups down helped damp down Poppy's anxiety and she felt even better once she was in the saddle. Cloud felt solid and familiar. She was also relieved that he seemed to be taking everything in his stride, whereas Red, normally so laid-back, was fizzing like a bath bomb and had already worked himself into a sweat. Scarlett was struggling to keep the rangy chestnut calm as they walked over to the outdoor school.

'There's Sam,' Poppy said, spotting Bella's grandson's blond head by the entrance. He was watching one of the posh girls cantering her dark bay mare around the school. Poppy hadn't seen Sam for a couple of months. She was taken aback to see that he seemed to have grown half a foot in that time. His face was different, too. More angular, less boyish. But when he saw them he grinned like a loon and loped over. Poppy found herself smiling back, despite her somersaulting stomach.

'Hey, you two,' he said. 'Gran's sent me over to sort you out. We'll start with some circles in trot and canter, shall we?'

As Poppy asked Cloud for a trot, she heard Scarlett muttering, 'What's your name, Bella Thompson?' and then cursing loudly as Red shied at the red wing of one of the practice fences.

With half a dozen other riders all warming up in the same school Poppy knew she needed to blank everyone else out. They circled on both reins until Cloud was listening to her aids and working in a nice outline. Poppy sat deeply in the saddle for a couple of strides and squeezed him into a canter.

'I'll put up a cross-pole,' called Sam. Poppy checked Cloud and he popped over the little jump with ease. Red crabbed up to the fence and, at the last minute, sprang forwards and leapt over it with feet to spare. The chestnut gelding gave a joyful buck. Scarlett, to her credit, hardly moved in the saddle.

By the time they'd both jumped a small upright on each leg Bella had reappeared.

'I've just been over to the collecting ring. The class is about to start. Scarlett, you're fifth to jump and Poppy, you're seventh. Walk them on a long rein for five minutes to give them a breather and then you'd better make your way over.'

Sam ran his hand down Cloud's neck and the Connemara nibbled the pockets of his jeans. 'Still nervous?' he asked Poppy.

'Utterly terrified,' she admitted.

He brushed a fleck of mud from her jodhpurs. 'You've really no need to be, Poppy. You're a great rider. We all think so. It's a shame you're the only one who can't see it.'

3

B uoyed by Sam's words, Poppy headed for the collecting ring. *You're a great rider,* he'd said. Did he mean it, or was he just being kind, trying to boost her confidence before she went into the ring? True, he'd let her ride Star, his prizewinning jumping pony, on more than one occasion. And he'd made it clear he didn't let just anyone ride her. He'd once described Poppy as a quiet rider. She hadn't known if that was good or bad. Surely quiet riders were feeble and ineffectual? But Bella had told her it was a compliment.

Cloud broke into a jog and Poppy tightened her reins. The last thing she needed was to fall off in front of everyone because she wasn't concentrating. She checked the Connemara, who snatched at the bit, impatient to jump.

'There you are,' said Caroline, appearing from behind a horse trailer. 'I've been looking for you everywhere. I've left Charlie and Tory in the spectators' gallery. Your class has just started.' She looked around. 'Where's Scarlett?'

'Gone to get her gloves. She won't be a minute.'

Caroline regarded her, her hands on her hips. 'You and Cloud look amazing. Like you've been competing together all your lives.'

Poppy gave her stepmum a grateful smile. She always knew exactly the right thing to say.

'Break a leg,' Caroline added. Then she clutched her head and grimaced. 'What a crazy thing to say. *Don't* break a leg. In fact, don't break anything. Go out there and jump your hearts out, both of you.'

Poppy was giggling despite her nerves. 'OK boss, we will.'

~

THERE WERE ELEVEN in the novice class, which was for ponies up to 148cm, or 14.2hh in old money, as Tory was fond of saying.

The first pair to jump, a skinny girl with a long, blonde plait and an excitable dun pony, whizzed around the course but in their haste knocked down both the planks and the gate.

'That's the trouble when you let your pony flatten,' said Bella in a voice loud enough to be heard in Tavistock. A woman clasping a sweat rug gave her a filthy look and Poppy could see Sam cringing. Bella had many attributes. Diplomacy was not one of them.

The second rider was a girl in Poppy and Scarlett's year at school. Her skewbald gelding looked balanced and focused as they trotted calmly into the ring.

'Good luck,' Scarlett called.

'I don't think she's going to need it,' said Poppy. And she was right. The skewbald jumped a faultless clear round.

'That's the one to beat,' bellowed Bella.

Two more riders had four faults apiece and then it was Scarlett's turn to jump. Poppy gave her the thumbs up and Bella gave Red such a hearty pat on the rump that he shot into the ring like a stone in one of Charlie's homemade catapults.

'I'm not going to put any pressure on him. I want him to enjoy today,' Scarlett had told Poppy as they'd tacked up. Poppy noticed how her best friend let the chestnut gelding have a good look at the fillers as she trotted him around the ring, waiting for the starting bell to sound.

When it did Scarlett squeezed Red into a canter and turned him towards the first fence. His chestnut ears were pricked as he leapt over it. He took off on the wrong leg but it didn't faze Scarlett, who slowed him to a trot and then asked him to canter on the right leg. Red popped over the second and third fences like an old pro but hesitated at the planks, which were painted in a garish green and red.

'Come on, kiddo,' said Scarlett and he made an enormous cat-leap over the jump to the amusement of the spectators. Scarlett checked him and he jumped the brush and rails neatly, his white socks tucked into his chest.

Poppy realised she was holding her breath as Red cantered towards the double. She could see he was getting strong. Scarlett did her best to bring him back on the bit but he misjudged his stride and knocked down the first part of the double.

'That's a shame. They were doing so well,' said a familiar voice. Jodie Morgan had slipped into the collecting ring to watch Red's round.

'How's Biscuit?' Poppy asked, her eyes still on Scarlett and Red as they popped over the wall. Biscuit was an adorable appaloosa pony who'd helped save Jodie's horse rescue centre from bankruptcy that summer when he was filmed by the local television station and his story went viral.

'The Mail on Sunday is sending Liz Jones over next week to write a feature on him. "A day in the life of Nethercote's famous laughing horse",' said Jodie, her gloved hands sketching apostrophes in the air.

'Don't knock it. All publicity is good publicity,' Poppy reminded her. 'Think of your winter food bill.'

They groaned as Red knocked down the second part of the final double. But Scarlett was beaming as she cantered out of the ring.

'Eight faults in his first ever class! He's such a clever boy,' she said. Even Jodie, who rarely showed her feelings, was smiling.

'Number forty-seven!' shouted the collecting ring steward and the posh girl on the dark bay gelding trotted past them into the ring. Poppy walked Cloud around in circles, trying to steady her racing pulse.

'And that's four faults for Fiona Cavanagh-Smythe,' announced the Tannoy what seemed like seconds later. 'And next to jump we have number thirty-two, Poppy McKeever riding Cloud Nine!'

Poppy looked around her in horror. After all the hard work, the endless jumping lessons, the books on riding techniques she'd pored over and the hours spent getting ready, and her worst nightmare had come true.

She looked at Scarlett in horror.

'I've forgotten the course!'

4

S carlett rode Red alongside Cloud and gave Poppy's arm a gentle
squeeze.

'No, you haven't. Picture us walking it together. It'll come back
to you once you start, I promise. And forget all about the people watching. It's just you and Cloud out there, OK? You can do it, Poppy.'

Poppy rammed her hat down low on her forehead and took a deep
breath. Scarlett was right. She could do this. She kicked Cloud into a
canter, nearly knocking the collecting ring steward flying. The lights in
the arena seemed bright after the murky December weather outside and
it took a moment for Poppy's eyes to adjust. She slowed Cloud to a trot
and dipped her head at the judge, as she'd seen the other riders do. Her
eyes scoured the arena for the first jump, the red and white upright. But
which jump was next? Poppy forced herself to concentrate. Scarlett had
held out her right arm as she'd measured the related distance to the green
and white upright. Of course. And then the spread and a right turn to the
planks. She could remember after all!

Poppy sat tall in the saddle and fixed her eyes on the first fence, as
Bella had taught her to do. The starting bell sounded and she asked Cloud
for a canter. His ears pricked, he met the upright perfectly. He landed
neatly and Poppy turned him towards the green and white upright and
the spread.

'Steady,' Poppy murmured as they approached the planks. But she needn't have worried. Cloud flew over with inches to spare. Mid-air, Poppy remembered they were changing direction and squeezed her left rein. The Connemara landed on the left leg and popped over the brush and rails as if it was a fallen log on the moor.

Four strides to the double, which Cloud cleared easily, and then a left turn to the wall. Poppy folded forwards, allowing her hands to go with him as he stretched over the jump.

For a second, as they landed, Poppy couldn't remember which jump was next, the white upright with the red fillers or the blue and white upright three strides before the double. Just in time she remembered and pointed Cloud at the white jump. Three long strides or four short ones to the blue and yellow parallel bar. Poppy opted for three and pushed Cloud on. He took off early and Poppy held her breath as his back legs rattled the pole in the cups. But it was their lucky day. The pole stayed where it was.

Jump ten was the solid-looking gate. Poppy pretended it was the small wattle gate she'd set up in Cloud and Chester's field as part of her home-made cross country course. Cloud jumped it easily. And then another left turn to the final three jumps, set up like a line of gridwork. Poppy remembered not to look down as Cloud jumped the first. Once he'd landed she sat down in the saddle and used her seat to push him forwards and he soared over the double.

Poppy shook her head in amazement as they cantered through the finish line. A clear round at their first show together! Her heart bursting with pride, she jumped off Cloud the minute they left the ring and threw her arms around him. Her legs felt as wobbly as pipe cleaners as the adrenalin flooded out of her system and she clung to her pony for support as first Bella and then Caroline, Scarlett, Sam, Tory, Charlie and Jodie all came up and clapped her on the shoulder and told her what a brilliant round it had been.

Poppy could have stayed where she was for several days, basking in all the attention, but the harassed-looking collecting ring steward marched over and asked them to move out of the way. Poppy ran up her stirrups and loosened Cloud's girth.

'I'll walk him around for you so you can go with Gran to look at the jump-off course,' said Sam, appearing by her side.

Poppy stared at him, wide-eyed. In her excitement she'd clean forgotten she would be jumping again, this time against the clock. She gave Cloud one last hug and watched Sam lead him away before following Bella and Scarlett to the spectators' gallery.

'There are only four clear rounds,' said Bella, as they leant on the rails and watched the stewards raise some fences and dismantle others. 'You jump the first then gallop to the third. The fourth and fifth are as before then it's a tight turn to the ninth.'

'Which one's that?' said Poppy, who was finding it hard to follow where Bella was pointing.

'The blue and yellow parallel bar that you demolished earlier,' said Scarlett helpfully.

'You can really make up some time with a tight turn to the gate, then it's a gallop down to the last two jumps. But don't let him flatten, whatever you do,' said Bella.

Poppy imagined she was riding the course. Ten fences. Nine if you were being pedantic. They all looked enormous.

'They've put them up at least four holes,' she groaned.

'They just look big because you're at ground level. Once you're in the saddle they'll look positively tiny,' said Scarlett.

Poppy was unconvinced.

'You're second to jump,' Bella announced. 'You'd better go and find your pony.'

≈

ONCE AGAIN POPPY waited in the collecting ring, trying to contain her nerves. The girl on the skewbald cantered out to a round of applause.

'And a second clear round from Lucy White and Patchwork in a time of fifty-nine seconds,' announced the Tannoy.

'Good luck!' called Lucy as she passed.

Poppy smiled her thanks and clicked her tongue. Cloud trotted merrily into the ring. He was so obviously enjoying himself that Poppy felt her nerves melt away.

The bell went and they cantered towards the first jump. Safely over it, Cloud lengthened his stride to the third. Poppy checked him so he was back on his hocks in time to jump the planks. Four strides to the brush and rails and then the Connemara turned on a sixpence to jump the blue and yellow parallel bar. Poppy sat back in the saddle and pulled him sharply to the left. Too late she realised she'd set him an impossible task. The angle they were approaching the gate was too tight. She half expected him to run out. But Cloud had the heart of a lion and he took off so close to the wing that Poppy clipped it with her boot.

It was enough to send the gate crashing to the ground. Poppy resisted the urge to look back and instead focused on maintaining her contact and looking for the next jump. They met the blue and white upright perfectly and flew over the double.

'Four faults for Poppy McKeever and Cloud Nine in an impressive time of fifty-two seconds,' crackled the Tannoy. Euphoria swept through Poppy as they cantered out of the ring.

Sam and Scarlett were waiting for her in the collecting ring.

'Bad luck,' commiserated Scarlett.

'Never mind,' said Sam, feeling in his pocket for a handful of pony nuts.

'Never mind?' said Poppy, her face flushed. 'That was brilliant! The gate was totally my fault but Cloud jumped like an angel. We made the jump-off. Who cares if we had four faults. I feel like a proper rider at last.'

Realising her voice had gone all squeaky, she slithered off Cloud and buried her face in his neck, drinking in the heady smell of sweaty horse. Scarlett watched in astonishment as she took off her hat and ran up her stirrups.

'What on earth are you doing?'

'Taking Cloud back to the trailer, what else?' said Poppy.

'You twit! You're going to come at least fourth. And by the sound of that,' - they listened to the thud of crashing poles echoing around the indoor arena - 'probably third. Get back on and go and get your first rosette.'

'Alright, bossy knickers,' countered Poppy. But a big grin had spread across her face and she rammed on her hat and jumped back into the saddle without another word.

Bella appeared beside them.

'There were two clear rounds in the end, and someone else had four faults too. But yours was the fastest time by seven seconds. Well done, Poppy. You came third.'

5

P oppy knew she would remember cantering around the indoor arena for her first ever lap of honour for the rest of her life. Even if she lived to one hundred and two. In fact she would bore the other residents at her old people's home silly with stories of the day she came home with a rosette from her first ever show.

Once she was satisfied that Cloud was settled, Poppy went in search of the others. She found them in the spectators' gallery, watching the stewards build the course for the open jumping. Angela Snell, Georgia's trainer and the Claydon livery yard manager, stood in the middle of the arena, consulting a clipboard and barking instructions.

'You think I'm bossy,' said Scarlett, pointing her thumb at Angela. The woman's hair was pulled back in a severe bun and the tight set of her shoulders and her thin-lipped expression spoke of imperious impatience.

'Crikey, Sam. I thought our jumps were big, but these are enormous,' said Poppy, as the course took shape.

But Sam wasn't looking. Instead he was staring at a man with salt and pepper hair and a matching handlebar moustache who was sitting four rows behind them.

Poppy nudged him. 'Who's that?'

'Peter Frampton,' he whispered. His face had frozen. Whether it was through fear or awe, Poppy couldn't be sure.

'Who's Peter Frampton?' she whispered back.

'Only the guy who runs the British Showjumping Pony European Championships squad.' The words fell over themselves in a jumble. Sam rocked back on his seat and stared at the ceiling. 'What's he doing here?'

'Come to watch you and Georgia, I expect,' said Jodie. 'I heard on the grapevine that one of his team had moved to seniors, so he must have a space to fill.'

'Wait, that was the team you were picked for, wasn't it?' Poppy asked Jodie. 'You were going to represent Britain at the championships in Sweden.'

Jodie scowled. 'Until my dad decided to fiddle the books at work and the police seized Nero as proceeds of crime. He was my jumping pony,' she explained to Sam. 'At least you won't have to worry about that when you get picked.'

'*If* I get picked.' Sam risked another glance over his shoulder. Peter Frampton was making notes in a small, leather-bound notebook. 'Georgia's pony Barley has been jumping out of his skin all winter. They've beaten us at the last two indoor shows.'

Scarlett gave a derisive snort.

Poppy punched Sam lightly on the shoulder and stood up. 'And people tell me I'm a pessimist. Come on, we'll keep you company while you walk the course.'

~

SAM NEEDN'T HAVE WORRIED. He and Star pulled off a flawless round, flying over the enormous fences as if they were cavalettis in a pony paddock. They were the epitome of grace and style, thought Poppy, as the black Connemara mare cantered out of the ring to rapturous applause.

'When's Georgia due to jump?' Jodie asked.

'Last, I believe,' said Bella, who, like the others, was on the edge of her plastic seat.

'Typical. I bet she bribed the show organisers,' said Scarlett, loudly enough for Peter Frampton's head to jerk up.

'Scarlett!' said Poppy, shocked. 'That's not fair.'

Scarlett's hazel eyes blazed dangerously. 'Why are you sticking up for the moody madam all of a sudden?'

'You're virtually accusing her of cheating without one iota of evidence. You can't do that.'

'Why are you so bothered? She's a spoilt little rich girl who'll do anything to win.'

Keen not to ruin her perfect day with an argument with her best friend, Poppy decided to humour her. 'I'm not bothered at all,' she shrugged.

They sat and watched half a dozen more rounds in silence. Two more riders jumped clear, but neither showed Sam's flair. Charlie announced he was bored and talked Caroline into giving him money for a hot dog. Tory showed Poppy and Scarlett her sleek new mobile.

'It's a clever phone,' the old woman whispered proudly. 'My nephew gave it to me in case of emergencies.'

'Clever phone?' said Scarlett, frowning.

'It's ingenious. It has the internet and emails and everything.'

'You mean smart phone,' giggled Poppy.

'Yes, that's what I said. I just wish I could remember how to switch the damn thing on.'

POPPY WAS ATTEMPTING to show Tory how to send a text when the Tannoy echoed around the cavernous arena, 'And the last to jump is number one, Georgia Canning on her pony Pearl Barley.'

There was a faint ripple of applause and Poppy stole a look behind her. Peter Frampton was drumming his fingers on his thigh, an unreadable expression on his face.

'Trust her to be number one,' Scarlett muttered.

Poppy felt her patience snap. 'For God's sake, Scarlett, will you give it a rest? You're doing my head in. Can we please just watch the jumping?'

Scarlett's eyebrows shot upwards. 'Alright, keep your hair on. I was just saying.'

'Well, don't.'

'Where is she, anyway?'

'How would I know?' Poppy craned her neck towards the entrance, but there was no sign of Georgia or her palomino gelding. People in the spectators' gallery were beginning to fidget.

'Calling number one, Georgia Canning on Pearl Barley,' blared the Tannoy. 'This is your final call.'

'They'll be eliminated at this rate,' remarked Bella with satisfaction. They watched the collecting ring steward scuttle over to the judge and whisper urgently into his ear. The judge nodded, wrote something on his clipboard and beckoned over the other stewards who began building the jump-off course.

'I bet she heard the European squad man's here and chickened out,' said Scarlett.

'Maybe,' said Poppy. But she didn't believe it. Georgia Canning was the most competitive rider she had ever met. Her blatant desire to win radiated off her in waves. She wouldn't be put off by the fact that Peter Frampton was here. Far from it. She'd be doing everything in her power to impress him.

So where was she?

$$\sim$$

POPPY AND SCARLETT bumped into Charlie as they made their way back to the trailer. He was holding Freddie's lead in one hand and a triple cone ice cream in the other.

'I thought you were getting a hot dog,' said Poppy.

'The stall had gone.' Charlie took a huge mouthful of ice cream and juddered. 'Urgh. Brain freeze. How did Sam do?'

Poppy smiled. 'He walked it.'

'Someone needs to tell him he's never going to win like that.'

'You are an idiot sometimes. It means he won. Really easily. Georgia Canning was a no show.'

Charlie took another slurp of his ice cream. 'Perhaps she got food poisoning from her dodgy hot dog after all.'

6

Poppy woke on the morning of the donkey auditions to a heavy hoar frost. Feathery wisps of ice like spun candyfloss clung to fences and branches and the grass was crunchy underfoot. She watched her breath unfurl like smoke from a chimney as she crossed the yard to the stables.

Charlie was already there, dressed in his pyjamas, wellies and Poppy's old parka. He had a bulging carrier bag beside him.

'What are you doing out here?' said Poppy suspiciously.

'Making Chester nice and festive for the auditions,' said Charlie, as though it was blindingly obvious.

Poppy let herself into the stable. Charlie pulled a length of silver tinsel from the bag. 'I thought this'd look nice in his mane. And I was going to try to hang a bauble from the top of his tail.'

'You're joking, right? He's not a flippin' Christmas tree,' said Poppy, rubbing the old donkey's ear.

Charlie's face fell. 'I know. I just wanted to make him stand out.'

Poppy knew how excited he was about the auditions. He had talked about little else all week.

'I don't think they had tinsel in those days, Charlie. But I tell you what, we can thread some of the tinsel around his headcollar and lead rope. How would that be?'

'That would be good,' said her brother. He eyed her hopefully. 'And maybe a couple of paperchains around his neck?'

Poppy rolled her eyes. 'Don't push your luck.'

~

THE AUDITIONS WERE BEING HELD in St Mary's Church after the Sunday morning service. Terrified about being late, Charlie had insisted they left Riverdale in plenty of time. As a result, the congregation was still singing a hymn as they rounded the lane to the tiny 12th century church.

Charlie let Chester graze on the verge opposite the entrance while they waited for the service to finish. He looked as pale as Poppy had on the morning of the show.

'I wonder what the competition will be like,' he said, hopping from one foot to the other.

'I can't think of any other donkeys in Waterby,' said Poppy.

'But the village website said 'Waterby *and surrounding villages*',' he fretted. 'There might be hundreds in the surrounding villages for all we know.'

'I don't suppose there are,' soothed Caroline.

'Look, here comes one,' said Poppy, pointing up the lane that led to the village shop.

Caroline and Charlie followed her gaze.

'That's not a donkey, it's a Shetland pony!' said Charlie, outraged.

'Maybe he's a method actor,' Poppy giggled. Charlie shot her a filthy look.

'Sorry Charlie. Oh look, here comes another one.'

They watched, speechless, as what was clearly two people in a slightly moth-eaten pantomime donkey suit lurched up the lane, fore and hind legs completely out of synch.

'He looks as though he's been at the Christmas sherry,' said Caroline finally. Poppy snorted loudly, causing the pantomime donkey to stand stock still and waggle his head at her.

Even Charlie was laughing when the donkey walked up to Caroline and offered her a hoof to shake.

Poppy was stroking the pantomime donkey's neck when she heard a muffled but familiar voice from inside the costume.

'My back's killing me, Scott. I need to stand up or I'll never walk upright again.'

'Sam, is that you in there?'

The donkey broke in two to reveal Sam in the hind legs and Bella's godson Scott at the front.

Sam grimaced as he stretched his back. 'Meet Delilah. As you can imagine, she was Scott's idea. Gran had the costume up in the attic. I think the last time she had an outing was before the war.'

'Hi Poppy, how's things?' said Scott, running his hands through his hair. 'And you must be Caroline and Charlie,' he said, flashing them a disarming smile.

Charlie seemed as immune to Scott's charms as Poppy had always been.

'You're here under false pretences. That's not a real donkey,' he said, pointing to Delilah's head, which was hanging lifelessly from the crook of Scott's arm.

'The poster didn't actually specify that the donkeys had to be real,' Scott pointed out.

Charlie rose to his full height. 'But that's not fair on the real donkeys!'

Sam stepped forward. 'It's OK, Charlie. We just came 'cos Scott wanted to see if we could make the front page of the Herald. We're not bothered about being in the actual Nativity, are we, Scott?' He elbowed Bella's godson in the ribs.

'God, no. I've got a hot date that night. And sorry to disappoint you, Samantha, it's not with you.'

Poppy caught Sam's eye and they exchanged a wry smile. Scott hadn't changed, it seemed.

The heavily-studded church doors swung open with a loud creak and the congregation began filing out. The last few were followed by a slim, bright-eyed woman in black vestments and a dog collar. She saw the small group waiting by the entrance and scuttled over, her hands outstretched.

'Welcome to our donkey auditions! Marvellous! I'm so pleased you could make it! As you know, our incumbent, Rusty, has retired so we are looking for someone with star quality to step into his shoes, or should I say hooves!'

Poppy couldn't help warming to Reverend Annette Kirton. She was one of those endlessly enthusiastic people whose speech was littered with exclamation marks.

'So, who do we have here? My goodness! Three lovely auditionees!' she trilled.

'I'm not sure that's actually a word,' said Poppy. But Reverend Kirton didn't hear. She was too busy shepherding Chester, the Shetland and Delilah into the church.

A car drew up outside and two men let themselves out. One was tall and stooped, the other short and stout. Poppy recognised them immediately as Henry Blossom and Sniffer Smith, the photographer and reporter from the Tavistock Herald.

Sniffer did a double take when he saw the three McKeevers. 'Small world, eh?' he said, whipping a pen from behind his ear and jotting something down in his battered notebook. Poppy had a horrible feeling it was something to do with the time she and Charlie had seen the big cat on the moor the first summer they'd moved to Riverdale. The wily old hack never missed an opportunity to embellish a story if there was a chance of flogging it to the nationals.

Henry strode over and shook their hands. 'Good to see you again. And how's that wrist of yours?' he asked Caroline.

'As good as new,' she smiled. Sniffer may have been a scheming chancer, but Henry was a genuinely nice man.

Reverend Kirton clapped her hands. 'We're all here. Wonderful! We need to know that our four-legged star is happy walking down the aisle of a packed church to the stable in front of the altar. So, if everyone not leading an auditionee can pretend to be in the congregation we'll make a start!'

'Who's going to lead us?' said a muffled voice from inside Delilah.

Poppy sighed. 'I suppose I can.' Her heart sank as Henry rattled off a couple of pictures of her holding the thin leather strap. 'You two owe me,' she hissed into the pantomime donkey's threadbare ear.

The Shetland went first. Despite his owner's best efforts he tried to nibble the flower arrangements on the end of each pew and refused point blank to walk up the two steps to the area in front of the altar.

'Well done!' said Reverend Kirton. 'Chester next, I think.'

Charlie scratched the old donkey's poll and led him quietly and without incident up the aisle. Chester stood serenely in front of the altar as if he had been attending church every Sunday all his life.

'Bravo!' cried the vicar. 'And finally, our pantomime dame, the delightful Delilah!'

Poppy gave the leather strap a vicious tug, ignoring the indignant cry from inside the costume. Delilah sashayed up the aisle as if she was on the catwalk of a Milan fashion show and when she reached the altar danced a little jig before collapsing on the stone floor in a tangle of legs.

The tiny congregation was laughing so hard at Delilah's antics that no-one heard the click of a latch. Poppy was the first to see a grey-haired man in a flat cap and a shabby Barbour jacket shove open the doors of the church. He was holding a frayed black lead rope, on the end of which was a thin grey donkey with the saddest eyes Poppy had ever seen.

The man swore loudly as the donkey registered Delilah, who was now taking a bow, and froze. He yanked the lead rope. 'Gerrup you stupid mule!' he growled, flicking the end of the rope at the donkey's bony rump. The donkey skittered forwards. The congregation fell silent.

The vicar fixed a smile to her face. 'A fourth auditionee! What a wonderful surprise!' She clapped her hands again. The donkey started shaking. 'And who have we here?'

The man shrugged. 'She don't have a name. I only picked 'er up from the market yesterday.'

'Oh!' said Reverend Kirton, for once lost for words.

Poppy stepped forward and held out her hand to the donkey, who was still quivering by the man's side.

'Female donkeys are called jennys. You could call her that,' she said softly, offering her a Polo. The donkey stretched out her neck to sniff the mint, but before she could take it the man yanked her head back.

'Hey, why did you do that?' Poppy cried. Caroline slid out of the pew and stood beside her.

'She needs to be taught some manners,' the man growled, winding the lead rope around his hand and pulling the donkey towards him.

Ignoring his filthy look, Poppy bent down and stroked the donkey's neck. She could feel how thin she was under her thick winter coat. One of her eyes was red and inflamed. It looked as though she was weeping. Poppy felt tears prick her own eyes.

Reverend Kirton finally found her voice and began telling the man what she wanted him to do. While his attention was focused on the vicar Poppy sneaked Jenny the Polo. The donkey snuffled it from her hand so gently that Poppy felt her heart break.

As she watched Jenny being dragged towards the altar she realised there was something familiar about the man's puffed out chest and wheezy voice. A memory of a grey-haired man tugged at her subconscious. A man wearing corduroy trousers and a brown hacking jacket as he talked to Hope Taylor's mum, Shelley, at the Waterby dog show.

Poppy shivered. Jenny's new owner was the man who had bought Cloud from Tory after Caitlyn was killed. The same man who had beaten the Connemara half to death after he had been rounded up in the drift. A man whose stinginess was legendary and whose cruelty had given Poppy nightmares.

Jenny's new owner was George Blackstone.

7

Poppy wrapped her coat tightly around her and huddled into the hedge as she waited for the school bus to trundle into view. The sky was granite grey and a bitterly cold wind was systematically stripping the trees of their few remaining leaves, whipping them into eddies at her feet.

She checked the time on her phone. Ten to eight. The bus was due any minute and Scarlett was nowhere to be seen. She'd miss it at this rate. As if on cue, Poppy heard the unmistakable hiss of air breaks as the bus rounded the corner.

'No Scarlett today?' asked the bus driver, a cheery woman called Val who was also secretary of the local Women's Institute.

Poppy shook her head. 'I don't think she's sick. She would have told me otherwise.'

'We'll give her a couple of minutes,' Val said, letting the engine idle.

Poppy smiled gratefully and found a seat. The window was clouded with condensation and she wiped the glass with her sleeve so she could watch for her best friend. She couldn't imagine buses in Twickenham waiting for anyone. The slower pace of life was one of the things she loved about Devon.

'Here she is,' said Val, throwing the gearstick into first.

Scarlett jumped onto the bus, her face pink with exertion. 'Thanks for waiting, Val,' she panted. Spying Poppy, she slid into the seat beside her.

'You were cutting it a bit fine,' said Poppy.

'I've run all the way. I wanted to show you this,' Scarlett said, fishing about in her school bag. 'It's today's Herald. You're famous!'

Poppy grabbed the paper and stared at the front page photo. There she was, holding Delilah the pantomime donkey's lead rope. Standing either side of them were Chester, Jenny and the Shetland.

'Sniffer Smith made us all line up for a photo at the end of the audition,' she said gloomily. 'Everyone's going to be taking the mickey at school.'

'Never mind that! You know who that is, don't you?' said Scarlett, her finger jabbing the newspaper.

'The one and only George Blackstone. I remembered seeing him talking to Shelley Taylor at the dog show. Speaking of which, I had an email from Hope this morning. She's got a two-day-a-week share in a pony at a barn near her dad's. She's so excited.'

Poppy scrolled down her phone to find the pictures of the bay gelding Hope had sent her and showed them to Scarlett.

'I also had a text from Sam.'

'Did you now?' said Scarlett, raising her eyebrows.

Poppy elbowed her best friend. 'Stop stirring. He was just letting me know he has been picked as first reserve for the Pony European Championships squad. There are six in the squad so he'll only get to travel to Denmark if one of them is dropped.'

'That's a shame.'

'He doesn't seem to mind. I think he's just pleased to make it onto the team. And there's always next year.'

'Georgia missed out. I wonder if she's recovered from her food poisoning,' said Scarlett.

'I have no idea,' said Poppy mildly. 'All I know is that I'm going to have to ride over to Claydon on Saturday to get my new gloves. I must have left them in the arena when we were watching Sam jump.'

Scarlett, who had got out a pen and was drawing horns and a beard on the photo of George Blackstone, tutted.

'Well, don't think I'm coming with you. I have absolutely no desire to go there, thank you very much. You're on your own.'

~

BY SATURDAY the bitter wind had blown itself out and the morning was mild and murky. The kind of damp, dank day that made your hair frizz like wire wool.

Poppy pulled on her best jodhpurs and gave her boots a quick polish before heading out to the stables. She'd turned Chester out after breakfast and the old donkey was grazing in the far corner of the field. Cloud, still in his stable, whinnied impatiently as she slammed the back door shut.

'I know. But you'd only have rolled in the muddiest mud you could find and I want you looking smart for our trip to Claydon,' Poppy said, offering him a carrot.

She undid his rug and set to work, humming to herself as she groomed him from head to foot. Jodie had brought her clippers to Ashworthy the previous month and given both Cloud and Red trace clips. Charlie called them their go faster stripes.

Poppy brushed the knots from Cloud's tail and gave his mane a quick pull. She scooted inside for a bucket of warm water and sponged his eyes and nostrils. Finally, she picked out his feet and oiled his hooves.

She wasn't really sure why she was making such an effort. She knew that having a grey pony meant it was pointless getting precious about yellow feathers or the odd stable stain. Sometimes Cloud was so filthy he could easily be mistaken for a skewbald. She was used to being covered in grey hairs and laughed hollowly when Scarlett complained about keeping Red's four white socks clean. She had long ago come to terms with the fact that she was never likely to win a best turned out class. But Georgia and her pony were always so immaculate they could have stepped out of the pages of a riding magazine, and they left Poppy feeling inadequate.

Not today, she thought with satisfaction as she tacked Cloud up and led him out of the stable. Today he looked a million dollars.

They set off through the gate that led to the moor. Cloud felt fresh and full of energy and once they'd left Riverdale behind she gave him his head, relishing the cold air on her cheeks as they galloped past black-faced sheep, huddles of Dartmoor ponies and one lone backpack-clad rambler, trudging along a faraway ridge. By Poppy's reckoning Claydon Manor was almost an hour's ride away so they should make it there and back before lunch.

Her feet were numb with cold by the time they reached the imposing electronic gates at the end of Claydon Manor's long drive. They had been open the day of the show but today they were firmly closed. A CCTV camera sat atop one of the stone gate posts, staring at her with its unblinking eye. Poppy peered up at it, wondering who was watching her on the other end. Set into the stone post at shoulder height was a cast iron letterbox, painted black. A triangle of white caught her eye. It was the corner of an envelope, which was wedged in the flap like a minnow trapped in the jaws of a pike.

Poppy brought Cloud alongside the letterbox, held her reins in her left hand and gave the envelope a tug. The corner tore off in her hand.

'Whoops,' she said under her breath. She slipped her hand inside the letterbox and pulled the rest of it out. Grubby and creased, it was one of those envelopes with a see-through window. Expecting the usual type-written address Poppy was surprised to see a lock of black hair. Scrawled above the window in almost undecipherable handwriting was one word. *Canning.*

'Bit weird,' she said, shoving the envelope in her pocket. Cloud shifted his weight onto his other foot and Poppy looked around for the keypad on a metal post she and Scarlett had seen on their first visit to Claydon Manor.

Cloud stood patiently while she leaned over and pressed the button on the keypad with the picture of a tiny bell on it. She patted his neck.

'You're such a good boy. You'd be a whizz at handy pony.'

She wriggled her toes and stared through the bars of the wrought iron gates as she waited to be let in. Claydon Manor, in all its extravagant Georgian grandeur, was straight out of a Jane Austen novel. Poppy quite expected to see a butler standing to attention outside, his hands clasped behind his back and a deferential expression on his face. She couldn't imagine what it must have been like to grow up in such a huge mansion. She had been dragged around enough National Trust properties to know that there would be dozens of bedrooms, vast reception rooms and green baize doors leading to poky servants' quarters in the attic.

It was unimaginable to think that the haughty Georgia with her plummy voice and easy arrogance hailed from much humbler beginnings. Until her parents came into money she'd lived in a modest three bedroomed semi. Her mum had been a checkout girl at the local supermarket and her dad had been a builder. And now, for the price of a lottery ticket and six lucky numbers, they had all this.

A crackle from the speaker on the keypad interrupted Poppy's thoughts. A high-pitched voice cried, 'Who is that?'

'Poppy McKeever. I left some black leather gloves when I came to the show here the other day. I've come to pick them up.'

Poppy cocked her head to listen. She thought she could hear urgent whispers, but it could have been static on the intercom.

Then the woman's disembodied voice cut through the background noise. 'You'd better come in.' And with a click the huge iron gates slowly began to swing open.

～

Poppy let her reins slide through her hands as Cloud walked up the gravel drive, his stride long and his eyes swivelling left and right at Claydon's sleek liveries grazing in the paddocks either side. They passed a blue van parked on the grass verge. Above a picture of an old-fashioned chimney sweep were the words *Bert's Clean Sweep*. It wasn't until they were alongside the driver's door that she realised a man in blue overalls was snoozing in the driver's seat, his blue beanie hat pulled down so low that the only part of his face that was visible was his double chin.

Poppy jumped off Cloud and led him over to the panelled front door. She was about to knock when she saw a wrought iron door pull to her right. She gave it a tug and heard an answering clang from somewhere deep inside the house.

A crunch of gravel behind them made Cloud start and Poppy turned to see Angela Snell just a few feet away. The livery yard manager was holding Poppy's gloves in one hand and a mobile phone in the other.

'Did you see anyone on your way in?' said Angela shortly, her eyes narrowed.

'Only the chimney sweep.'

'And no-one was watching you?'

'No.'

'Are you sure?'

Poppy frowned. 'I told you already. The only person I saw was the sweep. And he was fast asleep. Why?'

Ignoring her, Angela held out the gloves. 'Yours, I believe?'

'Thanks.' Poppy shoved them in her pocket. As she did she remembered the envelope. She pulled it from her pocket. 'Oh, and this was poking out of the letterbox.'

Angela stiffened and her eyes slid over to the chimney sweep's van.

'I thought I'd bring it over, save you the job,' said Poppy, holding out the envelope and wondering why the older woman was acting so strangely.

Angela looked at Poppy, who was wearing a pair of Caroline's red woolly gloves, and then at her own gloveless hands. 'Stay there,' she instructed, and turned on her heels and headed for the chimney sweep's van.

'Is it me, or is this all a bit *weird*?' Poppy whispered to Cloud. He snuffled her hand with his velvety nose. His head shot up as he heard the van door open.

Angela strode back over and held out her hand. 'I'll take him.'

Poppy took a step back until she was touching Cloud's shoulder and clutched his reins tightly. 'No, you won't.'

Angela exhaled loudly. 'It's OK. I'm just going to put him in the stable next to Barley while you speak to him.' She nodded to the middle-aged man climbing stiffly out of the van. His blue overalls strained across his sizeable midriff. An image of digestive biscuits popped, unbidden, into Poppy's head.

'I don't understand -' she said.

Angela took Cloud's reins. 'Don't worry. I'll put a rug on him and give him some hay.'

Poppy watched mutely as Angela led her pony away. A meaty hand in a white latex glove reached over her shoulder and plucked the envelope from her hands.

'I'll be having that, young lady.'

8

Poppy stared at Bert the chimney sweep. He looked uncannily like Inspector Bill Pearson, the digestive-loving police officer she'd spoken to the day she'd discovered Shelley Taylor was swindling people out of a small fortune by pretending her daughter Hope had cancer. Perhaps they were twins, Poppy wondered wildly. One caught criminals for a living, the other spent his days cleaning chimneys. Bert slipped the envelope into the deep pocket of his soot-covered overalls, peeled off his latex gloves and held out his hand.

'Hello again, Poppy,' he said, showing her his warrant card. Bert the chimney sweep was indeed Inspector Bill Pearson from Devon and Cornwall Police. 'I think it's time for a cuppa and a chat, don't you?'

Poppy's mind was working overtime as she followed him around the side of the house. She felt as though she'd stepped into a television drama without being given any lines. What was the portly inspector doing here, dressed as a chimney sweep? Were times so hard he'd had to find a second job? Why hadn't Angela just taken the letter and let Poppy go home? And why had she seemed so cagey? Nothing made sense.

'After you,' said Inspector Pearson, holding the back door open. Poppy heeled off her jodhpur boots and stepped into a cluttered boot room. Coats in various shades of khaki and brown hung from hooks on one wall, and on the other was a huge butler's sink. Above it was a pinboard covered with rosettes. Most of them were red.

'We'll talk in the library,' said the inspector. Poppy scurried after him down a wide, shadowy corridor with closed doors leading off either side. She felt like Alice, following the White Rabbit into the rabbit-hole.

Inspector Pearson stopped outside one of the doors. 'Won't be a moment.'

As the door opened Poppy caught a glimpse of a cavernous kitchen as big as Riverdale's entire downstairs. Dominating the room was a vast oak table, at the centre of which was a vase of dead roses. It was all Poppy registered before the door swung shut.

She rocked back on her heels, unsure what to do. Behind the huge, painted pine door she could hear the low rumble of voices. A shaft of light pierced the gloomy hallway. It was coming from the keyhole. Without thinking, Poppy sank to her knees and pressed her face against it.

A well-built man with close-cropped hair and a thick neck was sitting at the head of the table, tapping furiously into his phone. Next to him a woman stared blankly out of the window as she wound a pink hairband round and round her fingers. She had fair skin, ash-blonde hair, pale blue eyes and colourless lips. She was wearing a beige cashmere jumper. Everything about her looked muted, as though she'd been edited with a sepia filter.

A younger woman with shoulder-length brown hair, wearing jeans and a Jack Wills hoodie, had her back to them as she filled the kettle at the kitchen sink.

Inspector Pearson was talking to the couple at the table, showing them the scruffy white envelope, which was now in a police evidence bag. Curiouser and curiouser, thought Poppy, as she pressed her face closer to the keyhole.

The man stopped texting and said something in a gruff voice.

Inspector Pearson nodded, pulled on his latex gloves and used a kitchen knife to carefully prise open the envelope. He pulled out a single sheet of white paper and read it with raised eyebrows. He peered into the envelope, turned it upside down and gave it a shake.

The woman took one look at the lock of black hair on the table, buried her head in her hands and began keening softly. The sound was so wretched it made the hairs on the back of Poppy's neck stand up. Inspector Pearson cleared his throat and started speaking.

Poppy held her breath, straining to hear what was being said. But she only caught random words. *Letterbox. Fingerprints. Precious. Police.* It didn't make sense.

The thickset man thumped his fist on the table, making Poppy jump. Inspector Pearson slid his chair back and she scrambled to her feet. By the time the policeman had joined her in the hallway she was inspecting an antique map of Devon hanging over a mahogany console table.

'Sorry about that,' he said. 'I just need to ask you a couple of questions and then you can go.'

He pushed another door open to reveal a square room, lined floor to ceiling with books. It was north-facing and bitterly cold. The inspector switched on an electric fire between two chintzy armchairs and motioned Poppy to sit down. He took out a pocket notebook, a black ballpoint pen and the letter, which was back in its plastic evidence bag.

'So, Poppy, how did you come to be in possession of this letter?'

'It was in the letterbox.'

Inspector Pearson narrowed his eyes. 'If it was in the letterbox, how did you know it was there?'

'Sorry, I meant it was half in and half out. I thought I'd save someone a job by taking it down to the house. As I was going anyway.'

'So, you pulled it out of the letterbox. Were you wearing gloves?'

Poppy nodded.

'But I thought the reason you'd ridden over today was to pick up your gloves?'

'I'd left my new riding gloves here.' Poppy pulled the gloves out of her pocket and showed him. 'I borrowed my stepmum's gloves today.'

The inspector scribbled something down in his notebook. 'And did you see anyone outside the gates? Anyone at all?'

Poppy shook her head.

'Think very carefully, Poppy. This is important.'

Poppy pictured the ride to Claydon. She didn't think a single car had passed them. The only things they'd seen were sheep, Dartmoor ponies and the occasional buzzard.

'No, we didn't see anyone.'

'We?' he queried.

'Me and Cloud. My pony.'

'Right. And I gather from the Cannings that you're not a friend of Georgia's. So how did you come to leave your gloves here?'

'I was at the show last weekend. I left them in the arena by accident. They were new, else I probably wouldn't have bothered riding over.'

'Ah. You were at the show. Have you ever met Georgia before?'

'A few times, yes. Why?'

'Did you see her at the show?'

'She was there when we arrived, yes.'

'What time was that?'

'Um, about half eight, I suppose. Our class started at nine.'

'Did you speak to her?'

'Briefly.'

The inspector was watching her intently. 'What about?'

Poppy thought back. 'I asked her about the course. To see if she had any tips. It was my first show, you see.'

'She seemed OK to you? Not worried about anything?'

Georgia had seemed her usual snooty self. 'No.'

'Did you notice anything out of ordinary at the show? Anyone who looked out of place? Hanging around, asking questions?'

'I don't think so,' Poppy said. 'But I was concentrating on the jumping. I'm probably not the best person to ask.'

Inspector Pearson sighed.

'Wait, there was someone,' said Poppy.

'At the show?'

'No, this morning. I saw a walker, up on Barrow Ridge.'

'Man or woman?' he asked.

Poppy screwed up her eyes. 'A man, I think. Wearing camouflage gear and one of those massive backpacks students use when they're on a gap year.'

'Did you see his face?'

'He was too far away. But he just looked like a rambler. Sorry.'

There was a rap at the door and the woman in the Jack Wills hoodie walked in with a mug of tea and a plate of digestive biscuits.

'Hello Poppy.'

Poppy felt a jolt of recognition. The last time she'd seen this woman she'd been in police uniform, leading a man away in handcuffs.

Poppy looked from Inspector Pearson to PC Claire Bodiam and back again.

'Why are you dressed as a chimney sweep? Has something happened to Georgia? Is *that* why you're here?'

9

Inspector Pearson took a digestive biscuit and dunked it in his tea.

'I'm afraid we're not at liberty to tell you that.'

'We all thought she had food poisoning.'

His hand stopped in mid-air. A soggy corner of the biscuit fell into his tea with a soft plop.

'Why did you think that?'

'She was complaining about her hot dog. Said it was virtually raw. We assumed it had given her a gyppy tummy and that's why she didn't jump.'

A phone rang somewhere deep in the house. The inspector jumped to his feet. He was surprisingly nimble for someone of his size.

'Stay here,' he told Poppy, disappearing through the door with PC Bodiam close behind him.

This was getting weirder and weirder, Poppy thought. She wiggled her toes and gazed around the room. Hundreds, no thousands, of antique, leather-bound books lined the shelves. She padded across the room and studied the spines. An array of Encyclopaedia Britannicas with navy leather covers and gold-leaf lettering caught her eye and she pulled one from the shelf. To her surprise it wasn't an antique book at all – it was a moulded book panel designed to look like one. Poppy tried more. Every single book was a fake. They were all there for show, never to be read.

She sat back down and switched on her mobile. No phone signal here, let alone 3G. The wifi signal was strong but she didn't know the Cannings' passcode and she could hardly interrupt them to ask. She sighed, wondering how long Inspector Pearson was likely to be. And then she noticed the plastic evidence bag, which had slipped down the side of the armchair in his haste to leave.

Poppy knew she shouldn't look at the letter. But she also knew it would probably explain why the police were here, and what had happened to Georgia. It was becoming increasingly obvious that her disappearance had nothing to do with a dodgy hot dog. Poppy grappled with her conscience for all of thirty seconds. Inevitably curiosity won out. She checked that the door was closed and reached for the evidence bag.

The scruffy, white paper was blank on one side. Poppy turned it over, her mouth dry. Her eyes slid over the untidy lines of handwriting, scrawled in ugly capital letters:

THESE ARE OUR DEMANDS. TWO MILLION IN EXCHANGE FOR YOUR PRECIOUS DAUGHTER. WE'VE SENT A LITTLE GIFT TO SHOW WE MEAN BUSINESS. IT'LL BE A FINGER NEXT TIME. AND SHE'S DEAD IF YOU TELL THE POLICE. WAIT FOR THE NEXT INSTRUCTION.

Poppy's eyes widened. Was this a *ransom* note? Had Georgia been *kidnapped*? Common sense said no. Things like that happened in books and films, not real life. Real people didn't get kidnapped. But the Cannings were loaded. And why else were the police here?

Before Poppy had a chance to marshal her thoughts she heard footsteps in the hallway. She shoved the evidence bag back down the side of the armchair. She was sitting with her hands clasped demurely on her lap when PC Bodiam appeared moments later.

'You've been very helpful, Poppy. We won't take up any more of your time.'

'So, can I go home?' Poppy asked. Her eyes slid involuntarily to the armchair where a corner of plastic peeked out. She didn't notice the PC follow her gaze.

'You can. But Poppy – and this is really, really important – you must not tell a soul what you've seen, or think you've seen, here today. Lives could be in danger if even a whisper gets out that there are police at

Claydon Manor.' PC Bodiam's voice was gentle, but her expression was deadly serious.

'I haven't seen anything,' Poppy gabbled.

PC Bodiam stared at the letter and then at Poppy. 'Well, that's alright then. Come on, I'll show you out.'

As they walked into the yard Angela Snell was leading Cloud out of his borrowed stable. Poppy tightened his girth and pulled his stirrup leathers down. She was about to edge her toe into the stirrup when PC Bodiam laid a hand on her arm. 'Don't worry. We know what we're doing. But you must not tell anyone we were here, do you understand?'

Poppy didn't understand at all. But she nodded anyway. PC Bodiam smiled briefly.

'Thank you. Believe me, Georgia's life depends on it.'

$\sim$

ONCE THEY WERE on the moor Poppy kicked Cloud into a canter. She wanted to put as much distance as possible between them and the oppressive atmosphere that hung over the old Georgian manor house like smog. She wished she could turn back the clock. If only she'd hacked out with Scarlett and Red instead. What did a pair of gloves matter, in the grand scheme of things? If she hadn't ridden over to Claydon, hadn't let curiosity get the better of her, she'd be blissfully ignorant. She'd be looking forward to an afternoon in front of the fire, watching an old Christmas film with Caroline and Charlie.

Instead, her stomach churned with misgiving and her mind was whirring. Georgia had been kidnapped by goodness knows who. The police obviously had no clue, otherwise Inspector Pearson wouldn't have quizzed her at such length. Poppy pictured the scrawled note. The threat it contained was clear. What would happen to Georgia if her parents didn't hand over the two million pounds? Or if they discovered that the Cannings had called in the police? Organised criminals didn't make idle threats. PC Bodiam said Georgia's life was in danger. And she wouldn't say that unless it was true.

Poppy slowed Cloud to a walk and let him stretch his neck. His ears were pricked and he looked around the moor with interest, completely oblivious to the maelstrom of thoughts swirling in Poppy's head.

She had the horrible feeling that PC Bodiam knew she'd read the ransom note. Why else would the normally kindly PC have given her such a blunt warning to keep quiet? Poppy chastised herself for snooping. She should have minded her own business and she'd have been none the wiser. As it was she knew too much.

Would they kill Georgia? Surely not. She was worth more to them alive than dead. Alive, she was their only bargaining tool. Dead, she was a liability. Cutting off a lock of hair was an easy way to instil terror, and it had worked. The wretched look on the face of Georgia's mum was proof of that.

What if the kidnappers were watching the house and had seen Poppy arrive? Was she now in danger, too? Were they following her, to see where she lived? And what about Cloud? Chester? They were the two most important things in Poppy's life. What if the kidnappers hurt them to get at Poppy?

She halted the Connemara and wheeled him around, shielding her eyes from the low winter sun as she scoured the open moorland anxiously. A movement to her right caught her eye and her insides turned to ice. But it was only a solitary sheep, picking its way through a patch of boggy ground.

Cloud tossed his head with impatience. With a heavy heart, Poppy turned him towards home.

10

Charlie must have been watching for them from his bedroom window because she was still tying Cloud up outside his stable when he burst out of the kitchen door, his face flushed with excitement.

'Chester's been chosen for the Nativity! A pair of net curtains just phoned and told Mum!'

'Good,' said Poppy shortly, running up the stirrup leathers and loosening Cloud's girth.

'Good? Is that all you can say?' said Charlie. 'I thought you'd be as pleased as I was.'

Poppy glanced at her brother. If he suspected something was up she'd never hear the end of it. He was as tenacious as a terrier. He'd dig and probe until she gave in and told him about the kidnap. She had to pretend everything was fine. Even though it absolutely wasn't.

'Sorry Charlie, my feet are so cold I can't think properly. That's brilliant. Have you told him?'

Mollified, Charlie grinned. 'Of course! He was especially pleased to find out he'd beaten a pantomime donkey *and* a Shetland pony. But he said he wouldn't have minded if Jenny had been chosen. I think he quite liked her.'

'So did I. She's so sweet. But George Blackstone will be mad that she wasn't chosen. Scarlett says he hates to lose anything.'

The kitchen window opened, emitting a fug of steam. Caroline poked her head out. 'Good, you're back. Lunch will be five minutes. Did you get your gloves?'

Poppy felt in the pockets of her coat and groaned. What a numbskull. After all that she'd left them in the library at Claydon Manor.

THAT NIGHT POPPY dreamt about Witch Cottage, an abandoned croft deep on the moor towards Princetown that locals claimed was haunted. In her dream, someone had built an impenetrable barbed wire fence just inside the dry stone wall that circled the cottage, and had driven a dozen *No Trespassing* signs into the peaty ground.

Ignoring the signs, Poppy had reached in her pocket for the powerful wirecutters she had with her and had snip, snip, snipped away at the barbed wire until she'd made a gap big enough to slip through. She'd crept past the teardrop-shaped tarn to the croft's tiny front door. She heard voices inside, low and urgent. She knelt down and looked through the keyhole. A rheumy eye stared back at her. Stifling a scream, she scrabbled to her feet and sprinted for the fence. But the wire had grown back and the barbs tore at her clothes like the arms of a giant octopus. The harder she struggled, the tighter they held her. Behind her, the sound of heavy footsteps grew closer. She dared not look around. Desperate to reach the safety of the trees, she felt in her pocket for the wirecutters. But they had turned into a pair of nail scissors. Poppy opened her lungs and screamed.

She woke with a start, her heart pounding and her pillow damp. She rubbed her eyes and steadied her breathing. In through the nose, out through the mouth, concentrating on the feeling of her diaphragm slowly expanding and contracting, just as she had on the day of the show. Slowly the nightmare slipped back into her unconsciousness like a retreating tide.

But the picture of Witch Cottage stayed with her as she clumped downstairs in her pyjamas and fleece slipper boots. The old croft sat resolutely in her mind's eye as she poured milk over her cereals and sipped the mug of tea Caroline handed her. She stared vacantly into space, remembering the tiny attic under the catslide roof where pigeons nested and dust motes danced. It had been used to hide ill-gotten gains once before. Could someone be using it again?

'Earth to Poppy. Is anyone at home?' Caroline was standing in front of her, her hands on her hips.

Poppy brushed her fringe out of her eyes. 'Sorry, I was miles away. What is it?'

'I asked if you wanted another cup of tea.' Caroline sat down and fixed her cornflower-blue eyes on Poppy's. 'It was the third time I'd asked. Is everything OK?'

'Everything's fine.'

'Only you've seemed very preoccupied since you got back from Claydon Manor yesterday. You would tell me if anything was wrong, wouldn't you?'

Poppy wasn't normally secretive. Dad always said fondly that she wore her heart on her sleeve, just like Mum had. But lying by omission didn't really count, did it? She crossed her fingers under the table.

''Course I would. And, yes please. I'd love another cup of tea.'

～

CLOUD WHICKERED as she let herself out of the back door. Poppy ruffled his forelock and blew softly into his nose.

'Fancy a ride to Witch Cottage later?' she whispered. He rubbed against her, leaving a layer of white hairs on her coat. 'I'll see if Scarlett and Red can come too, shall I?'

But Scarlett was otherwise engaged. *Great Auntie Miriam's down from Bristol for the day. Mum said I've got to stay in and entertain her. It's so unfair! She talks to me like I'm five. AND she has more whiskers than a walrus!!! (Great Auntie Miriam, that is, not Mum. Although actually, come to mention it...)* read the gloomy reply when Poppy texted her.

She was pulling on an extra pair of thermal socks when Charlie burst into her room.

'Poppy, come and look at what I've made,' he said, tugging the sleeve of her fleece.

'If I must,' Poppy sighed, following him into his room. Lego was strewn all over the floor in a kaleidoscope of primary colours. She winced as she trod on a red brick. Charlie was pointing to a large construction on his chest of drawers.

Poppy peered over his shoulder at a tableau of Lego people and animals all gathered around a manger.

'It's a Nativity scene,' she said.

'Not any Nativity scene. It's the one at St Mary's. It's so I can practice what we're supposed to do. Like a dress rehearsal. Only in Lego.'

'It's very good. Although I'm not sure there were monkeys and baby elephants in the original Nativity,' said Poppy.

'They're all I had. I'm having to use a giraffe to play Chester. But I think a pair of net curtains will be impressed, don't you?'

'You can't keep calling her that,' said Poppy, her eyes falling on Charlie's binoculars, which were hanging from the door of his wardrobe. 'Mind if I borrow them?'

'What for?' said Charlie suspiciously.

Poppy looked around her breezily. 'A spot of bird-watching while I'm out riding,' she said.

'Since when have you been interested in bird-watching?'

Poppy swiped them from the door knob and flashed him an innocent smile. 'Since now.'

THE BINOCULARS safely stored in an old rucksack, Poppy and Cloud set off towards Witch Cottage. Poppy whistled tunelessly as her pony's long stride ate up the miles. A pale sun glimmered in the hazy winter sky and gulls swooped and soared overhead.

Eventually they reached the small band of evergreens that hid the cottage from view. Although Poppy had only discovered the old croft that summer, Cloud knew it of old, and she gave him his head so he could pick his own path through the trees.

As the gaps in the conifers widened and sunlight pierced the dark canopy once again, Poppy halted her pony.

'We need to be careful. Just in case,' she said, jumping to the ground and slipping the rucksack from her shoulders. As she undid the straps she realised her fingers were trembling.

Did she really think Georgia Canning was being held to ransom in the derelict cottage, watched over by a gang of faceless kidnappers? Despite all she'd seen at Claydon Manor it still seemed totally ridiculous that a fourteen-year-old girl could disappear without trace.

Poppy led Cloud to the edge of the trees and fiddled with the lens of the binoculars until the old stone building swam into focus. There was the teardrop-shaped tarn she and Charlie had picnicked by. Next to it was the dry stone wall that circled the cottage. Poppy tracked back and forth, taking in every detail. The front door was still hanging off its ancient hinges, although the battalion of nettles that had guarded it all summer had died down. The window frames were still rotting and the hole in the catslide roof was even bigger than she remembered.

Satisfied she had covered every foot of the cottage, Poppy shoved the binoculars back into her rucksack and pulled it on. There was no sign of Georgia, but she knew she had to check inside, just to be sure.

Glancing left and right, she led Cloud past the tarn and looped his reins over an old fence post. She pushed open the front door and stepped into the small, square room that must once have been the parlour. She was immediately transported back to the dramatic day Jodie had admitted she was planning to smuggle stolen mobile phones into Dartmoor Prison two and a half miles away.

Poppy still remembered the determined set of Jodie's jaw as she'd defended her decision, claiming it was the only way she could raise enough money to keep Nethercote open. Luckily Poppy had shown her another way and, with the help of Biscuit, the horse sanctuary's future was now secure.

Today the room was empty, apart from the decaying body of a dead pigeon in the fireplace. Poppy shivered, hoping it wasn't an omen.

The kitchen was empty, too. Poppy crept up the narrow staircase to the two tiny rooms in the eaves. But she knew before she poked her head around each door that there was no-one in them.

There was no doubt the place was deserted. She was an idiot for even thinking she'd find Georgia. Who did she think she was – Sherlock flippin' Holmes? If Devon and Cornwall Police had no inkling where the girl was, why should she, Poppy McKeever?

She ran lightly down the stairs, eager to be outside. She fished in her pocket for a handful of pony nuts and gave them to Cloud. 'That's for being patient while I was playing detective.'

She was tightening his girth when he stiffened and sniffed the wind.

'There's no-one here, silly,' she said.

But Cloud's nostrils flared and he wheeled around, wrenching the reins from her hands. She watched in horror as he weaved through the trees, stirrups flapping and his tail high.

'Cloud, come back!' she called, trying to keep her voice steady. He slid to a halt and watched her. 'That's it, good boy. Stand still and I'll come and get you. There's nothing to be frightened of.'

And then she heard the crackle of footsteps on the forest floor. Cloud, who was gawping at something over her right shoulder, gave a high-pitch whinny, spun on his hocks and cantered deeper into the trees. Fear crept down Poppy's spine like a droplet of icy water.

Her hand flew to her mouth and her rucksack dropped to the floor like a stone. She'd thought Witch Cottage was deserted. How wrong she'd been.

～

A BEAR of a man in camouflage fatigues and a green balaclava was standing four paces away. Poppy took two steps back, colliding with the solid trunk of a conifer.

Her eyes darted nervously to the large metal contraption in his left hand and then over her shoulder to Cloud. The Connemara had stopped on the edge of the small forest and was watching them intently.

Poppy chanced another look at the man, who was pulling off the bala-clava with his right hand. He shoved it in his pocket. He had a thatch of red hair and a nose that was squished to one side as though it had been broken and hadn't set straight. He was the walker she'd seen on Barrow Ridge, she was sure of it. The one Inspector Pearson had been so inter-ested in.

'Sorry for frightening your pony,' he said in a growly voice. 'Do you need a hand catching him?'

He waved the metal contraption towards Cloud. Poppy flinched, and edged around the conifer.

The man ducked into a small, square green canvas tent, covered with conifer branches, that Poppy hadn't noticed. He reappeared seconds later with a neatly-quartered apple in his hand. 'Will this help?'

Never take sweets from strangers, Caroline used to drill into Poppy and Charlie when they were little. Poppy dithered. Catching Cloud would be easier with an apple, but this gruff man could have escaped from Dartmoor Prison for all she knew.

Not waiting for an answer, he thrust the pieces of apple into Poppy's hand. She jumped as if she'd been scalded, muttered her thanks and fled through the trees. Once there was a safe distance between them she chanced a look over her shoulder. The man had turned his back to her and was on his knees, fiddling with the metal contraption. It had three legs and a black handle on the top.

Cloud was still watching her, his ears pricked. As Poppy edged towards him she breathed deeply, trying not to let her anxiety transmit to her pony. She held out a quarter of the apple and he extended his neck towards her. She stood still, letting him come to her. He snaffled the apple, his whiskers tickling her palm. Relief flooded her system as her hands tightened around his reins.

'Good boy,' she said, springing into the saddle and turning him for home.

As they retraced their steps across the moor Poppy wondered about the burly camouflage-clad man and what he was doing, camped out in the woods in the middle of winter. It seemed unlikely he had anything to do with Georgia's disappearance. Perhaps he was a rough sleeper, seeking shelter in Witch Cottage. Perhaps he lived off the land, a wild man of the woods, and that contraption was a trap in which he caught rabbits.

At least she now knew that Georgia wasn't being kept in the old croft. So much for her theory that the abductors were using it as their base. She was right back at square one.

Little did she know that within twenty four short hours, Georgia's whereabouts would be the least of her worries.

11

The alarm on Poppy's phone woke her at half six. She allowed herself two presses of the snooze button before she threw back the duvet and jumped out of bed. It wasn't until she'd started pulling on her leggings, ready to race out of the house to muck out, feed and turn out Cloud and Chester before breakfast and school, that she remembered it was the first day of the Christmas holidays. Bliss. Two whole weeks with nothing to do. Well, she had tons of coursework but that could wait until the New Year.

'Don't forget we're picking your dad up from Bristol airport today,' said Caroline, as Poppy wolfed down three slices of toast and raspberry jam. Charlie whooped and Poppy grinned. Once Dad was home Christmas could begin.

They sang along to the radio on the long drive to Bristol, stopping for hot chocolates at a motorway service station to break the journey. Dad's plane had not long landed as they walked into the arrivals lounge and soon he was enveloping them all in a big bear hug.

'So, tell me your news,' he said as they set off for home.

'Where do I start?' said Charlie.

'At the beginning?' he said.

'Well, first we had the donkey auditions for this year's Nativity, held by a pair of net curtains.'

'A pair of what?'

Caroline gave a wry smile. 'Charlie means Reverend *Annette* Kirton.'

'Obviously,' said Dad, his mouth twitching. 'And then what?'

'And then she only went and chose Chester for the starring role.'

'That's brilliant! And Poppy, what've you been up to?'

Poppy met her dad's eyes in the rear-view mirror. If only she could tell him what had really been happening. But she'd promised the police. She shrugged. 'Nothing much.'

Caroline turned around in her seat. 'Apart from coming third in your first ever show.'

'Oh yeah,' grinned Poppy. 'I forgot about that.'

TWO HOURS later Mike McKeever pulled into the Riverdale drive. 'D'you remember the day we moved in?'

'It seems like yesterday, and in other ways I feel like we've lived here all our lives,' said Caroline.

'Magpie was sick in his basket, I remember that. And Poppy was really, really grumpy,' said Charlie.

'No, she wasn't,' said Caroline loyally.

'I was,' admitted Poppy. 'I thought I didn't want to live here. How stupid was I? I'd hate to live in Twickenham now.'

'And do you remember, Tory was here to welcome us to Riverdale?'

'She's like our pretend granny now, isn't she?' said Charlie.

'She certainly is,' said Dad.

'And I thought Chester was a pony,' said Poppy.

Dad laughed. 'So you did. What you didn't realise was that there was a pony for you after all. You were just looking in the wrong place.'

He parked the car and Poppy and Charlie helped him unload his cases from the boot. Caroline opened the front door and Freddie bounded out, his plumy tail wagging frantically as he welcomed them all in turn.

Cloud was lying by the water trough, dozing.

'Where's the panto star?' said Dad.

Poppy scanned the field for Chester's familiar brown shape. 'Probably down by the wood.'

'I'm starving. When's lunch?' said Charlie.

'Now,' said Caroline. 'You carry Dad's cases in and I'll heat up the soup.'

~

AFTER LUNCH DAD brought the big cardboard box of Christmas decorations down from the loft and Poppy and Charlie decorated the tree.

'Can we watch *Home Alone* after?' Charlie was standing on a chair, reaching over to dangle a bauble on one of the high branches.

'You've seen it a million times,' said Poppy.

'Who cares? It's the best Christmas film ever.'

'If we must. But I need to put Cloud and Chester away first. I'll be twenty minutes, OK?'

'I love that bit where Kevin heats up the doorknob and the burglar burns his hand.' Charlie chuckled to himself. 'And when he leaves the cars and stuff at the bottom of the stairs. Genius.'

An orange sun was sliding below the horizon as Poppy made her way across the field, Cloud's headcollar slung casually over her shoulder. She never brought one for Chester – the old donkey always followed them back to the yard.

Cloud was still snoozing, his ears floppy and his bottom lip drooping, when Poppy reached him.

'Hello, sleepyhead,' she said.

He opened one eye and regarded her blearily. Poppy slipped the noseband of his headcollar over his nose and buckled the strap, calling over her shoulder to Chester as she did so.

A couple of burrs were caught in Cloud's mane and she spent several minutes teasing them out. His head drooped again and his eyes closed.

She tutted fondly. 'What's wrong with you today? Late night last night, was it?'

Satisfied she had managed to pull out every last barb, she combed through his mane with her fingers. There was still no sign of Chester. Usually he'd have wandered over by now and would be nibbling her pockets, hoping for a Polo or a handful of pony nuts.

'Where *is* he?' Poppy squinted into the half-light, searching the field's dips and hollows, tracking slowly along the band of trees that marked the start of the Riverdale wood. There was no sign of the old donkey.

'I did let him out this morning, didn't I?' Occasionally, if the weather forecast was really bad, she would leave him in the stable with plenty of hay. He didn't have the luxury of a thick New Zealand rug like Cloud. But no, she remembered turning them both out. Chester had been impatient to be out and had trodden on her foot in his hurry to trot through the field gate.

'We'd better check the fencing hasn't got a hole in it.' Poppy pulled the lead rope gently but Cloud didn't move. She clicked her tongue. 'Come on, lazybones.' He took a half-hearted couple of steps forwards. 'That's it. Good boy,' she said as he followed her unenthusiastically around the perimeter of the field. The post and rail fencing was intact. Apart from a couple of rabbits, which bobbed off into the wood with a flash of white tail, the field was empty.

Poppy gazed around her, a feeling of unease settling on her shoulders like mist on a soggy autumn night. Chester could be mischievous at times and Poppy wouldn't put it past him to untie a gate or push through a gap in a fence if the grass looked greener on the other side. But the gate had been shut when she'd let herself in and there weren't any holes in the fence. Usually by now he'd be standing by the gate, ready for his tea. So, where was he?

Her sense of unease growing, Poppy coaxed Cloud back across the field. She turned on the yard lights, hoping to see the donkey's chocolate brown eyes gazing guiltily back at her from the hay barn or tack room. Both were empty. So was the stable he shared with Cloud. Poppy left Cloud in the stable and sprinted to the back door with a hammering heart.

12

'Chester's disappeared!' she yelled at the top of her voice. Caroline, who was peeling potatoes at the sink, raised her eyebrows.

'What do you mean, disappeared?'

'He's not in the field. He's not in the yard. He's vanished!' Poppy could hear her voice climbing an octave and she took a deep breath. 'I've looked everywhere. He's gone.'

Caroline dropped the peeler in the sink and dried her hands on a tea towel. 'Grab the torches. I'll go and get your dad and Charlie. We'll come and have another look.'

'He wouldn't have run away, would he?' said Charlie in a small voice. They were walking four abreast across the field, having already searched the outbuildings and small paddock with no luck.

'Of course he wouldn't, sweetheart. I'm sure he's here somewhere. Try not to worry,' said Caroline.

They were walking past the water trough when Poppy stood on something sharp. She shone her torch down. A white plastic syringe was lying in the mud. She bent down to pick it up.

'Sedalin Gel,' she said, showing the syringe to Caroline. 'What on earth is that?'

Her stepmum shrugged. 'No idea.'

The rest of the label was obscured by mud. Poppy slipped it into her pocket and trudged on, the beam of her torch sweeping to and fro like a searchlight. Her disquiet grew with every step.

'I told you he wasn't here,' she said fretfully, when they reached the far side of the field and there was still no sign of the old donkey.

'Where *is* he, then?' demanded Charlie with a catch in his voice. 'Chester! *Chester*! Where are you?' he shouted.

Poppy would have given anything to have heard Chester's familiar wheezy hee-haw, but the moor was quiet, save for the sound of the westerly wind whipping through the trees.

'And you're absolutely sure you shut the gate properly this morning?' said her dad.

'OF COURSE I'M SURE!' Poppy wanted to yell at the top of her voice. But she took another deep breath and answered as calmly as she could. 'It was definitely closed. Anyway, if I'd left it open Cloud would have escaped, too, wouldn't he?'

'It's OK, Poppy. I believe you,' he said. 'The first thing we need to do is ring round all the neighbours, in case they've seen him.'

'And if they haven't?' asked Caroline.

'Let's cross that bridge when we come to it.'

Poppy fed Cloud and changed his rugs on autopilot. Her mind was focused on Chester. Where on earth could he be? Common sense told her he'd just wandered off, and would clip-clop back into the yard at any moment. She tried and failed to dismiss the nagging doubts that whispered darker scenarios to her subconscious.

'Where is he, Cloud?' Poppy whispered, running a frozen hand along his velvety neck. Ignoring her, he guzzled his tea noisily. At least he finally seemed to have perked up, she thought, as she let herself out of the stable and tramped wearily back to the house.

CAROLINE WAS SITTING at the kitchen table, the phone pressed against her ear.

'Thanks Pat. No, I understand. And yes, if you could keep an eye out for him that'd be great. Tell Scarlett not to worry. He'll turn up, I'm sure.

Thanks again. You too.' She ended the call and placed the phone carefully on the table.

'Pat and Bill haven't seen him. Neither have the Jennings or the Coreys. Just the Samsons to try and that's everyone within a mile of Riverdale.'

Poppy remembered the syringe in her pocket. She rinsed off the mud under the hot tap. 'Acepromazine,' she read to herself. 'Sedative. Oral gel.'

Her heartbeat quickening, she reached for her mobile phone and Googled Sedalin Gel. *Used for the sedation of horses and ponies. Has a general tranquilizing effect which lasts for up to six or seven hours.* Fear squeezed Poppy's insides like a vice.

'He's been stolen,' she said loudly. Caroline, in the middle of leaving a message on the Samsons' answerphone, trailed off and stared at Poppy.

'How d'you know?' Charlie demanded.

'I found this in the field, near to where Cloud was standing. He seemed really sleepy earlier. I didn't think anything of it. But this is a sedative for horses. Someone's given him it so they could take Chester.'

'Are you sure?' said her dad.

'How else do you explain this?' Poppy said, holding out the syringe. 'Someone has stolen him. We need to call the police.'

No-one really wanted the pork chops and mash Caroline had made for dinner. They sat in silence around the table, each busy with their own thoughts. Caroline sprang to her feet with an audible sigh of relief when there was a rap at the front door.

'It'll be the police. Poppy, perhaps you could you clear the table.'

Poppy was mindlessly scraping leftovers into the green food caddy when Caroline re-appeared with PC Claire Bodiam and a fresh-faced young officer she introduced as PC Gilligan. He looked as if he was straight out of training school.

Poppy met PC Bodiam's eye. It's alright, she wanted to say. I haven't told anyone about Georgia. PC Bodiam gave a tiny nod, as if she understood.

The two police officers sat down. 'We wouldn't normally attend a theft report but we were passing and it was a quiet shift. We thought we might as well look in,' said PC Bodiam. 'Just as a matter of interest, do you have a four by four?'

'No, we've just got the estate. Why?' asked Poppy's dad.

'There are some tyre tracks at the bottom of the drive. They look wider than a car's.'

'They must have belonged to the thieves!' cried Charlie, his face pale.

'Possibly,' said PC Bodiam.

'Are you going to send out the crime scene people, like you did at Redhall?' Poppy asked.

'Probably not. We don't even know he was definitely stolen yet.'

Poppy showed the two police officers the sedative.

'Whoever took him tranquilised Cloud so they could steal Chester,' she said.

'That's what I don't get,' PC Bodiam admitted. 'We do get the occasional horse theft, and sheep rustling is a fairly common problem out in the rural. We even had eight Limousin cattle stolen from a farm over Okehampton way the other week. But who would go out of their way to steal an elderly donkey? It doesn't make sense.'

13

Poppy was shaking fresh straw into the stable the next morning when she heard the clatter of hooves on concrete. Her heart leapt and she sprinted to the open door, hoping to see Chester's woolly face, but it was Scarlett on Red. Her best friend jumped off and led the chestnut gelding over.

'Any news?'

'No,' said Poppy glumly. 'PC Bodiam has told the Farm Watch people and Caroline's posted his photo on some local Facebook horse groups. It's had loads of shares, but no-one's seen him.'

'Let's go for a ride, see if we can find him.'

'I don't know, Scar. I don't really feel like it. Anyway, I should probably stay here. In case there's any news.'

Scarlett looked shocked. 'But what if he's on the moor? What if he's hurt himself and needs our help?'

Trying to ignore the burn of unshed tears, Poppy stared at her feet. 'Caroline phoned Tory this morning.'

'How did she take it?'

'She was OK. Worried, but OK. She's coming over this afternoon.'

'By then we might have found him! Come on, Poppy. Let's give it a try at least. It's got to be better than sitting waiting for the phone to ring.'

~

'WHERE DO WE START?' said Poppy helplessly, as they rode onto the moor. It was a clear day and Dartmoor lay before them in all its bleak winter glory.

'We'll ride around the Riverdale tor and then head south, along the other side of the Riverdale wood, just in case he's taken shelter there,' said Scarlett decisively.

Perhaps Cloud sensed Poppy's despair for he seemed subdued as he followed Red around the base of the tor. But he probably missed the old donkey even more than she did.

She said as much to Scarlett.

Scarlett shook her head. 'It's probably the after-effects of the sedative.'

But Poppy knew she was wrong and every time he stopped to sniff the wind and gave a plaintive whinny it broke her heart.

They scoured the horizon for Chester-shaped brown blobs. Once Scarlett shrieked with excitement, making Cloud and Red both jump.

'There he is!' she cried, pointing to the lower slopes of a far-off tor. Poppy followed her gaze.

'It's a stag. I can see the antlers from here,' she said flatly. 'This is useless. I'm going home.' She wheeled Cloud to the right and kicked him into a canter. He lengthened his stride until the wiry moorland grass blurred beneath his feet. Poppy leaned low over his neck and gripped the reins tightly as he galloped for home, not bothering to wipe the tears that poured down her cheeks.

~

TORY WAS SITTING in the armchair by the fire, her swollen knuckles pale as she gripped the head of her walking stick and stared into the flames that crackled and leapt in the hearth.

Poppy hesitated by the door. Caroline had told her not to worry, that Tory didn't blame her. But Poppy had promised she would look after Chester and she hadn't. Chester was goodness only knew where and Poppy had failed him, failed them both. Fresh tears trickled down her face and she wiped them away impatiently. Apologising to Tory was the least she could do. She straightened her shoulders and walked into the room.

'I'm so, so sorry.' She knelt at Tory's feet, feeling the heat of the fire scorch her wind-chapped cheek.

'Oh pet, you mustn't blame yourself. It's not your fault,' the old woman said firmly.

'But –'

'No buts, Poppy. No-one looked after Chester better than you. Someone had a reason to take him. We just need to work out why.'

Poppy remembered Georgia. 'You don't think he's been kidnapped, do you?'

'Kidnapped?' Tory said, bemused. 'Who would kidnap an old donkey?'

'Maybe they think because Dad's on the TV we're loaded. Like the Cannings.'

The wrinkles on Tory's forehead deepened. 'What have the Cannings got to do with anything?'

Poppy bit her lip. 'Nothing. Pets do get kidnapped, though. It happened in the book I just read. The kidnapper left ransom notes in an old churchyard.'

'That's fiction,' said Tory kindly. 'Things like that don't happen in real life.'

'They might,' said Poppy. She cocked her head. 'Was that the phone?'

'I didn't hear, pet.'

Poppy sprang to her feet. 'I'll go and check.'

Caroline was replacing the handset in its base when Poppy burst into the kitchen.

'Who was that?' she demanded.

'Reverend Kirton. I thought I'd better tell her she needed to find a new donkey. She was just phoning back.'

Poppy stared at her stepmother. 'Don't you think we'll have found him by then?'

Caroline smiled brightly. 'I'm sure we will have. But I needed to warn her. The Nativity's on Friday. She needs time to find a stand-in.'

Charlie appeared in the doorway, Freddie by his side. 'Find a stand-in for what?'

'For the Nativity donkey,' said Caroline. 'Reverend Kirton says she'll probably ask George Blackstone if Jenny can do it.'

'George Blackstone!' Poppy exploded.

'How could she?' cried Charlie, his face crumpling. 'That was Chester's job! He'll be back to do it, won't he?'

Caroline made to comfort him but Poppy beat her to it. She wrapped her arms around his skinny frame. 'He'll be back, Charlie,' she whispered into his tousled blond hair. He was getting so tall. 'I promise.'

~

CAROLINE HAD INVITED Tory to stay the night and Poppy carried her small suitcase up to the spare bedroom before dinner.

'Thank you,' said Tory. She sat down heavily on the bed. 'Charlie's upset, isn't he. I've never seen him so down.'

'He loves Chester to bits. We all do.' There was a catch in Poppy's throat. 'He was so looking forward to the Nativity. He'd even made a Lego model of the church. I'll show you later.'

'Annette hasn't given the job to Delilah, has she?' said Tory. She had hooted with laughter when Poppy had phoned to tell her about Sam and Scott's appearance at the donkey auditions.

'No, she's going to ask George Blackstone to bring his poor, skinny donkey, Jenny.'

'George Blackstone?' Tory asked sharply.

Poppy shrugged. 'Jenny was the vicar's second choice, apparently. That's what she told Caroline, anyway.'

'Who else did she tell?' Tory wondered aloud as she struggled to her feet.

'What do you mean?'

Ignoring her, Tory waggled her stick at her suitcase. 'Pass me my coat, please, Poppy. There's somewhere we need to go.'

14

The McKeevers' estate car snaked its way along the windy lanes towards the Blackstone farm. They reached a crossroads. Poppy's dad looked at Tory, who was sitting in the passenger seat, her handbag clutched to her chest and a determined look on her face.

'Straight across,' she said. 'And then second left. The farm's down a track on the right.'

Charlie had been desperate to come but Dad had put his foot down. 'First, we don't want to go in mob-handed. And second, you're eight, Charlie. You should be in bed.'

Charlie had stormed up to his bedroom in tears of anger and frustration.

'I'd better see if he's OK,' said Caroline. 'Phone me as soon as you can. And please be careful. In fact, I've changed my mind. I don't think Poppy should go, either. What if he's got a gun? We should call the police. Let them sort it out.'

Dad gave her a brief hug. 'We don't even know if he's taken Chester. Imagine the fall-out if we're wrong.'

'We're not wrong,' said Poppy. 'And I am going. Sorry, Caroline. But I have to, don't you see?'

Poppy had grabbed her coat and disappeared out of the house before Caroline could stop her.

'But you stay in the car, OK?' her dad said now. 'I mean it, Poppy. Caroline's right. Leave it to me and Tory. We'll sort it out.'

They drove past the pair of semi-detached farm cottages that stood on the edge of the Blackstone farm. Poppy had ridden past them more times than she could remember. They were on the route of her and Scarlett's favourite ride. Jimmy Flynn, George Blackstone's farm hand, lived in Rose Cottage with his mum and dad. Flint Cottage had stood empty since Hope Taylor and her mum Shelley moved out.

Tory pursed her lips. 'Margaret was telling me that George has thrown the Flynns out of their cottage. Says he wants to do them both up to sell.'

'But Rose Cottage doesn't need doing up,' said Poppy, grateful for anything to take her mind off what lay ahead, even if it was boring talk about people she didn't know. 'It always looks so immaculate.'

'They've had to move in with Jimmy's Auntie Flo in Tavistock until they find a new place closer to Waterby.'

Poppy stared out of the window but the two cottages were in darkness. 'That's sad.'

'It's wicked, that's what it is,' said Tory. 'All that Blackstone man ever thinks about is money. Money, money, money! And at his age! It's not like you can take it with you. His mother would turn in her grave if she could see him now.'

'Here we are,' said Poppy's dad, indicating right and turning onto a roughshod farm track. The car bumped along for what seemed like miles, but was probably only a couple of hundred yards. He winced as they hit a deep pothole, scraping the underside of the car.

Eventually the headlights picked out a handful of ramshackle farm buildings and an old farmhouse. He switched off the engine and turned to them both with a wry smile.

'Welcome, travellers. We have reached our destination.'

≈

'REMEMBER WHAT I SAID. You stay here,' said Dad. He held the door open for Tory, who heaved herself out, still gripping her handbag in front of her like a shield. The door closed with a soft clunk and Poppy scrambled into Tory's seat to get a better view.

The yard was in darkness, save for the pale yellow glow of a security light over the back door of the farmhouse. Two border collies had started a cacophony of barking the minute the car had turned into the yard, and they were now straining at their ropes in an excited frenzy. Poppy watched her dad approach them with an outstretched hand. She could see his lips moving and she wound down the window so she could hear what he was saying.

'That's it, take it easy my friends. We've just come to see a man about a donkey.'

The two dogs grovelled on the ground, their tails pumping as he rubbed their tummies. They may be good sheepdogs but as guard dogs they were about as much use as a chocolate teapot, Poppy reflected.

Tory, meanwhile, had hobbled across the farmyard and was rapping sharply on the back door with her stick. 'I know you're in there, George Blackstone! Open up. You and I need to talk!'

After an age the door swung inwards and Poppy saw the old farmer silhouetted in the doorway. She counted to ten and let herself silently out of the car. She slunk past the two collies, a finger pressed to her lips, but they were too busy whining at their master to pay her any attention.

She stole as close to the house as she dared, stopping in a pool of darkness by the side of a tumbledown barn.

George Blackstone was shouting, his raspy voice filled with malice. 'I haven't got your bliddy donkey! And I've a good mind to call the old bill, have you two done for trespass.'

'I think you'll find trespass is a civil, not a criminal matter,' said Poppy's dad in his smooth television correspondent's voice. 'But we're more than happy to get the police involved, aren't we, Tory?'

'We certainly are. Just tell me where Chester is, George.'

The wily old farmer glanced in Poppy's direction and she shrank further into the shadows. He turned back to Tory, pointing his finger at her aggressively.

'Now look here, you meddling old bat. You can stop sticking your nose in right now. I told you. I don't know where your donkey is and I don't care.'

'So, you won't mind if we have a quick look around?' said Poppy's dad cheerfully.

George Blackstone took two steps forward and prodded his chest with a nicotine-stained finger. 'I shan't say this again Mister Lah-di-dah McKeever. Oh yes, I see you on the telly all the time, all smarm and smiles. Well, you don't impress me. I haven't got your cretinous donkey, do you understand? I've got far bigger fish to fry.'

Poppy's dad held up his hands in a placatory manner. 'Calm down, there's no need to shout.'

But George Blackstone had a murderous look in his eyes. Spittle was gathering at the corners of his mouth and Poppy could see a vein throbbing in his temple. He rose to his full height, his bulbous red nose centimetres from her dad's face.

'Don't you patronise me, you arrogant fool. Clear off my land!'

Poppy's dad lay a hand on Tory's shoulder. 'Come on, Tory, we'd better do as the gentleman says. We can't search the place without his permission.'

Poppy frowned in the darkness. *Come on, Dad, stand up to him,* she willed him silently. But he and Tory were tramping back to the car. She looked back at George Blackstone. He was watching them go with a smirk.

Poppy clenched her fists, fighting the urge to cry. A warm nose nudged her leg. It was the older of the two collies. His coat was matted and his eyes were milky. Poppy knelt down and hugged him. 'Poor boy,' she whispered as his tail thumped against the ground. His master was a cruel and greedy man. She couldn't take a chance that Chester was somewhere on the Blackstone farm.

Her mind made up, she crept along the walls of the old barn looking for a way in. She found a pair of big double doors halfway down. A steel padlock glinted in the beam of the security light. Without much hope, Poppy gave it a sharp tug. To her surprise, the shackle came away from the body of the padlock. It hadn't been locked properly. Poppy glanced over her shoulder. George Blackstone had disappeared inside the farmhouse. Her dad and Tory were whispering urgently a few feet from the car. She knew she had a matter of seconds before they realised she'd gone.

Her heart in her mouth, she pushed the door open and slipped inside.

1 5

It was as dark as a starless night inside the old haybarn. Poppy was transported back to her seventh birthday party, to a game of blind-man's bluff in the lounge of their old home in Twickenham. Caroline had carefully tied a blindfold over her eyes and she'd had to feel her way around the room, trying to identify her friends through touch alone. She employed the same tactic now, cautiously inching forwards, her hands in front of her like a zombie.

She didn't see the old metal plough lying in her path and tripped right over it, landing face down in a heap of musty straw. Dust filled her nostrils and she pinched her nose in an attempt to stop an attack of the sneezes. But the tickle refused to go away. *Atishoo atishoo atishoo.* She scrabbled to her feet and listened carefully to see if anyone had heard her.

Nothing.

To her right, in the cavernous darkness of the barn, she heard a rustling sound. Hoping more than anything it wasn't rats, Poppy took a tentative step forwards. She sneezed again and stared into the velvet blackness.

At first, when Poppy heard the mournful hee-haw, she thought she was imagining it. That maybe her desire to hear Chester's call had somehow conjured the donkey out of the darkness. But when a second hee-haw sliced through the still air in the barn, she knew instinctively that it was him. She stumbled towards the sound.

'Chester!' she called. He hee-hawed back. Tripping over old farm machinery and colliding with milking pails, she headed deeper into the barn. 'Hey, boy, where are you?'

The answering hee-haw was so loud he could only be a few feet away. She remembered her phone, tucked in her back pocket.

'Idiot!' she told herself, turning on the phone's torch. Keeping the spindly beam low, she waved it around. There, to her right, were four hairy legs, the colour of milk chocolate. One leg was hobbled to one of the barn's woodworm-ridden oak pillars.

'Oh Chester,' Poppy cried, burying her face in his soft coat. He nibbled her pocket. 'Yes,' she said, half laughing, half crying. 'I've got some somewhere.'

As she offered him a Polo another nose appeared. This one was seal-grey. 'Jenny!' Poppy thumbed another Polo out of the packet and the donkey took it timidly.

'We need to get you two out of here,' she told them, ruffling Chester's bristly mane. She ran towards the barn doors and yelled as loudly as her lungs allowed, 'He's in here!'

POPPY and her dad untied the shackles and used the ropes to loop loosely around the necks of the two donkeys while Tory watched, a mixture of relief and fury on her face.

'Follow me,' she commanded. 'He's not going to get away with this.' She set off determinedly towards the open barn doors.

'I'd better take Jenny,' Poppy told her dad. She clicked her tongue and gave the rope a gentle pull. The grey donkey tottered after her.

Tory was already hammering her fist against the back door of the farmhouse when they emerged from the barn. The door swung open and the old farmer appeared, a pasty in one hand and a dollop of tomato ketchup on his chin.

'What the hell are you doing back?' he snarled.

'You're a liar, George Blackstone.' Tory stepped aside and Poppy and her dad led the two donkeys into the light.

Blackstone's rheumy eyes darted from Chester to Tory and back again. 'This is a set-up. You're trying to frame me for theft,' he blustered.

'Oh, come on, you really think we'd do that?' said Poppy's dad incredulously.

'Still want to call the police?' Tory said. 'Perhaps you'd like to explain to them how Chester came to be hidden in your barn.'

Like a cornered animal, Blackstone turned on her. 'Maybe I did take your precious donkey, but that makes us even, doesn't it? Don't think I don't know that you let that damn Connemara out of its stable all them years ago.' He laughed nastily. 'What comes around, goes around, old woman.'

'Is that why you took Chester, as revenge for something you think happened years ago?' said Poppy's dad, shaking his head in disbelief.

Blackstone wiped his chin on the sleeve of his filthy tweed jacket and hooted scornfully. 'I was never going to keep the mangy old nag. Like I need another mouth to feed.' He waved his hand at Jenny. 'I thought if she was in the Nativity I'd be able to sell her on for a bit of a profit. Then the vicar picks your donkey. Stupid woman. But if your donkey happened to disappear, she'd have to use mine, wouldn't she?'

Tory nodded. 'I thought as much. I know how your mind works, George Blackstone. It all boils down to money, doesn't it? Never a thought for anyone else. Your mother would turn in her grave if she could see you now, honestly she would.'

'Stop droning on, woman! You'd have got him back after Christmas, no harm done.'

Poppy's dad reached for his mobile.

For the first time Poppy saw a flicker of fear in George Blackstone's bloodshot eyes. 'Oi, you aren't phoning the cops, are you? I thought we'd sorted this out.'

'I probably should, but no, they've got better things to do with their time. I'm phoning Bill to ask him to drive over with the trailer so we can take Chester home.'

Poppy stepped forward. 'What about Jenny? We can't leave her with *him*,' she cried.

The old hill farmer stared at her with loathing. 'That's my donkey and I paid good money for her. You must be mad if you think she's going with you.'

'How much did you pay?' said Poppy, thinking of the balance in her building society account. She'd been saving for a jumping saddle for well over a year, but that could wait.

Blackstone paused. Poppy knew he was probably thinking of a number, doubling it and more than likely multiplying it by ten for good measure. She held her breath and waited.

'Three hundred,' he said eventually. 'Yes, that's what I paid.'

'I'll give you three hundred and fifty for her,' she said.

'Hold on, Poppy, we need to talk about this first,' said her dad.

Poppy looked beseechingly at him. 'Please Dad. Look at the state of her. She's half-starved to death. I've got the money in my savings. And we've got the room.'

Tory lay a hand on his arm. 'I'll pay for her keep, Mike. Poppy's right. We can't leave the poor thing here.'

Poppy's dad shook his head ruefully. 'Alright. If Mr Blackstone agrees, I'll write a cheque now and we'll take her with us.'

George Blackstone looked positively jubilant as Poppy loaded Jenny and Chester into the back of Bill's trailer less than half an hour later.

'I don't suppose he paid more than fifty pounds for that poor donkey,' said Tory, as they bumped back down the farm track towards home.

'No wonder he was looking so pleased with himself,' said Poppy's dad. 'I hope he doesn't renege on our deal and report us to the police for stealing her.'

'He won't,' said Poppy with conviction.

'How can you be so sure, pet? He's as slippery as they come,' said Tory.

Poppy held up her mobile. 'Because I recorded everything. Him admitting he took Chester, agreeing to sell Jenny. It's all on my phone. As a kind of insurance,' she added, beaming at them both.

Her dad grinned back. 'That'll teach him to mess with a McKeever. Atta girl, Poppy.'

16

Poppy was awake early the next day. She sat up in bed and consulted her long list of things to do. Caroline had promised to phone the vet first thing to see if she could pop over and check Jenny's eye, and Poppy wanted everything shipshape before she arrived.

They'd left Jenny in the small paddock with Chester the previous night, but Poppy's plan was to clear out the second stable so the two donkeys could share that. Cloud would stay in his own stable next door.

Poppy pulled on an old pair of jods and her thickest fleece and went downstairs in search of breakfast. Charlie was already dressed and was eating a bowl of cereal at the kitchen table. He'd been asleep when they'd finally arrived home but Poppy had crept into his room and woken him to tell him the good news.

He looked at her anxiously. 'It wasn't a dream, was it? Chester is definitely back? And poor Jenny, too?'

'They're here. And I have a heap of work to do. Fancy helping?'

He pushed his bowl away and stood up. 'Try and stop me.'

After she had fed Cloud she turned him out with the two donkeys. She and Charlie watched from the gate as the Connemara walked over to Jenny, his ears pricked and his neck extended.

'I hope they get on alright,' she muttered. But she needn't have worried. They touched noses and the grey donkey hee-hawed softly. Within minutes they were all grazing peacefully.

'That's one hurdle crossed. Now for the stable,' said Poppy.

They spent the next couple of hours lugging piles of old flower pots, ancient paint tins and tools out of the second stable. Charlie brushed away cobwebs and Poppy checked the wooden kickboards for loose nails. Satisfied everything was in order she laid a thick bed of straw and filled two water buckets.

The vet arrived just before lunch. 'I hear you've rescued another waif and stray,' she remarked, reaching into the back of her mud-splattered Land Rover for her medicine bag.

Caroline rolled her eyes and Poppy and Charlie grinned at each other.

The vet gave Jenny's poll a friendly scratch and examined her swollen eye. 'It looks like a straightforward case of equine conjunctivitis. I'll wash it out with some saline solution now and give you some antibiotic ointment to use three times a day. It should be looking better in a couple of days but keep using the ointment for two days after it's back to normal.'

Poppy nodded and stroked Jenny's neck while the vet listened to her heart, felt her legs, checked her feet and examined her teeth.

'How old do you think she is?' Poppy asked.

The vet straightened her back. 'Only about three, I'd say. Apart from the eye infection, and the fact that she's underweight, she's in good health. And I know how brilliant you are at putting condition on your animals. Cloud's looking great, by the way.'

Poppy flushed with pleasure. The vet had been one of the first people to see the Connemara when he'd come off the moor. He'd been skin and bone, a shadow of himself. Coaxing him back to good health had taken months of hard work.

'So, poor Jenny's going to be alright?' Charlie asked.

The vet smiled at them all. 'Poor Jenny? I'd say she's pretty lucky myself. Yes, Jenny's going to be absolutely fine.'

~

POPPY LAUGHED at Scarlett as they rode along one of the old railway tracks high on the moor later that afternoon. Clouds scudded across the periwinkle-blue sky and a bitter wind numbed their fingers and feet.

'Your face is a picture,' she said.

Scarlett had looked more and more astonished as Poppy had related the events of the previous evening.

'So, what will you tell the police?' she asked finally.

'Dad phoned them this morning to say Chester had come home. They're closing the crime report. We've got Chester back. George Blackstone's got his money. Everyone's happy.'

'Including poor Jenny.'

'Especially poor Jenny,' said Poppy with feeling. 'She's such a sweet donkey. You didn't see how rough Blackstone was with her at the church. I couldn't bear the thought of leaving her. She and Chester are like an old married couple already. Charlie's hoping for the patter of tiny donkey hooves.'

'But Chester's a gelding,' giggled Scarlett.

'And Charlie's eight. You can give him a talk on the birds and the bees if you like, but I'd rather not, thanks all the same. Come on, let's have a canter,' Poppy said. She felt carefree, as though an exam she'd been dreading for months had suddenly been cancelled. Chester was home, they'd saved Jenny from Blackstone's evil clutches and, now the sedative had worn off, Cloud was back to his normal, bouncy self.

She gathered her reins and the Connemara danced on the spot. Red crabbed sideways up the track. The two ponies were like coiled springs, waiting to be released.

Poppy laughed and gave Cloud his head. 'Race you to the tor,' she cried. Cloud sprang into a canter, Red matching him stride for stride. Soon both girls were crouched low over their ponies' necks as they galloped towards the rocky outcrop.

When the smooth grassy ride became peppered with scattered rocks they slowed to a walk and let their reins slip through their fingers so the ponies could stretch their necks. Poppy wiggled her toes.

'I can't feel my feet. Let's walk the last bit,' she said, jumping off Cloud. Scarlett followed suit, yelping as her frozen feet hit the ground. As they sidestepped granite boulders and dodged peaty puddles Poppy had never felt happier. They settled on a wide, basin-like rock at the top of the tor and let the ponies nibble at the wiry grass while they gazed across the moor.

'This is the life,' sighed Poppy contentedly. 'No school for almost a fortnight, Christmas in a few days' time. Chester back home. Perfect.'

'Isn't it just,' Scarlett agreed. 'Bet Princess Georgia never has this much fun on her posh showjumper.'

It was as if Scarlett had flipped a switch. At the mention of Georgia's name an anxious knot formed in Poppy's stomach. She had managed to push the kidnapping deep into her subconscious when Chester had gone missing. But it had popped up again, like an irksome jack-in-a-box.

She chewed a nail. The urge to tell Scarlett was overwhelming. She knew she could trust her best friend. And wasn't it true that a problem shared was a problem halved?

'Talking about Georgia, d'you think she's still sore that she wasn't picked for the showjumping team?' said Scarlett.

'I don't suppose it's the main thing on her mind right now.'

Scarlett looked puzzled. 'Why?'

Poppy clambered to her feet. 'Come on, let's go home. My backside's gone completely numb. I'll tell you why on the way.'

~

ONCE AGAIN SCARLETT'S face was a picture of disbelief as Poppy recounted her trip to Claydon Manor.

'Surely if her parents just hand over the two million quid they'll get her back?' she said.

But Poppy had thought long and hard about this. 'I don't think they can afford to, Scar. Think about it. Georgia had to sell most of her jumping ponies a while back, didn't she? Don't you remember Sam telling us that they'd spent their way through their lottery win and that's why they opened the livery yard? They had to start making the place pay. The house was absolutely freezing when I was there. And everything looked shabby. Not shabby chic, just shabby. They may live in that enormous house, but I think they're what you call property rich and cash poor.'

Scarlett raised her eyebrows. 'Are you saying the Cannings are skint? Crikey.'

'Try not to sound too pleased,' Poppy said reprovingly.

'Sorry.' Scarlett looked shamefaced. 'But there's nothing we can do, is there?'

'I rode over to Witch Cottage, to see if she was there.'

Scarlett was aghast. 'And what would you have done if she was? These are not the type of people to mess with, Poppy.'

'You're right,' Poppy sighed. 'I just can't help thinking that I've missed something. Something important.'

'Let the police deal with it,' her best friend said firmly. 'If they can't find Georgia no-one will.'

~

THEY RODE home past the Blackstone farm. Poppy hadn't wanted to – she would be happy never to clap eyes on the place again – but it was the most direct route back and the sun was beginning to sink below the horizon. It would be dark in half an hour.

'New people must have moved in,' said Scarlett, as they trotted past the two farm cottages. A beaten-up red pick-up truck was parked on the muddy track behind Flint Cottage.

'It probably belongs to the builders. Tory said George Blackstone's doing up both cottages to sell,' said Poppy absentmindedly.

Scarlett pulled a face. 'To more out-of-towners, I expect.'

'Like us, you mean?' joked Poppy. It wasn't so long ago that the McKeevers had made the move from London to Devon in search of a quieter life.

Scarlett grinned. 'I forgot you used to be a city girl. It feels like you've lived here forever.'

Poppy pretended to look affronted. 'In a good way, I hope?'

'Of course, you twit.'

Poppy smiled to herself. To be described as a local was a compliment indeed.

17

Poppy was in her bedroom wrapping presents the following morning when Caroline poked her head around the door. Poppy was surprised to see her normally calm stepmum looking harassed.

'What's up?' she said through a mouthful of sticky tape.

'The vicar's just called. She's holding a dress rehearsal for the Nativity and wants Chester there.'

'That's alright, isn't it?'

'It's this afternoon! We were supposed to be going to the supermarket. I haven't got any food in for Christmas yet!'

The thought of spending over an hour in a crowded supermarket a couple of days before Christmas did not sound much fun.

'That's OK. I'll walk Charlie and Chester down to the church. I'll see if Scarlett wants to come, too. It'll be fun,' said Poppy.

'But that's not all,' said Caroline. 'She's suddenly announced that she wants Charlie to dress as a shepherd. There's no way he's going to agree to that, you know what he's like. And, anyway, how on earth am I supposed to find a costume in the next two hours?'

'Leave it to me,' said Poppy firmly.

≈

SHE FOUND Charlie in the lounge, watching television.

'It's a supermoon tonight,' he told her. 'Biggest one for nearly seventy years. It's going to be amazing.'

'No time for supermoons now,' she said, depositing the armful of items she had spent the last half an hour collecting on the sofa.

'What's all that?' he said suspiciously.

'Your costume.'

'I'm not wearing a tea towel on my head. I'll look like an idiot.'

'But you used to love dressing up,' said Poppy.

'That was when I was seven,' scoffed Charlie. 'I'm eight now. And eight-year-old boys do not like dressing up.'

'But shepherds are cool. At least you don't have to be Angel Gabriel and wear a white sheet and tinsel.'

'And a brown pillowcase is any better?' Charlie crossed his arms and gave her a mutinous look. Poppy realised that going to the supermarket with Caroline might have been the easier option.

'I spent ages hunting through the airing cupboard looking for that,' she said, holding the offending pillowcase against her. 'I turned it into a tunic for you!'

'That is not a tunic. It's a pillowcase with holes cut out for my head and arms,' said Charlie.

'I thought you could wear it over your brown trousers and that khaki long-sleeved top Caroline got for you the other day. I've found some rope to tie around your waist and head. And I've made you a crook, look.'

Poppy was quite pleased with the hook she'd fashioned out of cardboard, painted brown and fixed to the end of an old curtain pole. But Charlie gave her a withering look and turned back to the television.

'I suppose I'd better wear it, then,' she said, pulling the pillowcase over her head and poking her arms through the holes. She tied the longer length of rope around her waist and smoothed the cotton underneath. 'Now for the headdress.' She tied the tea towel around her forehead with the rest of the rope and picked up the crook. 'There. Pretty authentic shepherd, huh?'

Charlie looked at her out of the corner of his eye and shrugged.

'It's a shame,' she continued.

'What's a shame?' he asked grumpily.

'That you won't be leading Chester in the Nativity. I thought you were looking forward to it.'

'Of course I'll be leading him! A pair of net curtains chose us.'

'The *Reverend Kirton* chose Chester, not you. And if you had read the small print in the contract you'd have seen that the chosen donkey's helper must wear a shepherd's costume.'

'What contract?' cried Charlie, the supermoon forgotten.

Poppy crossed her fingers. 'The one she gave to Caroline on the way out. You were talking to Sam at the time.'

'But that's not –'

'Fair?' said Poppy. 'Of course it's fair. But it's your decision. It's fine. I'm more than happy to do it instead. I think my costume is cool.' She pulled off the tea towel and pillowcase and folded them neatly on the floor beside Charlie. 'I'll go and get Chester ready and we'll leave in fifteen minutes, OK?'

Charlie muttered something under his breath.

'Sorry, I didn't quite catch that,' said Poppy.

'I said, alright, I'll wear your stupid shepherd's costume.'

'Ah, but will you wear it with good grace?' said Poppy, aware she was pushing her luck.

Charlie's expression was doubtful. 'Why, does it say that in the contract, too?'

'No, of course it doesn't. But if you march up the aisle with a face like thunder it's not exactly going to make the congregation feel Christmassy, is it?'

Charlie rolled his eyes. 'I promise to wear your stupid – sorry, *splendid* – shepherd's costume with good grace,' he intoned.

'Glad that's finally settled,' said Poppy. 'Be ready in fifteen minutes.'

Once she was safely in the hallway she fist-pumped the air. It wasn't often that she got the better of her eight-year-old brother. When she did, victory was sweet.

~

THE REVEREND KIRTON was in the church porch, welcoming the stars of the Nativity, both human and animal, as they arrived.

'Lovely! You made it!' she exclaimed as Poppy, Scarlett, Charlie and

Chester made their way into the nave. 'And what a wonderful costume, Charlie!'

Relieved to see that he wasn't the only one dressed in tea towels and bed linen, Charlie gave her a gracious smile. 'Thanks. It's just something I threw together at the last minute,' he said, neatly sidestepping an elbow in the ribs from his sister.

They joined the rest of the cast at the back of the church. As well as Chester, there were a couple of goats, a sheep and an alpaca called Nelly.

'I don't remember alpacas being in the Nativity,' giggled Scarlett, as Nelly yawned, showing two rows of yellowing teeth.

'I don't think Baby Jesus wore dungarees either,' observed Poppy. The vicar had clearly been unable to find a baby for this year's performance.

'Do we have a volunteer to lead Daisy the sheep?' asked Reverend Kirton. 'I'm told she's very friendly.'

'Oo, yes, I'll do it,' said Scarlett. 'I'm good with sheep. On account of us having a sheep farm,' she added.

'Marvellous!' cried the vicar, clapping her hands in delight.

Poppy settled in a pew at the back of the church and watched the proceedings with amusement. The animals conducted themselves impeccably. It was the children who ignored Reverend Kirton's entreaties to behave.

'No Matthew, pulling hair is *not nice*,' she told the smallest of the Three Kings, who had just given Mary's ponytail a violent tug. 'And Jasper, please be quiet when the innkeeper is saying his line. It is a rather important one, after all.'

A dark-haired woman slipped into the pew beside Poppy. 'How's it going?' she whispered.

Poppy did a double take. It was PC Bodiam, wearing a grey duffle coat over her police uniform.

'Has something happened?' said Poppy, aghast.

'No. I'm here as a mum, not a police officer. My daughter Meg is one of the angels. I'm working on Christmas Eve and won't get a chance to see the actual Nativity. I promised her I'd come to the rehearsal. Luckily I'm not on duty until three. What about you?'

'I brought Chester and Charlie.'

'I heard Chester came back. He must have found a way out of his field after all. It did seem a bit far-fetched that he'd been stolen,' said PC Bodiam.

Poppy coloured. Fortunately the police officer was too busy watching her daughter to notice. Keen to change the subject, she said, 'Any news on you-know-what?'

PC Bodiam glanced over her shoulder to check no-one was in earshot. 'She's still missing, if that's what you mean. You haven't told your parents, have you?'

'No,' said Poppy truthfully. 'Did her mum and dad not pay the ransom?'

'Ah, well there's a problem there. They've got a bit of a cash flow problem.'

So, she had been right. The Cannings were clean broke. 'What happens now?'

'We are following a number of lines of enquiry.' PC Bodiam smiled wryly. 'Sorry, that sounds a bit official, doesn't it? We've had some intel that looks like it might have legs.'

'Intel?'

'Sorry, more police speak. Intelligence. It means information. According to one of our sources, two women at Eastwood Park were overheard talking about a wealthy family who lived near Tavistock. They described the family as an 'easy target'.' PC Bodiam drew inverted commas in the air.

She fell silent as the angels shuffled to their feet and began singing *While Shepherds Watched Their Flocks*. Or, as Charlie preferred to call it, *While Shepherds Washed Their Socks*. A girl aged about six with a band of silver tinsel tied around her poker-straight blonde hair waved furtively in their direction. PC Bodiam waved back. 'That's Meg,' she said with barely-disguised pride.

The Three Kings walked solemnly up the aisle and deposited their gifts of gold, frankincense and myrrh unceremoniously at the toddler Jesus's trainer-clad feet.

An image of Georgia, locked in a dark room all on her own while the rest of the world opened presents and stuffed themselves with turkey and mince pies, crept into Poppy's head. She shivered.

'It's not going to be much of a Christmas for Georgia, is it?'

The police officer shook her head. 'But you mustn't worry. We're doing everything we can to find her.'

'D'you think she'll be alright?'

PC Bodiam smiled sadly. 'I hope so, Poppy, I really do.'

18

P oppy sat, cross-legged, on the end of her bed. Scarlett lay on the floor, teasing Magpie with a ball of screwed up wrapping paper. Every now and then the cat raised his paw and swatted the ball lazily.

'Tell me what she said again?'

Poppy tried to remember PC Bodiam's exact words. 'Two women in some park or other were talking about a family with loads of money who lived near Tavistock.'

'There are probably lots of families with loads of money who live near Tavistock.'

'I know. But it's a bit of a coincidence, isn't it?'

'Maybe,' said Scarlett. 'Which park was it?'

'I'd have thought that's neither here nor there,' said Poppy, parroting one of Tory's favourite expressions.

'You never know.' Scarlett tickled Magpie's enormous stomach and sat up. 'Try and remember, just in case.'

'Um.' Poppy shut her eyes. 'East something. Eastwell! I think that was it.'

'Google it,' ordered Scarlett, joining Poppy on her bed. Poppy reached for her phone and tapped in Eastwell Park. According to Wikipedia it was a country estate near a place called Ashford in Kent.

'But that's the other side of the country,' said Scarlett. 'Why would two women in a country park in Kent be talking about a rich family in Devon?'

'I have absolutely no idea.'

'Are you sure it was Eastwell?'

Poppy tapped her lips with her index finger. 'It could have been East-wood. I'll try that.'

They watched the screen as the search engine listed dozens of hits.

'OMG,' said Scarlett.

The two girls looked at each other in disbelief. Eastwood Park was a women's prison in Gloucestershire.

Poppy clutched Scarlett's arm. 'That's the prison Shelley Taylor was sent to!'

'You don't think –'

'She pretended her own daughter had cancer so she could con people out of hundreds of pounds. I wouldn't put anything past her, would you?'

'Are you sure that's where she went?'

'One hundred per cent. It was a women's prison in Gloucestershire. I remember thinking it was the same county as the Badminton Horse Trials.'

The two girls were silent. And then Poppy gasped. 'Do you know what I also remember? You know that day we took Hope to the show at Redhall? D'you remember how Shelley was quizzing you about the Cannings when we dropped Hope off?'

Scarlett's eyes widened. 'I told her they'd won the lottery and that their house was full of antiques!' The colour drained from her face so her freckles stood out more than ever. 'I told her Georgia's pony cost ten grand. I even told her the name of the house. Oh my God, Poppy. This is all my fault!'

'Scar, we don't even know if Shelley's behind it,' Poppy reasoned.

'It has to be her. We should phone the police right now.'

'Hold on, we can't prove anything. We don't even know if Shelley's still in prison.'

'How long did she get, can you remember?'

Poppy thought hard. 'Three and a half years, I think. But sometimes people get let out early for good behaviour, don't they? At least they do on the telly.'

Scarlett jumped to her feet. 'Let's phone the prison now and find out.'
'They won't tell us. Prisoner confidentiality and all that.'
Scarlett looked agonised. 'So how will we find out?'
'That's easy. We'll ask Hope.'

THEY DISCUSSED TELLING Hope their theory that her mum had master-minded a dastardly kidnap plot but decided against it.

'It's not fair on Hope,' Poppy said. 'Shelley Taylor has made her life miserable enough already. There's no point worrying her until we know for sure that she's behind all this, if she even is.'

Instead they sent an email full of stories about the Nativity, the ponies and the latest village gossip.

'Just ask her casually at the end whether she's still in touch with her mum,' said Scarlett, peering over Poppy's shoulder.

Poppy typed furiously, read the email through one last time and pressed send.

'What's the time difference between here and Toronto?'

'Um. I'll check.' Poppy's fringe fell over her face as she opened Google. 'We're five hours ahead. So, it's just after eleven in the morning over there.'

Scarlett hugged her knees. 'I hope she sees it soon. I promised Mum I'd be home by five.'

'I'm sure she will. She's usually really quick to reply,' soothed Poppy.

'And what if she says her mum has been let out of prison? What do we do then?'

'That,' said Poppy, 'is the million dollar question.'

BUT BY THE time Scarlett left at five, there was still no email from Hope.

'Text me if you hear. Promise,' Scarlett said, her hazel eyes serious. 'I'll never be able to sleep tonight, worrying it's all my fault.'

'Don't be silly. It wasn't you who kidnapped Georgia, was it?'

'Who's kidnapped who?' trilled a voice. Poppy's heart sank. Charlie was standing in the kitchen door watching Scarlett pull on her wellies.

'No-one has kidnapped anyone. We were just talking about a film we watched the other day, weren't we Scar?'

'Yep. It was about a boy called George who got kidnapped. We saw it at my house. It was really good.'

'You never asked me,' said Charlie, his bottom lip jutting out.

'We would have done, but it was a twelve certificate. And you're only eight.' Poppy smiled sweetly, ignoring the daggers look Charlie gave her. He stomped out of the room and Poppy exhaled slowly.

'That was a close shave. If Charlie finds out we're in serious trouble.'

POPPY FEIGNED a headache after dinner so she could stay in her bedroom, checking and re-checking her emails. At nine o'clock she gave up and got ready for bed.

'One last time,' she told herself, reaching for the laptop.

And there it was, sitting in her inbox. An email from Hope. She opened it and began to read.

Hi Poppy and Scarlett!

Great to hear from you! I'm glad the ponies (and Chester) are all well. I miss them heaps. It's been snowing for the last couple of days in Toronto so it feels really Christmassy. They have turkey for Christmas lunch over here, only they have it with mashed potatoes, not roast potatoes. And Dad says we'll probably go tobogganing on Christmas morning, which'll be really cool.

I love it here, but a little bit of me wishes I could come and watch Chester in the Nativity. It sounds fun! Maybe one day I can come over for a holiday? Or you both could come over to Canada. That would be awesome!

Mum's still in prison. Dad says she's got at least another year to go. She writes to me once a week. She's never actually said, but I think she's sorry about everything.

Anyway, write soon. Send me some pics of the Nativity.

And have a FANTASTIC Christmas!

Love,

Hope xx

Poppy closed the laptop, slipped under the duvet and lay staring at the ceiling, her mind racing. When they'd realised Eastwood Park was the very same prison Shelley Taylor had been sent to Poppy had been convinced she must be behind the kidnap. She knew about the Cannings and their lottery win. She certainly had no compunction when it came to conning people out of their hard-earned cash. She'd spun an elaborate web of deceit to dupe countless good-hearted people into handing over money once before. And then she'd squandered it all on designer clothes. It wasn't that great a leap from fraud to kidnap. Poppy remembered the bitterness in Shelley's voice when Scarlett had told her about Claydon Manor and its expensive antiques and works of art. It was too much of a coincidence to think she wasn't involved, wasn't it?

And yet, according to Hope, she was still in prison. Poppy had no reason to doubt her friend. Hope had been as much a victim of Shelley's greed as any of the people who had given money to her fictitious charity appeal, believing they were helping to send a girl with leukaemia to America for treatment.

Certain sleep was beyond her grasp, Poppy let her mind wander. She thought about her visit to Claydon Manor and how she'd stumbled on a real-life drama with the highest of stakes. She pictured Georgia's heart-broken mum sitting at the kitchen table with her head in her hands. The gruff voice of Inspector Pearson as he questioned Poppy about the ransom note. The sad look on PC Claire Bodiam's face when Poppy had asked her if Georgia would be OK.

She remembered the last time she'd seen Georgia. She'd been her usual scornful self, griping about her underdone hot dog and winding Scarlett up. Perhaps she was ordering her captors around in her usual superior way. Poppy hoped so. But she had long suspected that beneath the veneer of superiority Georgia was as insecure as she was. Perhaps, more likely, she had fallen apart.

Poppy wondered if the police felt as powerless as she did. What could they do, other than wait for the Cannings to scrabble together enough money to satisfy the kidnappers' demands? Had they searched outbuild-ings, followed every lead? Poppy remembered her own hunch that Georgia was being kept at Witch Cottage. It seemed ludicrous now, just silly schoolgirl speculation.

A vision of Dartmoor Prison's high granite walls lurked on the edge of Poppy's consciousness. The prison dominated the skyline on that part of the moor, vast and impenetrable. Did Eastwood Park look like HMP Dartmoor? Could Shelley have escaped? And then realisation pinged in her brain and she wondered how she could have been so blind. She knew from bitter experience that criminals still planned crimes inside jail. Look at Jodie's dad. He'd directed a phone smuggling operation from his cell after he'd been jailed for fiddling the books at work. Just because Shelley was in prison didn't mean she had nothing to do with Georgia's disappearance.

She had the local knowledge and the motive. And, thanks to her time inside, she also had the criminal contacts.

Poppy sat up in bed, all thought of sleep forgotten. If she was right, and Shelley was behind Georgia's kidnap, where would she hide her?

nippets of conversation floated around in Poppy's head. Tory telling her indignantly that Jimmy Flynn and his parents had been forced out of Rose Cottage. George Blackstone muttering he had bigger fish to fry. The old farmer was supposed to be doing up both cottages to sell. But did the beaten-up red truck parked behind Flint Cottage belong to the builders, or was there another, far more sinister reason for its presence?

She reached for her phone and texted Scarlett.

Are you still awake?

The phone pinged in seconds.

Yep. Can't sleep. Why?

Think I know where Georgia is.

You're kidding me. How?

Just put two and two together and came up with about forty-six.

Are you gonna call the police?

Poppy closed her eyes and deliberated. Should she head straight downstairs and tell her dad and Caroline her theory? Leave it to the police to sort out? That would be the sensible option. But what if the police didn't believe her? What if they did, and she was wrong? Poppy could imagine the toe-curling embarrassment if a fleet of patrol cars with their blue lights flashing screeched up to the place in the middle of the night only to find it glaringly empty. She needed hard evidence before she called them out on a wild goose chase.

No. I need to check I'm right first.

When're you going, tomorrow?

Poppy tapped without thinking.

Tonight.

But it's almost ten o'clock!

Poppy sprinted across her room to the window and peered outside. The stables and fields were bathed in the silver glow of an enormous moon. Of course, Charlie's supermoon! It was so bright Poppy could pick out every tree and boulder between the house and the Riverdale tor. She tapped out another text.

It'll be fine. It's as light as day out there. I'll wait until Dad and Caroline are asleep and take Cloud. He'll look after me.

Poppy grinned when she saw her best friend's reply.

You're not going without us, OK?

OK. We'll meet you by the gate to the moor in 40 mins.

Poppy dressed quickly and climbed back into bed. After twenty minutes she heard the lounge door click shut and the sound of her dad and Caroline climbing the stairs to bed. After another quarter of an hour she heard the familiar low rumble of her dad snoring.

Poppy padded across her bedroom, eased open the door and crept along the landing, tiptoeing to avoid the creaky floorboard outside her parents' room. In the kitchen she gave Freddie a treat, pulled on her coat, flicked off the security light and slipped out of the back door.

As Poppy crossed the yard Jenny's head appeared over her stable door and the donkey gave the softest hee-haw. Poppy rubbed her head and the donkey nibbled the sleeve of her coat. Chester, laying asleep in the straw, his legs tucked neatly beneath him, opened an eye, saw it was Poppy and went back to sleep.

Poppy could hear Cloud moving around in the stable next door. She grabbed his saddle and bridle from the tack room, shoved her hat on and let herself into his stable. He watched her calmly, as if nocturnal hacks were an everyday occurrence.

Once he was tacked up she led him out of the stable to the gate that led to the moor. Scarlett and Red were nowhere to be seen. Poppy tightened her girth a notch and swung into the saddle. She checked the time on her phone. It was a quarter to eleven. She hoped Scarlett hadn't got cold feet. Suddenly the idea of riding to George Blackstone's farm in the middle of the night seemed at best foolhardy, at worst downright dangerous. If the cantankerous old farmer caught them on his land there was no knowing what he might do.

Cloud's head shot up. He sniffed the air and gave a low whinny. Poppy ran a hand down his neck and peered into the gloom. In the distance she could just make out the shape of Scarlett and Red. The chestnut gelding skittered left and right but Scarlett sat calmly in the saddle. At four, Red was still a baby and could be nervous out hacking. Goodness only knew what he was making of their late night ride. Poppy could hear Scarlett talking to him in a low, soothing voice. He whinnied when he saw Cloud and the two ponies touched noses.

'He thinks I've totally lost the plot,' said Scarlett. She grinned at Poppy. 'And I think he's probably right. Why on earth couldn't this wait until the morning?'

Poppy wasn't sure herself. 'I suppose I thought it was best if we checked out the place under the cover of darkness. If there's no-one there, there's no harm done and we'll leave it to the police to find Georgia.'

'You still haven't told me where we're going.'

Cloud snatched at the bit and Poppy tightened her reins. He was as excited as Red to be out. She kicked him into a canter and called over her shoulder, 'Flint Cottage, of course. That's where we're going.'

～

IT WAS EXHILARATING to canter across the moonlit moor. Dartmoor ponies watched silently as they approached and sheep scattered like bowling pins. Now and then they heard the eerie screech of a barn owl. Once they saw the zebra-striped face of a badger peering out from a copse of trees. Poppy felt the thunder of their ponies' hooves in time with the blood pounding in her temples. What would they find when they reached the old farm cottage? She patted her pocket to reassure herself she had her mobile phone and made a silent pledge to call the police at the first sign of trouble.

When the ponies' flanks were steaming they pulled up and walked the last half a mile to the boundary of the Blackstone farm.

'What's the plan?' Scarlett whispered.

Poppy realised she didn't actually have one. She gave a helpless shrug. 'I guess we need to check if that truck's still parked there for starters.'

'We can't ride up the lane. They'll hear the hooves on the tarmac. We'll have to go around the back.'

'You're right.' Poppy wondered why she hadn't thought of that. 'So, which way should we go?'

Scarlett halted Red. The moonlight had turned the chestnut gelding the colour of burnished copper. He fidgeted while Scarlett found her bearings. 'I reckon if we follow that old stone wall it should bring us out at the back of the cottages, don't you?'

Poppy had no idea. 'Let's give it a go.'

Like everything on the Blackstone farm, the old dry stone wall had long fallen into disrepair and Cloud and Red were forced to pick their way carefully through fallen boulders that peppered the close-cropped grass. Scarlett was right. The wall led straight to the back of the two farm cottages. The two girls fell silent as they drew nearer.

The back garden of Rose Cottage was as neat as a pin. A rectangle of lawn was sandwiched between two long borders of winter-flowering pansies. Poppy felt her breathing quicken when she saw a shadowy shape in the middle of the lawn. She gripped Cloud's reins tightly and was about to call a warning to Scarlett when she realised it was only a washing line hiding inside a green plastic cover.

The back garden of Flint Cottage was a choking tangle of brambles and overgrown shrubs, edged by an ancient wire stock fence that sagged pathetically like an old string vest.

'Look!' hissed Scarlett, pointing to fresh tyre tracks that looped up to the back fence and stopped abruptly right in front of them.

Poppy halted Cloud, her eyes searching for the truck they'd seen parked behind the cottage the day before. Shapes shifted in the silver light. Two oil drums, rusty with age. A roll of roofing felt as black as bitumen, leaning against a towering pile of rubble. An antiquated lawnmower that looked as though it had spluttered and died decades before.

But no beaten-up red truck. Wherever it was, it wasn't here.

20

M oonlight glinted off the windows of the two farm cottages, but otherwise they were in darkness.

'What do we do now?' said Scarlett in a low voice.

'I'm going to take a closer look.' Poppy jumped out of the saddle and handed her reins to Scarlett.

'Be careful!' Scarlett's eyes were as round as orbs.

Poppy gave her a quick smile and headed for the back garden of Rose Cottage. She gave the wooden gate a tentative tug, exhaling softly as it swung open.

To her relief, the security light at the back of the house wasn't working and she slipped across the lawn like a sylph to the patio doors. Cupping her eyes, she stared into a long, thin room that stretched the length of the house. The Flynns had probably used it as a lounge diner but it was now completely empty. Poppy sidled along to the kitchen window and peered inside. There was no sign of life. The surfaces were clean but bare. The only sound came from the drip, drip, drip of the tap.

Poppy glanced at Scarlett. She had jumped off Red and was pointing to the back of Flint Cottage. Poppy ran over to her.

'There's no-one there, Scar. I'm going to check Hope's old house.'

'There's a hole in the back fence, look. We'll be waiting in the garden. Don't be long. I'm getting really creeped out.'

Poppy nodded and climbed over the fence dividing the two gardens. She remembered the first time she and Scarlett had visited Flint Cottage. They'd taken a tin of chocolate brownies, keen to welcome the newcomers to the village. Hope had soon become a friend, but Poppy had never trusted Shelley. And her instincts had proved right.

She forced her way through the waist-high weeds, tripping over an old milk crate, until she reached the kitchen window. To her frustration the blind was drawn. She crouched down and peeped through the microscopic gap between the window frame and the bottom of the blind. Unlike Rose Cottage, the work surfaces in Flint Cottage were strewn with empty food packets, old teabags and dirty mugs and plates. Poppy's breathing quickened. Had the builders left it like this? Or had someone else been here?

She edged along the back wall to the dining room window. The two rooms hadn't been knocked through like the ones in Rose Cottage. Poppy wasn't sure if she felt relieved or anxious when she realised the curtains were open. She took a deep breath and stared into the room. It was empty, save for a cheap dining room table and four chairs.

Poppy was so busy trying to see if she could peer into the hallway from the dining room window that she didn't hear Scarlett and the two ponies approach. The first she knew they behind her was when Cloud gave her a business-like nudge.

'Oh my God!' she shrieked, all thoughts of staying concealed forgotten. 'Why did you creep up on me like that?'

'Sorry,' said Scarlett defensively. 'And I wasn't creeping up on you. I was leading your pony over because I want to go home. My feet are frozen and I'm worried Red'll catch a chill and there's clearly no-one here. The place is deserted.'

'You're right,' Poppy sighed. 'Good job I didn't call the police, isn't it? I'd have looked a proper muppet. C'mon, let's go home.'

Poppy took Cloud's reins from Scarlett and was edging her toe into the stirrup when she froze.

'What's that noise?' she hissed.

'What noise?' said Scarlett impatiently. 'I can't hear a thing.'

'That noise. Listen!'

Poppy felt her insides turn to ice. From somewhere near her feet she could hear the unmistakable sound of someone's knuckles rapping against a window. She clutched Cloud's neck, shrinking into his solid bulk. Scarlett was hopping around on one foot while Red, terrified by the noise, spun round and round.

'Steady boy,' she coaxed, eventually managing to clamber on. 'Poppy, can we *please* go!'

But Poppy was leading Cloud towards the tapping sound. She couldn't leave until she knew what it was. It seemed to be coming from beneath her feet. And then she saw something she hadn't noticed before – a tiny window behind a metal grill a few inches from the ground.

'Did you know Flint Cottage had a cellar?' she asked Scarlett, who was still trying to calm Red.

She shook her head. 'Poppy –'

Ignoring her, Poppy bent down and reached through the grill. The wooden window frame was as rotten as old fruit. She ran her fingers under it and gave it a tug. It opened a fraction.

Poppy knelt on the ground. 'Georgia!' she whispered urgently. 'Is that you?'

21

For a moment, all Poppy could hear was the beating of her own heart. Then a croaky voice whispered back, 'Is that the police?'

'Er, not exactly. It's me, Poppy McKeever. And Scarlett,' she added.

'Brilliant,' muttered the voice. Poppy jumped as the window flapped open. And then her jaw dropped as she saw Georgia's face staring back at her through the bars of the grill. There were dark circles under her china-blue eyes and an angry red welt on her temple. Her normally glossy black hair was lank and greasy.

'Is it her?' called Scarlett.

'Of course it's me!' Georgia hissed. 'You need to get me out of here before they come back.'

Poppy found she was rooted to the spot. 'Before who comes back?'

'Ricky and Bev. They've gone to get a Chinese takeaway. I heard them talking about it. They've been gone ages. They could be back at any minute!'

'Meet me by the back door. I'll see if I can force it open,' said Poppy.

'I'm locked in the cellar, you idiot! Don't you think I might have tried to get out before now otherwise?'

It seemed that even being kidnapped hadn't rubbed away any of Georgia's prickliness. Poppy felt a fleeting sympathy for her captors. She scrambled to her feet and handed Scarlett her reins.

'Call the police, Scar, and I'll see if I can break in.'

The back door was half-glazed. Thanking her lucky stars it wasn't a new uPVC door with toughened glass, Poppy looked around frantically, pouncing on a broken brick laying half-hidden in the undergrowth. Turning her face away from the door, she smashed the brick against the glass. It shattered like ice, leaving a circle of jagged shards like the jaws of a great white shark.

'Be careful, Poppy!' Scarlett shouted. She had jumped off Red and was holding both ponies in one hand and her mobile in the other.

'Tell them it's an emergency,' Poppy panted, and turned back to the door. She used the brick to smash a bigger hole and felt inside for the door handle.

'Please let the key be in the lock,' she muttered. The fates were being kind. Her fingers closed around the key and she turned it carefully. The last thing she needed was for it to fall onto the floor out of reach. The door now unlocked, she pulled the handle and gave it a shove. It didn't budge.

Poppy shot an anxious look at Scarlett.

'It might be bolted,' Scarlett mouthed, pointing to the top of the door. Poppy groaned.

'Are you coming?' shouted Georgia. The supercilious tone had been replaced by one of rising panic.

Poppy ran back to the cellar window. 'Can you remember if the back door was bolted?'

Georgia was clutching the bars of the grill. Her knuckles were the same alabaster-white as her face. 'I don't know! They blindfolded me. Can't you kick it in?'

Poppy shook her head. 'I suppose I can try.'

She balanced on her left leg and jabbed with her right, but the door stayed stubbornly shut. This was useless. She needed to open the bolt.

She knocked the rest of the broken glass out of the window and stood on tiptoes, but the top of the door was tantalisingly out of reach. She remembered the milk crate. Huffing as she pulled it out of the brambles, she set it on its side against the back door, hopped onto it and scrabbled blindly for the bolt.

'Yesss!' said Poppy as the bolt slid open. She opened the door and ran into the house. 'Georgia!' she yelled. 'Where are you?'

Poppy couldn't ever remember seeing a cellar door in Flint Cottage. Where would it be? She ran into the kitchen and came face to face with a white painted door. She used two hands to haul it open. But it was a pantry, empty apart from an old kettle and a lonely tin of peaches.

She was on her way to the lounge when she noticed the cupboard under the stairs. It was bolted top and bottom. Her heart thumping in her chest, she slid the bolts across and wrenched open the door.

At once she was hit by a damp, musty smell and the welcome sight of steep brick steps leading down. Poppy took the steps two at a time. They led to a tiny cellar, no more than eight foot by six foot, lit by the single bar of an electric fire. Against one wall was a green camp bed. On the floor beside it was a half-empty two litre bottle of water and the remains of a microwave meal. Georgia was still gazing out of the tiny window, a cheap nylon sleeping bag around her shaking shoulders.

'Georgia?' said Poppy uncertainly. 'Are you OK?'

The older girl slowly turned to face Poppy. She was still wearing her show jacket and jodhpurs, although the once-white material was black with filth. Tears were coursing down her cheeks. 'I thought I was going to die in here. Ricky has a gun, you see. And he gets really angry.' She touched the mark on her temple and lowered her eyes.

'You're safe now,' Poppy said, with as much confidence as she could muster. 'Scarlett is on the phone to the police. They'll be here any minute. But we should get out of the cellar. Come on.'

Poppy was halfway up the steps when she heard the whine of an engine in the distance. Georgia cried out as if she'd been struck and cringed against the wall.

'They're back!' she whispered.

Her terror was infectious and Poppy's insides turned to liquid. But she couldn't afford to panic. 'Georgia! We've got to go!' she shouted.

They sprinted up the cellar steps towards the back door. Poppy doubled back and slid the bolts closed. As soon as they saw the smashed glass the kidnappers would know Georgia had gone, but anything that gave them even a few seconds' advantage was worth doing.

Scarlett flung Cloud's reins at Poppy and jumped on Red. 'I had no signal,' she shrieked. 'And I can see a car coming!'

Georgia was staring at the two ponies as if she was in a trance.

'I'll get on first, then you get on the back,' ordered Poppy. It was a good job Cloud was used to Charlie riding behind her, she thought, as she lowered a hand to Georgia and pulled her into the saddle.

Headlights snaked around the side of the house and Red whinnied in fear. Georgia's arms felt as tight as a seatbelt around Poppy's waist.

'OK?' she said.

'Please, just go,' Georgia begged.

Poppy kicked Cloud into a canter and he flew through the hole in the fence, Red on his tail.

As they fled down the dirt track behind the two cottages Poppy allowed herself to think for one foolish moment that they were safe.

Until the truck rounded the corner with a furious roar and the two fleeing ponies were caught in its headlights. The truck sped towards them, its engine whining under the strain. And she realised just how much danger they were in.

22

Poppy made a decision she hoped she wouldn't regret.

'We need to split up,' she shouted to Scarlett. 'You go straight to ours and call the police. We'll head for the Riverdale woods. They'll never get the truck in there.'

Scarlett was trying to control Red, who was plunging and leaping like a bucking bronco, the whites of his eyes showing. She nodded and gave the gelding his head. He galloped into the night, his flaxen tail streaming behind him like a wisp of smoke.

'Stay safe,' Poppy called, even though she knew Scarlett would never hear over the noise of the revving engine. She kicked Cloud into a canter.

Poppy had been grateful for the supermoon when they'd set off for Flint Cottage, but now she longed for cloudy skies. The moon shone with such luminosity the moor was bathed in silver light, and she felt as exposed as a field mouse being hunted by a kestrel. Behind them the truck's diesel engine whined and spluttered as the driver – Poppy assumed it was Ricky – floored the throttle.

'They're getting closer!' cried Georgia. Poppy crouched low over the saddle and Cloud lengthened his stride until he was galloping full pelt, his neck stretched in front of him like a racehorse.

She tried to remember the lie of the land. Was there a river they could cross to escape Georgia's kidnappers? A memory of Beau and their race through the night after the storm at Oaklands flickered on the edge of her consciousness. They had nearly drowned that night. Scrub the river idea, she thought wildly.

Georgia was clutching Poppy so tightly she felt as if all the air was being squeezed out of her lungs.

'Faster!' Georgia urged, her breath hot on Poppy's neck.

They were galloping alongside the old stone wall on the edge of the Blackstone farm. By Poppy's reckoning it petered out in half a mile or so, but if they veered sharp left and jumped it now they stood a chance of losing the truck and reaching the Riverdale wood and safety. Poppy knew Cloud could turn on a sixpence – hadn't he proved it in the jump-off at Claydon? – but could she ask him to jump a solid stone wall at a ridiculously-tight angle with two people on his back? Did she have any choice?

'Hold on tight,' she told Georgia. She sat down in the saddle and gave a half-halt. 'Steady boy,' she murmured. Cloud's ears flicked back and his pace slowed. 'Ready?' she asked. She felt the older girl nod. Poppy half-halted again and turned Cloud on his quarters. The wall loomed before them. He managed one short stride before tucking his legs under him and taking off. Poppy felt a whoosh of cold air as they flew over the wall. He landed neatly on the other side and picked up a canter. Georgia loosened her grip a fraction and Poppy sucked in air gratefully.

She held her reins in one hand and patted her pony's neck over and over. 'You clever, clever boy.'

It wasn't long before Poppy could see the dark outline of the Riverdale wood. Cloud was breathing hard and fast and she could tell he was beginning to tire. She chanced a look back. The headlights of the truck were half-hidden by the old stone wall.

'Nearly there,' she crooned to her pony. Still he thundered on. She stared at his pricked ears until they were blurry with tears. She had asked the impossible and he had willingly delivered. He always did.

He plunged into the darkness of the wood and Poppy slowed him to a walk. It would be beyond foolhardy to try to canter through the trees at this time of night. Cloud shook his head and Poppy let her reins slide through her fingers. He was still blowing hard.

'We should get off, give him a breather,' she told Georgia.

'But what if they find us?'

'I think we've lost them. I can't see the headlights any more, can you?'

Poppy halted Cloud and both girls slid off. Poppy ran the stirrups up and loosened the girth a couple of notches. She looked around, trying to get her bearings. In the distance she could hear the unmistakable sound of running water. They must be close to the stream. Georgia was shivering. Poppy took off her coat and handed it to the older girl, who took it gratefully. Poppy gave her what she hoped was a reassuring smile. 'It's not far now.'

They walked in silence through the trees, one either side of Cloud. When they reached the stream they turned left and followed it as it curved and dipped through the trees.

'This is where I first saw Cloud,' said Poppy, when they reached a small beach.

'What do you mean?'

'He was running wild on the moor. Had been for years. He escaped from the Blackstone farm, too.'

Georgia shuddered. Poppy thought she heard a small sob, but it could have been the soughing of the wind in the trees.

'You OK?' she asked.

Georgia gave a tiny shrug. 'Not really. How did you know where I was?'

'I didn't know for sure. It was a lucky guess.'

'But how did you even know I had been kidnapped? I heard Ricky on the phone to my parents. He said if they told anyone I'd be –' she left the sentence hanging in the air.

'The police know. And Angela.' Georgia's face was stricken. 'But no-one else,' Poppy added hastily. 'Apart from Scarlett. And she'd never tell.'

'Why didn't they come for me?' Georgia's usually clipped voice was pitifully feeble.

'They had no idea where you were.' They reached a fallen tree trunk Poppy recognised. 'We need to cross the stream here,' she said. 'It's not deep.'

Georgia gasped as they plunged into the icy water. Cloud stopped in the middle and drank thirstily.

'Not too much,' said Poppy, who could no longer feel her feet. He lifted his head and nudged her gently.

They scrambled up the bank on the other side. Poppy wanted answers to the many questions buzzing around in her head.

'Did they take you at the show?'

'How did you know?'

'You're still in your riding gear.'

'Remember when I saw you, just before your class? I was eating a hot dog.'

'I remember. You said it was raw. We thought you'd got food poisoning and that's why you didn't jump.'

Georgia laughed bitterly. 'If only I had. It was so disgusting I went to demand my money back. The man told me to wait in the back of the van while he found some change. The minute I stepped inside someone covered my mouth and nose with a handkerchief. I must have passed out because the next thing I knew I was locked in the cellar.'

'They sedated you, like George Blackstone sedated Cloud,' said Poppy wonderingly.

'I woke up with a thumping headache. I was so angry. I knew I'd missed my class. Someone had tipped off Angela that Peter Frampton was going to be there. I wanted so badly to impress him. Who won?'

'The open jumping? Sam.'

'And I suppose he was picked for the team?'

'First reserve,' said Poppy.

Georgia gave a derisive snort.

Poppy raised her eyes to the sky. 'What happened then?'

'I banged and banged on the door of the cellar until this woman told me to belt up else Ricky would do his nut,' mimicked Georgia in perfect Estuary English.

'That was Bev?' Poppy asked.

Georgia nodded. 'She told me I'd be alright as long as my parents paid the two million ransom. Two million!' She laughed hollowly. 'They had no idea we're stony broke.'

There's stony broke and stony broke, thought Poppy drily. Not being able to afford to heat your mansion didn't exactly mean you were penniless.

'Bev was alright, actually,' Georgia continued. 'She made sure I had plenty to eat and drink. She even bought me a pack of cards so I could play Solitaire to pass the time. But Ricky, he was horrible. I think Bev was terrified of him, too. He was always having a go at her.'

Poppy laced her fingers in Cloud's mane. 'I thought Hope's mum had something to do with it. That's why we came to Flint Cottage. That's where Hope and Shelley used to live.'

Georgia wheeled around to face her. 'Did you say Shelley?'

'Yes. Why?'

'I heard Bev talking on her mobile one morning while Ricky was out. She said, 'It's all going to plan, Shell. We should have the dough any day now." Once again Georgia had the harsh tone and glottal stops of Bev's accent to a tee.

Something clicked in Poppy's brain and everything became clear. 'Do you think Bev has been inside?'

'Inside what?' said Georgia irritably.

Poppy rolled her eyes. Georgia really had led a cosseted, sheltered life.

'Inside prison. Because Shelley's in a women's prison in Gloucestershire. She knows your mum and dad won the lottery. How's she to know they've spent all their winnings? What if she met Bev there? They could have concocted the plan to kidnap you and put it into action once Bev was released. With a little help from Bev's shady boyfriend. And once your parents coughed up they probably planned to split the proceeds three ways. Shelley provided the insider information and the house. Bev and Ricky were the team on the ground. And I bet George Blackstone was in on it, too. You were the bigger fish he was planning to fry.'

The trees were thinning out and Cloud had quickened his stride, keen to be home after his late-night adventure.

'Almost there,' said Poppy, stifling a yawn.

'How did you do in the end? At the show?' said Georgia.

'We were third,' said Poppy proudly. 'We had the fastest round in the jump-off but we clipped a fence and had four faults.'

'That pony of yours jumps like a dream. How he cleared that wall with us both on his back. I don't suppose you want to sell him, do you?'

'Georgia!' shrieked Poppy, outraged. 'Honestly, you've got a nerve, you really have. No, you can't buy my pony. He's not for sale. He never will be.'

Georgia shrugged and said testily, 'There's no need to throw a hissy fit. You should be flattered that I'm even asking.'

Poppy was speechless. Perhaps there was a direct correlation between money and manners. The more you had of one, the less you had of the other. It was no wonder Georgia rubbed so many people up the wrong way.

Blind to Poppy's chagrin, Georgia carried on. 'Well, if you ever change your mind –'

Poppy realised she was grinding her teeth. 'Don't worry, I won't,' she said grimly.

23

Poppy felt a wave of tiredness sweep over her as they trudged across the field to the house. When she and Scarlett had set off for Flint Cottage, Riverdale had been in darkness, but now lights blazed from almost every window and a police patrol car was parked outside. It looked as though Scarlett had successfully raised the alarm.

A small delegation of people was heading in their direction, led by her dad. Caroline walked alongside him. A couple of paces behind them strode Inspector Pearson and PC Bodiam with serious expressions on their faces. The inspector was talking urgently into a police radio.

Cloud stopped, his eyes boggling. 'It's OK,' Poppy whispered. 'They're just checking we're alright.'

Poppy's dad clasped her shoulders and looked her sternly in the eye. 'Don't ever, *ever* disappear like that again, Poppy McKeever. Goodness only knows what could have happened!'

'Sorry, Dad,' she said in a small voice.

'Come here,' he commanded, wrapping his arms around her. 'We're just glad you're safe.'

'Is Scarlett OK?' she mumbled into his coat.

'She's absolutely fine. Bill's taken her home. You can see her in the morning.'

Poppy clung to her dad. He felt safe and familiar. She felt weak with relief. Despite all the odds, they'd rescued Georgia and made it home in one piece.

She could hear PC Bodiam telling Georgia that her parents were on their way.

'Have you caught them?' Poppy asked.

Inspector Pearson broke away from his radio conversation to give her a reassuring smile. 'We certainly have. Fortunately for us Ricky isn't the sharpest tool in the box. He drove his truck into a patch of boggy ground and was quite literally stuck in the mud when our patrols arrived. He's on his way to the cells at Plymouth as we speak.'

'What about Bev?' asked Georgia.

'Officers found her in the cottage trying to cover up their tracks. It turns out she's on licence from prison so she'll be back behind bars before she knows it.'

'Was she at Eastwood Park?' Poppy asked.

Inspector Pearson nodded, surprised. 'How did you know that?'

Poppy caught PC Bodiam's eye and a look of understanding passed between them. 'Just a lucky guess,' she said.

$\sim$

BY THE TIME Cloud was snug in his stable with a fresh bucket of water and a full haynet, Poppy was drooping with exhaustion. Caroline settled her at the kitchen table with a mug of hot chocolate and a shortbread biscuit as though she was six. But Poppy didn't mind. She wrapped her fingers around the mug and watched her stepmum fill her hot water bottle.

Georgia's parents had screeched up the drive in their Range Rover and had whisked their daughter home. Not before the older girl had sought Poppy out in the tack room and thanked her for rescuing her.

'God knows what would have happened if the police had left it to my parents to pay up. I'd have died in that cellar.' She said it lightly, but there was a lingering fear in her eyes. Poppy couldn't imagine how Georgia had survived such a terrifying ordeal and guessed that the scars would take a long time to fade.

The two police officers had also gone, telling the McKeevers that statements could wait until the next day. Inspector Pearson had agreed to bring forward PC Bodiam's shift to the morning, which meant she would be able to watch her daughter in the Nativity after all.

Charlie had slept through the whole thing.

'He'll be gutted when he discovers he's missed all the excitement,' said Poppy. To her embarrassment her voice was all shaky.

Caroline sat beside her and put her arm around her shoulder. 'Hey, are you OK?'

She stared into her hot chocolate. 'I'm glad Georgia's safe, of course I am. But I was stupid, putting everyone in danger. What if Cloud was killed?'

'Well, he wasn't, was he?'

'And Dad's mad at me.'

'He was worried, Poppy. We all were. The first thing we knew something was wrong was when Scarlett started banging on the door yelling something about kidnappers. Your dad was all set to race off in his pyjamas but I convinced him to call the police and let them deal with it.'

The image of her dad sprinting across the moor in his stripy jimjams was enough to tease a smile out of her.

'That's better,' said Caroline, patting her arm. 'Inspector Pearson said he was going to nominate you and Scarlett for a Chief Constable's award for bravery. Imagine that!'

Poppy groaned. 'I really hope he doesn't. Fame and fortune are overrated. Look where it got Georgia Canning.'

24

The skies were heavy with the threat of snow when Poppy peered out of her bedroom window the next morning. Chester and Jenny were watching over their stable door, their long ears pricked and their eyes fixed firmly on the back door as they waited for her to arrive with their breakfast. Suddenly desperate to see her pony, Poppy eased the window open and whistled softly. Cloud appeared, looked up at her bedroom window and whinnied.

She was pulling on her jeans when Charlie flung open her bedroom door, his face a study of incredulity.

'Ever heard of knocking?' said Poppy pointedly.

Ignoring her, he sat on the end of the bed. 'Mum's just told me what happened last night. Why didn't you take me with you? I could have helped!'

Poppy grabbed her sweatshirt and made for the door, sighing inwardly as Charlie followed her.

She decided to appease him. 'I know. But there wasn't time to wake you. I will take you next time, I promise.'

'Oh, OK.' Charlie seemed to accept this. 'Don't forget what day it is.'

Poppy always lost track of the days during school holidays. 'Saturday?' she hazarded.

'I don't mean what day it is, I mean what *day* it is. It's Christmas Eve! It's *Nativity day*.'

So it was. Poppy had clean forgotten in all the excitement. 'Well, we'd better make sure Chester is looking his best, hadn't we?'

'And Jenny,' said Charlie. 'A pair of net curtains says she can come, too. The more the merrier, she told Mum.'

'Pity she didn't decide that after the donkey auditions. George Blackstone would have had no reason to take Chester.'

'But we'd have never got Jenny then, would we?' said Charlie, with the simple logic of an eight-year-old.

'True. But you really have got to stop calling her that.'

'Stop calling her Jenny?' said Charlie, his eyebrows knotted. 'But that's her name. It was your idea, remember.'

'No, you idiot. I mean the Reverend Curtains. I mean Kirton. See? You've got me doing it now!'

Charlie creased up laughing and Poppy batted him lightly on the arm. 'Come on, little brother. Let's go and groom those donkeys.'

~

THE NATIVITY WAS due to start at three o'clock and at half past two the McKeevers set off along the windy country lanes towards St Mary's Church with Chester and Jenny.

The two donkeys had stood patiently as Poppy and Charlie groomed them until their thick coats shone. Caroline had made Poppy a makeshift shepherd's costume to match Charlie's, which she was wearing over her black jeans and brown leather boots.

'Bill reckons it'll snow tonight,' said Poppy's dad, looking up at the leaden sky. 'I can almost smell it in the air, can't you?'

Caroline laughed. 'Crystallised water doesn't smell.'

'Yes, it does,' he said. 'What do you think, kids?'

Poppy breathed in deeply. The sharp, cold tang of snowflakes filled her nostrils. 'Definitely,' she said.

'Of course it does!' said Charlie.

Caroline made a show of sniffing and shaking her head. 'Nope, can't smell a thing.'

'What if we're snowed in for Christmas?' said Charlie.

'It won't be the first time, and I don't suppose it'll be the last. It'll be an adventure. We've enough food in to feed an army and I don't think a bit of snow will stop Father Christmas and his reindeer, do you?'

Charlie looked at his dad pityingly. 'He's not real, you know.'

But Mike McKeever was watching a burly man dressed in camouflage gear and carrying a video camera disappear into the church. 'I don't believe it!' he said, striding after the man and tapping him on the shoulder.

Poppy watched as the mysterious red-haired man she'd seen at Witch Cottage turned in surprise. His face split into a grin.

'Mike McKeever as I live and breathe! What are you doing here?' he said, pumping her dad's hand.

'I live up the road, old friend. The question is, what are *you* doing here?'

The man held up his camera. 'I bumped into the vicar in the pub yesterday and she asked if I could film the Nativity. She's planning to sell copies to raise money for the church roof appeal.'

Poppy's dad beckoned them over. 'Come and say hello to John. We worked together in the Middle East years ago. Until John decided that filming wild animals was more fun than filming war zones.'

Charlie was staring at the man slack-jawed. 'Are you John Dunne the wildlife cameraman?'

The bearlike man's eyes crinkled. 'The very same. And who are you, young man?'

'I'm your biggest fan,' said Charlie earnestly. 'I've watched your film on snow leopards like about a million times. And that's my sister, Poppy.'

Poppy gave the cameraman a quick smile. 'Actually, we've already met.'

John Dunne looked puzzled, and then his face cleared. 'The girl with the grey pony. Of course. I didn't recognise you without your hat.'

'You still haven't told us what you're doing here,' said Poppy's dad.

'I'm filming a pair of barn owls in an old croft near Princetown for a new documentary. I've been camped out for about a week, that's why I look a bit rough.' He scratched the stubble on his chin and grinned self-consciously. 'I think I probably gave Poppy a bit of a fright the other day, but she galloped off before I could tell her who I was.'

Poppy realised the three-legged contraption he'd been carrying in the woods must have been a tripod for his camera. Not a trap at all. She shook her head.

'No, you didn't scare me at all.'

~

SCARLETT WAS ALREADY at the back of the church with Daisy the sheep and the rest of the cast. They watched the congregation slowly file in. It seemed as though the whole village had turned out for the service. Even Barney Broomfield, who ran the village shop, was there in his trademark red sweater. With his white beard, twinkly blue eyes and generous stomach, he bore more than a passing resemblance to Father Christmas.

Poppy nudged her brother. 'Still think there's no such thing as Santa?'

Charlie grinned. 'Maybe I was wrong.'

'There's a first time for everything,' she said drily.

They waved to Bella, Tory and Sam. Poppy mouthed, 'Where's Delilah?'

'Back in the loft, thank God,' Sam mouthed back.

PC Bodiam, wearing a pretty teal dress, denim jacket and black leather boots, walked in hand-in-hand with her daughter Meg, who looked the picture of Christmas in her angel costume, albeit her tinsel halo was slightly askew. PC Bodiam straightened the halo and ushered her to the back of the church before sliding into a pew.

Poppy felt hot breath on the back of her neck.

'Charlie!' she admonished. But it was Nelly the alpaca nibbling her hood.

'Look, there's Georgia,' whispered Scarlett.

Sure enough, Georgia was stalking into the church with a man and woman flanking her like bodyguards protecting a film star. Poppy did a double take when she realised the smiley woman with rosy cheeks, bundled up in a damson-coloured quilted coat, was Georgia's mum. She bore no resemblance to the muted ghost of a woman Poppy had spied through the keyhole at Claydon Manor. Even Georgia's dad looked happy. Poppy was glad for them. It could have been such a different story.

Gradually the pews filled up and before long the church was packed to the rafters. The Reverend Kirton bustled over to see them.

'Everyone remember what to do?' They nodded. 'Marvellous! You are my Christmas stars, every one of you. Even you, Matthew,' she said, bestowing a benevolent smile on the smallest of the Three Kings, who was balancing a homemade gold ingot on his head.

The organ wheezed into life and the congregation shuffled to their feet as the first few bars of *O Little Town of Bethlehem* rang around the church.

Poppy glanced out of the small leaded window beside them and gasped. Snowflakes were falling, scurrying and whirling in the half-light of a late December afternoon.

'It's snowing!' she breathed. The gaggle of children stared out of the window, transfixed. They passed on the news in excited whispers. The words gained a momentum of their own and soon the entire congregation was laughing and smiling at the thought of a white Christmas.

Suddenly Poppy felt giddy with happiness. The horror of the last few days felt like a bad dream. Chester and Jenny were safe. Cloud was tucked up in his stable, waiting for her to come home. Tomorrow was Christmas. And Poppy had a feeling it was going be the best one ever.

AFTERWORD

Thank you for reading *The Riverdale Pony Stories*. If you enjoyed Poppy and Cloud's adventures it would be great if you could spare a couple of minutes to write a quick review on Amazon. I'd love to hear your feedback!

ABOUT THE AUTHOR

Amanda Wills is the Amazon bestselling author of The Riverdale Pony Stories, which follow the adventures of pony-mad Poppy McKeever and her beloved Connemara Cloud.

She is also the author of Flick Henderson and the Deadly Game, a fast-paced mystery about a super-cool new heroine who has her sights set on becoming an investigative journalist.

Amanda, a UK-based former journalist who now works part-time as a police press officer, lives in Kent with her husband and fellow indie author Adrian Wills and their sons Oliver and Thomas.

Find out more at www.amandawills.co.uk or at www.facebook.-com/riverdaleseries or follow amandawillsauthor on Instagram.

www.amandawills.co.uk
amanda@amandawills.co.uk

ALSO BY AMANDA WILLS

The Thirteenth Horse

Juno's Foal

The Midnight Pony

The Pony of Tanglewood Farm

Flick Henderson and the Deadly Game

Printed in Great Britain
by Amazon

48666443R00435